# The World of

BY STEVEN MARCUS

*The Other Victorians*

*Dickens: From Pickwick to Dombey*

EDITED BY STEVEN MARCUS

*The World of Modern Fiction*

*The Life and Work of Sigmund Freud* by Ernest Jones
(with Lionel Trilling)

# MODERN FICTION

## EUROPEAN

EDITED AND WITH AN INTRODUCTION
BY

## Steven Marcus

 SIMON AND SCHUSTER·NEW YORK

All possible care has been taken to trace the ownership of every selection included and to make full acknowledgment for its use. If any errors have accidentally occurred, they will be corrected in subsequent editions, provided notification is sent to the publisher.

THE CHILDHOOD OF A LEADER by Jean-Paul Sartre, translated from the French by Lloyd Alexander. From *Intimacy*. Copyright 1948 by New Directions. Reprinted by permission of New Directions Publishing Corporation.

THE RENEGADE by Albert Camus, translated from the French by Justin O'Brien. From *Exile and the Kingdom*. Copyright 1958 by Alfred A. Knopf, Inc. Reprinted by permission of Alfred A. Knopf, Inc.

STORIES AND TEXTS FOR NOTHING, III by Samuel Beckett, translated from the French by Anthony Bonner and Samuel Beckett. From *Textes pour rien*. Copyright 1958 by Les Editions de Minuit.

THE SECRET ROOM by Alain Robbe-Grillet, translated from the French by Richard Howard. From *Instantanés*. Copyright 1962 by Les Editions de Minuit. This translation was first published in *Esquire*.

ENTER AND EXIT by Heinrich Böll, translated from the German by Leila Vennewitz. From *Absent Without Leave*. Copyright © 1965 by Heinrich Böll. Reprinted by permission of the McGraw-Hill Book Company.

POTEMKIN'S CARRIAGE PASSES THROUGH by Reinhard Lettau, translated from the German by Ursule Molinaro. From *Obstacles*. Copyright © 1965 by Random House, Inc. Reprinted by permission of Pantheon Books, a Division of Random House, Inc.

THE BOUND MAN by Ilse Aichinger, translated from the German by Eric Mosbacher. From *The Bound Man and Other Stories*. Copyright 1956 by Ilse Aichinger. Reprinted by permission of Farrar, Straus & Giroux, Inc.

RESURRECTION by Jakov Lind, translated from the German by Ralph Mannheim. From *Soul of Wood and Other Stories*. Copyright © 1964 by Jonathan Cape Ltd., London. Reprinted by permission of Grove Press, Inc.

THE PRIME OF MISS JEAN BRODIE by Muriel Spark. Copyright © 1961 by Muriel Spark. Reprinted by special arrangement with the publishers, J. B. Lippincott Company, and the author's agents, Harold Ober Associates, Incorporated. A substantial portion of this novel appeared originally in *The New Yorker*.

TOTENTANZ by Angus Wilson. From

# TO GERTRUD

# CONTENTS

JEAN-PAUL SARTRE
*The Childhood of a Leader* 9

ALBERT CAMUS
*The Renegade* 67

SAMUEL BECKETT
*Stories and Texts for Nothing, III* 80

ALAIN ROBBE-GRILLET
*The Secret Room* 84

HEINRICH BÖLL
*Enter and Exit* 89

REINHARD LETTAU
*Potemkin's Carriage Passes Through* 118

ILSE AICHINGER
*The Bound Man* 121

JAKOV LIND
*Resurrection* 133

MURIEL SPARK
*The Prime of Miss Jean Brodie* 154

ANGUS WILSON
*Totentanz* 246

DORIS LESSING
*To Room Nineteen*  262

WILLEM F. HERMANS
*The House of Refuge*  292

ALBERTO MORAVIA
*Agostino*  323

TOMMASO LANDOLFI
*Gogol's Wife*  388

RAMÓN SENDER
*The Terrace*  399

JORGE-LUIS BORGES
*Tlön, Uqbar, Orbis Tertius*  429

DAZAI OSAMU
*Villon's Wife*  443

TADEUSZ BOROWSKI
*This Way for the Gas, Ladies and Gentlemen*  458

SLAWOMIR MROZEK
*On a Journey*  474

ALEXANDER SOLZHENITSYN
*Matryona's Home*  477

# Jean-Paul Sartre

## THE CHILDHOOD OF A LEADER

"I LOOK ADORABLE in my little angel's costume." Mme. Portier told mamma: "Your little boy looks good enough to eat. He's simply adorable in his little angel's costume." M. Bouffardier drew Lucien between his knees and stroked his arm: "A real little girl," he said, smiling. "What's your name? Jacqueline, Lucienne, Margot?" Lucien turned red and said, "My name is Lucien." He was no longer quite sure about not being a little girl: a lot of people had kissed him and called him "mademoiselle," everybody thought he was so charming with his gauze wings, his long blue robe, small bare arms and blond curls: he was afraid that the people would suddenly decide he wasn't a little boy any more; he would have protested in vain, no one would listen to him, they wouldn't let him take off his dress any more except to sleep and every morning when he woke up he would find it at the foot of his bed and when he wanted to wee-wee during the day, he'd have to lift it up like Nenette and sit on his heels. Everybody would say: my sweet little darling; maybe it's happened already and I *am* a little girl; he felt so soft inside that it made him a little sick and his voice came out of his mouth like a flute and he offered flowers to everybody in rounded, curved gestures; he wanted to kiss his soft upper arm. He thought: it isn't real. He liked things that weren't real, but he had a better time on Mardi Gras: they dressed him up as Pierrot, he ran and jumped and shouted with Riri and they hid under the tables. His mother gave him a light tap with her lorgnette. "I'm proud of my little boy." She was impressive and beautiful, the fattest and biggest of all these ladies. When he passed in front of the long buffet covered with a white tablecloth, his papa, who was drinking a glass of champagne, lifted him up and said, "Little man!" Lucien felt like crying and saying, "Nah!" He asked for orangeade because it was cold and they had forbidden him to drink it. But they poured him some in a tiny glass. It had a pithy taste and wasn't as cold as they said: Lucien began to think about the orangeade with castor oil he swallowed when he was sick. He burst out sobbing and found it comforting to sit between papa and mamma in the car. Mamma pressed Lucien against her, she was hot and perfumed and all in silk. From time to time the inside of the car grew white as chalk, Lucien blinked his eyes, the violets mamma was wearing on her corsage came out of the shadows and Lucien suddenly smelled their perfume. He was still sobbing a little but he felt moist and itchy, somewhat pithy like the orangeade; he would have liked to splash in his little bathtub and have mamma wash him with the rubber sponge. They let him sleep in papa and mamma's room because he was a little baby; he laughed and made the springs of his little bed jingle and papa said, "The child is over-excited." He drank a little orange-blossom water and saw papa in shirt-sleeves.

The next day Lucien was sure he had forgotten something. He remembered the dream he had very clearly: papa and mamma were wearing angels' robes, Lucien was sitting all naked on his pot beating a drum, papa and mamma flew around him; it was a nightmare. But there had been something before the dream, Lucien must have wakened. When he tried to remember, he saw a long black tunnel lit by a small blue lamp like the night-light they turned on in his parents' room every evening. At the very bottom of this dark blue night something went past—something white. He sat on the ground at mamma's feet and took his drum. Mamma asked him, 'Why are you looking at me like that, darling?" He lowered his eyes and beat on his drum, crying, "Boom, boom, tara-boom." But when she turned her head he began to scrutinize her minutely as if he were seeing her for the first time. He recognized the blue robe with the pink stuff and the face too. Yet it wasn't the same. Suddenly he thought he had it; if he thought about it a tiny bit more, he would find what he was looking for. The tunnel lit up with a pale gray light and he could see something moving. Lucien was afraid and cried out. The tunnel disappeared. "What's the matter, little darling?" mamma asked. She was kneeling close to him and looked worried. "I'm having fun," Lucien said. Mamma smelled good but he was afraid she would touch him: she looked funny to him, papa too. He decided he would never sleep in their room any more.

Mamma noticed nothing the following day. Lucien was always under her feet, as usual, and he gossiped with her like a real little man. He asked her to tell him Little Red Ridinghood and mamma took him on her knees. She talked about the wolf and Little Red Ridinghood's grandmother, with finger raised, smiling and grave, Lucien looked at her and said, "And then what?" And sometimes he touched the little hairs on the back of her neck; but he wasn't listening, he was wondering if she were his real mother. When she finished, he said, "Mamma, tell me about when you were a little girl." And mamma told him; but maybe she was lying. Maybe she was a little boy before and they put dresses on her—like Lucien, the other night—and she kept on wearing them to act like a little girl. Gently he felt her beautiful fat arms which were soft as butter under the silk. What would happen if they took off mamma's dress and she put on papa's pants? Maybe right away she'd grow a black mustache. He clasped mamma's arms with all his might; he had a feeling she was going to be transformed into a horrible beast before his eyes—or maybe turn into a bearded lady like the one in the carnival. She laughed, opening her mouth wide, and Lucien saw her pink tongue and the back of her throat: it was dirty, he wanted to spit in it. "Hahaha!" mamma said, "how you hug me, little man, Hug me tight. As tight as you love me." Lucien took one of her lovely hands with the silver rings on it and covered it with kisses. But the next day when she was sitting near him holding his hands while he was on the pot and said to him, "Push, Lucien, push, little darling . . . please," he suddenly stopped pushing and asked her, a little breathlessly, "But you're my real mother, aren't you?" She said, "Silly," and asked him if it wasn't going to come soon. From that day Lucien was sure she was playing a joke on him and he never again told her he would marry her when he grew up. But he was not quite sure what the joke was: maybe one night in the tunnel, robbers came and took papa and mamma and put those two in their place. Or maybe it was really papa and mama but during the day they played one part and at night they were all different. Lucien was hardly surprised on Christmas Eve when he suddenly woke up and saw them putting toys in front of the fireplace. The next day they talked about Père Noël and Lucien pretended he believed them: he thought it was their role, they must have stolen the toys. He had scarlatina in February and had a lot of fun.

After he was cured, he got in the habit of playing orphan. He sat under the chestnut tree in the middle of the lawn, filling his hands with earth, and thought: I'm an orphan. I'm going to call myself Louis. I haven't eaten for six days. Germaine, the maid, called him to lunch and at table he kept on playing; papa and mamma noticed nothing. He had been picked up by robbers who wanted to make a pick-pocket out of him. After he had eaten he would run away and denounce them. He ate and drank very little; he had read in *L'Auberge de l'Ange Gardien* that the first meal of a starving man should be light. It was amusing because everybody was playing. Papa and mamma were playing papa and mamma; mamma was playing worried because her little darling wasn't eating, papa was playing at reading the paper and sometimes shaking his finger in Lucien's face saying, "Badaboom, little man!" And Lucien was playing too, but finally he didn't know at what. Orphan? Or Lucien? He looked at the water bottle. There was a little red light dancing in the bottom of the water and he would have sworn papa's hand was in the water bottle, enormous, luminous, with little black hairs on the fingers. Lucien suddenly felt that the water bottle was playing at being a water bottle. He barely touched his food and he was so hungry in the afternoon that he stole a dozen plums and almost had indigestion. He thought he had enough of playing Lucien.

Still, he could not stop himself and it seemed to him that he was always playing. He wanted to be like M. Bouffardier who was so ugly and serious. When M. Bouffardier came to dinner, he bent over mamma's hand and said, "Your servant, dear madame," and Lucien planted himself in the middle of the salon and watched him with admiration. But nothing serious happened to Lucien. When he fell down and bumped himself, he sometimes stopped crying and wondered, "Do I really hurt?" Then he felt even sadder and his tears flowed more than ever. When he kissed mamma's hand and said, "Your servant, dear madame," she rumpled his hair and said, "It isn't nice, little mouse, you mustn't make fun of grown ups," and he felt all discouraged. The only important thing she could find were the first and third Fridays of the month. Those days a lot of ladies came to see mamma and two or three were always in mourning; Lucien loved ladies in mourning especially when they had big feet. Generally, he liked grown ups because they were so respectable—and you could never imagine they forgot themselves in bed or did all the other things little boys do, because they have so many dark clothes on their bodies and you can't imagine what's underneath. When they're all together they eat everything and talk and even their laughs are serious, it's beautiful, like at mass. They treated Lucien like a grown up person. Mme. Couffin took Lucien on her lap and felt his calves, declaring, "He's the prettiest, cutest one I've seen." Then she questioned him about his likes and dislikes, kissed him and asked him what he would do when he was big. And sometimes he answered he'd be a great general like Joan of Arc and he'd take back Alsace-Lorraine from the Germans, or sometimes he wanted to be a missionary. As he spoke, he believed what he said. Mme. Besse was a large, strong woman with a slight mustache. She romped with Lucien, tickled him and called him "my little doll." Lucien was overjoyed, he laughed easily and squirmed under the ticklings; he thought he was a little doll, a charming little doll for the grown ups, and he would have liked Mme. Besse to undress him and wash him like a rubber doll and send him bye-bye in a tiny little cradle. And sometimes Mme. Besse asked, "And does my little doll talk?" and she squeezed his stomach suddenly. Then Lucien pretended to be a mechanical doll and said "Crick!" in a muffled voice and they both laughed.

The curé who came to the house every Saturday asked him if he loved his mother. Lucien adored his pretty mamma and his papa who was so strong and good. He answered "Yes," looking the curé straight in the eyes with a little air of boldness that made everybody laugh. The curé had a face like a raspberry, red and lumpy with a hair on each lump. He told Lucien it was very nice and that he should always love his mamma; then he asked who Lucien preferred, his mother or God. Lucien could not guess the answer on the spot and he began to shake his curls and stamp his feet, shouting, "Baroom, tarataraboom!" and the grown ups continued their conversation as though he did not exist. He ran to the garden and slipped out by the back door; he had brought his little reed cane with him. Naturally, Lucien was never supposed to leave the garden, it was forbidden; usually Lucien was a good little boy but that day he felt like disobeying. He looked defiantly at the big nettle patch; you could see it was a forbidden place; the wall was black, the nettles were naughty, harmful plants, a dog had done his business just at the foot of the nettles; it smelled of plants, dog dirt and hot wine. Lucien lashed at the nettles with his cane, crying, "I love my mamma, I love my mamma." He saw the broken nettles hanging sadly, oozing a white juice, their whitish, down necks had unraveled in breaking, he heard a small solitary voice which cried "I love my mamma, I love my mamma"; a big blue fly was buzzing around: a horsefly, Lucien was afraid of it—and a forbidden, powerful odor, putrid and peaceful, filled his nostrils. He repeated, "I love my mamma," but his voice seemed strange, he felt deep terror and ran back into the salon, like a flash. From that day on, Lucien understood that he did not love his mamma. He did not feel guilty but redoubled his niceties because he thought he should pretend to love his parents all his life, or else he was a naughty little boy. Mme. Fleurier found Lucien more and more tender and just then there was the war and papa went off to fight and mamma was glad, in her sorrow, that Lucien was so full of attention; in the afternoons, when she rested on her beach chair in the garden because she was so full of sorrow, he ran to get her a cushion and slipped it beneath her head or put a blanket over her legs and she protested, laughing, "But I'll be too hot, my little man, how sweet you are." He kissed her furiously, all out of breath, saying, "My own mamma," and sat down at the foot of the chestnut tree.

He said "chestnut tree" and waited. But nothing happened. Mamma was stretched out on the verandah, all tiny at the bottom of a heavy stifling silence. There was a smell of hot grass, you could play explorer in the jungle; but Lucien did not feel like playing. The air trembled about the red crest of the wall and the sunlight made burning spots on the earth and on Lucien's hands. "Chestnut tree!" It was shocking: when Lucien told mamma, "My pretty little mamma," she smiled and when he called Germaine "stinkweed" she cried and went complaining to mamma. But when he said "chestnut tree" nothing at all happened. He muttered between his teeth "Nasty old tree" and was not reassured, but since the tree did not move he repeated, louder, "Nasty old tree, nasty old chestnut tree, you wait, you just wait and see!" and he kicked it. But the tree stayed still—just as though it were made of wood. That evening at dinner Lucien told mamma, "You know, mamma, the trees, well . . . they're made out of wood," making a surprised little face which mamma liked. But Mme. Fleurier had received no mail at noon. She said dryly, "Don't act like a fool." Lucien became a little roughneck. He broke his toys to see how they were made, he whittled the arm of a chair with one of papa's old razors, he knocked down a tanagra figure in the living room to see if it were hollow and if there were anything inside; when he walked he struck the heads from plants and flowers with his cane: each time he was deeply disappointed, things were stupid, nothing really and truly existed. Often mamma showed him flowers and asked him, "What's the name of this?" But Lucien shook his head and answered, "That isn't anything, that doesn't have any name." All that wasn't worth bothering with. It was much more fun to pull the legs off a grasshopper because they throbbed between your fingers like a top and a yellow cream came out when you pressed its stomach. But even so, the grasshoppers didn't make any noise. Lucien would have liked to torture an animal that cried when it was hurt, a chicken for instance, but he didn't dare go near them. M. Fleurier came back in March because he was a manager and the general told him he would be much more useful at the head of his factory than in the trenches like just anybody. He thought Lucien had changed very much and said he didn't recognize his little man any more. Lucien had fallen into a sort of somnolence; he answered quickly, he always had a finger in his nose or else he breathed on his fingers and smelled them and he had to be begged to do his little business. Now he went alone to the bathroom; he had only to leave the door half open and from time to time mamma or Germaine came to encourage him. He stayed whole hours on the throne and once he was so bored he went to sleep. The doctor said he was growing too quickly and prescribed a tonic. Mamma wanted to teach Lucien new games but Lucien thought he played enough as it was and anyhow all games were the same, it was always the same thing. He often pouted: it was also a game and rather amusing. It hurt mamma, you felt all sad and resentful, you got a little deaf and your mouth was pursed up and your eyes misty, inside it was warm and soft like when you're under the sheets at night and smell your own odor; you were alone in the world. Lucien could no longer leave his broodings and when papa put on his mocking voice to tell him "You're going to hatch chickens" Lucien rolled on the ground and sobbed. He still went to the salon when mamma was having visitors, but since they had cut off his curls the grown ups paid less attention to him unless it was to point out a moral for him and tell him instructive stories. When his cousin Riri and Aunt Berthe, his pretty mamma, came to Férolles because of the bombings, Lucien was very glad and tried to teach him how to play. But Riri was too busy hating the Boches and he still smelled like a baby even though he was six months older than Lucien; he had freckles and didn't always understand things very well. However, Lucien confided to him that he walked in his sleep. Some people get up at night and talk and walk around still sleeping: Lucien had read that in the *Petit Explorateur* and he thought there must be a real Lucien who talked, walked, and really loved his parents at night, only as soon as morning came, he forgot everything and began to pretend to be Lucien. In the beginning Lucien only half believed this story but one day they went near the nettles and Riri showed Lucien his wee-wee and told him, "Look how big it is, I'm a big boy. When it'll be all big I'll be a man and I'll go and fight the Boches in the trenches." Lucien thought Riri was funny and he burst out laughing. "Let's see yours," Riri said. They compared and Lucien's was smaller but Riri cheated: he pulled his to make it longer. "I have the biggest," Riri said. "Yes, but I'm a sleepwalker," Lucien said calmly. Riri didn't know what a sleepwalker was and Lucien had to explain it to him. When he finished, he thought, "Then it's true I'm a sleepwalker" and he had a terrible desire to cry. Since they slept in the same bed they agreed that Riri would stay up the next night and watch Lucien when Lucien got up and remember all he said. "You wake me up after a while," Lucien said, "to see if I remember anything I did." That night Lucien, unable to sleep, heard sharp snores and had to wake up Riri. "Zanzibar!" Riri said. "Wake up, Riri, you have to watch me when I get up." "Let me sleep," Riri said in a thick pasty voice. Lucien shook him and pinched him under his shirt and Riri began to jump around and he stayed awake, his eyes open and a funny smile on his lips. Lucien thought about a bicycle his father was to buy him, he heard a train whistle and suddenly the maid came in and opened the curtains, it was eight o'clock in the morning. Lucien never knew what he did during the night. But God knew because God knew everything. Lucien knelt on the pre-dieu and forced himself to behave so that his mamma would congratulate him after mass but he hated God: God knew more about Lucien than Lucien himself. God knew that Lucien didn't love his mamma or papa and that he pretended to be good and touched his wee-wee in bed at night. Luckily, God couldn't remember everything because there were so many little boys in the world. When Lucien tapped his forehead and said "Picotin" right away God forgot everything he had seen. Lucien also undertook to persuade God that he loved his mamma. From time to time he said in his head, "How I love my dear mamma!" There was always a little corner in him which wasn't quite persuaded and of course God saw that corner. In that case, He won. But sometimes you could absorb yourself so completely in what you were saying. You said very quickly, "Oh how I love my mamma," pronouncing it carefully, and you saw mamma's face and felt all tender, you thought vaguely, vaguely, that God was watching you and afterwards you didn't think about it any more, you were all creamy with tenderness and then there were words dancing in your ears; mamma, MAMMA MAMMA. That only lasted an instant, of course, it was like Lucien trying to balance a chair on his feet. But if, just at that moment, you said "Pacota" God had lost: He had only seen Good and what He saw engraved itself in His memory forever. But Lucien tired of this game because he had to make too much effort and besides you never knew whether God had won or lost. Lucien had nothing more to do with God. When he made his first communion, the curé said he was the best behaved little boy and the most pious of all the catechism class. Lucien grasped things quickly and he had a good memory but his head was full of fog.

Sundays were a bright spot. The fog lifted when Lucien went walking with his father on the Paris road. He had on his handsome sailor suit and they met workers who saluted papa and Lucien. Papa went up to them and they said, "Good morning, Monsieur Fleurier," and also "Good morning, Master Fleurier." Lucien liked the workers because they were grown ups but not like the others. First, they called him master. And they wore caps and had short nails and big hands which always looked chapped and hurt. They were responsible and respectful. You musn't pull old Bouligaud's mustache: papa would have scolded Lucien. But when he spoke to papa, old Bouligaud took off his cap and papa and Lucien kept their hats on and papa spoke in a loud voice, smiling and somewhat testy. "So, we're waiting for our boy, are we, Bouligaud? When does he get leave?" "At the end of the month, Monsieur Fleurier, thank you, Monsieur Fleurier." Old Bouligaud looked happy and he wasn't allowed to slap Lucien on the rear and call him Toad, like M. Bouffardier. Lucien hated M. Bouffardier because he was so ugly. But when he saw old Bouligaud he felt all tender and wanted to be good. Once, coming back from the walk, papa took Lucien on his knees and explained to him what it was to be a boss. Lucien wanted to know how papa talked to the workers when he was at the factory and papa showed him how you had to do it and his voice was all changed. "Will I be a boss too?" Lucien asked. "Yes, indeed, my little man, that's what I made you for." "And who will I command?" "Well, when I'm dead you'll be the boss of my factory and you'll command my workers." "But they'll be dead too." "Well, you'll command their children and you must know how to make yourself obeyed and liked." "And how will I make myself be liked, papa?" Papa thought a little and said, "First, you must know them all by name." Lucien was deeply touched and when the foreman Morel's son came to the house to announce that his father had two fingers cut off, Lucien spoke seriously and gently with him, looking him straight in the eye and calling him Morel. Mamma said she was proud to have such a good, sensitive little boy. After that came the armistice, papa read the papers aloud every evening, everybody was talking about the Russians and the German government and reparations and papa showed Lucien the countries on the map: Lucien spent the most boring year of his life, he liked it better when the war was still going on; now everybody looked lost and the light you saw in Mme. Couffin's eyes went out. In October 1919, Mme. Fleurier made him attend the Ecole Saint-Joseph as a day student.

It was hot in Abbé Geromet's office. Lucien was standing near the abbé's armchair, he had his hands clasped behind him and was deeply bored. "Isn't mamma going to go soon?" But Mme. Fleurier had not yet thought of leaving. She was seated on the very edge of a green armchair and stretched out her ample bosom to the abbé; she spoke quickly and she had her musical voice she used when she was angry and didn't want to show it. The abbé spoke slowly and the words seemed much longer in his mouth than in other people's, you might think he was sucking them the way you suck barley sugar before swallowing it. He explained to mamma that Lucien was a good little boy and polite and a good worker but so terribly indifferent to everything and Mme. Fleurier said that she was very disappointed because she thought a change would do him good. She asked if he played, at least, during recess. "Alas, madame," the old priest answered, "even games do not seem to interest him. He is sometimes turbulent and even violent but he tires quickly; I believe he lacks perseverance." Lucien thought: they're talking about me. They were two grown ups and he was the subject of their conversation, just like the war, the German government or M. Poincaré; they looked serious and they reasoned out his case. But even this thought did not please him. His ears were full of his mother's little singing words, the sucked and sticky words of the abbé, he wanted to cry. Luckily the bell rang and they let him go. But during geography class he felt enervated and asked Abbé Jacquin permission to leave the room because he needed to move around.

First, the coolness, the solitude and the good smell of the toilet calmed him. He squatted down simply to clear his conscience but he didn't feel like it; he raised his head and began reading the inscriptions which covered the door. Someone had written in blue pencil *Barataud is a louse*. Lucien smiled: it was true, Barataud was a louse, he was small and they said he'd grow a little but not much because his father was little, almost a dwarf. Lucien wondered if Barataud had read this inscription and he thought not: otherwise it would be rubbed out. Barataud would have wet his finger and rubbed the letters until they disappeared. Lucien rejoiced a little imagining that Barataud would go to the toilet around four o'clock and that he would take down his velvet pants and read *Barataud is a louse*. Maybe he had never thought he was so small . . . Lucien promised himself to call him a louse starting the next day at recess. He got up on the right hand wall, read another inscription written in the same blue pencil: *Lucien Fleurier is a big beanpole*. He wiped it out carefully and went back to class. It's true, he thought, looking around at his schoolmates, they're all smaller than I am. He felt uncomfortable. Big beanpole. He was sitting at his little desk of holly wood. Germaine was in the kitchen, mamma hadn't come home yet. He wrote "big beanstalk" on a sheet of white paper to re-establish the spelling. But the words seemed too well known and made no effect on him. He called, "Germaine! Germaine!" "What do you want now?"

Germaine asked. "Germaine, I'd like you to write on this paper: Lucien Fleurier is a big beanpole." "Have you gone out of your mind, Monsieur Lucien?" He put his arms around her neck. "Be nice, Germaine." Germaine began to laugh and wiped her fat fingers on her apron. He did not look while she was writing, but afterwards he carried the paper to his room and studied it for a long time. Germaine's writing was pointed, Lucien thought he heard a dry voice saying in his ear: big beanpole. He thought, "I'm big." He was crushed with shame: big as Barataud was small and the others laughed behind his back. It was as if someone had cast a spell over him: until then it had seemed natural to see his friends from above. But now it seemed he had been suddenly condemned to be big for the rest of his life. That evening he asked his father if a person could shrink if he wanted to with all his might. M. Fleurier said no: all the Fleuriers had been big and strong and Lucien would grow still bigger. Lucien was without hope. After his mother tucked him in he got up and went to look at himself in the mirror. "I'm big." But he looked in vain, he could not see it, he seemed neither big nor little. He lifted up his nightshirt a little and saw his legs; then he imagined Costil saying to Hébrard: Say, look at those long beanpoles, and it made him feel funny. He was cold, he shivered and someone said, the beanpole has gooseflesh! Lucien lifted his shirttail very high and they all saw his navel and his whole business and then he ran and slipped into bed. When he put his hand under his shirt he thought that Costil saw him and was saying, Look what the big beanpole's doing! He squirmed and turned in bed, breathing heavily. Big beanpole! Big beanpole! until he made a little acid itching come beneath his fingers.

The following days, he wanted to ask the abbé's permission to sit in the rear of the class. It was because of Boisset, Winckelmann and Costil who were behind him and could look at the back of his neck. Lucien felt the back of his neck but he could not see it and often even forgot about it. But while he was answering the abbé as well as he could and was reciting the tirade from *Don Diego*, the others were behind him watching the back of his neck and they could be laughing and thinking, "How thin he is, he has two cords in his neck." Lucien forced himself to make his voice swell and express the humiliation of Don Diego. He could do what he wanted with his voice; but the back of his neck was always there, peaceful, inexpressive, like someone resting and Boisset saw it. He dared not change his seat because the last row was reserved for the dunces, but the back of his neck and his shoulder blades were constantly itching and he was obliged to scratch unceasingly. Lucien invented a new game: in the morning, when he took his bath, he imagined someone was watching him through the keyhole, sometimes Costil, sometimes old Bouligaud, sometimes Germaine. Then he turned all around for them to see him from all sides and sometimes he turned his rear toward the door, going down on all fours so that it would look all plump and ridiculous; M. Bouffardier was coming on tiptoe to give him an enema. One day when he was in the bathroom he heard sounds; it was Germaine rubbing polish on the buffet in the hall. His heart stopped beating, he opened the door quietly and went out, his trousers round his heels, his shirt rolled up around his back. He was obliged to make little hops in order to go forward without losing his balance. Germaine looked at him calmly: "What are you doing, running a sack race?" she asked. Enraged, he pulled up his trousers and ran and threw himself on his bed. Mme. Fleurier was heartbroken. She often told her husband, "He was so graceful when he was little and now look how awkward he is, if that isn't a shame." M. Fleurier glanced carelessly at Lucien and answered, "It's his age." Lucien did not know what to do with his body; no matter what he did, he felt this body existing on all sides at once, without consulting him. Lucien indulged himself by imagining he was invisible and then he took the habit of looking through keyholes to see how the others were made without their knowing it. He saw his mother while she was washing. She was seated on the *bidet,* she seemed asleep and she had surely forgotten her body and her face, because she thought that no one saw her. The sponge went back and forth by itself over this abandoned flesh; she moved lazily and he felt she was going to stop somewhere along the way. Mamma rubbed a washcloth with a piece of soap and her hand disappeared between her legs. Her face was restful, almost sad, surely she was thinking of something else, about Lucien's education or M. Poincaré. But during this time she *was* this gross pink mass, this voluminous body hanging over the porcelain *bidet.* Another time, Lucien removed his shoes and climbed all the way up to the eaves. He saw Germaine. She had on a long green chemise which fell to her feet, she was combing her hair before a small round mirror and she smiled softly at her image. Lucien began to laugh uncontrolledly and had to climb down hurriedly. After that he smiled and made faces at himself in front of the mirror in the salon and after a moment was seized with terrible fears.

Lucien finally went completely asleep but no one noticed except Mme. Couffin who called him her sleeping beauty; a great air bubble he could neither swallow nor spit out was always in his half open mouth: it was his *yawning;* when he was alone the bubble grew larger, caressing his palate and tongue; his mouth opened wide and tears ran down his cheeks: these were very pleasant moments. He did not amuse himself as much in the bathroom but to make up for it he liked very much to sneeze, it woke him up and for an instant he looked around him, exhilarated, then dozed off again. He learned to recognize different sorts of sleep: in winter, he sat before the fireplace and stretched his head toward the blaze; when it was quite red and roasted it suddenly emptied; he called that "head sleeping." Sunday morning, on the other hand, he went to sleep by the feet: he got into his bath, slowly lowered himself and sleep climbed in ripples all along his legs and thighs. Above the sleeping body, all white and swollen like a stewed chicken at the bottom of the water, a little blond head was enthroned, full of wise words, templum, templi, templo, iconoclasts. In class sleep was white and riddled with flashes: First: Lucien Fleurier. "What was the third estate? Nothing." First, Lucien Fleurier, second, Winckelmann, Pellereau was first in algebra; he had only one testicle, the other one hadn't come down; he made them pay two sous to see and ten to touch. Lucien gave the ten sous, hesitated, stretched out his hand and left without touching, but afterwards his regrets were so great that sometimes they kept him awake for more than an hour. He was less good in geology than in history. First, Winckelmann, second, Fleurier. On Sundays he went bicycling with Costil and Winckelmann. Through russet, heat-crushed countrysides, the bicycles skidded in the marrowy dust; Lucien's legs were active and muscular but the sleepy odor of the roads went to his head, he bent over the handlebars, his eyes grew pink and half closed. He won the honor prize three times in a row. They gave him *Fabiola, or The Church in the Catacombs,* the *Génie du Christianisme* and the *Life of Cardinal Lavigerie.* Costil, back from the long vacation, taught them all *De Profondis Morpionibus* and the *Artilleur de Metz.* Lucien decided to do better and consulted his father's *Larousse Medical Dictionary* on the article "Uterus," then he explained to them how women were made, he even made a sketch on the board and Costil declared it disgusting: but after that they could hear no mention of "tubes" without bursting out laughing and Lucien thought with satisfaction that in all of France you couldn't find a second class student and perhaps even a rhetoric student who knew female organs as well as he.

It was like a flash of magnesium when the Fleuriers moved to Paris. Lucien could no longer sleep because of the movies, cars and streets. He learned to distinguish a Voisin from a Packard, a Hispano-Suiza from a Rolls and he spoke frequently of cars. He had been wearing long pants for more than a year. His father sent him to England as a reward for his success in the first part of the baccalaureate; Lucien saw plains swollen with water and white cliffs, he boxed with John Latimer and learned the over-arm stroke, but, one fine day, he woke up to find himself asleep, it had come back; he went somnolently back to Paris. The elementary mathematics class in the Lycée Condorcet had thirty-seven pupils. Eight of these pupils said they knew all about women and called the others virgins. The Enlightened scorned Lucien until the first of November, but on All Saint's Day Lucien went walking with Garry, the most experienced of all of them, and negligently showed him proof of such anatomical knowledge that Garry was astonished. Lucien did not enter the group of the Enlightened because his parents did not allow him out at night, but he had a deeper and deeper understanding.

On Thursday, Aunt Berthe and Riri came to lunch at Rue Raynouard. She had grown enormous and sad and spent her time sighing; but since her skin had remained very fine and white, Lucien would have liked to see her naked. He thought about it that night in bed; it would be a winter day, in the Bois de Boulogne, he would come upon her naked in a copse, her arms crossed on her breast, shivering with gooseflesh. He imagined that a nearsighted passer-by touched her with his cane and said, "Well, what can that be?" Lucien did not get along too well with his cousin: Riri had become a very handsome young man, a little too elegant. He was taking philosophy at Lakanal and understood nothing of mathematics. Lucien could not keep himself from thinking that Riri, seven years ago, still did number two in his pants and after that walked with his legs wide apart like a duck and looked at his mother with candid eyes, saying, "No, mamma, I didn't do it, I promise." And he had some repugnance about touching Riri's hand. Yet he was very nice to him and explained his mathematics course; sometimes he had to make a great effort not to lose patience because Riri was not very intelligent. But he never let himself be carried away and always kept a calm, poised voice. Mme. Fleurier thought Lucien had much tact but Aunt Berthe showed him no gratitude. When Lucien proposed to give Riri a lesson she blushed a little, moved about on her chair, saying, "No, you're very kind, my little Lucien, but Riri is too big a boy. He can if he wants; but he must not get in the habit of counting on others." One night Mme. Fleurier told Lucien brusquely, "You think Riri's grateful for what you're doing for him? Well, don't kid yourself, my boy: he thinks you're stuck-up, your Aunt Berthe told me so." She had assumed her musical voice and familiar air; Lucien realized she was mad with rage. He felt vaguely intrigued but could find nothing to answer. The next day and the day after that he had a lot of work and the whole episode left his mind.

Sunday morning he set his pen down brusquely and wondered "Am I stuck-up?" It was eleven o'clock; sitting in his study Lucien watched the pink cretonne designs of the curtains which lined the walls; on his left cheek he felt the dry and dusty warmth of the first April sunlight, on his right cheek he felt the heavy, stifling heat of the radiator. "Am I stuck-up?" It was hard to answer, Lucien first tried to remember his last conversation with Riri and to judge his own attitude impartially. He had bent over Riri and smiled at him, saying, "You get it? If you don't catch on, don't be afraid to say so, and we'll start over." A little later he had made an error in a delicate problem and said, gaily, "That's one on me." It was an expression he had taken from M. Fleurier which amused him: "But was I stuck-up when I said that?" By dint of searching, he suddenly made something round and white appear, soft as a bit of cloud: it was his thought of the other day: he had said "Do you get it?" and it was in his head but it couldn't be described. Lucien made desperate efforts to *look* at this bit of cloud and he suddenly felt as though he were falling into it head first, he found himself in the mist and became mist himself, he was no more than a damp white warmth which smelled of linen. He wanted to tear himself from this mist and come back but it came with him. He thought, "I'm Lucien Fleurier, I'm in my room, I'm doing a problem in physics, it's Sunday." But his thoughts melted into banks of white fog. He shook himself and began counting the cretonne characters, two shepherdesses, two shepherds and Cupid. Then suddenly he told himself, "I am . . ." and there was a slight click: he had awakened from his long somnolence.

It was not pleasant. The shepherds had jumped back, it seemed to Lucien that he was looking at them from the wrong end of a telescope. In place of his stupor so sweet to him and which lost itself in its own folds, there was now a small, wideawake perplexity which wondered, "Who am I?"

"Who am I? I look at the bureau, I look at the notebook. My name is Lucien Fleurier but that's only a name. I'm stuck-up. I'm not stuck-up. I don't know, but it doesn't make sense."

"I'm a good student. No. That's a lie: a good student likes to work—not me. I have good marks but I don't like to work. I don't hate it, either, I don't give a damn. I don't give a damn about anything. I'll never be a boss." He thought with anguish, "But what will I be?" A moment passed; he scratched his cheek and shut his left eye because the sun was in it: "What am I, I . . . ?" There was this fog rolling back on itself, indefinite. "I!" He looked into the distance; the word rang in his head and then perhaps it was possible to make out something, like the top of a pyramid whose side vanished, far off, into the fog. Lucien shuddered and his hands trembled. "Now I have it!" he thought, "now I have it! I was sure of it: I *don't exist!*"

During the months that followed, Lucien often tried to go back to sleep but did not succeed: he slept well and regularly nine hours a night and the rest of the time was more lively and more and more perplexed: his parents said he had never been so healthy. When he happened to think he did not have the stuff to make a boss he felt romantic and wanted to walk for hours under the moon; but his parents still did not allow him out at night. Often, then, he would stretch out on his bed and take his temperature: the thermometer showed 98.6 or 98.7 and Lucien thought with bitter pleasure that his parents found him looking fine. "I don't exist." He closed his eyes and let himself drift: "Existence is an illusion because I *know* I don't exist, all I have to do is plug my ears and not think about anything and I'll become nothingness." But the illusion was tenacious. Over other people, at least, he had the malicious superiority of possessing a secret: Garry, for instance, didn't exist any more than Lucien. But it was enough to see him snoring tempestuously in the midst of his admirers: you could see right away he thought his own existence as solid as iron. Neither did M. Fleurier exist—nor Riri—nor anyone— the world was a comedy without actors. Lucien, who had been given an "A" for his dissertation on "Morality and Science," dreamed of writing a "Treatise on Nothingness" and he imagined that people, reading it, would disappear one after the other like vampires at cockcrow. Before beginning this treatise, he wanted the advice of The Baboon, his philosophy prof. "Excuse me, sir," he said at the end of a class, "could anyone claim that we don't exist?" The Baboon said no. "Goghito," he said, "ergo zum. You exist because you doubt your existence." Lucien was not convinced but he gave up his work. In July, he was given, without fanfare, his baccalaureate in mathematics and left for Férolles with his parents. The perplexity still did not leave him: it was like wanting to sneeze.

Old Bouligaud had died and the mentality of M. Fleurier's workers had changed a lot. Now they were drawing large salaries and their wives bought silk stockings. Mme. Bouffardier cited frightful examples to Mme. Fleurier: "My maid tells me she saw that little Ansiaume girl in the cook-shop. She's the daughter of one of your husband's best workers, the one we took care of when she lost her mother. She married a fitter from Beaupertuis. Well, she ordered a twenty-franc chicken. And so arrogant! Nothing's good enough for them: they want to have everything we have." Now, when Lucien took short Sunday walks with his father, the workers barely touched their caps on seeing them and there were even some who crossed over so as not to salute them. One day Lucien met Bouligaud's son who did not even seem to recognize him. Lucien was a little excited about it: here was a chance to prove himself a boss. He threw an eagle eye on Jules Bouliguad and went toward him, his hands behind his back. But Bouligaud did not seem intimidated: he turned vacant eyes to Lucien and passed by him, whistling. "He didn't recognize me," Lucien told himself. But he was deeply disappointed and, in the following days, thought more than ever that the world did not exist.

Mme. Fleurier's little revolver was put away in the left hand drawer of her dressing table. Her husband made her a present of it in September 1914 before he left for the front. Lucien took it and turned it around in his hand for a long while: it was a little jewel, with a gilded barrel and a butt inlaid with mother of pearl. He could not rely on a philosophical treatise to persuade people they did not exist. Action was needed, a really desperate act which would dissolve appearances and show the nothingness of the world in full light. A shot, a young body bleeding on the carpet, a few words scribbled on a piece of paper: "I kill myself because I do not exist. And you too, my brothers, you are nothingness!" People would read the newspaper in the morning and would see "An adolescent has dared"; And each would feel himself terribly troubled and would wonder, "And what about me? Do I exist?" There had been similar epidemics of suicide in history, among others after the publication of *Werther*. Lucien thought how "martyr" in Greek meant "witness." He was too sensitive for a boss but not for a martyr. As a result, he often entered his mother's room and looked at the revolver; he was filled with agony. Once he even bit the gilded barrel, gripping his fingers tightly around the butt. The rest of the time he was very gay for he thought that all true leaders had known the temptation of suicide. Napoleon, for example. Lucien did not hide from himself the fact that he was touching the depths of despair but he hoped to leave this crisis with a tempered soul and he read the *Mémorial de Sainte-Hélène* with interest. Yet he had to make a decision: Lucien set the 30th of September as the end of his hesitations. The last days were extremely difficult: surely the crisis was salutary, but it required of Lucien a tension so strong that he thought he would break one day like a glass. He no longer dared to touch the revolver; he contented himself with opening the drawer, lifting up his mother's slips a little and studying at great length the icy, headstrong little monster which rested in a hollow of pink silk. Yet he felt a sharp disappointment when he decided to live and found himself completely unoccupied. Fortunately, the multiple cares of going back to school absorbed him: his parents sent him to the Lycée Saint-Louis to take preparatory courses for the Ecole Centrale. He wore a fine red-bordered cap with an insignia and sang:

> *C'est le piston qui fait marcher les machines*
> *C'est le piston qui fait marcher les wagons . . .*

This new dignity of *piston* filled Lucien with pride; and then his class was not like the others: it had traditions and a ceremonial; it was a force. For instance, it was the usual thing at the end of the French class for a voice to ask, "What's a *cyrard?*" and everybody answered softly, "A *con!*" After which the voice repeated, "What's an *agro?*" and they answered a little louder, "A *con!*" Then M. Béthune, who was almost blind and wore dark glasses, said wearily, "Please, gentlemen!" There were a few moments of absolute silence and the students looked at each other with smiles of intelligence, then someone shouted, "What's a *piston?*" and they all roared, "A great man!" At those times Lucien felt galvanized. In the evening he told his parents the various incidents of the day in great detail and when he said, "Then the whole class started laughing . . ." or "the whole class decided to put Meyrinez in quarantine" the words, in passing, warmed his mouth like a drink of liquor. Yet the first months were very hard: Lucien missed his math and physics and then, individually, his schoolmates were not too sympathetic: they were on scholarships, mostly grinds untidy and ill-mannered. "There isn't one," he told his father, "I could make a friend of." "Young men on scholarships," M. Fleurier said dreamily, "represent an intellectual elite and yet they're poor leaders: they have missed one thing." Hearing him talk about "poor leaders," Lucien felt a disagreeable pinching in his heart and again thought of killing himself during the weeks that followed, but he had not the same enthusiasm as he had during vacation. In January, a new student named Berliac scandalized the whole class: he wore coats ringed in green or purple, in the latest styles, little round collars and trousers that are seen in tailor's engravings, so narrow that one wondered how he could even get into them. From the beginning, he was classed last in mathematics. "I don't give a damn," he said, "I'm literary, I take math to mollify myself." After a month he had won everyone's heart: he distributed contraband cigarettes and told them he had women and showed letters they sent him. The whole class decided he was all right and it would be best to let him alone. Lucien greatly admired his elegance and manners, but Berliac treated Lucien with condescension and called him a "rich kid." "After all," Lucien said one day, "it's better than being a poor kid." Berliac smiled. "You're a little cynic!" he told him and the next day he let him read one of his poems: "Caruso gobbled raw eyes every evening, otherwise he was sober as a camel. A lady made a bouquet with the eyes of her family and threw it on the stage. Everyone bows before this exemplary gesture. But do not forget that her hour of glory lasts only twenty-seven minutes: precisely from the first bravo to the extinction of the great chandelier in the Opera (after that she must keep her husband on a leash, winner of several contests, who filled the pink cavities of his orbits with two croix-de-guerre). And note well: all those among us who eat too much canned human flesh shall perish with scurvy." "It's very good," Lucien said, taken aback. "I get them by a new technique called automatic writing." Some time later Lucien had a violent desire to kill himself and decided to ask Berliac's advice. "What must I do?" he asked after he had explained the case. Berliac listened attentively; he was in the habit of sucking his fingers and then coating the pimples on his face with saliva, so that his skin glistened in spots like a road after a rainstorm. "Do what you want," he said, "it makes absolutely no difference." Lucien was a little disappointed but he realized Berliac had been profoundly touched when he asked Lucien to have tea with his mother the next Thursday. Mme. Berliac was very friendly; she had warts and a wine-colored birthmark on her left cheek: "You see," Berliac told Lucien, "we are the real victims of the war." That was also the opinion of Lucien and they agreed that they both belonged to the same sacrificed generation. Night fell, Berliac was lying on his bed, his hands knotted behind his head. They smoked English cigarettes, played phonograph records and Lucien heard the voices of Sophie Tucker and Al Jolson. They grew melancholy and Lucien thought Berliac was his best friend. Berliac asked him if he knew about psychoanalysis; his voice was serious and he looked at Lucien with gravity. "I desired my mother until I was fifteen," he confided. Lucien felt uncomfortable; he was afraid of blushing and remembered Mme. Berliac's moles and could not understand how anyone could desire her. Yet when she came to bring them toast, he was vaguely troubled and tried to imagine her breasts through the yellow sweater she wore. When she left, Berliac said in a positive voice, "Naturally, you've wanted to sleep with your mother too." He did not question, he affirmed. Lucien shrugged. "Naturally," he said. The next day he was worried, he was afraid Berliac would repeat their conversation. But he reassured himself quickly: After all, he thought, he's compromised himself more than I. He was quite taken by the scientific turn their confidences had taken and on the following Thursday he read a book on dreams by Freud he found in the Sainte-Geneviève Library. It was a revelation. "So that's it," Lucien repeated, roaming the streets, "so that's it." Next he bought *Introduction to Psychoanalysis* and *Psychopathology of Everyday Life*, and everything became clear to him. This strange feeling of not existing, this long emptiness in his conscience, his somnolence, his perplexities, his vain efforts to know himself which met only a curtain of fog . . . "My God," he thought, "I have a complex." He told Berliac how he was when he was a child, imagining he was a sleepwalker and how objects never seemed quite real to him. "I must have," he concluded, "a very extraordinary complex." "Just like me," said Berliac, "we both have terrific complexes!" They got the habit of interpreting their dreams and their slightest gestures; Berliac always had so many stories to tell that Lucien suspected him of inventing them, or at least enlarging them. But they got along well and approached the most delicate subjects with objectivity; they confessed to each other that they wore a mask of gaiety to deceive their associates but at heart were terribly tormented. Lucien was freed from his worries. He threw himself greedily into psychoanalysis because he realized it was something that agreed with him and now he felt reassured, he no longer needed to worry or to be always searching his conscience for palpable manifestations of his character. The true Lucien was deeply buried in his subconscious; he had to dream of him without ever seeing him, as an absent friend. All day Lucien thought of his complexes and with a certain pride he imagined the obscure world, cruel and violent, that rumbled beneath the mists of his consciousness. "You understand," he told Berliac, "in appearance I was a sleepy kid, indifferent to everything, somebody not too interesting. And even inside, you know, it seemed to be so much like that that I almost let myself be caught. But I knew there was something else." "There's *always* something else." Berliac answered. They smiled proudly at each other, Lucien wrote a poem called *When the Fog Lifts* and Berliac found it excellent, but he reproached Lucien for having written it in regular verse. Still, they learned it by heart and when they wished to speak of their libidos they said willingly, "The great crabs wrapped in the mantle of fog," then simply "Crabs," winking an eye.

But after a while Lucien, when he was alone at night, began to find all that a little terrifying. He no longer dared look his mother in the face and when he kissed her before going to bed he was afraid some shadowy power would deviate his kiss and drop it on Mme. Fleurier's mouth, it was as if he carried a volcano within himself. Lucien treated himself with caution in order not to violate the sumptuous, sinister soul he had discovered. Now he knew the price of everything and dreaded the terrible awakening. "I'm afraid of myself," he said. For six months he had renounced solitary practices because they annoyed him and he had too much work but he returned to them: everyone had to follow their bents, the books of Freud were filled with stories of unfortunate young people who became neurotic because they broke too quickly with their habits. "Are we going to go crazy?" he asked Berliac. And in fact, on certain Thursdays they felt strange; shadows had cunningly slipped into Berliac's room, they smoked whole packs of scented cigarettes, and their hands trembled. Then one of them would rise without a word, tiptoe to the door and turn the switch. A yellow light flooded the room and they looked at each other with defiance.

Lucien was not late in noticing that his friendship with Berliac was based on a misunderstanding; surely no one was more sensitive than he to the pathetic beauty of the Oedipus complex but in it he saw especially the sign of a power for passion which later he would like to use toward different ends. On the other hand, Berliac seemed to be content with his state and had no desire to leave it. "We're screwed," he said proudly, "we're flops. We'll never do anything." "Never anything," Lucien answered in echo. But he was furious. After Easter vacation Berliac told him he had shared his mother's room in a hotel in Dijon: he had risen very early in the morning, went to the bed on which his mother still was sleeping and gently lifted up the covers. "Her nightgown was up," he grinned. Hearing these words, Lucien could not keep himself from scorning Berliac a little and he felt quite alone. It was fine to have complexes but you had to know how to get rid of them eventually. How would a man be able to assume responsibilities and take command if he still had an infantile sexuality? Lucien began to worry seriously: he would have liked to take the advice of some competent person but he did not know whom to see. Berliac often spoke to him about a surrealist named Bergère who was well versed in psychoanalysis and who seemed to have a great ascendancy over him; but he had never offered to introduce him to Lucien. Lucien was also very disappointed because he had counted on Berliac to get women for him; he thought that the possession of a pretty mistress would naturally change the course of his ideas. But Berliac spoke no more of his lady friends. Sometimes they went along the boulevards and followed women, never daring to speak to them: "What do you expect, old man," Berliac said, "we aren't the kind that pleases. Women feel something frightening in us." Lucien did not answer; Berliac began to annoy him. He often made jokes in very bad taste about Lucien's parents, he called them M. and Mme. Dumollet. Lucien understood very well that a surrealist scorned the bourgeoisie in general, but Berliac had been invited several times by Mme. Fleurier who had treated him with confidence and friendship: lacking gratitude, a simple attention to decency would have kept him from speaking of her in that manner. And then Berliac was terrible with his mania for borrowing money and never returning it, in a café he only proposed to pay the round once out of five. Lucien told him plainly one day that he didn't understand, and that, between friends, they should share all expenses. Berliac looked at him deeply and said, "I thought so: you're an anal," and he explained the Freudian relation to him; feces equal gold and the Freudian theory of guilt. "I'd like to know one thing," he said, "until what age did your mother wipe you?" They almost fought.

From the beginning of May, Berliac began to cut school: Lucien went to him after class, in a bar on Rue des Petits-Champs where they drank Crucifix Vermouths. One Tuesday afternoon Lucien found Berliac sitting in front of an empty glass. "Oh, there you are," Berliac said. "Listen, I've got to beat it, I have an appointment with the dentist at five. Wait for me, he lives near here and it'll only take a half hour." "OK," Lucien answered, dropping into a chair. "François, give me a white vermouth." Just then a man came into the bar and smiled surprisedly at seeing them. Berliac blushed and got up hurriedly. "Who can that be?" Lucien wondered. Berliac, shaking hands with the stranger, stood so as to hide Lucien; he spoke in a low, rapid voice, the other answered clearly, "Indeed not, my friend, you'll always be a fool." At the same time he raised himself on tiptoe and looked at Lucien over Berliac's head with calm assurance. He could have been thirty-five; he had a pale face and magnificent white hair: "It's surely Bergère," Lucien thought, his heart pounding, "how handsome he is."

Berliac had taken the man with white hair by the elbow with an air of timid authority.

"Come with me," he said, "I'm going to the dentist, just across the way."

"But you were with a friend, weren't you," the other answered, his eyes not leaving Lucien's face. "You should introduce us."

Lucien got up, smiling. "Caught!" he thought; his cheeks were burning. Berliac's neck disappeared into his shoulders and for a second Lucien thought he was going to refuse. "So introduce me," he said gaily. But as soon as he had spoken the blood rushed to his temples and he wished the ground would swallow him. Berliac turned around and without looking at anyone muttered, "Lucien Fleurier, a friend from the lycée, Monsieur Achille Bergère."

"I admire your works," Lucien said feebly. Bergère took his hand in his own long, delicate fingers and motioned him to sit down. Bergère enveloped Lucien with a tender, warm look; he was still holding his hand. "Are you worried?" he asked gently.

"I am worried," he answered distinctly. It seemed he had just undergone the trials of an initiation. Berliac hesitated an instant then angrily sat down again, throwing his hat on the table. Lucien burned with a desire to tell Bergère of his attempted suicide; this was someone to whom one had to speak of things abruptly and without preparation. He dared not say anything because of Berliac; he hated Berliac.

"Do you have any *raki?*" Bergère asked the waiter.

"No, they don't" Berliac said quickly. "It's a nice little place but all they have to drink is vermouth."

"What's that yellow stuff you have in the bottle?" Bergère asked with an ease full of softness.

"White Crucifix," the waiter answered.

"All right, I'll have some of that."

Berliac squirmed on his chair: he seemed caught between a desire to show off his friends and the fear of making Lucien shine at his expense. Finally, he said, in a proud and dismal voice, "He wanted to kill himself."

"My God!" Bergère said, "I should hope so!"

There was another silence: Lucien had lowered his eyes modestly but he wondered if Berliac wasn't soon going to clear out: Bergère suddenly looked at his watch. "What about your dentist?" he asked.

Berliac rose ungraciously. "Come with me, Bergère," he begged, "it isn't far."

"No, you'll be back. I'll keep your friend company."

Berliac stayed for another moment, shifting from one foot to the other.

"Go on," Bergère said imperiously. "You meet us here."

When Berliac had gone, Bergère got up and sat next to Lucien. Lucien told him of his suicide at great length; he also explained to him that he had desired his mother and that he was a sadico-anal and that fundamentally he didn't love anything and that everything in him was a comedy. Bergère listened without a word, watching him closely, and Lucien found it delicious to be understood. When he finished, Bergère passed his arm familiarly around his shoulders and Lucien smelled a scent of eau-de-cologne and English tobacco.

"Do you know, Lucien, how I would describe your condition?" Lucien looked at Bergère hopefully; he was not disappointed.

"I call it," Bergère said, "Disorder."

Disorder: the word had begun tender and white as moonlight but the final "order" had the coppered flash of a trumpet.

"Disorder," Lucien said.

He felt as grave and uneasy as the time he told Riri he was a sleepwalker. The bar was dark but the door opened wide on the street, on the luminous springtime mist; under the discreet perfume Bergère gave off, Lucien perceived the heavy odor of the obscure room, an odor of red wine and damp wood. "Disorder," he thought; "what good will that do me?" He did not know whether a dignity or new sickness had been discovered in him; near his eyes he saw the quick lips of Bergère veiling and unveiling incessantly the sparkle of a gold tooth.

"I like people in disorder," Bergère said, "and I think you are extraordinarily lucky. For after all, that has been given you. You see all these swine? They're pedestrian. You'd have to give them to the red ants to stir them up a little. Do you know they have the consciousness of beasts?"

"They eat men," Lucien said.

"Yes, they strip skeletons of their human meat."

"I see," Lucien said. He added, "And I? What must I do?"

"Nothing, for God's sake," Bergère said with a look of comic fear. "Above all, don't sit down. Unless," he said, laughing, "it's on a tack. Have you read Rimbaud?"

"N-no," Lucien said.

"I'll lend you *The Illuminations*. Listen, we must see each other again. If you're free Thursday, stop in and see me around three, I live in Montparnasse, 9 Rue Campagne-Première."

The next Thursday Lucien went to see Bergère and he went back almost every day throughout May. They agreed to tell Berliac that they saw each other once a week, because they wanted to be frank with him and yet avoid hurting his feelings. Berliac showed himself to be completely out of sorts; he asked Lucien, grinning, "So, are you going steady? He gave you the worry business and you gave him the suicide business: a great game, what?" Lucien protested, "I'd like to have you know that it was you who talked about my suicide first." "Oh," Berliac said, "it was only to spare you the shame of telling it yourself." Their meetings became more infrequent. "Everything I liked about him," Lucien told Bergère one day, "he borrowed from you, I realize it now." "Berliac is a monkey," Bergère said, laughing, "that's what always attracted me. Did you know his maternal grandmother was a Jewess? That explains a lot of things." "Rather," Lucien answered. After an instant he added, "Besides, he's very charming." Bergère's apartment was filled with strange and comical objects: hassocks whose red velvet seats rested on the legs of painted wooden women, Negro statuettes, a studded chastity belt of forged iron, plaster breasts in which little spoons had been planted, on the desk a gigantic bronze louse and a monk's skull stolen from the Mistra Ossuary served as paper weights. The walls were papered with notices announcing the death of the surrealist Bergère. In spite of all this, the apartment gave the impression of intelligent comfort and Lucien liked to stretch out on the deep divan in the den. What particularly surprised Lucien was the enormous quantity of practical jokes Bergère had accumulated on a shelf: solid liquids, sneezing powder, floating sugar, an imitation turd and a bride's garter. While Bergère spoke, he took the artificial turd between his fingers and considered it with gravity. "These jokes," he said, "have a revolutionary value. They disturb. There is more destructive power in them than in all the works of Lenin." Lucien, surprised and charmed, looked by turns at this handsome tormented face with hollow eyes and these long delicate fingers gracefully holding a perfectly imitated excrement. Bergère often spoke of Rimbaud and the "systematic disordering of all the senses." "When you will be able, in crossing the Place de la Concorde, to see distinctly and at will a kneeling Negress sucking the obelisk, you will be able to tell yourself that you have torn down the scenery and you are saved." He lent him *The Illuminations*, the *Chants de Maldoror* and the works of the Marquis de Sade. Lucien tried conscientiously to understand them, but many things escaped him and he was shocked because Rimbaud was a pederast. He told Bergère who began to laugh. "Why not, my little friend?" Lucien was very embarrassed. He blushed and for a minute began to hate Bergère with all his might, but he mastered it, raised his head and said with simple frankness, "I'm talking nonsense." Bergère stroked his hair; he seemed

moved; "These great eyes full of trouble," he said, "these doe's eyes
. . . Yes, Lucien, you talked nonsense. Rimbaud's pederasty is the
first and genial disordering of his sensitivity. We owe his poems to it.
To think that there are specific objects of sexual desire and that these
objects are women because they have a hole between their legs, is the
hideous and willful error of the pedestrian. Look!" He took from his
desk a dozen yellowing photos and threw them on Lucien's knees,
Lucien gazed on horrible naked whores, laughing with toothless
mouths, spreading their legs like lips and darting between their thighs
something like a mossy tongue. "I got the collection for three
francs at Bou-Saada," Bergère said. "If you kiss the behind of one of
those women, you're a regular guy and everybody will say you're a
he-man. Because they're women, do you understand? I tell you the
first thing to convince yourself of is that *everything* can be an object
of sexual desire, a sewing machine, a measuring glass, a horse or a
shoe. I," he smiled, "have made love with flies. I know a marine who
used to sleep with ducks. He put the head in a drawer, held them
firmly by the feet and hoop-la!" Bergère pinched Lucien's ear dis-
tractedly and concluded, "The duck died and the battalion ate it."
Lucien emerged from these conversations with his face on fire, he
thought Bergère was a genius but sometimes he woke up at night,
drenched in sweat, his head filled with monstrous obscene visions
and he wondered if Bergère was a good influence on him. "To be
alone," he cried, wringing his hands, "to have no one to advise me, to
tell me if I'm on the right path." If he went to the very end, if he
really practiced the disordering of the senses, would he lose his foot-
ing and drown? One day Bergère had spoken to him of André
Breton: Lucien murmured, as if in a dream, "Yes, but afterwards, if I
could never come back." Bergère started. "Come back? Who's talking about coming back? If you go insane, so much the better. After
that, as Rimbaud says, '*viendront d'autres horribles travailleurs*.' "
"That's what I thought," Lucien said sadly. He had noticed that
these long chats had the opposite effect from the one wished for by
Bergère: as soon as Lucien caught himself showing the beginnings of
a fine sensation or an original impression, he began to tremble: "Now
it's starting," he thought. He would willingly have wished to have
only the most banal, stupid perception; he only felt comfortable in
the evenings with his parents: that was his refuge. They talked about
Briand, the bad faith of the Germans, of cousin Jeanne's confine-
ments, and the cost of living; Lucien voluptuously exchanged good
common-sense with them. One day after leaving Bergère, he was
entering his room and mechanically locked the door and slid the bolt.

When he noticed this gesture he forced himself to laugh at it but that night he could not sleep; he had just understood he was afraid.

However, nothing in the world would have stopped him from seeing Bergère. "He fascinates me," he told himself. And then he had a lively appreciation of the friendship so delicate and so particular which Bergère had been able to establish between them. Without dropping a virile, almost rude tone of voice, Bergère had the artistry to make Lucien feel, and, in a way of speaking, touch his tenderness: for instance, he reknotted his tie and scolded him for being so untidy, he combed his hair with a gold comb from Cambodia. He made Lucien discover his own body and explained to him the harsh and pathetic beauty of Youth: "You are Rimbaud," he told him, "he had your big hands when he came to Paris to see Verlaine. He had this pink face of a young healthy peasant and this long slim body of a fair-haired girl." He made Lucien unbutton his collar and open his shirt, then led him, confused, before a mirror and made him admire the charming harmony of his red cheeks and white throat; then he caressed Lucien's hips with a light hand and added, sadly, "We should kill ourselves at twenty." Often now, Lucien looked at himself in mirrors and he learned to enjoy his awkward grace. "I am Rimbaud," he thought, in the evenings, removing his clothing with gestures full of gentleness, and he began to believe that he would have the short and tragic life of a too-beautiful flower. At these times, it seemed to him that he had known, long before, similar impressions and an absurd image came to his mind: he saw himself again, small, with a long robe and angel's wings, distributing flowers at a charity sale. He looked at his long legs. "Is it true I have such a soft skin?" he thought with amusement. And once he ran his lips over his forearm from the wrist to the elbow, along a charming blue vein.

One day, he had an unpleasant surprise going to Bergère's: Berliac was there, busy cutting with a knife fragments of a blackish substance that looked like a clod of earth. The two young people had not seen each other for ten days: they shook hands coldly. "See that?" Berliac said. "That's hasheesh. We're going to put it in these pipes, between two layers of light tobacco, it gives a surprising effect. There's some for you," he added. "No, thanks," Lucien said, "I don't care for it." The other two laughed and Berliac insisted, looking ugly: "But you're crazy, old man, you've got to take some. You can't imagine how pleasant it is." "I told you no," Lucien said. Berliac said no more, merely smiled with a superior air and Lucien saw Bergère was smiling too. He tapped his foot and said, "I don't want any, I don't want to knock myself out, I think it's crazy to

stupefy yourself with that stuff." He had let that go in spite of himself, but when he realized the range of what he had just said and
imagined what Bergère must think of him, he wanted to kill Berliac
and tears came to his eyes. "You're a bourgeois," said Berliac, shrugging his shoulders, "you pretend to swim but you're much too afraid
of going out of your depth." "I don't want to get in the drug habit,"
Lucien said in a calmer voice; "one slavery is like another and I want
to stay clear." "Say you're afraid to get into it," Berliac answered
violently. Lucien was going to slap him when he heard the imperious
voice of Bergère. "Let him alone, Charles," he told Berliac, "he's
right. His fear of being involved is *also* disorder." They both
smoked, stretched out on the divan, and an odor of Armenian paper
filled the room. Lucien sat on a red velvet hassock and watched them
in silence. After a time, Berliac let his head fall back and fluttered his
eyelids with a moist smile. Lucien watched him with rancor and felt
humiliated. At last Berliac got up and walked unsteadily out of the
room: to the end he had the funny, sleeping and voluptuous smile on
his lips. "Give me a pipe," Lucien said hoarsely. Bergère began to
laugh. "Don't bother," he said. "Don't worry about Berliac. Do you
know what he's doing now?" "I don't give a damn," Lucien said.
"Well, I'll tell you anyhow. He's vomiting," Bergère said calmly.
"That's the only effect hasheesh ever had on him. The rest is a joke,
but I make him smoke it sometimes because he wants to show off and
it amuses me." The next day Berliac came to the lycée and wanted to
show off in front of Lucien. "You don't exactly go out on a limb, do
you," he said. But he found out to whom he was talking. "You're a
little show-off," Lucien answered, "maybe you think I don't know
what you were doing in the bathroom yesterday? You were puking,
old man!" Berliac grew livid. "Bergère told you?" "Who do you
think?" "All right," Berliac stammered, "but I wouldn't have
thought Bergère would screw his old friends with new ones." Lucien
was a little worried. He had promised Bergère not to repeat anything. "All right, all right," he said, "he didn't screw you, he just
wanted to show me it didn't work." But Berliac turned his back and
left without shaking hands. Lucien was not too glad when he met
Bergère. "What did you say to Berliac?" Bergère asked him neu-
trally. Lucien lowered his head without answering: he felt overwhelmed. But suddenly he felt Bergère's hand on his neck: "It
doesn't make any difference. In any case, it had to end: comedians
don't amuse me very long." Lucien took heart; he raised his head and
smiled: "But I'm a comedian too," he said, blinking his eyes. "Yes,
but you're pretty," Bergère answered, drawing him close. Lucien let

himself go; he felt soft as a girl and tears were in his eyes. Bergère kissed his cheeks and bit his ear, sometimes calling him "my lovely little scoundrel" and sometimes "my little brother," and Lucien thought it was quite pleasant to have a big brother who was so indulgent and understanding.

M. and Mme. Fleurier wanted to meet this Bergère of whom Lucien spoke so much and they invited him to dinner. Everyone found him charming, including Germaine who had never seen such a handsome man; M. Fleurier had known General Nizan who was Bergère's uncle and he spoke of him at great length. Also, Mme. Fleurier was only too glad to confide Lucien to Bergère for the spring vacation. They went to Rouen by car; Lucien wanted to see the cathedral and the hôtel-de-ville, but Bergère flatly refused. "That rubbish?" he asked insolently. Finally, they spent two hours in a brothel on Rue des Cordeliers and Bergère was a scream: he called all the chippies "mademoiselle," nudging Lucien under the table, then he agreed to go up with one of them but came back after five minutes: "Get the hell out," he gasped, "it's going to be rough." They paid quickly and left. In the street Bergère told what happened: while the woman had her back turned he threw a handful of itching powder on the bed, then told her he was impotent and came down again. Lucien had drunk two whiskies and was a little tight; he sang the *Artilleur de Metz* and *De Profondis Morpionibus;* he thought it wonderful that Bergère was at the same time so profound and so childish.

"I only reserved one room," Bergère said when they arrived at the hotel, "but there's a big bathroom." Lucien was not surprised: he had vaguely thought during the trip that he would share the room with Bergère without dwelling too much on the idea. Now that he could no longer retreat he found the thing a little disagreeable, especially because his feet were not clean. As the bags were being brought up, he imagined that Bergère would tell him, "How dirty you are, you'll make the sheets black." And he would answer insolently, "Your ideas of cleanliness are really bourgeois." But Bergère shoved him into the bathroom with his bag, saying, "Get yourself ready in there, I'm going to undress in the room." Lucien took a footbath and a sitz bath. He wanted to go to the toilet but he did not dare and contented himself with urinating in the washbasin; then he put on his nightshirt and the slippers his mother lent him (his own were full of holes) and knocked. "Are you ready?" he asked. "Yes, yes, come in." Bergère had slipped a black dressing gown over sky blue pajamas. The room smelled of eau-de-cologne. "Only one bed?" Lucien asked. Bergère did not answer: he looked at Lucien with a stupor that ended in a great burst of laughter. "Look at that shirt!" he said, laughing. "What did you do with your nightcap? Oh no, that's really too funny. I wish you could see yourself." "For two years," Lucien said, angrily, "I've been asking my mother to buy me pajamas." Bergère came toward him. "That's all right. Take it off," he said in a voice to which there was no answer, "I'll give you one of mine. It'll be a little big but it'll be better than that." Lucien stayed rooted in the middle of the room, his eyes riveted on the red and green lozenges of the wallpaper. He would have preferred to go back into the bathroom but he was afraid to act like a fool and with a brisk motion tossed the shirt over his head. There was a moment of silence: Bergère looked at Lucien, smiling, and Lucien suddenly realized he was naked in the middle of the room wearing his mother's pom-pommed slippers. He looked at his hands—the big hands of Rimbaud—he wanted to clutch them to his stomach and cover that at least, but he pulled himself together and put them bravely behind his back. On the walls, between two rows of lozenges, there was a small violet square going back further and further. "My word," said Bergère, "he's as chaste as a virgin: look at yourself in the mirror, Lucien, you're blushing as far as your chest. But you're still better like that than in a nightshirt." "Yes," Lucien said with effort, "but you never look good when you're naked. Quick, give me the pajamas." Bergère threw him silk pajamas that smelled of lavender and they went to bed. There was a heavy silence: "I'm sick," Lucien said, "I want to puke." Bergère did not answer and Lucien smelled whiskey in his throat. "He's going to sleep with me," he thought. And the lozenges on the wallpaper began to spin while the stifling smell of eau-de-cologne gagged him. "I shouldn't have said I'd take the trip." He had no luck; twenty times, these last few days, he had almost discovered what Bergère wanted of him and each time, as if on purpose, something happened to turn away his thought. And now he was there, in this man's bed, waiting his good pleasure. I'll take my pillow and go and sleep in the bathroom. But he did not dare; he thought of Bergère's ironic look. He began to laugh. "I'm thinking about the whore a while ago," he said, "she must be scratching now." Bergère still did not answer him; Lucien looked at him out of the corner of his eye: he was stretched out innocently on his back, his hands under his head. Then a violent fury seized Lucien, he raised himself on one elbow and asked him, "Well, what are you waiting for? You didn't bring me here to string beads!"

It was too late to regret his words: Bergère turned to him and studied him with an amused eye. "Look at that angel-faced little tart. Well, baby, I didn't make you say it: I'm the one you're counting on to disorder your little senses." He looked at him an instant longer, their faces almost touching, then he took Lucien in his arms and caressed his breast beneath the pajama shirt. It was not unpleasant, it tickled a little, only Bergère was frightening: He looked foolish and repeated with effort, "You aren't ashamed, little pig, you aren't ashamed little pig?" like the phonograph records in a train station announcing the arrivals and departures. On the contrary, Bergère's hand was swift and light and seemed to be an entire person. It gently grazed Lucien's breast as a caress of warm water in a bath. Lucien wanted to catch this hand, tear it from him and twist it, but Bergère would have laughed: look at that virgin. The hand slid slowly along his belly, stopped a moment to untie the knot of the drawstring which held the trousers. He let him continue: he was heavy and soft as a wet sponge and he was terribly afraid. Bergère had thrown back the covers and put his head on Lucien's breast as though he were listening for a heart beat. Lucien belched twice in a row and he was afraid of vomiting on the handsome, silver hair so full of dignity. "You're leaning on my stomach," he said. Bergère raised himself a little and passed his hand under Lucien's back; the other hand caressed no longer, it teased. "You have beautiful little buttocks," Bergère said suddenly. Lucien thought he was having a nightmare. "Do you like them?" he said cutely. But Bergère suddenly let him go and raised his head with a spiteful look. "Damned little bluffer," he said angrily, "wants to play Rimbaud and I've been playing with him for an hour and can't even excite him." Tears of rage came to Lucien's eyes and he pushed Bergère away with all his might. "It isn't my fault," he hissed, "you made me drink too much, I want to puke." "All right, go! Go!" Bergère said, "and take your time." Between his teeth he added, "Charming evening." Lucien pulled up his trousers, slipped on the black dressing gown and left. When he had closed the bathroom door he felt so alone and abandoned that he burst out sobbing. There were no handkerchiefs in the pocket of the dressing gown so he wiped his eyes and nose with toilet paper. In vain he pushed his fingers down his throat, he could not vomit. Then he dropped his trousers mechanically and sat down on the toilet, shivering. "The bastard," he thought, "the bastard." He was atrociously humiliated but he did not know whether he was ashamed for having submitted to Bergère's caresses or for not getting excited. The corridor on the other side of the door cracked and Lucien started at each sound but could not decide to go back into the room. "I have to go

back," he thought, "I must, or else he'll laugh at me—with Berliac!"
and he rose halfway, but as soon as he pictured the face of Bergère
and his stupid look, and heard him saying, "You aren't ashamed, little
pig?" he fell back on the seat in despair. After a while he was seized
with violent diarrhea which soothed him a little: "It's going out by
the back," he thought, "I like that better." In fact, he had no further
desire to vomit. "He's going to hurt me," he thought suddenly and
thought he was going to faint. Finally, he got so cold his teeth began
to chatter: he thought he was going to be sick and stood up
brusquely. Bergère watched him constrainedly when he went back;
he was smoking a cigarette and his pajamas were open and showed
his thin torso. Lucien slowly removed his slippers and dressing gown
and slipped under the covers without a word. "All right?" asked
Bergère. Lucien shrugged. "I'm cold." "Want me to warm you up?"
"You can try," Lucien said. At that instant he felt himself crushed
by an enormous weight. A warm, soft mouth, like a piece of raw
beefsteak, was thrust against his own. Lucien understood nothing
more, he no longer knew where he was and he was half smothering,
but he was glad because he was warm. He thought of Mme. Besse
who pressed her hand against his stomach and called him "my little
doll" and Hébrard who called him "big beanpole" and the baths he
took in the morning imagining that M. Bouffardier was going to
come in and give him an enema and he told himself, "I'm his little
doll!" Then Bergère shouted in triumph. "At last!" he said, "you've
decided. All right," he added, breathing heavily, "we'll make something out of you." Lucien slipped out of his pajamas.

The next day they awoke at noon. The bellboy brought them
breakfast in bed and Lucien thought he looked haughty. "He thinks
I'm a fairy," he thought with a shudder of discomfort. Bergère was
very nice, he dressed first and went and smoked a cigarette in the old
market place while Lucien took his bath. "The thing is," he thought,
rubbing himself carefully with a stiff brush, "that it's boring." Once
the first moment of terror had passed and he realized that it did not
hurt as much as he expected, he had sunk into dismal boredom. He
kept hoping it would be over and he could sleep but Bergère had not
left him a moment's peace before four in the morning. "I've got to
finish my trig problem, anyhow," he told himself. And he forced himself not to think of his work any more. The day was long. Bergère
told him about the life of Lautréamont, but Lucien did not pay much
attention; Bergère annoyed him a little. That night they slept in
Caudebec and naturally Bergère disturbed him for a good while, but,
around one in the morning, Lucien told him sharply that he was

sleepy and Bergère, without getting angry, let him be. They returned to Paris toward the end of the afternoon. All in all, Lucien
was not displeased with himself.

His parents welcomed him with open arms: "I hope you at least
said thank you to M. Bergère?" his mother asked. He stayed a while
to chat with them about the Normandy countryside and went to
bed early. He slept like an angel, but on awakening the next day he
seemed to be shivering inside. He got up and studied his face for a
long time in the mirror. "I'm a pederast," he told himself. And his
spirits sank. "Get up, Lucien," his mother called through the door,
"you go to school this morning." "Yes, mamma," he answered do-
cilely, but let himself drop back onto the bed and began to stare at
his toes. "It isn't right, I didn't realize, I have no experience." A man
had sucked those toes one after the other. Lucien violently turned his
face away: "He knew. What he made me do has a name. It's called
sleeping with a man and he knew it." It was funny—Lucien smiled
bitterly—for whole days you could ask yourself: am I intelligent, am
I stuck-up and you can never decide. And on top of that there were
labels which got stuck onto you one fine morning and you had to
carry them for the rest of your life: for instance, Lucien was tall and
blond, he looked like his father, he was the only son and, since yesterday, he was a pederast. They'd say about him: "Fleurier, you
know, the tall blond who loves men?" And people would answer,
"Oh yes, the big fairy? Sure, I know who he is."

He dressed and went out but he did not have the heart to go to
the lycée. He went down Avenue Lamballe as far as the Seine and
followed the quais. The sky was pure, the streets smelled of green
leaves, tar and English tobacco. A dreamed-of time to wear clean
clothes on a well-washed body and new soul. The people had a
moral look; Lucien alone felt suspicious and unusual in this springtime. "The fatal bent," he thought. "I started with an Oedipus complex, after that I became sadicoanal and now the payoff, I'm a pederast; where am I going to stop?" Evidently, his case was not yet
very grave: he did not derive much pleasure from Bergère's caresses.
"But suppose I get in the habit?" he thought with anguish. "I could
never do without it, it'll be like morphine!" He would become a
tarnished man, no one would have anything to do with him, his father's workers would laugh when he gave them orders. Lucien imagined his frightful destiny with complacency. He saw himself at 35,
gaunt, painted, and already an old gentleman with a mustache and
the Legion of Honor raising his cane with a terrible look: "Your
presence here, sir, is an insult to my daughters." Then suddenly he

hesitated and stopped playing: he had just remembered a phrase of Bergère's. At Caudebec during the night, Bergère had said, "So tell me—are you beginning to get a taste for it?" What did he mean? Naturally, Lucien was not made of wood and after so much caressing . . . "But that doesn't prove anything," he said, worried. But they said that men like that were amazing when it came to spotting other people like them, almost a sixth sense. For a long while Lucien watched a policeman directing traffic at the Pont d'Iéna. "Could that policeman excite me?" He stared at the blue trousers of the agent and imagined muscular, hairy thighs. "Does that do anything to me?" He left, very much comforted. "It's not too bad," he thought, "I can still escape. He took advantage of my disorder but I'm not *really* a pederast." He tried the experiment with every man who crossed his path and each time the result was negative. "Ouf!" he thought, "it was close!" It was a warning, nothing more. He must never start again because a bad habit is taken quickly and then he must absolutely cure himself of these complexes. He resolved to have himself psychoanalyzed by a specialist without telling his parents. Then he would find a mistress and become a man like the others.

Lucien was beginning to reassure himself when suddenly he thought of Bergère: even now, at this very moment, Bergère was existing somewhere in Paris, delighted with himself and his head full of memories. "He knows how I'm made, he knows my mouth, he said, 'you have an odor I shall not forget'; he'll go and brag to his friends and say, 'I had him,' as if I were a girl. Maybe even now he's telling about his nights to"—Lucien's heart stopped beating—"to Berliac! If he does that I'll kill him. Berliac hates me, he'll tell the whole class, and I'll be sunk, they won't even shake my hand. I'll say it isn't true." Lucien told himself wildly, "I'll bring charges, I'll say he raped me!" Lucien hated Bergère with all his strength: without him, without this scandalous irremediable conscience, everything would have been all right, no one would have known and even Lucien himself would eventually have forgotten it. "If he would die suddenly! Dear God, I pray you make him die tonight without telling anybody. Dear God, let this whole business be buried, you don't want me to be a pederast. But he's got me!" Lucien thought with rage. "I'll have to go back to him and do whatever he wants and tell him I like it or else I'm lost!" He took a few more steps, then added, as a measure of precaution, "Dear God, make Berliac die, too."

Lucien could not take it upon himself to return to Bergère's house. During the weeks that followed, he thought he met him at every step and, when he was working in his room, he jumped at the

sound of a bell; at night he had fearful nightmares: Bergère was rap-
ing him in the middle of the Lycée Saint-Louis schoolyard, all the
*pistons* were there watching and laughing. But Bergère made no attempt to see him again and gave no sign of life. "He only wanted my
body," Lucien thought vexedly. Berliac had disappeared as well and
Guigard, who sometimes went to the races with him on Sundays,
told Lucien he had left Paris after a nervous breakdown. Lucien
grew a little calmer: his trip to Rouen affected him as an obscure,
grotesque dream attached to nothing; he had almost forgotten the
details, he kept only the impression of a dismal odor of flesh and eau-
de-cologne and an intolerable weariness. M. Fleurier sometimes
asked what had happened to his friend Bergère: "We'll have to invite him to Férolles to thank him." "He went to New York," Lucien
finally answered. Sometimes he went boating on the Marne with
Guigard and Guigard's sister taught him to dance. "I'm waking up,"
he thought, "I'm being reborn." But he still often felt something
weighing on his back like a heavy burden: his complexes: he wondered if he should go to Vienna and see Freud: "I'll leave without
any money, on foot if I have to, I'll tell him I haven't a cent but I'm a
case." One hot afternoon in June, he met The Baboon, his old philosophy prof, on the Boulevard Saint-Michel. "Well, Fleurier," The
Baboon said, "you're preparing for Centrale?" "Yessir," Lucien
said. "You should be able," The Baboon said, "to orient yourself
toward a study of literature. You were good in philosophy—" "I
haven't given it up," Lucien said, "I've done a lot of reading this
year, Freud, for instance. By the way," he added, inspired. "I'd like
to ask you, monsieur, what do you think about psychoanalysis?"
The Baboon began to laugh: "A fad," he said, "which will pass. The
best part of Freud you will find already in Plato. For the rest," he
added, in a voice that brooked no answer, "I'll tell you I don't have
anything to do with that nonsense. You'd be better off reading Spinoza." Lucien felt himself delivered of an enormous weight and he
returned home on foot, whistling. "It was a nightmare," he thought,
"nothing more is left of it." The sun was hard and hot that day, but
Lucien raised his eyes and gazed at it without blinking: it was the
sun of the whole world and Lucien had the right to look at it in the
face; he was saved! "Nonsense," he thought, "it was nonsense! They
tried to drive me crazy but they didn't get me." In fact he had never
stopped resisting: Bergère had tripped him up in his reasoning, but
Lucien had sensed, for instance, that the pederasty of Rimbaud was a
stain, and when that little shrimp Berliac wanted to make him smoke
hasheesh Lucien had dressed him down properly: "I risked losing

myself," he thought, "but what protected me was my moral health!" That evening, at dinner, he looked at his father with sympathy. M. Fleurier had square shoulders and the slow heavy gestures of a peasant with something racial in them and his gray boss's eyes, metallic and cold. "I look like him," Lucien thought. He remembered that the Fleuriers, father and son, had been captains of industry for four generations: "Say what you want, the family exists!" And he thought proudly of the moral health of the Fleuriers.

Lucien did not present himself for the examinations at the Ecole Centrale that year and the Fleuriers left very shortly for Férolles. He was charmed to find the house again, the garden, the factory, the calm and poised little town. It was another world: he decided to get up early in the mornings and take long walks through the country. "I want," he told his father, "to fill my lungs with pure air and store up health for next year." He accompanied his mother to the Bouffardiers' and the Besses' and everyone thought he had become a big, well-poised and reasonable boy. Hébrard and Winckelmann, who were taking law courses in Paris, had come back to Férolles for a vacation. Lucien went out with them several times and they talked about the jokes they used to play on Abbé Jacquemart, their long bicycle trips and they sang the *Artilleur de Metz* in harmony. Lucien keenly appreciated the rough frankness and solidity of his old friends and he reproached himself for having neglected them. He confessed to Hébrard that he did not care much for Paris, but Hébrard could not understand it: his parents had entrusted him to an abbé and he was very much held in check; he was still dazzled by his visits to the Louvre and the evening he had spent at the Opera. Lucien was touched by his simplicity; he felt himself the elder brother of Hébrard and Winckelmann and he began to tell himself he did not regret having had such a tormented life: he had gained experience. He told them about Freud and psychoanalysis and amused himself by shocking them a little. They violently criticized the theory of complexes but their objections were naïve and Lucien pointed it out to them, then he added that from a philosophical viewpoint it was easy to refute the errors of Freud. They admired him greatly but Lucien pretended not to notice it.

M. Fleurier explained the operation of the factory to Lucien. He took him on a visit through the central buildings and Lucien watched the workers at great length. "If I should die," M. Fleurier said, "you'd have to take command of the factory at a moment's notice." Lucien scolded him and said, "Don't talk like that, will you please, papa." But he was serious for several days in a row thinking of the responsibilities which would fall on him sooner or later. They had long talks about the duties of the boss and Mr. Fleurier showed him that ownership was not a right but a duty:"What are they trying to give us, with their class struggle," he said, "as though the interests of the bosses and the workers were just the opposite. Take my case, Lucien, I'm a little boss, what they call small fry. Well, I make a living for a hundred workers and their families. If I do well, they're the first ones to profit. But if I have to close the plant, there they are in the street. *I don't have a right,*" he said forcefully, "to do bad business. And that's what I call the solidarity of classes."

All went well, for more than three weeks he almost never thought of Bergère; he had forgiven him: he simply hoped never to see him again for the rest of his life. Sometimes, when he changed his shirt, he went to the mirror and looked at himself with astonishment: "A man has desired this body," he thought. He passed his hands slowly over his legs and thought: "A man was excited by these legs." He touched his back and regretted not being another person to be able to caress his own flesh like a piece of silk. Sometimes he missed his complexes: they had been solid, heavy, their enormous somber mass had balanced him. Now it was finished, Lucien no longer believed in it and he felt terribly unstable. It was not so unpleasant, though; rather, it was a sort of very tolerable disenchantment, a little upsetting, which could, if necessary, pass for *ennui.* "I'm nothing," he thought, "but it's because nothing has soiled me. Berliac was soiled and caught. I can stand a little uncertainty: it's the price of purity."

During a walk, he sat down on a hillock and thought: "For six years I slept, and then one fine day I came out of my cocoon." He was animated and looked affably around the countryside. "I'm built for action," he thought. But in an instant his thought of glory faded. He whispered, "Let them wait a while and they'll see what I'm worth." He had spoken with force but the words rolled on his lips like empty shells. "What's the matter with me?" He did not want to recognize this odd inquietude, it had hurt him too much before. He thought, "It's this silence . . . this land . . ." Not a living being, save crickets laboriously dragging their black and yellow bellies in the dust. Lucien hated crickets because they always looked half dead. On the other side of the road, a grayish stretch of land, crushed, creviced, ran as far as the river. No one saw Lucien, no one heard him; he sprang to his feet and felt that his movements would meet with no resistance, not even that of gravity. Now he stood beneath a curtain of gray clouds; it was as though he existed in a vac-

uum. "This silence . . ." he thought. It was more than silence, it was
nothingness. The countryside was extraordinarily calm and soft about
Lucien, inhuman: it seemed that it was making itself tiny and was
holding its breath so as not to disturb him. *"Quand l'artilleur de
Metz revint en garnison . . ."* The sound died on his lips as a flame
in a vacuum: Lucien was alone, without a shadow and without echo,
in the midst of this too discreet nature which meant nothing. He
shook himself and tried to recapture the thread of his thought. "I'm
built for action. First, I can bounce back: I can do a lot of foolishness
but it doesn't go far because I always spring back." He thought. "I
have moral health." But he stopped, making a grimace of disgust, it
seemed so absurd to him to speak of "moral health" on this white
road crossed by dying insects. In rage, Lucien stepped on a cricket,
under his sole he felt a little elastic ball and, when he raised his foot,
the cricket was still alive: Lucien spat on it. "I'm perplexed. I'm perplexed. It's like last year." He began to think about Winckelmann
who called him "the ace of aces," about M. Fleurier who treated him
like a man, Mme. Besse who told him, "This is the big boy I used to
call my little doll, I wouldn't dare say it now, he frightens me." But
they were far, far away and it seemed the real Lucien was lost, that
there was only a white and perplexed larva. "What am I?" Miles and
miles of land, a flat, chapped soil, grassless, odorless, and then, suddenly springing straight from this gray crust, the beanpole, so un-
wonted that there was even no shadow behind it. "What am I?" The
question had not changed since the past vacation, it was as if it
waited for Lucien at the very spot he had left it; or, it wasn't a question, but a condition. Lucien shrugged his shoulders. "I'm too scrupulous," he thought, "I analyze myself too much."

The following days he forced himself to stop analyzing: he
wanted to let himself be fascinated by things; lengthily he studied
egg cups, napkin rings, trees, and store fronts; he flattered his mother
very much when he asked her if she would like to show him her
silver service, he thought he was looking at silver and behind the
look throbbed a little living fog. In vain Lucien absorbed himself in
conversation with M. Fleurier, this abundant, tenacious mist, whose
opaque inconsistency falsely resembled light, slipped *behind* the attention he gave his father's words: this fog was himself. From time to
time, annoyed, Lucien stopped listening, turned away, tried to catch
the fog and look it in the face: he found only emptiness, the fog was
still *behind*.

Germaine came in tears to Mme. Fleurier: her brother had bron-
cho-pneumonia. "My poor Germaine," Mme. Fleurier said. "And

you always said how strong he was!" She gave her a month's vacation and, to replace her, brought in the daughter of one of the factory workers, little Berthe Mozelle who was seventeen. She was small, with blond plaits rolled about her head; she limped slightly. Since she came from Concarneau, Mme. Fleurier begged her to wear a lace coif: "That would be much nicer." From the first days, each time she met Lucien, her wide blue eyes reflected a humble and passionate adoration and Lucien realized she worshiped him. He spoke to her familiarly and often asked her, "Do you like it here?" In the hallways he amused himself making passes at her to see if they had an effect. But she touched him deeply and he drew a precious comfort from this love; he often thought with a sting of emotion of the image Berthe must make of him. "By the simple fact that I hardly look like the young workers she goes out with." On a pretext he took Winckelmann into the pantry and Winckelmann thought she was well built: "You're a lucky dog," he concluded, "I'd look into it if I were you." But Lucien hesitated: she smelled of sweat and her black blouse was eaten away under the arms. One rainy day in September M. Fleurier drove into Paris and Lucien stayed in his room alone. He lay down on his bed and began to yawn. He seemed to be a cloud, capricious and fleeting, always the same, always something else, always diluting himself in the air. "I wonder why I exist?" He was there, he digested, he yawned, he heard the rain tapping on the windowpanes and the white fog was unraveling in his head; and then? His existence was a scandal and the responsibilities he would assume later would barely be enough to justify it. "After all, I didn't ask to be born," he said. And he pitied himself. He remembered his childhood anxieties, his long somnolences and they appeared to him in a new light: fundamentally, he had not stopped being embarrassed with his life, with this voluminous, useless gift, and he had carried it in his arms without knowing what to do with it or where to set it down. "I have spent my time regretting I was born." But he was too depressed to push his thoughts further; he rose, lit a cigarette and went down into the kitchen to ask Berthe to make some tea.

She did not see him enter. He touched her shoulder and she started violently. "Did I frighten you?" he asked. She looked at him fearfully, leaning both hands on the table and her breast heaved: after a moment she smiled and said, "It scared me, I didn't think anybody was there." Lucien returned her smile with indulgence and said, "It would be very nice if you'd make a little tea for me." "Right away, Monsieur Lucien," the girl answered and she went to the stove: Lucien's presence seemed to make her uncomfortable. Lucien remained on the doorstep, uncertain. "Well," he asked paternally, "do you like it here with us?" Berthe turned her back on him and filled a pan at the spigot. The sound of the water covered her answer. Lucien waited a moment and when she had set the pan on the gas range he continued, "Have you ever smoked?" "Sometimes," the girl answered, warily. He opened his pack of cigarettes and held it out to her. He was not too pleased: he felt he was compromising himself; he shouldn't make her smoke. "You want . . . me to smoke?" she asked, surprised. "Why not?" "Madame will scold me." Lucien had an unpleasant impression of complicity. He began to laugh and said, "We won't tell her." Berthe blushed, took a cigarette with the tips of her fingers and put it in her mouth. Should I offer to light it? That wouldn't be right. He said to her, "Well, aren't you going to light it?" She annoyed him; she stood there, her arms stiff, red and docile, her lips bunched around the cigarette like a thermometer stuck in her mouth. She finally took a sulphur match from the tin box, struck it, smoked a few puffs with her eyes half shut and said, "It's mild." Then she hurriedly took the cigarette from her mouth and clutched it awkwardly between her five fingers. "A born victim," Lucien thought. Yet, she thawed a little when he asked her if she liked her Brittany, she described the different sorts of Breton coifs to him and even sang a song from Rosporden in a soft, off-key voice. Lucien teased her gently but she did not understand the joke and looked at him fearfully: at those times she looked like a rabbit. He was sitting on a stool and felt quite at ease: "Sit down," he told her . . . "Oh no, Monsieur Lucien, not before Monsieur Lucien." He took her under the arms and drew her to his knees. "And like that?" he asked. She let herself go, murmuring, "On your knees!" with an air of ecstasy and reproach with a funny accent and Lucien thought wearily, "I'm getting too much involved, I shouldn't have gone so far." He was silent: she stayed on his knees, hot, quiet, but Lucien felt her heart beating. "She belongs to me," he thought, "I can do anything I want with her." He let her go, took the teapot and went back to his room: Berthe did not make a move to stop him. Before drinking the tea, Lucien washed his hands with his mother's scented soap because they smelled of armpits.

"Am I going to sleep with her?" In the following days Lucien was absorbed in this small problem; Berthe was always putting herself in his way, looking at him with the great sad eyes of a spaniel. Morality won out: Lucien realized he risked making her pregnant because he did not have enough experience (impossible to buy contraceptives in Férolles, he was too well known) and he would cause

M. Fleurier much worry. He also told himself that later he would have less authority in the factory if one of the workers' daughters could brag he had slept with her. "I don't have the right to touch her." He avoided being alone with Berthe during the last days of September. "So," Winkelmann asked him, "What are you waiting for?" "I'm not going to bother," Lucien answered dryly, "I don't like ancillary love." Winckelmann, who heard the words "ancillary love" for the first time, gave a low whistle and was silent.

Lucien was very satisfied with himself: he had conducted himself like a *chic type* and that repaid many errors. "She was ripe for it," he told himself with a little regret, but on reconsidering it, he thought, "It's the same as though I had her: she offered herself and I didn't want her." And henceforth he no longer considered himself a virgin. These slight satisfactions occupied his mind for several days. Then they, too, melted into the fog. Returning to school in October, he felt as dismal as at the beginning of the previous year.

Berliac had not come back and no one had heard anything about him. Lucien noticed several unknown faces. His right hand neighbor whose name was Lemordant had taken a year of special mathematics in Poitiers. He was even bigger than Lucien and, with his black mustache, already looked like a man. Lucien met his friends again without pleasure: they seemed childish to him and innocently boisterous: schoolboys. He still associated himself with their collective manifestation but with nonchalance, as was permitted him by his position of *carré*. Lemordant would have attracted him more, because he was mature; but, unlike Lucien, he did not seem to have acquired that maturity through multiple and painful experiences: he was an adult by birth. Lucien often contemplated with a full satisfaction that voluminous, pensive head, neckless, planted awry on the shoulders: it seemed impossible to get anything into it, neither through the ears nor through the tiny slanting eyes, pink and glassy: "Man with convictions," Lucien thought with respect; and he wondered, not without jealousy, what that certitude could be that gave Lemordant such a full consciousness of self. "That's how I should be; a rock." He was even a little surprised that Lemordant should be accessible to mathematical reasoning; but M. Husson convinced him when he gave back the first papers: Lucien was seventh and Lemordant had been given a "5" and 78th place; all was in order. Lemordant gave no sign, he seemed to expect the worst. His tiny mouth, his heavy cheeks, yellow and smooth, were not made to express feelings: he was a Buddha. They saw him angry only once, the day Loewy bumped into him in the cloakroom. First he gave a dozen sharp little growls, and blinked his eyes; "Back to Poland," he said at last, "to Poland you dirty kike and don't come crapping around here with us." He dominated Loewy with his whole form and his massive chest swayed on his long legs. He finished up by slapping him and little Loewy apologized: the affair ended there.

On Thursdays, Lucien went out with Guigard who took him dancing with his sister's girl friends. But Guigard finally confessed that these hops bored him. "I've got a girl," he confided, "a *première* in Plisnier's, Rue Royale. She has a friend who doesn't have anybody: you ought to come with us Saturday night." Lucien made a scene with his parents and got permission to go out every Saturday; they left the key under the mat for him. He met Guigard around nine o'clock in a bar on the Rue Saint-Honoré. "You wait and see," Guigard said, "Fanny is charming and what's nice about her is she really knows how to dress." "What about mine?" "I don't know her; I know she's an apprentice dressmaker and she's just come to Paris from Angoulême. By the way," he added, "don't pull any boners. My name's Pierre Daurat. You, because you're blond, I said you were part English, it's better. Your name's Lucien Bonnières." "But why?" asked Lucien, intrigued. "My boy," Guigard answered, "it's a rule. You can do what you like with these girls but never tell your name." "All right," Lucien said, "what do I do for a living?" "You can say you're a student, that's better, you understand, it flatters them and then you don't have to spend much money. Of course, we share the expenses; but let me pay this evening; I'm in the habit: I'll tell you what you owe me on Monday." Immediately Lucien thought Guigard was trying to get a rake-off. "God, how distrustful I've gotten!" he thought with amusement. Just then Fanny came in: a tall, thin brunette with long thighs and a heavily rouged face. Lucien found her intimidating. "Here's Bonnières I was telling you about," Guigard said. "Pleased to meet you," Fanny said with a myopic look. "This is my girl friend Maud." Lucien saw an ageless little woman wearing a hat that looked like an overturned flower pot. She was not rouged and appeared grayish after the dazzling Fanny. Lucien was bitterly disappointed but he saw she had a pretty mouth—and then there was no need to be embarrassed with her. Guigard had taken care to pay for the beers in advance so that he could profit from the commotion of their arrival to push the two girls gaily toward the door without allowing them the time for a drink. Lucien was grateful to him: M. Fleurier only gave him 125 francs a week and out of this money he had to pay carfare. The evening was amusing; they went dancing in the Latin Quarter in a hot, pink little place with dark corners and where a cocktail cost five francs. There were many students with girls of the same type as Fanny but not as good-looking. Fanny was superb: she looked straight in the eyes of a big man with a beard who smoked a pipe and said very loudly, "I hate people who smoke pipes at dances." The man turned crimson and put the lighted pipe back in his pocket. She treated Guigard and Lucien with a certain condescension and sometimes told them, "You're a couple of kids" with a gentle, maternal air. Lucien felt full of ease and sweetness; he told Fanny several amusing little things and smiled while telling them. Finally, the smile never left his face and he was able to hit on a refined tone of voice with touches of devil-may-care and tender courtesy tinged with irony. But Fanny spoke little to him; she took Guigard's chin and pulled his cheeks to make his mouth stand out; when the lips were full and drooling a little, like fruit swollen with juice or like snails, she licked them, saying "Baby." Lucien was horribly annoyed and thought Guigard was ridiculous: Guigard had rouge near his lips and fingermarks on his cheeks. But the behavior of the other couples was even more negligent: everyone kissed; from time to time the girl from the checkroom passed among them with a little basket, throwing streamers and multicolored balls shouting, "*Olé, mes enfants, amusez-vous, olé, olé!*" and everybody laughed. At last Lucien remembered the existence of Maud and he said to her, smiling, "Look at those turtle doves . . ." He pointed to Fanny and Guigard and added, "*Nous autres, nobles viellards . . .*" He did not finish the phrase but smiled so drolly that Maud smiled too. She removed her hat and Lucien saw with pleasure that she was somewhat better than the other women in the dance hall; then he asked her to dance and told her the jokes he played on his professors the year of his baccalaureate. She danced well, her eyes were black and serious and she had an intelligent look. Lucien told her about Berthe and said he was full of remorse. "But," he added, "it was better for her." Maud thought the story about Berthe was poetic and sad, she asked how much Berthe earned from Lucien's parents. "It's not always funny," she added, "for a young girl to be in the family way." Guigard and Fanny paid no more attention to them, they caressed each other and Guigard's face was covered with moisture. From time to time Lucien repeated, "Look at those turtle doves, just look at them!" and he had his sentence ready, "They make me feel like doing it too." But he dared not say it and contented himself with smiling, then he pretended that he and Maud were old friends, disdainful of love, and he called her "brother" and made as if to slap her on the back. Suddenly, Fanny turned her head and looked at them

with surprise, "Well," she said, "first graders, how're you doing?
Why don't you kiss, you're dying to." Lucien took Maud in his
arms; he was a little annoyed because Fanny was watching them: he
wanted the kiss to be long and successful but he wondered how people breathed. Finally, it was not as difficult as he thought, it was
enough to kiss on an angle, leaving the nostrils clear. He heard Guigard counting "one-two-three-four-" and he let go of Maud at 52.
"Not bad for a beginning," Guigard said. "I can do better." Lucien
looked at his wrist watch and counted: Guigard left Fanny's mouth
at the 159th second. Lucien was furious and thought the contest was
stupid. "I let go of Maud just to be safe," he thought, "but that's
nothing, once you know how to breathe you can keep on forever."
He proposed a second match and won. When it was all over, Maud
looked at Lucien and said seriously, "You kiss well." Lucien blushed
with pleasure. "At your service," he answered, bowing. Still he
would rather have kissed Fanny. They parted around half past
twelve because of the last métro. Lucien was joyful; he leaped and
danced in the Rue Raynouard and thought, "It's in the bag." The
corner of his mouth hurt because he had smiled so much.

He saw Maud every Thursday at six and on Saturday evening. She
let herself be kissed but nothing more. Lucien complained to Guigard who reassured him, "Don't worry," Guigard said, "Fanny's
sure she'll lay; but she's young and only had two boys; Fanny says
for you to be very tender with her." "Tender?" Lucien said, "Get a
load of that!" They both laughed and Guigard concluded, "That's
what you've got to do." Lucien was very tender. He kissed Maud a
lot and told her he loved her, but after a while it became a little
monotonous and then he was not too proud of going out with her:
he would have liked to give her advice on how she should dress, but
she was full of prejudices and angered quickly. Between kisses, they
were silent, gazing at each other and holding hands. "God knows
what she's thinking with those strict eyes she has." Lucien still
thought of the same thing: this small existence, sad and vague,
which was his own, and told himself, "I wish I were Lemordant,
there's a man who's found his place!" During those times he saw
himself as though he were another person: sitting near a woman who
loved him, his hand in hers, his lips still wet from kisses, refusing the
humble happiness she offered him: alone. Then he clasped Maud's
fingers tightly and tears came to his eyes: he would have liked to
make her happy.

One morning in December, Lemordant came up to Lucien; he
held a paper. "You want to sign?" he asked. "What is it?" "Because

of the kikes at the Normale Sup; they sent the *Oeuvre* a petition against compulsory military training with two hundred signatures. So we're protesting; we need a thousand names at least: we're going to get the *cyrards*, the *flottards*, the *agros*, the *X's*, and the whole works." Lucien was flattered. "Is it going to be printed?" "Surely in *Action*. Maybe in *Echo de Paris* besides." Lucien wanted to sign on the spot but he thought it would not be wise. He took the paper and read it carefully. Lemordant added, "I hear you don't have anything to do with politics; that's your business. But you're French and you've got a right to have your say." Lucien felt an inexplicable and rapid joy. He signed. The next day he bought *Action Française* but the proclamation was not there. It didn't appear until Thursday, Lucien found it on the second page under the headline: YOUTH OF FRANCE SCORES IN TEETH OF INTERNATIONAL JEWRY. His name was there, compressed, definitive, not far from Lemordant's, almost as strange as the names *Flèche* and *Flipot* which surrounded it; it looked unreal. "Lucien Fleurier," he thought. "A peasant name, a real French name." He read the whole series of names starting with F aloud and when it came to his turn he pronounced it as if he did not recognize it. Then he stuffed the newspaper in his pocket and went home happily.

A few days later he sought out Lemordant. "Are you active in politics?" he asked. "I'm in the League," Lemordant said. "Ever read *Action Française*?" "Not much," Lucien confessed. "Up to now it didn't interest me but I think I'm changing my mind." Lemordant looked at him without curiosity, with his impenetrable air. Lucien told him in a few words what Bergère had called his "Disorder." "Where do you come from?" Lemordant asked. "Férolles. My father has a factory there." "How long did you stay there?" "Till second form." "I see," Lemordant said, "it's very simple, you're uprooted. Have you read Barrès?" "I read *Colette Baudoche*." "Not that," Lemordant said impatiently, "I'll bring you the *Déracinés* this afternoon. That's your story. You'll find the cause and cure." The book was bound in green leather. On the first page was an "*ex libris* André Lemordant" in Gothic letters. Lucien was surprised; he had never dreamed Lemordant could have a first name.

He began reading it with much distrust: it had been explained to him so many times: so many times had he been lent books with a "Read this, it fits you perfectly." Lucien thought with a sad smile that he was not someone who could be set down in so many pages. The Oedipus complex, the Disorder: what childishness, and so far away! But, from the very first, he was captivated: in the first place, it was not psychology—Lucien had a bellyful of psychology—the young people Barrès described were not abstract individuals or declassed like Rimbaud or Verlaine, nor sick like the unemployed Viennese who had themselves psychoanalyzed by Freud. Barrès began by placing them in their milieu, in their family: they had been well brought up, in the provinces, in solid traditions. Lucien thought Sturel resembled himself. "It's true," he said, "I'm uprooted." He thought of the moral health of the Fleuriers, a health acquired only in the land, their physical strength (his grandfather used to twist a bronze sou between his fingers); he remembered with emotion the dawns in Férolles: he rose, tiptoed down the stairs so as not to wake his family, straddled his bicycle and the soft countryside of the Ile de France enveloped him in its discreet caresses. "I've always hated Paris," he thought with force. He also read the *Jardin de Bérénice* and, from time to time, stopped reading and began to ponder, his eyes vague; thus they were again offering him a character and a destiny, a means of escaping the inexhaustible gossip of his conscience, a method of defining and appreciating himself. And how much he preferred the unconscious, reeking of the soil, which Barrès gave him, to the filthy, lascivious images of Freud. To grasp it Lucien had only to turn himself away from a sterile and dangerous contemplation of self: he must study the soil and subsoil of Férolles, he must decipher the sense of the rolling hills which descended as far as the Sernette, he must apply himself to human geography and history. Or, simply return to Férolles and live there: he would find it harmless and fertile at his feet, stretched across the countryside, mixed in the woods, the springs, and the grass like nourishing humus from which Lucien could at last draw the strength to become a leader. Lucien left these long dreams exalted, and sometimes felt as if he had found his road. Now he was silent close to Maud, his arm about her waist, the words, the scraps of sentences resounding in him: "renew tradition," "the earth and the dead"; deep, opaque words, inexhaustible. "How tempting it is," he thought. Yet he dared not believe it: he had already been disappointed too often. He opened up his fears to Lemordant: "It would be too good." "My boy," Lemordant answered, "you don't believe everything you want to right away: you need practice." He thought a little and said, "You ought to come with us." Lucien accepted with an open heart, but he insisted on keeping his liberty. "I'll come," he said, "but I won't be involved. I want to see and think about it."

Lucien was captivated by the camaraderies of the young *camelots;* they gave him a cordial, simple welcome and he immediately felt at ease in their midst. He soon knew Lemordant's "gang," about twenty students, almost all of whom wore velvet berets. They held their meetings on the second floor of the Polder beerhall where they played bridge and billiards. Lucien often went there to meet them and soon he realized they had adopted him for he was always greeted with shouts of "*Voilà le plus beau!*" or "Our National Fleurier!" But it was their good humor which especially captured Lucien: nothing pedantic or austere; little talk of politics. They laughed and sang, that was all, they shouted or beat the tables in honor of the student youth. Lemordant himself smiled without dropping an authority which no one would have dared question. Lucien was more often silent, his look wandering over these boisterous, muscular young people. "This is strength," he thought. Little by little he discovered the true sense of youth in the midst of them: it was not in the affected grace Bergère appreciated; youth was the future of France. However, Lemordant's friends did not have the troubled charm of adolescence: they were adults and several wore beards. Looking closely he found an air of parenthood in all of them: they had finished with the wanderings and uncertainties of their age, they had nothing more to learn, they were made. In the beginning their lighthearted, ferocious jokes somewhat shocked Lucien: one might have thought them without conscience. When Rémy announced that Mme. Dubus, the wife of the radical leader, had her legs cut off by a truck, Lucien expected them to render a brief homage to their unfortunate adversary. But they all burst out laughing and slapped their legs, saying: "The old carrion!" and "What a fine truck driver!" Lucien was a little taken aback but suddenly he understood that this great, purifying laughter was a refusal: they had scented danger, they wanted no cowardly pity and they were firm. Lucien began to laugh too. Little by little their pranks appeared to him in their true light: there was only the shell of frivolity; at heart it was the affirmation of a right: their conviction was so deep, so religious, that it gave them the right to appear frivolous, to dismiss all that was not essential with a whim, a pirouette. Between the icy humor of Charles Maurras and the jokes of Desperreau, for instance (he carried in his pocket an old condom end which he called Blum's foreskin), there was only a difference of degree. In January the University announced a solemn meeting in the course of which the degree of *doctor honoris causa* was to be bestowed on two Swedish mineralogists. "You're going to see something good," Lemordant told Lucien, giving him an invitation card. The big amphitheater was packed. When Lucien saw the President of the Republic and the Rector enter at the sound of the *Marseillaise*, his heart began to pound, he was afraid for his friends. Just then a few young people rose from their seats and began to shout. With sympathy Lucien recognized Rémy, red as a beet, struggling between two men who were pulling his coat, shouting, "France for the French!" But he was especially pleased to see an old gentleman, with the air of a precocious child, blowing a little horn. "How healthy it is," he thought. He keenly tasted this odd mixture of headstrong gravity and turbulence which gave the youngest an air of maturity and the oldest an impish air. Soon Lucien himself tried to joke. He had some success and when he said of Herriot, "There's no more God if he dies in his bed," he felt the birth of a sacred fury in him. Then he gritted his teeth and, for a moment, felt as convinced, as strict, as powerful as Rémy or Desperreau. "Lemordant is right," he thought, "you need practice, it's all there." He also learned to avoid discussions: Guigard, who was only a republican, overwhelmed him with objections. Lucien listened to him politely but, after a while, shut up. Guigard was still talking but Lucien did not even look at him any more: he smoothed the fold in his trousers and amused himself by blowing smoke rings with his cigarette and looking at women. Nevertheless, he heard a few of Guigard's objections, but they quickly lost their weight and slipped off him, light and futile. Guigard finally was quiet, quite impressed. Lucien told his parents about his new friends and M. Fleurier asked him if he was going to be a *camelot*. Lucien hesitated and gravely said, "I'm tempted, I'm really tempted." "Lucien, I beg you, don't do it," his mother said, "they're very excitable and something bad can happen so quickly. Don't you see you can get in trouble or be put in prison? Besides, you're much too young to be mixed up in politics." Lucien answered her only with a firm smile and M. Fleurier intervened. "Let him alone, dear," he said gently, "let him follow his own ideas; he has to pass through it." From that day on it seemed to Lucien that his parents treated him with a certain consideration. Yet he did not decide; these few weeks had taught him much: by turn he considered the benevolent curiosity of his father, Mme. Fleurier's worries, the growing respect of Guigard, the insistence of Lemordant and the impatience of Rémy and, nodding his head, he told himself, "This is no small matter." He had a long conversation with Lemordant and Lemordant well understood his reasons and told him not to hurry. Lucien still was nostalgic: he had the impression of being only a small gelatinous transparency trembling on the seat in a café and the boisterous agitation of the *camelots* seemed absurd to him. But at other times he felt hard and heavy as a rock and he was almost happy.

He got along better and better with the whole gang. He sang them the *Noce à Rebecca* which Hébrard had taught him the previous vacation and everyone thought it was tremendously amusing. Lucien threw out several biting reflections about the Jews and spoke of Berliac who was so miserly: "I always asked myself: why is he so cheap, it isn't possible to be that cheap. Then one day I understood: he was one of the tribe." Everybody began to laugh and a sort of exaltation came over Lucien: he felt truly furious about the Jews and the memory of Berliac was deeply unpleasant to him. Lemordant looked him in the eyes and said, "You're a real one, you are." After that they often asked Lucien: "Fleurier, tell us a good one about the kikes." And Lucien told the Jewish jokes he learned from his father; all he had to do was begin, "Vun day Levy met Bloom . . ." to fill his friends with mirth. One day Rémy and Patenôtre told how they had come across an Algerian Jew by the Seine and how they had almost frightened him to death by acting as if they were going to throw him in the water: "I said to myself," Rémy concluded, "what a shame it was Fleurier wasn't with us." "Maybe it was better he wasn't there," Desperreau interrupted, "he'd have chucked him in the water for good!" There was no one like Lucien for recognizing a Jew from the nose. When he went out with Guigard he nudged his elbow: "Don't turn around now: the little short one, behind us, he's one of them!" "For that," Guigard said, "you can really smell 'em out." Fanny could not stand the Jews either; all four of them went to Maud's room one Thursday and Lucien sang the *Noce à Rebecca*. Fanny could stand no more, she said, "Stop, stop, or I'll wet my pants." And when he had finished, she gave him an almost tender look. They played jokes on him in the Polder beerhall. There was always someone to say, negligently, "Fleurier who likes the Jews so much . . ." or "Léon Blum, the great friend of Fleurier . . ." and the others waited, in stitches, holding their breath, openmouthed. Lucien grew red and struck the table, shouting, "God damn . . . !" and they burst out laughing and said, "He bit! He bit! He didn't bite—he swallowed it!"

He often went to political meetings with them and heard Professor Claude and Maxime Réal del Sarte. His work suffered a little from these new obligations, but, since Lucien could not count on winning the Centrale scholarship anyhow, that year, M. Fleurier was indulgent. "After all," he told his wife, "Lucien must learn the job of being a man." After these meetings Lucien and his friends felt hot-headed and were given to playing tricks. Once about ten of them came across a little, olive-skinned man who was crossing the Rue

Saint-André-des-Arts, reading *Humanité*. They shoved him into a wall and Rémy ordered, "Throw down that paper." The little man wanted to act up but Desperreau slipped behind him and grabbed him by the waist while Lemordant ripped the paper from his grasp with a powerful fist. It was very amusing. The little man, furious, kicked the air and shouted, "Let go of me! Let go!" with an odd accent and Lemordant, quite calm, tore up the paper. But things were spoiled when Desperreau wanted to let the man go: he threw himself on Lemordant and would have struck him if Rémy hadn't landed a good punch behind his ear just in time. The man fell against the wall and looked at them all evilly, saying, *"Sales Français!"* "Say that again," Marchesseau demanded coldly. Lucien realized there was going to be some dirty work: Marchesseau could not take a joke when it was a question of France. *"Sales Français!"* the dago said. He was slapped again and threw himself forward, his head lowered. *"Sales Français, sales bourgeois,* I hate you, I hope you croak, all of you, all of you!" and a flood of other filthy curses with a violence that Lucien never imagined possible. Then they lost patience and all had to step in and give him a good lesson. After a while they let him go and the man dropped against the wall: his breath was a whistle, one punch had closed his left eye and they were all around him, tired of striking him, waiting for him to fall. The man twisted his mouth and spat: *"Sales Français, sales Français."* There was a moment of hesitation and Lucien realized his friends were going to give it up. Then it was stronger than he was, he leaped forward and struck with all his might. He heard something crack and the little man looked at him with surprise and weakness. *"Sales . . ."* he muttered, but his puffed eye began to open on a red, sightless globe; he fell to his knees and said nothing more. "Get the hell out," Rémy hissed. They ran, stopping only at Place Saint-Michel: no one was following them. They straightened their ties and brushed each other off.

The evening passed without mention of the incident and the young men were especially nice to each other: they had abandoned the modest brutality which usually veiled their feelings. They spoke politely to each other and Lucien thought that for the first time they were acting as they acted with their families; but he was enervated: he was not used to fighting thugs in the middle of the street. He thought tenderly of Maud and Fanny.

He could not sleep. "I can't go on," he thought, "following them like an amateur. Everything has been weighed, I *must* join!" He felt grave and almost religious when he announced the good news to Lemordant. "It's decided," he said, "I'm with you." Lemordant slapped him on the shoulder and the gang celebrated the event by polishing off several bottles. They had recovered their gay and brutal tone and talked only about the incident of the night before. As they were about to leave, Marchesseau told Lucien simply, "You've got a terrific punch!" and Lucien answered, "He was a Jew."

The day after that he went to see Maud with a heavy malacca cane he had bought in a store on the Boulevard Saint-Michel. Maud understood immediately: she looked at the cane and said, "So you did it?" "I did it," Lucien smiled. Maud seemed flattered; personally, she favored the ideas of the Left, but she was broad-minded. "I think," she said, "there's good in all parties." In the course of the evening, she scratched his neck several times and called him "My little *camelot*." A little while after that, one Saturday night, Maud felt tired. "I think I'll go back," she said, "but you can come up with me if you're good: you can hold my hand and be real nice to your little Maud who's so tired, and you can tell her stories." Lucien was hardly enthusiastic: Maud's room depressed him with its careful poverty: it was like a maid's room. But it would have been criminal to let such an opportunity pass by. Hardly in the room, Maud threw herself on the bed, saying, "Whew! It feels so good!" Then she was silent, gazing into Lucien's eyes, and puckered her lips. He stretched himself out near her and she put her hand over his eyes, spreading her fingers and saying, "Peekaboo, I see you, you know I see you, Lucien!" He felt soft and heavy, she put her fingers in his mouth and he sucked them, then spoke to her tenderly, "Poor little Maud's sick, does little Maud have a pain?" and he caressed her whole body; she had closed her eyes and was smiling mysteriously. After a moment he raised her skirt and they made love; Lucien thought, "What a break!" When it was over Maud said, "Well, if I'd thought that!" She looked at Lucien with a tender reproach. "Naughty boy, I thought you were going to be good!" Lucien said he was as surprised as she was. "That's the way it happens," he said. She thought a little and then told him seriously, "I don't regret anything. Before maybe it was purer but it wasn't so complete."

In the métro, Lucien thought, "I have a mistress." He was empty and tired, saturated with a smell of absinthe and fresh fish; he sat down, holding himself stiffly to avoid contact with his sweat-soaked shirt; he felt his body to be curdled milk. He repeated forcefully, "I have a mistress." But he felt frustrated: what he desired in Maud the night before was her narrow, closed face which seemed so unattainable, her slender silhouette, her look of dignity, her reputation for being a serious girl, her scorn of the masculine sex, all those things that made her a strange being, truly *someone else*, hard and definitive, always out of reach, with her clean little thoughts, her modesties, her silk stockings and crepe dresses, her permanent wave. And all this veneer had melted under his embrace, the flesh remained, he had stretched his lips toward an eyeless face, naked as a belly, he had possessed a great flower of moist flesh. Again he saw the blind beast throbbing in the sheets with rippling, hairy yawns and he thought: that was *us two*. They had made a single one, he could no longer distinguish his flesh from that of Maud; no one had ever given him that feeling of sickening intimacy, except possibly Riri, when Riri showed him his wee-wee behind a bush or when he had forgotten himself and stayed resting on his belly, bouncing up and down, his behind naked, while they dried out his pants. Lucien felt some comfort thinking about Guigard: tomorrow he would tell him: "I slept with Maud, she's a sweet little kid, old man, it's in her blood." But he was uncomfortable, and felt naked in the dusty heat of the métro, naked beneath a thin film of clothing, stiff and naked beside a priest, across from two mature women, like a great, soiled beanpole.

Guigard congratulated him vehemently. He was getting a little tired of Fanny. "She really has a rotten temper. Yesterday she gave me dirty looks all evening." They both agreed: there have to be women like that, because, after all, you couldn't stay chaste until you got married and then they weren't in love and they weren't sick but it would be a mistake to get attached to them. Guigard spoke of real girls with delicacy and Lucien asked him news of his sister. "She's fine," said Guigard. "She says you're a quitter. You know," he added, with a little abandon, "I'm not sorry I have a sister: you find out things you never could imagine." Lucien understood him perfectly. As a result they spoke often of girls and felt full of poetry and Guigard loved to recite the words of one of his uncles who had had much success with women: "Possibly I haven't always done the right thing in my dog's life, but there's one thing God will witness: I'd rather cut my hands off than touch a virgin." Sometimes they went to see Pierrette, Guigard's sister. Lucien liked Pierrette a lot, he talked to her like a big brother, teased her a little and was grateful to her because she had not cut her hair. He was completely absorbed in his political activities; every Sunday morning he went to sell *Action Française* in front of the church in Neuilly. For more than two hours, Lucien walked up and down, his face hard. The girls coming out of mass sometimes raised beautiful frank eyes toward him; then Lucien relaxed a little and felt pure and strong; he smiled at them. He explained to the gang that he respected women and he was glad to find in them the understanding he had hoped for. Besides, they almost all had sisters.

On the 17th of April, the Guigards gave a dance for Pierrette's eighteenth birthday and naturally Lucien was invited. He was already quite good friends with Pierrette, she called him her dancing partner and he suspected her of being a little bit in love with him. Mme. Guigard had brought in a caterer and the afternoon promised to be quite gay. Lucien danced with Pierrette several times, then went to see Guigard who was receiving his friends in the smoking room. "Hello," Guigard said, "I think you all know each other: Fleurier, Simon, Vanusse, Ledoux." While Guigard was naming his friends, Lucien saw a tall young man with red, curly hair, milky skin and hard black eyelashes, approaching them hesitantly and he was overcome with rage. "What's this fellow doing here," he wondered, "Guigard knows I can't stand Jews!" He spun on his heels and withdrew rapidly to avoid introduction. "Who is that Jew?" he asked Pierrette a moment later. "It's Weill, he's at the Hautes Etudes Commerciales; my brother met him in fencing class." "I hate Jews," Lucien said. Pierrette gave a little laugh. "This one's a pretty good chap," she said. "Take me in to the buffet." Lucien drank a glass of champagne and only had time to set it down when he found himself nose to nose with Guigard and Weill. He glared at Guigard and turned his back, but Pierrette took his arm and Guigard approached him openly: "My friend Fleurier, my friend Weill," he said easily, "there, you're introduced." Weill put out his hand and Lucien felt miserable. Luckily, he suddenly remembered Desperreau: "Fleurier would have chucked the Jew in the water for good." He thrust his hands in his pockets, turned his back on Guigard and walked away. "I can never set foot in this house again," he thought, getting his coat. He felt a bitter pride. "That's what you call keeping your ideals; you can't live in society any more." Once in the street his pride melted and Lucien grew worried. "Guigard must be furious!" He shook his head and tried to tell himself with conviction, "He didn't have the right to invite a Jew if he invited me!" But his rage had left him; he saw the surprised face of Weill again with discomfort, his outstretched hand, and he felt he wanted a reconciliation: "Pierrette surely thinks I'm a heel. I should have shaken hands with him. After all, it didn't involve me in anything. Say hello to him and afterwards go right away: that's what I should have done." He wondered if he had time to go back to Guigard's. He would go up to Weill and say, "Excuse me, I wasn't feeling well." He would shake hands and say a few nice words. No. It was too late, his action was irreparable. He thought with irritation, "Why did I need to show my opinions to people who can't understand them?" He shrugged his shoulders nervously: it was a disaster. At that very instant Guigard and Pierrette were commenting on his behavior, Guigard was saying, "He's completely crazy!" Lucien clenched his fists. "Oh God," he thought, "how I hate them! God, how I hate Jews!" and he tried to draw strength from the contemplation of this immense hatred. But it melted away under his look, in vain he thought of Léon Blum who got money from Germany and hated the French, he felt nothing more than a dismal indifference. Lucien was lucky to find Maud home. He told her he loved her and possessed her several times with a sort of rage. "It's all screwed up," he told himself, "I'll never be *anybody*." "No, no," Maud said, "stop that, my big darling, it's forbidden!" But at last she let herself go: Lucien wanted to kiss her everywhere. He felt childish and perverse; he wanted to cry.

At school, next morning, Lucien's heart tightened when he saw Guigard. Guigard looked sly and pretended not to see him. Lucien was so enraged that he could not take notes: "The bastard," he thought, "the bastard!" At the end of the class, Guigard came up to him, he was pale. "If he says a word," thought Lucien, "I'll knock his teeth in." They stayed side by side for an instant, each looking at the toes of their shoes. Finally, Guigard said in an injured voice, "Excuse me, old man, I shouldn't have done that to you." Lucien started and looked at him with distrust. But Guigard went on painfully, "I met him in the class, you see, so I thought . . . we fenced together and he invited me over to his place, but I understand, you know, I shouldn't have . . . I don't know how it happened, but when I wrote the invitations I didn't think for a second . . ." Lucien still said nothing because the words would not come out, but he felt indulgent. Guigard, his head bowed, added, "Well, what a boner . . ." "You big hunk of baloney!" Lucien said, slapping his shoulder, "of course I know you didn't do it on purpose." He said generously, "I was wrong, too. I acted like a heel. But what do you expect—it's stronger than I am. I can't stand them—it's physical. I feel as though they had scales on their hands. What did Pierrette say?" "She laughed like mad," Guigard said pitifully. "And the guy?" "He caught on. I said what I could, but he took off fifteen minutes later." Still humble, he added, "My parents say you were right and you couldn't have done otherwise because of your convictions." Lucien savored the word "convictions"; he wanted to hug Guigard: "It's nothing, old man," he told him. "It's nothing because we're still friends." He walked down the Boulevard Saint-Michel in a state of extraordinary exaltation: he seemed to be himself no longer.

He told himself, "It's funny, it isn't *me* any more. I don't recognize myself!" It was hot and pleasant; people strolled by, wearing the first astonished smile of springtime on their faces; Lucien thrust himself into this soft crowd like a steel wedge; he thought, "It's not me any more. Only yesterday I was a big, bloated bug like the crickets in Férolles." Now Lucien felt clean and sharp as a chronometer. He went into La Source and ordered a pernod. The gang didn't hang around the Source because the place swarmed with dagos; but dagos and Jews did not disturb Lucien that day. He felt unusual and threatening in the midst of these olive-tinted bodies which rustled like a field of oats in the wind; a monstrous clock leaning on the bar, shining red. He recognized with amusement a little Jew the J.P. had roughed up last semester in the Faculté de Droit corridors. The fat and pensive little monster had not kept the mark of the blows, he must have stayed laid up for a while and then regained his round shape; but there was a sort of obscene resignation in him.

He was happy for the time being: he yawned voluptuously; a ray of sunlight tickled his nostrils; he scratched his nose and smiled. Was it a smile? Or rather a little oscillation which had been born on the outside, somewhere in a corner of the place, and which had come to die on his mouth? All the dagos were floating in dark, heavy water whose eddies jolted their flabby flesh, raised their arms, agitated their fingers and played a little with their lips. Poor bastards! Lucien almost pitied them. What did they come to France for? What sea currents had brought them and deposited them here? They could dress in clothes from tailors on the Boulevard Saint-Michel in vain; they were hardly more than jellyfish, Lucien thought, he was not a jellyfish, he did not belong to that humiliated race, he told himself, "I'm a diver." Then he suddenly forgot the Source and the dagos, he only saw a back, a wide back hunched with muscles going further and further away, losing itself, implacable, in the fog. He saw Guigard: Guigard was pale, he followed the back with his eyes and said to an invisible Pierrette, "Well, what a boner . . . !" Lucien was flooded with an almost intolerable joy: this powerful, solitary back was *his own!* And the scene happened yesterday! For an instant, at the cost of a violent effort, he was Guigard, he saw the humility of Guigard and felt himself deliciously terrified. "Let that be a lesson to them!" he thought. The scene changed; it was Pierrette's boudoir, it was happening in the future, Pierrette and Guigard were pointing out a name on the list of invitations. Lucien was not there but his power was

over them. Guigard was saying, "Oh no! Not that one! That would
be fine for Lucien. Lucien can't stand Jews." Lucien studied himself
once more; he thought, "I am Lucien! Somebody who can't stand
Jews." He had often pronounced this sentence but today was unlike
all other times. Not at all like them. Of course, it was apparently a
simple statement, as if someone had said, "Lucien doesn't like oysters"
or "Lucien likes to dance." But there was no mistaking it: love of
dancing might be found in some little Jew who counted no more
than a fly: all you had to do was look at that damned kike to know
that his likes and dislikes clung to him like his odor, like the reflections of his skin, that they disappeared with him like the blinking of
his heavy eyelids, like his sticky, voluptuous smiles. But Lucien's
anti-Semitism was of a different sort; unrelenting and pure, it stuck
out of him like a steel blade menacing other breasts. "It's . . . sacred,"
he thought. He remembered his mother when he was little, sometimes speaking to him in a certain special tone of voice: "Papa is
working in his office." This sentence seemed a sacramental formula
to him which suddenly conferred a halo of religious obligations on
him, such as not playing with his air gun and shouting "Tarara-
boom!"; he walked down the hall on tiptoes as if he were in a cathedral. "Now it's my turn," he thought with satisfaction. Lowering
their voices, they said, "Lucien doesn't like Jews," and people would
feel paralyzed, their limbs transfixed by a swarm of aching little ar-
rows. "Guigard and Pierrette," he said tenderly, "are children." They
had been guilty but it sufficed for Lucien to show his teeth and they
were filled with remorse, they had spoken in a low voice and walked
on tiptoe.

Lucien felt full of self-respect for the second time. But this time
he no longer needed the eyes of Guigard: he appeared respectable in
his own eyes—in his own eyes which had finally pierced his envelope
of flesh, of likes and dislikes, habits and humors. "Where I sought
myself," he thought, "I could not find myself." In good faith he took
a detailed counting of all he *was*. "But if I could only be what I am I
wouldn't be worth any more than that little kike." What could one
discover searching in this mucous intimacy if not the sorrow of flesh,
the ignoble lie of equality and disorder? "First maxim," Lucien said,
"Not to try and see inside yourself; there is no mistake more dangerous." The real Lucien—he knew now—had to be sought in the eyes
of others, in the frightened obedience of Pierrette and Guigard, the
hopeful waiting of all those beings who grew and ripened for him,
these young apprentice girls who would become *his* workers, people
of Férolles, great and small, of whom he would one day be the mas-

ter. Lucien was almost afraid, he felt almost too great for himself. So
many people were waiting for him, at attention: and he was and always would be this immense waiting of others. "That's a leader," he
thought. And he saw a hunched, muscular back reappear, then, immediately afterwards, a cathedral. He was inside, walking on tiptoe
beneath the sifted light that fell from the windows. "Only this time I
am the cathedral!" He stared intently at his neighbor, a tall Cuban,
brown and mild as a cigar. He must absolutely find words to express
this extraordinary discovery. Quietly, cautiously, he raised his hand
to his forehead, like a lighted candle, then drew into himself for an
instant, thoughtful and holy, and the words came of themselves. "I
HAVE RIGHTS!" Rights! Something like triangles and circles: it
was so perfect that it didn't exist, you could trace thousands of circles
with a compass in vain, you could never make a single circle. Generations of workers could even scrupulously obey the commands of Lucien, they would never exhaust his right to command, rights were
beyond existence, like mathematical objects and religious dogma.
And now Lucien was just that: an enormous bouquet of responsibilities and rights. He had believed that he existed by chance for a long
time, but it was due to a lack of sufficient thought. His place in the
sun was marked in Férolles long before his birth. They were *waiting*
for him long before his father's marriage: if he had come into the
world it was to occupy that place: "I exist," he thought, "because I
have the right to exist." And, perhaps for the first time, he had a
flashing, glorious vision of his destiny. Sooner or later he would go
to the Centrale (it made no difference). Then he would drop Maud
(she always wanted to sleep with him, it was tiresome, their confused flesh giving off an odor of scorched rabbit stew in the
torrid heat of springtime. "And then, Maud belongs to everybody.
Today me, tomorrow somebody else, none of it makes any sense");
he would go and live in Férolles. Somewhere in France there was a
bright young girl like Pierrette, a country girl with eyes like flowers
who would stay chaste for him: sometimes she tried to imagine her
future master, this gentle and terrible man; but she could not. She was
a virgin; in the most secret part of her body she recognized the right
of Lucien alone to possess her. He would marry her, she would be
*his* wife, the tenderest of his rights. When, in the evening, she would
undress with slender, sacred gestures, it would be like a holocaust.
He would take her in his arms with the approval of everyone, and
tell her, "You belong to me!" What she would show him she would
have the right to show him alone and for him the act of love would be
a voluptuous counting of his goods. His most tender right, his most

intimate right: the right to be respected to the very flesh, obeyed to the very bed. "I'll marry young," he thought. He thought too that he would like to have many children; then he thought of his father's work; he was impatient to continue it and wondered if M. Fleurier was not going to die soon.

A clock struck noon; Lucien rose. The metamorphosis was complete: a graceful, uncertain adolescent had entered this café one hour earlier; now a man left, a leader among Frenchmen. Lucien took a few steps in the glorious light of a French morning. At the corner of Rue des Ecoles and the Boulevard Saint-Michel he went toward a stationery shop and looked at himself in the mirror: he would have liked to find on his own face the impenetrable look he admired on Lemordant's. But the mirror only reflected a pretty, headstrong, little face that was not yet terrible. "I'll grow a mustache," he decided.

*Translated from the French by Lloyd Alexander*

# Albert Camus

## THE RENEGADE

WHAT A JUMBLE! What a jumble! I must tidy up my mind. Since they cut out my tongue, another tongue, it seems, has been constantly wagging somewhere in my skull, something has been talking, or someone, that suddenly falls silent and then it all begins again—oh, I hear too many things I never utter, what a jumble, and if I open my mouth it's like pebbles rattling together. Order and method, the tongue says, and then goes on talking of other matters simultaneously—yes, I always longed for order. At least one thing is certain, I am waiting for the missionary who is to come and take my place. Here I am on the trail, an hour away from Taghâsa, hidden in a pile of rocks, sitting on my old rifle. Day is breaking over the desert, it's still very cold, soon it will be too hot, this country drives men mad and I've been here I don't know how many years. . . . No, just a little longer. The missionary is to come this morning, or this evening. I've heard he'll come with a guide, perhaps they'll have but one camel between them. I'll wait, I am waiting, it's only the cold making me shiver. Just be patient a little longer, filthy slave!

But I have been patient for so long. When I was home on that high plateau of the Massif Central, my coarse father, my boorish mother, the wine, the pork soup every day, the wine above all, sour and cold, and the long winter, the frigid wind, the snowdrifts, the revolting bracken—oh, I wanted to get away, leave them all at once and begin to live at last, in the sunlight, with fresh water. I believed the priest, he spoke to me of the seminary, he tutored me daily, he had plenty of time in that Protestant region, where he used to hug the walls as he crossed the village. He told me of the future and of the sun, Catholicism is the sun, he used to say, and he would get me to read, he beat Latin into my hard head ("The boy's bright but he's pig-headed"), my head was so hard that, despite all my falls, it has never once bled in my life: "Bull-headed," my pig of a father used to say. At the seminary they were proud as punch, a recruit from the Protestant region was a victory, they greeted me like the sun at Austerlitz.

The sun was pale and feeble, to be sure, because of the alcohol, they have drunk sour wine and the children's teeth are set on edge, *gra gra*, one really ought to kill one's father, but after all there's no danger that *he*'ll hurl himself into missionary work since he's now long dead, the tart wine eventually cut through his stomach, so there's nothing left but to kill the missionary.

I have something to settle with him and with his teachers, with my teachers who deceived me, with the whole of lousy Europe, everybody deceived me. Missionary work, that's all they could say, go out to the savages and tell them: "Here is my Lord, just look at him, he never strikes or kills, he issues his orders in a low voice, he turns the other cheek, he's the greatest of masters, choose him, just see how much better he's made me, offend me and you will see." Yes, I believed, *gra gra*, and I felt better, I had put on weight, I was almost handsome, I wanted to be offended. When we would walk out in tight black rows, in summer, under Grenoble's hot sun and would meet girls in cotton dresses, *I* didn't look away, I despised them, I waited for them to offend me, and sometimes they would laugh. At such times I would think: "Let them strike me and spit in my face," but their laughter, to tell the truth, came to the same thing, bristling with teeth and quips that tore me to shreds, the offense and the suffering were sweet to me! My confessor couldn't understand when I used to heap accusations on myself: "No, no, there's good in you!" Good! There was nothing but sour wine in me, and that was all for the best, how can a man become better if he's not bad, I had grasped that in everything they taught me. That's the only thing I did grasp, a single idea, and, pig-headed bright boy, I carried it to its logical conclusion, I went out of my way for punishments, I groused at the normal, in short I too wanted to be an example in order to be noticed and so that after noticing me people would give credit to what had made me better, through me praise my Lord.

Fierce sun! It's rising, the desert is changing, it has lost its mountain-cyclamen color, O my mountain, and the snow, the soft enveloping snow, no, it's a rather grayish yellow, the ugly moment before the great resplendence. Nothing, still nothing from here to the horizon over yonder where the plateau disappears in a circle of still soft colors. Behind me, the trail climbs to the dune hiding of Taghàsa, whose iron name has been beating in my head for so many years. The first to mention it to me was the half-blind old priest who had retired to our monastery, but why do I say the first, he was the only one, and it wasn't the city of salt, the white walls under the blinding sun, that struck me in his account but the cruelty of the savage inhabitants and the town closed to all outsiders, only one of those who had tried to get in, one alone, to his knowledge, had lived to relate what he had seen. They had whipped him and driven him out into the desert after having put salt on his wounds and in his mouth, he had met nomads who for once were compassionate, a stroke of luck, and since then I had been dreaming about his tale, about the fire of the salt and the sky, about the House of the Fetish and his slaves, could anything more barbarous, more exciting be imagined, yes, that was my mission and I had to go and reveal to them my Lord.

They all expatiated on the subject at the seminary to discourage me, pointing out the necessity of waiting, that it was not missionary country, that I wasn't ready yet, I had to prepare myself specially, know who I was, and even then I had to go through tests, then they would see! But go on waiting, ah, no!—yes, if they insisted, for the special preparation and the tryouts because they took place at Algiers and brought me closer, but for all the rest I shook my pig-head and repeated the same thing, to get among the most barbarous and live as they did, to show them at home, and even in the House of the Fetish, through example, that my Lord's truth would prevail. They would offend me, of course, but I was not afraid of offenses, they were essential to the demonstration, and as a result of the way I endured them I'd get the upper hand of those savages like a strong sun. Strong, yes, that was the word I constantly had on the tip of my tongue, I dreamed of absolute power, the kind that makes people kneel down, that forces the adversary to capitulate, converts him in short, and the blinder, the crueler he is, the more he's sure of himself, mired in his own conviction, the more his consent establishes the royalty of whoever brought about his collapse. Converting good folk who had strayed somewhat was the shabby ideal of our priests, I despised them for daring so little when they could do so much, they lacked faith and I had it, I wanted to be acknowledged by the torturers themselves, to fling them on their knees and make them say: "O Lord, here is thy victory," to rule in short by the sheer force of words over an army of the wicked. Oh, I was sure of reasoning logically on that subject, never quite sure of myself otherwise, but once I get an idea I don't let go of it, that's my strong point, yes the strong point of the fellow they all pitied!

The sun has risen higher, my forehead is beginning to burn. Around me the stones are beginning to crack open with a dull sound, the only cool thing is the rifle's barrel, cool as the fields, as the evening rain long ago when the soup was simmering, they would wait for me, my father and mother who would occasionally smile at me,

perhaps I loved them. But that's all in the past, a film of heat is beginning to rise from the trail, come on, missionary, I'm waiting for you,
now I know how to answer the message, my new masters taught me,
and I know they are right, you have to settle accounts with that
question of love. When I fled the seminary in Algiers I had a different
idea of the savages and only one detail of my imaginings was true,
they are cruel. I had robbed the treasurer's office, cast off my habit,
crossed the Atlas, the upper plateaus and the desert, the bus-driver of
the Trans-Sahara line made fun of me: "Don't go there," he too,
what had got into them all, and the gusts of sand for hundreds of
wind-blown kilometers, progressing and backing in the face of the
wind, then the mountains again made up of black peaks and ridges
sharp as steel, and after them it took a guide to go out on the endless
sea of brown pebbles, screaming with heat, burning with the fires of a
thousand mirrors, to the spot on the confines of the white country
and the land of the blacks where stands the city of salt. And the
money the guide stole from me, ever naïve I had shown it to him,
but he left me on the trail—just about here, it so happens—after having struck me: "Dog, there's the way, the honor's all mine, go ahead,
go on, they'll show you," and they did show me, oh yes, they're like
the sun that never stops, except at night, beating sharply and
proudly, that is beating me hard at this moment, too hard, with a
multitude of lances burst from the ground, oh shelter, yes shelter,
under the big rock, before everything gets muddled.

The shade here is good. How can anyone live in the city of salt,
in the hollow of that basin full of dazzling heat? On each of the sharp
right-angle walls cut out with a pickaxe and coarsely planed, the
gashes left by the pickaxe bristle with blinding scales, pale scattered
sand yellows them somewhat except when the wind dusts the upright walls and terraces, then everything shines with dazzling whiteness under a sky likewise dusted even to its blue rind. I was going
blind during those days when the stationary fire would crackle for
hours on the surface of the white terraces that all seemed to meet as
if, in the remote past, they had all together tackled a mountain of
salt, flattened it first, and then had hollowed out streets, the insides of
houses and windows directly in the mass, or as if—yes, this is more
like it—they had cut out their white, burning hell with a powerful jet
of boiling water just to show that they could live where no one ever
could, thirty days' travel from any living thing, in this hollow in the
middle of the desert where the heat of day prevents any contact
among creatures, separates them by a portcullis of invisible flames and
of searing crystals, where without transition the cold of night con-

geals them individually in their rock-salt shells, nocturnal dwellers in a dried-up icefloe, black Eskimos suddenly shivering in their cubical igloos. Black because they wear long black garments, and the salt that collects even under their nails, that they continue tasting bitterly and swallowing during the sleep of those polar nights, the salt they drink in the water from the only spring in the hollow of a dazzling groove, often spots their dark garments with something like the trail of snails after a rain.

Rain, O Lord, just one real rain, long and hard, rain from your heaven! Then at last the hideous city, gradually eaten away, would slowly and irresistibly cave in and, utterly melted in a slimy torrent, would carry off its savage inhabitants towards the sands. Just one rain, Lord. But what do I mean, what Lord, they are the lords and masters! They rule over their sterile homes, over their black slaves that they work to death in the mines and each slab of salt that is cut out is worth a man in the region to the south, they pass by, silent, and at night, when the whole town looks like a milky phantom, they wearing their mourning veils in the mineral whiteness of the streets, stoop down and enter the shade of their homes, where the salt walls shine dimly. They sleep with a weightless sleep and, as soon as they wake, they give orders, they strike, they say they are a united people, that their god is the true god, and that one must obey. They are my masters, they are ignorant of pity and, like masters, they want to be alone, to progress alone, to rule alone, because they alone had the daring to build in the salt and the sands a cold torrid city. And I . . .

What a jumble when the heat rises, I'm sweating, they never do, now the shade itself is heating up, I feel the sun on the stone above me, it's striking, striking like a hammer on all the stones and it's the music, the vast music of noon, air and stones vibrating over hundreds of kilometers, *gra*, I hear the silence as I did once before. Yes, it was the same silence, years ago, that greeted me when the guards led me to them, in the sunlight, in the center of the square, whence the concentric terraces rose gradually towards the lid of hard blue sky sitting on the edge of the basin. There I was, thrown on my knees in the hollow of that white shield, my eyes corroded by the swords of salt and fire issuing from all the walls, pale with fatigue, my ear bleeding from the blow given by my guide, and they, tall and black, looked at me without saying a word. The day was at its midcourse. Under the blows of the iron sun the sky resounded at length, a sheet of white-hot tin, it was the same silence, and they stared at me, time passed, they kept on staring at me, and I couldn't face their stares, I panted more and more violently, eventually I wept, and suddenly they turned their backs on me in silence and all together went off in the same direction. On my knees, all I could see, in the red-and-black sandals, was their feet sparkling with salt as they raised the long black gowns, the tip rising somewhat, the heel striking the ground lightly, and when the square was empty I was dragged to the House of the Fetish.

Squatting, as I am today in the shelter of the rock and the fire above my head pierces the rock's thickness, I spent several days within the dark of the House of the Fetish, somewhat higher than the others, surrounded by a wall of salt, but without windows, full of a sparkling night. Several days, and I was given a basin of brackish water and some grain that was thrown before me the way chickens are fed, I picked it up. By day the door remained closed and yet the darkness became less oppressive, as if the irresistible sun managed to flow through the masses of salt. No lamp, but by feeling my way along the walls I touched garlands of dried palms decorating the walls and, at the end, a small door, coarsely fitted, of which I could make out the bolt with my fingertips. Several days, long after—I couldn't count the days or the hours, but my handful of grain had been thrown me some ten times and I had dug out a hole for my excrements that I covered up in vain, the stench of an animal den hung on anyway—long after, yes, the door opened wide and they came in.

One of them came towards me where I was squatting in a corner. I felt the burning salt against my cheek, I smelled the dusty scent of the palms, I watched him approach. He stopped a yard away from me, he stared at me in silence, a signal, and I stood up, he stared at me with his metallic eyes that shone without expression in his brown horse-face, then he raised his hand. Still impassive, he seized me by the lower lip, which he twisted slowly until he tore my flesh and, without letting go, made me turn around and back up to the center of the room, he pulled on my lip to make me fall on my knees there, mad with pain and my mouth bleeding, then he turned away to join the others standing against the walls. They watched me moaning in the unbearable heat of the unbroken daylight that came in the wide-open door, and in that light suddenly appeared the Sorcerer with his raffia hair, his chest covered with a breastplate of pearls, his legs bare under a straw skirt, wearing a mask of reeds and wire with two square openings for the eyes. He was followed by musicians and women wearing heavy motley gowns that revealed nothing of their bodies. They danced in front of the door at the end, but a coarse, scarcely rhythmical dance, they just barely moved, and finally the

Sorcerer opened the little door behind me, the masters did not stir, they were watching me, I turned around and saw the Fetish, his double axe-head, his iron nose twisted like a snake.

I was carried before him, to the foot of the pedestal, I was made to drink a black, bitter, bitter water, and at once my head began to burn, I was laughing, that's the offense, I have been offended. They undressed me, shaved my head and body, washed me in oil, beat my face with cords dipped in water and salt, and I laughed and turned my head away, but each time two women would take me by the ears and offer my face to the Sorcerer's blows while I could see only his square eyes, I was still laughing, covered with blood. They stopped, no one spoke but me, the jumble was beginning in my head, then they lifted me up and forced me to raise my eyes towards the Fetish, I had ceased laughing. I knew that I was now consecrated to him to serve him, adore him, no, I was not laughing any more, fear and pain stifled me. And there, in that white house, between those walls that the sun was assiduously burning on the outside, my face taut, my memory exhausted, yes, I tried to pray to the Fetish, he was all there was and even his horrible face was less horrible than the rest of the world. Then it was that my ankles were tied with a cord that permitted just one step, they danced again, but this time in front of the Fetish, the masters went out one by one.

The door once closed behind them, the music again, and the Sorcerer lighted a bark fire around which he pranced, his long silhouette broke on the angles of the white walls, fluttered on the flat surfaces, filled the room with dancing shadows. He traced a rectangle in a corner to which the women dragged me, I felt their dry and gentle hands, they set before me a bowl of water and a little pile of grain and pointed to the Fetish, I grasped that I was to keep my eyes fixed on him. Then the Sorcerer called them one after the other over to the fire, he beat some of them who moaned and who then went and prostrated themselves before the Fetish my god, while the Sorcerer kept on dancing and he made them all leave the room until only one was left, quite young, squatting near the musicians and not yet beaten. He held her by a shock of hair which he kept twisting round his wrist, she dropped backward with eyes popping until she finally fell on her back. Dropping her, the Sorcerer screamed, the musicians turned to the wall, while behind the square-eyed mask the scream rose to an impossible pitch, and the woman rolled on the ground in a sort of fit and, at last on all fours, her head hidden in her locked arms, she too screamed, but with a hollow, muffled sound, and in this posi-tion, without ceasing to scream and to look at the Fetish, the Sorcerer took her nimbly and nastily, without the woman's face being visible, for it was covered with the heavy folds of her garment. And, wild as a result of the solitude, *I* screamed too, yes, howled with fright towards the Fetish until a kick hurled me against the wall, biting the salt as I am biting this rock today with my tongueless mouth, while waiting for the man I must kill.

Now the sun has gone a little beyond the middle of the sky. Through the breaks in the rock I can see the hole it makes in the white-hot metal of the sky, a mouth voluble as mine, constantly vomiting rivers of flame over the colorless desert. On the trail in front of me, nothing, no cloud of dust on the horizon, behind me they must be looking for me, no, not yet, it's only in the late afternoon that they opened the door and I could go out a little, after having spent the day cleaning the House of the Fetish, set out fresh offerings, and in the evening the ceremony would begin, in which I was sometimes beaten, at others not, but always I served the Fetish, the Fetish whose image is engraved in iron in my memory and now in my hope also. Never had a god so possessed or enslaved me, my whole life day and night was devoted to him, and pain and the absence of pain, wasn't that joy, were due to him and even, yes, desire, as a result of being present, almost every day, at that impersonal and nasty act which I heard without seeing it inasmuch as I now had to face the wall or else be beaten. But, my face up against the salt, obsessed by the bestial shadows moving on the wall, I listened to the long scream, my throat was dry, a burning sexless desire squeezed my temples and my belly as in a vice. Thus the days followed one another, I barely distinguished them as if they had liquefied in the torrid heat and the treacherous reverberation from the walls of salt, time had become merely a vague lapping of waves in which there would burst out, at regular intervals, screams of pain or possession, a long ageless day in which the Fetish ruled as this fierce sun does over my house of rocks, and now, as I did then, I weep with unhappiness and longing, a wicked hope consumes me, I want to betray, I lick the barrel of my gun and its soul inside, its soul, only guns have souls— oh, yes! the day they cut out my tongue, I learned to adore the immortal soul of hatred!

What a jumble, what a rage, *gra gra*, drunk with heat and wrath, lying prostrate on my gun. Who's panting here? I can't endure this endless heat, this waiting, I must kill him. Not a bird, not a blade of grass, stone, an arid desire, their screams, this tongue within me talking, and, since they mutilated me, the long, flat, deserted suffering deprived even of the water of night, the night of which I would dream, when locked in with the god, in my den of salt. Night alone with its cool stars and dark fountains could save me, carry me off at last from the wicked gods of mankind, but ever locked up I could not contemplate it. If the newcomer tarries more, I shall see it at least rise from the desert and sweep over the sky, a cold golden vine that will hang from the dark zenith and from which I can drink at length, moisten this black dried hole that no muscle of live flexible flesh revives now, forget at last that day when madness took away my tongue.

How hot it was, really hot, the salt was melting or so it seemed to me, the air was corroding my eyes, and the Sorcerer came in without his mask. Almost naked under grayish tatters, a new woman followed him and her face, covered with a tattoo reproducing the mask of the Fetish, expressed only an idol's ugly stupor. The only thing alive about her was her thin flat body that flopped at the foot of the god when the Sorcerer opened the door of the niche. Then he went out without looking at me, the heat rose, I didn't stir, the Fetish looked at me over that motionless body whose muscles stirred gently and the woman's idol-face didn't change when I approached. Only her eyes enlarged as she stared at me, my feet touched hers, the heat then began to shriek, and the idol, without a word, still staring at me with her dilated eyes, gradually slipped on to her back, slowly drew her legs up and raised them as she gently spread her knees. But, immediately afterwards, *gra*, the Sorcerer was lying in wait for me, they all entered and tore me from the woman, beat me dreadfully on the sinful place, what sin, I'm laughing, where is it and where is virtue, they clapped me against a wall, a hand of steel gripped my jaws, another opened my mouth, pulled on my tongue until it bled, was it I screaming with that bestial scream, a cool cutting caress, yes cool at last, went over my tongue. When I came to, I was alone in the night, glued to the wall, covered with hardened blood, a gag of strange-smelling dry grasses filled my mouth, it had stopped bleeding, but it was vacant and in that absence the only living thing was a tormenting pain. I wanted to rise, I fell back, happy, desperately happy to die at last, death too is cool and its shadow hides no god.

I did not die, a new feeling of hatred stood up one day, at the same time I did, walked towards the door of the niche, opened it, closed it behind me, I hated my people, the Fetish was there and from the depths of the hole in which I was I did more than pray to him, I believed in him and denied all I had believed up to then. Hail! he was strength and power, he could be destroyed but not converted, he stared over my head with his empty, rusty eyes. Hail! he was the master, the only lord, whose indisputable attribute was malice, there are no good masters. For the first time, as a result of offenses, my whole body crying out a single pain, I surrendered to him and approved his maleficent order, I adored in him the evil principle of the world. A prisoner of his kingdom—the sterile city carved out of a mountain of salt, divorced from nature, deprived of those rare and fleeting flowerings of the desert, preserved from those strokes of chance or marks of affection such as an unexpected cloud or a brief violent downpour that are familiar even to the sun or the sands, the city of order in short, right-angles, square rooms, rigid men—I freely became its tortured, hate-filled citizen, I repudiated the long history that had been taught me. I had been misled, solely the reign of malice was devoid of defects, I had been misled, truth is square, heavy, thick, it does not admit distinctions, good is an idle dream, an intention constantly postponed and pursued with exhausting effort, a limit never reached, its reign is impossible. Only evil can reach its limits and reign absolutely, it must be served to establish its visible kingdom, then we shall see, but what does "then" mean, only evil is present, down with Europe, reason, honor, and the cross. Yes, I was to be converted to the religion of my masters, yes indeed, I was a slave, but if I too become vicious I cease to be a slave, despite my shackled feet and my mute mouth. Oh, this heat is driving me crazy, the desert cries out everywhere under the unbearable light, and he, the Lord of kindness, whose very name revolts me, I disown him, for I know him now. He dreamed and wanted to lie, his tongue was cut out so that his word would no longer be able to deceive the world, he was pierced with nails even in his head, his poor head, like mine now, what a jumble, how weak I am, and the earth didn't tremble, I am sure, it was not a righteous man they had killed, I refuse to believe it, there are no righteous men but only evil masters who bring about the reign of relentless truth. Yes, the Fetish alone has power, he is the sole god of this world, hatred is his commandment, the source of all life, the cool water, cool like mint that chills the mouth and burns the stomach.

Then it was that I changed, they realized it, I would kiss their hands when I met them, I was on their side, never wearying of admiring them, I trusted them, I hoped they would mutilate my people as they had mutilated me. And when I learned that the missionary was to come, I knew what I was to do. That day like all the others, the same blinding daylight that had been going on so long! Late in the afternoon a guard was suddenly seen running along the edge of the basin, and, a few minutes later, I was dragged to the House of the

Fetish and the door closed. One of them held me on the ground in the dark, under threat of his cross-shaped sword, and the silence lasted for a long time until a strange sound filled the ordinarily peaceful town, voices that it took me some time to recognize because they were speaking my language, but as soon as they rang out the point of the sword was lowered towards my eyes, my guard stared at me in silence. Then two voices came closer and I can still hear them, one asking why that house was guarded and whether they should break in the door, Lieutenant, the other said: "No" sharply, then added, after a moment, that an agreement had been reached, that the town accepted a garrison of twenty men on condition that they would camp outside the walls and respect the customs. The private laughed, "They're knuckling under," but the officer didn't know, for the first time in any case they were willing to receive someone to take care of the children and that would be the chaplain, later on they would see about the territory. The other said they would cut off the chaplain's you know what if the soldiers were not there. "Oh, no!" the officer answered. "In fact, Father Beffort will come before the garrison; he'll be here in two days." That was all I heard, motionless, lying under the sword, I was in pain, a wheel of needles and knives was whirling in me. They were crazy, they were crazy, they were allowing a hand to be laid on the city, on their invincible power, on the true god, and the fellow who was to come would not have his tongue cut out, he would show off his insolent goodness without paying for it, without enduring any offense. The reign of evil would be postponed, there would be doubt again, again time would be wasted dreaming of the impossible good, wearing oneself out in fruitless efforts instead of hastening the realization of the only possible kingdom and I looked at the sword threatening me, O sole power to rule over the world! O power, and the city gradually emptied of its sounds, the door finally opened, I remained alone, burned and bitter, with the Fetish, and I swore to him to save my new faith, my true masters, my despotic God, to betray well, whatever it might cost me.

*Gra*, the heat is abating a little, the stone has ceased to vibrate, I can go out of my hole, watch the desert gradually take on yellow and ocher tints that will soon be mauve. Last night I waited until they were asleep, I had blocked the lock on the door, I went out with the same step as usual, measured by the cord, I knew the streets, I knew where to get the old rifle, what gate wasn't guarded, and I reached here just as the night was beginning to fade around a handful of stars while the desert was getting a little darker. And now it seems days and days that I have been crouching in these rocks. Soon, soon, I hope he comes soon! In a moment they'll begin to look for me, they'll speed over the trails in all directions, they won't know that I left for them and to serve them better, my legs are weak, drunk with hunger and hate. Oh! over there, *gra*, at the end of the trail, two camels are growing bigger, ambling along, already multiplied by short shadows, they are running with that lively and dreamy gait they always have. Here they are, here at last!

Quick, the rifle and I load it quickly. O Fetish, my god over yonder, may your power be preserved, may the offense be multiplied, may hate rule pitilessly over a world of the damned, may the wicked forever be masters, may the kingdom come, where in a single city of salt and iron black tyrants will enslave and possess without pity! And now, *gra gra*, fire on pity, fire on impotence and its charity, fire on all that postpones the coming of evil, fire twice, and there they are toppling over, falling, and the camels flee towards the horizon, where a geyser of black birds has just risen in the unchanged sky. I laugh, I laugh, the fellow is writhing in his detested habit, he is raising his head a little, he sees me—me his all-powerful shackled master, why does he smile at me, I'll crush that smile! How pleasant is the sound of a rifle butt on the face of goodness, today, today at last, all is consummated and everywhere in the desert, even hours away from here, jackals sniff the non-existent wind, then set out in a patient trot towards the feast of carrion awaiting them. Victory! I raise my arms to a heaven moved to pity, a lavender shadow is just barely suggested on the opposite side, O nights of Europe, home, childhood, why must I weep in the moment of triumph?

He stirred, no the sound comes from somewhere else, and from the other direction here they come rushing like a flight of dark birds, my masters, who fall upon me, seize me, ah yes! strike, they fear their city sacked and howling, they fear the avenging soldiers I called forth, and this is only right, upon the sacred city. Defend yourselves now, strike! strike me first, you possess the truth! O my masters, they will then conquer the soldiers, they'll conquer the word and love, they'll spread over the deserts, cross the seas, fill the light of Europe with their black veils—strike the belly, yes, strike the eyes— sow their salt on the continent, all vegetation, all youth will die out, and dumb crowds with shackled feet will plod beside me in the world-wide desert under the cruel sun of the true faith, I'll not be alone. Ah! the pain, the pain they cause me, their rage is good and on this cross-shaped war-saddle where they are now quartering **me,** pity! I'm laughing, I love the blow that nails me down **crucified.**

\* \* \*

How silent the desert is! Already night and I am alone. I'm thirsty. Still waiting, where is the city, those sounds in the distance, and the soldiers perhaps the victors, no, it can't be, even if the soldiers are victorious, they're not wicked enough, they won't be able to rule, they'll still say one must become better, and still millions of men between evil and good, torn, bewildered, O Fetish, why hast thou forsaken me? All is over, I'm thirsty, my body is burning, a darker night fills my eyes.

This long, this long dream, I'm awaking, no, I'm going to die, dawn is breaking, the first light, daylight for the living, and for me the inexorable sun, the flies. Who is speaking, no one, the sky is not opening up, no, no, God doesn't speak in the desert, yet whence comes that voice saying: "If you consent to die for hate and power, who will forgive us?" Is it another tongue in me or still that other fellow refusing to die, at my feet, and repeating: "Courage! courage! courage!"? Ah! supposing I were wrong again! Once fraternal men, sole recourse, O solitude, forsake me not! Here, here who are you, torn, with bleeding mouth, is it you, Sorcerer, the soldiers defeated you, the salt is burning over there, it's you my beloved master! Cast off that hate-ridden face, be good now, we were mistaken, we'll begin all over again, we'll rebuild the city of mercy, I want to go back home. Yes, help me, that's right, give me your hand. . . .

A handful of salt fills the mouth of the garrulous slave.

*Translated from the French by Justin O'Brien*

# Samuel Beckett

## STORIES AND TEXTS FOR NOTHING, III

L EAVE, I was going to say leave all that. What matter who's speaking, someone said what matter who's speaking. There's going to be a departure, I'll be there, it won't be me, I'll be here, I'll say I'm far, it won't be me, I won't say anything, there's going to be a story, someone's going to try and tell a story. Yes, enough denials, all is false, there's no one, it's agreed, there's nothing, enough phrases, let's be dupes, dupes of time, all time, until it's over, all over, and the voices are stilled, they're only voices, only lies. Here, leave here and go elsewhere, or stay here, but coming and going. Move first, there must be a body, as of old, I don't say no, I won't say no any more, I'll say I have a body, a body that moves, forward, backward, up and down, as required. With a clutter of limbs and organs, all that's needed to live once again, to hold out, a short spell, I'll call that living, I'll say it's me, I'll stand up, I'll think no more, I'll be too taken up, standing up, keeping standing up, moving about, holding out, getting to the next day, the next week, that will be enough, a week will be enough, a week in spring, that will be bracing. It's enough to will, I'm going to will, will myself a body, will myself a head, a little strength, a little courage, I'm going to start, a week is soon over, then back here, this inextricable place, far from the days, the days are far, it's not going to be easy. And why, after all, no no, leave it, don't start that again, don't listen to everything, don't say everything, all is old, all one, that's settled. There you are up, I give you my word, I swear it's mine, work your hands, palp your skull, seat of the understanding, without it nothing doing, then the rest, the lower parts, can't do without them, and say what you are, what kind of man, have a guess, there must be a man, or a woman, feel between your legs, no need of beauty, or strength, a week is soon over, no one's going to love you, don't worry. No, not like that, too sudden, I gave myself a fright. And to start with stop panting, no one's going to kill you, oh no, no one's going to love you and no one's going to kill you. You may emerge in the high depression of Gobi, there you'll feel at home.

I'll wait for you here, my mind at rest, at rest for you, no, I'm alone,
I alone am, it's I must go, this time it's I. I know what I'll do, I'll be a
man, I must, a kind of man, a kind of old infant, I'll have a nurse,
she'll be fond of me, she'll give me her hand, to cross over, she'll let
me loose in gardens, I'll be good, I'll sit in a corner and comb my
beard, smooth it down, to be nicer looking, a little nicer, if it could
be like that. She'll say to me, Come, lamb, it's time for home. I won't
have any responsibility, she'll have all the responsibility, her name
will be Nanny, I'll call her Nanny, if it could only be like that. Come,
pet, it's time for bottle. Who taught me all I know, I alone, when I
was still a wanderer, I deduced it all, from nature, with the aid of an
all-in-one, I know it's not true, but it's too late now, too late to deny
it, the knowledge is there, items of knowledge, gleaming in turn, far
and near, flickering over the abyss, allies. Leave it and go, I must go,
I must say so anyway, the moment is come, one doesn't know why.
What does it matter where you say you are, here or elsewhere, fixed
or movable, shapeless or oblong like man, without light or in the
light of heaven, I don't know, it seems to matter, it's not going to be
easy. If I went back to where all went out and then on from there,
no, that wouldn't lead anywhere, that never led anywhere, the memory of it has gone out too, a great flame and then blackness, a great
spasm and then no more bulk or traversable space, I don't know. I
tried to have me fall, off the cliff, in the street in the midst of
mortals, that led nowhere, I gave up. Travel the road again that
cast me up here, before going back the way I came, or on, wise
advice. That's so that I'll never stir again, dribble on here till time is
done, murmuring every ten centuries, It's not me, it's not true, it's
not me, I'm far. No no, I'll speak now of the future, I'll speak in
the future, as in the days when I said to myself, in the night, Tomorrow I'll put on my blue tie, the one with the stars, and put it on, when
the night was past. Quick quick before I weep. I'll have a friend, my
own age, my own bog, an old warrior, we'll fight our battles over
again and compare our scratches. Quick quick. He had served in the
navy, perhaps under Jellicoe, while I was potting at the invader from
behind a barrel of Guinness, with my arquebus. We have not long,
that's right, in the present, not long to live, it's our last winter of all,
halleluiah. We wonder what will carry us off finally. He's gone in
the wind, I in the bladder rather. We envy each other, he envies me,
I envy him, on and off. I catheterize myself unaided, with trembling
hand, standing in the public pisshouse, bent double, under cover of
my cape, people take me for a dirty old man. Meanwhile he waits for
me on a bench, coughing up his guts, spitting into a snuff-box which

no sooner overflows than he empties it into the canal, out of public-spiritedness. We have deserved well of our motherland, she'll get us into hospital before we die. We spend our life, it's ours, trying to unite in the same instant a ray of sunshine and a free bench, in an oasis of public greenery, we have taken to a love of nature, in our sere and yellow, it belongs to one and all, in places. He reads to me in choking murmur from the paper of the day before, he had better been the blind one. Our passion is horse-racing, dog-racing too, we have no political opinions, just limply republican. But we also have a warm spot for the Windsors, the Hanoverians, I forget, the Hohen-zollerns is it. Nothing human is foreign to us, once we have digested the dogs and horses. No, alone, I'd be better off alone, it would be quicker. He'd feed me, he had a friend, a pork-butcher, he'd ram my soul back down my gullet with black pudding. With his consola-tions, allusions to cancer, recollections of imperishable raptures, he'd prevent discouragement from sapping my foundations. And I, instead of concentrating on my own horizons, which might have en-abled me to throw them under a lorry, would have my mind dis-tracted by his. I'd say to him, Come on, son, leave all that, think no more about it, and it's I would think no more about it, besotted with brotherliness. And the obligations, I have in mind particularly the appointments at ten o'clock in the morning, rain, hail or shine, in front of Duggan's, thronging already with sporting men in a hurry to get their bets out of harm's way before the bars opened. We were, there we are past and gone again, so  much the better, so much the better, most punctual, I must say. To see the remains of Vincent arriv-ing in sheets of rain, with the brave involuntary swagger of the old tar, his head swathed in a bloody clout and a gleam in his eye, was for the acute observer an example of what man is capable of, in his thirst for enjoyment. With one hand he sustained his sternum, with the heel of the other his spinal column, no, that's all memories, last shifts more ancient than the flood. To see what's happening here, where there's no one, where nothing happens, to get something to happen here, someone to be here, then put an end to it, make silence, enter silence, or another noise, a noise of other voices than those of life and death, of lives and deaths that never will be mine, enter my story, in order to leave it, no, that's all fiddle-faddle. Is it possible I'll sprout a head in the end, all my own, in which to brew some poisons worthy of me, and legs to kick my heels, I'd be there at last, I could go, it's all I ask, no, I can't ask anything. Nothing but the head and the two legs, or just one, in the middle, I'd go hopping. Or nothing but the head, nice and round, nice and smooth, no need of features,

I'd roll, downhill, almost a pure spirit, no, that wouldn't work, all's uphill from here, there'd have to be a leg, or the equivalent, an annular joint or so, contractile, with them you go a long way. To set forth from Duggan's door, on a spring morning of rain and shine, not knowing if you'll ever come to evening, what's wrong there? It would be so easy. To be buried in that flesh or in another, in that arm held by a friendly hand, and in that hand, without arms, without hands, and without soul in those trembling souls, through the crowd, the hoops, the toy balloons, what's wrong there? I don't know, I'm here, that's all I know, and that it's still not me, that's what you have to make the best of. There's no flesh anywhere, nor any means of dying, leave all that, to want to leave all that, without knowing what that means, all that, it's soon said, soon done, in vain, nothing has stirred, no one spoken. Here, nothing will happen, there will be no one here, for many a long day. Departures, stories, they're not for tomorrow. And the voices, wherever they come from, are stone dead.

*Translated from the French by Anthony Bonner and Samuel Beckett*

# Alain Robbe-Grillet

## THE SECRET ROOM

F IRST THERE IS a red spot, bright red, shiny but dark, shading to almost black. It forms an irregular, clearly outlined rosette, extended on several sides by wide streaks of varying lengths which then divide and dwindle until they are no more than meandering threads. The entire area stands out against the pallor of a smooth, rounded, dull and yet pearly surface, a half-sphere gently curving to an expanse of the same pale hue—a whiteness attenuated by the gloom of the place: dungeon, crypt or cathedral—gleaming with a diffused luster in the darkness.

Beyond, the space is occupied by the cylindrical shafts of columns that grow more numerous and blurred in the distance, where the beginning of a huge stone staircase can be made out, gradually turning and narrowing as it rises toward the high vaulting into which it vanishes.

The whole of this scene is empty, staircase and colonnades. Alone in the foreground, glimmers the prone body, on which the red spot is spreading—a white body suggesting the luminous, supple, doubtless fragile and vulnerable flesh. Beside the bloodstained half-sphere, another identical though intact globe can be seen from almost the same angle; but the darker ringed tip crowning it is here quite recognizable, whereas the first is almost completely destroyed, or at least concealed, by the wound.

In the background, toward the bend of the stairs, a black figure is vanishing from sight, a man wrapped in a long, loose cape, who mounts the last steps without turning around, his crime committed. A faint vapor rises in intertwining spirals from a kind of incense burner set on a high, silvery-metal stand. Quite near lies the milky body where wide rivulets of blood are flowing from the left breast, down the side and over the hip.

It is a woman's body, its forms opulent but not heavy, completely naked, lying on its back, the bust half-raised by thick cushions laid on the floor, which is covered by rugs of Oriental design. The waist is very narrow, the neck long and slender, curved to one side, the head thrown back into a darker area where the features of the face can still be discerned, the mouth half open, the large eyes wide, gleaming with a fixed luster, and the mass of the long black hair spread out in waves of formal disorder on the heavy folds of some fabric, velvet perhaps, on which the arm and shoulder also rest.

It is a smooth, dark-violet velvet, or seems to be in this light. But violet, brown and blue also seem to prevail in the colors of the cushions—of which only a small part is concealed by the velvet material and which extend farther down under the bust and the waist—as well as in the Oriental patterns of the rugs on the floor. Beyond, these same colors recur in the stone of the slabs and columns, the arches of the vaulting, the staircase, the vaguer surfaces where the limits of the room are lost to view.

It is difficult to specify the latter's dimensions; the slaughtered young woman seems at first glance to occupy a considerable place in it, but the vast proportions of the staircase descending toward her would suggest, on the contrary, that she does not take up the whole room, for a noticeable area must actually extend to the right and the left, as well as toward those distant browns and blues in the various rows of columns, perhaps toward other sofas, heavy rugs, piles of cushions and fabrics, other tortured bodies, other incense burners.

It is also difficult to say where the light is coming from. Nothing, on the columns or on the floor, suggests the direction of its source. Moreover, there is no window in sight, and no torch. It is the milky body itself that seems to illuminate the scene, the neck and the swelling breasts, the curve of the hips, the belly, the full thighs, the legs stretched out, wide apart, and the black fleece of the sex exposed— provocative, proffered, henceforth useless.

The man has already moved several strides away. Now he is already on the first steps of the staircase which he is about to mount. The lower steps are long and deep, like the shallow stairs leading to some public edifice, temple or theatre; they then gradually diminish in size as they rise, and at the same time begin a broad spiral movement, so gradual that the staircase has not yet effected a half-turn when, reduced to an awkward narrow passageway without a railing, even vaguer in the deepening darkness, it disappears toward the top of the vaulting.

But the man is not looking in this direction, where his steps will nonetheless carry him; his left foot on the second step and his right already set on the third, knee bent, he has turned around to take a look at the scene. The long loose cape which he has hastily thrown over his shoulders, and which he holds at his waist with one hand, has been swept by the rotation which has just brought his head and upper body around to face away from the direction he is going, a flap of material raised in the air as though by the effect of a gust of wind; the corner, which folds back on itself in a loose S, reveals the gold-embroidered, red-satin lining.

The man's features are impassive, but strained, as though in anticipation—fear perhaps—of some sudden event, or rather reassuring himself as to the total immobility of the scene. Although he looks back in this way, his whole body has remained leaning slightly forward, as though he were still continuing his ascent. His right arm —the one not holding the edge of the cape—is half extended to the left, toward a point in space where the railing would be if there were one on this staircase, an interrupted, almost incomprehensible gesture, unless it is an instinctive impulse to catch hold of the missing support?

As for the direction of his gaze, it is unquestionably toward the body of the victim lying exposed on the cushions, the limbs extended in a cross, the bust raised slightly, the head thrown back. But perhaps the face is hidden from the man's eyes by one of the columns which rises at the foot of the stairs. The young woman's right hand touches the floor just at this column's base. A thick iron fetter encircles the delicate wrist. The arm is almost in shadow, the hand alone receiving enough light for the slender, spread fingers to be clearly visible against the circular rim that forms a base for the stone shaft. A black-metal chain is fastened around the shaft and passes through a ring on the fetter, closely attaching the wrist to the column.

At the arm's other end, a round shoulder, raised by the cushions, is also plainly lighted, as are the neck, the throat and the other shoulder, the armpit and its down, the left arm stretched behind the body too and its wrist attached in the same way to the base of another column, quite close to the foreground; here the iron ring and the chain are clearly seen, drawn with great distinctness down to the smallest detail.

Seen in the same way, still in the foreground but on the other side, is a similar though somewhat lighter chain which twice encircles the ankle directly, attaching it to a heavy ring set in the floor. About a yard or so behind it, the right foot is chained in the same manner. But it is the left foot and its chain that are represented with the most precision.

The foot is small, delicate, finely modeled. The chain has bruised the flesh in places, making noticeable though small depressions. Its links are oval, thick and about the size of an eye. The ring is like those used for hitching horses; it is lying almost flat on the stone slab, in which it is held by a massive spike. The edge of a rug begins an inch or so away; it is raised here by a fold produced, no doubt, by the victim's convulsive though necessarily limited movements when she attempted to struggle.

The man is still half leaning over her, standing about a yard away. He examines her face tilted back, the dark eyes enlarged by cosmetics, the mouth wide as if in a scream. The man's position reveals only one-quarter of his face, but he is evidently in the grip of violent excitement, despite his rigid position, silence, and immobility. His back is bent slightly. His left hand, the only one that can be seen, holds away from his body a piece of fabric, some dark garment which trails on the rug and which must be the long cape with its gold-embroidered lining.

This massive figure greatly conceals the naked flesh where the red spot, which has spread over the bulge of the breast, flows in long rivulets which branch out as they grow thinner, against the pale background of the torso and the whole side. One of them has reached the armpit and traces a fine, almost straight line the length of the arm; others have run down toward the waist and drawn a more arbitrary network, which is already congealing over the belly, the hip and the top of the thigh. Three or four veinules have reached as far as the hollow of the groin and formed a meandering line which joins the point of the V formed by the parted legs and vanishes in the black fleece.

There, now the flesh is still intact, the black fleece and the white belly, the gentle curve of the hips, the slender waist and, above, the pearly breasts which rise in time to the rapid breathing, whose rhythm grows faster. The man, close beside her, one knee on the ground, bends farther forward. The head with the long wavy hair, which alone has kept some freedom of movement, stirs, struggles; finally the girl's mouth opens and twists, while the flesh yields, the blood spurts out over the tender, smooth skin, the skillfully painted black eyes widen enormously, the mouth opens still further, the head is flung from right to left, violently, one last time, then more gently, finally falling back motionless in the mass of black hair spread out on the velvet.

At the very top of the stone staircase, the little door is open, releasing a yellow, sustained light, against which the dark figure of the man wrapped in his long cape is silhouetted. He has no more than a few steps to climb in order to reach the threshold.

Then the whole scene is empty, the enormous violet-shadowed room with its stone columns extending on all sides, the monumental staircase with no railing that turns as it rises, growing narrower and vaguer as it mounts into the darkness toward the top of the vaulting, where it vanishes.

Near the supine body whose wound has congealed, whose luster is already fading, the faint vapor from the incense burner forms complicated volutes in the calm air: at first it is a strand inclined to the left, then rises and increases slightly in height, then returns toward the axis of its point of departure, exceeds it on the right, again starts in the other direction, only to return once more, thus tracing an irregular, gradually fading sinusoid, which rises vertically toward the top of the canvas.

*Translated from the French by Richard Howard*

# Heinrich Böll

## ENTER AND EXIT

### WHEN THE WAR BROKE OUT

I WAS LEANING out of the window, my arms resting on the sill, I had rolled up my shirtsleeves and was looking beyond the main gate and guardroom across to the divisional headquarters telephone exchange, waiting for my friend Leo to give me the prearranged signal: come to the window, take off his cap, and put it on again. Whenever I got the chance I would lean out of the window, my arms on the sill; whenever I got the chance I would call a girl in Cologne and my mother—at army expense—and when Leo came to the window, took off his cap, and put it on again, I would run down to the barrack square and wait in the public callbox till the phone rang.

The other telephone operators sat there bareheaded, in their undershirts, and when they leaned forward to plug in or unplug, or to push up a flap, their identity disks would dangle out of their undershirts and fall back again when they straightened up. Leo was the only one wearing a cap, just so he could take it off to give me the signal. He had a heavy, pink face, very fair hair, and came from Oldenburg. The first expression you noticed on his face was guileless; the second was: incredibly guileless, and no one paid enough attention to Leo to notice more than those two expressions; he looked as uninteresting as the boys whose faces appear on advertisements for cheese.

It was hot, afternoon; the alert that had been going on for days had become stale, transforming all time as it passed into stillborn Sunday hours. The barrack square lay there blind and empty, and I was glad I could at least keep my head out of the camaraderie of my roommates. Over there the operators were plugging and unplugging, pushing up flaps, wiping off sweat, and Leo was sitting there among them, his cap on his thick fair hair.

All of a sudden I noticed the rhythm of plugging and unplugging had altered; arm movements were no longer routine, mechanical, they became hesitant, and Leo threw his arms up over his head three times: a signal we had not arranged but from which I could tell that something out of the ordinary had happened; then I saw an operator take his steel helmet from the switchboard and put it on; he looked ridiculous, sitting there sweating in his undershirt, his identity disk dangling, his steel helmet on his head—but I couldn't laugh at him; I realized that putting on a steel helmet meant something like "ready for action," and I was scared.

The ones who had been dozing on their beds behind me in the room got up, lit cigarettes, and formed the two customary groups: three probationary teachers, who were still hoping to be discharged as being "essential to the nation's educational system," resumed their discussion of Ernst Jünger; the other two, an orderly and an office clerk, began discussing the female form; they didn't tell dirty stories, they didn't laugh, they discussed it just as two exceptionally boring geography teachers might have discussed the conceivably interesting topography of the Ruhr valley. Neither subject interested me. Psychologists, those interested in psychology, and those about to complete an adult education course in psychology, may be interested to learn that my desire to call the girl in Cologne became more urgent than in previous weeks; I went to my locker, took out my cap, put it on, and leaned out of the window, my arms on the sill, wearing my cap: the signal for Leo that I had to speak to him at once. To show he understood, he waved to me, and I put on my tunic, went out of the room, down the stairs, and stood at the entrance to headquarters, waiting for Leo.

It was hotter than ever, quieter than ever, the barrack squares were even emptier, and nothing has ever approximated my idea of hell as closely as hot, silent, empty barrack squares. Leo came very quickly; he was also wearing his steel helmet now, and was displaying one of his other five expressions which I knew: dangerous for everything he didn't like; this was the face he sat at the switchboard with when he was on evening or night duty, listened in on secret official calls, told me what they were about, suddenly jerked out plugs, cut off secret official calls so as to put through an urgent secret call to Cologne, for me to talk to the girl; then it would be my turn to work the switchboard, and Leo would first call his girl in Oldenburg, then his father; meanwhile Leo would cut thick slices from the ham his mother had sent him, cut these into cubes, and we would eat cubes of ham. When things were slack, Leo would teach me the art of recognizing the caller's rank from the way the flaps fell; at first I thought it was enough to be able to tell the rank simply by the force with which the flap fell: corporal, sergeant, etc., but Leo could tell exactly whether it was an officious corporal or a tired colonel demanding a line; from the way the flap fell he could even distinguish between angry captains and annoyed lieutenants—nuances which are very hard to tell apart, and as the evening went on his other expressions made their appearance: fixed hatred; primordial malice; with these faces he would suddenly become pedantic, articulate his "Are you still talking?", his "Yessirs," with great care, and with unnerving rapidity switch plugs so as to turn an official call about boots into one about boots and ammunition, and the other call about ammunition into one about ammunition and boots, or the private conversation of a sergeant-major with his wife might be suddenly interrupted by a lieutenant's voice saying: "I insist the man be punished, I absolutely insist." With lightning speed Leo would then switch the plugs over so that the boot partners were talking about boots again and the others about ammunition, and the sergeant-major's wife could resume discussion of her stomach trouble with her husband. When the ham was all gone, Leo's relief had arrived, and we were walking across the silent barrack square to our room, Leo's face would wear its final expression: foolish, innocent in a way that had nothing to do with childlike innocence.

Any other time I would have laughed at Leo, standing there wearing his steel helmet, that symbol of inflated importance. He looked past me, across the first, the second barrack square, to the stables; his expressions alternated from three to five, from five to four, and with his final expression he said: "It's war, war, war—they finally made it." I said nothing, and he said: "I guess you want to talk to her?" "Yes," I said.

"I've already talked to mine," he said. "She's not pregnant, I don't know whether to be glad or not. What d'you think?" "You can be glad," I said, "I don't think it's a good idea to have kids in wartime."

"General mobilization," he said, "state of alert, this place is soon going to be swarming—and it'll be a long while before you and I can go off on our bikes again." (When we were off duty we used to ride our bikes out into the country, onto the moors, the farmers' wives used to fix us fried eggs and thick slices of bread and butter.) "The first joke of the war has already happened," said Leo: "In view of my special skills and services in connection with the telephone system, I have been made a corporal—now go over to the public callbox, and if it doesn't ring in three minutes I'll demote myself for incompetence."

In the callbox I leaned against the "Münster Area" phone book,

lit a cigarette, and looked out through a gap in the frosted glass across
the barrack square; the only person I could see was a sergeant-
major's wife, in Block 4 I think; she was watering her geraniums
from a yellow jug; I waited, looked at my wristwatch: one minute,
two, and I was startled when it actually rang, and even more startled
when I immediately heard the voice of the girl in Cologne: "May-
bach's Furniture Company," and I said: "Marie, it's war, it's war"
—and she said: "No." I said: "Yes it is," then there was silence
for half a minute, and she said: "Shall I come?", and before I could
say spontaneously, instinctively, "Yes, please do," the voice of what
was probably a fairly senior officer shouted: "We need ammunition, and we need it urgently." The girl said: "Are you still there?"
The officer yelled: "God damn it!" Meanwhile I had had time to
wonder about what it was in the girl's voice that had sounded unfamiliar, ominous almost: her voice had sounded like marriage, and
I suddenly knew I didn't feel like marrying her. I said: "We're probably pulling out tonight." The officer yelled: "God damn it, God
damn it!" (evidently he couldn't think of anything better to say),
the girl said: "I could catch the four o'clock train and be there just
before seven," and I said, more quickly than was polite: "It's too
late, Marie, too late"—then all I heard was the officer, who seemed to
be on the verge of apoplexy. He screamed: "Well, do we get the
ammunition or don't we?" And I said in a steely voice (I had learned
that from Leo): "No, no, you don't get any ammunition, even if it
chokes you." Then I hung up.

It was still daylight when we loaded boots from railway cars onto
trucks, but by the time we were loading boots from trucks onto railway cars it was dark, and it was still dark when we loaded boots
from railway cars onto trucks again, then it was daylight again, and
we loaded bales of hay from trucks onto railway cars, and it was still
daylight, and we were still loading bales of hay from trucks onto
railway cars; but then it was dark again, and for exactly twice as long
as we had loaded bales of hay from trucks onto railway cars, we
loaded bales of hay from railway cars onto trucks. At one point a
field kitchen arrived, in full combat rig, we were given large helpings
of goulash and small helpings of potatoes, and we were given real
coffee and cigarettes which we didn't have to pay for; that must have
been at night, for I remember hearing a voice say: real coffee and
cigarettes for free, the surest sign of war; I don't remember the face
belonging to this voice. It was daylight again when we marched back
to barracks, and as we turned into the street leading past the barracks

we met the first battalion going off. It was headed by a marching band playing "Must I then, must I then," followed by the first company, then their armored vehicles, then the second, third and finally the fourth with the heavy machine guns. On not one face, not one single face, did I see the least sign of enthusiasm; of course there were some people standing on the sidewalks, some girls too, but not once did I see anybody stick a bunch of flowers onto a soldier's rifle; there was not even the merest trace of a sign of enthusiasm in the air.

Leo's bed was untouched; I opened his locker (a degree of familiarity with Leo which the probationary teachers, shaking their heads, called "going too far"); everything was in its place: the photo of the girl in Oldenburg, she was standing, leaning against her bicycle, in front of a birch tree; photos of Leo's parents; their farmhouse. Next to the ham there was a message: "Transferred to area headquarters. In touch with you soon, take all the ham, I've taken what I need. Leo." I didn't take any of the ham, and closed the locker; I was not hungry, and the rations for two days had been stacked up on the table: bread, cans of liver sausage, butter, cheese, jam and cigarettes. One of the probationary teachers, the one I liked least, announced that he had been promoted to Pfc and appointed room senior for the period of Leo's absence; he began to distribute the rations; it took a very long time; the only thing I was interested in was the cigarettes, and these he left to the last because he was a nonsmoker. When I finally got the cigarettes I tore open the pack, lay down on the bed in my clothes and smoked; I watched the others eating. They spread liver sausage an inch thick on the bread and discussed the "excellent quality of the butter," then they drew the black-out blinds and lay down on their beds; it was very hot, but I didn't feel like undressing; the sun shone into the room through a few cracks, and in one of these strips of light sat the newly promoted Pfc sewing on his Pfc's chevron. It isn't so easy to sew on a Pfc's chevron: it has to be placed at a certain prescribed distance from the seam of the sleeve; moreover, the two open sides of the chevron must be absolutely straight; the probationary teacher had to take off the chevron several times, he sat there for at least two hours, unpicking it, sewing it back on, and he did not appear to be running out of patience; outside the band came marching by every forty minutes, and I heard the "Must I then, must I then," from Block 7, Block 2, from Block 9, then from over by the stables—it would come closer, get very loud, then softer again; it took almost exactly three "Must I thens" for the Pfc to sew on his chevron, and it still wasn't quite straight; by that time I had smoked the last of my cigarettes and fell asleep.

That afternoon we didn't have to load either boots from trucks onto railway cars or bales of hay from railway cars onto trucks; we had to help the quartermaster-sergeant; he considered himself a genius at organization; he had requisitioned as many assistants as there were items of clothing and equipment on his list, except that for the groundsheets he needed two; he also required a clerk. The two men with the groundsheets went ahead and laid them out, flicking the corners nice and straight, neatly on the cement floor of the stable; as soon as the groundsheets had been spread out, the first man started off by laying two neckties on each groundsheet; the second man, two handkerchiefs; I came next with the mess kits, and while all the articles in which, as the sergeant said, size was not a factor were being distributed, he was preparing, with the aid of the more intelligent members of the detachment, the objects in which size was a factor: tunics, boots, trousers, and so on; he had a whole pile of paybooks lying there, he selected the tunics, trousers and boots according to measurements and weight, and he insisted everything would fit, "unless the bastards have got too fat as civilians"; it all had to be done at great speed, in one continuous operation, and it was done at great speed, in one continuous operation, and when everything had been spread out the reservists came in, were conducted to their groundsheets, tied the ends together, hoisted their bundles onto their backs, and went to their rooms to put on their uniforms. Only occasionally did something have to be exchanged, and then it was always because someone had got too fat as a civilian. It was also only occasionally that something was missing: a shoe-cleaning brush or a spoon or fork, and it always turned out that someone else had two shoe-cleaning brushes or two spoons or forks, a fact which confirmed the sergeant's theory that we did not work mechanically enough, that we were "still using our brains too much." I didn't use my brain at all, with the result that no one was short a mess kit. While the first man of each company being equipped was hoisting his bundle onto his shoulder, the first of our own lot had to start spreading out the next groundsheet; everything went smoothly; meanwhile the newly promoted Pfc sat at the table and wrote everything down in the paybooks; most of the time he had only to enter a one in the paybook, except with the neckties, socks, handkerchiefs, undershirts and underpants, where he had to write a two.

In spite of everything, though, there were occasionally some dead minutes, as the quartermaster-sergeant called them, and we were allowed to use these to fortify ourselves; we would sit on the bunks in the grooms' quarters and eat bread and liver sausage, sometimes bread and cheese or bread and jam, and when the sergeant had a few dead minutes himself he would come over and give us a lecture about the difference between rank and appointment; he found it tremendously interesting that he himself was a quartermaster-sergeant—"that's my appointment"—and yet had the rank of a corporal, "that's my rank," in this way, so he said, there was no reason, for example, why a Pfc should not act as a quartermaster-sergeant, indeed even an ordinary private might; he found the theme endlessly fascinating and kept on concocting new examples, some of which betokened a well-nigh treasonable imagination: "It can actually happen, for instance," he said, "that a Pfc is put in command of a company, of a battalion even."

For ten hours I laid mess kits on groundsheets, slept for six hours, and again for ten hours laid mess kits on groundsheets; then I slept another six hours and had still heard nothing from Leo. When the third ten hours of laying out mess kits began, the Pfc started entering a two wherever there should have been a one, and a one wherever there should have been a two. He was relieved of his post, and now had to lay out neckties, and the second probationary teacher was appointed clerk. I stayed with the mess kits during the third ten hours too, the sergeant said he thought I had done surprisingly well.

During the dead minutes, while we were sitting on the bunks eating bread and cheese, bread and jam, bread and liver sausage, strange rumors were beginning to be peddled around. A story was being told about a rather well-known retired general who received orders by phone to go to a small island in the North Sea where he was to assume a top-secret, extremely important command; the general had taken his uniform out of the closet, kissed his wife, children and grandchildren goodbye, given his favorite horse a farewell pat, and taken the train to some station on the North Sea and from there hired a motorboat to the island in question; he had been foolish enough to send back the motorboat before ascertaining the nature of his command; he was cut off by the rising tide and—so the story went —had forced the farmer on the island at pistol point to risk his life and row him back to the mainland. By afternoon there was already a variation to the tale: some sort of a struggle had taken place in the boat between the general and the farmer, they had both been swept overboard and drowned. What I couldn't stand was that this story— and a number of others—was considered criminal all right, but funny as well, while to me they seemed neither one nor the other; I couldn't accept the grim accusation of sabotage, which was being used like some kind of moral tuning-fork, nor could I join in the laughter or grin with the others. The war seemed to deprive what was funny of its funny side.

At any other time the "Must I thens" which ran through my dreams, my sleep, and my few waking moments, the countless men who got off the streetcars and came hurrying into the barracks with their cardboard boxes and went out again an hour later with "Must I then"; even the speeches which we sometimes listened to with half an ear, speeches in which the words "united effort" were always occurring—all this I would have found funny, but everything which would have been funny before was not funny any more, and I could no longer laugh or smile at all the things which would have seemed laughable; not even the sergeant, and not even the Pfc, whose chevron was still not quite straight and who sometimes laid out three neckties on the groundsheet instead of two.

It was still hot, still August, and the fact that three times sixteen hours are only forty-eight, two days and two nights, was something I didn't realize until I woke up about eleven on Sunday and for the first time since Leo had been transferred was able to lean out of the window, my arms on the sill; the probationary teachers, wearing their walking-out dress, were ready for church and looked at me in a challenging kind of way, but all I said was: "Go ahead, I'll follow you," and it was obvious that they were glad to be able to go without me for once. Whenever we had gone to church they had looked at me as if they would like to excommunicate me, because something or other about me or my uniform was not quite up to scratch in their eyes: the way my boots were cleaned, the way I had tied my tie, my belt or my hair-cut; they were indignant not as fellow-soldiers (which, objectively speaking, I agree would have been justified), but as Catholics; they would rather I had not made it so unmistakably clear that we were actually going to one and the same church; it embarrassed them, but there wasn't a thing they could do about it, because my paybook is marked: R.C.

This Sunday there was no mistaking how glad they were to be able to go without me, I had only to watch them marching off to town, past the barracks, clean, upright, and brisk. Sometimes, when I felt bouts of pity for them, I was glad for their sakes that Leo was a Protestant: I think they simply couldn't have borne it if Leo had been a Catholic too.

The office clerk and the orderly were still asleep; we didn't have to be at the stable again till three that afternoon. I stood leaning out of the window for a while, till it was time to go, so as to get to church just in time to miss the sermon. Then, while I was dressing, I opened Leo's locker again: to my surprise it was empty, except for a piece of paper and a big chunk of ham; Leo had locked the cupboard again to be sure I would find the message and the ham. On the paper was written: "This is it—I'm being sent to Poland—did you get my message?" I put the paper in my pocket, turned the key in the locker, and finished dressing; I was in a daze as I walked into town and entered the church, and even the glances of the three probationary teachers, who turned round to look at me and then back to the altar again, shaking their heads, failed to rouse me completely. Probably they wanted to make sure quickly whether I hadn't come in *after* the Elevation of the Host so they could apply for my excommunication; but I really had arrived *before* the Elevation, there was nothing they could do, besides I wanted to remain a Catholic. I thought of Leo and was scared, I thought too of the girl in Cologne and had a twinge of conscience, but I was sure her voice had sounded like marriage. To annoy my roommates, I undid my collar while I was still in church.

After Mass I stood outside leaning against the church wall in a shady corner between the vestry and the door, took off my cap, lit a cigarette, and watched the faithful as they left the church and walked past me. I wondered how I could get hold of a girl with whom I could go for a walk, have a cup of coffee, and maybe go to a movie; I still had three hours before I had to lay out mess kits on groundsheets again. It would be nice if the girl were not too silly and reasonably pretty. I also thought about dinner at the barracks, which I was missing now, and that perhaps I ought to have told the office clerk he could have my chop and dessert.

I smoked two cigarettes while I stood there, watching the faithful standing about in twos and threes, then separating again, and just as I was lighting the third cigarette from the second a shadow fell across me from one side, and when I looked to the right I saw that the person casting the shadow was even blacker than the shadow itself: it was the chaplain who had read Mass. He looked very kind, not old, thirty perhaps, fair and just a shade too well-fed. First he looked at my open collar, then at my boots, then at my bare head, and finally at my cap, which I had put next to me on a ledge where it had slipped off onto the paving; last of all he looked at my cigarette, then my face, and I had the feeling that he didn't like anything he saw there. "What's the matter?" he finally asked. "Are you in trouble?" And hardly had I nodded in reply to this question when he said: "Do you wish to confess?" Damn it, I thought, all they ever think of is confession, and only a certain part of that even. "No," I said, "I don't wish to confess." "Well, then," he said, "what's on your mind?" He might just as well have been asking about my stomach as my mind. He was obviously very impatient, looked at my cap, and I felt he was annoyed that I hadn't picked it up yet. I would have liked to turn his impatience into patience, but after all it wasn't I who had spoken to him, but he who had spoken to me, so I asked—to my annoyance, somewhat falteringly—whether he knew of some nice girl who would go for a walk with me, have a cup of coffee and maybe go to a movie in the evening; she didn't have to be a beauty queen, but she must be reasonably pretty, and if possible not from a good family, as these girls are usually so silly. I could give him the address of a chaplain in Cologne where he could make inquiries, call up if necessary, to satisfy himself I was from a good Catholic home. I talked a lot, toward the end a bit more coherently, and noticed how his face altered: at first it was almost kind, it had almost looked benign, that was in the early stage when he took me for a highly interesting, possibly even fascinating case of feeblemindedness and found me psychologically quite amusing. The transitions from kind to almost benign, from almost benign to amused were hard to distinguish, but then all of a sudden—the moment I mentioned the physical attributes the girl was to have—he went purple with rage. I was scared, for my mother had once told me it is a sign of danger when overweight people suddenly go purple in the face. Then he began to shout at me, and shouting has always put me on edge. He shouted that I looked a mess, with my "field tunic" undone, my boots unpolished, my cap lying next to me "in the dirt, yes in the dirt," and how undisciplined I was, smoking one cigarette after another, and whether perhaps I couldn't tell the difference between a Catholic priest and a pimp. With my nerves strung up as they were I had stopped being scared of him, I was just plain angry. I asked him what my tie, my boots, my cap, had to do with him, whether he thought maybe he had to do my corporal's job, and: "Anyway," I said, "you fellows tell us all the time to come to you with our troubles, and when someone really tells you his troubles you get mad." "You fellows, eh?" he said, gasping with rage, "since when are we on such familiar terms?" "We're not on any terms at all," I said. I picked up my cap, put it on without looking at it, and left, walking straight across the church square. He called after me to at least do up my tie, and I shouldn't be so stubborn; I very nearly turned round and shouted that *he* was the stubborn one, but then I remembered my mother telling me it was all right to be frank with a priest but you should try and avoid being impertinent—and so, without looking back, I went on into town. I left my tie dangling and thought about Catholics; there was a war on, but the first thing they looked at was your tie, then your boots. They said you should tell them your troubles, and when you did they got mad.

I walked slowly through town, on the lookout for a café where I wouldn't have to salute anyone; this stupid saluting spoiled all cafés for me; I looked at all the girls I passed, I turned round to look at them, at their legs even, but there wasn't one whose voice would not have sounded like marriage. I was desperate, I thought of Leo, of the girl in Cologne, I was on the point of sending her a telegram; I was almost prepared to risk getting married just to be alone with a girl. I stopped in front of the window of a photographer's studio, so I could think about Leo in peace. I was scared for him. I saw my reflection in the shop window—my tie undone and my black boots unpolished, I raised my hands to button up my collar, but then it seemed too much trouble, and I dropped my hands again. The photographs in the studio window were very depressing. They were almost all of soldiers in walking-out dress; some had even had their pictures taken wearing their steel helmets, and I was wondering whether the ones in steel helmets were more depressing than the ones in peak caps when a sergeant came out of the shop carrying a framed photograph: the photo was fairly large, at least twenty-four by thirty, the frame was painted silver, and the picture showed the sergeant in walking-out dress and steel helmet; he was quite young, not much older than I was, twenty-one at most; he was just about to walk past me, he hesitated, stopped, and I was wondering whether to raise my hand and salute him, when he said: "Forget it—but if I were you I'd do up your collar, and your tunic too, the next guy might be tougher than I am." Then he laughed and went off, and ever since then I have preferred (relatively, of course) the ones who have their pictures taken in steel helmets to the ones who have their pictures taken in peak caps.

Leo would have been just the person to stand with me in front of the photo studio and look at the pictures; there were also some bridal couples, first communicants, and students wearing colored ribbons and fancy fobs over their stomachs, and I stood there wondering why they didn't wear ribbons in their hair; some of them wouldn't have looked bad in them at all. I needed company and had none.

Probably the chaplain thought I was suffering from lust, or that I was an anticlerical Nazi; but I was neither suffering from lust nor was I anticlerical or a Nazi. I simply needed company, and not male company either, and that was so simple that it was terribly complicated; of course there were loose women in town as well as prostitutes (it was a Catholic town), but the loose women and the prostitutes were always offended if you weren't suffering from lust.

I stood for a long time in front of the photo studio; to this day I still always look at photo studios in strange cities; they are all much the same, and all equally depressing, although not everywhere do you find students with colored ribbons. It was nearly one o'clock when I finally left, on the lookout for a café where I didn't have to salute anyone, but in all the cafés they were sitting around in their uniforms, and I ended up by going to a movie anyway, to the first show at one-fifteen. All I remember was the newsreel: some very ignoble-looking Poles were maltreating some very noble-looking Germans; it was so empty in the movie that I could risk smoking during the show; it was hot that last Sunday in August 1939.

When I got back to barracks it was way past three; for some reason the order to put down groundsheets at three o'clock and spread out mess kits and neckties on them had been countermanded; I came in just in time to change, have some bread and liver sausage, lean out of the window for a few minutes, listen to snatches of the discussion about Ernst Jünger and the other one about the female form; both discussions had become more serious, more boring; the orderly and the office clerk were now weaving Latin expressions into their remarks, and that made the whole thing even more repulsive than it was in the first place.

At four we were called out, and I had imagined we would be loading boots from trucks onto railways cars again or from railway cars onto trucks, but this time we loaded cases of soap powder, which were stacked up in the gym, onto trucks, and from the trucks we unloaded them at the parcel post office, where they were stacked up again. The cases were not heavy, the addresses were typewritten; we formed a chain, and so one case after another passed through my hands; we did this the whole of Sunday afternoon right through till late at night, and there were scarcely any dead minutes when we could have had a bite to eat; as soon as a truck was fully loaded, we drove to the main post office, formed a chain again, and unloaded the cases. Sometimes we overtook a Must-I-then column, or met one coming the other way; by this time they had three bands, and it was all going much faster. It was late, after midnight, when we had driven off with the last of the cases, and my hands remembered the number of mess kits and decided there was very little difference between cases of soap powder and mess kits.

I was very tired and wanted to throw myself on the bed fully dressed, but once again there was a great stack of bread and cans of liver sausage, jam and butter, on the table, and the others insisted it be distributed; all I wanted was the cigarettes, and I had to wait till everything had been divided up exactly, for of course the Pfc left the cigarettes to the last again; he took an abnormally long time about it, perhaps to teach me moderation and discipline and to convey his contempt for my craving; when I finally got the cigarettes, I lay down on the bed in my clothes and smoked and watched them spreading their bread with liver sausage, listened to them praising the excellent quality of the butter, and arguing mildly as to whether the jam was made of strawberries, apples and apricots, or of strawberries and apples only. They went on eating for a long time, and I couldn't fall asleep; then I heard footsteps coming along the passage and knew they were for me: I was afraid, and yet relieved, and the strange thing was that they all, the office clerk, the orderly and the three probationary teachers who were sitting round the table, stopped their chewing and looked at me as the footsteps drew closer; now the Pfc found it necessary to shout at me; he got up and yelled, calling me by my surname: "Damn it, take your boots off when you lie down."

There are certain things one refuses to believe, and I still don't believe it, although my ears remember quite well that all of a sudden he called me by my surname; I would have preferred it if we had used surnames all along, but coming so suddenly like that it sounded so funny that, for the first time since the war started, I had to laugh. Meanwhile the door had been flung open and the company clerk was standing by my bed; he was pretty excited, so much so that he didn't bawl me out, although he was a corporal, for lying on the bed with my boots and clothes on, smoking. He said: "You there, in twenty minutes in full marching order in Block 4, understand?" I said: "Yes" and got up. He added: "Report to the sergeant-major over there," and again I said yes and began to clear out my locker. I hadn't realized the company clerk was still in the room; I was just putting the picture of the girl in my trouser pocket when I heard him say: "I have some bad news, it's going to be tough on you but it should make you proud too; the first man from this regiment to be killed in action was your roommate, Corporal Leo Siemers."

I had turned round during the last half of this sentence, and they were all looking at me now, including the corporal; I had gone quite pale, and I didn't know whether to be furious or silent; then I said in a low voice: "But war hasn't been declared yet, he can't have been killed—and he wouldn't have been killed," and I shouted suddenly: "Leo wouldn't get killed, not him . . . you know he wouldn't." No one said anything, not even the corporal, and while I cleared out my locker and crammed all the stuff we were told to take with us into my pack, I heard him leave the room. I piled up all the things on the stool so I didn't have to turn around; I couldn't hear a sound from the others, I couldn't even hear them chewing. I packed all my stuff very quickly; the bread, liver sausage, cheese and butter I left in the locker and turned the key. When I had to turn around I saw they had managed to get into bed without a sound; I threw my locker key onto the office clerk's bed, saying: "Clear out everything that's still in there, it's all yours." I didn't care for him much, but I liked him best of the five; later on I was sorry I hadn't left without saying a word, but I was not yet twenty. I slammed the door, took my rifle from the rack outside, went down the stairs and saw from the clock over the office door downstairs that it was nearly three in the morning. It was quiet and still warm that last Monday of August 1939. I threw Leo's locker key somewhere onto the barrack square as I went across to Block 4. They were all there, the band was already moving into position at the head of the company, and some officer who had given the united effort speech was walking across the square, he took off his cap, wiped the sweat from his forehead and put his cap on again. He reminded me of a streetcar conductor who takes a short break at the terminus.

The sergeant-major came up to me and said: "Are you the man from staff headquarters?" and I said: "Yes." He nodded; he looked pale and very young, somewhat at a loss; I looked past him toward the dark, scarcely distinguishable mass; all I could make out was the gleaming trumpets of the band. "You wouldn't happen to be a telephone operator?" asked the sergeant-major. "We're short one here." "As a matter of fact I am," I said quickly and with an enthusiasm which seemed to surprise him, for he looked at me doubtfully. "Yes, I'm one," I said, "I've had practical training as a telephone operator." "Good," he said, "you're just the man I need, slip in somewhere there at the end, we'll arrange everything en route." I went over toward the right where the dark gray was getting a little lighter; as I got closer I even recognized some faces. I took my place at the end of the company. Someone shouted: "Right turn—forward march!" and I had hardly lifted my foot when they started playing their "Must I then."

### WHEN THE WAR WAS OVER

It was just getting light when we reached the German border: to our left, a broad river, to our right a forest, even from its edges you could tell how deep it was; silence fell in the boxcar; the train passed slowly over patched-up rails, past shelled houses, splintered telegraph poles. The little guy sitting next to me took off his glasses and polished them carefully.

"Christ," he whispered to me, "d'you have the slightest idea where we are?"

"Yes," I said, "the river you've just seen is known here as the Rhine, the forest you see over there on the right is called the Reich Forest—and we'll soon be getting into Cleves."

"D'you come from around here?"

"No, I don't." He was a nuisance; all night long he had driven me crazy with his high-pitched schoolboy's voice, he had told me how he had secretly read Brecht, Tucholsky and Walter Benjamin, as well as Proust and Karl Kraus; that he wanted to study sociology, and theology too, and help create a new order for Germany, and when we stopped at Nimwegen at daybreak and someone said we were just coming to the German border, he nervously asked us all if there was anyone who would trade some thread for two cigarette butts, and when no one said anything I offered to rip off my collar tabs known—I believe—as insignia and turn them into dark-green thread; I took off my tunic and watched him carefully pick the things off with a bit of metal, unravel them, and then actually start using the thread to sew on his ensign's piping around his shoulder straps. I asked him whether I might attribute this sewing job to the influence of Brecht, Tucholsky, Benjamin or Karl Kraus, or was it perhaps the subconscious influence of Jünger which made him restore his rank with Tom Thumb's weapon; he had flushed and said he was through with Jünger, he had written him off; now, as we approached Cleves, he stopped sewing and sat down on the floor beside me, still holding Tom Thumb's weapon.

"Cleves doesn't convey anything to me," he said, "not a thing. How about you?"

"Oh yes," I said, "Lohengrin, 'Swan' margarine, and Anne of Cleves, one of Henry the Eighth's wives."

"That's right," he said, "Lohengrin—although at home we always had 'Sanella.' Don't you want the butts?"

"No," I said, "take them home for your father. I hope he'll punch you in the nose when you arrive with that piping on your shoulder."

"You don't understand," he said, "Prussia, Kleist, Frankfurt-on-the-Oder, Potsdam, Prince of Homburg, Berlin."

"Well," I said, "I believe it was quite a while ago that Prussia took Cleves—and somewhere over there on the other side of the Rhine there is a little town called Wesel."

"Oh of course," he said, "that's right, Schill."

"The Prussians never really established themselves beyond the Rhine," I said, "they only had two bridgeheads: Bonn and Koblenz."

"Prussia," he said.

"Blomberg," I said. "Need any more thread?" He flushed and was silent.

The train slowed down, everyone crowded round the open sliding door and looked at Cleves; English guards on the platform, casual and tough, bored yet alert: we were still prisoners; in the street a sign: To Cologne. Lohengrin's castle up there among the autumn trees. October on the Lower Rhine, Dutch sky; my cousins in Xanten, aunts in Kevelaer; the broad dialect and the smugglers' whispering in the taverns; St. Martin's Day processions, gingerbread men, Breughelesque carnival, and everywhere the smell, even where there was none, of honey cakes.

"I wish you'd try and understand," said the little guy beside me.

"Leave me alone," I said; although he wasn't a man yet, no doubt he soon would be, and that was why I hated him; he was offended and sat back on his heels to add the final stitches to his braid; I didn't even feel sorry for him: clumsily, his thumb smeared with blood, he pushed the needle through the blue cloth of his air force tunic; his glasses were so misted over I couldn't make out whether he was crying or whether it just looked like it; I was close to tears myself: in two hours, three at most, we would be in Cologne, and from there it was not far to the one I had married, the one whose voice had never sounded like marriage.

The woman emerged suddenly from behind the freight shed, and before the guards knew what was happening she was standing by our boxcar and unwrapping a blue cloth from what I first took to be a baby: a loaf of bread; she handed it to me, and I took it; it was heavy, I swayed for a moment and almost fell forward out of the train as it started moving; the bread was dark, still warm, and I wanted to call out "Thank you, thank you," but the words seemed ridiculous, and the train was moving faster now, so I stayed there on

my knees with the heavy loaf in my arms; to this day all I know
about the woman is that she was wearing a dark headscarf and was
no longer young.

When I got up, clasping the loaf, it was quieter than ever in the
boxcar; they were all looking at the bread, and under their stares it
got heavier and heavier; I knew those eyes, I knew the mouths belonged to those eyes, and for months I had been wondering where
the borderline runs between hatred and contempt, and I hadn't
found the borderline; for a while I had divided them up into sewers-
on and non-sewers-on, when we had been transferred from an American camp (where the wearing of rank insignia was prohibited) to an
English one (where the wearing of rank insignia was permitted), and
I had felt a certain fellow-feeling with the non-sewers-on till I found
out they didn't even have any ranks whose insignia they could have
sewn on; one of them, Egelhecht, had even tried to drum up a kind
of court of honor that was to deny me the quality of being German
(and I had wished that this court, which never convened, had actually had the power to deny me this quality). What they didn't know
was that I hated them, Nazis and non-Nazis, not because of their
sewing and their political views but because they were men, men of
the same species as those I had had to spend the last six years with;
the words *man* and *stupid* had become almost identical for me.

In the background Egelhecht's voice said: "The first German
bread—and he of all people is the one to get it."

He sounded as if he was almost sobbing, I wasn't far off it myself
either, but they would never understand that it wasn't just because
of the bread, or because by now we had crossed the German border,
it was mainly because, for the first time in eight months, I had for
one moment felt a woman's hand on my arm.

"No doubt," said Egelhecht in a low voice, "you will even deny
the bread the quality of being German."

"Yes indeed," I said, "I shall employ a typical intellectual's trick
and ask myself whether the flour this bread is made of doesn't perhaps come from Holland, England or America. Here you are," I
said, "divide it up if you like."

Most of them I hated, many I didn't care about one way or the
other, and Tom Thumb, who was now the last to join the ranks of
the sewers-on, was beginning to be a nuisance, yet I felt it was the
right thing to do, to share this loaf with them, I was sure it hadn't
been meant only for me.

Egelhecht made his way slowly toward me: he was tall and thin,
like me, and he was twenty-six, like me; for three months he had

tried to make me see that a nationalist wasn't a Nazi, that the words
*honor, loyalty, fatherland, decency,* could never lose their value—
and I had always countered his impressive array of words with just
five: Wilhelm II, Papen, Hindenburg, Blomberg, Keitel, and it had
infuriated him that I never mentioned Hitler, not even that first of
May when the sentry ran through the camp blaring through a megaphone: "Hitler's dead, Hitler's dead!"

"Go ahead," I said, "divide up the bread."

"Number off," said Egelhecht. I handed him the loaf, he took off
his coat, laid it on the floor of the boxcar with the lining uppermost,
smoothed the lining, placed the bread on it, while the others num-
bered off around us. "Thirty-two," said Tom Thumb, then there
was a silence. "Thirty-two," said Egelhecht, looking at me, for it
was up to me to say thirty-three; but I didn't say it, I turned away
and looked out: the highway with the old trees: Napoleon's poplars,
Napoleon's elms, like the ones I had rested under with my brother
when we rode from Weeze to the Dutch border on our bikes to buy
chocolate and cigarettes cheap.

I could sense that those behind me were terribly offended; I saw
the yellow road signs: To Kalkar, to Xanten, to Geldern, heard behind me the sounds of Egelhecht's tin knife, felt the offendedness
swelling like a thick cloud; they were always being offended for
some reason or other, they were offended if an English guard offered
them a cigarette, and they were offended if he did not; they were
offended when I cursed Hitler, and Egelhecht was mortally offended
when I did not curse Hitler; Tom Thumb had secretly read Benjamin and Brecht, Proust, Tucholsky and Karl Kraus, and when we
crossed the German border he was sewing on his ensign's piping. I
took the cigarette out of my pocket I had got in exchange for
my staff Pfc chevron, turned around, and sat down beside Tom
Thumb. I watched Egelhecht dividing up the loaf: first he cut it in
half, then the halves in quarters, then each quarter again in eight
parts. This way there would be a nice fat chunk for each man, a dark
cube of bread which I figured would weigh about sixty grams.

Egelhecht was just quartering the last eighth, and each man,
every one of them, knew that the ones who got the center pieces
would get at least ten to five grams extra, because the loaf bulged in
the middle and Egelhecht had cut the slices all the same thickness.
But then he cut off the bulge of the two center slices and said:
"Thirty-three—the youngest starts." Tom Thumb glanced at me,
blushed, bent down, took a piece of bread and put it directly into his

mouth; everything went smoothly till Bouvier, who had almost driven me crazy with his planes he was always talking about, had taken his piece of bread; now it should have been my turn, followed by Egelhecht, but I didn't move. I would have liked to light my cigarette, but I had no matches and nobody offered me one. Those who already had their bread were scared and stopped chewing; the ones who hadn't got their bread yet had no idea what was happening, but they understood: I didn't want to share the loaf with them; they were offended, while the others (who already had their bread) were merely embarrassed; I tried to look outside: at Napoleon's poplars, Napoleon's elms, at the tree-lined road with its gaps, with Dutch sky caught in the gaps, but my attempt to look unconcerned was not successful; I was scared of the fight which was bound to start now; I wasn't much good in a fight, and even if I had been it wouldn't have helped, they would have beaten me up the way they did in the camp near Brussels when I had said I would rather be a dead Jew than a live German. I took the cigarette out of my mouth, partly because it felt ridiculous, partly because I wanted to get it through the fight intact, and I looked at Tom Thumb who, his face scarlet, was squatting on his heels beside me. Then Gugeler, whose turn it would have been after Egelhecht, took his piece of bread, put it directly into his mouth, and the others took theirs; there were three pieces left when the man came toward me whom I scarcely knew; he had not joined our tent till we were in the camp near Brussels; he was already old, nearly fifty, short, with a dark, scarred face, and whenever we began to quarrel he wouldn't say a word, he used to leave the tent and run along beside the barbed-wire fence like someone to whom this kind of trotting up and down is familiar. I didn't even know his first name; he wore some sort of faded tropical uniform, and civilian shoes. He came from the far end of the boxcar straight toward me, stopped in front of me and said in a surprisingly gentle voice: "Take the bread"—and when I didn't he shook his head and said: "You fellows have one hell of a talent for turning everything into a symbolic event. It's just bread, that's all, and the woman gave it to you, the woman—here you are." He picked up a piece of bread, pressed it into my right hand, which was hanging down helplessly, and squeezed my hand around it. His eyes were quite dark, not black, and his face wore the look of many prisons. I nodded, got my hand muscles moving so as to hold onto the bread; a deep sigh went through the car, Egelhecht took his bread, then the old man in the tropical uniform. "Damn it all," said the old fellow, "I've been away from Germany for twelve years, you're a crazy bunch, but I'm just beginning to understand you." Before I could put the bread into my mouth the train stopped, and we got out.

Open country, turnip fields, no trees; a few Belgian guards with the lion of Flanders on their caps and collars ran along beside the train calling: "All out, everybody out!"

Tom Thumb remained beside me; he polished his glasses, looked at the station sign, and said: "Weeze—does this also convey something to you?"

"Yes," I said, "it lies north of Kevelaer and west of Xanten."

"Oh yes," he said, "Kevelaer, Heinrich Heine."

"And Xanten: Siegfried, in case you've forgotten."

Aunt Helen, I thought. Weeze. Why hadn't we gone straight through to Cologne? There wasn't much left of Weeze other than a spattering of red bricks showing through the treetops. Aunt Helen had owned a fair-sized shop in Weeze, a regular village store, and every morning she used to slip some money into our pockets so we could go boating on the River Niers or ride over to Kevelaer on our bikes; the sermons on Sunday in church, roundly berating the smugglers and adulterers.

"Let's go," said the Belgian guard, "get a move on, or don't you want to get home?"

I went into the camp. First we had to file past an English officer who gave us a twenty-mark bill, for which we had to sign a receipt. Next we had to go to the doctor; he was a German, young, and grinned at us; he waited till twelve or fifteen of us were in the room, then said: "Anyone who is so sick that he can't go home today need only raise his hand." A few of us laughed at this terribly witty remark; then we filed past his table one by one, had our release papers stamped, and went out by the other door. I waited for a few moments by the open door and heard him say: "Anyone who is so sick that—," then moved on, heard the laughter when I was already at the far end of the corridor, and went to the next check point: this was an English corporal, standing out in the open next to an uncovered latrine. The corporal said: "Show me your paybooks and any papers you still have." He said this in German, and when they pulled out their paybooks he pointed to the latrine and told them to throw the books into it, adding, "Down the hatch!" and then most of them laughed at this witticism. It had struck me anyway that Germans suddenly seemed to have a sense of humor, so long as it was foreign humor: in camp even Egelhecht had laughed at the American captain who had pointed to the barbed-wire entanglement and said: "Don't take it so hard, boys, now you're free at last."

The English corporal asked me too about my papers, but all I had was my release; I had sold my paybook to an American for two cigarettes; so I said: "No papers"—and that made him as angry as the American corporal had been when I had answered his question: "Hitler Youth, S.A., or Party?" with: "No." He had yelled at me and put me on K.P., he had sworn at me and accused my grandmother of various sexual offenses the nature of which, due to my insufficient knowledge of the American language, I was unable to ascertain; it made them furious when something didn't fit into their stereotyped categories. The English corporal went purple with rage, stood up and began to frisk me, and he didn't have to search long before he had found my diary: it was thick, cut from paperbags, stapled together, and in it I had written down everything that had happened to me from the middle of April till the end of September: from being taken prisoner by the American sergeant Stevenson to the final entry I had made in the train as we went through dismal Antwerp and I read on walls: *Vive le Roi!* There were more than a hundred paperbag pages, closely written, and the furious corporal took it from me, threw it into the latrine, and said: "Didn't I ask you for your papers?" Then I was allowed to go.

We stood crowded around the camp gate waiting for the Belgian trucks which were supposed to take us to Bonn. Bonn? Why Bonn, of all places? Someone said Cologne was closed off because it was contaminated by corpses, and someone else said we would have to clear away rubble for thirty or forty years, rubble, ruins, "and they aren't even going to give us trucks, we'll have to carry away the rubble in baskets." Luckily there was no one near me whom I had shared a tent or sat in the boxcar with. The drivel coming from mouths I did not know was a shade less disgusting than if it had come from mouths I knew. Someone ahead of me said: "But then he didn't mind taking the loaf of bread from the Jew," and another voice said: "Yes, they're the kind of people who are going to set the tone." Someone nudged me from behind and asked: "A hundred grams of bread for a cigarette, how about it, eh?" and from behind he thrust his hand in front of my face, and I saw it was one of the pieces of bread Egelhecht had divided up in the train. I shook my head. Someone else said: "The Belgians are selling cigarettes at ten marks apiece." To me that seemed very cheap: in camp the Germans had sold cigarettes for a hundred and twenty marks apiece. "Cigarettes, anyone?" "Yes," I said, and put my twenty-mark bill into an anonymous hand.

Everyone was trading with everyone else. It was the only thing that seriously interested them. For two thousand marks and a threadbare uniform someone got a civilian suit, the deal was concluded and clothes were changed somewhere in the waiting crowd, and suddenly I heard someone call out: "But of *course* the underpants go with the suit—and the tie too." Someone sold his wristwatch for three thousand marks. The chief article of trade was soap. Those who had been in American camps had a lot of soap, twenty cakes some of them, for they had been given soap every week but never any water to wash in, and the ones who had been in the English camps had no soap at all. The green and pink cakes of soap went back and forth. Some of the men had discovered their artistic aspirations and shaped the soap into little dogs, cats, and gnomes, and now it turned out that the artistic aspirations had lowered the exchange value: unsculptured soap rated higher than sculptured, a loss of weight being suspected in the latter.

The anonymous hand into which I had placed the twenty-mark bill actually reappeared and pressed two cigarettes into my left hand, and I was almost touched by so much honesty (but I was only almost touched till I found out that the Belgians were selling cigarettes for five marks; a hundred-per-cent profit was evidently regarded as a fair mark-up, especially among "comrades"). We stood there for about two hours, jammed together, and all I remember is hands: trading hands, passing soap from right to left, from left to right, money from left to right and again from right to left; it was as if I had fallen into a snakepit; hands from all sides moved every which way, passing goods and money over my shoulders and over my head in every direction.

Tom Thumb had managed to get close to me again. He sat beside me on the floor of the Belgian truck driving to Kevelaer, through Kevelaer, to Krefeld, around Krefeld to Neuss; there was silence over the fields, in the towns, we saw hardly a soul and only a few animals, and the dark autumn sky hung low; on my left sat Tom Thumb, on my right the Belgian guard, and we looked out over the tailboard at the road I knew so well: my brother and I had often ridden our bicycles along it. Tom Thumb kept trying to justify himself, but I cut him off every time, and he kept trying to be clever; there was no stopping him. "But Neuss," he said, "that can't remind you of anything. What on earth could Neuss remind anybody of?"

"Novesia Chocolate," I said, "sauerkraut and Quirinus, but I don't suppose you ever heard of the Thebaic Legion."

"No, I haven't," he said, and blushed again.

I asked the Belgian guard if it was true that Cologne was closed off, contaminated by corpses, and he said: "No—but it's a mess all right, is that where you're from?"

"Yes," I said.

"Be prepared for the worst . . . do you have any soap left?"

"Yes, I have," I said.

"Here," he said, pulling a pack of tobacco out of his pocket; he opened it and held out the pale-yellow, fresh fine-cut tobacco for me to smell. "It's yours for two cakes of soap—fair enough?"

I nodded, felt around in my coat pocket for the soap, gave him two cakes and put the tobacco in my pocket. He gave me his submachine gun to hold while he hid the soap in his pockets; he sighed as I handed it back to him. "These lousy things," he said, "we'll have to go on carrying them around for a while yet. You fellows aren't half as badly off as you think. What are you crying about?"

I pointed toward the right: the Rhine. We were approaching Dormagen. I saw that Tom Thumb was about to open his mouth and said quickly: "For God's sake shut up, can't you? Shut up." He had probably wanted to ask me whether the Rhine reminded me of anything. Thank God he was deeply offended now and said no more till we got to Bonn.

In Cologne there were actually some houses still standing; somewhere I even saw a moving streetcar, some people too, women even: one of them waved to us; from the Neuss-Strasse we turned into the Ring avenues and drove along them, and I was waiting all the time for the tears, but they didn't come; even the insurance buildings on the avenue were in ruins, and all I could see of the Hohenstaufen Baths was a few pale-blue tiles. I was hoping all the time the truck would turn off somewhere to the right, for we had lived on the Carolingian Ring; but the truck did not turn, it drove down the Rings: Barbarossa Square, Saxon Ring, Salian Ring, and I tried not to look, and I wouldn't have looked if the truck convoy had not got into a traffic jam up front at Clovis Square and we hadn't stopped in front of the house we used to live in, so I did look. The term "totally destroyed" is misleading; only in rare cases is it possible to destroy a house totally: it has to be hit three or four times and, to make certain, it should then burn down; the house we used to live in was actually, according to official terminology, totally destroyed, but not in the technical sense. That is to say, I could still recognize it, the front door and the doorbells, and I submit that a house where it is still possible to recognize the front door and the doorbells has not, in the strict technical sense, been totally destroyed; but of the house we used to live in there was more to be recognized than the doorbells and the front door: two rooms in the basement were almost intact, on the mezzanine, absurdly enough, even three: a fragment of wall was supporting the third room which would probably not have passed a spirit-level test; our apartment on the second floor had only one room intact, but it was gaping open in front, toward the street; above this, a high, narrow gable reared up, bare, with empty window sockets; however, the interesting thing was that two men were moving around in our living-room as if their feet were on familiar ground; one of the men took a picture down from the wall, the Terborch print my father had been so fond of, walked to the front, carrying the picture, and showed it to a third man who was standing down below in front of the house, but this third man shook his head like someone who is not interested in an object being auctioned, and the man up above walked back with the Terborch and hung it up again on the wall; he even straightened the picture; I was touched by this mark of neatness—he even stepped back to make sure the picture was really hanging straight, then nodded in a satisfied way. Meanwhile the second man took the other picture off the wall: an engraving of Lochner's painting of the Cathedral, but this one also did not appear to please the third man standing down below; finally the first man, the one who had hung the Terborch back on the wall, came to the front, formed a megaphone with his hands and shouted: "Piano in sight!" and the man below laughed, nodded, likewise formed a megaphone with hands and shouted: "I'll get the straps." I could not see the piano, but I knew where it stood: on the right in the corner I couldn't see into and where the man with the Lochner picture was just disappearing.

"Whereabouts in Cologne did you live?" asked the Belgian guard.

"Oh, somewhere over there," I said, gesturing vaguely in the direction of the western suburbs.

"Thank God, now we're moving again," said the guard. He picked up his submachine gun, which he had placed on the floor of the truck, and straightened his cap. The lion of Flanders on the front of his cap was rather dirty. As we turned into Clovis Square I could see why there had been a traffic jam: some kind of raid seemed to be going on. English military police cars were all over the place, and civilians were standing in them with their hands up, surrounded by a sizable crowd, quiet yet tense: a surprisingly large number of people in such a silent, ruined city.

"That's the black market," said the Belgian guard. "Once in a while they come and clean it up."

Before we were even out of Cologne, while we were still on the Bonn-Strasse, I fell asleep and I dreamed of my mother's coffee mill: the coffee mill was being let down on a strap by the man who had offered the Terborch without success, but the man below rejected the coffee mill; the other man drew it up again, opened the hall door and tried to screw the coffee mill onto where it had hung before: immediately to the left of the kitchen door, but now there was no wall there for him to screw it onto, and still the man kept on trying (this mark of tidiness touched me even in my dream). He searched with the forefinger of his right hand for the pegs, couldn't find them and raised his fist threateningly to the gray autumn sky which offered no support for the coffee mill; finally he gave up, tied the strap around the mill again, went to the front, let down the coffee mill and offered it to the third man, who again rejected it, and the other man pulled it up again, untied the strap and hid the coffee mill under his jacket as if it were a valuable object; then he began to wind up the strap, rolled it into a coil and threw it down into the third man's face. All this time I was worried about what could have happened to the man who had offered the Lochner without success, but I couldn't see him anywhere; something was preventing me from looking into the corner where the piano was, my father's desk, and I was upset at the thought that he might be reading my father's diaries. Now the man with the coffee mill was standing by the living room door trying to screw the coffee mill onto the door panel, he seemed absolutely determined to give the coffee mill a permanent resting place, and I was beginning to like him, even before I discovered he was one of our many friends whom my mother had comforted while they sat on the chair beneath the coffee mill, one of those who had been killed right at the beginning of the war in an air raid.

Before we got to Bonn the Belgian guard woke me up. "Come on," he said, "rub your eyes, freedom is at hand," and I straightened up and thought of all the people who had sat on the chair beneath my mother's coffee mill: truant schoolboys, whom she helped to overcome their fear of exams, Nazis whom she tried to enlighten, non-Nazis whom she tried to fortify: they had all sat on the chair beneath the coffee mill, had received comfort and censure, defense and respite, bitter words had destroyed their ideals and gentle words had offered them those things which would outlive the times: mercy to the weak, comfort to the persecuted.

The old cemetery, the market square, the university. Bonn. Through the Koblenz Gate and into the park. "So long," said the Belgian guard, and Tom Thumb with his tired child's face said: "Drop me a line some time." "All right," I said. "I'll send you my complete Tucholsky."

"Wonderful," he said, "and your Kleist too?"

"No," I said, "only the ones I have duplicates of."

On the other side of the barricade, through which we were finally released, a man was standing between two big laundry baskets; in one he had a lot of apples, in the other a few cakes of soap; he shouted: "Vitamins, my friends, one apple—one cake of soap!" And I could feel my mouth watering; I had quite forgotten what apples looked like; I gave him a cake of soap, was handed an apple, and bit into it at once; I stood there watching the others come out; there was no need for him to call out now: it was a wordless exchange; he would take an apple out of the basket, be handed a cake of soap, and throw the soap into the empty basket; there was a dull thud when the soap landed; not everyone took an apple, not everyone had any soap, but the transaction was as swift as in a self-service store, and by the time I had just finished my apple he already had his soap basket half full. The whole thing took place swiftly and smoothly and without a word, and even the ones who were very economical and very calculating couldn't resist the sight of the apples, and I began to feel sorry for them. Home was welcoming its homecomers so warmly with vitamins.

It took me a long time to find a phone in Bonn; finally a girl in the post office told me that the only people to get phones were doctors and priests, and even then only those who hadn't been Nazis. "They're scared stiff of the Nazi Werewolf underground," she said. "I s'pose you wouldn't have a cigarette for me?" I took my pack of tobacco out of my pocket and said: "Shall I roll one for you?", but she said no, she could do it herself, and I watched her take a cigarette paper out of her coat pocket and quickly and deftly roll herself a firm cigarette. "Who do you want to call?" she said, and I said: "My wife," and she laughed and said I didn't look married at all. I also rolled myself a cigarette and asked her whether there was any chance of selling some soap; I needed money, train fare, and didn't have a pfennig. "Soap," she said, "let's have a look." I felt around in my coat lining and pulled out some soap, and she snatched it out of my hand, sniffed it, and said: "Real Palmolive! That's worth—worth— I'll give you fifty marks for it." I looked at her in amazement, and she said: "Yes, I know, you can get as much as eighty for it, but I can't afford that." I didn't want to take the fifty marks, but she insisted, she thrust the note into my coat pocket and ran out of the post office; she was quite pretty, with that hungry prettiness which lends a girl's voice a certain sharpness.

What struck me most of all, in the post office and as I walked slowly on through Bonn, was the fact that nowhere was there a student wearing colored ribbons, and the smells: everyone smelled terrible, all the rooms smelled terrible, and I could see why the girl was so crazy about the soap; I went to the station, tried to find out how I could get to Oberkerschenbach (that was where the one I married lived), but nobody could tell me; all I knew was that it was a little place somewhere in the Eifel district not too far from Bonn; there weren't any maps anywhere either, where I could have looked it up; no doubt they had been banned on account of the Nazi Werewolves. I always like to know where a place is, and it bothered me that I knew nothing definite about this place Oberkerschenbach and couldn't find out anything definite. In my mind I went over all the Bonn addresses I knew but there wasn't a single doctor or a single priest among them; finally I remembered a professor of theology I had called on with a friend just before the war; he had had some sort of trouble with Rome and the Index, and we had gone to see him simply to give him our moral support; I couldn't remember the name of the street, but I knew where it was, and I walked along the Poppelsdorf Avenue, turned left, then left again, found the house and was relieved to read the name on the door.

The professor came to the door himself; he had aged a great deal, he was thin and bent, his hair quite white. I said: "You won't remember me, Professor, I came to see you some years ago when you had that stink with Rome and the Index—can I speak to you for a moment?" He laughed when I said stink, and said: "Of course," when I had finished, and I followed him into his study; I noticed it no longer smelled of tobacco, otherwise it was still just the same with all the books, files, and house plants. I told the professor I had heard that the only people who got phones were priests and doctors, and I simply had to call my wife; he heard me out—a very rare thing—then said that, although he was a priest, he was not one of those who had a phone, for: "You see," he said, "I am not a pastor." "Perhaps you're a Werewolf," I said; I offered him some tobacco, and I felt sorry for him when I saw how he looked at my tobacco; I am always sorry for old people who have to go without something they like. His hands trembled as he filled his pipe, and they did not tremble just because he was old. When he had at last got it lit—I had no matches and couldn't help him—he told me that doctors and priests were not the only people with phones. "These night clubs they're opening up everywhere for the soldiers," they had them, too, and I might try in one of these night clubs; there was one just around the corner. He wept when I put a few pipefuls of tobacco on his desk as I left, and he asked me as his tears fell whether I knew what I was doing, and I said, yes, I knew, and I suggested he accept the few pipefuls of to-bacco as a belated tribute to the courage he had shown toward Rome all those years ago. I would have liked to give him some soap as well, I still had five or six pieces in my coat lining, but I was afraid his heart would burst with joy; he was so old and frail.

"Night club" was a nice way of putting it; but I didn't mind that so much as the English sentry at the door of this night club. He was very young and eyed me severely as I stopped beside him. He pointed to the notice prohibiting Germans from entering this night club, but I told him my sister worked there, I had just returned to my beloved fatherland and my sister had the house key. He asked me what my sister's name was, and it seemed safest to give the most Ger-man of all German girls' names, and I said: "Gretchen"; oh yes, he said, that was the blonde one, and let me go in; instead of bothering to describe the interior, I refer the reader to the pertinent "Fräulein literature" and to movies and TV; I won't even bother to describe Gretchen (see above); the main thing was that Gretchen was sur-prisingly quick in the uptake and, in exchange for a cake of Palm-olive, was willing to make a phone call to the priest's house in Ker-schenbach (which I hoped existed) and have the one I had married called to the phone. Gretchen spoke fluent English on the phone and told me her boy friend would try to do it through the army ex-change; it would be quicker. While we were waiting I offered her some tobacco, but she had something better; I tried to pay her the agreed fee of a cake of soap in advance, but she said no, she didn't want it after all, she would rather not take anything, and when I insisted on paying she began to cry and confided that one of her brothers was a prisoner of war, the other one dead, and I felt sorry for her, for it is not pleasant when girls like Gretchen cry; she even let on that she was a Catholic, and just as she was about to get her first communion picture out of a drawer the phone rang, and Gretchen lifted the receiver and said: "Reverend," but I had already heard that it was not a man's voice. "Just a moment," Gretchen said and handed me the receiver. I was so excited I couldn't hold the receiver, in fact I dropped it, fortunately onto Gretchen's lap; she picked it up, held it against my ear, and I said: "Hallo—is that you?"

"Yes," she said. "—Darling, where are you?"

"I'm in Bonn," I said. "The war's over—for me."

"My God," she said, "I can't believe it. No—it's not true."

"It is true," I said, "it is—did you get my postcard?"

"No," she said, "what postcard?"

"When we were taken prisoner—we were allowed to write one postcard."

"No," she said, "for the last eight months I haven't had the slightest idea where you were."

"Those bastards," I said, "those dirty bastards—listen, just tell me where Kerschenbach is."

"I—" She was crying so hard she couldn't speak, I heard her sobbing and gulping till at last she was able to whisper: "—at the station in Bonn, I'll meet you," then I could no longer hear her, someone said something in English that I didn't understand.

Gretchen put the receiver to her ear, listened a moment, shook her head and replaced it. I looked at her and knew I couldn't offer her the soap now. I couldn't even say "Thank you," the words seemed ridiculous. I lifted my arms helplessly and went out.

I walked back to the station, in my ear the woman's voice which had never sounded like marriage.

*Translated from the German by Leila Vennewitz*

# Reinhard Lettau

POTEMKIN'S CARRIAGE PASSES THROUGH

April 11, 1784

L AST NIGHT we received orders from Sebastopol to remain here and await further instructions. It seems that we are to be kept here even after the carriage has passed through. It makes sense; we have traveled a great distance from our native villages, and even before we began building this village we had to prepare regular sleeping accommodations for ourselves. We began by building simple huts, for which we used part of the government material slated for the construction of the make-believe village. Then we built the housefronts of the village they had ordered onto our modest lodgings on either side of the road. My quarters, for instance, are situated directly behind a rather high wooden wall that creates the illusion of being a town hall when seen from the road. If one opens the front door of the town hall, one stands right outside my hut. I spend the days and nights lying here, listening to the reports of my foremen. Most of them are just painters. "Little Father Overseer," they say to me, "what shall we do now?" And I tell them.

Of course the roofers are really painters, and so are the glaziers who insert windows with deft brushes. The bricklayers are painters and so are the masons; the only people who work at their true trade here are the stagehands who put up the scaffoldings and lent a hand with our lodgings. But since then no one's seen them do any work. I am told that they are lying around drinking behind the wooden wall that looks like a tavern from the road. One of them supposedly had the idea of throwing a stone through one of the not-so-well-painted windows in the village, the other day, and replacing it with real glass. If this practice spreads, I almost fear for the success of my mission.

April 12, 1784

The meaning of my last sentence in yesterday's annotations can best be illustrated by the fact that more and more fake window fronts have, since then, been replaced by real ones. One of the glaziers, a certain Popov from Nicolaiev, a painter in reality, complained to me today. "Our honest work is being disfigured," he cried. "One hardly has time to lay down one's brush before people replace our paintings with real windows."

Sometimes I can't help feeling that we are in reality building two villages: a false one and a real one, without actually wanting to build the real one, as though it were growing by itself out of the false one, as if by necessity.

### April 13, 1784

A nightmare shocked me from my nap after lunch today. I dreamed that the carriage was finally passing through the village, but that the Empress was fast asleep and even the prince did not dare rouse her. I tell myself she might also happen to be in the arms of her lover, that very same Prince Potemkin, just as the carriage races through our street. Perhaps she'll look out for the flick of an eyelid. I'm aware that all of us are here for nothing but the possibility of this one blink. I have asked Pravdin to subject the gables particularly to another critical examination, in view of her possible glance.

Petrov just came to me, all out of breath, and told me confidentially that real smoke was rising from a chimney he had just finished painting. Since I have no time to check up on the matter myself, I sent him back and asked him to take a look at the various housefronts from the rear. Someone has extended the front toward the back and made a house of it, he called to me from the door of my hut. By all the saints! I wouldn't be surprised if church bells rang for mass tomorrow morning.

### April 17, 1784

The dream I mentioned earlier seems to be undergoing curious transformations, especially when one compares it to the anxiety fantasies I had when I first learned of my mission. At the time I thought, "What if Catherine expressed the wish to dismount? What if she were to be led behind empty façades rather than into a cozy room?"

Lieutenant Chuchotatsky called on me yesterday, or the day before, just as I was lying down for a nap; he's being transferred from Odessa to one of the new garrisons on Crimea. "Where do you intend to build the make-believe village, Little Father?" he asked me. Although I know that he's fond of joking, I'd almost jumped to my feet and rushed outside. For days now I've been plagued by a fantasy of the prince asking me the same question. The church bells did ring this morning and Petrov tells me that smoke is now rising from every chimney and that one can see one's reflection in countless windows behind which one can see real flowers standing in real vases. Supposedly the locksmiths, glaziers, roofers, bricklayers, *et al.*, no longer have paint stains on their overalls, and very close to my lodgings, wall to wall so to speak, I can hear men at work. I wouldn't be surprised if I discovered one of these days that my hut is a room in the town hall.

## April 19, 1784

I can't get the thought out of my mind, especially since I hear sounds above my hut, as if people were running about. The temptation to get up and look into the matter is great. There is the danger of the prince's taking this village for a real village. And then he'll ask me where I built the fake one he ordered. He might even suspect me of having sold the material entrusted to me by the government. At any rate, I've hurriedly issued instructions to give the housefronts along the village road the outright dillettantish look of stage settings. While I write this, the glaziers and the roofers, the masons and the locksmiths are as busy as ants, painting over their handiwork.

## April 21, 1784

I am particularly interested in the successful conclusion of this task since yesterday I was informed of my unanimous election to the position of town elder. My appointment is not far off, since the town hall is practically finished. Within the hour, a second door will be broken into my hut which, were I to get up, would lead me into the corridor of the town hall and into a suite of pleasant rooms that have supposedly been installed there for me.

I am forced to interrupt these notes. The approach of the imperial carriage has just been announced.

## April 29, 1784

Breaking through the wall caused a most dreadful noise. I was obliged to get up and retreat to the opposite corner of the room. The sound still rings in my ears. I am told that it often takes weeks to get over that kind of experience. Absolute rest and especially sleep, that healer of all ills, are recommended.

The prefect came to make his report to me. The long-awaited carriage bearing the imperial arms has recently passed through. Work on the schoolhouse is progressing.

*Translated from the German by Ursule Molinaro*

# Ilse Aichinger

## THE BOUND MAN

SUNLIGHT ON HIS FACE woke him, but made him shut his eyes again; it streamed unhindered down the slope, collected itself into rivulets, attracted swarms of flies, which flew low over his forehead, circled, sought to land, and were overtaken by fresh swarms. When he tried to whisk them away, he discovered that he was bound. A thin rope cut into his arms. He dropped them, opened his eyes again, and looked down at himself. His legs were tied all the way up to his thighs; a single length of rope was tied round his ankles, criss-crossed up his legs, and encircled his hips, his chest and his arms. He could not see where it was knotted. He showed no sign of fear or hurry, though he thought he was unable to move, until he discovered that the rope allowed his legs some free play and that round his body it was almost loose. His arms were tied to each other but not to his body, and had some free play too. This made him smile, and it occurred to him that perhaps children had been playing a practical joke on him.

He tried to feel for his knife, but again the rope cut softly into his flesh. He tried again, more cautiously this time, but his pocket was empty. Not only his knife, but the little money that he had on him, as well as his coat, were missing. His shoes had been pulled from his feet and taken too. When he moistened his lips he tasted blood, which had flowed from his temples down his cheeks, his chin, his neck, and under his shirt. His eyes were painful; if he kept them open for long he saw reddish stripes in the sky.

He decided to stand up. He drew his knees up as far as he could, rested his hands on the fresh grass and jerked himself to his feet. An elder-branch stroked his cheek, the sun dazzled him, and the rope cut into his flesh. He collapsed to the ground again, half out of his mind with pain, and then tried again. He went on trying until the blood started flowing from his hidden weals. Then he lay still again for a long while and let the sun and the flies do what they liked.

When he awoke for the second time the elder-bush had cast its shadow over him, and the coolness stored in it was pouring from between its branches. He must have been hit on the head. Then they must have laid him down carefully, just as a mother lays her baby behind a bush when she goes to work in the fields.

His chances all lay in the amount of free play allowed him by the rope. He dug his elbows into the ground and tested it. As soon as the rope tautened he stopped, and tried again more cautiously. If he had been able to reach the branch over his head he could have used it to drag himself to his feet, but he could not reach it. He laid his head back on the grass, rolled over, and struggled to his knees. He tested the ground with his toes, and then managed to stand up almost without effort.

A few paces away lay the path across the plateau, and in the grass were wild pinks and thistles in bloom. He tried to lift his foot to avoid trampling on them, but the rope round his ankles prevented him. He looked down at himself.

The rope was knotted at his ankles, and ran round his legs in a kind of playful pattern. He carefully bent and tried to loosen it, but, loose though it seemed to be, he could not make it any looser. To avoid treading on the thistles with his bare feet he hopped over them like a bird.

The cracking of a twig made him stop. People in this district were very prone to laughter. He was alarmed by the thought that he was in no position to defend himself. He hopped on until he reached the path. Bright fields stretched far below. He could see no sign of the nearest village, and if he could move no faster than this, night would fall before he reached it.

He tried walking, and discovered that he could put one foot before another if he lifted each foot a definite distance from the ground and then put it down again before the rope tautened. In the same way he could actually swing his arms a little.

After the first step he fell. He fell right across the path, and made the dust fly. He expected this to be a sign for the long-suppressed laughter to break out, but all remained quiet. He was alone. As soon as the dust had settled he got up and went on. He looked down and watched the rope slacken, grow taut, and then slacken again.

When the first glow-worms appeared he managed to look up. He felt in control of himself again, and his impatience to reach the nearest village faded.

Hunger made him light-headed, and he seemed to be going so fast that not even a motor-cycle could have overtaken him; alternatively he felt as if he were standing still and that the earth was rushing past him, like a river flowing past a man swimming against the stream. The stream carried branches which had been bent southward by the north wind, stunted young trees, and patches of grass with bright, long-stalked flowers. It ended by submerging the bushes and the young trees, leaving only the sky and the man above water-level. The moon had risen, and illuminated the bare, curved summit of the plateau, the path, which was overgrown with young grass, the bound man making his way along it with quick, measured steps, and two hares, which ran across the hill just in front of him and vanished down the slope. Though the nights were still cool at this time of the year, before midnight the bound man lay down at the edge of the escarpment and went to sleep.

In the light of morning the animal-tamer who was camping with his circus in the field outside the village saw the bound man coming down the path, gazing thoughtfully at the ground. The bound man stopped and bent down. He held out one arm to help keep his balance and with the other picked up an empty wine-bottle. Then he straightened himself and stood erect again. He moved slowly, to avoid being cut by the rope, but to the circus proprietor what he did suggested the voluntary limitations of an enormous swiftness of movement. He was enchanted by its extraordinary gracefulness, and while the bound man looked about for a stone on which to break the bottle, so that he could use the splintered neck to cut the rope, the animal-tamer walked across the field and approached him. The first leaps of a young panther had never filled him with such delight.

"Ladies and gentlemen, the bound man!" His very first movements let loose a storm of applause, which out of sheer excitement caused the blood to rush to the cheeks of the animal-tamer standing at the edge of the arena. The bound man rose to his feet. His surprise whenever he did this was like that of a four-footed animal which has managed to stand on its hind-legs. He knelt, stood up, jumped, and turned cart-wheels. The spectators found it as astonishing as if they had seen a bird which voluntarily remained earthbound, and confined itself to hopping.

The bound man became an enormous draw. His absurd steps and little jumps, his elementary exercises in movement, made the rope-dancer superfluous. His fame grew from village to village, but the motions he went through were few and always the same; they were really quite ordinary motions, which he had continually to practice in the daytime in the half-dark tent in order to retain his shackled freedom. In that he remained entirely within the limits set by his rope he was free of it, it did not confine him, but gave him wings and endowed his leaps and jumps with purpose; just as the flights of birds of passage have purpose when they take wing in the warmth of summer and hesitantly make small circles in the sky.

All the children of the neighborhood started playing the game of "bound man." They formed rival gangs, and one day the circus people found a little girl lying bound in a ditch, with a cord tied round her neck so that she could hardly breathe. They released her, and at the end of the performance that night the bound man made a speech. He announced briefly that there was no sense in being tied up in such a way that you could not jump. After that he was regarded as a comedian.

Grass and sunlight, tent-pegs driven into the ground and then pulled up again, and on to the next village. "Ladies and gentlemen, the bound man!" The summer mounted toward its climax. It bent its face deeper over the fish-ponds in the hollows, taking delight in its dark reflection, skimmed the surface of the rivers, and made the plain into what it was. Everyone who could walk went to see the bound man.

Many wanted a close-up view of how he was bound. So the circus proprietor announced after each performance that anyone who wanted to satisfy himself that the knots were real and the rope not made of rubber was at liberty to do so. The bound man generally waited for the crowd in the area outside the tent. He laughed or remained serious, and held out his arms for inspection. Many took the opportunity to look him in the face, others gravely tested the rope, tried the knots on his ankles, and wanted to know exactly how the lengths compared with the length of his limbs. They asked him how he had come to be tied up like that, and he answered patiently, always saying the same thing. Yes, he had been tied up, he said, and when he awoke he found that he had been robbed as well. Those who had done it must have been pressed for time, because they had tied him up somewhat too loosely for someone who was not supposed to be able to move and somewhat too tightly for someone who was expected to be able to move. But he did move, people pointed out. Yes, he replied, what else could he do?

Before he went to bed he always sat for a time in front of the fire. When the circus proprietor asked him why he didn't make up a better story he always answered that he hadn't made up that one, and blushed. He preferred staying in the shade.

The difference between him and the other performers was that when the show was over he did not take off his rope. The result was that every movement that he made was worth seeing, and the villagers used to hang about the camp for hours, just for the sake of seeing him get up from in front of the fire and roll himself in his blanket. Sometimes the sky was beginning to lighten when he saw their shadows disappear.

The circus proprietor often remarked that there was no reason why he should not be untied after the evening performance and tied up again next day. He pointed out that the rope-dancers, for instance, did not stay on their rope overnight. But no one took the idea of untying him seriously.

For the bound man's fame rested on the fact that he was always bound, that whenever he washed himself he had to wash his clothes too and vice versa, and that his only way of doing so was to jump in the river just as he was every morning when the sun came out, and that he had to be careful not to go too far out for fear of being carried away by the stream.

The proprietor was well aware that what in the last resort protected the bound man from the jealousy of the other performers was his helplessness; he deliberately left them the pleasure of watching him groping painfully from stone to stone on the river bank every morning with his wet clothes clinging to him. When the proprietor's wife pointed out that even the best clothes would not stand up indefinitely to such treatment (and the bound man's clothes were by no means of the best), he replied curtly that it was not going to last forever. That was his answer to all objections—it was for the summer season only. But when he said this he was not being serious; he was talking like a gambler who has no intention of giving up his vice. In reality he would have been prepared cheerfully to sacrifice his lions and his rope-dancers for the bound man.

He proved this on the night when the rope-dancers jumped over the fire. Afterward he was convinced that they did it, not because it was midsummer's day, but because of the bound man, who as usual was lying and watching them with that peculiar smile that might have been real or might have been only the effect of the glow on his face. In any case no one knew anything about him because he never talked about anything that had happened to him before he emerged from the wood that day.

But that evening two of the performers suddenly picked him up by the arms and legs, carried him to the edge of the fire and started playfully swinging him to and fro, while two others held out their arms to catch him on the other side. In the end they threw him, but too short. The two men on the other side drew back—they explained afterward that they did so the better to take the shock. The result was that the bound man landed at the very edge of the flames and would have been burned if the circus proprietor had not seized his arms and quickly dragged him away to save the rope which was starting to get singed. He was certain that the object had been to burn the rope. He sacked the four men on the spot.

A few nights later the proprietor's wife was awakened by the sound of footsteps on the grass, and went outside just in time to prevent the clown from playing his last practical joke. He was carrying a pair of scissors. When he was asked for an explanation he insisted that he had had no intention of taking the bound man's life, but only wanted to cut his rope because he felt sorry for him. He was sacked too.

These antics amused the bound man because he could have freed himself if he had wanted to whenever he liked, but perhaps he wanted to learn a few new jumps first. The children's rhyme: "We travel with the circus, we travel with the circus" sometimes occurred to him while he lay awake at night. He could hear the voices of spectators on the opposite bank who had been driven too far downstream on the way home. He could see the river gleaming in the moonlight, and the young shoots growing out of the thick tops of the willow trees, and did not think about autumn yet.

The circus proprietor dreaded the danger that sleep involved for the bound man. Attempts were continually made to release him while he slept. The chief culprits were sacked rope-dancers, or children who were bribed for the purpose. But measures could be taken to safeguard against these. A much bigger danger was that which he represented to himself. In his dreams he forgot his rope, and was surprised by it when he woke in the darkness of morning. He would angrily try to get up, but lose his balance and fall back again. The previous evening's applause was forgotten, sleep was still too near, his head and neck too free. He was just the opposite of a hanged man—his neck was the only part of him that was free. You had to make sure that at such moments no knife was within his reach. In the early hours of the morning the circus proprietor sometimes sent his wife to see whether the bound man was all right. If he was asleep she would bend over him and feel the rope. It had grown hard from dirt and damp. She would test the amount of free play it allowed him, and touch his tender wrists and ankles.

The most varied rumors circulated about the bound man. Some said he had tied himself up and invented the story of having been

robbed, and toward the end of the summer that was the general opinion. Others maintained that he had been tied up at his own request,
perhaps in league with the circus proprietor. The hesitant way in
which he told his story, his habit of breaking off when the talk got
round to the attack on him, contributed greatly to these rumors.
Those who still believed in the robbery-with-violence story were
laughed at. Nobody knew what difficulties the circus proprietor had
in keeping the bound man, and how often he said he had had enough
and wanted to clear off, for too much of the summer had passed.

Later, however, he stopped talking about clearing off. When the
proprietor's wife brought him his food by the river and asked him
how long he proposed to remain with them, he did not answer. She
thought he had got used, not to being tied up, but to remembering
every moment that he was tied up—the only thing that anyone in his
position could get used to. She asked him whether he did not think it
ridiculous to be tied up all the time, but he answered that he did not.
Such a variety of people—clowns, freaks, and comics, to say nothing
of elephants and tigers—traveled with circuses that he did not see
why a bound man should not travel with a circus too. He told her
about the movements he was practicing, the new ones he had discovered, and about a new trick that had occurred to him while he was
whisking flies from the animals' eyes. He described to her how he
always anticipated the effect of the rope and always restrained his
movements in such a way as to prevent it from ever tautening; and
she knew that there were days when he was hardly aware of the
rope, when he jumped down from the wagon and slapped the flanks
of the horses in the morning as if he were moving in a dream. She
watched him vault over the bars almost without touching them, and
saw the sun on his face, and he told her that sometimes he felt as if he
were not tied up at all. She answered that if he were prepared to be
untied, there would never be any need for him to feel tied up. He
agreed that he could be untied whenever he felt like it.

The woman ended by not knowing whether she was more concerned with the man or with the rope that tied him. She told him that
he could go on traveling with the circus without his rope, but she did
not believe it. For what would be the point of his antics without his
rope, and what would he amount to without it? Without his rope he
would leave them, and the happy days would be over. She would no
longer be able to sit beside him on the stones by the river without
arousing suspicion, and she knew that his continued presence, and
her conversations with him, of which the rope was the only subject,
depended on it. Whenever she agreed that the rope had its advan-

tages, he would start talking about how troublesome it was, and whenever he started talking about its advantages, she would urge him to get rid of it. All this seemed as endless as the summer itself.

At other times she was worried at the thought that she was herself hastening the end by her talk. Sometimes she would get up in the middle of the night and run across the grass to where he slept. She wanted to shake him, wake him up and ask him to keep the rope. But then she would see him lying there; he had thrown off his blanket, and there he lay like a corpse, with his legs outstretched and his arms close together, with the rope tied round them. His clothes had suffered from the heat and the water, but the rope had grown no thinner. She felt that he would go on traveling with the circus until the flesh fell from him and exposed the joints. Next morning she would plead with him more ardently than ever to get rid of his rope.

The increasing coolness of the weather gave her hope. Autumn was coming, and he would not be able to go on jumping into the river with his clothes on much longer. But the thought of losing his rope, about which he had felt indifferent earlier in the season, now depressed him.

The songs of the harvesters filled him with foreboding. "Summer has gone, summer has gone." But he realized that soon he would have to change his clothes, and he was certain that when he had been untied it would be impossible to tie him up again in exactly the same way. About this time the proprietor started talking about traveling south that year.

The heat changed without transition into quiet, dry cold, and the fire was kept going all day long. When the bound man jumped down from the wagon he felt the coldness of the grass under his feet. The stalks were bent with ripeness. The horses dreamed on their feet and the wild animals, crouching to leap even in their sleep, seemed to be collecting gloom under their skins which would break out later.

On one of these days a young wolf escaped. The circus proprietor kept quiet about it, to avoid spreading alarm, but the wolf soon started raiding cattle in the neighborhood. People at first believed that the wolf had been driven to these parts by the prospect of a severe winter, but the circus soon became suspect. The proprietor could not conceal the loss of the animal from his own employees, so the truth was bound to come out before long. The circus people offered the burgomasters of the neighboring villages their aid in tracking down the beast, but all their efforts were in vain. Eventually the circus was openly blamed for the damage and the danger, and spectators stayed away.

The bound man went on performing before half-empty seats without losing anything of his amazing freedom of movement. During the day he wandered among the surrounding hills under the thin-beaten silver of the autumn sky, and, whenever he could, lay down where the sun shone longest. Soon he found a place which the twilight reached last of all, and when at last it reached him he got up most unwillingly from the withered grass. In coming down the hill he had to pass through a little wood on its southern slope, and one evening he saw the gleam of two little green lights. He knew that they came from no church window, and was not for a moment under any illusion about what they were.

He stopped. The animal came toward him through the thinning foliage. He could make out its shape, the slant of its neck, its tail which swept the ground, and its receding head. If he had not been bound, perhaps he would have tried to run away, but as it was he did not even feel fear. He stood calmly with dangling arms and looked down at the wolf's bristling coat under which the muscles played like his own underneath the rope. He thought the evening wind was still between him and the wolf when the beast sprang. The man took care to obey his rope.

Moving with the deliberate care that he had so often put to the test, he seized the wolf by the throat. Tenderness for a fellow-creature arose in him, tenderness for the upright being concealed in the four-footed. In a movement that resembled the drive of a great bird (he felt a sudden awareness that flying would be possible only if one were tied up in a special way) he flung himself at the animal and brought it to the ground. He felt a slight elation at having lost the fatal advantage of free limbs which causes men to be worsted.

The freedom he enjoyed in this struggle was having to adapt every movement of his limbs to the rope that tied him—the freedom of panthers, wolves, and the wild flowers that sway in the evening breeze. He ended up lying obliquely down the slope, clasping the animal's hind-legs between his own bare feet and its head between his hands. He felt the gentleness of the faded foliage stroking the backs of his hands, and he felt his own grip almost effortlessly reaching its maximum, and he felt too how he was in no way hampered by the rope.

As he left the wood light rain began to fall and obscured the setting sun. He stopped for a while under the trees at the edge of the wood. Beyond the camp and the river he saw the fields where the cattle grazed, and the places where they crossed. Perhaps he would travel south with the circus after all. He laughed softly. It was against all reason. Even if he continued to put up with the sores that covered his joints and opened and bled when he made certain movements, his clothes would not stand up much longer to the friction of the rope.

The circus proprietor's wife tried to persuade her husband to announce the death of the wolf without mentioning that it had been killed by the bound man. She said that even at the time of his greatest popularity people would have refused to believe him capable of it, and in their present angry mood, with the nights getting cooler, they would be more incredulous than ever. The wolf had attacked a group of children at play that day, and nobody would believe that it had really been killed; for the circus proprietor had many wolves, and it was easy enough for him to hang a skin on the rail and allow free entry. But he was not to be dissuaded. He thought that the announcement of the bound man's act would revive the triumphs of the summer.

That evening the bound man's movements were uncertain. He stumbled in one of his jumps, and fell. Before he managed to get up he heard some low whistles and catcalls, rather like birds calling at dawn. He tried to get up too quickly, as he had done once or twice during the summer, with the result that he tautened the rope and fell back again. He lay still to regain his calm, and listened to the boos and catcalls growing into an uproar. "Well, bound man, and how did you kill the wolf?" they shouted, and: "Are you the man who killed the wolf?" If he had been one of them, he would not have believed it himself. He thought they had a perfect right to be angry: a circus at this time of year, a bound man, an escaped wolf, and all ending up with this. Some groups of spectators started arguing with others, but the greater part of the audience thought the whole thing a bad joke. By the time he had got to his feet there was such a hubbub that he was barely able to make out individual words.

He saw people surging up all round him, like faded leaves raised by a whirlwind in a circular valley at the center of which all was yet still. He thought of the golden sunsets of the last few days; and the sepulchral light which lay over the blight of all that he had built up during so many nights, the gold frame which the pious hang round dark, old pictures, this sudden collapse of everything, filled him with anger.

They wanted him to repeat his battle with the wolf. He said that such a thing had no place in a circus performance, and the proprietor declared that he did not keep animals to have them slaughtered in front of an audience. But the mob stormed the ring and forced them toward the cages. The proprietor's wife made her way between the seats to the exit and managed to get round to the cages from the other side. She pushed aside the attendant whom the crowd had forced to open a cage door, but the spectators dragged her back and prevented the door from being shut.

"Aren't you the woman who used to lie with him by the river in the summer?" they called out. "How does he hold you in his arms?" She shouted back at them that they needn't believe in the bound man if they didn't want to, they had never deserved him. Painted clowns were good enough for them.

The bound man felt as if the bursts of laughter were what he had been expecting ever since early May. What had smelled so sweet all through the summer now stank. But, if they insisted, he was ready to take on all the animals in the circus. He had never felt so much at one with his rope.

Gently he pushed the woman aside. Perhaps he would travel south with them after all. He stood in the open doorway of the cage, and he saw the wolf, a strong young animal, rise to its feet, and he heard the proprietor grumbling again about the loss of his exhibits. He clapped his hands to attract the animal's attention, and when it was near enough he turned to slam the cage door. He looked the woman in the face. Suddenly he remembered the proprietor's warning to suspect of murderous intentions anyone near him who had a sharp instrument in his hand. At the same moment he felt the blade on his wrists, as cool as the water of the river in autumn, which during the last few weeks he had been barely able to stand. The rope curled up in a tangle beside him while he struggled free. He pushed the woman back, but there was no point in anything he did now. Had he been insufficiently on his guard against those who wanted to release him, against the sympathy in which they wanted to lull him? Had he lain too long on the river bank? If she had cut the cord at any other moment it would have been better than this.

He stood in the middle of the cage, and rid himself of the rope like a snake discarding its skin. It amused him to see the spectators shrinking back. Did they realize that he had no choice now? Or that fighting the wolf now would prove nothing whatever? At the same time he felt all his blood rush to his feet. He felt suddenly weak.

The rope, which fell at its feet like a snare, angered the wolf more than the entry of a stranger into its cage. It crouched to spring.

The man reeled, and grabbed the pistol that hung ready at the side of the cage. Then, before anyone could stop him, he shot the wolf between the eyes. The animal reared, and touched him in falling.

On the way to the river he heard the footsteps of his pursuers—spectators, the rope-dancers, the circus proprietor, and the proprietor's wife, who persisted in the chase longer than anyone else. He hid in a clump of bushes and listened to them hurrying past, and later on streaming in the opposite direction back to the camp. The moon shone on the meadow; in that light its color was both of growth and of death.

When he came to the river his anger died away. At dawn it seemed to him as if lumps of ice were floating in the water, and as if snow had fallen, obliterating memory.

*Translated from the German by Eric Mosbacher*

# Jakov Lind

## RESURRECTION

"D EUM JESUM CHRISTUM in gloriam eternam est. Nu." Goldschmied turned over on the other side, put down the
prayer book and tried to sleep. He pulled his coat over his head and
nearly suffocated, he took it off and the light hurt his eyes. He
turned from side to side, but cautiously, so as not to touch either of
the walls. His head touched the wall behind him (it was padded) and
his toes pressed against the chair between the bed and the fourth
wall. He couldn't sleep a wink. They won't let you have your rest,
not even in the coffin, you'd expect there'd at least be room to stretch
your legs six foot underground. Not a chance. Psiakrew Pieronie!
It was only in Polish that he dared. As a Protestant he wasn't allowed
to swear. I hope he's a midget, I'll put him under the bed. How can
two people sleep in this place? A hundred guilders a week and he
won't let me breathe. Meine goyim. Czort!

Swiss Alpine Club. Holiday at Arosa. Altitude 6,000 feet. First-
class hotels. Reduced prices out of season. It's out of season all right.
Who wants to go to Switzerland in October? Too early for skiing,
too late for sun-bathing. Now would be the time to go, if I could.
The calendar won't mind. He himself had brought the calendar.
Every day a stroke. So far he had struck off 184 days, 184 years.
Only the pencil had stayed untouched by it all. It hung on its nail, its
point as sharp as on the first day.

The motto for October: In golden splendor flows the wine—and
the picture: vintner carrying a basket full of grapes, clinking glasses
with a young couple. Carriage, vines, women, a team of oxen in the
background. Young woman smiles merrily. Husband smacks lips.
Vintner holds one hand over his paunch.

I could stand it in Switzerland right now. Not too hot, not too
cold.

In November they plow, in December they sing Holy Night,
Silent Night beside the Savior's cradle, in January skiing, in February
too, in March they take the cable car up the Matterhorn (does it

133

have to be March?), in April the young lambs playing in the meadow, in May a nightingale singing in the trees, in June they ski and swim.

But how will I live through such troubles?

Nothing about it in the calendar. A book tumbled down from over the bed. *Introduction to Inorganic Chemistry*, Dr. K. Kluisenhart, Groningen 1902. In 1902 I was still in Cracow. Do I need inorganic chemistry? I'm inorganic enough already. He put the book down and took paper and pen to write van Tuinhout a letter. Dear Mr. van Tuinhout: Nothing doing. I can barely stand it by myself, if there are two of us I'll go mad. I'll give you a hundred guilders, but don't do that to me. Find him another place.

I'm a sociable man, but how can two live in this hole without killing each other? Besides, there's the difference in denomination. Try to understand.

He didn't write the letter, he didn't have time. Van Tuinhout was outside the wall. He gave the prearranged knock. Without having to get up, Goldschmied opened the two hooks.

The trap door was pushed up slightly from outside and van Tuinhout climbed through the opening. Now what does he want? Has he found two more?

As usual van Tuinhout sat down on the bed without a word and for a time said nothing. Van Tuinhout was a pale man, about forty-two, thin hair, short straight nose and small brown eyes. When he spoke, he usually stuck his tongue out as though to give his words a last lick before he let them go; when he was silent, he played with his false teeth.

Meneer Goldschmied, he said finally: not tomorrow, tonight he'll be here. Right after dark.

Thank God, said Goldschmied, I would have had a sleepless night. Van Tuinhout eyed Goldschmied with suspicion. He had taken in roomers for fifteen years, but a Protestant, religious too, by the name of Efraim Goldschmied, origin unknown except that he was a mof, a German—that was a new one.

Whatever Goldschmied said in his mixture of Yiddish and Dutch sounded suspicious to van Tuinhout.

How old is he? asked Goldschmied.

Not more than thirty. Maybe twenty.

You mean there's no difference? Nu, we'll see. But remember, you promised. A week at the most, it'll get to be three—then I'll kill myself.

Meneer Goldschmied, it isn't my fault. I have to do what they tell me. It's only a week, then they'll put him somewhere else.

Did you protest at least, van Tuinhout?

Of course. But that's how it is. We can't be finicky. It's getting more dangerous every day. And the Jews have got to be helped.

You're telling me? Of course they've got to be helped, but does that mean putting two grown men in a box? Why, this isn't a room, van Tuinhout, it's a coffin.

It's not a coffin, Mr. Goldschmied, you're always dramatizing, it's a closet. Where one can live, so can two—don't get me wrong—but that's how Mr. Jaap and Mr. Tinus want it. You think I have anything to say about it?

Suppose something terrible happens, Mr. van Tuinhout. You'll be responsible.

Responsible? In the first place the Germans are responsible, in the second place Mr. Jaap and Mr. Tinus. I'm just carrying out orders.

Silence set in. What can I do with this goy? He's an idiot. Goldschmied rubbed his three-day beard. (Every three days he was allowed to use the bathroom in the rear hallway.) It can only end in disaster. That much he knew. A hundred and eighty-four days he had lived through it—and what's to prevent the war from going on for another twenty years? Cholera! He'd never live to see the end. A young fellow in the same hole? Two corpses in one coffin would have more room; besides, corpses wouldn't mind. Van Tuinhout didn't budge. He sat there with his hands in his pockets (it's not that cramped in here), stared straight ahead and seemed frozen. He didn't smoke, he didn't seem to be looking at anything, he just sat there. After four minutes Goldschmied began to feel uncomfortable. He knew exactly what was going on, but now that he had something to complain about, he didn't want to play along. He too waited four minutes, he too put his hands in his pockets and stared at the wall. I can outlast him at this any time. Goldschmied said his twelve Our Fathers. That's more than he can do. How can that man think nothing so long? He gave himself another dozen Our Fathers. Still van Tuinhout didn't budge.

Till the Last Judgment I'll let him sit, Goldschmied decided. He'll get his money anyway, but this time he can beg for it. Van Tuinhout gave a slight cough. Ah, he's starting in. Goldschmied gave a little cough too. (In this hole "coughing" meant an almost inaudible clearing of the throat, and "talking" meant a barely intelligible whispering.)

So make up your mind. Spit it out.

Van Tuinhout would rather have hanged himself than remind Goldschmied of his rent. Goldschmied knew the ritual by heart.

It was up to him to start in about the homework. Then came lamentations about Kees, the poor motherless boy, followed by a short speech about the moral degradation of children in wartime, and finally a word of consolation and encouragement. But today he would not start in, Goldschmied had made up his mind to that. The stubborn *mof*, thought van Tuinhout, he knows damn well I won't ask him for money. I can wait. After the third dozen Our Fathers Goldschmied had enough. To hell with him, he'll never be as generous as me.

All right, Goldschmied broke the silence, how's the homework going? Van Tuinhout was overjoyed. He still had the rabbits to feed and the supper to prepare. Perfect. He got the best mark in everything. How do you do it? Why, it's at least forty years since you went to school. I don't understand a word of it. Neither does Kees. Not even the teachers, if you ask me. You must be a genius. Every single answer was right. To tell the truth, the work is much too hard. He's only twelve. Yes, I know he's lazy. Maybe not lazy, but neglected. It's always that way without a mother. I can't keep after him all day long. And he takes advantage. It's lucky we have curfew at eight, or he wouldn't get home until morning. You should see the friends he bums around with all day. A bunch of thugs. Juvenile delinquents the whole lot of them. Every day I expect him to be locked up for theft or murder. He's capable of anything these days. In the street? The kind of people you find in the streets these days. Riffraff, soldiers, and whores. Respectable people don't go out. Don't exaggerate, said Goldschmied in whom this subject (streets, going out) touched a sore point. Look here, Meneer Goldschmied, war breeds criminals—what they see now they imitate later. Wait and see what happens after the war (I should live so long, thought Goldschmied). And said aloud: I should live so long, Mr. van Tuinhout.

What do you mean, Mr. Goldschmied, you think I'm telling fairy tales? What do you know? Sitting night and day in this hole. Have you any idea what's going on outside?

Have I any idea what's going on outside? asked Goldschmied with a slight shake of his head. (Why are the goyim so dumb? After all, I'm a Christian myself, so it can't be the religion: Goldschmied's everlasting puzzle.) That's it, Mr. Goldschmied. You just sit here. Sometimes I envy you. Would you like to change places, van Tuinhout? I didn't mean it that way—but it's hard. Every day new regulations, sometimes you don't know if you're still allowed to use the pavement, because some of the regulations aren't posted. People vanish into thin air for no reason at all. Yes, you can consider yourself fortunate, Meneer Goldschmied, you're out of the rain at least.

So it's raining too?

Van Tuinhout looked at him with suspicion. With Jews you can talk, with Protestants you can talk (he himself was a member of the Brethren of the Blessed Virgin), but with a Christian Jew, a Jewish Christian, you don't know where you are. The Christians are hypocrites, most of all the Protestants, the Jews are too smart. To be on the safe side, he took Goldschmied's question literally.

This morning the weather was good, he said, but it may very well rain tonight. Get on with it, said Goldschmied impatiently, he couldn't stand it any more.

As I was saying, Kees is getting to be more of a gangster every day. Do you know what he did yesterday? He took the ferry across the Ij and found himself a girl, a child, maybe ten years old . . .

Nu? (Goldschmied was growing more and more impatient.) He's only a kid himself—you want him to sleep with an old woman?

Believe it or not, Meneer Goldschmied, he really did sleep with the child, but the police caught him in the act. I'll be surprised if they don't put him in jail.

He is a little young, Goldschmied admitted. At his age I was apprenticed already. Sixteen hours a day. We supplied umbrellas all the way to Budapest. No, for such things I didn't have time.

That's what I've been telling you, you're living here like in a hothouse, so sheltered. You can be glad you haven't any children.

Glad, no. Except maybe right now. Children, that's all I need.

Anyway, Meneer Goldschmied, everything is getting more expensive and the money is worthless.

That was the cue. Goldschmied took out his wallet and gave him the hundred guilders rent he was going to give him anyway. But van Tuinhou had certain principles. And one of them was: You can't ask these poor persecuted people for money. Renting rooms was his profession, hiding people was patriotism. If his protégé wished to contribute something of his own free will, he couldn't refuse. But never in all the world would he have asked.

Bring me the next batch of homework soon, said Goldschmied, or the boy will be left behind.

Just one question. Doesn't the teacher notice that his homework is right and his answers in class wrong?

The teachers these days, Mr. Goldschmied, aren't teachers: they're students who've flunked their exams. Today you could be a professor at the university.

I ask you, Goldschmied shook his head. Is it such an honor to be a professor at a university? My umbrellas are more interesting and it's a better living. But if the war keeps on much longer and the homework keeps coming, I'll be ruined. After the war, I'll need a flood to put me back on my feet.

Meneer Goldschmied, I'd like you to do me a favor.

What? You're asking me a favor?

The gentleman who's coming today, van der Waal his name is, he doesn't know you're paying me one hundred guilders a week. If it's all the same to you, please don't tell him. I have my reasons.

Don't worry, Mr. van Tuinhout. I'll be silent like a tomb. I don't think I'll speak to him anyway. I'll just ignore him.

You promise, Meneer Goldschmied.

I promise. All day I'll look at the wall and pretend he's not there. You can rely on me. You have your reasons and I don't even want to know them. But now you must excuse me, I'm busy.

Between ten and twelve. All right?

A few minutes more or less don't matter, van Tuinhout, and in case you decide to put him somewhere else, it'll be all right with me too. I can manage for money, but the air here is another matter. I could do a good business in air if I had some, it's fantastic.

The knock came at about half past ten. Goldschmied looked up from his book. There he is. Exactly between ten and twelve. You can trust van Tuinhout. Van der Waal, said Goldschmied to himself, that means either Birnbaum or Wollman. But he was mistaken. The young man who crawled in, Goldschmied guessed him to be nineteen, was called Weintraub.

To err is human. Weintraub had red cheeks, sweaty hands, and short-cropped hair. He had big blue eyes, a fleshy nose (poor boy, the bone is missing, thought Goldschmied) that looked Jewish at the end, but only at the end. He was short and thick-set. Had on a blue sweater and corduroy trousers, introduced himself as van der Waal, and tossed his small suitcase deftly under the bed.

Van Tuinhout showed his face for another two minutes in the opening, darting glances intended to impress it once again upon Goldschmied that the matter of the hundred guilders was a private arrangement between van Tuinhout and Goldschmied.

Goldschmied bent down to van Tuinhout and whispered: Don't worry. We practically won't see each other.

Van Tuinhout handed him two copybooks. These are for next week. I'll bring the other two tomorrow.

Goldschmied took the copybooks and put them too under the bed. The wall was closed and the two sat on the bed.

Goldschmied looked the young man up and down, decided the

view was incomplete, and said: Stand up. Weintraub stood up. Goldschmied got up too and stood beside him.

Good. You get the shorter blanket.

Maybe the young man was shy, he said nothing and looked the
other way. How do you like it here, Goldschmied interrupted. Isn't
it cozy?

Weintraub, his first name was Egon, saw the one chair, the book-
shelf over the bed, the calendar of the Swiss Alpine Club with the
pencil hanging from a nail, and at the foot end of the bed (he couldn't
believe his eyes) a cross a foot high with a crucified Jesus on it. He
couldn't take his eyes off it.

That, Mr. van de Waal, is mine. So are the calendar and the pencil. But the blankets belong to the landlord. No talking in here except
in a whisper, even if it wrecks your voice, and don't breathe too much
either. Air is very important, we've got to economize. What you ex-
hale I inhale and vice versa, so I hope your teeth are good.

Still not a word out of Weintraub. He just looked at Goldschmied.

Goldschmied had sagging cheeks, a bald head, an enormous nose,
and a chin that receded like a flight of steps. His lips were two thin
lines, drawn down at the ends. Weintraub put his age at sixty. Actually he was only fifty-two. His hands were large and broad, he had
sunken shoulders and a paunch. Two fingers of his right hand, pointer
and middle finger, seemed to be crooked. Reminders of a wound in
the First War.

With these fingers, said Goldschmied, I swore allegiance to Franz
Josef; God punished me by making them crooked. My name, by the
way, is Hubertus Alphons Brederode of Utrecht, but you can call me
Efraim Goldschmied, that's what I call myself to show sympathy for
the Jews.

Otherwise I'm a Christian, a real Christian, as you probably noticed right away.

(Still no sign of life from Weintraub.) A Christian, see, a goy, not
one of us, one of them. Now do you see what I mean?

But baptized?

Thank God, you can talk. I was beginning to think they had cut
your tongue out. Yes, baptized. Disgusting, isn't it?

Weintraub shrugged his shoulders. It's a question of taste. But are
you hiding as a Jew or as a Christian?

Ha, a khokhem yet. Both, my young friend. This isn't only the
cave of the Maccabees, it's also the catacombs of Amsterdam. I'm hiding double, so to speak. You see, I'm not an ordinary baptized Jew,

I'm a convinced and pious Christian. I'd have had tsores either way.

Either way? Why as a Christian?

Some day I'll tell you the story of my life, but there's no hurry, because I will have the honor of seeing you again. But in a nutshell: I am the deacon of a congregation in the Nederlandsche Gereformeerde Kerk. You know the church on the Overtoom, the Church of Saints Peter and Paul? Well, I, Goldschmied, am the deacon. Yes, the Catholic name is misleading, a leftover from before the Reformation—after the war we'll change it with God's help. And you, Weintraub? You're a Jew, I hope. Because two goyim in here would be too much. And I wouldn't be able to convert you.

Nobody can convert me. I'm not interested in such things. I'm of Polish origin.

Polish? Goldschmied could hardly contain himself. He almost shouted. Polish—don't say another word. Jescze Polska niezginela. He nearly fell on Weintraub's neck.

But, said Weintraub, I was only a baby when I came to Holland.

Doesn't mean a thing. Once a Pole always a Pole. What luck!

What's so lucky, you want to know? It's not so quick to explain. Polish isn't just a nationality. It's not so simple. The Poles are the chosen people the Jews would have liked to be. And why davke the Poles? Because the Poles have what the Jews haven't got. Sense and faith.

The Jews have no sense and faith? You're joking.

Pan Weintraub, I ask you, if the Jews had sense would they have gone on being Jews? Not a chance. They would have gone over to the new religion long ago. And because they have no true faith, they are the worst heathen in the world in my opinion. Absolutely.

But, Mr. Goldschmied, Weintraub protested . . .

Don't interrupt me just because I'm right, that's how it is . . . They're always talking about God, but they don't really believe in anything, except money. Sure, they are good at making up ethical laws in God's name, for everything they've got a law, but what's all this got to do with religion? Nothing. The whole Jewish religion is full of practical advice, but the sense of mystery, the feeling for holiness, that they haven't got; just like the Germans and that's not the only reason.

The Germans? What are you talking about?

Goldschmied didn't like to be interrupted. You want to know what I'm talking about? Listen and you'll find out. Why do the Germans shout so loud about nation and blood? Because they're not a united nation. It's exactly the same with the Jews; they shout too loud about their Jehovah and His chosen people. There's something fishy about that. So you'll ask what's fishy? Well, I'll tell you: their religion, that's where it begins. That's where everything begins. Between you and me, Weintraub, the Jewish religion is no good. What do I mean, religion? And what do I mean no good? I'll tell you, and Goldschmied whispered mysteriously: Because Jews have no religion and because they stopped being a nation thousands of years ago, that's why they have such a lousy time.

Moralizing, that's what they do. Philosophizing. The Greeks, the Romans and the English, they got somewhere in this world—except as individuals, the Jews never accomplished a thing, not where it counts, and what counts is to find a union between man's need of faith and his individual humanity. The Jews are still what they always were, scattered tribes of merchants and Bedouins with a small group of intellectuals, from a little, insignificant Mediterranean country. Super-chauvinists, all their national feeling is nothing but primitive clannishness—like the Indians. And their racial purity? Racism, my dear Wentraub, was invented by the Jews, not the Germans. Azoi it is. And only azoi.

Goldschmied leaned back against the wall, exhausted but happy. Come to think of it, thought Goldschmied, a fool is better to talk to than a wall.

Weintraub was a kind of Palestine pioneer—a quarter Zionist, a quarter orthodox Jew (by upbringing), and the other half Dutchman. Until driven underground, that was two years before, he had worked on a farm as a hired hand. He had graduated from secondary school, though very late. Illness had delayed everything in his short life. He had been tubercular since the age of thirteen. Work and fresh air on the farm had done him good—the coughing fits had stopped; and he had been lucky during his two years in hiding, always somewhere in the country—his last hiding place had been raided, someone had denounced him, he had escaped at the last moment. Van Tuinhout's hideout was only temporary; the friends in the underground who were helping him were well aware that a consumptive in a wall was a danger to everybody.

A temporary solution, for a week or two at the most, until they could find him a new hideout with a peasant or gardener.

He had expected it to be small, but not this small; he had expected a bed of his own. How could he share a bed with this old codger when he didn't share a single one of his opinions?

But his ups and downs had made Weintraub philosophical. Well, he said to himself, it's an experience. I only hope he's not homosexual. That I couldn't stand.

Goldschmied was not homosexual—sex seemed never even to occur to him. Sex is not for me, he would say, it's for women and children. What interests me is my business, making umbrellas, and theology. Everything else is playing around.

They lived through the night, each rolled in his blanket, back to back (twice Weintraub woke up because he thought he was going to suffocate, but somehow he survived) until the gray dawn trickled in through a pipe connected with the chimney. When Weintraub sat up and rubbed the sleep from his eyes, Goldschmied was already sitting on the other side of the bed, his back turned to him, an open book on his knees and muttering something. He swayed his body, fell into a soft sing-song—reminding Weintraub in every way of his father chanting his morning prayers.

Goldschmied prayed in Dutch and Latin—both with the same Yiddish accent—crossed himself three times at the end, kissed the book, and put it back with the others above the bed.

Of course you don't pray. You heathen—now come the exercises, then comes breakfast, such a breakfast you won't get in Krasnopolsky—everything here is home-made—even the scrambled eggs. Stand as thin as possible against the wall—good. And now, one, two, three, four—Goldschmied lay down on the bed, propped up his back and began to bicycle in the air. After five minutes he said: That's for the legs. Now for the arms. He thrust his hands out to both sides a dozen times, each time hitting Weintraub in the stomach. (You hippopotamus, can't you make yourself thinner?) In conclusion a few knee bends.

That's that, said Goldschmied, it's healthier than tennis, and it doesn't make you perspire so much. Now it's your turn. Goldschmied stood on the chair and beat time.

One, two, three, four, one, two, three, four. And so on. That's enough. Save the rest for tomorrow.

At nine van Tuinhout brought in a basin of water.

Mr. van Tuinhout, the young man has to have his own water. We're not married. Goldschmied handed him the urinal to empty. He needs his own bottle too. What you Dutchmen need is a little of our Polish tidiness.

Goldschmied washed from head to foot, showing thin white legs, a blubbery back, and sunken buttocks.

Van Tuinhout came back five minutes later with Goldschmied's breakfast, a large cup of black coffee sweetened with saccharine, two slices of bread and margarine, and a dark-yellow mush on the edge of the plate—fried egg-powder.

He took away the basin and brought it back five minutes later with fresh water. Weintraub, who had decided to spend three days at a public bath after the war, dipped a corner of his towel and rubbed his face with it. Goldschmied looked up: Oh no, my friend, that won't do. After all, we sleep together. You wash yourself properly from top to bottom, or you can move to a hotel.

Weintraub mustered him. The hell with him, he thought. Not even my father had the nerve to tell me to wash and where.

But as a newcomer, he could only give in to the elderly goy.

Breakfast was cleared away, the bed made, and they sat on the bed, Weintraub with his legs crossed, Goldschmied with his elbows on his knees and the book on his chair.

Three weeks later. Weintraub was still there. I predicted it, Mr. van Tuinhout, in six months he'll still be here—with God's help we'll move to the old people's home together. Van Tuinhout had nothing but curses for the situation. The underground had hoodwinked him. As it turned out, Weintraub was penniless. What should I do, Mr. Goldschmied? I can't put him out in the street. He can't pay. What should I do?

I'll make you a proposition, Meneer van Tuinhout. Just forget about the few cents he would have paid you. Put it on my bill. Give me twice as much homework.

Now what does he want? Van Tuinhout sucked his teeth. Does he think he can pull my leg?

I'll speak to my aunt—she has money, I can't ask persecuted people for money. I'll speak to my aunt, that's the best way.

Are you sure?

My aunt is obligated to us. My wife took care of her when she was down with varicose veins. She's got to help. She has more money than you and Weintraub put together.

Weintraub, said Goldschmied, we've known each other now for three weeks—and it looks like we'll be together forever. To tell you the truth, I've almost got used to it; it's been like a change of air. But now, seriously, if you want to be my friend, you've got to stop coughing like that. That cough will cost us our lives. Coughing is all right in peacetime—you should have done all your coughing before, because now it can cost us our necks. Weintraub flushed. I thought, he said, it had stopped. But now it's started again. I doubt if I have six months to live. Six months, Weintraub, six months is a long time.

Yes, but the end can come any day. I never told you, Mr. Goldschmied, but now I've got to tell you. I have tuberculosis. I can die
any day. Goldschmied looked at his new friend sharply. If you're
telling me the truth I won't be so hard on you any more. A man
marked by death deserves consideration, special consideration.
Marked by death? What does that mean in times like these? Weintraub couldn't stand it. What do you think will happen to you if you
stick your head out of the door? Marked by death. It sounds so tragic
—actually I may live to be seventy. But you, Goldschmied, how long
do you expect to live—without tuberculosis?

Goldschmied didn't like the way this conversation was going. He
was willing to feel sorry for a poor sick man, but that the candidate
for death should predict an early end for him, Goldschmied, that was
too much.

Weintraub, said Goldschmied—he wanted to get this thing settled once and for all. I'm not afraid, you see I'm living in the grace of
our Lord Jesus Christ. My Jesus loves me, He'll see me through, His
mercy is great, His will be done, as it says in our prayer. We'll see.

Now, after three weeks, Weintraub had ceased to live in a dream.
The wall had become reality; actually he was very happy to be with
this fellow Goldschmied.

He was ashamed of his coughing. Coughing was a sickness and he
was ashamed of being sick. At the approach of a coughing fit—Goldschmied had learned to recognize the signs—he wrapped his young
friend's head in a blanket, which he removed ten minutes later.

Every day there were three or four fits and the previous night had
been especially bad. Something's got to be done about you, Weintraub. Maybe I should keep watch at night.

Weintraub didn't know what to say. Yesterday he had spat blood
again. He felt the cough tearing his lungs to pieces, he was simply
spitting them out. That cough is deplorable, disgraceful. What could
be done?

Van Tuinhout is bound to turn up with good news any day. He's
got to get out of this wall—if he doesn't, he'll die and everybody will
be in danger. What day is it? he asked.

Goldschmied scrutinized Weintraub. He took the calendar (peasants plowing a field. The Alpine Club's motto: He who sows will
reap). Your twenty-fourth day, Weintraub. It's my two hundred
and eighth. You don't catch up with me. This is the last winter. Next
year you'll be in Jerusalem and I in my church. One more winter, Pan
Weintraub. What's one winter? I'm too old for skiing anyway. I'll
stay here.

Knocking. Goldschmied pushed the hooks aside. Van Tuinhout appeared in the opening; a stranger was with him. One after another, they crawled in.

The stranger was large and broad-shouldered, with protuberant cheekbones and a wide chin. He wore glasses and a cap.

He looked like a repair man from the telephone company. This is Verhulst, van Tuinhout introduced him. He knows a peasant in Frisia who'll put van der Waal up.

But it won't be cheap, understand, said Verhulst. Goldschmied understood. How much is not cheap?

Fifteen hundred guilders. We're not getting anything from the underground.

Fifteen hundred guilders. That's a lot of money. Van der Waal hasn't got any. The underground is broke too. So what will we do?

Yes, what will we do? Hasn't he somebody he can borrow from? asked Verhulst.

Have you somebody, van der Waal? Goldschmied looked at him sternly. My parents are gone, said Weintraub. I have relatives, but where they are I don't know. I'll make you a proposition. I'll give you a pledge. He looked through his suitcase and brought out a small tin wrapped in paper. The three looked on eagerly. A pocket watch came to light.

It had a modern dial and was chrome-plated.

It's worth three guilders, said Weintraub and looked from one to the other. He was ashamed of his childish treasure. But it's worth a million to me. After the war I'll give you fifteen hundred guilders for it. It means a great deal to me.

Verhulst looked at him under his glasses. Goldschmied looked away. Van Tuinhout played with his false teeth. A short silence.

Weintraub put the watch back in its box, wrapped it in the same paper and replaced the rubber band around it. He put it in his suitcase and shoved the suitcase under the bed.

Goldschmied was first to speak. In this wallet—he took the wallet from his jacket—there's still a hundred guilders. The last. Until my committee sends me some more money, that's all. He handed van Tuinhout the wallet. Van Tuinhout turned it over twice, thought of opening it to have a look, because he couldn't believe his ears, and decided to let well enough alone. He put the wallet down beside Goldschmied. Verhulst gave him a glance.

Van Tuinhout stood up, followed by Verhulst, they opened the trap, and Verhulst climbed out first. For a few seconds van Tuinhout's head remained in the opening. He gave Goldschmied a look of

reproach and astonishment. My aunt won't do it, Meneer Goldschmied. She can't right now.

Goldschmied reached under the bed and gave van Tuinhout two
copybooks: Here is the homework, Meneer van Tuinhout. The last.
The trap closed. They were alone.

Weintraub, it's hopeless. You can see that. No money no life. I
can't keep myself any longer and you're done for too. Weintraub—
Goldschmied looked at him out of eyes in which this world was already extinguished—Weintraub, my friend, I think it's all over.

Weintraub's voice had a nervous flutter and seemed to come from
far away: I won't survive it, neither here nor in Poland, Mr. Goldschmied, but you, no children and baptized, all you have to do is get
yourself sterilized, and you're free.

Goidschmied's whole body swayed and he spoke louder than
usual: Jesus suffered more, and that's why He understands. He's got
to help, because no one else will. He, the Anointed One, is the only
God. How do we know? Do you know the Talmud?

Why so serious, Goldschmied? You forgotten how to laugh?
What kind of laughter, young man, did I ever have? Goldschmied
continued:

He and He alone is the Anointed One; it is written in your holy
Talmud, but one has to know how to read it:

When a man stands up and the others remain seated, does it mean
that those who remain seated, as I am seated here, are inferior to the
one who stands up? Or does the one who stands up wish to dissociate
himself from those who are seated? People stand up for various reasons. For instance, to mention only three: a man stands up because he
has something to say and wishes to be seen; or he stands up because
he wants to see something that he can't see when he is seated (for instance, if I want to see what is written on the Cross—as it happens I
know it by heart—I have to stand up), or he stands up simply because he doesn't want to sit down any more.

In the first case—he wants to speak and be seen, in other words,
he wishes to exalt his spirit, but to exalt one's spirit means to come
closer to the Holy One, may He be praised. This standing up is
therefore a good work.

In the second case, however—when a man stands up because he
wants to see what he can't see sitting down—it means that his soul
thirsts for wisdom, for wisdom does not come down to a man who is
seated.

Therefore this standing up is also good.

And now to the third case—if a man stands up because he doesn't wish to be seated any longer, he is likewise doing a good work, for the heart in which dwells the love of the Almighty, holy is His name, is filled with joy and jubilation and wishes to be seated no longer. To sit, is it not to mourn? Therefore it is good to stand up: but what does this mean?

It means that the spirit, the soul, and the heart lift themselves out of their abasement, and standing up is to sitting as life is to death. When Rabbi Gershon ben Yehuda asked his student Rabbi Naphtali: Why do some stand up while others remain seated? he was really asking: How is it that some rise up from the dead and others do not? What does this mean? It means above all one thing: Some can rise up from the dead and others cannot. So you see, Rabbi Gershon admits (would he otherwise have asked such a question?) that there is such a thing as standing up, or resurrection, from the dead. But who can rise from the dead before he is judged? Who doesn't have to wait until the Prophet Eliyahu announces the Messiah? Who? Only someone who doesn't have to wait for the Messiah. But if someone can stand up from the dead without waiting for the Messiah, can he be an ordinary man? Not in the least. Can he be an extraordinary man? No, because an extraordinary man is still a man. Therefore he must be what no one else can be, namely, the Messiah Himself. Therefore He who has stood up from the dead is the Anointed One. His name is Jesus Christ. Who else?

As a baptized Jew without children, Mr. Goldschmied, you'd only have to be sterilized and you'll be a Messiah yourself. You'll be able to stand up as much as you please—even in the tram, in the train, anywhere. And when you go to the cinema, you can take standing room.

Young man, Goldschmied gave him a friendly tug on the ear, you are making fun of me. But sterilization is no joke.

Take it from me, Mr. Goldschmied, if they'd let me. This very minute. But they won't let me. They need me the way I am, half dead. But you? Goldschmied, who had grown fond of his young Polish friend, looked at him with a fatherly tenderness. They don't exactly need you, and aren't you being a little frivolous, van der Waal? Tuberculosis isn't enough for you, you want to be sterilized too?

Anything, Mr. Goldschmied, anything is better than to die before your time. Even if they left me nothing but a mouth and a lung, believe me . . .

Goldschmied wagged his head: Yes, I admit, in your case breathing is the most important thing in life, and maybe if I had your

. . . maybe if I, myself, well, you know what I mean—maybe I'd talk the same as you. But as it is? Am I a mad dog? Weintraub, who had come to love Goldschmied like his own uncle, was dismayed. The moment Verhulst disappeared through the trap, he saw himself getting out of the train at Westerbork. Westerbork, stopover on the way to the end. This has been going on for two years and twenty-four days. The Germans aren't to blame, or the Nazis, or the Verhulsts; it's this disease that's come down in my family. He died of TB, they'll say, nobody has him on his conscience, they'll say. Nobody will have me on his conscience, said Weintraub aloud, he died of TB, they'll say. A lump rose in Weintraub's throat.

But Weintraub, Goldschmied laid a hand on his shoulder, what do you care what they're going to say? Who dies for his obituary? Do you really think this world still needs more examples of murdered innocents? There's no shortage. No one will miss you except a few friends and relatives. Sad, but that's how it is.

Although Weintraub had his eyes on Goldschmied's lips as he was saying these words, his thoughts were far away: It's all an accident, pure chance that there was no other place that week; chance that I had to fall in with this van Tuinhout, who has to make his little deals. The fifteen hundred guilders wouldn't have done me any good either, or would they? The J is the meat hook. Everybody has to carry his own—if you've got it, they gas you right away, if you haven't they kick you and torture you until you admit you've got the hook. And then they hang you up on it.

It's not the J that matters, even without it you can be sentenced to death, it's the admission that counts. Admit you're a Jew. If it comes to that, what will Goldschmied do with his Jesus and his Talmud? He can live. He has only to say the word. He's not a Jew. He doesn't want children. He doesn't bother with sex, or not very much. Has he a martyr complex? Why does he want to die when he can live? If they find him here, that's an admission in itself. They'll smash the Cross over his head. As deacon of a Christian congregation, he had no need to hide.

He looked at Goldschmied, who was passing a finger over the mountain ranges on his calendar, and tried to read his thoughts.

The word sterilization had but one effect on Goldschmied, to throw him into utter confusion.

The possibility of saving his life was more than his nerves could stand. How could he explain this to Weintraub? But he had to explain (or Weintraub would die with mistaken ideas and false hopes).

The essential difference is between killing and being killed. Murderers after their deed need human mercy—but the murdered need divine mercy in advance. Goldschmied also knew it was all over, not with life, that would be no problem, but with hiding. Two hundred and eight is a cabalistic magic number, if you could only discover its meaning. Goldschmied knew the Talmud, Rashi's commentaries, and of course his Old Testament (how he had time left for his umbrellas was a mystery to his closest friends); when he wanted to start on the Cabala, it was impossible to find either teachers or books.

How easy it is to miscount, Weintraub. The years were too short. Two hundred and eight is a mysterious number. Why just two hundred and eight? Is two hundred and twenty better, or two hundred and fifty? The highest number is best, but is there such a thing as the highest number? There is only infinity. But I've taken out my insurance on that. Is there any better life-insurance, with lower premiums, than Christ? If there were, Weintraub, wouldn't I have taken it out? A Jew who takes up Christianity has lost nothing and gained everything. For good Christians such a Jew is a Christian, but for anti-Semites I'm still a Jew. So I turn anti-Semite; that way I can go on seeing myself as a Jew (between you and me, I was an anti-Semite before and as a Jewish anti-Semite I couldn't stand myself). So now you know why I turned Christian. It makes everything so simple. With one exception: the regulation about the childless baptized. On one rotten condition they let me live—as a Jew, no conditions, they just kill me. They let me choose something I wouldn't wish on a dog. You have no choice. You don't have to turn into a dog; you can die like a normal, healthy human being.

That's why I don't want the day to come, because tomorrow I'll have to make up my mind and I can't choose. Because if a normal, healthy human being lets himself be killed when he has a choice—is that normal and healthy? And I'll tell you what's sick about the Jews: their religion. As Christians or Mohammedans they could have trampled on the world and established the Jewish justice they're always raving about. But no, they didn't want to. They didn't have the imagination or the power; to succeed they'd have to become Christians. But they didn't feel like it. Instead of martyring, they let themselves be martyred; looking on is impossible. For Jews. Now I'll tell you the truth. I didn't hide because I'm a Jew, I hid to avoid choosing.

Then you can stand and look on, Mr. Goldschmied: Weintraub was furious at the Talmudic complications with which Goldschmied tried to talk himself out of his fear. Why won't he admit it? The

Nazis are to blame that a man like Goldschmied has to think such thoughts. By hair-splitting he had turned their guilt into a guilt of his own.

Jewish conceit, Mr. Goldschmied; you won't even let the other fellow keep his guilt. How can anybody know where he stands if the victims take the guilt for themselves? No wonder they all climb into the trains of their own free will; they think it serves them right, and not that they're wronged.

Maybe we all of us suffer injustice, but does it really matter, Weintraub? If tomorrow I decide to be sterilized, I can look on as they finish you off.

The Nazis would have fired their ovens in any case, believe me, if not with Jews, then with Poles, Russians, gypsies. If they had let the Jews, God forbid, look on, or even worse, if they had let them help make the fire, not one, Weintraub, but the majority would have gone over to the Nazis. When it comes to anti-Semitism and organization, the Nazis could learn plenty from some Jews. But how could such a thing have been justified in the eyes of God?

Mr. Goldschmied, you talk like that because you're scared stiff.

I talk the way I do because tomorrow you'll lose your life and I my sanity. To tell you the truth, I've considered it from time to time —but for the last three weeks, since you came, my last chance is gone too.

Do you love me as much as that? asked Weintraub bewildered.

Like my own flesh.

Just admit you're a Jew, Goldschmied, and we'll go together.

What's that, Weintraub? You know I am a pious Christian. My mazel!

Frankly, Mr. Goldschmied, I have no sympathy for you. I'd rather be a live onlooker than a dead victim. You talk and talk. Religion, holiness, the Jews' mission. All a lot of phrases, slogans. Choice, dog, guilt. I don't give a shit about all that. In a few days they'll strangle me and burn me like a leper, and that's the end of Sholem Weintraub. They'll give me a number on a mass grave, colored with gold dust, and I'll never be alive again. Resurrection is nothing but Talmudic hair-splitting, mystery, smoke and sulphur, hocus-pocus, theological speculation. There is no second time, not before and not after the Messiah, and He doesn't exist anyway. I want to live, Mr. Goldschmied, I want to live and breathe and I don't care how—like a dog or a frog or a bedbug, it's all the same to me. I want to live and breathe, to live.

Weintraub's face turned dark-red and his glands swelled. Goldschmied reached for the blanket and threw it over Weintraub's head. But Weintraub shook it off. His eyes glittered, sweat stood out on his forehead, and his hands trembled as he shouted: Live, breathe, I want to live, live. Goldschmied flung himself on Weintraub, and tried to put his hand over his mouth, but Weintraub flailed like a wild beast and went on shouting. Live, live, I don't want to die like a dog. Cut off my balls and my cock with it, cut off my hands and feet, but let me live and breathe!

Weintraub broke into a coughing fit, and he spat and wheezed blood. Goldschmied sat stiff and pale on the chair and watched his young friend Weintraub who was beginning to decompose even before he was dead. Goldschmied's eyes stared into the void. There was a knocking and drumming on all four walls. Shouts were heard and a car stopping. Weintraub flailed about on the bed and seemed to choke with coughing. The drumming grew louder, angrier.

Goldschmied stood up, climbed on the chair, and tore the Cross off the wall.

Shouts and stamping feet were heard, followed by unexpected silence, then boots pounded through the corridor, the trap was pushed up with rifle butts and a voice under a helmet shouted: Come on out, or I'll take the lead out of your ass.

An ambulance, Goldschmied heard himself saying from far off, he wants to live, but he's going to die on us.

Goldschmied crawled out first, he stood with upraised hands, the Cross protruding from his coat pocket, waiting for them to bring out Weintraub.

Two of them reached through the opening and picked Weintraub off the bed like a sack. Goldschmied was unobserved for a moment: running isn't in my line, he decided.

In the living-room stood two more men in uniform, through the window a small crowd and a patrol car could be seen. Van Tuinhout sat there with bowed head, staring into space.

The policeman with the most stripes was in Dutch uniform. He turned to Goldschmied.

You can take your things, of course, or just wait here and I'll get them. The first to come down was Weintraub, looking pale and sick —escorted by a policeman. Then came the Dutchman and his German colleague.

Each carried a small suitcase. I'll take them to the car, gentlemen, your friend seems unwell.

He carried the suitcases to the car. Yes, Meneer, said the Dutchman, it's disgusting work, but what can you do. I'm only doing my duty. I have a wife and three children. One of my sons is just about your age, he said to Weintraub. Just lie down on the bench and if we drive too fast for you, please knock and we'll slow down a bit. There's no hurry. Goldschmied had recovered from his terror and Weintraub too felt newborn in the fresh air, even though it was damp and cold. So you know what it's like to feel sick? he asked the Dutchman.

I know plenty. O.K., he said to the German driver, but not too fast. The Dutchman turned round to Goldschmied: I've been suffering from headaches for years and this work is driving me crazy. I've got a good recipe for headache, Inspector, you should try it sometime, said Goldschmied. Sugar water, bring it to a quick boil, mix it with honey and melted butter, and drink it down while it's still hot.

You don't say? And it helps? I'll have to tell my wife about that, she'll make me some up tomorrow. We menfolks are lost when it comes to cooking and such. Am I right? Ha-ha-ha.

Yes, that's a good idea, the German driver put in. I'll have to try it. I'm crazy about sweet things. Chocolate, candy, and all that kind of stuff, that's for me. I used to work in a chocolate factory, that was a few years back, it belonged to a Jew, but not any more. I should have known you then, called one of the policemen in the rear, a ramrod of a man in his forties. I'm crazy about chocolate myself. A nice piece of chocolate, as I always say, is as good as a meal. You can keep your chocolate, said the second policeman, who was standing with his rifle beside van Tuinhout. What I like best is fresh dill pickles and marinated herring. Naw, sweets ain't for me.

Why argue, Goldschmied interrupted. It's all a matter of taste. One likes sweet, another likes sour.

That's the truth, the Dutchman agreed. How's your friend? he asked Goldschmied. I hope he's feeling better.

Weintraub listened to the whole conversation with closed eyes—chocolate, dill pickles, sugar water with honey—they're talking about normal things. In the last three weeks the conversation was all about religion and Jews and guilt. I almost died in that hole. If Goldschmied hadn't got me so riled with his high-flown speeches, maybe we'd still be sitting in that hell.

Suddenly life seemed to him reasonable and simple again, and he was ashamed of acting like a madman. Now that there was air to breathe, all his fear had left him. The air has done you good, said Goldschmied, glad to see Weintraub looking normal again. Get a good lungful. You never know when there'll be more.

Van Tuinhout, who had so far sat silent and motionless, turned to the Dutch police officer: Who's going to take care of my boy when I'm gone?

The state, I suppose, I don't know exactly how it works—but the Germans always look after the younger generation, you've got to hand it to them.

They were taken to Gestapo headquarters. Don't be afraid, said Goldschmied to the livid Weintraub next day as he was carried from the cell to a waiting ambulance, we'll meet again, I'll take bets on it.

Weintraub didn't have one word to say for himself—his case was clear. After a lengthy cross-examination Goldschmied's case was also settled, and a week after his arrest he too arrived at the transit camp. No sooner had he passed through the gate than he ran into his friend, looking healthy and cheerful. They hugged each other. There were tears of joy in Weintraub's eyes. I can breathe again, Goldschmied, he cried with joy, what do you say to that, I can breathe again.

Well, said Goldschmied, the air here isn't bad (it was a warm autumn day and the children were playing in the sun), it's nice in the outside world. You look newborn.

You look much better too, Goldschmied. Why, you stand up straight as a soldier. I always thought you had a hump.

Yes, Weintraub, if they just leave you alone, if they just let you stand and sit and walk up and down . . . it's like a second life.

I've missed you, Weintraub. When are you leaving?

Weintraub said blandly: My train leaves today. At five o'clock.

Today? When I've just come? Can't you take a later train? What's the hurry?

Today, Mr. Goldschmied. Today at five. We shall meet again.

Still in this world?

Why, naturally, in this world, Mr. Goldschmied, do you really believe those stories about Poland? Now that I'm feeling better, I don't believe them any more. Sick people get such crazy fears.

Goldschmied looked at Weintraub for a long moment, then turned and left him. As he left he said: You're right, Weintraub, we've got to keep our health, with all this fear we might as well be dead. Keep healthy, have a good trip, and make sure you get there all right. We shall meet again.

A week after this conversation the two did indeed meet. Weintraub was climbing the steep stairs to his holy Jerusalem and Goldschmied to his Jesus on the Cross. For to tell the truth, the city of Jerusalem is not so very big.

*Translated from the German by Ralph Mannheim*

# Muriel Spark

## THE PRIME OF MISS JEAN BRODIE

### CHAPTER ONE

T HE BOYS, as they talked to the girls from Marcia Blaine School, stood on the far side of their bicycles holding the handlebars, which established a protective fence of bicycle between the sexes, and the impression that at any moment the boys were likely to be away.

The girls could not take off their panama hats because this was not far from the school gates and hatlessness was an offense. Certain departures from the proper set of the hat on the head were overlooked in the case of fourth-form girls and upwards so long as nobody wore their hat at an angle. But there were other subtle variants from the ordinary rule of wearing the brim turned up at the back and down at the front. The five girls, standing very close to each other because of the boys, wore their hats each with a definite difference.

These girls formed the Brodie set. That was what they had been called even before the headmistress had given them the name, in scorn, when they had moved from the Junior to the Senior school at the age of twelve. At that time they had been immediately recognizable as Miss Brodie's pupils, being vastly informed on a lot of subjects irrelevant to the authorized curriculum, as the headmistress said, and useless to the school as a school. These girls were discovered to have heard of the Buchmanites and Mussolini, the Italian Renaissance painters, the advantages to the skin of cleansing cream and witch-hazel over honest soap and water, and the word "menarche"; the interior decoration of the London house of the author of *Winnie the Pooh* had been described to them, as had the love lives of Charlotte Brontë and of Miss Brodie herself. They were aware of the existence of Einstein and the arguments of those who considered the Bible to be untrue. They knew the rudiments of astrology but not the date of the Battle of Flodden or the capital of Finland. All of the Brodie set, save one, counted on its fingers, as had Miss Brodie, with accurate results more or less.

By the time they were sixteen, and had reached the fourth form, and loitered beyond the gates after school, and had adapted themselves to the orthodox regime, they remained unmistakably Brodie, and were all famous in the school, which is to say they were held in suspicion and not much liking. They had no team spirit and very little in common with each other outside their continuing friendship with Jean Brodie. She still taught in the Junior department. She was held in great suspicion.

Marcia Blaine School for Girls was a day school which had been partially endowed in the middle of the nineteenth century by the wealthy widow of an Edinburgh book-binder. She had been an admirer of Garibaldi before she died. Her manly portrait hung in the great hall, and was honored every Founder's Day by a bunch of hard-wearing flowers such as chrysanthemums or dahlias. These were placed in a vase beneath the portrait, upon a lectern which also held an open Bible with the text underlined in red ink, "Oh where shall I find a virtuous woman, for her price is above rubies."

The girls who loitered beneath the tree, shoulder to shoulder, very close to each other because of the boys, were all famous for something. Now, at sixteen, Monica Douglas was a prefect, famous mostly for mathematics which she could do in her brain, and for her anger which, when it was lively enough, drove her to slap out to right and left. She had a very red nose, winter and summer, long dark plaits, and fat, peg-like legs. Since she had turned sixteen, Monica wore her panama hat rather higher on her head than normal, perched as if it were too small and as if she knew she looked grotesque in any case.

Rose Stanley was famous for sex. Her hat was placed quite unobtrusively on her blonde short hair, but she dented in the crown on either side.

Eunice Gardiner, small, neat and famous for her spritely gymnastics and glamorous swimming, had the brim of her hat turned up at the front and down at the back.

Sandy Stranger wore it turned up all round and as far back on her head as it could possibly go; to assist this, she had attached to her hat a strip of elastic which went under the chin. Sometimes Sandy chewed this elastic and when it was chewed down she sewed on a new piece. She was merely notorious for her small, almost nonexistent eyes, but she was famous for her vowel sounds which, long ago in the long past, in the Junior school, had enraptured Miss Brodie. "Well, come and recite for us, please, because it has been a tiring day."

> She left the web, she left the loom,
> She made three paces thro' the room,
> She saw the water-lily bloom,
> She saw the helmet and the plume,
>         She look'd down to Camelot.

"It lifts one up," Miss Brodie usually said, passing her hand outward from her breast towards the class of ten-year-old girls who were listening for the bell which would release them. "Where there is no vision," Miss Brodie had assured them, "the people perish. Eunice, come and do a somersault in order that we may have comic relief."

But now, the boys with their bicycles were cheerfully insulting Jenny Gray about her way of speech which she had got from her elocution classes. She was going to be an actress. She was Sandy's best friend. She wore her hat with the front brim bent sharply downward; she was the prettiest and most graceful girl of the set, and this was her fame. "Don't be a lout, Andrew," she said with her uppish tone. There were three Andrews among the five boys, and these three Andrews now started mimicking Jenny: "Don't be a lout, Andrew," while the girls laughed beneath their bobbing panamas.

Along came Mary Macgregor, the last member of the set, whose fame rested on her being a silent lump, a nobody whom everybody could blame. With her was an outsider, Joyce Emily Hammond, the very rich girl, their delinquent, who had been recently sent to Blaine as a last hope, because no other school, no governess, could manage her. She still wore the green uniform of her old school. The others wore deep violet. The most she had done, so far, was to throw paper pellets sometimes at the singing master. She insisted on the use of her two names, Joyce Emily. This Joyce Emily was trying very hard to get into the famous set, and thought the two names might establish her as a something, but there was no chance of it and she could not see why.

Joyce Emily said, "There's a teacher coming out," and nodded towards the gates.

Two of the Andrews wheeled their bicycles out on to the road and departed. The other three boys remained defiantly, but looking the other way as if they might have stopped to admire the clouds on the Pentland Hills. The girls crowded round each other as if in discussion.

"Good afternoon," said Miss Brodie when she approached the group. "I haven't seen you for some days. I think we won't detain these young men and their bicycles. Good afternoon, boys." The famous set moved off with her, and Joyce, the new delinquent, followed. "I think I haven't met this new girl," said Miss Brodie, looking closely at Joyce. And when they were introduced she said: "Well, we must be on our way, my dear."

Sandy looked back as Joyce Emily walked, and then skipped, leggy and uncontrolled for her age, in the opposite direction, and the Brodie set was left to their secret life as it had been six years ago in their childhood.

"I am putting old heads on your young shoulders," Miss Brodie had told them at that time, "and all my pupils are the crème de la crème."

Sandy looked with her little screwed-up eyes at Monica's very red nose and remembered this saying as she followed the set in the wake of Miss Brodie.

"I should like you girls to come to supper tomorrow night," Miss Brodie said. "Make sure you are free."

"The Dramatic Society . . ." murmured Jenny.

"Send an excuse," said Miss Brodie. "I have to consult you about a new plot which is afoot to force me to resign. Needless to say, I shall not resign." She spoke calmly as she always did in spite of her forceful words.

Miss Brodie never discussed her affairs with the other members of the staff, but only with those former pupils whom she had trained up in her confidence. There had been previous plots to remove her from Blaine, which had been foiled.

"It has been suggested again that I should apply for a post at one of the progressive schools, where my methods would be more suited to the system than they are at Blaine. But I shall not apply for a post at a crank school. I shall remain at this education factory. There needs must be a leaven in the lump. Give me a girl at an impressionable age, and she is mine for life."

The Brodie set smiled in understanding of various kinds.

Miss Brodie forced her brown eyes to flash as a meaningful accompaniment to her quiet voice. She looked a mighty woman with her dark Roman profile in the sun. The Brodie set did not for a moment doubt that she would prevail. As soon expect Julius Caesar to apply for a job at a crank school as Miss Brodie. She would never resign. If the authorities wanted to get rid of her she would have to be assassinated.

"Who are the gang, this time?" said Rose, who was famous for sex-appeal.

"We shall discuss tomorrow night the persons who oppose me," said Miss Brodie. "But rest assured they shall not succeed."

"No," said everyone. "No, of course they won't."

"Not while I am in my prime," she said. "These years are still the years of my prime. It is important to recognize the years of one's prime, always remember that. Here is my tram car. I daresay I'll not get a seat. This is nineteen-thirty-six. The age of chivalry is past."

Six years previously, Miss Brodie had led her new class into the garden for a history lesson underneath the big elm. On the way through the school corridors they passed the headmistress's study. The door was wide open, the room was empty.

"Little girls," said Miss Brodie, "come and observe this."

They clustered round the open door while she pointed to a large poster pinned with drawing-pins on the opposite wall within the room. It depicted a man's big face. Underneath were the words "Safety First."

"This is Stanley Baldwin who got in as Prime Minister and got out again ere long," said Miss Brodie. "Miss Mackay retains him on the wall because she believes in the slogan 'Safety First.' But Safety does not come first. Goodness, Truth and Beauty come first. Follow me."

This was the first intimation, to the girls, of an odds between Miss Brodie and the rest of the teaching staff. Indeed, to some of them, it was the first time they had realized it was possible for people glued together in grown-up authority to differ at all. Taking inward note of this, and with the exhilarating feeling of being in on the faint smell of row, without being endangered by it, they followed danger-ous Miss Brodie into the secure shade of the elm.

Often, that sunny autumn, when the weather permitted, the small girls took their lessons seated on three benches arranged about the elm.

"Hold up your books," said Miss Brodie quite often that autumn, "prop them up in your hands, in case of intruders. If there are any intruders, we are doing our history lesson . . . our poetry . . . English grammar."

The small girls held up their books with their eyes not on them, but on Miss Brodie.

"Meantime I will tell you about my last summer holiday in Egypt . . . I will tell you about care of the skin, and of the hands . . . about the Frenchman I met in the train to Biarritz . . . and I must tell you about the Italian painting I saw. Who is the greatest Italian painter?"

"Leonardo da Vinci, Miss Brodie."

"That is incorrect. The answer is Giotto, he is my favorite."

Some days it seemed to Sandy that Miss Brodie's chest was flat, no bulges at all, but straight as her back. On other days her chest was breast-shaped and large, very noticeable, something for Sandy to sit and peer at through her tiny eyes while Miss Brodie on a day of lessons indoors stood erect, with her brown head held high, staring out of the window like Joan of Arc as she spoke.

"I have frequently told you, and the holidays just past have convinced me, that my prime has truly begun. One's prime is elusive. You little girls, when you grow up, must be on the alert to recognize your prime at whatever time of your life it may occur. You must then live it to the full. Mary, what have you got under your desk, what are you looking at?"

Mary sat lump-like and too stupid to invent something. She was too stupid ever to tell a lie, she didn't know how to cover up.

"A comic, Miss Brodie," she said.

"Do you mean a comedian, a droll?"

Everyone tittered.

"A comic paper," said Mary.

"A comic paper, forsooth. How old are you?"

"Ten, ma'am."

"You are too old for comic papers at ten. Give it to me."

Miss Brodie looked at the colored sheets. "*Tiger Tim's* forsooth," she said, and threw it into the wastepaper basket. Perceiving all eyes upon it she lifted it out of the basket, tore it up beyond redemption and put it back again.

"Attend to me, girls. One's prime is the moment one was born for. Now that my prime has begun—Sandy, your attention is wandering. What have I been talking about?"

"Your prime, Miss Brodie."

"If anyone comes along," said Miss Brodie, "in the course of the following lesson, remember that it is the hour for English grammar. Meantime I will tell you a little of my life when I was younger than I am now, though six years older than the man himself."

She leaned against the elm. It was one of the last autumn days when the leaves were falling in little gusts. They fell on the children who were thankful for this excuse to wriggle and for the allowable movements in brushing the leaves from their hair and laps.

"Season of mists and mellow fruitfulness. I was engaged to a young man at the beginning of the war but he fell on Flanders Field," said Miss Brodie. "Are you thinking, Sandy, of doing a day's washing?"

"No, Miss Brodie."

"Because you have got your sleeves rolled up. I won't have to do with girls who roll up the sleeves of their blouses, however fine the weather. Roll them down at once, we are civilized beings. He fell the week before Armistice was declared. He fell like an autumn leaf, although he was only twenty-two years of age. When we go indoors we shall look on the map at Flanders, and the spot where my lover was laid before you were born. He was poor. He came from Ayrshire, a countryman, but a hard-working and clever scholar. He said, when he asked me to marry him, 'We shall have to drink water and walk slow.' That was Hugh's country way of expressing that we would live quietly. We shall drink water and walk slow. What does the saying signify, Rose?"

"That you would live quietly, Miss Brodie," said Rose Stanley who six years later had a great reputation for sex.

The story of Miss Brodie's felled fiancé was well on its way when the headmistress, Miss Mackay, was seen to approach across the lawn. Tears had already started to drop from Sandy's little pig-like eyes and Sandy's tears now affected her friend Jenny, later famous in the school for her beauty, who gave a sob and groped up the leg of her knickers for her handkerchief. "Hugh was killed," said Miss Brodie, "a week before the Armistice. After that there was a general election and people were saying, 'Hang the Kaiser!' Hugh was one of the Flowers of the Forest, lying in his grave." Rose Stanley had now begun to weep. Sandy slid her wet eyes sideways, watching the advance of Miss Mackay, head and shoulders forward, across the lawn.

"I am come to see you and I have to be off," she said. "What are you little girls crying for?"

"They are moved by a story I have been telling them. We are having a history lesson," said Miss Brodie, catching a falling leaf neatly in her hand as she spoke.

"Crying over a story at ten years of age!" said Miss Mackay to the girls who had stragglingly risen from the benches, still dazed with Hugh the warrior. "I am only come to see you and I must be off. Well, girls, the new term has begun. I hope you all had a splendid summer holiday and I look forward to seeing your splendid essays on how you spent them. You shouldn't be crying over history at the age of ten. My word!"

"You did well," said Miss Brodie to the class, when Miss Mackay had gone, "not to answer the question put to you. It is well, when in difficulties, to say never a word, neither black nor white. Speech is silver but silence is golden. Mary, are you listening? What was I saying?"

Mary Macgregor, lumpy, with merely two eyes, a nose and a mouth like a snowman, who was later famous for being stupid and always to blame and who, at the age of twenty-three, lost her life in a hotel fire, ventured, "Golden."

"What did I say was golden?"

Mary cast her eyes around her and up above. Sandy whispered, "The falling leaves."

"The falling leaves," said Mary.

"Plainly," said Miss Brodie, "you were not listening to me. If only you small girls would listen to me I would make you the crème de la crème."

CHAPTER TWO

Mary Macgregor, although she lived into her twenty-fourth year, never quite realized that Jean Brodie's confidences were not shared with the rest of the staff and that her love-story was given out only to her pupils. She had not thought much about Jean Brodie, certainly never disliked her, when, a year after the outbreak of the Second World War, she joined the Wrens, and was clumsy and incompetent, and was much blamed. On one occasion of real misery—when her first and last boy friend, a corporal whom she had known for two weeks, deserted her by failing to turn up at an appointed place and failing to come near her again—she thought back to see if she had ever really been happy in her life; it occurred to her then that the first years with Miss Brodie, sitting listening to all those stories and opinions which had nothing to do with the ordinary world, had been the happiest time of her life. She thought this briefly, and never again referred her mind to Miss Brodie, but had got over her misery, and had relapsed into her habitual slow bewilderment, before she died while on leave in Cumberland in a fire in the hotel. Back and forth along the corridors ran Mary Macgregor, through the thickening smoke. She ran one way; then, turning, the other way; and at either end the blast furnace of the fire met her. She heard no screams, for the roar of the fire drowned the screams; she gave no scream, for the smoke was choking her. She ran into somebody on her third turn, stumbled and died. But at the beginning of the nineteen-thirties, when Mary Macgregor was ten, there she was sitting blankly among Miss Brodie's pupils. "Who has spilled ink on the floor—was it you, Mary?"

"I don't know, Miss Brodie."

"I daresay it was you. I've never come across such a clumsy girl. And if you can't take an interest in what I am saying, please try to look as if you did."

These were the days that Mary Macgregor, on looking back, found to be the happiest days of her life.

Sandy Stranger had a feeling at the time that they were supposed to be the happiest days of her life, and on her tenth birthday she said so to her best friend Jenny Gray who had been asked to tea at Sandy's house. The speciality of the feast was pineapple cubes with cream, and the speciality of the day was that they were left to themselves. To Sandy the unfamiliar pineapple had the authentic taste and appearance of happiness and she focused her small eyes closely on the pale gold cubes before she scooped them up in her spoon, and she thought the sharp taste on her tongue was that of a special happiness, which was nothing to do with eating, and was different from the happiness of play that one enjoyed unawares. Both girls saved the cream to the last, then ate it in spoonfuls.

"Little girls, you are going to be the crème de la crème," said Sandy, and Jenny spluttered her cream into her handkerchief.

"You know," Sandy said, "these are supposed to be the happiest days of our lives."

"Yes, they are always saying that," Jenny said. "They say, make the most of your schooldays because you never know what lies ahead of you."

"Miss Brodie says prime is best," Sandy said.

"Yes, but she never got married like our mothers and fathers."

"They don't have primes," said Sandy.

"They have sexual intercourse," Jenny said.

The little girls paused, because this was still a stupendous thought, and one which they had only lately lit upon; the very phrase and its meaning were new. It was quite unbelievable. Sandy said, then, "Mr. Lloyd had a baby last week. He must have committed sex with his wife." This idea was easier to cope with and they laughed screamingly into their pink paper napkins. Mr. Lloyd was the art master to the Senior girls.

"Can you *see* it happening?" Jenny whispered.

Sandy screwed her eyes even smaller in the effort of seeing with her mind. "He would be wearing his pyjamas," she whispered back.

The girls rocked with mirth, thinking of one-armed Mr. Lloyd, in his solemnity, striding into school.

Then Jenny said, "You do it on the spur of the moment. That's how it happens."

Jenny was a reliable source of information, because a girl employed by her father in his grocer shop had recently been found to be pregnant, and Jenny had picked up some fragments of the ensuing fuss. Having confided her finds to Sandy, they had embarked on a course of research which they called "research," piecing together clues from remembered conversations illicitly overheard, and passages from the big dictionaries.

"It all happens in a flash," Jenny said. "It happened to Teenie when she was out walking at Puddocky with her boy friend. Then they had to get married."

"You would think the urge would have passed by the time she got her *clothes* off," Sandy said. By "clothes," she definitely meant to imply knickers, but "knickers" was rude in this scientific context.

"Yes, that's what I can't understand," said Jenny.

Sandy's mother looked round the door and said, "Enjoying yourselves, darlings?" Over her shoulder appeared the head of Jenny's mother. "My word," said Jenny's mother, looking at the tea-table, "they've been tucking in!"

Sandy felt offended and belittled by this; it was as if the main idea of the party had been the food.

"What would you like to do now?" Sandy's mother said.

Sandy gave her mother a look of secret ferocity which meant: you promised to leave us all on our own, and a promise is a promise, you know it's very bad to break a promise to a child, you might ruin all my life by breaking your promise, it's my birthday.

Sandy's mother backed away bearing Jenny's mother with her. "Let's leave them to themselves," she said. "Just enjoy yourselves, darlings."

Sandy was sometimes embarrassed by her mother being English and calling her "darling," not like the mothers of Edinburgh who said "dear." Sandy's mother had a flashy winter coat trimmed with fluffy fox fur like the Duchess of York's, while the other mothers wore tweed or, at the most, musquash that would do them all their days.

It had been raining and the ground was too wet for them to go and finish digging the hole to Australia, so the girls lifted the tea-table with all its festal relics over to the corner of the room. Sandy opened the lid of the piano stool and extracted a notebook from be-tween two sheaves of music. On the first page of the notebook was written,

## The Mountain Eyrie

### by

### Sandy Stranger and Jenny Gray

This was a story, still in the process of composition, about Miss Brodie's lover, Hugh Carruthers. He had not been killed in the war, that was a mistake in the telegram. He had come back from the war and called to enquire for Miss Brodie at school, where the first per-son whom he encountered was Miss Mackay, the headmistress. She had informed him that Miss Brodie did not desire to see him, she loved another. With a bitter, harsh laugh, Hugh went and made his abode in a mountain eyrie, where, wrapped in a leathern jacket, he had been discovered one day by Sandy and Jenny. At the present stage in the story Hugh was holding Sandy captive but Jenny had escaped by night and was attempting to find her way down the mountainside in the dark. Hugh was preparing to pursue her.

Sandy took a pencil from a drawer in the sideboard and contin-ued:

"Hugh!" Sandy beseeched him, "I swear to you before all I hold sacred that Miss Brodie has never loved another, and she awaits you below, praying and hoping in her prime. If you will let Jenny go, she will bring back your lover Jean Brodie to you and you will see her with your own eyes and hold her in your arms after these twelve long years and a day."

His black eye flashed in the lamplight of the hut. "Back, girl!" he cried, "and do not bar my way. Well do I know that yon girl Jenny will report my whereabouts to my mocking erst-while fiancée. Well do I know that you are both spies sent by her that she might mock. Stand back from the door, I say!"

"Never!" said Sandy, placing her young lithe body squarely

in front of the latch and her arm through the bolt. Her large eyes flashed with an azure light of appeal.

Sandy handed the pencil to Jenny. "It's your turn," she said.

Jenny wrote: "With one movement he flung her to the farthest end of the hut and strode out into the moonlight and his strides made light of the drifting snow."

"Put in about his boots," said Sandy.

Jenny wrote: "His high boots flashed in the moonlight."

"There are too many moonlights," Sandy said, "but we can sort that later when it comes to publication."

"Oh, but it's a secret, Sandy!" said Jenny.

"I know that," Sandy said. "Don't worry, we won't publish it till our prime."

"Do you think Miss Brodie ever had sexual intercourse with Hugh?" said Jenny.

"She would have had a baby, wouldn't she?"

"I don't know."

"I don't think they did anything like that," said Sandy. "Their love was above all that."

"Miss Brodie said they clung to each other with passionate abandon on his last leave."

"I don't think they took their clothes off, though," Sandy said, "do you?"

"No. I can't see it," said Jenny.

"I wouldn't like to have sexual intercourse," Sandy said.

"Neither would I. I'm going to marry a pure person."

"Have a toffee."

They ate their sweets, sitting on the carpet. Sandy put some coal on the fire and the light spurted up, reflecting on Jenny's ringlets. "Let's be witches by the fire, like we were at Hallowe'en."

They sat in the twilight eating toffees and incanting witches' spells. Jenny said, "There's a Greek god at the museum standing up with nothing on. I saw it last Sunday afternoon but I was with Auntie Kate and I didn't have a chance to *look* properly."

"Let's go to the museum next Sunday," Sandy said. "It's research."

"Would you be allowed to go alone with me?"

Sandy, who was notorious for not being allowed to go out and about without a grown-up person, said, "I don't think so. Perhaps we could get someone to take us."

"We could ask Miss Brodie."

Miss Brodie frequently took the little girls to the art galleries and museums, so this seemed feasible.

"But suppose," said Sandy, "she won't let us look at the statue if it's naked."

"I don't think she would notice that it was naked," Jenny said. "She just wouldn't see its thingummyjig."

"I know," said Sandy. "Miss Brodie's above all that."

It was time for Jenny to go home with her mother, all the way in the tram car through the haunted November twilight of Edinburgh across the Dean Bridge. Sandy waved from the window, and wondered if Jenny, too, had the feeling of leading a double life, fraught with problems that even a millionaire did not have to face. It was well known that millionaires led double lives. The evening paper rattle-snaked its way through the letter box and there was suddenly a six-o'clock feeling in the house.

Miss Brodie was reciting poetry to the class at a quarter to four, to raise their minds before they went home. Miss Brodie's eyes were half shut and her head was thrown back:

> In the stormy east wind straining
> The pale yellow woods were waning,
> The broad stream in his banks complaining,
> Heavily the low sky raining
>            Over tower'd Camelot.

Sandy watched Miss Brodie through her little pale eyes, screwed them smaller and shut her lips tight.

Rose Stanley was pulling threads from the girdle of her gym tunic. Jenny was enthralled by the poem, her lips were parted, she was never bored. Sandy was never bored, but she had to lead a double life of her own in order never to be bored.

> Down she came and found a boat
> Beneath a willow left afloat,
> And round about the prow she wrote
> *The Lady of Shalott.*

"By what means did your Ladyship write these words?" Sandy enquired in her mind with her lips shut tight.

"There was a pot of white paint and a brush which happened to be standing upon the grassy verge," replied the Lady of Shalott graciously. "It was left there no doubt by some heedless member of the Unemployed."

"Alas, and in all that rain!" said Sandy for want of something better to say, while Miss Brodie's voice soared up to the ceiling, and curled round the feet of the Senior girls upstairs.

The Lady of Shalott placed a white hand on Sandy's shoulder and gazed at her for a space. "That one so young and beautiful should be so ill-fated in love!" she said in low sad tones.

"What can be the meaning of these words?" cried Sandy in alarm, with her little eyes screwed on Miss Brodie and her lips shut tight.

Miss Brodie said: "Sandy, are you in pain?"

Sandy looked astonished.

"You girls," said Miss Brodie, "must learn to cultivate an expression of composure. It is one of the best assets of a woman, an expression of composure, come foul, come fair. Regard the Mona Lisa over yonder!"

All heads turned to look at the reproduction which Miss Brodie had brought back from her travels and pinned on the wall. Mona Lisa in her prime smiled in steady composure even though she had just come from the dentist and her lower jaw was swollen.

"She is older than the rocks on which she sits. Would that I had been given charge of you girls when you were seven. I sometimes fear it's too late, now. If you had been mine when you were seven you would have been the crème de la crème. Sandy, come and read some stanzas and let us hear your vowel sounds."

Sandy, being half-English, made the most of her vowels, it was her only fame. Rose Stanley was not yet famous for sex, and it was not she but Eunice Gardiner who had approached Sandy and Jenny with a Bible, pointing out the words, "The babe leapt in her womb." Sandy and Jenny said she was dirty and threatened to tell on her. Jenny was already famous for her prettiness and had a sweet voice, so that Mr. Lowther, who came to teach singing, would watch her admiringly as she sang "Come see where golden-hearted spring . . ."; and he twitched her ringlets, the more daringly since Miss Brodie always stayed with her pupils during the singing lesson. He twitched her ringlets and looked at Miss Brodie like a child showing off its tricks and almost as if testing Miss Brodie to see if she were at all willing to conspire in his un-Edinburgh conduct.

Mr. Lowther was small, with a long body and short legs. His hair and moustache were red-gold. He curled his hand round the back of his ear and inclined his head towards each girl to test her voice. "Sing ah!"

"Ah!" sang Jenny, high and pure as the sea maiden of the Hebrides whom Sandy had been talking about. But her eyes swiveled over to catch Sandy's.

Miss Brodie ushered the girls from the music room and, gathering them about her, said, "You girls are my vocation. If I were to receive a proposal of marriage tomorrow from the Lord Lyon King-of-Arms I would decline it. I am dedicated to you in my prime. Form a single file, now, please, and walk with your heads up, *up* like Sybil Thorndike, a woman of noble mien."

Sandy craned back her head, pointed her freckled nose in the air and fixed her little pig-like eyes on the ceiling as she walked along in the file.

"What are you doing, Sandy?"

"Walking like Sybil Thorndike, ma'am."

"One day, Sandy, you will go too far."

Sandy looked hurt and puzzled.

"Yes," said Miss Brodie, "I have my eye upon you, Sandy. I observe a frivolous nature. I fear you will never belong to life's élite or, as one might say, the crème de la crème."

When they had returned to the classroom Rose Stanley said, "I've got ink on my blouse."

"Go to the science room and have the stain removed; but remember it is very bad for the tussore."

Sometimes the girls would put a little spot of ink on a sleeve of their tussore silk blouses so that they might be sent to the science room in the Senior school. There a thrilling teacher, a Miss Lockhart, wearing a white overall, with her gray short hair set back in waves from a tanned and weathered golfer's face, would pour a small drop of white liquid from a large jar on to a piece of cotton wool. With this, she would dab the ink-spot on the sleeve, silently holding the girl's arm, intently absorbed in the task. Rose Stanley went to the science room with her inky blouse only because she was bored, but Sandy and Jenny got ink on their blouses at discreet intervals of four weeks, so that they could go and have their arms held by Miss Lockhart who seemed to carry six inches of pure air around her person wherever she moved in that strange-smelling room. This long room was her natural setting and she had lost something of her quality when Sandy saw her walking from the school in her box-pleat tweeds over to her sports car like an ordinary teacher. Miss Lockhart in the science room was to Sandy something apart, surrounded by three lanes of long benches set out with jars half-full of colored crystals and powders and liquids, ocher and bronze and metal gray and cobalt blue, glass vessels of curious shapes, bulbous, or with pipe-like stems. Only once when Sandy went to the science room was there a lesson in progress. The older girls, big girls, some with bulging chests, were standing in couples at the benches, with gas jets burning before them. They held a glass tube full of green stuff in their hands and were dancing the tube in the flame, dozens of dancing green tubes and flames, all along the benches. The bare winter top branches of the trees brushed the windows of this long room, and beyond that was the cold winter sky with a huge red sun. Sandy, on that occasion, had the presence of mind to remember that her school-days were supposed to be the happiest days of her life and she took the compelling news back to Jenny that the Senior school was going to be marvelous and Miss Lockhart was beautiful.

"All the girls in the science room were doing just as they liked." said Sandy, "and that's what they were supposed to be doing."

"We do a lot of what we like in Miss Brodie's class," Jenny said. "My mummy says Miss Brodie gives us too much freedom."

"She's not supposed to give us freedom, she's supposed to give us lessons," said Sandy. "But the science class is supposed to be free, it's allowed."

"Well, I like being in Miss Brodie's," Jenny said.

"So do I," Sandy said. "She takes an interest in our general knowledge, my mother says."

All the same, the visits to the science room were Sandy's most secret joy, and she calculated very carefully the intervals between one ink-spot and another, so that there should be no suspicion on Miss Brodie's part that the spots were not an accident. Miss Lockhart would hold her arm and carefully dab the inkstain on her sleeve while Sandy stood enthralled by the long room which was this science teacher's rightful place, and by the lawful glamour of everything there. It was on the occasion when Rose Stanley, after the singing lesson, was sent to the science room to get ink off her blouse that Miss Brodie told her class:

"You must be more careful with your ink. I can't have my girls going up and down to the science room like this. We must keep our good name."

She added, "Art is greater than science. Art comes first, and then science."

The large map had been rolled down over the blackboard because they had started the geography lesson. Miss Brodie turned with her pointer to show where Alaska lay. But she turned again to the class and said: "Art and religion first; then philosophy; lastly science. That is the order of the great subjects of life, that's their order of importance."

This was the first winter of the two years that this class spent with Miss Brodie. It had turned nineteen-thirty-one. Mis Brodie had already selected her favorites, or rather those whom she could trust; or rather those whose parents she could trust not to lodge complaints about the more advanced and seditious aspects of her educational policy, these parents being either too enlightened to complain or too unenlightened, or too awed by their good fortune in getting their girls' education at endowed rates, or too trusting to question the value of what their daughters were learning at this school of sound reputation. Miss Brodie's special girls were taken home to tea and bidden not to tell the others, they were taken into her confidence, they understood her private life and her feud with the headmistress and the allies of the headmistress. They learned what troubles in her career Miss Brodie encountered on their behalf. "It is for the sake of you girls—my influence, now, in the years of my prime." This was the beginning of the Brodie set.

Eunice Gardiner was so quiet at first, it was difficult to see why she had been drawn in by Miss Brodie. But eventually she cut capers for the relief and amusement of the tea-parties, doing cart-wheels on the carpet. "You are an Ariel," said Miss Brodie. Then Eunice began to chatter. She was not allowed to do cart-wheels on Sundays, for in many ways Miss Brodie was an Edinburgh spinster of the deepest dye. Eunice Gardiner did somersaults on the mat only at Saturday gatherings before high teas, or afterwards on Miss Brodie's kitchen linoleum, while the other girls were washing up and licking honey from the depleted comb off their fingers as they passed it over to be put away in the food cupboard. It was twenty-eight years after Eunice did the splits in Miss Brodie's flat that she, who had become a nurse and married a doctor, said to her husband one evening:

"Next year when we go for the Festival——"

"Yes?"

She was making a wool rug, pulling at a different stitch.

"Yes?" he said.

"When we go to Edinburgh," she said, "remind me while we're there to go and visit Miss Brodie's grave."

"Who was Miss Brodie?"

"A teacher of mine, she was full of culture. She was an Edinburgh Festival all on her own. She used to give us teas at her flat and tell us about her prime."

"Prime what?"

"Her prime of life. She fell for an Egyptian courier once, on her travels, and came back and told us all about it. She had a few favorites. I was one of them. I did the splits and made her laugh, you know."

"I always knew your upbringing was a bit peculiar."

"But she wasn't mad. She was as sane as anything. She knew exactly what she was doing. She told us all about her love life, too."

"Let's have it then."

"Oh, it's a long story. She was just a spinster. I must take flowers to her grave—I wonder if I could find it?"

"When did she die?"

"Just after the war. She was retired by then. Her retirement was rather a tragedy, she was forced to retire before time. The head never liked her. There's a long story attached to Miss Brodie's retirement. She was betrayed by one of her own girls, we were called the Brodie set. I never found out which one betrayed her."

It is time now to speak of the long walk through the old parts of Edinburgh where Miss Brodie took her set, dressed in their deep violet coats and black velour hats with the green and white crest, one Friday in March when the school's central heating system had broken down and everyone else had been muffled up and sent home. The wind blew from the icy Forth and the sky was loaded with forthcoming snow. Mary Macgregor walked with Sandy because Jenny had gone home. Monica Douglas, later famous for being able to do real mathematics in her head, and for her anger, walked behind them with her dark red face, broad nose and dark pigtails falling from her black hat and her legs already shaped like pegs in their black wool stockings. By her side walked Rose Stanley, tall and blonde with a yellow-pale skin, who had not yet won her reputation for sex, and whose conversation was all about trains, cranes, motor cars, Meccanos and other boys' affairs. She was not interested in the works of engines or the constructive powers of the Meccanos, but she knew their names, the variety of colors in which they came, the makes of motor cars and their horse-power, the various prices of the Meccano sets. She was also an energetic climber of walls and trees. And although these concerns at Rose Stanley's eleventh year marked her as a tomboy, they did not go deep into her femininity and it was her superficial knowledge of these topics alone, as if they had been a conscious preparation, which stood her in good stead a few years later with the boys.

With Rose walked Miss Brodie, head up, like Sybil Thorndike, her nose arched and proud. She wore her loose brown tweed coat with the beaver collar tightly buttoned, her brown felt hat with the brim up at one side and down at the other. Behind Miss Brodie, last in the group, little Eunice Gardiner who, twenty-eight years later, said of Miss Brodie, "I must visit her grave," gave a skip between each of her walking steps as if she might even break into pirouettes on the pavement, so that Miss Brodie, turning round, said from time to time, "Now, Eunice!" And, from time to time again, Miss Brodie would fall behind to keep Eunice company.

Sandy, who had been reading *Kidnapped*, was having a conversation with the hero, Alan Breck, and was glad to be with Mary Macgregor because it was not necessary to talk to Mary.

"Mary, you may speak quietly to Sandy."

"Sandy won't talk to me," said Mary who later, in that hotel fire, ran hither and thither till she died.

"Sandy cannot talk to you if you are so stupid and disagreeable. Try to wear an agreeable expression at least, Mary."

"Sandy, you must take this message o'er the heather to the Macphersons," said Alan Breck. "My life depends upon it, and the Cause no less."

"I shall never fail you, Alan Breck," said Sandy. "Never."

"Mary," said Miss Brodie, from behind, "please try not to lag behind Sandy."

Sandy kept pacing ahead, fired on by Alan Breck whose ardor and thankfulness, as Sandy prepared to set off across the heather, had reached touching proportions.

Mary tried to keep up with her. They were crossing the Meadows, a gusty expanse of common land, glaring green under the snowy sky. Their destination was the Old Town, for Miss Brodie had said they should see where history had been lived; and their route had brought them to the Middle Meadow Walk.

Eunice, unaccompanied at the back, began to hop to a rhyme which she repeated to herself:

> Edinburgh, Leith,
> Portobello, Musselburgh
> *And* Dalkeith.

Then she changed to the other foot.

Edinburgh, Leith. . .

Miss Brodie turned round and hushed her, then called forward to Mary Macgregor who was staring at an Indian student who was approaching,

"Mary, don't you *want* to walk tidily?"

"Mary," said Sandy, "stop staring at the brown man."

The nagged child looked numbly at Sandy and tried to quicken her pace. But Sandy was walking unevenly, in little spurts forward and little halts, as Alan Breck began to sing to her his ditty before she took to the heather to deliver the message that was going to save Alan's life. He sang:

> This is the song of the sword of Alan:
> The smith made it,
> The fire set it;
> Now it shines in the hand of Alan Breck.

Then Alan Breck clapped her shoulder and said, "Sandy, you are a brave lass and want nothing in courage that any King's man might possess."

"Don't walk so fast," mumbled Mary.

"You aren't walking with your head up," said Sandy. "Keep it up, up."

Then suddenly Sandy wanted to be kind to Mary Macgregor, and thought of the possibilities of feeling nice from being nice to Mary instead of blaming her. Miss Brodie's voice from behind was saying to Rose Stanley, "You are all heroines in the making. Britain must be a fit country for heroines to live in. The League of Nations . . ." The sound of Miss Brodie's presence, just when it was on the tip of Sandy's tongue to be nice to Mary Macgregor, arrested the urge. Sandy looked back at her companions, and understood them as a body with Miss Brodie for the head. She perceived herself, the absent Jenny, the ever-blamed Mary, Rose, Eunice and Monica, all in a frightening little moment, in unified compliance to the destiny of Miss Brodie, as if God had willed them to birth for that purpose.

She was even more frightened then, by her temptation to be nice to Mary Macgregor, since by this action she would separate herself, and be lonely, and blameable in a more dreadful way than Mary who, although officially the faulty one, was at least inside Miss Brodie's category of heroines in the making. So, for good fellowship's sake, Sandy said to Mary, "I wouldn't be walking with *you* if Jenny was here." And Mary said, "I know." Then Sandy started to hate herself again and to nag on and on at Mary, with the feeling that if you did a thing a lot of times, you made it into a right thing. Mary started to cry, but quietly, so that Miss Brodie could not see. Sandy was unable to cope and decided to stride on and be a married lady having an argument with her husband:

"Well, Colin, it's rather hard on a woman when the lights have fused and there isn't a man in the house."

"Dearest Sandy, *how* was I to know . . ."

As they came to the end of the Meadows a group of Girl Guides came by. Miss Brodie's brood, all but Mary, walked past with eyes ahead. Mary stared at the dark blue big girls with their regimented vigorous look and broader accents of speech than the Brodie girls used when in Miss Brodie's presence. They passed, and Sandy said to Mary, "It's rude to stare." And Mary said, "I wasn't staring." Meanwhile Miss Brodie was being questioned by the girls behind on the question of the Brownies and the Girl Guides, for quite a lot of the other girls in the Junior school were Brownies.

"For those who like that sort of thing," said Miss Brodie in her best Edinburgh voice, "that is the sort of thing they like."

So Brownies and Guides were ruled out. Sandy recalled Miss Brodie's admiration for Mussolini's marching troops, and the picture she had brought back from Italy showing the triumphant march of the black uniforms in Rome.

"These are the fascisti," said Miss Brodie, and spelled it out. "What are these men, Rose?"

"The fascisti, Miss Brodie."

They were dark as anything and all marching in the straightest of files, with their hands raised at the same angle, while Mussolini stood on a platform like a gym teacher or a Guides mistress and watched them. Mussolini had put an end to unemployment with his fascisti and there was no litter in the streets. It occurred to Sandy, there at the end of the Middle Meadow Walk, that the Brodie set was Miss Brodie's fascisti, not to the naked eye, marching along, but all knit together for her need and in another way, marching along. That was all right, but it seemed, too, that Miss Brodie's disapproval of the Girl Guides had jealousy in it, there was an inconsistency, a fault. Perhaps the Guides were too much a rival fascisti, and Miss Brodie could not bear it. Sandy thought she might see about joining the Brownies. Then the group-fright seized her again, and it was necessary to put the idea aside, because she loved Miss Brodie.

"We make good company for each other, Sandy," said Alan Breck, crunching beneath his feet the broken glass in the blood on the floor of the ship's round-house. And taking a knife from the table, he cut off one of the silver buttons from his coat. "Wherever you show that button," he said, "the friends of Alan Breck will come around you."

"We turn to the right," said Miss Brodie.

They approached the Old Town which none of the girls had properly seen before, because none of their parents was so historically minded as to be moved to conduct their young into the reeking network of slums which the Old Town constituted in those years. The Canongate, The Grassmarket, The Lawnmarket, were names which betokened a misty region of crime and desperation: "Lawnmarket Man Jailed."

Only Eunice Gardiner and Monica Douglas had already traversed the High Street on foot on the Royal Mile from the Castle or Holyrood. Sandy had been taken to Holyrood in an uncle's car and had seen the bed, too short and too broad, where Mary Queen of Scots had slept, and the tiny room, smaller than their own scullery at home, where the Queen had played cards with Rizzio.

Now they were in a great square, the Grassmarket, with the Castle, which was in any case everywhere, rearing between a big gap in the houses where the aristocracy used to live. It was Sandy's first experience of a foreign country, which intimates itself by its new smells and shapes and its new poor. A man sat on the icy-cold pavement, he just sat. A crowd of children, some without shoes, were playing some fight game, and some boys shouted after Miss Brodie's violet-clad company, with words that the girls had not heard before, but rightly understood to be obscene. Children and women with shawls came in and out of the dark closet. Sandy found she was holding Mary's hand in her bewilderment, all the girls were holding hands, while Miss Brodie talked of history. Into the High Street, and "John Knox," said Miss Brodie, "was an embittered man. He could never be at ease with the gay French Queen. We of Edinburgh owe a lot to the French. We are Europeans." The smell was amazingly terrible. In the middle of the road farther up the High Street a crowd was gathered. "Walk past quietly," said Miss Brodie.

A man and a woman stood in the midst of the crowd which had formed a ring around them. They were shouting at each other and the man hit the woman twice across the head. Another woman, very little, with cropped black hair, a red face and a big mouth, came forward and took the man by the arm. She said:

"I'll be your man."

From time to time throughout her life Sandy pondered this, for she was certain that the little woman's words were "I'll be your man," not "I'll be your woman," and it was never explained.

And many times throughout her life Sandy knew with a shock, when speaking to people whose childhood had been in Edinburgh, that there were other people's Edinburghs quite different from hers, and with which she held only the names of districts and streets and monuments in common. Similarly, there were other people's nineteen-thirties. So that, in her middle age, when she was at last allowed all those visitors to the convent—so many visitors being against the Rule, but a special dispensation was enforced on Sandy because of her Treatise—when a man said, "I must have been at school in Edinburgh at the same time as you, Sister Helena," Sandy, who was now some years Sister Helena of the Transfiguration, clutched the bars of the grille as was her way, and peered at him through her little faint eyes and asked him to describe his schooldays and his school, and the Edinburgh he had known. And it turned out, once more, that his was a different Edinburgh from Sandy's. His school, where he was a boarder, had been cold and gray. His teachers had been supercilious Englishmen, "or near-Englishmen," said the visitor, "with third-rate degrees." Sandy could not remember ever having questioned the quality of her teachers' degrees, and the school had always been lit with the sun or, in winter, with a pearly north light. "But Edinburgh," said the man, "was a beautiful city, more beautiful then than it is now. Of course, the slums have been cleared. The Old Town was always my favorite. We used to love to explore the Grassmarket and so on. Architecturally speaking, there is no finer sight in Europe."

"I once was taken for a walk through the Canongate," Sandy said, "but I was frightened by the squalor."

"Well, it was the 'thirties," said the man. "Tell me, Sister Helena, what would you say was your greatest influence during the 'thirties? I mean, during your teens. Did you read Auden and Eliot?"

"No," said Sandy.

"We boys were very keen on Auden and that group of course. We wanted to go and fight in the Spanish Civil War. On the Republican side, of course. Did you take sides in the Spanish Civil War at your school?"

"Well, not exactly," said Sandy. "It was all different for us."

"You weren't a Catholic then, of course?"

"No," said Sandy.

"The influences of one's teens are very important," said the man.

"Oh yes," said Sandy, "even if they provide something to react against."

"What was your biggest influence, then, Sister Helena? Was it political, personal? Was it Calvinism?"

"Oh no," said Sandy. "But there was a Miss Jean Brodie in her prime." She clutched the bars of the grille as if she wanted to escape from the dim parlor beyond, for she was not composed like the other nuns who sat, when they received their rare visitors, well back in the darkness with folded hands. But Sandy always leaned forward and peered, clutching the bars with both hands, and the other sisters remarked it and said that Sister Helena had too much to bear from the world since she had published her psychological book which was so unexpectedly famed. But the dispensation was forced upon Sandy, and she clutched the bars and received the choice visitors, the psychologists and the Catholic seekers, and the higher journalist ladies and the academics who wanted to question her about her odd psychological treatise on the nature of moral perception, called "The Transfiguration of the Commonplace."

"We will not go into St. Giles'," said Miss Brodie, "because the day draws late. But I presume you have all been to St. Giles' Cathedral?"

They had nearly all been in St. Giles' with its tattered bloodstained banners of the past. Sandy had not been there, and did not want to go. The outsides of old Edinburgh churches frightened her, they were of such dark stone, like presences almost the color of the Castle Rock, and were built so warningly with their upraised fingers.

Miss Brodie had shown them a picture of Cologne Cathedral, like a wedding cake, which looked as if it had been built for pleasure and festivities, and parties given by the Prodigal Son in his early career. But the insides of Scottish churches were more reassuring because during the services they contained people, and no ghosts at all. Sandy, Rose Stanley and Monica Douglas were of believing though not church-going families. Jenny Gray and Mary Macgregor were Presbyterians and went to Sunday School. Eunice Gardiner was Episcopalian and claimed that she did not believe in Jesus, but in the Father, Son and Holy Ghost. Sandy, who believed in ghosts, felt that the Holy Ghost was a feasible proposition. The whole question was, during this winter term, being laid open by Miss Brodie who, at the same time as adhering to the strict Church of Scotland habits of her youth, and keeping the Sabbath, was now, in her prime, attending evening classes in comparative religion at the University. So her pupils heard all about it, and learned for the first time that some honest people did not believe in God, nor even Allah. But the girls were set to study the Gospels with diligence for their truth and goodness, and to read them aloud for their beauty.

Their walk had brought them into broad Chambers Street. The group had changed its order, and was now walking three abreast, with Miss Brodie in front between Sandy and Rose. "I am summoned to see the headmistress at morning break on Monday," said Miss Brodie. "I have no doubt Miss Mackay wishes to question my methods of instruction. It has happened before. It will happen again. Meanwhile, I follow my principles of education and give of my best in my prime. The word 'education' comes from the root *e* from *ex*, out, and *duco*, I lead. It means a leading out. To me education is a leading out of what is already there in the pupil's soul. To Miss Mackay it is a putting in of something that is not there, and that is not what I call education, I call it intrusion, from the Latin root prefix *in* meaning in and the stem *trudo*, I thrust. Miss Mackay's method is to thrust a lot of information into the pupil's head; mine is a leading out of knowledge, and that is true education as is proved by the root meaning. Now Miss Mackay has accused me of putting ideas into my girls' heads, but in fact that is *her* practice and mine is quite the opposite. Never let it be said that I put ideas into your heads. What is the meaning of education, Sandy?"

"To lead out," said Sandy who was composing a formal invitation to Alan Breck, a year and a day after their breath-taking flight through the heather.

Miss Sandy Stranger requests the pleasure of Mr. Alan Breck's company at dinner on Tuesday the 6th of January at 8 o'clock.

That would surprise the hero of *Kidnapped* coming unexpectedly from Sandy's new address in the lonely harbor house of the coast of Fife—described in a novel by the daughter of John Buchan—of which Sandy had now by devious means become the mistress. Alan Breck would arrive in full Highland dress. Supposing that passion struck upon them in the course of the evening and they were swept away into sexual intercourse? She saw the picture of it happening in her mind, and Sandy could not stand for this spoiling. She argued with herself, surely people have to *think*, they have to stop to think while they are taking their clothes off, and if they stop to think, how can they be swept away?

"That is a Citroën," said Rose Stanley about a motor car that had passed by. "They are French."

"Sandy, dear, don't rush. Take my hand," said Miss Brodie. "Rose, your mind is full of motor cars. There is nothing wrong with motor cars, of course, but there are higher things. I'm sure Sandy's mind is not on motor cars, she is paying attention to my conversation like a well-mannered girl."

And if people take their clothes off in front of each other, thought Sandy, it is so rude, they are bound to be put off their passion for a moment. And if they are put off just for a single moment, *how* can they be swept away in the urge? If it all happens in a flash . . .

Miss Brodie said, "So I intend simply to point out to Miss Mackay that there is a radical difference in our principles of education. Radical is a word pertaining to roots—Latin *radix*, a root. We differ at root, the headmistress and I, upon the question whether we are employed to educate the minds of girls or to intrude upon them. We have had this argument before, but Miss Mackay is not, I may say, an outstanding logician. A logician is one skilled in logic. Logic is the art of reasoning. What is logic, Rose?"

"To do with reasoning, ma'am," said Rose, who later, while still in her teens, was to provoke Miss Brodie's amazement and then her awe and finally her abounding enthusiasm for the role which Rose then appeared to be enacting: that of a great lover, magnificently elevated above the ordinary run of lovers, above the moral laws, Venus incarnate, something set apart. In fact, Rose was not at the time in question engaged in the love affair which Miss Brodie thought she was, but it seemed so, and Rose was famous for sex. But in her mere eleventh year, on the winter's walk, Rose was taking note of the motor cars and Miss Brodie had not yet advanced far enough into her prime to speak of sex except by veiled allusion, as when she said of her warrior lover, "He was a pure man," or when she read from James Hogg's poem "Bonnie Kilmeny,"

> Kilmeny was pure as pure could be

and added, "Which is to say, she did not go to the glen in order to mix with men."

"When I see Miss Mackay on Monday morning," said Miss Brodie, "I shall point out that by the terms of my employment my methods cannot be condemned unless they can be proved to be in any part improper or subversive, and so long as the girls are in the least equipped for the end-of-term examination. I trust you girls to work hard and try to scrape through, even if you learn up the stuff and forget it next day. As for impropriety, it could never be imputed to me except by some gross distortion on the part of a traitor. I do not think ever to be betrayed. Miss Mackay is younger than I am and higher salaried. That is by accident. The best qualifications available at the University in my time were inferior to those open to Miss Mackay. That is why she holds the senior position. But her reasoning power is deficient, and so I have no fears for Monday."

"Miss Mackay has an awfully red face, with the veins all showing," said Rose.

"I can't permit that type of remark to pass in my presence, Rose," said Miss Brodie, "for it would be disloyal."

They had come to the end of Lauriston Place, past the fire station, where they were to get on a tram car to go to tea with Miss Brodie in her flat at Churchill. A very long queue of men lined this part of the street. They were without collars, in shabby suits. They were talking and spitting and smoking little bits of cigarette held between middle finger and thumb.

"We shall cross here," said Miss Brodie and herded the set across the road.

Monica Douglas whispered, "They are the Idle."

"In England they are called the Unemployed. They are waiting to get their dole from the labor bureau," said Miss Brodie. "You must all pray for the Unemployed, I will write you out the special prayer for them. You all know what the dole is?"

Eunice Gardiner had not heard of it.

"It is the weekly payment made by the State for the relief of the Unemployed and their families. Sometimes they go and spend their dole on drink before they go home, and their children starve. They are our brothers. Sandy, stop staring at once. In Italy the unemployment problem has been solved."

Sandy felt that she was not staring across the road at the endless queue of brothers, but that it was pulling her eyes towards it. She felt once more very frightened. Some of the men looked over at the girls, but without seeing them. The girls had reached the tram stop. The men were talking and spitting a great deal. Some were laughing with hacking laughs merging into coughs and ending up with spits.

As they waited for the tram car Miss Brodie said, "I had lodgings in this street when first I came to Edinburgh as a student. I must tell you a story about the landlady, who was very frugal. It was her habit to come to me every morning to ask what I would have for breakfast, and she spoke like this: 'Wud ye have a red herrin?—no ye wouldn't. Could ye eat a boilt egg?—no ye couldn't.' The result was, I never had but bread and butter to my breakfast all the time I was in those lodgings, and very little of that."

The laughter of the girls met that of the men opposite, who had now begun to file slowly by fits and starts into the labor bureau. Sandy's fear returned as soon as she had stopped laughing. She saw the slow jerkily moving file tremble with life, she saw it all of a piece like one dragon's body which had no right to be in the city and yet would not go away and was unslayable. She thought of the starving children. This was a relief to her fear. She wanted to cry as she always did when she saw a street singer or a beggar. She wanted Jenny to be there, because Jenny cried easily about poor children. But the snaky creature opposite started to shiver in the cold and made Sandy tremble again. She turned and said to Mary Macgregor who had brushed against her sleeve, "Stop pushing."

"Mary, dear, you mustn't push," said Miss Brodie.

"I wasn't pushing," said Mary.

In the tram car Sandy excused herself from tea with Miss Brodie on the plea that she thought she had a cold coming on. Indeed she shivered. She wanted at that moment to be warmly at home, outside which even the corporate Brodie set lived in a colder sort of way.

But later, when Sandy thought of Eunice doing somersaults and splits on Miss Brodie's kitchen linoleum while the other girls washed up, she rather wished she had gone to tea at Miss Brodie's after all. She took out her secret notebook from between the sheets of music and added a chapter to "The Mountain Eyrie," the true love story of Miss Jean Brodie.

CHAPTER THREE

The days passed and the wind blew from the Forth.

It is not to be supposed that Miss Brodie was unique at this point of her prime; or that (since such things are relative) she was in any way off her head. She was alone, merely, in that she taught in a school like Marcia Blaine's. There were legions of her kind during the nineteen-thirties, women from the age of thirty and upwards, who crowded their war-bereaved spinsterhood with voyages of discovery into new ideas and energetic practices in art or social welfare, education or religion. The progressive spinsters of Edinburgh did not teach in schools, especially in schools of traditional character like Marcia Blaine's School for Girls. It was in this that Miss Brodie was, as the rest of the staff spinsterhood put it, a trifle out of place. But she was not out of place amongst her own kind, the vigorous daughters of dead or enfeebled merchants, of ministers of religion, University professors, doctors, big warehouse owners of the past, or the owners of fisheries who had endowed these daughters with shrewd wits, high-colored cheeks, constitutions like horses, logical educations, hearty spirits and private means. They could be seen leaning over the democratic counters of Edinburgh grocers' shops arguing with the Manager at three in the afternoon on every subject from the authenticity of the Scriptures to the question what the word "guaranteed" on a jam-jar really meant. They went to lectures, tried living on honey and nuts, took lessons in German and then went walking in Germany; they bought caravans and went off with them into the hills among the lochs; they played the guitar, they supported all the new little theatre companies; they took lodgings in the slums and, distributing pots of paint, taught their neighbors the arts of simple interior decoration; they preached the inventions of Marie Stopes; they attended the meetings of the Oxford Group and put Spiritualism to their hawk-eyed test. Some assisted in the Scottish Nationalist Movement; others, like Miss Brodie, called themselves Europeans and Edinburgh a European capital, the city of Hume and Boswell.

They were not, however, committee women. They were not schoolteachers. The committee spinsters were less enterprising and not at all rebellious, they were sober churchgoers and quiet workers. The schoolmistresses were of a still more orderly type, earning their keep, living with aged parents and taking walks on the hills and holidays at North Berwick.

But those of Miss Brodie's kind were great talkers and feminists and, like most feminists, talked to men as man-to-man.

"I tell you this, Mr. Geddes, birth control is the only answer to the problem of the working class. A free issue to every household . . ."

And often in the thriving grocers' shops at three in the afternoon:

"Mr. Logan, Elder though you are, I am a woman in my prime of life, so you can take it from me that you get a sight more religion out of Professor Tovey's Sunday concerts than you do out of your kirk services."

And so, seen in this light, there was nothing outwardly odd about Miss Brodie. Inwardly was a different matter, and it remained to be seen towards what extremities her nature worked her. Outwardly she differed from the rest of the teaching staff in that she was still in a state of fluctuating development, whereas they had only too understandably not trusted themselves to change their minds, particularly on ethical questions, after the age of twenty. There was nothing Miss Brodie could not yet learn, she boasted of it. And it was not a static Miss Brodie who told her girls, "These are the years of my prime. You are benefiting by my prime," but one whose nature was growing under their eyes, as the girls themselves were under formation. It extended, this prime of Miss Brodie's, still in the making when the girls were well on in their teens. And the principles governing the end of her prime would have astonished herself at the beginning of it.

The summer holidays of nineteen-thirty-one marked the first anniversary of the launching of Miss Brodie's prime. The year to come was in many ways the most sexual year of the Brodie set, who were now turned eleven and twelve; it was a crowded year of stirring revelations. In later years, sex was only one of the things in life. That year it was everything.

The term opened vigorously as usual. Miss Brodie stood bronzed before her class and said, "I have spent most of my summer holidays in Italy once more, and a week in London, and I have brought back a great many pictures which we can pin on the wall. Here is a Cimabue. Here is a larger formation of Mussolini's fascisti, it is a better view of them than that of last year's picture. They are doing splendid things as I shall tell you later. I went with my friends for an audience with the Pope. My friends kissed his ring but I thought it proper only to bend over it. I wore a long black gown with a lace mantilla, and looked magnificent. In London my friends who are well-to-do—their small girl has two nurses, or nannies as they say in England—took me to visit A. A. Milne. In the hall was hung a reproduction of Botticelli's *Primavera* which means The Birth of Spring. I wore my silk dress with the large red poppies which is just right for my coloring. Mussolini is one of the greatest men in the world, far more so than Ramsay MacDonald, and his fascisti——"

"Good morning, Miss Brodie. Good morning, sit down, girls," said the headmistress who had entered in a hurry, leaving the door wide open.

Miss Brodie passed behind her with her head up, up, and shut the door with the utmost meaning.

"I have only just looked in," said Miss Mackay, "and I have to be off. Well, girls, this is the first day of the new session. Are we downhearted? No. You girls must work hard this year at every subject and pass your qualifying examination with flying colors. Next year you will be in the Senior school, remember. I hope you've all had a nice summer holiday, you all look nice and brown. I hope in due course of time to read your essays on how you spent them."

When she had gone Miss Brodie looked hard at the door for a long time. A girl, not of her set, called Judith, giggled. Miss Brodie said to Judith, "That will do." She turned to the blackboard and rubbed out with her duster the long division sum she always kept on the blackboard in case of intrusions from outside during any arithmetic period when Miss Brodie should happen not to be teaching arithmetic. When she had done this she turned back to the class and said, "Are we downhearted no, are we downhearted no. As I was saying, Mussolini has performed feats of magnitude and unemployment is even farther abolished under him than it was last year. I shall be able to tell you a great deal this term. As you know, I don't believe in talking down to children, you are capable of grasping more than is generally appreciated by your elders. Education means a leading out, from *e*, out, and *duco*, I lead. Qualifying examination or no qualifying examination, you will have the benefit of my experiences in Italy. In Rome I saw the Forum and I saw the Colosseum where the gladiators died and the slaves were thrown to the lions. A vulgar American remarked to me, 'It looks like a mighty fine quarry.' They talk nasally. Mary, what does to talk nasally mean?"

Mary did not know.

"Stupid as ever," said Miss Brodie. "Eunice?"

"Through your nose," said Eunice.

"Answer in a complete sentence, please," said Miss Brodie. "This year I think you should all start answering in complete sentences, I must try to remember this rule. Your correct answer is 'To talk nasally means to talk through one's nose.' The American said, 'It looks like a mighty fine quarry.' Ah! It was there the gladiators fought. 'Hail Caesar!' they cried. 'These about to die salute thee!'"

Miss Brodie stood in her brown dress like a gladiator with raised arm and eyes flashing like a sword. "Hail Caesar!" she cried again, turning radiantly to the window light, as if Caesar sat there. "Who opened the window?" said Miss Brodie, dropping her arm.

Nobody answered.

"Whoever has opened the window has opened it too wide," said Miss Brodie. "Six inches is perfectly adequate. More is vulgar. One should have an innate sense of these things. We ought to be doing history at the moment according to the timetable. Get out your history books and prop them up in your hands. I shall tell you a little more about Italy. I met a young poet by a fountain. Here is a picture of Dante meeting Beatrice—it is pronounced Beatrichay in Italian which makes the name very beautiful—on the Ponte Vecchio. He fell in love with her at that moment. Mary, sit up and don't slouch. It was a sublime moment in a sublime love. By whom was the picture painted?"

Nobody knew.

"It was painted by Rossetti. Who was Rosetti, Jenny?"

"A painter," said Jenny.

Miss Brodie looked suspicious.

"And a genius," said Sandy, to come to Jenny's rescue.

"A friend of——?" said Miss Brodie.

"Swinburne," said a girl.

Miss Brodie smiled. "You have not forgotten," she said, looking round the class. "Holidays or no holidays. Keep your history books propped up in case we have any further intruders." She looked disapprovingly towards the door and lifted her fine dark Roman head with dignity. She had often told the girls that her dead Hugh had admired her head for its Roman appearance.

"Next year," she said, "you will have the specialists to teach you history and mathematics and languages, a teacher for this and a teacher for that, a period of forty-five minutes for this and another for that. But in this your last year with me and you will receive the fruits of my prime. They will remain with you all your days. First, however, I must mark the register for today before we forget. There are two new girls. Stand up the two new girls."

They stood up with wide eyes while Miss Brodie sat down at her desk.

"You will get used to our ways. What religions are you?" said Miss Brodie with her pen poised on the page while, outside in the sky, the gulls from the Firth of Forth wheeled over the school and the green and golden tree-tops swayed towards the windows.

> "Come autumn sae pensive, in yellow and gray,
> And soothe me wi' tidings o' nature's decay

—Robert Burns," said Miss Brodie when she had closed the register. "We are now well into the nineteen-thirties. I have four pounds of rosy apples in my desk, a gift from Mr. Lowther's orchard, let us eat them now while the coast is clear—not but what the apples do not come under my own jurisdiction, but discretion is . . . discretion is . . . Sandy?"

"The better part of valor, Miss Brodie." Her little eyes looked at Miss Brodie in a slightly smaller way.

Even before the official opening of her prime Miss Brodie's colleagues in the Junior school had been gradually turning against her. The teaching staff of the Senior school was indifferent or mildly amused, for they had not yet felt the impact of the Brodie set; that was to come the following year, and even then these Senior mistresses were not unduly irritated by the effects of what they called Miss Brodie's experimental methods. It was in the Junior school, among the lesser paid and lesser qualified women, with whom Miss Brodie had daily dealings, that indignation seethed. There were two exceptions on the staff, who felt neither resentment nor indifference towards Miss Brodie, but were, on the contrary, her supporters on every count. One of these was Mr. Gordon Lowther, the singing master for the whole school, Junior and Senior. The other was Mr. Teddy Lloyd, the Senior girls' art master. They were the only men on the staff. Both were already a little in love with Miss Brodie, for they found in her the only scx-bestirred object in their daily environment, and although they did not realize it, both were already beginning to act as rivals for her attention. But so far, they had not engaged her attention as men, she knew them only as supporters, and was proudly grateful. It was the Brodie set who discerned, before she did, and certainly these men did, that Mr. Lowther and Mr. Lloyd were at pains to appear well, each in his exclusive right before Miss Brodie.

To the Brodie set Gordon Lowther and Teddy Lloyd looked rather like each other until habitual acquaintance proved that they looked very different. Both were red-gold in coloring. Teddy Lloyd, the art master, was by far the better-shaped, the better-featured and the more sophisticated. He was said to be half Welsh, half English. He spoke with a hoarse voice as if he had bronchitis all the time. A golden forelock of his hair fell over his forehead into his eyes. Most wonderful of all, he had only one arm, the right, with which he painted. The other was a sleeve tucked into his pocket. He had lost the contents of the sleeve in the Great War.

Miss Brodie's class had only once had an opportunity to size him up closely, and then it was in a dimmed light, for the blinds of the art room had been drawn to allow Mr. Lloyd to show his lantern slides. They had been marched into the art room by Miss Brodie, who was going to sit with the girls on the end of a bench, when the art master came forward with a chair for her held in his one hand and presented in a special way with a tiny inflection of the knees, like a flunkey. Miss Brodie seated herself nobly like Britannia with her legs apart under her loose brown skirt which came well over her knees. Mr. Lloyd showed his pictures from an exhibition of Italian art in London. He had a pointer with which he indicated the design of the picture in accompaniment to his hoarse voice. He said nothing of what the pictures represented, only followed each curve and line as the artist had left it off, perhaps at the point of an elbow, and picked it up, perhaps at the edge of a cloud or the back of a chair. The ladies of the *Primavera*, in their netball-playing postures, provided Mr. Lloyd with much pointer work. He kept on passing the pointer along the lines of their bottoms which showed through the drapery. The third time he did this a collective quiver of mirth ran along the front row of girls, then spread to the back rows. They kept their mouths shut tight against these convulsions, but the tighter their lips, the more did the little gusts of humor escape through their noses. Mr. Lloyd looked round with offended exasperation.

"It is obvious," said Miss Brodie, "that these girls are not of cultured homes and heritage. The Philistines are upon us, Mr. Lloyd."

The girls, anxious to be of cultured and sexless antecedents, were instantly composed by the shock of this remark. But immediately Mr. Lloyd resumed his demonstration of artistic form, and again dragged his pointer all round the draped private parts of one of Botticelli's female subjects, Sandy affected to have a fit of spluttering coughs, as did several girls behind her. Others groped under their seat as if looking for something they had dropped. One or two frankly leaned against each other and giggled with hands to their helpless mouths.

"I am surprised at *you*, Sandy," said Miss Brodie. "I thought you were the leaven in the lump."

Sandy looked up from her coughs with a hypocritical blinking of her eyes. Miss Brodie, however, had already fastened on Mary Macgregor who was nearest to her. Mary's giggles had been caused by contagion, for she was too stupid to have any sex-wits of her own, and Mr. Lloyd's lesson would never have affected her unless it had first affected the rest of the class. But now she was giggling openly like a dirty-minded child of an uncultured home. Miss Brodie grasped Mary's arm, jerked her to her feet and propelled her to the door where she thrust her outside and shut her out, returning as one who had solved the whole problem. As indeed she had, for the violent action sobered the girls and made them feel that, in the official sense, an unwanted ring-leader had been apprehended and they were no longer in the wrong.

As Mr. Lloyd had now switched his equipment to a depiction of the Madonna and Child, Miss Brodie's action was the more appreciated, for no one in the class would have felt comfortable at being seized with giggles while Mr. Lloyd's pointer was tracing the outlines of this sacred subject. In fact, they were rather shocked that Mr. Lloyd's hoarse voice did not change its tone in the slightest for this occasion, but went on stating what the painter had done with his brush; he was almost defiant in his methodical tracing of lines all over the Mother and the Son. Sandy caught his glance towards Miss Brodie as if seeking her approval for his very artistic attitude and Sandy saw her smile back as would a goddess with superior understanding smile to a god away on the mountain tops.

It was not long after this that Monica Douglas, later famous for mathematics and anger, claimed that she had seen Mr. Lloyd in the act of kissing Miss Brodie. She was very definite about it in her report to the five other members of the Brodie set. There was a general excited difficulty in believing her.

"When?"

"Where?"

"In the art room after school yesterday."

"What were you doing in the art room?" said Sandy who took up the role of cross-examiner.

"I went to get a new sketch pad."

"Why? You haven't finished your old sketch pad yet."

"I have," said Monica.

"When did you use up your old sketch pad?"

"Last Saturday afternoon when you were playing golf with Miss Brodie."

It was true that Jenny and Sandy had done nine holes on the Braid Hills course with Miss Brodie on the previous Saturday, while the rest of the Brodie set wandered afield to sketch.

"Monica used up all her book. She did the Tee Woods from five angles," said Rose Stanley in verification.

"What part of the art room were they standing in?" Sandy said.

"The far side," Monica said. "I know he had his arm round her and was kissing her. They jumped apart when I opened the door."

"Which arm?" Sandy snapped.

"The right of course, he hasn't got a left."

"Were you inside or outside the room when you saw them?" Sandy said.

"Well, in and out. I *saw* them, I tell you."

"What did they say?" Jenny said.

"They didn't see me," said Monica. "I just turned and ran away."

"Was it a long and lingering kiss?" Sandy demanded, while Jenny came closer to hear the answer.

Monica cast the corner of her eye up to the ceiling as if doing mental arithmetic. Then when her calculation was finished she said, "Yes it was."

"How do you know if you didn't stop to see how long it was?"

"I know," said Monica, getting angry, "by the bit that I did see. It was a small bit of a good long kiss that I saw, I could see it by his arm being round her, and——"

"I don't believe all this," Sandy said squeakily, because she was excited and desperately trying to prove the report true by eliminating the doubts. "You must have been dreaming," she said.

Monica pecked with the fingers of her right hand at Sandy's arm, and pinched the skin of it with a nasty half-turn. Sandy screamed. Monica, whose face was becoming very red, swung the attaché case which held her books, so that it hit the girls who stood in its path and made them stand back from her.

"She's losing her temper," said Eunice Gardiner, skipping.

"I don't believe what she says," said Sandy, desperately trying to visualize the scene in the art room and to goad factual Monica into describing it with due feeling.

"I believe it," said Rose. "Mr. Lloyd is an artist and Miss Brodie is artistic too."

Jenny said, "Didn't they see the door opening?"

"Yes," said Monica, "they jumped apart as I opened the door."

"How did you know they didn't see you?" Sandy said.

"I got away before they turned round. They were standing at the far end of the room beside the still-life curtain." She went to the classroom door and demonstrated her quick get-away. This was not dramatically satisfying to Sandy who went out of the classroom, opened the door, looked, opened her eyes in a startled way, gasped and retreated in a flash. She seemed satisfied by her experimental re-enactment but it so delighted her friends that she repeated it. Miss Brodie came up behind her on her fourth performance which had reached a state of extreme flourish.

"What are you doing, Sandy?" said Miss Brodie.

"Only playing," said Sandy, photographing this new Miss Brodie
with her little eyes.

The question of whether Miss Brodie was actually capable of being kissed and of kissing occupied the Brodie set till Christmas. For
the war-time romance of her life had presented to their minds a Miss
Brodie of hardly flesh and blood, since that younger Miss Brodie
belonged to the prehistory of before their birth. Sitting under the
elm last autumn, Miss Brodie's story of "when I was a girl" had
seemed much less real, and yet more believable than this report by
Monica Douglas. The Brodie set decided to keep the incident to
themselves lest, if it should spread to the rest of the class, it should
spread wider still and eventually to someone's ears who would get
Monica Douglas into trouble.

There was, indeed, a change in Miss Brodie. It was not merely
that Sandy and Jenny, recasting her in their minds, now began to try
to imagine her as someone called "Jean." There was a change in herself. She wore newer clothes and with them a glowing amber necklace which was of such real amber that, as she once showed them, it
had magnetic properties when rubbed and then applied to a piece of
paper.

The change in Miss Brodie was best discerned by comparison
with the other teachers in the Junior school. If you looked at them
and then looked at Miss Brodie it was more possible to imagine her
giving herself up to kissing.

Jenny and Sandy wondered if Mr. Lloyd and Miss Brodie had
gone further that day in the art room, and had been swept away by
passion. They kept an eye on Miss Brodie's stomach to see if it
showed signs of swelling. Some days, if they were bored, they decided it had begun to swell. But on Miss Brodie's entertaining days
they found her stomach as flat as ever and at these times even agreed
together that Monica Douglas had been telling a lie.

The other Junior schoolteachers said good morning to Miss Brodie, these days, in a more than Edinburgh manner, that is to say it
was gracious enough, and not one of them omitted to say good
morning at all; but Sandy, who had turned eleven, perceived that the
tone of "morning" in "Good morning" made the word seem purposely
to rhyme with "scorning," so that these colleagues of Miss Brodie's
might just as well have said, "I scorn you," instead of "Good morning." Miss Brodie's reply was more anglicized in its accent than was its
usual proud wont. "Good mawning," she replied, in the corridors,
flattening their scorn beneath the chariot wheels of her superiority,

and deviating her head towards them no more than an insulting half-inch. She held her head up, up, as she walked, and often, when she reached and entered her own classroom, permitted herself to sag gratefully against the door for an instant. She did not frequent the staff common rooms in the free periods when her class was taking its singing or sewing lessons, but accompanied them.

Now the two sewing teachers were somewhat apart from the rest of the teaching staff and were not taken seriously. They were the two younger sisters of a third, dead, eldest sister whose guidance of their lives had never been replaced. Their names were Miss Ellen and Miss Alison Kerr; they were incapable of imparting any information whatsoever, so flustered were they, with their fluffed-out hair, dry blue-gray skins and birds' eyes; instead of teaching sewing they took each girl's work in hand, one by one, and did most of it for her. In the worst cases they unstitched what had been done and did it again, saying, "This'll not do," or, "That's never a run and fell seam." The sewing sisters had not as yet been induced to judge Miss Brodie since they were by nature of the belief that their scholastic colleagues were above criticism. Therefore the sewing lessons were a great relaxation to all, and Miss Brodie in the time before Christmas used the sewing period each week to read *Jane Eyre* to her class who, while they listened, pricked their thumbs as much as was bearable so that interesting little spots of blood might appear on the stuff they were sewing, and it was even possible to make blood-spot designs.

The singing lessons were far different. Some weeks after the report of her kissing in the art room it gradually became plain that Miss Brodie was agitated before, during, and after the singing lessons. She wore her newest clothes on singing days.

Sandy said to Monica Douglas, "Are you sure it was Mr. Lloyd who kissed her? Are you sure it wasn't Mr. Lowther?"

"It was Mr. Lloyd," said Monica, "and it was in the art room, not the music room. What would Mr. Lowther have been doing in the art room?"

"They look alike, Mr. Lloyd and Mr. Lowther," Sandy said.

Monica's anger was rising in her face. "It was Mr. Lloyd with his one arm round her," she said. "I saw them. I'm sorry I ever told you. Rose is the only one that believes me."

Rose Stanley believed her, but this was because she was indifferent. She was the least of all the Brodie set to be excited by Miss Brodie's love affairs, or by anyone else's sex. And it was always to be the same. Later, when she was famous for sex, her magnificently appealing qualities lay in the fact that she had no curiosity about sex at all, she never reflected upon it. As Miss Brodie was to say, she had instinct.

"Rose is the only one who believes me," said Monica Douglas.

When she visited Sandy at the nunnery in the late nineteen-fifties, Monica said, "I really did see Teddy Lloyd kiss Miss Brodie in the art room one day."

"I know you did," said Sandy.

She knew it even before Miss Brodie had told her so one day after the end of the war, when they sat in the Braid Hills Hotel eating sandwiches and drinking tea which Miss Brodie's rations at home would not run to. Miss Brodie sat shriveled and betrayed in her long-preserved dark musquash coat. She had been retired before time. She said, "I am past my prime."

"It was a good prime," said Sandy.

They looked out of the wide windows at the little Braid Burn trickling through the fields and at the hills beyond, so austere from everlasting that they had never been capable of losing anything by the war.

"Teddy Lloyd was greatly in love with me, as you know," said Miss Brodie, "and I with him. It was a great love. One day in the art room he kissed me. We never became lovers, not even after you left Edinburgh, when the temptation was strongest."

Sandy stared through her little eyes at the hills.

"But I renounced him," said Miss Brodie. "He was a married man. I renounced the great love of my prime. We had everything in common, the artistic nature."

She had reckoned on her prime lasting till she was sixty. But this, the year after the war, was in fact Miss Brodie's last and fifty-sixth year. She looked older than that, she was suffering from an internal growth. This was her last year in the world and in another sense it was Sandy's.

Miss Brodie sat in her defeat and said, "In the late autumn of nineteen-thirty-one—are you listening, Sandy?"

Sandy took her eyes from the hills.

In the late autumn of nineteen-thirty-one Miss Brodie was away from school for two weeks. It was understood she had an ailment. The Brodie set called at her flat after school with flowers and found no one at home. On enquiring at school next day they were told she had gone to the country to stay with a friend until she was better.

In the meantime Miss Brodie's class was dispersed, and squashed in among the classes of her colleagues. The Brodie set stuck together and were placed with a gaunt woman who was, in fact, a Miss Gaunt from the Western Isles who wore a knee-length skirt made from what looked like gray blanket stuff; this had never been smart even in the knee-length days; Rose Stanley said it was cut short for economy. Her head was very large and bony. Her chest was a slight bulge flattened by a bust bodice, and her jersey was a dark forbidding green. She did not care at all for the Brodie set who were stunned by a sudden plunge into industrious learning and very put out by Miss Gaunt's horrible sharpness and strict insistence on silence throughout the day.

"Oh dear," said Rose out loud one day when they were settled to essay writing, "I can't remember how you spell 'possession.' Are there two s's or——?"

"A hundred lines of *Marmion*," Miss Gaunt flung at her.

The black-marks book, which eventually reflected itself on the end-of-term reports, was heavily scored with the names of the Brodie set by the end of the first week. Apart from enquiring their names for this purpose Miss Gaunt did not trouble to remember them. "You, girl," she would say to every Brodie face. So dazed were the Brodie girls that they did not notice the omission during that week of their singing lesson which should have been on Wednesday.

On Thursday they were herded into the sewing room in the early afternoon. The two sewing teachers, Miss Alison and Miss Ellen Kerr, seemed rather cowed by gaunt Miss Gaunt, and applied themselves briskly to the sewing machines which they were teaching the girls to use. The shuttle of the sewing machines went up and down, which usually caused Sandy and Jenny to giggle, since at that time everything that could conceivably bear a sexual interpretation immediately did so to them. But the absence of Miss Brodie and the presence of Miss Gaunt had a definite subtracting effect from the sexual significance of everything, and the trepidation of the two sewing sisters contributed to the effect of grim realism.

Miss Gaunt evidently went to the same parish church as the Kerr sisters, to whom she addressed remarks from time to time while she embroidered a tray cloth.

"My brothurr . . ." she kept saying, "my brothurr says . . ."

Miss Gaunt's brother was apparently the minister of the parish, which accounted for the extra precautions Miss Alison and Miss Ellen were taking about their work today, with the result that they got a lot of the sewing mixed up.

"My brothurr is up in the morning at five-thirty . . . My brothurr organized a . . ."

Sandy was thinking of the next installment of *Jane Eyre*, which Miss Brodie usually enlivened this hour by reading. Sandy had done with Alan Breck and had taken up with Mr. Rochester, with whom she now sat in the garden.

"You are afraid of me, Miss Sandy."

"You talk like the Sphinx, sir, but I am not afraid."

"You have such a grave, quiet manner, Miss Sandy—you are going?"

"It has struck nine, sir."

A phrase of Miss Gaunt's broke upon the garden scene: "Mr. Lowther is not at school this week."

"So I hear," Miss Alison said.

"It seems he will be away for another week at least."

"Is he ill?"

"I understand so, unfortunately," said Miss Gaunt.

"Miss Brodie is ailing, too," said Miss Ellen.

"Yes," said Miss Gaunt. "She too is expected to be absent for another week."

"What is the trouble?"

"That I couldn't say," said Miss Gaunt. She stuck her needle in and out of her embroidery. Then she looked up at the sisters. "It may be Miss Brodie has the same complaint as Mr. Lowther," she said.

Sandy saw her face as that of the housekeeper in *Jane Eyre*, watching her carefully and knowingly as she entered the house, late, from the garden where she had been sitting with Mr. Rochester.

"Perhaps Miss Brodie is having a love affair with Mr. Lowther," Sandy said to Jenny, merely in order to break up the sexless gloom that surrounded them.

"But it was Mr. Lloyd who kissed her. She must be in love with Mr. Lloyd or she wouldn't have let him kiss her."

"Perhaps she's working it off on Mr. Lowther. Mr. Lowther isn't married."

It was a fantasy worked up between them, in defiance of Miss Gaunt and her forbidding brother, and it was understood in that way. But Sandy, remembering Miss Gaunt's expression as she remarked, "It may be Miss Brodie has the same complaint as Mr. Lowther," was suddenly not sure that the suggestion was not true. For this reason she was more reticent than Jenny about the details of the imagined love affair. Jenny whispered, "They go to bed. Then he puts out the light. Then their toes touch. And then Miss Brodie . . . Miss Brodie . . ." She broke into giggles.

"Miss Brodie yawns," said Sandy in order to restore decency, now that she suspected it was all true.

"No, Miss Brodie says, 'Darling.' She says——"

"Quiet," whispered Sandy, "Eunice is coming."

Eunice Gardiner approached the table where Jenny and Sandy sat, grabbed the scissors and went away. Eunice had lately taken a religious turn and there was no talking about sex in front of her. She had stopped hopping and skipping. The phase did not last long, but while it did she was nasty and not to be trusted. When she was well out of the way Jenny resumed:

"Mr. Lowther's legs are shorter than Miss Brodie's, so I suppose she winds hers round his, and——"

"Where does Mr. Lowther live, do you know?" Sandy said.

"At Cramond. He's got a big house with a housekeeper."

In that year after the war when Sandy sat with Miss Brodie in the window of the Braid Hills Hotel, and brought her eyes back from the hills to show she was listening, Miss Brodie said:

"I renounced Teddy Lloyd. But I decided to enter into a love affair, it was the only cure. My love for Teddy was an obsession, he was the love of my prime. But in the autumn of nineteen-thirty-one I entered an affair with Gordon Lowther, he was a bachelor and it was more becoming. That is the truth and there is no more to say. Are you listening, Sandy?"

"Yes, I'm listening."

"You look as if you were thinking of something else, my dear. Well, as I say, that is the whole story."

Sandy was thinking of something else. She was thinking that it was not the whole story.

"Of course the liaison was suspected. Perhaps you girls knew about it. You, Sandy, had a faint idea . . . but nobody could prove what was between Gordon Lowther and myself. It was never proved. It was not on those grounds that I was betrayed. I should like to know who betrayed me. It is incredible that it should have been one of my own girls. I often wonder if it was poor Mary. Perhaps I should have been nicer to Mary. Well, it was tragic about Mary, I picture that fire, that poor girl. I can't see how Mary could have betrayed me, though."

"She had no contact with the school after she left," Sandy said.

"I wonder, was it Rose who betrayed me?"

The whine in her voice—". . . betrayed me, betrayed me"—bored and afflicted Sandy. It is seven years, thought Sandy, since I betrayed this tiresome woman. What does she mean by "betray"?

She was looking at the hills as if to see there the first and unbetrayable Miss Brodie, indifferent to criticism as a crag.

After her two weeks' absence Miss Brodie returned to tell her class that she had enjoyed an exciting rest and a well-earned one. Mr. Lowther's singing class went on as usual and he beamed at Miss Brodie as she brought them proudly into the music room with their heads up, up. Miss Brodie now played the accompaniment, sitting very well at the piano and sometimes, with a certain sadness of countenance, richly taking the second soprano in "How sweet is the shepherd's sweet lot," and other melodious preparations for the annual concert. Mr. Lowther, short-legged, shy and golden-haired, no longer played with Jenny's curls. The bare branches brushed the windows and Sandy was almost as sure as could be that the singing master was in love with Miss Brodie and that Miss Brodie was in love with the art master. Rose Stanley had not yet revealed her potentialities in the working-out of Miss Brodie's passion for one-armed Teddy Lloyd, and Miss Brodie's prime still flourished unbetrayed.

It was impossible to imagine Miss Brodie sleeping with Mr. Lowther, it was impossible to imagine her in a sexual context at all, and yet it was impossible not to suspect that such things were so.

During the Easter term Miss Mackay, the headmistress, had the girls in to tea in her study in small groups and, later, one by one. This was a routine of enquiry as to their intentions for the Senior school, whether they would go on the Modern side or whether they would apply for admission to the Classical.

Miss Brodie had already prompted them as follows: "I am not saying anything against the Modern side. Modern and Classical, they are equal, and each provides for a function in life. You must make your free choice. Not everyone is capable of a Classical education. You must make your choice quite freely." So that the girls were left in no doubt as to Miss Brodie's contempt for the Modern side.

From among her special set only Eunice Gardiner stood out to be a Modern, and that was because her parents wanted her to take a course in domestic science and she herself wanted the extra scope for gymnastics and games which the Modern side offered. Eunice, preparing arduously for Confirmation, was still a bit too pious for Miss Brodie's liking. She now refused to do somersaults outside of the gymnasium, she wore lavender water on her handkerchief, declined a try of Rose Stanley's aunt's lipstick, was taking a suspiciously healthy interest in international sport and, when Miss Brodie herded her set to the Empire Theatre for their first and last opportunity to witness the dancing of Pavlova, Eunice was absent, she had pleaded off because of something else she had to attend which she described as "a social."

"Social what?" said Miss Brodie, who always made difficulties about words when she scented heresy.

"It's in the Church Hall, Miss Brodie."

"Yes, yes, but social what? Social is an adjective and you are using it as a noun. If you mean a social gathering, by all means attend your social gathering and we shall have our own social gathering in the presence of the great Anna Pavlova, a dedicated woman who, when she appears on the stage, makes the other dancers look like elephants. By all means attend your social gathering. We shall see Pavlova doing the death of the Swan, it is a great moment in eternity."

All that term she tried to inspire Eunice to become at least a pioneer missionary in some deadly and dangerous zone of the earth, for it was intolerable to Miss Brodie that any of her girls should grow up not largely dedicated to some vocation. "You will end up as a Girl Guide leader in a suburb like Corstorphine," she said warningly to Eunice, who was in fact secretly attracted to this idea and who lived in Corstorphine. The term was filled with legends of Pavlova and her dedicated habits, her wild fits of temperament and her intolerance of the second-rate. "She screams at the chorus," said Miss Brodie, "which is permissible in a great artist. She speaks English fluently, her accent is charming. Afterwards she goes home to meditate upon the swans which she keeps on a lake in the grounds."

"Sandy," said Anna Pavlova, "you are the only truly dedicated dancer, next to me. Your dying Swan is perfect, such a sensitive, final tap of the claw upon the floor of the stage . . ."

"I know it," said Sandy (in considered preference to "Oh, I do my best"), as she relaxed in the wings.

Pavlova nodded sagely and gazed into the middle distance with the eyes of tragic exile and of art. "Every artist knows," said Pavlova, "is it not so?" Then, with a voice desperate with the menace of hysteria, and a charming accent, she declared, "I have never been understood. Never. Never."

Sandy removed one of her ballet shoes and cast it casually to the other end of the wings where it was respectfully retrieved by a member of the common chorus. Pausing before she removed the other shoe, Sandy said to Pavlova, "I am sure I understand you."

"It is true," exclaimed Pavlova, clasping Sandy's hand, "because you are an artist and will carry on the torch."

Miss Brodie said: "Pavlova contemplates her swans in order to perfect her swan dance, she studies them. That is true dedication. You must all grow up to be dedicated women as I have dedicated myself to you."

A few weeks before she died, when, sitting up in bed in the nursing home, she learned from Monica Douglas that Sandy had gone to a convent, she said: "What a waste. That is not the sort of dedication I meant. Do you think she has done this to annoy me? I begin to wonder if it was not Sandy who betrayed me."

The headmistress invited Sandy, Jenny and Mary to tea just before the Easter holidays and asked them the usual questions about what they wanted to do in the Senior school and whether they wanted to do it on the Modern or the Classical side. Mary Macgregor was ruled out of the Classical side because her marks did not reach the required standard. She seemed despondent on hearing this.

"Why do you want so much to go on the Classical side, Mary? You aren't cut out for it. Don't your parents realize that?"

"Miss Brodie prefers it."

"It has nothing to do with Miss Brodie," said Miss Mackay, settling her great behind more firmly in her chair. "It is a question of your marks or what you and your parents think. In your case, your marks don't come up to the standard."

When Jenny and Sandy opted for Classical, she said: "Because Miss Brodie prefers it, I suppose. What good will Latin and Greek be to you when you get married or take a job? German would be more useful."

But they stuck out for Classical, and when Miss Mackay had accepted their choice she transparently started to win over the girls by praising Miss Brodie. "What we would do without Miss Brodie, I don't know. There is always a difference about Miss Brodie's girls, and the last two years I may say a *marked* difference."

Then she began to pump them. Miss Brodie took them to the theatre, the art galleries, for walks, to Miss Brodie's flat for tea? How kind of Miss Brodie. "Does Miss Brodie pay for all your theatre tickets?"

"Sometimes," said Mary.

"Not for all of us every time," said Jenny.

"We go up to the gallery," Sandy said.

"Well, it is most kind of Miss Brodie. I hope you are appreciative."

"Oh, yes," they said, united and alert against anything unfavorable to the Brodie idea which the conversation might be leading up to. This was not lost on the headmistress.

"That's splendid," she said. "And do you go to concerts with Miss Brodie? Miss Brodie is very musical, I believe?"

"Yes," said Mary, looking at her friends for a lead.

"We went to the opera with Miss Brodie last term to see *La Traviata*," said Jenny.

"Miss Brodie is musical?" said Miss Mackay again, addressing Sandy and Jenny.

"We saw Pavlova," said Sandy.

"Miss Brodie is musical?" said Miss Mackay.

"I think Miss Brodie is more interested in art, ma'am," said Sandy.

"But music is a form of art."

"Pictures and drawings, I mean," said Sandy.

"Very enlightening," said Miss Mackay. "Do you girls take piano lessons?"

They all said yes.

"From whom? From Mr. Lowther?"

They answered variously, for Mr. Lowther's piano lessons were not part of the curriculum and these three girls had private arrangements for the piano at home. But now, at the mention of Mr. Lowther, even slow-minded Mary suspected what Miss Mackay was driving at.

"I understand Miss Brodie plays the piano for your singing lessons. So what makes you think she prefers art to music, Sandy?"

"Miss Brodie told us so. Music is an interest to her but art is a passion, Miss Brodie said."

"And what are *your* cultural interests? I'm sure you are too young to have passions."

"Stories, ma'am," Mary said.

"Does Miss Brodie tell you stories?"

"Yes," said Mary.

"What about?"

"History," said Jenny and Sandy together, because it was a question they had foreseen might arise one day and they had prepared the answer with a brainracking care for literal truth.

Miss Mackay paused and looked at them in the process of moving the cake from the table to the tray; their reply had plainly struck her as being on the ready side.

She asked no further questions, but made the following note-worthy speech:

"You are very fortunate in Miss Brodie. I could wish your arithmetic papers had been better. I am always impressed by Miss Brodie's girls in one way or another. You will have to work hard at ordinary humble subjects for the qualifying examinations. Miss Brodie is giving you an excellent preparation for the Senior school. Culture cannot compensate for lack of hard knowledge. I am happy to see you are devoted to Miss Brodie. Your loyalty is due to the school rather than to any one individual."

Not all of this conversation was reported back to Miss Brodie.

"We told Miss Mackay how much you liked art," said Sandy, however.

"I do indeed," said Miss Brodie, "but 'like' is hardly the word; pictorial art is my passion."

"That's what I said," said Sandy.

Miss Brodie looked at her as if to say, as in fact she had said twice before, "One day, Sandy, you will go too far for my liking."

"Compared to music," said Sandy, blinking up at her with her little pig-like eyes.

Towards the end of the Easter holidays, to crown the sex-laden year, Jenny, out walking alone, was accosted by a man joyfully exposing himself beside the Water of Leith. He said, "Come and look at this."

"At what?" said Jenny, moving closer, thinking to herself he had picked up a fallen nestling from the ground or had discovered a strange plant. Having perceived the truth, she escaped unharmed and unpursued though breathless, and was presently surrounded by solicitous, horrified relations and was coaxed to sip tea well sugared against the shock. Later in the day, since the incident had been reported to the police, came a wonderful policewoman to question Jenny.

These events contained enough exciting possibilities to set the rest of the Easter holidays spinning like a top and to last out the whole of the summer term. The first effect on Sandy was an adverse one, for she had been on the point of obtaining permission to go for walks alone in just such isolated spots as that in which Jenny's encounter had taken place. Sandy was now still forbidden lone walks, but this was a mere by-effect of the affair. The rest brought nothing but good. The subject fell under two headings: first, the man himself and the nature of what he had exposed to view, and secondly the policewoman.

The first was fairly quickly exhausted.

"He was a horrible creature," said Jenny.

"A terrible beast," said Sandy.

The question of the policewoman was inexhaustible, and although Sandy never saw her, nor at that time any policewoman (for these were in the early days of the women police), she quite deserted Alan Breck and Mr. Rochester and all the heroes of fiction for the summer term, and fell in love with the unseen policewoman who had questioned Jenny; and in this way she managed to keep alive Jenny's enthusiasm too.

"What did she look like? Did she wear a helmet?"

"No, a cap. She had short, fair, curly hair curling under the cap. And a dark blue uniform. She said, 'Now tell me all about it.'"

"And what did you say?" said Sandy for the fourth time.

For the fourth time Jenny replied: "Well, I said, 'The man was walking along under the trees by the bank, and he was holding something in his hand. And then when he saw me he laughed out loud and said, come and look at this. I said, at what? And I went a bit closer and I saw . . .'—but I couldn't tell the policewoman what I saw, could I? So the policewoman said to me, 'You saw something nasty?' And I said, 'Yes.' Then she asked me what the man was like, and . . ."

But this was the same story all over again. Sandy wanted new details about the policewoman, she looked for clues. Jenny had pronounced the word "nasty" as "nesty," which was unusual for Jenny.

"Did she say 'nasty' or 'nesty'?" said Sandy on this fourth telling.

"Nesty."

This gave rise to an extremely nasty feeling in Sandy and it put her off the idea of sex for months. All the more as she disapproved of the pronunciation of the word, it made her flesh creep, and she plagued Jenny to change her mind and agree that the policewoman had pronounced it properly.

"A lot of people say nesty," said Jenny.

"I know, but I don't like them. They're neither one thing nor another."

It bothered Sandy a great deal, and she had to invent a new speaking-image for the policewoman. Another thing that troubled her was that Jenny did not know the policewoman's name, or even whether she was addressed as "constable," "sergeant," or merely "miss." Sandy decided to call her Sergeant Anne Grey. Sandy was Anne Grey's right-hand woman in the Force, and they were dedicated to eliminate sex from Edinburgh and environs. In the Sunday newspapers, to which Sandy had free access, the correct technical phrases were to be found, such as "intimacy took place" and "plaintiff was in a certain condition." Females who were up for sex were not called "Miss" or "Mrs.," they were referred to by their surnames: "Willis was remanded in custody . . . ," "Roebuck, said Counsel, was discovered to be in a certain condition."

So Sandy pushed her dark blue police force cap to the back of her head and sitting on a stile beside Sergeant Anne Grey watched the spot between the trees by the Water of Leith where the terrible beast had appeared who had said, "Look at this," to Jenny, but where, in fact, Sandy never was.

"And another thing," said Sandy, "we've got to find out more about the case of Brodie and whether she is yet in a certain condition as a consequence of her liaison with Gordon Lowther, described as singing master, Marcia Blaine School for Girls."

"Intimacy has undoubtedly taken place," said Sergeant Anne, looking very nice in her dark uniform and short-cropped curls blondely fringing her cap. She said. "All we need are a few incriminating documents."

"Leave all that to me, Sergeant Anne," said Sandy, because she was at that very time engaged with Jenny in composing the love correspondence between Miss Brodie and the singing master. Sergeant Anne pressed Sandy's hand in gratitude; and they looked into each other's eyes, their mutual understanding too deep for words.

At school after the holidays the Water of Leith affair was kept a secret between Jenny and Sandy, for Jenny's mother had said the story must not be spread about. But it seemed natural that Miss Brodie should be told in a spirit of sensational confiding.

But something made Sandy say to Jenny on the first afternoon of the term: "Don't tell Miss Brodie."

"Why?" said Jenny.

Sandy tried to work out the reason. It was connected with the undecided state of Miss Brodie's relationship to cheerful Mr. Lowther, and with the fact that she had told her class, first thing: "I have spent Easter at the little Roman village of Cramond." That was where Mr. Lowther lived all alone in a big house with a housekeeper.

"Don't tell Miss Brodie," said Sandy.

"Why?" said Jenny.

Sandy made an effort to work out her reasons. They were also connected with something that had happened in the course of the morning, when Miss Brodie, wanting a supply of drawing books and charcoal to start the new term, sent Monica Douglas to fetch them from the art room, then called her back, and sent Rose Stanley instead. When Rose returned, laden with drawing books and boxes of chalks, she was followed by Teddy Lloyd, similarly laden. He dumped his books and asked Miss Brodie if she had enjoyed her holiday. She gave him her hand, and said she had been exploring Cramond, one should not neglect these little nearby seaports.

"I shouldn't have thought there was much to *explore* at Cramond," said Mr. Lloyd, smiling at her with his golden forelock falling into his eye.

"It has quite a lot of charm," she said. "And did you go away at all?"

"I've been painting," he said in his hoarse voice. "Family portraits."

Rose had been stacking the drawing books into their cupboard and now she had finished. As she turned, Miss Brodie put her arm round Rose's shoulder and thanked Mr. Lloyd for his help, as if she and Rose were one.

"N'tall," said Mr. Lloyd, meaning, "Not at all," and went away. It was then Jenny whispered, "Rose has changed in the holidays, hasn't she?"

This was true. Her fair hair was cut shorter and was very shiny. Her cheeks were paler and thinner, her eyes less wide open, set with the lids half-shut as if she were posing for a special photograph.

"Perhaps she has got the Change," said Sandy. Miss Brodie called it the Menarche but so far when they tried to use this word amongst themselves it made them giggle and feel shy.

Later in the afternoon after school, Jenny said: "I'd better tell Miss Brodie about the man I met."

Sandy replied, "Don't tell Miss Brodie."

"Why not?" said Jenny.

Sandy tried, but could not think why not, except to feel an unfinished quality about Miss Brodie and her holiday at Cramond, and her sending Rose to Mr. Lloyd. So she said, "The policewoman said to try to forget what happened. Perhaps Miss Brodie would make you remember it."

Jenny said, "That's what I think, too."

And so they forgot the man by the Water of Leith and remembered the policewoman more and more as the term wore on.

During the last few months of Miss Brodie's teaching she made herself adorable. She did not exhort or bicker and even when hard pressed was irritable only with Mary Macgregor. That spring she monopolized with her class the benches under the elm from which could be seen an endless avenue of dark pink May trees, and heard the trotting of horses in time to the turning wheels of light carts returning home empty by a hidden lane from their early morning rounds. Not far off, like a promise of next year, a group of girls from the Senior school were doing first-form Latin. Once, the Latin mistress was moved by the spring of the year to sing a folk-song to fit the clip-clop of the ponies and carts, and Miss Brodie held up her index finger with delight so that her own girls should listen too.

> *Nundinarum adest dies,*
> *Mulus ille nos vehet*
> *Eie, curre, mule, mule,*
> *I tolutari gradu.*

That spring Jenny's mother was expecting a baby, there was no rain worth remembering, the grass, the sun and the birds lost their self-centered winter mood and began to think of others. Miss Brodie's old love story was newly embroidered, under the elm, with curious threads: it appeared that while on leave from the war, her late fiancé had frequently taken her out sailing in a fishing boat and that they had spent some of their merriest times among the rocks and pebbles of a small seaport. "Sometimes Hugh would sing, he had a rich tenor voice. At other times he fell silent and would set up his easel and paint. He was very talented at both arts, but I think the painter was the real Hugh."

This was the first time the girls had heard of Hugh's artistic leanings. Sandy puzzled over this and took counsel with Jenny, and it came to them both that Miss Brodie was making her new love story fit the old. Thereafter the two girls listened with double ears, and the rest of the class with single.

Sandy was fascinated by this method of making patterns with facts, and was divided between her admiration for the technique and the pressing need to prove Miss Brodie guilty of misconduct.

"What about those incriminating documents?" said Sergeant Anne Grey in her jolly friendly manner. She really was very thrilling.

Sandy and Jenny completed the love correspondence between Miss Brodie and the singing master at half-term. They were staying in the small town of Crail on the coast of Fife with Jenny's aunt who showed herself suspicious of their notebook; and so they took it off to a neighboring village along the coast by bus, and sat at the mouth of a cave to finish the work. It had been a delicate question how to present Miss Brodie in both a favorable and an unfavorable light, for now, as their last term with Miss Brodie drew to a close, nothing less than this was demanded.

That intimacy had taken place was to be established. But not on an ordinary bed. That had been a thought suitable only for the enlivening of a sewing period, but Miss Brodie was entitled to something like a status. They placed Miss Brodie on the lofty lion's back of Arthur's Seat, with only the sky for roof and bracken for a bed. The broad parkland rolled away beneath the gaze to the accompanying flash and crash of a thunderstorm. It was here that Gordon Lowther, shy and smiling, small, with a long body and short legs, his red-gold hair and moustache, found her.

"Took her," Jenny had said when they had first talked it over.

"Took her—well, no. She gave herself to him."

"She gave herself to him," Jenny said, "although she would fain have given herself to another."

The last letter in the series, completed at mid-term, went as follows:

My Own Delightful Gordon,

Your letter has moved me deeply as you may imagine. But alas, I must ever decline to be Mrs. Lowther. My reasons are twofold. I am dedicated to my Girls as is Madame Pavlova, and there is another in my life whose mutual love reaches out to me beyond the bounds of Time and Space. He is Teddy Lloyd! Intimacy has never taken place with him. He is married to another. One day in the art room we melted into each other's arms and knew the truth. But I was proud of giving myself to you when you came and took me in the bracken on Arthur's Seat while the storm raged about us. If I am in a certain condition I shall place the infant in the care of a worthy shepherd and his wife, and we can discuss it calmly as platonic acquaintances. I may permit misconduct to occur again from time to time as an outlet because I am in my Prime. We can also have many a breezy day in the fishing boat at sea.

I wish to inform you that your housekeeper fills me with

anxiety like John Knox. I fear she is rather narrow, which arises from an ignorance of culture and the Italian scene. Pray ask her not to say, "You know your way up," when I call at your house at Cramond. She should take me up and show me in. Her knees are not stiff. She is only pretending that they are.

I love to hear you singing "Hey Johnnie Cope." But were I to receive a proposal of marriage tomorrow from the Lord Lyon King of Arms I would decline it.

Allow me, in conclusion, to congratulate you warmly upon your sexual intercourse, as well as your singing.

With fondest joy,<br>Jean Brodie

When they had finished writing this letter they read the whole correspondence from beginning to end. They were undecided then whether to cast this incriminating document out to sea or to bury it. The act of casting things out to sea from the shore was, as they knew, more difficult than it sounded. But Sandy found a damp hole half-hidden by a stone at the back of the cave and they pressed into it the notebook containing the love correspondence of Miss Jean Brodie, and never saw it again. They walked back to Crail over the very springy turf full of fresh plans and fondest joy.

CHAPTER FOUR

"I have enough gunpowder in this jar to blow up this school," said Miss Lockhart in even tones.

She stood behind her bench in her white linen coat, with both hands on a glass jar three-quarters full of a dark gray powder. The extreme hush that fell was only what she expected, for she always opened the first science lesson with these words and with the gunpowder before her, and the first science lesson was no lesson at all, but a naming of the most impressive objects in the science room. Every eye was upon the jar. Miss Lockhart lifted it and placed it carefully in a cupboard which was filled with similar jars full of different-colored crystals and powders.

"These are bunsen burners, this is a test-tube, this is a pipette, that's a burette, that is a retort, a crucible . . ."

Thus she established her mysterious priesthood. She was quite the nicest teacher in the Senior school. But they were all the nicest teachers in the school. It was a new life altogether, almost a new school. Here were no gaunt mistresses like Miss Gaunt, those many who had stalked past Miss Brodie in the corridors saying good morning with predestination in their smiles. The teachers here seemed to have no thoughts of anyone's personalities apart from their speciality in life, whether it was mathematics, Latin or science. They treated the new first-formers as if they were not real, but only to be dealt with, like symbols of algebra, and Miss Brodie's pupils found this refreshing at first. Wonderful, too, during the first week was the curriculum of dazzling new subjects, and the rushing to and from room to room to keep to the time-table. Their days were now filled with unfamiliar shapes and sounds which were magically disso- ciated from ordinary life, the great circles and triangles of geometry, the hieroglyphics of Greek on the page and the curious hisses and spits some of the Greek sounds made from the teacher's lips—"psst . . . psooch . . ."

A few weeks later, when meanings appeared from among these sights and sounds, it was difficult to remember the party-game effect of that first week, and that Greek had ever made hisses and spits or that "mensarum" had sounded like something out of nonsense verse. The Modern side, up to the third form, was distinguished from the Classical only by modern or ancient languages. The girls on the Mod- ern side were doing German and Spanish, which, when rehearsed between periods, made the astonishing noises of foreign stations got in passing on the wireless. A mademoiselle with black frizzy hair, who wore a striped shirt with real cufflinks, was pronouncing French in a foreign way which never really caught on. The science room smelled unevenly of the Canongate on that day of the winter's walk with Miss Brodie, the bunsen burners, and the sweet autumnal smoke that drifted in from the first burning leaves. Here in the science room—strictly not to be referred to as a laboratory—lessons were called experiments, which gave everyone the feeling that not even Miss Lockhart knew what the result might be, and anything might occur between their going in and coming out, and the school might blow up.

Here, during that first week, an experiment was conducted which involved magnesium in a test-tube which was made to tickle a bunsen flame. Eventually, from different parts of the room, great white magnesium flares shot out of the test-tubes and were caught in larger glass vessels which waited for the purpose. Mary Macgregor took fright and ran along a single lane between two benches, met with a white flame, and ran back to meet another brilliant tongue of fire. Hither and thither she ran in panic between the benches until she was caught and induced to calm down, and she was told not to be so stupid by Miss Lockhart, who already had learned the exasperation of looking at Mary's face, its two eyes, nose and mouth, with nothing more to say about it.

Once, in later years, when Sandy was visited by Rose Stanley, and they fell to speaking of dead Mary Macgregor, Sandy said,

"When any ill befalls me I wish I had been nicer to Mary."

"How were we to know?" said Rose.

And Miss Brodie, sitting in the window of the Braid Hills Hotel with Sandy, had said: "I wonder if it was Mary Macgregor betrayed me? Perhaps I should have been kinder to Mary."

The Brodie set might easily have lost its identity at this time, not only because Miss Brodie had ceased to preside over their days which were now so brisk with the getting of knowledge from unsoulful experts, but also because the headmistress intended them to be dispersed.

She laid a scheme and it failed. It was too ambitious, it aimed at ridding the school of Miss Brodie and breaking up the Brodie set in the one stroke.

She befriended Mary Macgregor, thinking her to be gullible and bribable, and underrating her stupidity. She remembered that Mary had, in common with all Miss Brodie's girls, applied to go on the Classical side, but had been refused. Now Miss Mackay changed her mind and allowed her to take at least Latin. In return she expected to be informed concerning Miss Brodie. But as the only reason that Mary wanted to learn Latin was to please Miss Brodie, the headmistress got no further. Give the girl tea as she might, Mary simply did not understand what was required of her and thought all the teachers were in league together, Miss Brodie and all.

"You won't be seeing much of Miss Brodie," said Miss Mackay, "now that you are in the Senior school."

"I see," said Mary, taking the remark as an edict rather than a probing question.

Miss Mackay laid another scheme and the scheme undid her. There was a highly competitive house system in the Senior school, whose four houses were named Holyrood, Melrose, Argyll and Biggar. Miss Mackay saw to it that the Brodie girls were as far as possible placed in different houses. Jenny was put in Holyrood, Sandy with Mary Macgregor in Melrose, Monica and Eunice went into Argyll and Rose Stanley into Biggar. They were therefore obliged to compete with each other in every walk of life within the school and on the wind-swept hockey fields which lay like the graves of the martyrs exposed to the weather in an outer suburb. It was the team spirit, they were told, that counted now, every house must go all out for the shield and turn up on Saturday mornings to yell encouragement to the house. Inter-house friendships must not suffer, of course, but the team spirit . . .

This phrase was enough for the Brodie set who, after two years at Miss Brodie's, had been well directed as to its meaning.

"Phrases like 'the team spirit' are always employed to cut across individualism, love and personal loyalties," she had said. "Ideas like 'the team spirit,' " she said, "ought not to be enjoined on the female sex, especially if they are of that dedicated nature whose virtues from time immemorial have been utterly opposed to the concept. Florence Nightingale knew nothing of the team spirit, her mission was to save life regardless of the team to which it belonged. Cleopatra knew nothing of the team spirit if you read your Shakespeare. Take Helen of Troy. And the Queen of England, it is true she attends international sport, but she has to, it is all empty show, she is concerned only with the King's health and antiques. Where would the team spirit have got Sybil Thorndike? *She* is the great actress and the rest of the cast have got the team spirit. Pavlova . . ."

Perhaps Miss Brodie had foreseen this moment of the future when her team of six should be exposed to the appeal of four different competing spirits, Argyll, Melrose, Biggar and Holyrood. It was impossible to know how much Miss Brodie planned by deliberation, or how much she worked by instinct alone. However, in this, the first test of her strength, she had the victory. Not one of the senior house-prefects personified an argument to touch Sybil Thorndike and Cleopatra. The Brodie set would as soon have entered the Girl Guides as the team spirit. Not only they, but at least ten other girls who had passed through Brodie hands kept away from the playing grounds except under compulsion. No one, save Eunice Gardiner, got near to being put in any team to try her spirit upon. Everyone agreed that Eunice was so good on the field, she could not help it.

On most Saturday afternoons Miss Brodie entertained her old set to tea and listened to their new experiences. Herself, she told them, she did not think much of her new pupils' potentialities, and she described some of her new little girls and made the old ones laugh, which bound her set together more than ever and made them feel chosen. Sooner or later she enquired what they were doing in the art class, for now the girls were taught by golden-locked, one-armed Teddy Lloyd.

There was always a great deal to tell about the art lesson. Their

first day, Mr. Lloyd found difficulty in keeping order. After so
many unfamiliar packed hours and periods of different exact subjects, the girls immediately felt the relaxing nature of the art room,
and brimmed over with relaxation. Mr. Lloyd shouted at them in his
hoarse voice to shut up. This was most bracing.

He was attempting to explain the nature and appearance of an
ellipse by holding up a saucer in his one right hand, high above his
head, then lower. But his romantic air and his hoarse "Shut up" had
produced a reaction of giggles varying in tone and pitch.

"If you girls don't shut up I'll smash this saucer to the floor," he
said.

They tried but failed to shut up.

He smashed the saucer to the floor.

Amid the dead silence which followed he picked on Rose Stanley
and indicating the fragments of saucer on the floor, he said, "You
with the profile—pick this up."

He turned away and went and did something else at the other
end of the long room for the rest of the period, while the girls looked
anew at Rose Stanley's profile, marveled at Mr. Lloyd's style, and
settled down to drawing a bottle set up in front of a curtain. Jenny
remarked to Sandy that Miss Brodie really had good taste.

"He has an artistic temperament, of course," said Miss Brodie
when she was told about the saucer. And when she heard that he had
called Rose "you with the profile," she looked at Rose in a special
way, while Sandy looked at Miss Brodie.

The interest of Sandy and Jenny in Miss Brodie's lovers had entered a new phase since they had buried their last composition and
moved up to the Senior school. They no longer saw everything in a
sexual context, it was now rather a question of plumbing the deep
heart's score. The world of pure sex seemed years away. Jenny had
turned twelve. Her mother had recently given birth to a baby boy,
and the event had not moved them even to speculate upon its origin.

"There's not much time for sex research in the Senior school,"
Sandy said.

"I feel I'm past it," said Jenny. This was strangely true, and she
did not again experience her early sense of erotic wonder in life until
suddenly one day when she was nearly forty, an actress of moderate
reputation married to a theatrical manager. It happened she was
standing with a man whom she did not know very well outside a
famous building in Rome, waiting for the rain to stop. She was surprised by a reawakening of that same buoyant and airy discovery of
sex, a total sensation which it was impossible to say was physical or

mental, only that it contained the lost and guileless delight of her eleventh year. She supposed herself to have fallen in love with the man, who might, she thought, have been moved towards her in his own way out of a world of his own, the associations of which were largely unknown to her. There was nothing whatever to be done about it, for Jenny had been contentedly married for sixteen years past; but the concise happening filled her with astonishment whenever it came to mind in later days, and with a sense of the hidden possibilities in all things.

"Mr. Lowther's housekeeper," said Miss Brodie one Saturday afternoon, "has left him. It is most ungrateful, that house at Cramond is easily run. I never cared for her as you know. I think she resented my position as Mr. Lowther's friend and confidante, and seemed dissatisfied by my visits. Mr. Lowther is composing some music for a song at the moment. He ought to be encouraged."

The next Saturday she told the girls that the sewing sisters, Miss Ellen and Miss Alison Kerr, had taken on the temporary task of housekeepers to Mr. Lowther, since they lived near Cramond.

"I think those sisters are inquisitive," Miss Brodie remarked. "They are too much in with Miss Gaunt and the Church of Scotland."

On Saturday afternoons an hour was spent on her Greek lessons, for she had insisted that Jenny and Sandy should teach her Greek at the same time as they learned it. "There is an old tradition for this practice," said Miss Brodie. "Many families in the olden days could afford to send but one child to school, whereupon that one scholar of the family imparted to the others in the evening what he had learned in the morning. I have long wanted to know the Greek language, and this scheme will also serve to impress your knowledge on your own minds. John Stuart Mill used to rise at dawn to learn Greek at the age of five, and what John Stuart Mill could do as an infant at dawn, I too can do on a Saturday afternoon in my prime."

She progressed in Greek, although she was somewhat muddled about the accents, being differently informed by Jenny and Sandy who took turns to impart to her their weekly intake of the language. But she was determined to enter and share the new life of her special girls, and what she did not regard as humane of their new concerns, or what was not within the scope of her influence, she scorned.

She said: "It is witty to say that a straight line is the shortest distance between two points, or that a circle is a plane figure bounded by one line, every point of which is equidistant from a fixed center.

It is plain witty. Everyone knows what a straight line and a circle are."

When, after the examinations at the end of the first term, she looked at the papers they had been set, she read some of the more vulnerable of the questions aloud with the greatest contempt: "A window cleaner carries a uniform 60-lb. ladder 15 ft. long, at one end of which a bucket of water weighing 40 lb. is hung. At what point must he support the ladder to carry it horizontally? Where is the c.g. of his load?" Miss Brodie looked at the paper, after reading out this question, as if to indicate that she could not believe her eyes. Many a time she gave the girls to understand that the solution to such problems would be quite useless to Sybil Thorndike, Anna Pavlova and the late Helen of Troy.

But the Brodie set were on the whole still dazzled by their new subjects. It was never the same in later years when the languages of physics and chemistry, algebra and geometry had lost their elemental strangeness and formed each an individual department of life with its own accustomed boredom, and become hard work. Even Monica Douglas, who later developed such a good brain for mathematics, was plainly never so thrilled with herself as when she first subtracted $x$ from $y$ and the result from $a$; she never afterwards looked so happy.

Rose Stanley sliced a worm down the middle with the greatest absorption during her first term's biology, although in two terms' time she shuddered at the thought and had dropped the subject. Eunice Gardiner discovered the Industrial Revolution, its right and wrongs, to such an extent that the history teacher, a vegetarian communist, had high hopes of her which were dashed within a few months when Eunice reverted to reading novels based on the life of Mary Queen of Scots. Sandy, whose handwriting was bad, spent hours forming the Greek characters in neat rows in her notebooks while Jenny took the same pride in drawing scientific apparatus for her chemistry notes. Even stupid Mary Macgregor amazed herself by understanding Caesar's Gallic Wars which as yet made no demands on her defective imagination and the words of which were easier to her than English to spell and pronounce, until suddenly one day it appeared, from an essay she had been obliged to write, that she believed the document to date from the time of Samuel Pepys; and then Mary was established in the wrong again, being tortured with probing questions, and generally led on to confess to the mirth-shaken world her notion that Latin and shorthand were one.

Miss Brodie had a hard fight of it during those first few months when the Senior school had captivated her set, displaying as did the set that capacity for enthusiasm which she herself had implanted. But having won the battle over the team spirit, she did not despair. It was evident even then that her main concern was lest the girls should become personally attached to any one of the Senior teachers, but she carefully refrained from direct attack because the teachers themselves seemed so perfectly indifferent to her brood.

By the summer term, the girls' favorite hours were those spent unbrainfully in the gymnasium, swinging about on parallel bars, hanging upside down on wall bars or climbing ropes up to the ceiling, all competing with agile Eunice to heave themselves up by hands, knees, and feet like monkeys climbing a tropical creeper, while the gym teacher, a thin gray-haired little wire, showed them what to do and shouted each order in a broad Scots accent interspersed by her short cough, on account of which she was later sent to a sanatorium in Switzerland.

By the summer term, to stave off the onslaughts of boredom, and to reconcile the necessities of the working day with their love for Miss Brodie, Sandy and Jenny had begun to apply their new-found knowledge to Miss Brodie in a merry fashion. "If Miss Brodie was weighed in air and then in water . . ." And, when Mr. Lowther seemed not quite himself at the singing lesson, they would remind each other that an immersed Jean Brodie displaces its own weight of Gordon Lowther.

Presently, in the late spring of nineteen-thirty-three, Miss Brodie's Greek lessons on a Saturday afternoon came to an end, because of the needs of Mr. Lowther who, in his house at Cramond which the girls had not yet seen, was being catered for quite willingly by those sewing mistresses, Miss Ellen and Miss Alison Kerr. Living on the coast nearby, it was simple for them to go over turn by turn and see to Mr. Lowther after school hours, and prepare his supper and lay out provision for his breakfast; it was not only simple, it was enjoyable to be doing good, and it was also profitable in a genteel way. On Saturdays either Miss Ellen or Miss Alison would count his laundry and keep house for him. On some Saturday mornings both were busy for him; Miss Ellen supervised the woman who came to clean while Miss Alison did the week's shopping. They never had been so perky or useful in their lives before, and especially not since the eldest sister had died, who had always told them what to do with their spare time as it cropped up, so that Miss Alison could never get

used to being called Miss Kerr and Miss Ellen could never find it in
her to go and get a book from the library, wanting the order from
the late Miss Kerr.

But the minister's sister, gaunt Miss Gaunt, was secretly taking
over the dead sister's office. As it became known later, Miss Gaunt
approved of their arrangement with Gordon Lowther and encouraged them to make it a permanent one for their own good and also
for private reasons connected with Miss Brodie.

Up to now, Miss Brodie's visits to Mr. Lowther had taken place
on Sundays. She always went to church on Sunday mornings, she
had a rota of different denominations and sects which included the
Free Churches of Scotland, the Established Church of Scotland, the
Methodist and the Episcopalian churches and any other church outside the Roman Catholic pale which she might discover. Her disapproval of the Church of Rome was based on her assertions that it was
a church of superstition, and that only people who did not want to
think for themselves were Roman Catholics. In some ways, her attitude was a strange one, because she was by temperament suited only
to the Roman Catholic Church; possibly it could have embraced,
even while it disciplined, her soaring and diving spirit, it might even
have normalized her. But perhaps this was the reason that she
shunned it, lover of Italy though she was, bringing to her support a
rigid Edinburgh-born side of herself when the Catholic Church was
in question, although this side was not otherwise greatly in evidence.
So she went round the various non-Roman churches instead, hardly
ever missing a Sunday morning. She was not in any doubt, she let
everyone know she was in no doubt, that God was on her side whatever her course, and so she experienced no difficulty or sense of hypocrisy in worship while at the same time she went to bed with the
singing master. Just as an excessive sense of guilt can drive people to
excessive action, so was Miss Brodie driven to it by an excessive lack
of guilt.

The side-effects of this condition were exhilarating to her special
girls in that they in some way partook of the general absolution she
had assumed to herself, and it was only in retrospect that they could
see Miss Brodie's affair with Mr. Lowther for what it was, that is to
say, in a factual light. All the time they were under her influence she
and her actions were outside the context of right and wrong. It was
twenty-five years before Sandy had so far recovered from a creeping
vision of disorder that she could look back and recognize that Miss
Brodie's defective sense of self-criticism had not been without its

beneficent and enlarging effects; by which time Sandy had already betrayed Miss Brodie and Miss Brodie was laid in her grave.

It was after morning church on Sundays that Miss Brodie would go to Cramond, there to lunch and spend the afternoon with Mr. Lowther. She spent Sunday evenings with him also, and more often than not the night, in a spirit of definite duty, if not exactly martyrdom, since her heart was with the renounced teacher of art.

Mr. Lowther, with his long body and short legs, was a shy fellow who smiled upon nearly everyone from beneath his red-gold moustache, and who won his own gentle way with nearly everybody, and who said little and sang much.

When it became certain that the Kerr sisters had taken over permanently the housekeeping for this bashful, smiling bachelor, Miss Brodie fancied he was getting thin. She announced this discovery just at a time when Jenny and Sandy had noticed a slimmer appearance in Miss Brodie and had begun to wonder, since they were nearly thirteen and their eyes were more focused on such points, if she might be physically beautiful or desirable to men. They saw her in a new way, and decided she had a certain deep romantic beauty, and that she had lost weight through her sad passion for Mr. Lloyd, and this noble undertaking of Mr. Lowther in his place, and that it suited her.

Now Miss Brodie was saying: "Mr. Lowther is looking thin these days. I have no faith in those Kerr sisters, they are skimping him, they have got skimpy minds. The supplies of food they leave behind on Saturdays are barely sufficient to see him through Sunday, let alone the remainder of the week. If only Mr. Lowther could be persuaded to move from that big house and take a flat in Edinburgh, he would be so much easier to look after. He needs looking after. But he will not be persuaded. It is impossible to persuade a man who does not disagree, but smiles."

She decided to supervise the Kerr sisters on their Saturdays at Cramond when they prepared for Mr. Lowther's domestic week ahead. "They get well paid for it," said Miss Brodie. "I shall go over and see that they order the right stuff, and sufficient." It might have seemed an audacious proposition, but the girls did not think of it this way. They heartily urged Miss Brodie to descend upon the Kerrs and to interfere, partly in anticipation of some eventful consequence, and partly because Mr. Lowther would somehow smile away any fuss; and the Kerr sisters were fairly craven; and above all, Miss Brodie was easily the equal of both sisters together, she was the

square on the hypotenuse of a right-angled triangle and they were
only the squares on the other two sides.

The Kerr sisters took Miss Brodie's intrusion quite meekly, and
that they were so unquestioning about any authority which imposed
itself upon them was the very reason why they also did not hesitate
later on to answer the subsequent questions of Miss Gaunt. Meantime Miss Brodie set about feeding Mr. Lowther up, and, since this
meant her passing Saturday afternoons at Cramond, the Brodie set
was invited to go, two by two, one pair every week, to visit her in
Mr. Lowther's residence where he smiled and patted their hair or
pulled pretty Jenny's ringlets, looking meanwhile for reproof or approval, or some such thing, at brown-eyed Jean Brodie. She gave
them tea while he smiled; and he frequently laid down his cup and
saucer, went and sat at the piano and burst into song. He sang:

> March, march, Ettrick and Teviotdale,
> *Why* the de'il dinna ye march *forward* in order?
> March, march, Eskdale and Liddesdale,
> All the Blue Bonnets are bound for the Border.

At the end of the song he would smile his overcome and bashful
smile and take his teacup again, looking up under his ginger eyebrows at Jean Brodie to see what she felt about him at the current
moment. She was Jean to him, a fact that none of the Brodie set
thought proper to mention to anyone.

She reported to Sandy and Jenny: "I made short work of those
Kerr sisters. They were starving him. Now it is I who see to the
provisions. I am a descendant, do not forget, of Willie Brodie, a man
of substance, a cabinet maker and designer of gibbets, a member of
the Town Council of Edinburgh and a keeper of two mistresses who
bore him five children between them. Blood tells. He played much
dice and fighting cocks. Eventually he was a wanted man for having
robbed the Excise Office—not that he needed the money, he was a
night burglar only for the sake of the danger in it. Of course, he was
arrested abroad and was brought back to the Tolbooth prison, but
that was mere chance. He died cheerfully on a gibbet of his own
devising in seventeen-eighty-eight. However all this may be, it is the
stuff I am made of, and I have brooked and shall brook no nonsense
from Miss Ellen and Miss Alison Kerr."

Mr. Lowther sang:

> O mother, mother, make my bed,
> O make it soft and narrow,
> For my true love died for me today.
> I'll die for him tomorrow.

Then he looked at Miss Brodie. She was, however, looking at a chipped rim of a teacup. "Mary Macgregor must have chipped it," she said. "Mary was here last Sunday with Eunice and they washed up together. Mary must have chipped it."

Outside on the summer lawn the daisies sparkled. The lawn spread wide and long, one could barely see the little wood at the end of it and even the wood belonged to Mr. Lowther, and the fields beyond. Shy, musical and gentle as he was, Mr. Lowther was a man of substance.

Now Sandy considered Miss Brodie not only to see if she was desirable, but also to find out if there was any element of surrender about her, since this was the most difficult part of the affair to realize. She had been a dominant presence rather than a physical woman like Norma Shearer or Elisabeth Bergner. Miss Brodie was now forty-three and this year when she looked so much thinner than when she had stood in the classroom or sat under the elm, her shape was pleasanter, but it was still fairly large compared with Mr. Lowther's. He was slight and he was shorter than Miss Brodie. He looked at her with love and she looked at him severely and possessively.

By the end of the summer term, when the Brodie set were all turned, or nearly turned, thirteen, Miss Brodie questioned them in their visiting pairs each week about their art lesson. The girls always took a close interest in Teddy Lloyd's art classes and in all he did, making much of details, so as to provide happy conversation with Miss Brodie when their turn came to visit her at Gordon Lowther's house at Cramond.

It was a large gabled house with a folly-turret. There were so many twists and turns in the wooded path leading up from the road, and the front lawn was so narrow, that the house could never be seen from the little distance that its size demanded and it was necessary to crane one's neck upward to see the turret at all. The back of the house was quite plain. The rooms were large and gloomy with Venetian blinds. The banisters began with a pair of carved lions' heads and carried up and up, round and round, as far as the eye could reach. All the furniture was large and carved, dotted with ornaments of silver and rose-colored glass. The library on the ground floor where Miss Brodie entertained them held a number of glass bookcases so dim in their interiors that it was impossible to see the titles of the books without peering close. A grand piano was placed across one corner of the room, and on it, in summer, stood a bowl of roses.

This was a great house to explore and on days when Miss Brodie was curiously occupied in the kitchen with some enormous preparation for the next day's eating—in those months when her obsession with Mr. Lowther's food had just begun—the girls were free to roam up the big stairs, hand-in-hand with awe, and to open the doors and look into the dust-sheeted bedrooms and especially into two rooms that people had forgotten to furnish properly, one of which had nothing in it but a large desk, not even a carpet, another of which was empty except for an electric light bulb and a large blue jug. These rooms were icy cold, whatever the time of year. On their descending the stairs after these expeditions, Mr. Lowther would often be standing waiting for them, shyly smiling in the hall with his hands clasped together as if he hoped that everything was to their satisfaction. He took roses from the bowl and presented one each to the girls before they went home.

Mr. Lowther never seemed quite at home in his home, although he had been born there. He always looked at Miss Brodie for approval before he touched anything or opened a cupboard as if, really, he was not allowed to touch without permission. The girls decided that perhaps his mother, now four years dead, had kept him under all his life, and he was consequently unable to see himself as master of the house.

He sat silently and gratefully watching Miss Brodie entertain the two girls whose turn it was to be there, when she had already started on her project of fattening him up which was to grow to such huge proportions that her food-supplying mania was the talk of Miss Ellen and Miss Alison Kerr, and so of the Junior school. One day, when Sandy and Jenny were on the visiting rota, she gave Mr. Lowther, for tea alone, an admirable lobster salad, some sandwiches of liver paste, cake and tea, followed by a bowl of porridge and cream. These were served to him on a tray for himself alone, you could see he was on a special diet. Sandy was anxious to see if Mr. Lowther would manage the porridge as well as everything else. But he worked his way through everything with impassive obedience while she questioned the girls: "What are you doing in the art class just now?"

"We're at work on the poster competition."

"Mr. Lloyd—is he well?"

"Oh yes, he's great fun. He showed us his studio two weeks ago."

"Which studio, where? At his house?"—although Miss Brodie knew perfectly well.

"Yes, it's a great long attic, it——"

"Did you meet his wife, what was she like? What did she say, did she give you tea? What are the children like, what did you do when you got there? . . ."

She did not attempt to conceal from her munching host her keen interest in the art master. Mr. Lowther's eyes looked mournful and he ate on. Sandy and Jenny knew that similar questions had been pressed upon Mary Macgregor and Eunice Gardiner the previous week, and upon Rose Stanley and Monica Douglas the week before. But Miss Brodie could not hear enough versions of the same story if it involved Teddy Lloyd, and now that the girls had been to his house—a large and shabby, a warm and unconventional establishment in the north of Edinburgh—Miss Brodie was in a state of high excitement by very contact with these girls who had lately breathed Lloyd air.

"How many children?" said Miss Brodie, her teapot poised.

"Five, I think," said Sandy.

"Six, I think," said Jenny, "counting the baby."

"There are lots of babies," said Sandy.

"Roman Catholics, of course," said Miss Brodie, addressing this to Mr. Lowther.

"But the littlest baby," said Jenny, "you've forgotten to count the wee baby. That makes six."

Miss Brodie poured tea and cast a glance at Gordon Lowther's plate.

"Gordon," she said, "a cake."

He shook his head and said softly, as if soothing her, "Oh, no, no."

"Yes, Gordon. It is full of goodness." And she made him eat a Chester cake, and spoke to him in a slightly more Edinburgh way than usual, so as to make up to him by both means for the love she was giving to Teddy Lloyd instead of to him.

"You must be fattened up, Gordon," she said. "You must be two stone the better before I go my holidays."

He smiled as best he could at everyone in turn, with his drooped head and slowly moving jaws. Meanwhile Miss Brodie said:

"And Mrs. Lloyd—is she a woman, would you say, in her prime?"

"Perhaps not yet," said Sandy.

"Well, Mrs. Lloyd may be past it," Jenny said. "It's difficult to say with her hair being long on her shoulders. It makes her look young although she may not be."

"She looks really like as if she won't have any prime," Sandy said.

"The word 'like' is redundant in that sentence. What is Mrs. Lloyd's Christian name?"

"Deirdre," said Jenny, and Miss Brodie considered the name as if it were new to her although she had heard it last week from Mary and Eunice, and the week before that from Rose and Monica, and so had Mr. Lowther. Outside, light rain began to fall on Mr. Lowther's leaves.

"Celtic," said Miss Brodie.

Sandy loitered at the kitchen door waiting for Miss Brodie to come for a walk by the sea. Miss Brodie was doing something to an enormous ham prior to putting it into a huge pot. Miss Brodie's new ventures into cookery in no way diminished her previous grandeur, for everything she prepared for Gordon Lowther seemed to be large, whether it was family-sized puddings to last him out the week, or joints of beef or lamb, or great angry-eyed whole salmon.

"I must get this on for Mr. Lowther's supper," she said to Sandy, "and see that he gets his supper before I go home tonight."

She always so far kept up the idea that she went home on these week-end nights and left Mr. Lowther alone in the big house. So far the girls had found no evidence to the contrary, nor were they ever to do so; a little later Miss Ellen Kerr was brought to the headmistress by Miss Gaunt to testify to having found Miss Brodie's nightdress under a pillow of the double bed on which Mr. Lowther took his sleep. She had found it while changing the linen; it was the pillow on the far side of the bed, nearest the wall, under which the nightdress had been discovered folded neatly.

"How do you know the nightdress was Miss Brodie's?" demanded Miss Mackay, the sharp-minded woman, who smelled her prey very near and yet saw it very far. She stood with a hand on the back of her chair, bending forward full of ears.

"One must draw one's own conclusions," said Miss Gaunt.

"I am addressing Miss Ellen."

"Yes, one must draw one's own conclusions," said Miss Ellen, with her tight-drawn red-veined cheeks looking shiny and flustered. "It was crêpe de Chine."

"It is non proven," said Miss Mackay, sitting down to her desk. "Come back to me," she said, "if you have proof positive. What did you do with the garment? Did you confront Miss Brodie with it?"

"Oh, no, Miss Mackay," said Miss Ellen.

"You should have confronted her with it. You should have said, 'Miss Brodie, come here a minute, can you explain this?' That's what you should have said. Is the nightdress still there?"

"Oh, no, it's gone."

"She's that brazen," said Miss Gaunt.

All this was conveyed to Sandy by the headmistress herself at that subsequent time when Sandy looked at her distastefully through her little eyes and, evading the quite crude question which the coarse-faced woman asked her, was moved by various other considerations to betray Miss Brodie.

"But I must organize the dear fellow's food before I go home tonight," Miss Brodie said in the summer of nineteen-thirty-three while Sandy leaned against the kitchen door with her legs longing to be running along the sea shore. Jenny came and joined her, and together they waited upon Miss Brodie, and saw on the vast old kitchen table the piled-up provisions of the morning's shopping. Outside on the dining-room table stood large bowls of fruit with boxes of dates piled on top of them, as if this were Christmas and the kitchen that of a holiday hotel.

"Won't all this give Mr. Lowther a stoppage?" Sandy said to Jenny.

"Not if he eats his greens," said Jenny.

While they waited for Miss Brodie to dress the great ham like the heroine she was, there came the sound of Mr. Lowther at the piano in the library singing rather slowly and mournfully:

> All people that on earth do dwell,
> Sing to the Lord with cheerful voice.
> Him serve with mirth, his praise forth tell,
> Come ye before him and rejoice.

Mr. Lowther was the choir-master and an Elder of the church, and had not yet been quietly advised to withdraw from these offices by Mr. Gaunt the minister, brother of Miss Gaunt, following the finding of the nightdress under the pillow next to his.

Presently, as she put the ham on a low gas and settled the lid on the pot, Miss Brodie joined in the psalm richly, contralto-wise, giving the notes more body:

O enter then his gates with praise,
Approach with joy his courts unto.

The rain had stopped and was only now hanging damply within the salt air. All along the sea front Miss Brodie questioned the girls, against the rhythm of the waves, about the appointments of Teddy Lloyd's house, the kind of tea they got, how vast and light was the studio, and what was said.

"He looked very romantic in his own studio," Sandy said.

"How was that?"

"I think it was his having only one arm," said Jenny.

"But he always has only one arm."

"He did more than usual with it," said Sandy.

"He was waving it about," Jenny said. "There was a lovely view from the studio window. He's proud of it."

"The studio is in the attic, I presume?"

"Yes, all along the top of the house. There is a new portrait he has done of his family, it's a little bit amusing, it starts with himself, very tall, then his wife. Then all the little children graded downwards to the baby on the floor, it makes a diagonal line across the canvas."

"What makes it amusing?" said Miss Brodie.

"They are all facing square and they all look serious," Sandy said. "You are supposed to laugh at it."

Miss Brodie laughed a little at this. There was a wonderful sunset across the distant sky, reflected in the sea, streaked with blood and puffed with avenging purple and gold as if the end of the world had come without intruding on every-day life.

"There's another portrait," Jenny said, "not finished yet, of Rose."

"He has been painting Rose?"

"Yes."

"Rose has been sitting for him?"

"Yes, for about a month."

Miss Brodie was very excited. "Rose didn't mention this," she said.

Sandy halted. "Oh, I forgot. It was supposed to be a surprise. You aren't supposed to know."

"What, the portrait, I am to see it?"

Sandy looked confused, for she was not sure how Rose had meant her portrait to be a surprise to Miss Brodie.

Jenny said, "Oh, Miss Brodie, it is the fact that she's sitting for

Mr. Lloyd that she wanted to keep for a surprise." Sandy realized, then, that this was right.

"Ah," said Miss Brodie, well pleased. "That is thoughtful of Rose."

Sandy was jealous, because Rose was not supposed to be thoughtful.

"What is she wearing for her portrait?" said Miss Brodie.

"Her gym tunic," Sandy said.

"Sitting sideways," Jenny said.

"In profile," said Miss Brodie.

Miss Brodie stopped a man to buy a lobster for Mr. Lowther. When this was done she said:

"Rose is bound to be painted many times. She may well sit for Mr. Lloyd on future occasions, she is one of the crème de la crème."

It was said in an enquiring tone. The girls understood she was trying quite hard to piece together a whole picture from their random remarks.

Jenny accordingly let fall, "Oh, yes, Mr. Lloyd wants to paint Rose in red velvet."

And Sandy added, "Mrs. Lloyd has a bit of red velvet to put round her, they were trying it round her."

"Are you to return?" said Miss Brodie.

"Yes, all of us," Sandy said. "Mr. Lloyd thinks we're a jolly nice set."

"Have you not thought it remarkable," said Miss Brodie, "that it is you six girls that Mr. Lloyd has chosen to invite to his studio?"

"Well, we're a set," said Jenny.

"Has he invited any other girls from the school?"—but Miss Brodie knew the answer.

"Oh, no, only us."

"It is because you are mine," said Miss Brodie. "I mean of my stamp and cut, and I am in my prime."

Sandy and Jenny had not given much thought to the fact of the art master's inviting them as a group. Indeed, there was something special in his acceptance of the Brodie set. There was a mystery here to be worked out, and it was clear that when he thought of them he thought of Miss Brodie.

"He always asks about you," Sandy said to Miss Brodie, "as soon as he sees us."

"Yes, Rose did tell me that," said Miss Brodie.

Suddenly, like migrating birds, Sandy and Jenny were of one mind for a run and without warning they ran along the pebbly beach into the air which was full of sunset, returning to Miss Brodie to hear of her forthcoming summer holiday when she was going to leave the fattened-up Mr. Lowther, she was afraid, to fend for himself with the aid of the Misses Kerr, and was going abroad, not to Italy this year but to Germany, where Hitler was become Chancellor, a prophet-figure like Thomas Carlyle, and more reliable than Mussolini; the German brownshirts, she said, were exactly the same as the Italian black, only more reliable.

Jenny and Sandy were going to a farm for the summer holidays, where in fact the name of Miss Brodie would not very much be on their lips or in their minds after the first two weeks, and instead they would make hay and follow the sheep about. It was always difficult to realize during term times that the world of Miss Brodie might be half forgotten, as were the worlds of the school houses, Holyrood, Melrose, Argyll and Biggar.

"I wonder if Mr. Lowther would care for sweetbreads done with rice," Miss Brodie said.

### CHAPTER FIVE

"Why, it's like Miss Brodie!" said Sandy. "It's terribly like Miss Brodie." Then, perceiving that what she had said had accumulated a meaning between its passing her lips and reaching the ears of Mr. and Mrs. Lloyd, she said, "Though of course it's Rose, it's more like Rose, it's terribly like Rose."

Teddy Lloyd shifted the new portrait so that it stood in a different light. It still looked like Miss Brodie.

Deirdre Lloyd said, "I haven't met Miss Brodie I don't think. Is she fair?"

"No," said Teddy Lloyd in his hoarse way, "she's dark."

Sandy saw that the head on the portrait was fair, it was Rose's portrait all right. Rose was seated in profile by a window in her gym dress, her hands palm-downwards, one on each knee. Where was the resemblance to Miss Brodie? It was the profile perhaps; it was the forehead, perhaps; it was the type of stare from Rose's blue eyes, perhaps, which was like the dominating stare from Miss Brodie's brown. The portrait was very like Miss Brodie.

"It's Rose, all right," Sandy said, and Deirdre Lloyd looked at her.

"Do you like it?" said Teddy Lloyd.

"Yes, it's lovely."

"Well, that's all that matters."

Sandy continued looking at it through her very small eyes, and while she was doing so Teddy Lloyd drew the piece of sheeting over the portrait with a casual flip of his only arm.

Deirdre Lloyd had been the first woman to dress up as a peasant whom Sandy had ever met, and peasant women were to be fashionable for the next thirty years or more. She wore a fairly long full-gathered dark skirt, a bright green blouse with the sleeves rolled up, a necklace of large painted wooden beads and gipsy-looking earrings. Round her waist was a bright red wide belt. She wore dark brown stockings and sandals of dark green suède. In this, and various other costumes of similar kind, Dierdre was depicted on canvas in different parts of the studio. She had an attractive near-laughing voice. She said:

"We've got a new one of Rose. Teddy, show Sandy the new one of Rose."

"It isn't quite at a stage for looking at."

"Well, what about Red Velvet? Show Sandy that—Teddy did a splendid portrait of Rose last summer, we swathed her in red velvet, and we've called it Red Velvet."

Teddy Lloyd had brought out a canvas from behind a few others. He stood it in the light on an easel. Sandy looked at it with her tiny eyes which it was astonishing that anyone could trust.

The portrait was like Miss Brodie. Sandy said, "I like the colors."

"Does it resemble Miss Brodie?" said Deirdre Lloyd with her near-laughter.

"Miss Brodie is a woman in her prime," said Sandy, "but there is a resemblance now you mention it."

Deirdre Lloyd said: "Rose was only fourteen at the time; it makes her look very mature, but she is very mature."

The swathing of crimson velvet was so arranged that it did two things at once, it made Rose look one-armed like the artist himself, and it showed the curves of her breast to be more developed than they were, even now, when Rose was fifteen. Also, the picture was like Miss Brodie, and this was the main thing about it and the main mystery. Rose had a large-boned pale face. Miss Brodie's bones were small, although her eyes, nose and mouth were large. It was difficult to see how Teddy Lloyd had imposed the dark and Roman face of Miss Brodie on that of pale Rose, but he had done so.

Sandy looked again at the other recent portraits in the studio, Teddy Lloyd's wife, his children, some unknown sitters. They were none of them like Miss Brodie.

Then she saw a drawing lying on top of a pile on the work-table. It was Miss Brodie leaning against a lamp post in the Lawnmarket with a working woman's shawl around her; on closer inspection it proved to be Monica Douglas with the high cheekbones and long nose. Sandy said:

"I didn't know Monica sat for you."

"I've done one or two preliminary sketches. Don't you think that setting's rather good for Monica? Here's one of Eunice in her harlequin outfit, I thought she looked rather well in it."

Sandy was vexed. These girls, Monica and Eunice, had not said anything to the others about their being painted by the art master. But now they were all fifteen there was a lot they did not tell each other. She looked more closely at this picture of Eunice.

Eunice had worn the harlequin dress for a school performance. Small and neat and sharp-featured as she was, in the portrait she looked like Miss Brodie. In amongst her various bewilderments Sandy was fascinated by the economy of Teddy Lloyd's method, as she had been four years earlier by Miss Brodie's variations on her love story, when she had attached to her first, war-time lover the attributes of the art master and the singing master who had then newly entered her orbit. Teddy Lloyd's method of presentation was similar, it was economical, and it always seemed afterwards to Sandy that where there was a choice of various courses, the most economical was the best, and that the course to be taken was the most expedient and most suitable at the time for all the objects in hand. She acted on this principle when the time came for her to betray Miss Brodie.

Jenny had done badly in her last term's examinations and was mostly, these days, at home working up her subjects. Sandy had the definite feeling that the Brodie set, not to mention Miss Brodie herself, was getting out of hand. She thought it perhaps a good thing that the set might split up.

From somewhere below one of the Lloyd children started to yell, and then another, and then a chorus. Deirdre Lloyd disappeared with a swing of her peasant skirt to see to all her children. The Lloyds were Catholics and so were made to have a lot of children by force.

"One day," said Teddy Lloyd as he stacked up his sketches before taking Sandy down to tea, "I would like to do all you Brodie girls, one by one and then all together." He tossed his head to move back the golden lock of his hair from his eyes. "It would be nice to do you all together," he said, "and see what sort of a group portrait I could make of you."

Sandy thought this might be an attempt to keep the Brodie set together at the expense of the newly glimpsed individuality of its members. She turned on him in her new manner of sudden irritability and said, "We'd look like one big Miss Brodie, I suppose."

He laughed in a delighted way and looked at her more closely, as if for the first time. She looked back just as closely through her little eyes, with the near-blackmailing insolence of her knowledge. Whereupon he kissed her long and wetly. He said in his hoarse voice, "That'll teach you to look at an artist like that."

She started to run to the door, wiping her mouth dry with the back of her hand, but he caught her with his one arm and said: "There's no need to run away. You're just about the ugliest little thing I've ever seen in my life." He walked out and left her standing in the studio, and there was nothing for her to do but to follow him downstairs. Deirdre Lloyd's voice called from the sitting-room. "In here, Sandy."

She spent most of the tea time trying to sort out her preliminary feelings in the matter, which was difficult because of the children who were present and making demands on the guest. The eldest boy, who was eight, turned on the wireless and began to sing in mincing English tones, "Oh play to me, Gipsy" to the accompaniment of Henry Hall's Band. The other three children were making various kinds of din. Above this noise Dierdre Lloyd requested Sandy to call her Deirdre rather than Mrs. Lloyd. And so Sandy did not have much opportunity to discover how she was feeling inside herself about Teddy Lloyd's kiss and his words, and to decide whether she was insulted or not. He now said, brazenly, "And you can call me Teddy outside of school." Amongst themselves, in any case, the girls called him Teddy the Paint. Sandy looked from one to the other of the Lloyds.

"I've heard such a lot about Miss Brodie from the girls," Deirdre was saying. "I really must ask her to tea. D'you think she'd like to come?"

"No," said Teddy.

"Why?" said Deirdre, not that it semed to matter, she was so languid and long armed, lifting the plate of biscuits from the table and passing them round without moving from the low stool on which she sat.

"You kids stop that row or you leave the room," Teddy declared.

"Bring Miss Brodie to tea," Deirdre said to Sandy.

"She won't come," Teddy said, "—will she, Sandy?"

"She's awfully busy," Sandy said.

"Pass me a fag," said Deirdre.

"Is she still looking after Lowther?" said Teddy.

"Well, yes, a bit——"

"Lowther," said Teddy, waving his only arm, "must have a way with women. He's got half the female staff of the school looking after him. Why doesn't he employ a housekeeper?—He's got plenty of money, no wife, no kids, no rent to pay, it's his own house. Why doesn't he get a proper housekeeper?"

"I think he likes Miss Brodie," Sandy said.

"But what does she see in him?"

"He sings to her," Sandy said, suddenly sharp.

Deirdre laughed. "Miss Brodie sounds a bit queer, I must say. What age is she?"

"Jean Brodie," said Teddy, "is a magnificent woman in her prime." He got up, tossing back his lock of hair, and left the room.

Deirdre blew a cloud of reflective smoke and stubbed out her cigarette, and Sandy said she would have to go now.

Mr. Lowther had caused Miss Brodie a good deal of worry in the past two years. There had been a time when it seemed he might be thinking of marrying Miss Alison Kerr, and another time when he seemed to favor Miss Ellen, all the while being in love with Miss Brodie herself, who refused him all but her bed-fellowship and her catering.

He tired of food, for it was making him fat and weary and putting him out of voice. He wanted a wife to play golf with and to sing to. He wanted a honeymoon on the Hebridean island of Eigg, near Rum, and then to return to Cramond with the bride.

In the midst of this dissatisfaction had occurred Ellen Kerr's finding of a nightdress of quality folded under the pillow next to Mr. Lowther's in that double bed on which, to make matters worse, he had been born.

Still Miss Brodie refused him. He fell into a melancholy mood upon his retirement from the offices of choirmaster and Elder, and the girls thought he brooded often upon the possibility that Miss Brodie could not take to his short legs, and was all the time pining for Teddy Lloyd's long ones.

Most of this Miss Brodie obliquely confided in the girls as they grew from thirteen to fourteen and from fourteen to fifteen. She did not say, even obliquely, that she slept with the singing master, for she was still testing them out to see whom she could trust, as it would be her way to put it. She did not want any alarming suspicions to arise in the minds of their parents. Miss Brodie was always very careful to impress the parents of her set and to win their approval and gratitude. So she confided according to what seemed expedient at the time, and was in fact now on the look-out for a girl amongst her set in whom she could confide entirely, whose curiosity was greater than her desire to make a sensation outside, and who, in the need to gain further confidences from Miss Brodie, would never betray what had been gained. Of necessity there had to be but one girl; two would be dangerous. Almost shrewdly, Miss Brodie fixed on Sandy, and even then it was not of her own affairs that she spoke.

In the summer of nineteen-thirty-five the whole school was forced to wear rosettes of red, white and blue ribbon in the lapels of its blazers, because of the Silver Jubilee. Rose Stanley lost hers and said it was probably in Teddy Lloyd's studio. This was not long after Sandy's visit to the art master's residence.

"What are you doing for the summer holidays, Rose?" said Miss Brodie.

"My father's taking me to the Highlands for a fortnight. After that, I don't know. I suppose I'll be sitting for Mr. Lloyd off and on."

"Good," said Miss Brodie.

Miss Brodie started to confide in Sandy after the next summer holidays. They played rounds of golf in the sunny early autumn after school.

"All my ambitions," said Miss Brodie, "are fixed on yourself and Rose. You will not speak of this to the other girls, it would cause envy. I had hopes of Jenny, she is so pretty; but Jenny has become insipid, don't you think?"

This was a clever question, because it articulated what was already growing in Sandy's mind. Jenny had bored her this last year, and it left her lonely.

"Don't you think?" said Miss Brodie, towering above her, for Sandy was playing out of a bunker. Sandy gave a hack with her niblick and said, "Yes, a bit," sending the ball in a little backward half-circle.

"And I had hopes of Eunice," Miss Brodie said presently, "but she seems to be interested in some boy she goes swimming with."

Sandy was not yet out of the bunker. It was sometimes difficult to follow Miss Brodie's drift when she was in her prophetic moods. One had to wait and see what emerged. In the meantime she glanced up at Miss Brodie who was standing on the crest of the bunker which was itself on a crest of the hilly course. Miss Brodie looked admirable in her heather-blue tweed with the brown of a recent holiday in Egypt still warming her skin. Miss Brodie was gazing out over Edinburgh as she spoke.

Sandy got out of the bunker. "Eunice," said Miss Brodie, "will settle down and marry some professional man. Perhaps I have done her some good. Mary, well, Mary. I never had any hopes of Mary. I thought when you were young children that Mary might be something. She was a little pathetic. But she's really a most irritating girl, I'd rather deal with a rogue than a fool. Monica will get her B.Sc. with honors I've no doubt, but she has no spiritual insight, and of course that's why she's——"

Miss Brodie was to drive off now and she had decided to stop talking until she had measured her distance and swiped her ball. Which she did. "——that's why she has a bad temper, she understands nothing but signs and symbols and calculations. Nothing infuriates people more than their own lack of spiritual insight, Sandy, that is why the Moslems are so placid, they are full of spiritual insight. My dragoman in Egypt would not have it that Friday was their Lord's Day. 'Every day is the Lord's day,' he said to me. I thought that very profound, I felt humbled. We had already said our farewells on the day before my departure, Sandy, but lo and behold when I was already seated in the train, along the platform came my dragoman with a beautiful bunch of flowers for me. He had true dignity. Sandy, you will never get anywhere by hunching over your putter, hold your shoulders back and bend from the waist. He was a very splendid person with a great sense of his bearing."

They picked up their balls and walked to the next tee. "Have you ever played with Miss Lockhart?" Sandy said.

"Does she play golf?"

"Yes, rather well." Sandy had met the science mistress surprisingly on the golf course one Saturday morning playing with Gordon Lowther.

"Good shot, Sandy. I know very little of Miss Lockhart," said Miss Brodie. "I leave her to her jars and gases. They are all gross materialists, these women in the Senior school, they all belong to the Fabian Society and are pacifists. That's the sort of thing Mr. Lowther, Mr. Lloyd and myself are up against when we are not up against the narrow-minded, half-educated crowd in the Junior departments. Sandy, I'll swear you are short-sighted, the way you peer at people. You must get spectacles."

"I'm not," said Sandy irritably, "it only seems so."

"It's unnerving," said Miss Brodie. "Do you know, Sandy dear, all my ambitions are for you and Rose. You have got insight, perhaps not quite spiritual, but you're a deep one, and Rose has got instinct, Rose has got instinct."

"Perhaps not quite spiritual," said Sandy.

"Yes," said Miss Brodie, "you're right. Rose has got a future by virtue of her instinct."

"She has an instinct how to sit for her portrait," said Sandy.

"That's what I mean by your insight," said Miss Brodie. "I ought to know, because my prime has brought me instinct and insight, both."

Fully to savor her position, Sandy would go and stand outside St. Giles' Cathedral of the Tolbooth, and contemplate these emblems of a dark and terrible salvation which made the fires of the damned seem very merry to the imagination by contrast, and much preferable. Nobody in her life, at home or at school, had ever spoken of Calvinism except as a joke that had once been taken seriously. She did not at the time understand that her evironment had not been on the surface peculiar to the place, as was the environment of the Edinburgh social classes just above or, even more, just below her own. She had no experience of social class at all. In its outward forms her fifteen years might have been spent in any suburb of any city in the British Isles; her school, with its alien house system, might have been in Ealing. All she was conscious of now was that some quality of life peculiar to Edinburgh and nowhere else had been going on unbeknown to her all the time, and however undesirable it might be she felt deprived of it; however undersirable, she desired not to know what it was, and to cease to be protected from it by enlightened people.

In fact, it was the religion of Calvin of which Sandy felt deprived, or rather a specified recognition of it. She desired this birthright; something definite to reject. It pervaded the place in proportion as it was unacknowledged. In some ways the most real and rooted people whom Sandy knew were Miss Gaunt and the Kerr sisters who made no evasions about their belief that God had planned for practically everybody before they were born a nasty surprise when they died. Later, when Sandy read John Calvin, she found that although popular conceptions of Calvinism were sometimes mistaken, in this particular there was no mistake, indeed it was but a mild understanding of the case, he having made it God's pleasure to implant in certain people an erroneous sense of joy and salvation, so that their surprise at the end might be the nastier.

Sandy was unable to formulate these exciting propositions; nevertheless she experienced them in the air she breathed, she sensed them in the curiously defiant way in which the people she knew broke the Sabbath, and she smelled them in the excesses of Miss Brodie in her prime. Now that she was allowed to go about alone, she walked round the certainly forbidden quarters of Edinburgh to look at the blackened monuments and hear the unbelievable curses of drunken men and women, and, comparing their faces with the faces from Morningside and Merchisten with which she was familiar, she saw, with stabs of new and exciting Calvinistic guilt, that there was not much difference.

In this oblique way, she began to sense what went to the makings of Miss Brodie who had elected herself to grace in so particular a way and with more exotic suicidal enchantment than if she had simply taken to drink like other spinsters who couldn't stand it any more.

It was plain that Miss Brodie wanted Rose with her instinct to start preparing to be Teddy Lloyd's lover, and Sandy with her insight to act as informant on the affair. It was to this end that Rose and Sandy had been chosen as the crème de la crème. There was a whiff of sulphur about the idea which fascinated Sandy in her present mind. After all, it was only an idea. And there was no pressing hurry in the matter, for Miss Brodie liked to take her leisure over the unfolding of her plans, most of her joy deriving from the preparation, and moreover, even if these plans were as clear to her own mind as they were to Sandy's, the girls were too young. All the same, by the time the girls were sixteen Miss Brodie was saying to her set at large: "Sandy will make an excellent Secret Service agent, a great spy"; and to Sandy alone she had started saying, "Rose will be a great lover. She is above the common moral code, it does not apply to her. This is a fact which it is not expedient for anyone to hear about who is not endowed with insight."

For over a year Sandy entered into the spirit of this plan, for she visited the Lloyds' frequently, and was able to report to Miss Brodie how things were going with the portraits of Rose which so resembled Miss Brodie.

"Rose," said Miss Brodie, "is like a heroine from a novel by D. H. Lawrence. She has got instinct."

But in fact the art master's interest in Rose was simply a professional one, she was a good model; Rose had an instinct to be satisfied with this role, and in the event it was Sandy who slept with Teddy Lloyd and Rose who carried back the information.

It was some time before these things came to pass, and meanwhile Miss Brodie was neglecting Mr. Lowther at Cramond and spending as much time as possible with Rose and Sandy discussing art, and then the question of sitting for an artist, and Rose's future as a model, and the necessity for Rose to realize the power she had within her, it was a gift and she an exception to all the rules, she was the exception that proved the rule. Miss Brodie was too cautious to be more precise and Rose only half-guessed at Miss Brodie's meaning, for she was at this time, as Sandy knew, following her instinct and becoming famous for sex among the schoolboys who stood awkwardly with their bicycles at a safe distance from the school gates. Rose was greatly popular with these boys, which was the only reason why she was famed for sex, although she did not really talk about sex, far less indulge it. She did everything by instinct, she even listened to Miss Brodie as if she agreed with every word.

"When you are seventeen or eighteen, Rose, you will come to the moment of your great fulfilment."

"Yes, honestly I think so, Miss Brodie."

Teddy Lloyd's passion for Jean Brodie was greatly in evidence in all the portraits he did of the various members of the Brodie set. He did them in a group during one summer term, wearing their panama hats each in a different way, each hat adorning, in a magical transfiguration, a different Jean Brodie under the forms of Rose, Sandy, Jenny, Mary, Monica and Eunice. But mostly it was Rose, because she was instinctively a good model and Teddy Lloyd paid her five shillings a sitting, which Rose found useful, being addicted to the cinema.

Sandy felt warmly towards Miss Brodie at these times when she saw how she was misled in her idea of Rose. It was then that Miss Brodie looked beautiful and fragile, just as dark heavy Edinburgh itself could suddenly be changed into a floating city when the light was a special pearly white and fell upon one of the gracefully fashioned streets. In the same way Miss Brodie's masterful features became clear and sweet to Sandy when viewed in the curious light of the woman's folly, and she never felt more affection for her in her later years than when she thought upon Miss Brodie silly.

But Miss Brodie as the leader of the set, Miss Brodie as a Roman matron, Miss Brodie as an educational reformer were still prominent. It was not always comfortable, from the school point of view, to be associated with her. The lack of team spirit alone, the fact that the Brodie set preferred golf to hockey or netball if they preferred anything at all, were enough to set them apart, even if they had not dented in the crowns of their hats and tilted them backwards or forwards. It was impossible for them to escape from the Brodie set because they were the Brodie set in the eyes of the school. Nominally, they were members of Holyrood, Melrose, Argyll and Biggar, but it had been well known that the Brodie set had no team spirit and did not care which house won the shield. They were not allowed to care. Their disregard had now become an institution, to be respected like the house system itself. For their own part, and without this reputation, the six girls would have gone each her own way by the time she was in the fourth form and had reached the age of sixteen.

But it was irrevocable, and they made the most of it, and saw that their position was really quite enviable. Everyone thought the Brodie set had more fun than anyone else, what with visits to Cramond, to Teddy Lloyd's studio, to the theatre and teas with Miss Brodie. And indeed it was so. And Miss Brodie was always a figure of glamorous activity even in the eyes of the non-Brodie girls.

Miss Brodie's struggles with the authorities on account of her educational system were increasing throughout the years, and she made it a moral duty for her set to rally round her each time her battle reached a crisis. Then she would find them, perhaps, loitering with the bicycle boys after school, and the bicycles would rapidly bear the boys away, and they would be bidden to supper the following evening.

They went to the tram-car stop with her. "It has been suggested again that I should apply for a post at one of the progressive, that is to say, crank schools. I shall not apply for a post at a crank school. I shall remain at this education factory where my duty lies. There needs must be a leaven in the lump. Give me a girl at an impressionable age and she is mine for life. The gang who oppose me shall not succeed."

"No," said everyone. "No, of course they won't."

The headmistress had not quite given up testing the girls of the Brodie set to see what they knew. In her frustration she sometimes took reprisals against them when she could do so under the guise of fair play, which was not often.

"If they do not try to unseat me on the grounds of my educational policy, they attempt personal calumny," said Miss Brodie one day. "It is unfortunate, but true, that there have been implications against my character in regard to my relations with poor Mr. Lowther. As you girls well know, I have given much of my energy to Mr. Lowther's health. I am fond of Mr. Lowther. Why not? Are we not bidden to love one another? I am Gordon Lowther's closest friend, his confidante. I have neglected him of late I am afraid, but still I have been all things to Gordon Lowther, and I need only lift my little finger and he would be at my side. This relationship has been distorted . . ."

It was some months, now, that Miss Brodie had neglected the singing master, and the girls no longer spent Saturday afternoons at Cramond. Sandy assumed that the reason why Miss Brodie had stopped sleeping with Gordon Lowther was that her sexual feelings were satisfied by proxy; and Rose was predestined to be the lover of Teddy Lloyd. "I have had much calumny to put up with on account of my good offices at Cramond," said Miss Brodie. "However, I shall survive it. If I wished I could marry him tomorrow."

The morning after this saying, the engagement of Gordon Lowther to Miss Lockhart, the science teacher, was announced in *The Scotsman*. Nobody had expected it. Miss Brodie was greatly taken aback and suffered untimely, for a space, from a sense of having been betrayed. But she seemed to recall herself to the fact that the true love of her life was Teddy Lloyd whom she had renounced; and Gordon Lowther had merely been useful. She subscribed with the rest of the school to the china tea-set which was presented to the couple at the last assembly of the term. Mr. Lowther made a speech in which he called them "you girlies," glancing shyly from time to time at Miss Brodie who was watching the clouds through the window. Sometimes he looked towards his bride to be, who stood quietly by the side of the headmistress half-way up the hall waiting till he should be finished and they could join him on the platform. He had confidence in Miss Lockhart, as everyone did, she not only played golf well and drove a car, she could also blow up the school with her jar of gunpowder and would never dream of doing so.

Miss Brodie's brown eyes were fixed on the clouds, she looked quite beautiful and frail, and it occurred to Sandy that she had possibly renounced Teddy Lloyd only because she was aware that she could not keep up this beauty; it was a quality in her that came and went.

Next term, when Mr. Lowther returned from his honeymoon on the island of Eigg, Miss Brodie put her spare energy into her plan for

Sandy and Rose, with their insight and instinct; and what energy she had to spare from that she now put into political ideas.

CHAPTER SIX

Miss Mackay, the headmistress, never gave up pumping the Brodie set. She knew it was useless to do so directly, her approach was indirect, in the hope that they would be tricked into letting fall some piece of evidence which could be used to enforce Miss Brodie's retirement. Once a term, the girls went to tea with Miss Mackay.

But in any case there was now very little they could say without implicating themselves. By the time their friendship with Miss Brodie was of seven years' standing, it had worked itself into their bones, so that they could not break away without, as it were, splitting their bones to do so.

"You still keep up with Miss Brodie?" said Miss Mackay, with a gleaming smile. She had new teeth.

"Oh, yes, rather . . ."

"Yes, oh yes, from time to time . . ."

Miss Mackay said to Sandy confidentially when her turn came round—because she treated the older girls as equals, which is to say, as equals definitely wearing school uniform—"Dear Miss Brodie, she sits on under the elm, telling her remarkable life story to the Junior children. I mind when Miss Brodie first came to the school, she was a vigorous young teacher, but now—" She sighed and shook her head. She had a habit of putting the universal wise saws into Scots dialect to make them wiser. Now she said, "What canna be cured maun be endured. But I fear Miss Brodie is past her best. I doubt her class will get through its qualifying examination this year. But don't think I'm criticizing Miss Brodie. She likes her wee drink, I'm sure. After all, it's nobody's business, so long as it doesn't affect her work and you girls."

"She doesn't drink," said Sandy, "except for sherry on her birthday, half a bottle between the seven of us."

Miss Mackay could be observed mentally scoring drink off her list of things against Miss Brodie. "Oh, that's all I meant," said Miss Mackay.

The Brodie girls, now that they were seventeen, were able to detach Miss Brodie from her aspect of teacher. When they conferred amongst themselves on the subject they had to admit, at last, and without doubt, that she was really an exciting woman as a woman.

Her eyes flashed, her nose arched proudly, her hair was still brown, and coiled matriarchally at the nape of her neck. The singing master, well satisfied as he was with Miss Lockhart, now Mrs. Lowther and lost to the school, would glance at Miss Brodie from under his ginger eyebrows with shy admiration and memories whenever he saw her.

One of her greatest admirers was the new girl called Joyce Emily Hammond who had been sent to Blaine School as a last hope, having been obliged to withdraw from a range of expensive schools north and south of the border, because of her alleged delinquency which so far had not been revealed, except once or twice when she had thrown paper pellets at Mr. Lowther and succeeded only in hurting his feelings. She insisted on calling herself Joyce Emily, was brought to school in the morning by a chauffeur in a large black car, though she was obliged to make her own way home; she lived in a huge house with a stables in the near environs of Edinburgh. Joyce Emily's parents, wealthy as they were, had begged for a trial period to elapse before investing in yet another set of school uniform clothing for their daughter. So Joyce Emily still went about in dark green, while the rest wore deep violet, and she boasted five sets of discarded colors hanging in her wardrobe at home besides such relics of governesses as a substantial switch of hair cut off by Joyce Emily's own hand, a post office savings book belonging to a governess called Miss Michie, and the charred remains of a pillow-case upon which the head of yet another governess called Miss Chambers had been resting when Joyce Emily had set fire to it.

The rest of the girls listened to her chatter, but in general she was disapproved of not only because of her green stockings and skirt, her shiny car and chauffeur, but because life was already exceedingly full of working for examinations and playing for the shield. It was the Brodie set to which Joyce Emily mostly desired to attach herself, perceiving their individualism; but they, less than anybody, wanted her. With the exception of Mary Macgregor, they were, in fact, among the brightest girls in the school, which was somewhat a stumbling-block to Miss Mackay in her efforts to discredit Miss Brodie.

The Brodie set, moreover, had outside interests. Eunice had a boy friend with whom she practiced swimming and diving. Monica Douglas and Mary Macgregor went slum-visiting together with bundles of groceries, although Mary was reported to be always making remarks like, "Why don't they eat cake?" (What she actually said was, "Well, why don't they send their clothes to the laundry?" when she heard complaints of the prohibitive price of soap.) Jenny was already showing her dramatic talent and was all the time rehearsing for something in the school dramatic society. Rose modeled for Teddy Lloyd and Sandy occasionally joined her, and was watchful, and sometimes toyed with the idea of inducing Teddy Lloyd to kiss her again just to see if it could be done by sheer looking at him insolently with her little eyes. In addition to these activities the Brodie set were meeting Miss Brodie by twos and threes, and sometimes all together after school. It was at this time, in nineteen-thirty-seven, that she was especially cultivating Rose, and questioning Sandy, and being answered as to the progress of the great love affair presently to take place between Rose and the art master.

So that they had no time to do much about a delinquent whose parents had dumped her on the school by their influence, even if she was apparently a delinquent in name only. Miss Brodie, however, found time to take her up. The Brodie girls slightly resented this but were relieved that they were not obliged to share the girl's company, and that Miss Brodie took her to tea and the theatre on her own.

One of Joyce Emily's boasts was that her brother at Oxford had gone to fight in the Spanish Civil War. This dark, rather mad girl wanted to go too, and to wear a white blouse and black skirt and march with a gun. Nobody had taken this seriously. The Spanish Civil War was something going on outside in the newspapers and only once a month in the school debating society. Everyone, including Joyce Emily, was anti-Franco if they were anything at all.

One day it was realized that Joyce Emily had not been at school for some days, and soon someone else was occupying her desk. No one knew why she had left until, six weeks later, it was reported that she had run away to Spain and had been killed in an accident when the train she was traveling in had been attacked. The school held an abbreviated form of remembrance service for her.

Mary had gone to be a shorthand typist and Jenny had gone to a school of dramatic art. Only four remained of the Brodie set for the last year. It was hardly like being at school at all, there was so much free time, so many lectures and so much library research outside the school building for the sixth-form girls that it was just a matter of walking in and out. They were deferred to and consulted, and had the feeling that they could, if they wished, run the place.

Eunice was to do modern languages, although she changed her mind a year later and became a nurse. Monica was destined for science, Sandy for psychology. Rose had hung on, not for any functional reason, but because her father thought she should get the best out of her education, even if she was only going to the art school later on, or at the worst, become a model for artists or dress designers. Rose's father played a big part in her life, he was a huge widower, as handsome in his masculine way as was Rose in her feminine, proudly professing himself a cobbler; that was to say, he now owned an extensive shoe-making business. Some years ago, on meeting Miss Brodie he had immediately taken a hearty male interest in her, as so many men did, not thinking her to be ridiculous as might have been expected, but she would have none of Mr. Stanley, for he was hardly what she would call a man of culture. She thought him rather carnal. The girls, however, had always guiltily liked Rose's father. And Rose, instinctive as she undoubtedly was, followed her instinct so far as to take on his hard-headed and merry carnality, and made a good marriage soon after she left school. She shook off Miss Brodie's influence as a dog shakes pond-water from its coat.

Miss Brodie was not to know that this would be, and meantime Rose was inescapably famous for sex and was much sought after by sixth-form schoolboys and first-year University students. And Miss Brodie said to Sandy: "From what you tell me I should think that Rose and Teddy Lloyd will soon be lovers." All at once Sandy realized that this was not all theory and a kind of Brodie game, in the way that so much of life was unreal talk and game-planning, like the prospects of a war and other theories that people were putting about in the air like pigeons, and one said, "Yes, of course, it's inevitable." But this was not theory, Miss Brodie meant it. Sandy looked at her, and perceived that the woman was obsessed by the need for Rose to sleep with the man she herself was in love with; there was nothing new in the idea, it was the reality that was new. She thought of Miss Brodie eight years ago sitting under the elm tree telling her first simple love story and wondered to what extent it was Miss Brodie who had developed complications throughout the years, and to what extent it was her own conception of Miss Brodie that had changed.

During the year past Sandy had continued seeing the Lloyds. She went shopping with Deirdre Lloyd and got herself a folkweave skirt like Deirdre's. She listened to their conversation, at the same time calculating their souls by signs and symbols, as was the habit in those days of young persons who had read books of psychology when listening to older persons who had not. Sometimes, on days when Rose was required to pose naked, Sandy sat with the painter and his model in the studio, silently watching the strange mutations of the flesh on the canvas as they represented an anonymous nude figure, and at the same time resembled Rose, and more than this, resembled

Miss Brodie. Sandy had become highly interested in the painter's mind, so involved with Miss Brodie as it was, and not accounting her ridiculous.

"From what you tell me I should think that Rose and Teddy Lloyd will soon be lovers." Sandy realized that Miss Brodie meant it. She had told Miss Brodie how peculiarly all his portraits reflected her. She had said so again and again, for Miss Brodie loved to hear it. She had said that Teddy Lloyd wanted to give up teaching and was preparing an exhibition, and was encouraged in this course by art critics and discouraged by the thought of his large family.

"I am his Muse," said Miss Brodie. "But I have renounced his love in order to dedicate my prime to the young girls in my care. I am his Muse but Rose shall take my place."

She thinks she is Providence, thought Sandy, she thinks she is the God of Calvin, she sees the beginning and the end. And Sandy thought, too, the woman is an unconscious Lesbian. And many theories from the books of psychology categorized Miss Brodie, but failed to obliterate her image from the canvases of one-armed Teddy Lloyd.

When she was a nun, sooner or later one and the other of the Brodie set came to visit Sandy, because it was something to do, and she had written her book of psychology, and everyone likes to visit a nun, it provides a spiritual sensation, a catharsis to go home with, especially if the nun clutches the bars of the grille. Rose came, now long since married to a successful business man who varied in his line of business from canned goods to merchant banking. They fell to talking about Miss Brodie.

"She talked a lot about dedication," said Rose, "but she didn't mean your sort of dedication. But don't you think she was dedicated to her girls in a way?"

"Oh yes, I think she was," said Sandy.

"Why did she get the push?" said Rose. "Was it sex?"

"No, politics."

"I didn't know she bothered about politics."

"It was only a side line," Sandy said, "but it served as an excuse."

Monica Douglas came to visit Sandy because there was a crisis in her life. She had married a scientist and in one of her fits of anger had thrown a live coal at his sister. Whereupon the scientist demanded a separation, once and for all.

"I'm not much good at that sort of problem," said Sandy. But Monica had not thought she would be able to help much, for she knew Sandy of old, and persons known of old can never be of much help. So they fell to talking of Miss Brodie.

"Did she ever get Rose to sleep with Teddy Lloyd?" said Monica.

"No," said Sandy.

"Was she in love with Teddy Lloyd herself?"

"Yes," said Sandy, "and he was in love with her."

"Then it was a real renunciation in a way," said Monica.

"Yes, it was," said Sandy. "After all, she was a woman in her prime."

"You used to think her talk about renunciation was a joke," said Monica.

"So did you," said Sandy.

In the summer of nineteen-thirty-eight, after the last of the Brodie set had left Blaine, Miss Brodie went to Germany and Austria, while Sandy read psychology and went to the Lloyds' to sit for her own portrait. Rose came and kept them company occasionally.

When Deirdre Lloyd took the children into the country Teddy had to stay on in Edinburgh because he was giving a summer course at the art school. Sandy continued to sit for her portrait twice a week, and sometimes Rose came and sometimes not.

One day when they were alone, Sandy told Teddy Lloyd that all his portraits, even that of the littlest Lloyd baby, were now turning out to be likenesses of Miss Brodie, and she gave him her insolent blackmailing stare. He kissed her as he had done three years before when she was fifteen, and for the best part of five weeks of the summer they had a love affair in the empty house, only sometimes answering the door to Rose, but at other times letting the bell scream on.

During that time he painted a little, and she said: "You are still making me look like Jean Brodie." So he started a new canvas, but it was the same again.

She said: "Why are you obsessed with that woman? Can't you see she's ridiculous?"

He said, yes, he could see Jean Brodie was ridiculous. He said, would she kindly stop analyzing his mind, it was unnatural in a girl of eighteen.

Miss Brodie telephoned for Sandy to come to see her early in September. She had returned from Germany and Austria which were now magnificently organized. After the war Miss Brodie admitted to Sandy, as they sat in the Braid Hills Hotel, "Hitler *was* rather naughty," but at this time she was full of her travels and quite sure the new regime would save the world. Sandy was bored, it did not seem necessary that the world should be saved, only that the poor people in the streets and slums of Edinburgh should be relieved. Miss Brodie said there would be no war. Sandy never had thought so, anyway. Miss Brodie came to the point: "Rose tells me you have become his lover."

"Yes, does it matter which one of us it is?"

"Whatever possessed you?" said Miss Brodie in a very Scottish way, as if Sandy had given away a pound of marmalade to an English duke.

"He interests me," said Sandy.

"Interests you, forsooth," said Miss Brodie. "A girl with a mind, a girl with insight. He is a Roman Catholic and I don't see how you can have to do with a man who can't think for himself. Rose was suitable. Rose has instinct but no insight."

Teddy Lloyd continued reproducing Jean Brodie in his paintings. "You have instinct," Sandy told him, "but no insight, or you would see that the woman isn't to be taken seriously."

"I know she isn't," he said. "You are too analytical and irritable for your age."

The family had returned and their meetings were dangerous and exciting. The more she discovered him to be still in love with Jean Brodie, the more she was curious about the mind that loved the woman. By the end of the year it happened that she had quite lost interest in the man himself, but was deeply absorbed in his mind, from which she extracted, among other things, his religion as a pith from a husk. Her mind was as full of his religion as a night sky is full of things visible and invisible. She left the man and took his religion and became a nun in the course of time.

But that autumn, while she was still probing the mind that invented Miss Brodie on canvas after canvas, Sandy met Miss Brodie several times. She was at first merely resigned to Sandy's liaison with the art master. Presently she was exultant, and presently again enquired for details, which she did not get.

"His portraits still resemble me?" said Miss Brodie.

"Yes, very much," said Sandy.

"Then all is well," said Miss Brodie. "And after all, Sandy," she said, "you are destined to be the great lover, although I would not have thought it. Truth is stranger than fiction. I wanted Rose for him, I admit, and sometimes I regretted urging young Joyce Emily to go to Spain to fight for Franco, she would have done admirably for him, a girl of instinct, a——"

"Did she go to fight for Franco?" said Sandy.

"That was the intention. I made her see sense. However, she didn't have the chance to fight at all, poor girl."

When Sandy returned, as was expected of her, to see Miss Mackay that autumn, the headmistress said to this rather difficult old girl with the abnormally small eyes, "You'll have been seeing something of Miss Brodie, I hope. You aren't forgetting your old friends, I hope."

"I've seen her once or twice," said Sandy.

"I'm afraid she put ideas into your young heads," said Miss Mackay with a knowing twinkle, which meant that now Sandy had left school it would be all right to talk openly about Miss Brodie's goings-on.

"Yes, lots of ideas," Sandy said.

"I wish I knew what some of them were," said Miss Mackay, slumping a little and genuinely worried. "Because it is still going on, I mean class after class, and now she has formed a new set, and they are so out of key with the rest of the school, Miss Brodie's set. They are precocious. Do you know what I mean?"

"Yes," said Sandy. "But you won't be able to pin her down on sex. Have you thought of politics?"

Miss Mackay turned her chair so that it was nearly square with Sandy's. This was business.

"My dear," she said, "what do you mean? I didn't know she was attracted by politics."

"Neither she is," said Sandy, "except as a side interest. She's a born fascist, have you thought of that?"

"I shall question her pupils on those lines and see what emerges, if that is what you advise, Sandy. I had no idea you felt so seriously about the state of world affairs, Sandy, and I'm more than delighted——"

"I'm not really interested in world affairs," said Sandy, "only in putting a stop to Miss Brodie."

It was clear the headmistress thought this rather unpleasant of Sandy. But she did not fail to say to Miss Brodie, when the time came, "It was one of your own girls who gave me the tip, one of your set, Miss Brodie."

Sandy was to leave Edinburgh at the end of the year and when she said goodbye to the Lloyds she looked round the studio at the canvases on which she had failed to put a stop to Miss Brodie. She congratulated Teddy Lloyd on the economy of his method. He congratulated her on the economy of hers, and Dierdre looked to see whatever did he mean? Sandy thought, if he knew about my stopping of Miss Brodie, he would think me more economical still. She was more fuming, now, with Christian morals, than John Knox.

Miss Brodie was forced to retire at the end of the summer term of nineteen-thirty-nine, on the grounds that she had been teaching Fascism. Sandy, when she heard of it, thought of the marching troops of black shirts in the pictures on the wall. By now she had entered the Catholic Church, in whose ranks she had found quite a number of fascists much less agreeable than Miss Brodie.

"Of course," said Miss Brodie when she wrote to tell Sandy the news of her retirement, "this political question was only an excuse. They tried to prove personal immorality against me on many occasions and failed. My girls were always reticent on these matters. It was my educational policy they were up against which had reached its perfection in my prime. I was dedicated to my girls, as you know. But they used this political excuse as a weapon. What hurts and amazes me most of all is the fact, if Miss Mackay is to be believed, that it was one of my own set who betrayed me and put the enquiry in motion.

"You will be astonished. I can write to you of this, because you of all my set are exempt from suspicion, you had no *reason* to betray me. I think first of Mary Macgregor. Perhaps Mary has nursed a grievance, in her stupidity of mind, against me—she is such an exasperating young woman. I think of Rose. It may be that Rose resented my coming first with Mr. L. Eunice—I cannot think it could be Eunice, but I did frequently have to come down firmly on her commonplace ideas. She wanted to be a Girl Guide, you remember. She was attracted to the Team Spirit—could it be that Eunice bore a grudge? Then there is Jenny. Now you know Jenny, how she went *off* and was never the same after she wanted to be an actress. She became so dull. Do you think she minded my telling her that she would never be a Fay Compton, far less a Sybil Thorndike? Finally, there is Monica. I half incline to suspect Monica. There is very little Soul behind the mathematical brain, and it may be that, in a fit of rage against that Beauty, Truth and Goodness which was beyond her grasp, she turned and betrayed me.

"You, Sandy, as you see, I exempt from suspicion, since you had no reason whatsoever to betray me, indeed you have had the best part of me in my confidences and in the man I love. Think, if you can, who it could have been. I must know which one of you betrayed me . . ."

Sandy replied like an enigmatic Pope: "If you did not betray us it is impossible that you could have been betrayed by us. The word betrayed does not apply . . ."

She heard again from Miss Brodie at the time of Mary Macgregor's death, when the girl ran hither and thither in the hotel fire and was trapped by it. "If this is a judgment on poor Mary for betraying me, I am sure I would not have wished . . ."

"I'm afraid," Jenny wrote, "Miss Brodie is past her prime. She keeps wanting to know who betrayed her. It isn't at all like the old Miss Brodie, she was always so full of fight."

Her name and memory, after her death, flitted from mouth to mouth like swallows in summer, and in winter they were gone. It was always in summer time that the Brodie set came to visit Sandy, for the nunnery was deep in the country.

When Jenny came to see Sandy, who now bore the name Sister Helena of the Transfiguration, she told Sandy about her sudden falling in love with a man in Rome and there being nothing to be done about it. "Miss Brodie would have liked to know about it," she said, "sinner as she was."

"Oh, she was quite an innocent in her way," said Sandy, clutching the bars of the grille.

Eunice, when she came, told Sandy, "We were at the Edinburgh Festival last year. I found Miss Brodie's grave, I put some flowers on it. I've told my husband all the stories about her, sitting under the elm and all that; he thinks she was marvelous fun."

"So she was, really, when you think of it."

"Yes, she was," said Eunice, "when she was in her prime."

Monica came again. "Before she died," she said, "Miss Brodie thought it was you who betrayed her."

"It's only possible to betray where loyalty is due," said Sandy.

"Well, wasn't it due to Miss Brodie?"

"Only up to a point," said Sandy.

And there was that day when the enquiring young man came to see Sandy because of her strange book of psychology, *The Transfiguration of the Commonplace*, which had brought so many visitors that Sandy clutched the bars of her grille more desperately than ever.

"What were the main influences of your schooldays, Sister Helena? Were they literary or political or personal? Was it Calvinism?"

Sandy said: "There was a Miss Jean Brodie in her prime."

# Angus Wilson

## TOTENTANZ

THE NEWS of the Cappers' good fortune first became generally known at the Master's garden party. It was surprisingly well received, in view of the number of their enemies in the University, and for this the unusually fine weather was largely responsible. In their sub-arctic isolation, cut off from the main stream of Anglo-Saxon culture and its preferments, sodden with continual mists, pinched by perpetual north-east gales, kept always a little at bay by the natives with their self-satisfied homeliness and their smugly traditional hospitality, the dons and their wives formed a phalanx against spontaneous gaiety that would have satisfied John Knox himself. But rare though days of sunshine were, they transformed the town as completely as if it had been one of those scenes in a child's painting book on which you had only to sprinkle water for the brighter colors to emerge. The Master's lawns, surfeited with rain and mist, lay in flaunting spring green beneath the even deep blue of the July sky. The neat squares of the eighteenth-century burghers' houses and the twisted shapes of the massive gray lochside ruins recovered their designs from the blurring mists. The clumps of wallflowers, gold and copper, filling the crevices of the walls, seemed to mock the solemnity of the covenanting crows that croaked censoriously above them. The famous pale blue silk of the scholars' gowns flashed like silver airships beneath the deeper sky. On such a day even the most mildewed and disappointed of the professors, the most blue and deadening of their wives felt impulses of generosity, or at any rate a freedom from bitterness, that allowed them to rejoice at a fellow prisoner's release. Only the youngest and most naïve research students could be deceived by the sun into brushing the mold off their *own* hopes and ideals, but if others had found a way back to their aims, well, good luck to them!—in any case the Cappers, especially Mrs. Capper, had only disturbed the general morass with their futile struggles and most people would be glad to see them go.

The Master's wife, always so eccentric in her large fringed cape, said in her deep voice, "It's come just in time. Just in time that is for Isobel."

"Just in time," squeaked little Miss Thurkill, the assistant French lecturer, "I should have thought any time was right for a great legacy like that," and she giggled, really the old woman said such odd, personal things.

"Yes, just in time," repeated the Master's wife, she prided herself on understanding human beings and lost no opportunity of expounding them. "A few months more and she would have rotted away."

In the wide opening between the points of his old-fashioned, high Gladstone collar, the Master's protrusive Adam's apple wobbled, gulped. In Oxford or Cambridge his wife's eccentricity would have been an assistance; up here, had he not known exactly how to isolate her, it might have been an embarrassment.

"How typical of women," he said in the unctuous but incisive voice that convinced so many business men and baillies that they were dealing with a scholar whose head was screwed on the right way. "How typical of women to consider only the legacy. Very nice of course, a great help in their new sphere." There was a trace of bitterness, for his own wife's fortune, so important when they had started, had vanished through his unfortunate investments. "But Capper's London Chair is the important thing. A new chair, too, Professor of the History of Technics and Art. Here, of course, we've come to accept so many of Capper's ideas into our everyday thoughts, as a result of his immense powers of persuasion and . . . and his great enthusiasm"—he paused, staring eagle-like beneath his bushy white eyebrows, the scholar who was judge of men—"that we forget how revolutionary some of them are." He had indeed the vaguest conception of anything that his subordinates thought, an administrator has to keep above detail. "No doubt there'll be fireworks, but I venture to suggest that Capper's youth and energy will win the day, don't you agree with me, Todhurst?"

Mr. Todhurst's white suet pudding face tufted with sandy hair was unimpressed. He was a great deal younger than Capper and still determined to remember what a backwater he was stranded in. "Capper's not so young," he said, ostentatiously Yorkshire. "Maybe they'll have heard it all before, and happen they'll tell him so too."

But the Master was conveniently able to ignore Todhurst, for red-faced Sir George was approaching, the wealthiest, most influential business man on the University Board. A tough and rough diamond with his Glaswegian accent and his powerful whiskied breath, Sir George was nevertheless impressed by the size of the legacy. "Five hundred thousand pounds." He gave a whistle. "That's not so bad a sum. Though, mind you, this Government of robbers'll be taking a tidy part of it away in taxation. But still I'm glad for the sake of his missus." Perhaps, he thought, Mrs. Capper would help in getting Margaret presented at Court. How little he knew Isobel Capper, his wife would not have made the mistake.

"And this magnificent appointment coming along at the same time," said the Master.

"Aye," said Sir George, he did not understand that so well, "there's no doubt Capper's a smart young chap." Perhaps, he thought, the Board has been a bit slow, the Master was getting on and they might need a level-headed warm young fellow.

"Oh, there they are," squeaked Miss Thurkill excitedly. "I must say Isobel certainly looks . . ." But she could find no words to describe Isobel's appearance, it was really so very outré.

Nothing could have fitted Isobel Capper's combination of chic and Liberty artiness better than the ultra-smart dressing-gown effect of her New Look dress, the floating flimsiness of her little flowered hat. Her long stride was increased with excitement, even her thin white face had relaxed its tenseness and her amber eyes sparkled with triumph. Against the broad pink and black stripes of her elaborate, bustled dress, her red hair clashed like fire. She was a little impatient with the tail-end of an episode that she was glad to close, her mind was crowded with schemes, but still this victory parade, though petty and provincial, would be a pleasant start to a new life. Brian, too, looked nearer twenty than forty, most of his hard, boyish charm, his emphasized friendliness and sincerity had returned with the prospect of his new appointment. He tossed his brown curly hair back from his forehead as, loose-limbed, athletic, he leaped a deck chair to speak to Sir George. "Hope so very much to see something of you and Lady Maclean if all those company meetings permit." Before the Master he stood erect, serious, a little abashed. "So impossible to speak adequately of what I shall carry away from here . . ." There was no doubt that Brian was quite himself again. His even white teeth gleamed as he smiled at the Master's wife. To her he presented himself almost with a wink as the professional charmer, because after all she was not a woman you could fool. "The awful thing is that my first thought about it is for all the fun we're going to have." With Todhurst he shared their contempt for the backwater. "Not going to say I wish you'd got the appointment, because I don't. Besides kunstgeschichte, old man! you and I know what a bloody fraud the whole thing is. Not that I don't intend to make something useful out of it all and that's exactly why I've got to pick your brains before I go South." It was really amazing, Isobel thought, how the news had revived him—alive, so terribly keen and yet modest withal, and behind everything steady as a rock, a young chap of forty, in fact, who would go far.

Her own method was far more direct, she had never shared her husband's spontaneous sense of salesmanship, at times even found it nauseating. There was no need to bother about these people any more and she did not intend to do so. "Silly to say we shall meet again, Sir George," she told him, before he could get round to asking. "It's only in the bonny North that the arts are conducted on purely business lines." Todhurst, like all the other junior dons, she ignored. "You must be so happy," said Jessie Colquhoun, the poetess of the lochs. "I shan't be *quite* happy," Isobel replied, "until we've crossed the Border." "Of *course* we shall lose touch," she said to the Master's wife, "but I'm not so pleased as you think I am." And really, she thought, if the old woman's eccentricity had not been quite so provincial and frowsty it might have been possible to invite her to London. Her especial venom was reserved for the Master himself. "Dear Mrs. Capper," he intoned. "What a tremendous loss you will be to us, and Capper, too, the ablest man on the Faculty." "I wonder what you'll say to the Board when they wake up to their loss, as I'm sure they will," replied Isobel. "It'll take a lot of explaining."

And yet the Master's wife was quite right, it was only just in time for both of them. Brian had begun to slip back badly in the last few years. His smile, the very center of his charm, had grown too mechanical, gum recession was giving him an equine look. His self-satisfaction which had once made him so friendly to all—useful and useless alike—had begun to appear as heavy indifference. When he had first come North he had danced like a shadow-boxer from one group to another, making the powerful heady with praise, giving to the embittered a cherished moment of flattery, yet never committing himself; engaging all hearts by his youthful belief in Utopia, so much more acceptable because he was obviously so fundamentally sound. But with the years his smiling sincerity had begun to change to dogmatism; he could afford his own views and often they were not interesting, occasionally very dull. Younger colleagues annoyed him, he knew that they thought him out of date. Though he still wanted always to be liked, he had remained "a young man" too long to have any technique for charming the *really* young. Faced by their contempt, he was often rude and sulky. The long apprenticeship in pleasing—the endless years of scholarships and examinations, of being the outstanding student of the year—were now too far behind to guard him from the warping atmosphere of the town. Commonwealths and Harmsworths were becoming remote memories, the Dulwich trams of his schooldays, the laurel bushes of his suburban childhood were closer to him now than the dreams and ambitions of Harvard, Oxford and McGill. Had the chair come a year later he would probably have refused it. He had been such a success at thirty-three, it would have been easy to forget that at forty he was no longer an infant phenomenon.

If Brian had been rescued from the waters of Lethe in the nick of time, Isobel had been torn from the flames of hell. Her hatred of the University and the heat of her ambition had begun to burn her from within, until the strained, white face with cheekbones almost bursting through the skin and the over-intense eyes recalled some witch in death agonies. It did not take long for the superiority of her wit and taste to cease to bother a world in which they were unintelligible, depression and a lack of audience soon gave her irony a "governessy" flavor, until at last the legend of Mrs. Capper's sharp tongue had begun to bore herself as much as others. The gold and white satin, the wooden Negro page of her Regency room had begun to fret her nerves with their shabbiness, yet it seemed pointless to furnish anew, even if she could have afforded it, for a world she so much despised. She made less and less pretense of reading or listening to music, and yet for months she would hardly stir outside. Everything that might have been successful in a more sophisticated society was misunderstood here: her intellectual Anglicanism was regarded as dowdy churchgoing, her beloved Caravaggio was confused with Greuze, her Purcell enthusiasm thought to be a hangover from the time when *The Beggar's Opera* was all the rage; she would have done far better, been thought more daring with Medici, van Goghs and some records of the *Bolero*. She had come to watch all Brian's habits with horror, his little provincial don's sarcasms, his tobacco-jarred, golfey homeliness, his habit of pointing with his pipe and saying: "Now hold on a minute. I want to examine this average man or woman of yours more carefully"; or "Anarchism, now that's a very interesting word, but are we *quite* sure we know what it means?" She became steadily more afraid of "going to pieces," knew herself to be toppling on the edge of a neurotic apathy from which she would never recover.

It was not surprising therefore that as she said good-bye for the third time to old Professor Green, who was so absent-minded, she blessed the waves that had sucked Aunt Gladys down in a confusion of flannel petticoats and straggling gray hair, or the realistic sailor who had cut Uncle Joseph's bony fingers from the side of an over-loaded lifeboat. She was rich, rich enough to realize her wildest am-bitions; beside this Brian's professorship seemed of little importance. And yet in Isobel's growing schemes it had its place, for she had determined to storm London and she was quite shrewd enough to realize that she would never take that citadel by force of cash alone, far better to enter by the academic gate she knew so well.

By January six months of thick white mists and driving rain had finally dissipated the faint traces of July's charity, and with them all interest in the Cappers' fortunes. The Master's wife, dragged along by her two French bulldogs, was fighting her way through Aidan's arch against a battery of hail when she all but collided with Miss Thurkill returning from lunch at the British Restaurant. She would have passed on with a nod but Miss Thurkill's red fox-terrier nose was quivering with news.

"The Cappers' good fortune seems to have been quite a sell," she yelped. "They've got that great house of her uncle's on their hands."

"From all I hear about London conditions Pentonville prison would be a prize these days," boomed the Master's wife.

"Oh, but that isn't all. It's quite grisly," giggled Miss Thurkill. "They've got to have the bodies in the house for ever and ever. It's part of the conditions of the will."

Boredom had given the Master's wife a conviction of psychic as well as psychological powers and she suddenly "felt aware of evil."

"I was wrong when I said that silly little woman was saved in time. Pathetic creature with her cheap ambitions and her dressing-up clothes, she's in for a very bad time."

Something of the old woman's prophetic mood was communi-cated to Miss Thurkill and she found herself saying:

"I know. Isn't it horrible?"

For a moment they stood outlined against the gray stormy sky, the Master's wife, her great black mackintosh cape billowing out behind, like an evil bat, Miss Thurkill sharp and thin like a barking jackal. Then the younger woman laughed nervously.

"Well, I must rush on or I'll be drenched to the skin."

She could not hear the other's reply for the howling of the wind, but it sounded curiously like "Why not?"

Miss Thurkill was, of course, exaggerating wildly when she spoke of "bodies" in the house, because the bones of Uncle Joseph and Aunt Gladys were long since irrevocably Atlantic coral or on the way to it. But there was a clause in the will that was troublesome enough to give Isobel great cause for anxiety in the midst of her triumphant campaign for power.

A very short time had been needed to prove that the Cappers were well on the way to a brilliant success. Todhurst had proved a false prophet, Brian had been received with acclamations in the London academic world, not only within the University, but in the smart society of the Museums and Art Galleries, and in the houses of rich connoisseurs, art dealers, smart sociologists and archaeologists with chic that lay around its periphery. It has to be remembered that many of those with Brian's peculiar brand of juvenile careerist charm were now getting a little passé and tired, whilst the post-war generation were somehow too total in outlook, too sure of their views to achieve the necessary flexibility, the required chameleon character. Brian might have passed unnoticed in 1935, in 1949 he appeared as a refreshing draught from the barbaric North. Already his name was current at the high tables of All Souls and King's—a man to watch. He talked on the Third Programme and on the Brains Trust—Isobel was a bid doubtful about this—he reviewed for smart weeklies and monthlies, he was commissioned to write a Pelican book.

Isobel was pleased with all this, but she aimed at something more than an academical sphere however chic—she was incurably romantic and over Brian's shoulder she saw a long line of soldier-mystics back from Persia, introvert explorers, able young Conservatives, important Dominicans, and Continental novelists with international reputations snatched from the jaws of O.G.P.U.—and at the center, herself, the woman who counted. Brian's success would be a help, their money more so. For the moment her own role was a passive one, she was content if she "went down," and for this her chic Anglo-Catholicism—almost Dominican in theological flavor, almost Jesuit Counter Reformation in aesthetic taste—combined with her spiteful wit, power of mimicry and interesting appearance, sufficed. Meanwhile she was watching and learning, entertaining lavishly, being pleasant to everyone and selecting carefully the important few who were to carry them on to the next stage—the most influential people within their present circle, but not, and here she was most careful, people who were too many jumps ahead; they would come later. By the time that this ridiculous, this insane clause in the will had been definitely proved, she had already chosen the four people who must be cultivated.

First and most obviously Professor Cadaver, that long gaunt old man with his corseted figure, his military mustache and his almost too beautiful clothes; foremost of archaeologists, author of *Digging Up the Dead*, *The Tomb My Treasurehouse* and *Where Grave Thy Victory?* It was not only the tombs of the ancient world on which he was a final authority, for in the intervals between his expeditions to the Near East and North Africa, he had familiarized himself with all the principal cemeteries of the British Isles and had formed a remarkable collection of photographs of unusual graves. His enthusiasm for the ornate masonry of the nineteenth century had given him *réclame* among the devotees of Victorian art. He enthusiastically supported Brian's views on the sociological importance of burial customs, though he often irritated his younger colleague by the emphasis he seemed to lay upon the state of preservation of the bodies themselves. Over embalming in particular he would wax very enthusiastic—"Every feature, every limb preserved in their lifetime beauty," he would say, "and yet over all the odor of decay, the sweet stillness of death." A strange old man! For Isobel, too, he seemed to have a great admiration, he would watch her with his old reptilian eyes for hours on end—"What wonderful bone-structure," he would say; "one can almost *see* the cheek bones." "How few people one sees today, Mrs. Capper, with your perfect pallor, at times it seems almost livid."

Over Lady Maude she hesitated longer, there were so many old women—well-connected and rich—who were interested in art history and of these Lady Maude was physically the least prepossessing. With her little myopic pig's eyes, her wide-brimmed hats insecurely pinned to falling coils of hennaed hair and her enormous body encased in musquash, she might have been passed over by any eye less sharp than Isobel's. But Lady Maude had been everywhere and seen everything. Treasures locked from all other Western gaze by Soviet secrecy or Muslim piety had been revealed to her. American millionaires had shown her masterpieces of provenance so dubious that they could not be publicly announced without international complications. She had spent many hours watching the best modern fakers at work. Her memory was detailed and exact, and though her eyesight was failing daily, her strong glasses still registered what she saw as though it had been photographed by the camera. Outside her knowledge of the arts she was intensely stupid and thought only of her food. This passionate greed she tried to conceal, but Isobel soon discovered it, and set out to win her with every delicacy that the Black Market could provide.

With Taste and Scholarship thus secured, Isobel began to cast

about for a prop outside the smart academic world, a stake embedded
deep in café society. The thorns that surrounded the legacy were beginning to prick. She still refused to believe that the fantastic, the
wicked clause, could really be valid and had set all London's lawyers
to refute it. But even so there were snags. It was necessary, for example, that they should leave the large furnished flat which they had
taken in Cadogan Street and occupy Uncle Joseph's rambling mansion in Portman Square, with its mass of miscellaneous middle-class
junk assembled since 1890; so much the will made perfectly clear.
The district, she felt, might do. But before the prospect of filling the
house, and filling it correctly, with furniture, servants, and above all,
guests, she faltered. It was at this moment that she met Guy Rice.
Since coming to London she had seen so many beautiful pansy
young men, all with the same standard voices, jargon, bow-ties
and complicated hair-do's, that she tended now to ignore them. That
some of them were important, she felt no doubt, but it was difficult
to distinguish amid such uniformity and she did not wish to make a
mistake. Guy Rice, however, decided to know *her*. He sensed at
once her insecurity, her hardness and her determination. She was just
the wealthy peg he needed on which to hang his great flair for pastiche, which he saw with alarm was in danger of becoming a drug on
the market. Mutual robbery, after all, was fair exchange, he thought,
as he watched her talking to a little group before the fire.

"I can never understand," she was saying, "why people who've
made a mess of things should excuse themselves by saying that they
can't accept authority. But then *I* don't think insanity's a very good
plea." It was one of her favorite themes. Guy patted the couch beside him.

"Come and sit here, dearie," he said in the flat cockney whine he
had always refused to lose—it was, after all, a distinction.

"You *do* try hard, dear, don't you? But you know it won't do."
And then he proceeded to lecture and advise her on how to behave. Amazingly, Isobel did not find herself at all annoyed. As he
said, "You could be so cosy, dear, if you tried, and that would be nice,
wouldn't it? All this clever talk's very well, but what people want is a
good old-fashioned bit of fun. What they want is parties, great big
slap-up do's like we had in the old days," for Guy was a rather old
young man. "Lots of fun, childish, you know, elaborate and a wee
bit nasty; and you're just the girl to give it to them." He looked
closely at her emaciated, white face. "The skeleton at the feast, dear,
that's you."

Their rather surprising friendship grew daily—shopping, lunching, but mostly just sitting together over a cup of tea, for they both dearly loved a good gossip. He put her wise about everyone, hard-boiled estimates with a dash of good scout sentimentality—it was "I shouldn't see too much of them, dear, they're on the out. Poor old dears! They say they were ever such naughties once," or, "Cling on for dear life. She's useful. Let her talk, duckie, that's the thing. She likes it. Gets a bit lonely sometimes, I expect, like we all do." He reassured her, too, about her husband.

"What do you think of Brian?" she had asked.

"Same as you do, dear. He bores me dizzy. But don't you worry, there's thousands love that sort of thing. Takes all sorts to make a world."

He put her clothes right for her, saying with a sigh, "Oh, Isobel, dear, you *do* look tatty," until she left behind that touch of outré-artiness that the Master's wife had been so quick to see. With his help she made a magnificent, if somewhat over-perfect, spectacle of the Portman Square Mansion. His knowledge of interior decoration was very professional and with enough money and rooms he let his love of pastiche run wild. He was wise enough to leave the show pieces—the Zurbarán, the Fragonard, the Samuel Palmers and the Bracques—to the Professor and Lady Maude, but for the rest he just let rip. There were Regency bedrooms, a Spanish Baroque dining room, a Second Empire room, a Victorian study, something amusing in Art Nouveau; but his greatest triumph of all was a large lavatory with tubular furniture, American cloth and cacti in pots. "Let's have a dear old prewar lav in the nice old-fashioned Munich style," he had said and the Cappers, wondering, agreed.

On one point only did they differ, Isobel was adamant in favor of doing things as economically as possible, both she and Brian had an innate taste for saving. With this aspect of her life Guy refused to be concerned, but he introduced her to her fourth great prop—Tanya Mule.

"She's the biggest bitch unhung, duckie," he said, "but she'll touch propositions no one else will. She's had it all her own way ever since the war, when 'fiddling' began in a big way."

Mrs. Mule had been very beautiful in the style of Gladys Cooper, but now her face was ravaged into a million lines and wrinkles from which two large and deep blue eyes stared in dead appeal; she wore her hair piled up very high and colored very purple; she always dressed in the smartest black of Knightsbridge with a collar of pearls. She was of the greatest help to Isobel, for although she charged a high commission, she knew every illegal avenue for getting servants and furniture and decorator's men and unrationed food; she could smell out bankruptcy over miles of territory and was always first at the sale; she knew every owner of objets d'art who was in distress and exactly how little they could be made to take. No wonder, then, that with four such allies Isobel felt sure of her campaign.

Suddenly, however, in the flush of victory the great blow struck her—the lawyers decided that the wicked, criminal lunatic clause in Uncle Joseph's will must stand. Even Brian was forced up from beneath his life of lectures, and talks, and dinners to admit that the crisis was serious. Isobel was in despair. She looked at the still unfurnished drawing-room—they had decided on Louis Treize—and thought of the horrors that must be perpetrated there. Certainly the issue was too big to be decided alone, they must call a council of their allies.

Isobel paced up and down in front of the great open fire as she talked, pulling her cigarette out of her tautened mouth and blowing quick angry puffs of smoke. She looked now at the Zurbarán friar with his ape and his owl, now at the blue and buff tapestried huntsmen who rode among the fleshy nymphs and satyrs, occasionally she glanced at Guy as he lay sprawled on the floor, twirling a Christmas rose, but never at Brian, or Lady Maude, Mrs. Mule or the Professor as they sat upright on their high-backed tapestried chairs. "I had hoped never to have to tell you," she said. "Of course, it's absolutely clear that Uncle Joseph and Aunt Gladys were completely insane at the time when the will was made, but apparently the law doesn't care about that. Oh! it's so typical of a country where sentimentalism reigns supreme without regard for God's authority or even for the Natural law for that matter. A crazy, useless old couple, steeped in some nonconformist nonsense, decide on an act of tyrannous interference with the future and all the lawyers can talk about is the liberty of an Englishman to dispose of his money as he wishes. Just because of that, the whole of our lives—Brian's and mine—are to be ruined, we're to be made a laughingstock. Just listen to this: 'If the great Harvester should see fit to gather my dear wife and me to Him when we are on the high seas or in any other manner by which our mortal remains may not be recovered for proper Christian burial and in places where our dear niece and nephew, or under God, other heirs may decently commune with us and in other approved ways show us their respect and affection, then I direct that two memorials, which I have already caused to be made, shall be set in that room in our house in Portman Square in which they entertain their friends, that we may in some way share, assist and participate in their happy pastimes. This is absolutely to be carried out, so that if they shall not agree the whole of our estate shall pass to the charities hereinafter named.' And that," Isobel cried, "*that* is what the law says we shall have to do." She paused, dramatically waving the document in the air. "Well," said Guy, "I'm not partial to monuments myself, but they can be very nice, Isobel dear." "Nice," cried Isobel, "nice. Come and look"; and she threw open the great double doors into the drawing-room. The little party followed her solemnly.

It was perfectly true that the monuments could not be called nice. In the first place they were each seven feet high. Then they were made in white marble—not solid mid-Victorian, something could have been done with that; nor baroque, with angels and gold trumpets, which would have been better still. They were in the most exaggeratedly simple modern good taste by an amateur craftsman, a long way after Eric Gill. "My dear," said Guy, "they're horrors"; and Lady Maude remarked that they were not the kind of thing one ever wanted to see. The lettering, too, was bold, modern and very artful—one read "Joseph Briggs. Ready at the call," and the other "Gladys Briggs. Steel true, blade straight, the Great Artificer made my mate." Professor Cadaver was most distressed by them, "Really, without *any*thing in them," he kept on saying. "Nothing, not even ashes. It all seems most unfortunate." He appeared to feel that a great opportunity had been missed. No one had any suggestion to make. Mrs. Mule knew the names of many crooked lawyers and even a criminal undertaker, but this did not seem to be quite in their line. Lady Maude privately thought that as long as the dining room and kitchen could function there was really very little reason for anxiety. They all stood about in gloom, when suddenly Guy cried, "What did you say the lawyers were called?" "Robertson, Naismith and White," said Isobel, "but it's no good, we've gone over all that." "Trust little Guy, dear," said her friend. Soon his voice could be heard excitedly talking over the telephone. He was there for more than twenty minutes, they could hear little of what he said, though once he screamed rather angrily, "Never said I did say I did say I did," and at least twice he cried petulantly, "Aow, pooh!" When he returned he put his hand on Isobel's shoulder. "It's all right, ducks," he said. "I've fixed it. Now we can all be cosy and that's nice, isn't it?" Sitting tailor-wise on the floor, he produced his solution with reasonable pride. "You see," he said, "it only says in the will 'set in that room in which they entertain their friends.' But it doesn't say you need entertain with those great horrors in the room more than once, and after a great deal of tiresome talk those lawyers have

agreed that I'm right. For that one entertainment we'll build our setting round the horrors, Isobel dear, everything morbid and ghostly.
Your first big reception, duckie, shall be a Totentanz. It's just the
sort of special send-off you need. After that, pack the beastly things
off, and presto, dear, back to normal."

The Totentanz was Isobel's greatest, alas! her last, triumph. The
vast room was swathed in black and purple, against which the huge
white monuments and other smaller tombstones specially designed
for the occasion stood out in bold relief. The waiters and barmen
were dressed as white skeletons or elaborate Victorian mutes with
black ostrich plumes. The open fireplace was arranged as a crematorium fire, and the chairs and tables were coffins made in various
woods. Musical archives had been ransacked for funeral music of
every age and clime. A famous Jewish contralto wailed like the
ghetto, an African beat the tomtom as it is played at human sacri-
fices, an Irish tenor made everyone weep with his wake songs. Supper was announced by "The Last Post" on a bugle and hearses were
provided to carry the guests home.

Some of the costumes were most original. Mrs. Mule came tritely
but aptly enough as a Vampire. Lady Maude with her hair screwed
up in a handkerchief and dressed in a shapeless gown was strikingly
successful as Marie Antoinette shaved for the guillotine. Professor
Cadaver dressed up as a Corpse Eater was as good as Boris Karloff;
he clearly enjoyed every minute of the party, indeed his snake-like
slit eyes darted in every direction at the many beautiful young
women dressed as corpses and his manner became so incoherent and
excited before he left that Isobel felt quite afraid to let him go home
alone. Guy had thought at first of coming as Millais's Ophelia, but he
remembered the harm done to the original model's health and decided against it. With flowing hair and marbled features, however,
he made a very handsome "Suicide of Chatterton." Isobel thought he
seemed a little melancholy during the evening, but when she asked
him if anything was wrong he replied quite absently, "No, dear,
nothing really. Half in love with easeful death, I s'pose. I mean all
this fun *is* rather hell when it comes to the point, isn't it?" But when
he saw her face cloud, he said, "Don't you worry, ducks, you've
arrived," and, in fact, Isobel was too happy to think of anyone but
herself. For many hours after the last guests had departed, she sat
happily chipping away at the monuments with a hammer. She sang a
little to herself: "I've beaten you, Uncle and Auntie dear, I hope it's
the last time you'll bother us here."

Guy felt very old and weary as he let himself into his one-roomed luxury flat. He realized that Isobel would not be needing him much longer, soon she would be on the way to spheres beyond his ken. There were so many really young men who could do his stuff now and they didn't get bored or tired in the middle like he did. Suddenly he saw a letter in the familiar, uneducated handwriting lying on the mat. He turned giddy for a moment and leaned against the wall. It would be impossible to go on finding money like this for ever. Perhaps this time he could get it from Isobel, after all she owed most of her success to him, but it would hasten the inevitable break with her. And even if he had the courage to settle this, there were so many more demands in different uneducated hands, so much more past sentimentalism turned to fear. He lay for a long time in the deep green bath, then sat in front of his double mirror to perform a complicated routine with creams and powders. At last he put on a crimson and white silk dressing gown and hung his Chatterton wig and costume in the wardrobe. He wished so much that Chatterton were there to talk to. Then going to the white painted medicine cupboard, he took out his bottle of luminal. "In times like these," he said aloud, "there's nothing like a good old overdose to pull one through."

Lady Maude enjoyed the party immensely. The funeral baked meats were delicious and Isobel had seen that the old lady had all she wanted. She sat on the edge of her great double bed, with her gray hair straggling about her shoulders, and swung her thick white feet with their knobby blue veins. The caviar and chicken mayonnaise and Omelette Surprise lay heavy upon her, but she found, as usual, that indigestion only made her the more hungry. Suddenly she remembered the game pie in the larder. She put on her ancient padded pink dressing gown and tiptoed downstairs—it would not do for the Danbys to hear her, servants could make one look so foolish. But when she opened the larder, she was horrified to find that someone had forestalled her, the delicious, rich game pie had been removed. The poor, cheated lady was not long in finding the thief. She padded into the kitchen and there, seated at the table, noisily guzzling the pie, was a very young man with long fair hair, a red and blue checked shirt and a white silk tie with girls in scarlet bathing costumes on it; he looked as though he suffered from adenoids. Lady Maude had read a good deal in her favorite newspapers about spivs and burglars so that she was not greatly surprised. Had he been in the act of removing the silver, she would have fled in alarm, but as it was she felt nothing but anger. Her whole social foundation seemed to shake beneath the wanton looting of her favorite food. She immediately rushed towards him, shouting for help. The man—he was little more than a youth and very frightened—struck at her wildly with a heavy iron bar. Lady Maude fell backwards upon the table, almost unconscious and bleeding profusely. Then the boy completely lost his head and, seizing up the kitchen meat axe, with a few wild strokes he severed her head from her body. She died like a queen.

Only the moon lit the vast spaces of Brompton Cemetery, showing up here a tomb and there a yew tree. Professor Cadaver's eyes were wild and his hands shook as he glided down the central pathway. His head still whirled with the fumes of the party and a thousand beautiful corpses danced before his eyes. An early underground train rattled in the distance and he hurried his steps. At last he reached his objective—a freshly dug grave on which wooden planks and dying wreaths were piled. The Professor began feverishly to tear these away, but he was getting old and neither his sight nor his step was as sure as it had been, he caught his foot in a rope and fell nine or ten feet into the tomb. When they found him in the morning his neck was broken. The papers hushed up the affair, and a Sunday newspaper in an article entitled "Has Science the Right?" only confused the matter by describing him as a professor of anatomy and talking obscurely of Burke and Hare.

It was the end of Isobel's hopes. True, Mrs. Mule still remained to play the vampire, but without the others she was as nothing. Indeed, the position for Isobel was worse than when she arrived in London, for it would take a long time to live down her close association with the Professor and Guy. Brian was a little nonplussed at first, but there was so much to do at the University that he had little time to think of what might have been. He was now the center of a circle of students and lecturers who listened to his every word. As Isobel's social schemes faded, he began to fill the house with his friends. Sometimes she would find him standing full square before the Zurbarán pointing the end of his pipe at a party of earnest young men sitting bolt upright on the tapestried chairs. "Ah," he would be saying jocosely, "but you haven't yet proved to me that your famous average man or woman is anything but a fiction," or, "But look here, Wotherspoon, you can't just throw words like 'beauty' or 'formal design' about like that. We must define our terms." Once she discovered a tobacco pouch and a Dorothy Sayers detective novel on a tubular chair in the "dear old lav." But if Brian had turned the house into a W.E.A. lecture center, Isobel would not have protested now. Her thoughts were too much with the dead. She sat all day in the vast empty drawing-room, where the two great monuments threw their giant shadows over her. Here she would smoke an endless chain of cigarettes and drink tea off unopened packing cases. Occasionally she would glance up at the inscriptions with a look of mute appeal, but she never seemed to find an answer. She made less and less pretense of reading and listening to good music, and yet for months on end would hardly stir from the house.

A faint April sun shone down upon the wet pavements of the High Street, casting a faint and melancholy light upon the pools of rain that had gathered here and there among the cobblestones. It was a deceptive gleam, however, for the wind was piercingly cold. Miss Thurkill drew her B.A. gown tightly around her thin frame as she emerged from the lecture hall and hurried off to the Heather Café. Turning the corner by Strachan's bookshop, he saw the Master's wife advancing upon her. Despite the freezing weather, the old lady moved slowly, for the bitter winter's crop of influenza and bronchitis had weakened her heart; she seemed now as fat and waddling as her bulldogs.

"Did you get the London appointment?" she shouted; it was a cruel question, for she knew already the negative reply. "Back to the tomb, eh?" she went on. "Ah well! at least we know we're dead here."

Miss Thurkill giggled nervously. "London didn't seem very alive," she said. "I went to see the Cappers, but I couldn't get any reply. The whole house seemed to be shut up."

"Got the plague, I expect," said the Master's wife; "took it from here," and as she laughed to herself, she crouched forward like some huge, squat toad.

"Isobel certainly hasn't been the success she supposed," hissed Miss Thurkill, writhing like a malicious snake. "Well, I shall catch my death of cold if I stay here," she added, and hurried on.

The old lady's voice came to her in the gale that blew down the street: "No one would notice the difference," it seemed to cry.

# Doris Lessing

## TO ROOM NINETEEN

Tʜɪs ɪs ᴀ sᴛᴏʀʏ, I suppose, about a failure in intelligence: the Rawlings' marriage was grounded in intelligence.

They were older when they married than most of their married friends: in their well-seasoned late twenties. Both had had a number of affairs, sweet rather than bitter; and when they fell in love—for they did fall in love—had known each other for some time. They joked that they had saved each other "for the real thing." That they had waited so long (but not too long) for this real thing was to them a proof of their sensible discrimination. A good many of their friends had married young, and now (they felt) probably regretted lost opportunities; while others, still unmarried, seemed to them arid, self-doubting, and likely to make desperate or romantic marriages.

Not only they, but others, felt they were well matched: their friends' delight was an additional proof of their happiness. They had played the same roles, male and female, in this group or set, if such a wide, loosely connected, constantly changing constellation of people could be called a set. They had both become, by virtue of their moderation, their humour, and their abstinence from painful experience people to whom others came for advice. They could be, and were, relied on. It was one of those cases of a man and a woman linking themselves whom no one else had ever thought of linking, probably because of their similarities. But then everyone exclaimed: Of course! How right! How was it we never thought of it before!

And so they married amid general rejoicing, and because of their foresight and their sense for what was probable, nothing was a surprise to them.

Both had well-paid jobs. Matthew was a subeditor on a large London newspaper, and Susan worked in an advertising firm. He was not the stuff of which editors or publicized journalists are made, but he was much more than "a subeditor," being one of the essential background people who in fact steady, inspire and make possible the people in the limelight. He was content with this position. Susan had a talent for commercial drawing. She was humorous about the advertisements she was responsible for, but she did not feel strongly about them one way or the other.

Both, before they married, had had pleasant flats, but they felt it unwise to base a marriage on either flat, because it might seem like a submission of personality on the part of the one whose flat it was not. They moved into a new flat in South Kensington on the clear understanding that when their marriage had settled down (a process they knew would not take long, and was in fact more a humorous concession to popular wisdom than what was due to themselves) they would buy a house and start a family.

And this is what happened. They lived in their charming flat for two years, giving parties and going to them, being a popular young married couple, and then Susan became pregnant, she gave up her job, and they bought a house in Richmond. It was typical of this couple that they had a son first, then a daughter, then twins, son and daughter. Everything right, appropriate, and what everyone would wish for, if they could choose. But people did feel these two had chosen; this balanced and sensible family was no more than what was due to them because of their infallible sense for *choosing* right.

And so they lived with their four children in their gardened house in Richmond and were happy. They had everything they had wanted and had planned for.

*And yet . . .*

Well, even this was expected, that there must be a certain flatness. . . .

Yes, yes, of course, it was natural they sometimes felt like this. Like what?

Their life seemed to be like a snake biting its tail. Matthew's job for the sake of Susan, children, house, and garden—which caravanserai needed a well-paid job to maintain it. And Susan's practical intelligence for the sake of Matthew, the children, the house and the garden—which unit would have collapsed in a week without her.

But there was no point about which either could say: "For the sake of *this* is all the rest." Children? But children can't be a center of life and a reason for being. They can be a thousand things that are delightful, interesting, satisfying, but they can't be a wellspring to live from. Or they shouldn't be. Susan and Matthew knew that well enough.

Matthew's job? Ridiculous. It was an interesting job, but scarcely a reason for living. Matthew took pride in doing it well; but he could hardly be expected to be proud of the newspaper: the newspaper he read, *his* newspaper, was not the one he worked for.

Their love for each other? Well, that was nearest it. If this wasn't a centre, what was? Yes, it was around this point, their love, that the whole extraordinary structure revolved. For extraordinary it certainly was. Both Susan and Matthew had moments of thinking so, of looking in secret disbelief at this thing they had created: marriage, four children, big house, garden, charwomen, friends, cars . . . and this *thing*, this entity, all of it had come into existence, been blown into being out of nowhere, because Susan loved Matthew and Matthew loved Susan. Extraordinary. So that was the central point, the wellspring.

And if one felt that it simply was not strong enough, important enough, to support it all, well, whose fault was that? Certainly neither Susan's nor Matthew's. It was in the nature of things. And they sensibly blamed neither themselves nor each other.

On the contrary, they used their intelligence to preserve what they had created from a painful and explosive world: they looked around them, and took lessons. All around them, marriages collapsing, or breaking, or rubbing along (even worse, they felt). They must not make the same mistakes, they must not.

They had avoided the pitfall so many of their friends had fallen into—of buying a house in the country *for the sake of the children;* so that the husband became a weekend husband, a weekend father, and the wife always careful not to ask what went on in the town flat which they called (in joke) a bachelor flat. No, Matthew was a full-time husband, a full-time father, and at nights, in the big married bed in the big married bedroom (which had an attractive view of the river) they lay beside each other talking and he told her about his day, and what he had done, and whom he had met; and she told him about her day (not as interesting, but that was not her fault) for both knew of the hidden resentments and deprivations of the woman who has lived her own life—and above all, has earned her own living —and is now dependent on a husband for outside interests and money.

Nor did Susan make the mistake of taking a job for the sake of her independence, which she might very well have done, since her old firm, missing her qualities of humour, balance, and sense, invited her often to go back. Children needed their mother to a certain age, that both parents knew and agreed on; and when these four healthy wisely brought-up children were of the right age, Susan would work again, because she knew, and so did he, what happened to women of fifty at the height of their energy and ability, with grown-up children who no longer needed their full devotion.

So here was this couple, testing their marriage, looking after it, treating it like a small boat full of helpless people in a very stormy sea. Well, of course, so it was. . . . The storms of the world were bad, but not too close—which is not to say they were selfishly felt: Susan and Matthew were both well-informed and responsible people. And the inner storms and quicksands were understood and charted. So everything was all right. Everything was in order. Yes, things were under control.

So what did it matter if they felt dry, flat? People like themselves, fed on a hundred books (psychological, anthropological, sociological) could scarcely be unprepared for the dry, controlled wistfulness which is the distinguishing mark of the intelligent marriage. Two people, endowed with education, with discrimination, with judgment, linked together voluntarily from their will to be happy together and to be of use to others—one sees them everywhere, one knows them, one even is that thing oneself: sadness because so much is after all so little. These two, unsurprised, turned towards each other with even more courtesy and gentle love: this was life, that two people, no matter how carefully chosen, could not be everything to each other. In fact, even to say so, to think in such a way, was banal, they were ashamed to do it.

It was banal, too, when one night Matthew came home late and confessed he had been to a party, taken a girl home and slept with her. Susan forgave him, of course. Except that forgiveness is hardly the word. Understanding, yes. But if you understand something you don't forgive it, you are the thing itself: forgiveness is for what you *don't* understand. Nor had he *confessed*—what sort of word is that?

The whole thing was not important. After all, years ago they had joked: Of course I'm not going to be faithful to you, no one can be faithful to one other person for a whole lifetime. (And there was the word *faithful*—stupid, all these words, stupid, belonging to a savage old world.) But the incident left both of them irritable. Strange, but they were both bad-tempered, annoyed. There was something unassimilable about it.

Making love splendidly after he had come home that night, both had felt that the idea that Myra Jenkins, a pretty girl met at a party, could be even relevant was ridiculous. They had loved each other for over a decade, would love each other for years more. Who, then, was Myra Jenkins?

Except, thought Susan, unaccountably bad-tempered, she was (is?) the first. In ten years. So either the ten years' fidelity was not important, or she isn't. (No, no, there is something wrong with this way of thinking, there must be.) But if she isn't important, presumably it wasn't important either when Matthew and I first went to bed with each other that afternoon whose delight even now (like a very long shadow at sundown) lays a long, wandlike finger over us. (Why did I say sundown?) Well, if what we felt that afternoon was not important, nothing is important, because if it hadn't been for what we felt, we wouldn't be Mr. and Mrs. Rawlings with four children, etc., etc. The whole thing is *absurd*—for him to have come home and told me was absurd. For him not to have told me was absurd. For me to care, or for that matter not to care, is absurd . . . and who is Myra Jenkins? Why, no one at all.

There was only one thing to do, and of course these sensible people did it: they put the thing behind them, and consciously, knowing what they were doing, moved forward into a different phase of their marriage, giving thanks for past good fortune as they did so.

For it was inevitable that the handsome, blond, attractive, manly man, Matthew Rawlings, should be at times tempted (oh, what a word!) by the attractive girls at parties she could not attend because of the four children; and that sometimes he would succumb (a word even more repulsive, if possible) and that she, a good-looking woman in the big well-tended garden at Richmond, would sometimes be pierced as by an arrow from the sky with bitterness. Except that bitterness was not in order, it was out of court. Did the casual girls touch the marriage? They did not. Rather it was they who knew defeat because of the handsome Matthew Rawlings' marriage body and soul to Susan Rawlings.

In that case why did Susan feel (though luckily not for longer than a few seconds at a time) as if life had become a desert, and that nothing mattered, and that her children were not her own?

Meanwhile her intelligence continued to assert that all was well. What if her Matthew did have an occasional sweet afternoon, the odd affair? For she knew quite well, except in her moments of aridity, that they were very happy, that the affairs were not important.

Perhaps that was the trouble? It was in the nature of things that the adventures and delights could no longer be hers, because of the four children and the big house that needed so much attention. But perhaps she was secretly wishing, and even knowing that she did, that the wildness and the beauty could be his. But he was married to her. She was married to him. They were married inextricably. And therefore the gods could not strike him with the real magic, not really. Well, was it Susan's fault that after he came home from an adventure he looked harassed rather than fulfilled? (In fact, that was how she knew he had been *unfaithful*, because of his sullen air, and his glances at her, similar to hers at him: What is it that I share with this person that shields all delight from me?) But none of it by any-body's fault. (But what did they feel ought to be somebody's fault?) Nobody's fault, nothing to be at fault, no one to blame, no one to offer or to take it . . . and nothing wrong, either, except that Mat-thew never was really struck, as he wanted to be, by joy; and that Susan was more and more often threatened by emptiness. (It was usually in the garden that she was invaded by this feeling: she was coming to avoid the garden, unless the children or Matthew were with her.) There was no need to use the dramatic words, *unfaithful*, *forgive*, and the rest: intelligence forbade them. Intelligence barred, too, quarrelling, sulking, anger, silences of withdrawal, accusations and tears. Above all, intelligence forbids tears.

A high price has to be paid for the happy marriage with the four healthy children in the large white gardened house.

And they were paying it, willingly, knowing what they were doing. When they lay side by side or breast to breast in the big civi-lized bedroom overlooking the wild sullied river, they laughed, often, for no particular reason; but they knew it was really because of these two small people, Susan and Matthew, supporting such an edifice on their intelligent love. The laugh comforted them; it saved them both, though from what, they did not know.

They were now both fortyish. The older children, boy and girl, were ten and eight, at school. The twins, six, were still at home. Susan did not have nurses or girls to help her: childhood is short; and she did not regret the hard work. Often enough she was bored, since small children can be boring; she was often very tired; but she regretted nothing. In another decade, she would turn herself back into being a woman with a life of her own.

Soon the twins would go to school, and they would be away from home from nine until four. These hours, so Susan saw it, would be the preparation for her own slow emancipation away from the role of hub-of-the-family into woman-with-her-own life. She was already planning for the hours of freedom when all the children would be "off her hands." That was the phrase used by Matthew and by Susan and by their friends, for the moment when the youngest child went off to school. "They'll be off your hands, darling Susan, and you'll have time to yourself." So said Matthew, the intelligent husband, who had often enough commended and consoled Susan, standing by her in spirit during the years when her soul was not her own, as she said, but her children's.

What it amounted to was that Susan saw herself as she had been at twenty-eight, unmarried; and then again somewhere about fifty, blossoming from the root of what she had been twenty years before. As if the essential Susan were in abeyance, as if she were in cold storage. Matthew said something like this to Susan one night: and she agreed that it was true—she did feel something like that. What, then, was this essential Susan? She did not know. Put like that it sounded ridiculous, and she did not really feel it. Anyway, they had a long discussion about the whole thing before going off to sleep in each other's arms.

So the twins went off to their school, two bright affectionate children who had no problems about it, since their older brother and sister had trodden this path so successfully before them. And now Susan was going to be alone in the big house, every day of the school term, except for the daily woman who came in to clean.

It was now, for the first time in this marriage, that something happened which neither of them had foreseen.

This is what happened. She returned, at nine-thirty, from taking the twins to the school by car, looking forward to seven blissful hours of freedom. On the first morning she was simply restless, worrying about the twins "naturally enough" since this was their first day away at school. She was hardly able to contain herself until they came back. Which they did happily, excited by the world of school, looking forward to the next day. And the next day Susan took them, dropped them, came back, and found herself reluctant to enter her big and beautiful home because it was as if something was waiting for her there that she did not wish to confront. Sensibly, however, she parked the car in the garage, entered the house, spoke to Mrs. Parkes the daily woman about her duties, and went up to her bedroom. She was possessed by a fever which drove her out again, downstairs, into the kitchen, where Mrs. Parkes was making cake and did not need her, and into the garden. There she sat on a bench and tried to calm herself, looking at trees, at a brown glimpse of the river. But she was filled with tension, like a panic: as if an enemy was in the garden with her. She spoke to herself severely, thus: All this is quite natural. First, I spent twelve years of my adult life working, *living my own life*. Then I married, and from the moment I became pregnant for the first time I signed myself over, so to speak, to other people. To the children. Not for one moment in twelve years have I been alone, had time to myself. So now I have to learn to be myself again. That's all.

And she went indoors to help Mrs. Parkes cook and clean, and found some sewing to do for the children. She kept herself occupied every day. At the end of the first term she understood she felt two contrary emotions. First: secret astonishment and dismay that during those weeks when the house was empty of children she had in fact been more occupied (had been careful to keep herself occupied) than ever she had been when the children were around her needing her continual attention. Second: that now she knew the house would be full of them, and for five weeks, she resented the fact she would never be alone. She was already looking back at those hours of sewing, cooking (but by herself), as at a lost freedom which would not be hers for five long weeks. And the two months of term which would succeed the five weeks stretched alluringly open to her—freedom. But what freedom—when in fact she had been so careful *not* to be free of small duties during the last weeks? She looked at herself, Susan Rawlings, sitting in a big chair by the window in the bedroom, sewing shirts or dresses, which she might just as well have bought. She saw herself making cakes for hours at a time in the big family kitchen: yet usually she bought cakes. What she saw was a woman alone, that was true, but she had not felt alone. For instance, Mrs. Parkes was always somewhere in the house. And she did not like being in the garden at all, because of the closeness there of the enemy —irritation, restlessness, emptiness, whatever it was, which keeping her hands occupied made less dangerous for some reason.

Susan did not tell Matthew of these thoughts. They were not sensible. She did not recognize herself in them. What should she say to her dear friend and husband Matthew? "When I go into the garden, that is, if the children are not there, I feel as if there is an enemy there waiting to invade me." "What enemy, Susan darling?" "Well, I don't know, really. . . ." "Perhaps you should see a doctor?"

No, clearly this conversation should not take place. The holidays began and Susan welcomed them. Four children, lively, energetic, intelligent, demanding: she was never, not for a moment of her day, alone. If she was in a room, they would be in the next room, or waiting for her to do something for them; or it would soon be time for lunch or tea, or to take one of them to the dentist. Something to do: five weeks of it, thank goodness.

On the fourth day of these so welcome holidays, she found she was storming with anger at the twins, two shrinking beautiful children who (and this is what checked her) stood hand in hand looking at her with sheer dismayed disbelief. This was their calm mother, shouting at them. And for what? They had come to her with some game, some bit of nonsense. They looked at each other, moved closer for support, and went off hand in hand, leaving Susan holding on to the windowsill of the living room, breathing deep, feeling sick. She went to lie down, telling the older children she had a headache. She heard the boy Harry telling the little ones: "It's all right, Mother's got a headache." She heard that *It's all right* with pain.

That night she said to her husband: "Today I shouted at the twins, quite unfairly." She sounded miserable, and he said gently: "Well, what of it?"

"It's more of an adjustment than I thought, their going to school."

"But Susie, Susie darling . . ." For she was crouched weeping on the bed. He comforted her: "Susan, what is all this about? You shouted at them? What of it? If you shouted at them fifty times a day it wouldn't be more than the little devils deserve." But she wouldn't laugh. She wept. Soon he comforted her with his body. She became calm. Calm, she wondered what was wrong with her, and why she should mind so much that she might, just once, have behaved unjustly with the children. What did it matter? They had forgotten it all long ago: Mother had a headache and everything was all right.

It was a long time later that Susan understood that that night, when she had wept and Matthew had driven the misery out of her with his big solid body, was the last time, ever in their married life, that they had been—to use their mutual language—with each other. And even that was a lie, because she had not told him of her real fears at all.

The five weeks passed, and Susan was in control of herself, and good and kind, and she looked forward to the holidays with a mixture of fear and longing. She did not know what to expect. She took the twins off to school (the elder children took themselves to school) and she returned to the house determined to face the enemy wherever he was, in the house, or the garden or—where?

She was again restless, she was possessed by restlessness. She cooked and sewed and worked as before, day after day, while Mrs. Parkes remonstrated: "Mrs. Rawlings, what's the need for it? I can do that, it's what you pay me for."

And it was so irrational that she checked herself. She would put the car into the garage, go up to her bedroom, and sit, hands in her lap, forcing herself to be quiet. She listened to Mrs. Parkes moving around the house. She looked out into the garden and saw the branches shake the trees. She sat defeating the enemy, restlessness. Emptiness. She ought to be thinking about her life, about herself. But she did not. Or perhaps she could not. As soon as she forced her mind to think about Susan (for what else did she want to be alone for?) it skipped off to thoughts of butter or school clothes. Or it thought of Mrs. Parkes. She realized that she sat listening for the movements of the cleaning woman, following her every turn, bend, thought. She followed her in her mind from kitchen to bathroom, from table to oven, and it was as if the duster, the cleaning cloth, the saucepan, were in her own hand. She would hear herself saying: No, not like that, don't put that there. . . . Yet she did not give a damn what Mrs. Parkes did, or if she did it at all. Yet she could not prevent herself from being conscious of her, every minute. Yes, this was what was wrong with her: she needed, when she was alone, to be really alone, with no one near. She could not endure the knowledge that in ten minutes or in half an hour Mrs. Parkes would call up the stairs: "Mrs. Rawlings, there's no silver polish. Madam, we're out of flour."

So she left the house and went to sit in the garden where she was screened from the house by trees. She waited for the demon to appear and claim her, but he did not.

She was keeping him off, because she had not, after all, come to an end of arranging herself.

She was planning how to be somewhere where Mrs. Parkes would not come after her with a cup of tea, or a demand to be allowed to telephone (always irritating since Susan did not care who she telephoned or how often), or just a nice talk about something. Yes, she needed a place, or a state of affairs, where it would not be necessary to keep reminding herself: In ten minutes I must telephone Matthew about . . . and at half past three I must leave early for the children because the car needs cleaning. And at ten o'clock tomorrow I must remember. . . . She was possessed with resentment that the seven hours of freedom in every day (during weekdays in the school term) were not free, that never, not for one second, ever, was she free from the pressure of time, from having to remember this or that. She could never forget herself; never really let herself go into forgetfulness.

Resentment. It was poisoning her. (She looked at this emotion and thought it was absurd. Yet she felt it.) She was a prisoner. (She looked at this thought too, and it was no good telling herself it was a ridiculous one.) She must tell Matthew—but what? She was filled with emotions that were utterly ridiculous, that she despised, yet that nevertheless she was feeling so strongly she could not shake them off.

The school holidays came round, and this time they were for nearly two months, and she behaved with a conscious controlled decency that nearly drove her crazy. She would lock herself in the bathroom, and sit on the edge of the bath, breathing deep, trying to let go into some kind of calm. Or she went up into the spare room, usually empty, where no one would expect her to be. She heard the children calling "Mother, Mother," and kept silent, feeling guilty. Or she went to the very end of the garden, by herself, and looked at the slow-moving brown river; she looked at the river and closed her eyes and breathed slow and deep, taking it into her being, into her veins.

Then she returned to the family, wife and mother, smiling and responsible, feeling as if the pressure of these people—four lively children and her husband—were a painful pressure on the surface of her skin, a hand pressing on her brain. She did not once break down into irritation during these holidays, but it was like living out a prison sentence, and when the children went back to school, she sat on a white stone seat near the flowing river, and she thought: It is not even a year since the twins went to school, since *they were off my hands* (What on earth did I think I meant when I used that stupid phrase?) and yet I'm a different person. I'm simply not myself. I don't understand it.

Yet she had to understand it. For she knew that this structure—big white house, on which the mortgage still cost four hundred a year, a husband, so good and kind and insightful, four children, all doing so nicely, and the garden where she sat, and Mrs. Parkes the cleaning woman—all this depended on her, and yet she could not understand why, or even what it was she contributed to it.

She said to Matthew in their bedroom: "I think there must be something wrong with me."

And he said: "Surely not, Susan? You look marvellous—you're as lovely as ever."

She looked at the handsome blond man, with his clear, intelligent, blue-eyed face, and thought: Why is it I can't tell him? Why not? And she said: "I need to be alone more than I am."

At which he swung his slow blue gaze at her, and she saw what she had been dreading: Incredulity. Disbelief. And fear. An incredulous blue stare from a stranger who was her husband, as close to her as her own breath.

He said: "But the children are at school and off your hands."

She said to herself: I've got to force myself to say: Yes, but do you realize that I never feel free? There's never a moment I can say to myself: There's nothing I have to remind myself about, nothing I have to do in half an hour, or an hour, or two hours. . . .

But she said: "I don't feel well."

He said: "Perhaps you need a holiday."

She said, appalled: "But not without you, surely?" For she could not imagine herself going off without him. Yet that was what he meant. Seeing her face, he laughed, and opened his arms, and she went into them, thinking: Yes, yes, but why can't I say it? And what *is* it I have to say?

She tried to tell him, about never being free. And he listened and said: "But Susan, what sort of freedom can you possibly want—short of being dead! Am I ever free? I go to the office, and I have to be there at ten—all right, half past ten, sometimes. And I have to do this or that, don't I? Then I've got to come home at a certain time—I don't mean it, you know I don't—but if I'm not going to be back home at six I telephone you. When can I ever say to myself: I have nothing to be responsible for in the next six hours?"

Susan, hearing this, was remorseful. Because it was true. The good marriage, the house, the children, depended just as much on his voluntary bondage as it did on hers. But why did he not feel bound? Why didn't he chafe and become restless? No, there was something really wrong with her and this proved it.

And that word *bondage*—why had she used it? She had never felt marriage, or the children, as bondage. Neither had he, or surely they wouldn't be together lying in each other's arms content after twelve years of marriage.

No, her state (whatever it was) was irrelevant, nothing to do with her real good life with her family. She had to accept the fact that after all, she was an irrational person and to live with it. Some people had to live with crippled arms, or stammers, or being deaf. She would have to live knowing she was subject to a state of mind she could not own.

Nevertheless, as a result of this conversation with her husband, there was a new regime next holidays.

The spare room at the top of the house now had a cardboard sign saying: PRIVATE! DO NOT DISTURB! on it. (This sign had been drawn in colored chalks by the children, after a discussion between the parents in which it was decided this was psychologically the right thing.) The family and Mrs. Parkes knew this was "Mother's Room" and that she was entitled to her privacy. Many serious conversations took place between Matthew and the children about not taking Mother for granted. Susan overheard the first, between father and Harry, the older boy, and was surprised at her irritation over it. Surely she could have a room somewhere in that big house and retire into it without such a fuss being made? Without it being so solemnly discussed? Why couldn't she simply have announced: "I'm going to fit out the little top room for myself, and when I'm in it I'm not to be disturbed for anything short of fire"? Just that, and finished; instead of long earnest discussions. When she heard Harry and Matthew explaining it to the twins with Mrs. Parkes coming in—"Yes, well, a family sometimes gets on top of a woman"—she had to go right away to the bottom of the garden until the devils of exasperation had finished their dance in her blood.

But now there was a room, and she could go there when she liked, she used it seldom: she felt even more caged there than in her bedroom. One day she had gone up there after a lunch for ten children she had cooked and served because Mrs. Parkes was not there, and had sat alone for a while looking into the garden. She saw the children stream out from the kitchen and stand looking up at the window where she sat behind the curtains. They were all—her children and their friends—discussing Mother's Room. A few minutes later, the chase of children in some game came pounding up the stairs, but ended as abruptly as if they had fallen over a ravine, so sudden was the silence. They had remembered she was there, and had gone silent in a great gale of "Hush! Shhhhhh! Quiet, you'll disturb her. . . ." And they went tiptoeing downstairs like criminal conspirators. When she came down to make tea for them, they all apologized. The twins put their arms around her, from front and back, making a human cage of loving limbs, and promised it would never occur again. "We forgot, Mummy, we forgot all about it!"

What it amounted to was that Mother's Room, and her need for privacy, had become a valuable lesson in respect for other people's rights. Quite soon Susan was going up to the room only because it was a lesson it was a pity to drop. Then she took sewing up there, and the children and Mrs. Parkes came in and out: it had become another family room.

She sighed, and smiled, and resigned herself—she made jokes at her own expense with Matthew over the room. That is, she did from the self she liked, she respected. But at the same time, something inside her howled with impatience, with rage. . . . And she was frightened. One day she found herself kneeling by her bed and praying: "Dear God, keep it away from me, keep him away from me." She meant the devil, for she now thought of it, not caring if she were irrational, as some sort of demon. She imagined him, or it, as a youngish man, or perhaps a middle-aged man pretending to be young. Or a man young-looking from immaturity? At any rate, she saw the young-looking face which, when she drew closer, had dry lines about mouth and eyes. He was thinnish, meagre in build. And he had a reddish complexion, and ginger hair. That was he—a gingery, energetic man, and he wore a reddish hairy jacket, unpleasant to the touch.

Well, one day she saw him. She was standing at the bottom of the garden, watching the river ebb past, when she raised her eyes and saw this person, or being, sitting on the white stone bench. He was looking at her, and grinning. In his hand was a long crooked stick, which he had picked off the ground, or broken off the tree above him. He was absent-mindedly, out of an absent-minded or freakish impulse of spite, using the stick to stir around in the coils of a blind-worm or a grass snake (or some kind of snakelike creature: it was whitish and unhealthy to look at, unpleasant). The snake was twisting about, flinging its coils from side to side in a kind of dance of protest against the teasing prodding stick.

Susan looked at him thinking: Who is the stranger? What is he doing in our garden? Then she recognized the man around whom her terrors had crystallized. As she did so, he vanished. She made herself walk over to the bench. A shadow from a branch lay across thin emerald grass, moving jerkily over its roughness, and she could see why she had taken it for a snake, lashing and twisting. She went back to the house thinking: Right, then, so I've seen him with my own eyes, so I'm not crazy after all—there *is* a danger because I've seen him. He is lurking in the garden and sometimes even in the house, and he wants *to get into me and to take me over.*

She dreamed of having a room or a place, anywhere, where she could go and sit, by herself, no one knowing where she was.

Once, near Victoria, she found herself outside a news agent that had Rooms to Let advertised. She decided to rent a room, telling no one. Sometimes she could take the train in from Richmond and sit alone in it for an hour or two. Yet how could she? A room would cost three or four pounds a week, and she earned no money, and how could she explain to Matthew that she needed such a sum? What for? It did not occur to her that she was taking it for granted she wasn't going to tell him about the room.

Well, it was out of the question, having a room; yet she knew she must.

One day, when a school term was well established, and none of the children had measles or other ailments, and everything seemed in order, she did the shopping early, explained to Mrs. Parkes she was meeting an old school friend, took the train to Victoria, searched until she found a small quiet hotel, and asked for a room for the day. They did not let rooms by the day, the manageress said, looking doubtful, since Susan so obviously was not the kind of woman who needed a room for unrespectable reasons. Susan made a long explanation about not being well, being unable to shop without frequent rests for lying down. At last she was allowed to rent the room provided she paid a full night's price for it. She was taken up by the manageress and a maid, both concerned over the state of her health . . . which must be pretty bad if, living at Richmond (she had signed her name and address in the register), she needed a shelter at Victoria.

The room was ordinary and anonymous, and was just what Susan needed. She put a shilling in the gas fire, and sat, eyes shut, in a dingy armchair with her back to a dingy window. She was alone. She was alone. She was alone. She could feel pressures lifting off her. First the sounds of traffic came very loud; then they seemed to vanish; she might even have slept a little. A knock on the door: it was Miss Townsend the manageress, bringing her a cup of tea with her own hands, so concerned was she over Susan's long silence and possible illness.

Miss Townsend was a lonely woman of fifty, running this hotel with all the rectitude expected of her, and she sensed in Susan the possibility of understanding companionship. She stayed to talk. Susan found herself in the middle of a fantastic story about her illness, which got more and more improbable as she tried to make it tally with the large house at Richmond, well-off husband, and four children. Suppose she said instead: Miss Townsend, I'm here in your hotel because I need to be alone for a few hours, above all *alone and with no one knowing where I am.* She said it mentally, and saw, mentally, the look that would inevitably come on Miss Townsend's elderly maiden's face. "Miss Townsend, my four children and my husband are driving me insane, do you understand that? Yes, I can see from the gleam of hysteria in your eyes that comes from loneliness controlled but only just contained that I've got everything in the world you've ever longed for. Well, Miss Townsend, I don't want any of it. You can have it, Miss Townsend. I wish I was absolutely alone in the world, like you. Miss Townsend, I'm besieged by seven devils, Miss Townsend, Miss Townsend, let me stay here in your hotel where the devils can't get me. . . ." Instead of saying all this, she described her anemia, agreed to try Miss Townsend's remedy for it, which was raw liver, minced, between whole-meal bread, and said yes, perhaps it would be better if she stayed at home and let a friend do shopping for her. She paid her bill and left the hotel, defeated.

At home Mrs. Parkes said she didn't really like it, no, not really, when Mrs. Rawlings was away from nine in the morning until five. The teacher had telephoned from school to say Joan's teeth were paining her, and she hadn't known what to say; and what was she to make for the children's tea, Mrs. Rawlings hadn't said.

All this was nonsense, of course. Mrs. Parkes's complaint was that Susan had withdrawn herself spiritually, leaving the burden of the big house on her.

Susan looked back at her day of "freedom" which had resulted in her becoming a friend to the lonely Miss Townsend, and in Mrs. Parkes's remonstrances. Yet she remembered the short blissful hour of being alone, really alone. She was determined to arrange her life, no matter what it cost, so that she could have that solitude more often. An absolute solitude, where no one knew her or cared about her.

But how? She thought of saying to her old employer: I want to back you up in a story with Matthew that I am doing part-time work for you. The truth is that . . . but she would have to tell him a lie too, and which lie? She could not say: I want to sit by myself three or four times a week in a rented room. And besides, he knew Matthew, and she could not really ask him to tell lies on her behalf, apart from his being bound to think it meant a lover.

Suppose she really took a part-time job, which she could get through fast and efficiently, leaving time for herself. What job? Addressing envelopes? Canvassing?

And there was Mrs. Parkes, working widow, who knew exactly what she was prepared to give to the house, who knew by instinct when her mistress withdrew in spirit from her responsibilities. Mrs. Parkes was one of the servers of this world, but she needed someone to serve. She had to have Mrs. Rawlings, her madam, at the top of the house or in the garden, so that she could come and get support from her: "Yes, the bread's not what it was when I was a girl. . . . Yes, Harry's got a wonderful appetite, I wonder where he puts it all. . . . Yes, it's lucky the twins are so much of a size, they can wear each other's shoes, that's a saving in these hard times. . . . Yes, the cherry jam from Switzerland is not a patch on the jam from Poland, and three times the price. . . ." And so on. That sort of talk Mrs. Parkes must have, every day, or she would leave, not knowing herself why she left.

Susan Rawlings, thinking these thoughts, found that she was prowling through the great thicketed garden like a wild cat: she was walking up the stairs, down the stairs, through the rooms, into the garden, along the brown running river, back, up through the house, down again. . . . It was a wonder Mrs. Parkes did not think it strange. But on the contrary, Mrs. Rawlings could do what she liked, she could stand on her head if she wanted, provided she was *there*. Susan Rawlings prowled and muttered through her house, hating Mrs. Parkes, hating poor Miss Townsend, dreaming of her hour of solitude in the dingy respectability of Miss Townsend's hotel bedroom, and she knew quite well she was mad. Yes, she was mad.

She said to Matthew that she must have a holiday. Matthew agreed with her. This was not as things had been once—how they had talked in each other's arms in the marriage bed. He had, she knew, diagnosed her finally as *unreasonable*. She had become someone outside himself that he had to manage. They were living side by side in this house like two tolerably friendly strangers.

Having told Mrs. Parkes, or rather, asked for her permission, she went off on a walking holiday in Wales. She chose the remotest place she knew of. Every morning the children telephoned her before they went off to school, to encourage and support her, just as they had over Mother's Room. Every evening she telephoned them, spoke to each child in turn, and then to Matthew. Mrs. Parkes, given permission to telephone for instructions or advice, did so every day at lunchtime. When, as happened three times, Mrs. Rawlings was out on the mountainside, Mrs. Parkes asked that she should ring back at such and such a time, for she would not be happy in what she was doing without Mrs. Rawlings' blessing.

Susan prowled over wild country with the telephone wire holding her to her duty like a leash. The next time she must telephone, or wait to be telephoned, nailed her to her cross. The mountains themselves seemed trammelled by her unfreedom. Everywhere on the mountains, where she met no one at all, from breakfast time to dusk, excepting sheep, or a shepherd, she came face to face with her own craziness which might attack her in the broadest valleys, so that they seemed too small; or on a mountain-top from which she could see a hundred other mountains and valleys, so that they seemed too low, too small, with the sky pressing down too close. She would stand gazing at a hillside brilliant with ferns and bracken, jewelled with running water, and see nothing but her devil, who lifted inhuman eyes at her from where he leaned negligently on a rock, switching at his ugly yellow boots with a leafy twig.

She returned to her home and family, with the Welsh emptiness at the back of her mind like a promise of freedom.

She told her husband she wanted to have an *au pair* girl.

They were in their bedroom, it was late at night, the children slept. He sat, shirted and slippered, in a chair by the window, looking out. She sat brushing her hair and watching him in the mirror. A time-hallowed scene in the connubial bedroom. He said nothing, while she heard the arguments coming into his mind, only to be rejected because every one was *reasonable*.

"It seems strange to get one now, after all, the children are in school most of the day. Surely the time for you to have help was when you were stuck with them day and night. Why don't you ask Mrs. Parkes to cook for you? She's even offered to—I can understand if you are tired of cooking for six people. But you know that an *au pair* girl means all kinds of problems, it's not like having an ordinary char in during the day. . . ."

Finally he said carefully: "Are you thinking of going back to work?"

"No," she said, "no, not really." She made herself sound vague, rather stupid. She went on brushing her black hair and peering at herself so as to be oblivious of the short uneasy glances her Matthew kept giving her. "Do you think we can't afford it?" she went on vaguely, not at all the old efficient Susan who knew exactly what they could afford.

"It's not that," he said, looking out of the window at dark trees, so as not to look at her. Meanwhile she examined a round, candid, pleasant face with clear dark brows and clear gray eyes. A sensible face. She brushed thick healthy black hair and thought: Yet that's the reflection of a madwoman. How very strange! Much more to the point if what looked back at me was the gingery green-eyed demon with his dry meagre smile. . . . Why wasn't Matthew agreeing? After all, what else could he do? She was breaking her part of the bargain and there was no way of forcing her to keep it: that her spirit, her soul, should live in this house, so that the people in it could grow like plants in water, and Mrs. Parkes remain content in their service. In return for this, he would be a good loving husband, and responsible towards the children. Well, nothing like this had been true of either of them for a long time. He did his duty, perfunctorily; she did not even pretend to do hers. And he had become like other husbands, with his real life in his work and the people he met there, and very likely a serious affair. All this was her fault.

At last he drew heavy curtains, blotting out the trees, and turned to force her attention: "Susan, are you really sure we need a girl?" But she would not meet his appeal at all: She was running the brush over her hair again and again, lifting fine black clouds in a small hiss of electricity. She was peering in and smiling as if she were amused at the clinging hissing hair that followed the brush.

"Yes, I think it would be a good idea on the whole," she said, with the cunning of a madwoman evading the real point.

In the mirror she could see her Matthew lying on his back, his hands behind his head, staring upwards, his face sad and hard. She felt her heart (the old heart of Susan Rawlings) soften and call out to him. But she set it to be indifferent.

He said: "Susan, the children?" It was an appeal that *almost* reached her. He opened his arms, lifting them from where they had lain by his sides, palms up, empty. She had only to run across and fling herself into them, onto his hard, warm chest, and melt into herself, into Susan. But she could not. She would not see his lifted arms. She said vaguely: "Well, surely it'll be even better for them? We'll get a French or a German girl and they'll learn the language."

In the dark she lay beside him, feeling frozen, a stranger. She felt as if Susan had been spirited away. She disliked very much this woman who lay here, cold and indifferent beside a suffering man, but she could not change her.

Next morning she set about getting a girl, and very soon came Sophie Traub from Hamburg, a girl of twenty, laughing, healthy, blue-eyed, intending to learn English. Indeed, she already spoke a good deal. In return for a room—"Mother's Room"—and her food, she undertook to do some light cooking, and to be with the children when Mrs. Rawlings asked. She was an intelligent girl and understood perfectly what was needed. Susan said: "I go off sometimes, for the morning or for the day—well, sometimes the children run home from school, or they ring up, or a teacher rings up. I should be here, really. And there's the daily woman. . . ." And Sophie laughed her deep fruity *Fräulein's* laugh, showed her fine white teeth and her dimples, and said: "You want some person to play mistress of the house sometimes, not so?"

"Yes, that is just so," said Susan, a bit dry, despite herself, thinking in secret fear how easy it was, how much nearer to the end she was than she thought. Healthy Fräulein Traub's instant understanding of their position proved this to be true.

The *au pair* girl, because of her own common sense, or (as Susan said to herself with her new inward shudder) because she had been *chosen* so well by Susan, was a success with everyone, the children liking her, Mrs. Parkes forgetting almost at once that she was German, and Matthew finding her "nice to have around the house." For he was now taking things as they came, from the surface of life, withdrawn both as a husband and a father from the household.

One day Susan saw how Sophie and Mrs. Parkes were talking and laughing in the kitchen, and she announced that she would be away until teatime. She knew exactly where to go and what she must look for. She took the District Line to South Kensington, changed to the Circle, got off at Paddington, and walked around looking at the smaller hotels until she was satisfied with one which had FRED'S HOTEL painted on windowpanes that needed cleaning. The façade was a faded shiny yellow, like unhealthy skin. A door at the end of a passage said she must knock; she did, and Fred appeared. He was not at all attractive, not in any way, being fattish, and run-down, and wearing a tasteless striped suit. He had small sharp eyes in a white creased face, and was quite prepared to let Mrs. Jones (she chose the farcical name deliberately, staring him out) have a room three days a week from ten until six. Provided of course that she paid in advance each time she came? Susan produced fifteen shillings (no price had been set by him) and held it out, still fixing him with a bold unblinking challenge she had not known until then she could use at will. Looking at her still, he took up a ten-shilling note from her palm between thumb and forefinger, fingered it; then shuffled up two half crowns, held out his own palm with these bits of money displayed thereon, and let his gaze lower broodingly at them. They were standing in the passage, a red-shaded light above, bare boards beneath, and a strong smell of floor polish rising about them. He shot his gaze up at her over the still-extended palm, and smiled as if to say: What do you take me for? "I shan't," said Susan, "be using this room for the purposes of making money." He still waited. She added another five shillings, at which he nodded and said: "You pay, and I ask no questions." "Good," said Susan. He now went past her to the stairs, and there waited a moment: the light from the street door being in her eyes, she lost sight of him momentarily. Then she saw a sober-suited, white-faced, white-balding little man trotting up the stairs like a waiter, and she went after him. They proceeded in utter silence up the stairs of this house where no questions were asked—Fred's Hotel, which could afford the freedom for its visitors that poor Miss Townsend's hotel could not. The room was hideous. It had a single window, with thin green brocade curtains, a three-quarter bed that had a cheap green satin bedspread on it, a fireplace with a gas fire and a shilling meter by it, a chest of drawers, and a green wicker armchair.

"Thank you," said Susan, knowing that Fred (if this was Fred, and not George, or Herbert or Charlie) was looking at her, not so much with curiosity, an emotion he would not own to, for professional reasons, but with a philosophical sense of what was appropriate. Having taken her money and shown her up and agreed to everything, he was clearly disapproving of her for coming here. She did not belong here at all, so his look said. (But she knew, already, how very much she did belong: the room had been waiting for her to join it.) "Would you have me called at five o'clock, please?" and he nodded and went downstairs.

It was twelve in the morning. She was free. She sat in the armchair, she simply sat, she closed her eyes and sat and let herself be alone. She was alone and no one knew where she was. When a knock came on the door she was annoyed, and prepared to show it: but it was Fred himself, it was five o'clock and he was calling her as ordered. He flicked his sharp little eyes over the room—bed, first. It was undisturbed. She might never have been in the room at all. She thanked him, said she would be returning the day after tomorrow, and left. She was back home in time to cook supper, to put the children to bed, to cook a second supper for her husband and herself later. And to welcome Sophie back from the pictures where she had gone with a friend. All these things she did cheerfully, willingly. But she was thinking all the time of the hotel room, she was longing for it with her whole being.

Three times a week. She arrived promptly at ten, looked Fred in the eyes, gave him twenty shillings, followed him up the stairs, went into the room, and shut the door on him with gentle firmness. For Fred, disapproving of her being here at all, was quite ready to let friendship, or at least acquaintanceship, follow his disapproval, if only she would let him. But he was content to go off on her dismissing nod, with the twenty shillings in his hand.

She sat in the armchair and shut her eyes.

What did she *do* in the room? Why, nothing at all. From the chair, when it had rested her, she went to the window, stretching her arms, smiling, treasuring her anonymity, to look out. She was no longer Susan Rawlings, mother of four, wife of Matthew, employer of Mrs. Parkes and of Sophie Traub, with these and those relations with friends, schoolteachers, tradesmen. She no longer was mistress of the big white house and garden, owning clothes suitable for this and that activity or occasion. She was Mrs. Jones, and she was alone, and she had no past and no future. Here I am, she thought, after all these years of being married and having children and playing those roles of responsibility—and I'm just the same. Yet there have been times I thought that nothing existed of me except the roles that went with being Mrs. Matthew Rawlings. Yes, here I am, and if I never saw any of my family again, here I would still be . . . how very strange that is! And she leaned on the sill, and looked into the street, loving the men and women who passed, because she did not know them. She looked at the downtrodden buildings over the street, and at the sky, wet and dingy, or sometimes blue, and she felt she had never seen buildings or sky before. And then she went back to the chair, empty, her mind a blank. Sometimes she talked aloud, saying nothing—an exclamation, meaningless, followed by a comment about the floral pattern on the thin rug, or a stain on the green satin coverlet. For the most part, she wool-gathered—what word is there for it?—brooded, wandered, simply went dark, feeling emptiness run deliciously through her veins like the movement of her blood.

This room had become more her own than the house she lived in. One morning she found Fred taking her a flight higher than usual. She stopped, refusing to go up, and demanded her usual room, Number 19. "Well, you'll have to wait half an hour then," he said. Willingly she descended to the dark disinfectant-smelling hall, and sat waiting until the two, man and woman, came down the stairs, giving her swift indifferent glances before they hurried out into the street, separating at the door. She went up to the room, *her* room, which they had just vacated. It was no less hers, though the windows were set wide open, and a maid was straightening the bed as she came in.

After these days of solitude, it was both easy to play her part as mother and wife, and difficult—because it was so easy: she felt an impostor. She felt as if her shell moved here, with her family, answering to Mummy, Mother, Susan, Mrs. Rawlings. She was surprised no one saw through her, that she wasn't turned out of doors, as a fake. On the contrary, it seemed the children loved her more; Matthew and she "got on" pleasantly, and Mrs. Parkes was happy in her work under (for the most part, it must be confessed) Sophie Traub. At night she lay beside her husband, and they made love again, apparently just as they used to, when they were really married. But she, Susan, or the being who answered so readily and improbably to the name of Susan, was not there: she was in Fred's Hotel, in Paddington, waiting for the easing hours of solitude to begin.

Soon she made a new arrangement with Fred and with Sophie. It was for five days a week. As for the money, five pounds, she simply asked Matthew for it. She saw that she was not even frightened he might ask what for: he would give it to her, she knew that, and yet it was terrifying it could be so, for this close couple, these partners, had once known the destination of every shilling they must spend. He agreed to give her five pounds a week. She asked for just so much, not a penny more. He sounded indifferent about it. It was as if he were paying her, she thought: *paying her off*—yes, that was it. Terror came back for a moment, when she understood this, but she stilled it: things had gone too far for that. Now, every week, on Sunday nights, he gave her five pounds, turning away from her before their eyes could meet on the transaction. As for Sophie Traub, she was to be somewhere in or near the house until six at night, after which she was free. She was not to cook, or to clean, she was simply to be there. So she gardened or sewed, and asked friends in, being a person who was bound to have a lot of friends. If the children were sick, she nursed them. If teachers telephoned, she answered them sensibly. For the five daytimes in the school week, she was altogether the mistress of the house.

One night in the bedroom, Matthew asked: "Susan, I don't want to interfere—don't think that, please—but are you sure you are well?"

She was brushing her hair at the mirror. She made two more strokes on either side of her head, before she replied: "Yes, dear, I am sure I am well."

He was again lying on his back, his big blond head on his hands, his elbows angled up and part-concealing his face. He said: "Then, Susan, I have to ask you this question, though you must understand,

I'm not putting any sort of pressure on you." (Susan heard the word "pressure" with dismay, because this was inevitable, of course she could not go on like this.) "Are things going to go on like this?"

"Well," she said, going vague and bright and idiotic again, so as to escape: "Well, I don't see why not."

He was jerking his elbows up and down, in annoyance or in pain, and, looking at him, she saw he had got thin, even gaunt; and restless angry movements were not what she remembered of him. He said: "Do you want a divorce, is that it?"

At this, Susan only with the greatest difficulty stopped herself from laughing: she could hear the bright bubbling laughter she *would* have emitted, had she let herself. He could only mean one thing: she had a lover, and that was why she spent her days in London, as lost to him as if she had vanished to another continent.

Then the small panic set in again: she understood that he hoped she did have a lover, he was begging her to say so, because otherwise it would be too terrifying.

She thought this out, as she brushed her hair, watching the fine black stuff fly up to make its little clouds of electricity, hiss, hiss, hiss. Behind her head, across the room, was a blue wall. She realized she was absorbed in watching the black hair making shapes against the blue. She should be answering him. "Do *you* want a divorce, Matthew?"

He said: "That surely isn't the point, is it?"

"You brought it up, I didn't," she said, brightly, suppressing meaningless tinkling laughter.

Next day she asked Fred: "Have enquiries been made for me?"

He hesitated, and she said: "I've been coming here a year now. I've made no trouble, and you've been paid every day. I have a right to be told."

"As a matter of fact, Mrs. Jones, a man did come asking."

"A man from a detective agency?"

"Well, he could have been, couldn't he?"

"I was asking you. . . . Well, what did you tell him?"

"I told him a Mrs. Jones came every weekday from ten until five or six and stayed in Number Nineteen by herself."

"Describing me?"

"Well, Mrs. Jones, I had no alternative. Put yourself in my place."

"By rights I should deduct what that man gave you for the information."

He raised shocked eyes: she was not the sort of person to make jokes like this! Then he chose to laugh: a pinkish wet slit appeared across his white crinkled face: his eyes positively begged her to laugh, otherwise he might lose some money. She remained grave, looking at him.

He stopped laughing and said: "You want to go up now?"—returning to the familiarity, the comradeship, of the country where no questions are asked, on which (and he knew it) she depended completely.

She went up to sit in her wicker chair. But it was not the same. Her husband had searched her out. (The world had searched her out.) The pressures were on her. She was here with his connivance. He might walk in at any moment, here, into Room 19. She imagined the report from the detective agency: "A woman calling herself Mrs. Jones, fitting the description of your wife (etc., etc., etc.), stays alone all day in Room No. 19. She insists on this room, waits for it if it is engaged. As far as the proprietor knows, she receives no visitors there, male or female." A report something on these lines, Matthew must have received.

Well, of course he was right: things couldn't go on like this. He had put an end to it all simply by sending the detective after her.

She tried to shrink herself back into the shelter of the room, a snail pecked out of its shell and trying to squirm back. But the peace of the room had gone. She was trying consciously to revive it, trying to let go into the dark creative trance (or whatever it was) that she had found there. It was no use, yet she craved for it, she was as ill as a suddenly deprived addict.

Several times she returned to the room, to look for herself there, but instead she found the unnamed spirit of restlessness, a prickling fevered hunger for movement, an irritable self-consciousness that made her brain feel as if it had colored lights going on and off inside it. Instead of the soft dark that had been the room's air, were now waiting for her demons that made her dash blindly about, muttering words of hate; she was impelling herself from point to point like a moth dashing herself against a windowpane, sliding to the bottom, fluttering off on broken wings, then crashing into the invisible barrier again. And again and again. Soon she was exhausted, and she told Fred that for a while she would not be needing the room, she was going on holiday. Home she went, to the big white house by the river. The middle of a weekday, and she felt guilty at returning to her own home when not expected. She stood unseen, looking in at the kitchen window. Mrs. Parkes, wearing a discarded floral overall of Susan's, was stooping to slide something into the oven. Sophie, arms folded, was leaning her back against a cupboard and laughing at some joke made by a girl not seen before by Susan—a dark foreign girl, Sophie's visitor. In an armchair Molly, one of the twins, lay curled, sucking her thumb and watching the grownups. She must have some sickness, to be kept from school. The child's listless face, the dark circles under her eyes, hurt Susan: Molly was looking at the three grownups working and talking in exactly the same way Susan looked at the four through the kitchen window: she was remote, shut off from them.

But then, just as Susan imagined herself going in, picking up the little girl, and sitting in an armchair with her, stroking her probably heated forehead, Sophie did just that: she had been standing on one leg, the other knee flexed, its foot set against the wall. Now she let her foot in its ribbon-tied red shoe slide down the wall, stood solid on two feet, clapping her hands before and behind her, and sang a couple of lines in German, so that the child lifted her heavy eyes at her and began to smile. Then she walked, or rather skipped, over to the child, swung her up, and let her fall into her lap at the same moment she sat herself. She said "Hopla! Hopla! Molly . . ." and began stroking the dark untidy young head that Molly laid on her shoulder for comfort.

*Well.* . . . Susan blinked the tears of farewell out of her eyes, and went quietly up the house to her bedroom. There she sat looking at the river through the trees. She felt at peace, but in a way that was new to her. She had no desire to move, to talk, to do anything at all. The devils that had haunted the house, the garden, were not there; but she knew it was because her soul was in Room 19 in Fred's Hotel; she was not really here at all. It was a sensation that should have been frightening: to sit at her own bedroom window, listening to Sophie's rich young voice sing German nursery songs to her child, listening to Mrs. Parkes clatter and move below, and to know that all this had nothing to do with her: she was already out of it.

Later, she made herself go down and say she was home: it was unfair to be here unannounced. She took lunch with Mrs. Parkes, Sophie, Sophie's Italian friend Maria, and her daughter Molly, and felt like a visitor.

A few days later, at bedtime, Matthew said: "Here's your five pounds," and pushed them over at her. Yet he must have known she had not been leaving the house at all.

She shook her head, gave it back to him, and said, in explanation, not in accusation: "As soon as you knew where I was, there was no point."

He nodded, not looking at her. He was turned away from her: thinking, she knew, how best to handle this wife who terrified him.

He said: "I wasn't trying to . . . it's just that I was worried."

"Yes, I know."

"I must confess that I was beginning to wonder . . ."

"You thought I had a lover?"

"Yes, I am afraid I did."

She knew that he wished she had. She sat wondering how to say: "For a year now I've been spending all my days in a very sordid hotel room. It's the place where I'm happy. In fact, without it I don't exist." She heard herself saying this, and understood how terrified he was that she might. So instead she said: "Well, perhaps you're not far wrong."

Probably Matthew would think the hotel proprietor lied: he would want to think so.

"Well," he said, and she could hear his voice spring up, so to speak, with relief: "in that case I must confess I've got a bit of an affair on myself."

She said, detached and interested: "Really? Who is she?" and saw Matthew's startled look because of this reaction.

"It's Phil. Phil Hunt."

She had known Phil Hunt well in the old unmarried days. She was thinking: No, she won't do, she's too neurotic and difficult. She's never been happy yet. Sophie's much better: Well, Matthew will see that himself, as sensible as he is.

This line of thought went on in silence, while she said aloud: "It's no point telling you about mine, because you don't know him."

Quick, quick, invent, she thought. Remember how you invented all that nonsense for Miss Townsend.

She began slowly, careful not to contradict herself: "His name is Michael"—(*Michael What?*)—"Michael Plant." (What a silly name!) "He's rather like you—in looks, I mean." And indeed, she could imagine herself being touched by no one but Matthew himself. "He's a publisher." (Really? Why?) "He's got a wife already and two children."

She brought out this fantasy, proud of herself.

Matthew said: "Are you two thinking of marrying?"

She said, before she could stop herself: "Good God, *no!*"

She realized, if Matthew wanted to marry Phil Hunt, that this was too emphatic, but apparently it was all right, for his voice sounded relieved as he said: "It is a bit impossible to imagine oneself married to anyone else, isn't it?" With which he pulled her to him, so that her head lay on his shoulder. She turned her face into the dark of his flesh, and listened to the blood pounding through her ears saying: I am alone, I am alone, I am alone.

In the morning Susan lay in bed while he dressed.

He had been thinking things out in the night, because now he said: "Susan, why don't we make a foursome?"

Of course, she said to herself, of course he would be bound to say that. If one is sensible, if one is reasonable, if one never allows oneself a base thought or an envious emotion, naturally one says: Let's make a foursome!

"Why not?" she said.

"We could all meet for lunch. I mean, it's ridiculous, you sneaking off to filthy hotels, and me staying late at the office, and all the lies everyone has to tell."

What on earth did I say his name was?—she panicked, then said: "I think it's a good idea, but Michael is away at the moment. When he comes back though—and I'm sure you two would like each other."

"He's away, is he? So that's why you've been . . ." Her husband put his hand to the knot of his tie in a gesture of male coquetry she would not before have associated with him; and he bent to kiss her cheek with the expression that goes with the words: Oh you naughty little puss! And she felt its answering look, naughty and coy, come onto her face.

Inside she was dissolving in horror at them both, at how far they had both sunk from honesty of emotion.

So now she was saddled with a lover, and he had a mistress! How ordinary, how reassuring, how jolly! And now they would make a foursome of it, and go about to theatres and restaurants. After all, the Rawlings could well afford that sort of thing, and presumably the publisher Michael Plant could afford to do himself and his mistress quite well. No, there was nothing to stop the four of them developing the most intricate relationship of civilized tolerance, all enveloped in a charming afterglow of autumnal passion. Perhaps they would all go off on holidays together? She had known people who did. Or perhaps Matthew would draw the line there? Why should he, though, if he was capable of talking about "foursomes" at all?

She lay in the empty bedroom, listening to the car drive off with Matthew in it, off to work. Then she heard the children clattering off to school to the accompaniment of Sophie's cheerfully ringing voice. She slid down into the hollow of the bed, for shelter against her own irrelevance. And she stretched out her hand to the hollow where her husband's body had lain, but found no comfort there: he was not her husband. She curled herself up in a small tight ball under the clothes: she could stay here all day, all week, indeed, all her life.

But in a few days she must produce Michael Plant, and—but how? She must presumably find some agreeable man prepared to impersonate a publisher called Michael Plant. And in return for which she would—what? Well, for one thing they would make love. The idea made her want to cry with sheer exhaustion. Oh no, she had finished with all that—the proof of it was that the words "make love," or even imagining it, trying hard to revive no more than the pleasures of sensuality, let alone affection, or love, made her want to run away and hide from the sheer effort of the thing. . . . Good Lord, why make love at all? Why make love with anyone? Or if you are going to make love, what does it matter who with? Why shouldn't she simply walk into the street, pick up a man and have a roaring sexual affair with him? Why not? Or even with Fred? What difference did it make?

But she had let herself in for it—an interminable stretch of time with a lover, called Michael, as part of a gallant civilized foursome. Well, she could not, and she would not.

She got up, dressed, went down to find Mrs. Parkes, and asked her for the loan of a pound, since Matthew, she said, had forgotten to leave her money. She exchanged with Mrs. Parkes variations on the theme that husbands are all the same, they don't think, and without saying a word to Sophie, whose voice could be heard upstairs from the telephone, walked to the underground, travelled to South Kensington, changed to the Inner Circle, got out at Paddington, and walked to Fred's Hotel. There she told Fred that she wasn't going on holiday after all, she needed the room. She would have to wait an hour, Fred said. She went to a busy tearoom-cum-restaurant around the corner, and sat watching the people flow in and out the door that kept swinging open and shut, watched them mingle and merge and separate, felt her being flow into them, into their movement. When the hour was up she left a half crown for her pot of tea, and left the place without looking back at it, just as she had left her house, the big, beautiful white house, without another look, but silently dedicating it to Sophie. She returned to Fred, received the key of No. 19, now free, and ascended the grimy stairs slowly, letting floor after floor fall away below her, keeping her eyes lifted, so that floor after floor descended jerkily to her level of vision, and fell away out of sight.

No. 19 was the same. She saw everything with an acute, narrow, checking glance: the cheap shine of the satin spread, which had been replaced carelessly after the two bodies had finished their convulsions under it; a trace of powder on the glass that topped the chest of drawers; an intense green shade in a fold of the curtain. She stood at the window, looking down, watching people pass and pass and pass until her mind went dark from the constant movement. Then she sat in the wicker chair, letting herself go slack. But she had to be careful, because she did not want, today, to be surprised by Fred's knock at five o'clock.

The demons were not here. They had gone forever, because she was buying her freedom from them. She was slipping already into the dark fructifying dream that seemed to caress her inwardly, like the movement of her blood . . . but she had to think about Matthew first. Should she write a letter for the coroner? But what should she say? She would like to leave him with the look on his face she had seen this morning—banal, admittedly, but at least confidently healthy. Well, that was impossible, one did not look like that with a wife dead from suicide. But how to leave him believing she was dying because of a man—because of the fascinating publisher Michael Plant? Oh, how ridiculous! How absurd! How humiliating! But she decided not to trouble about it, simply not to think about the living. If he wanted to believe she had a lover, he would believe it. And he *did* want to believe it. Even when he had found out that there was no publisher in London called Michael Plant, he would think: Oh poor Susan, she was afraid to give me his real name.

And what did it matter whether he married Phil Hunt or Sophie? Though it ought to be Sophie, who was already the mother of those children . . . and what hypocrisy to sit here worrying about the children, when she was going to leave them because she had not got the energy to stay.

She had about four hours. She spent them delightfully, darkly, sweetly, letting herself slide gently, gently, to the edge of the river. Then, with hardly a break in her consciousness, she got up, pushed the thin rug against the door, made sure the windows were tight shut, put two shillings in the meter, and turned on the gas. For the first time since she had been in the room she lay on the hard bed that smelled stale, that smelled of sweat and sex.

She lay on her back on the green satin cover, but her legs were chilly. She got up, found a blanket folded in the bottom of the chest of drawers, and carefully covered her legs with it. She was quite content lying there, listening to the faint soft hiss of the gas that poured into the room, into her lungs, into her brain, as she drifted off into the dark river.

# Willem F. Hermans

## THE HOUSE OF REFUGE

THE LARGE LIMB, nearly the whole top, suddenly lay under the tree, without my hearing any sound of cracking. It was drowned by the explosion of earth clods in a short-lived growth of scrub, not far from the tree.

Other explosions followed, though I did not see their effect. I did not look back. No one walked ahead of me. Perhaps I was the first. There were few trees and I must have been quite easy to spot. Still it seemed as though the firing was being done at random. I turned my ankles with every step on the hard clods of earth. The incline was high and steep. On the other side of the hill lay the Germans. I hoped they would come to meet us. I would seek cover, creep quietly away somewhere. From thirst alone I could hardly go on. My canteen was empty. I looked around at the others. No one was near enough to ask for water. Then the sergeant blew his whistle. We gathered by a sunken road and fell down to rest. I raised my empty canteen. But those who saw it shook their heads. In fact almost no one paid any attention to it. The sergeant, lying nearest to me, had shoved his helmet over his face to shut out the heat and the light; with his hands crossed on his breast, it looked as if he were sleeping. The sun was glaring; it had not rained for days. The yellow ground was so dry that the dust raised by the exploding shells did not settle again.

I looked at my wrist watch. It was half-past one. A silence had fallen; everyone who participated in the war seemed to have relaxed, as if the war were a huge sick body that had been given a morphine injection. The only thing that happened: three fighters in action at a great height. I looked at them, a dry blade of grass between my teeth. They drew a pattern of white loops on the blue of the sky, as advertisement writers do. It looked as if they were doing it to amuse us, only for that. Do not try to read what they write, or you'll go crazy. Coca-Cola. They need both of their hands, I thought, but perhaps they have a rubber tube in their mouth, through which they can suck in a drink. The bullets from their machine guns hit the ground near us. Right now they could get me, I thought, and I just sit here, I do nothing. I am thirsty. Right now I could be hit, as if there were a death sentence for sitting. But everyone dies, even if there never were a war. What difference does war make? Just imagine myself as someone who has no memory, who can think of nothing but what he sees, hears and feels . . . For him no war exists. He sees the hill, the sky, he feels the dry tissue of his throat shrink, he hears the explosions of . . . he would have to have a memory to know of what. He hears explosions. He sees people lying here and there. It is warm. The sun is shining. Three airplanes are practicing advertisement writing. Nothing is happening. War does not exist.

I thought about a Spaniard who had asked me for a match that morning. He knew a few words of French. In the company, which consisted of Bulgarian, Czech, Hungarian and Rumanian partisans, there was no one that I could understand.

How long I have been away from the Netherlands, I thought, always in different foreign countries, everywhere the same darkness at evening in the towns and then no one at all to whom I can talk. In Germany I could at least listen to the conversations of others. But now everything I heard was mere sound. Rumbling of motors, explosions, buzzing of bullets, shrieking of animals, rustling, cracking, thumping, barking. From people too, there came only sounds. "Proletarians of all countries, unite!" But they are not able to exchange one single word with one another.

Sometimes I did not even understand the commands. That made no difference to the officers. Three days ago our platoon lay under its own fire. A special Russian detachment also came and picked out five men whom they took behind the shed where we were lying, and shot. One had tried to run away. The following morning he lay, face upward, in the middle of the road. No one dared to shove him aside. We marched over him, putting our feet down on him so as not to lose step. I walked behind in the column. When I reached him, his head was already crushed and unrecognizable. I could not tell who it was. I must have seen him daily for the past three months. Still I would not have known what his name was.

While one of the fighters began to lose altitude, I thought about the Spaniard who spoke French. I would have liked to talk to him now.

The airplane changed into a comet of soot and struck the ground somewhere behind me. The explosion sounded as though the world had made a sound of ingurgitation, increased a millionfold. There was satisfaction in that sound, as if the earth had lain in wait for that airplane as a frog does for a fly. Then a black cloud of soot began gradually to obstruct the view on the road. Suddenly through the smoke I saw the Spaniard coming toward me bareheaded. It was as if the plane that crashed had brought him here, as if he had appeared from the wreck unhurt.

I wanted to call something to him. I wanted to call: I was just thinking about you! But I did not know how to formulate that so quickly.

Perhaps I had completely forgotten how to speak.

That is why I did not even take the trouble to raise my arm to him. But still he seemed to have recognized me. He squatted next to me. He laid his helmet, which he had been carrying in his hand like a pail, over his knee.

"Where from?" he asked.

"Holland! Already four years away! November 1940!"

"Ah! Is nothing! I eight years!" He swatted a horsefly on his cheek. "Eight years!" He stuck up eight fingers.

Now there was no more shooting anywhere. The only thing that could be heard was the crackle of the burning airplane behind our backs. "I spy," I said, "a bit." With my hands I showed what a bit of a spy I had been, while I was considering the following sentence. "Arrested by Germans. Jail. Sentenced. Three years. Prison. Escaped on way to other prison. Then arrested again. Concentration camp. Strellwitz. You know Strellwitz? Six months. Escaped again. Caught just at Swiss border. Jumped off train in Saxony. Walked, kept on and on walking, toward the east."

I looked at him without noticing anything. I would not even know now what color eyes he had. I looked at him the way you mostly look at others: without really knowing anything about them, obliged, by a lack of proof, to assume that they are about the same as yourself.

Words are nothing more than currents of air in a hermetically closed room which change nothing essential, incessantly restoring balances without ever having disturbed them.

"I out Spain when civil war," he said. "I Communist. Taken by French. In camp. Then escape. On ship. Turkey, Russia."

Having got that far with the story, he began speaking more rapidly and using more Spanish words. I understood that Russia had not been what he expected. That is why I said, for the first time since I had been outside the sphere of German influence: "I no Communist!" He laughed.

"Merde! Tout ça, merde!"

"Kameraad! Give me a cigarette!"

Talking had made me still thirstier. He had no canteen with him either.

He broke his last cigarette in two and stretched out on one elbow.

"What do you do?" he asked. He made it clear to me that he wanted to know what I had done formerly, before the war.

"School," I said. "Technical school."

"Yo yesero," he answered, "moi yesero!" Because I shrugged my shoulders, he repeated the strange word several times, as if by doing that it would become a new idea for me: something which he was, for once and always, as a horse is a horse and not a tiger. "Yesero!" Our conversation must have ended about there. I remember quite well that we did not tell each other our names. When I thought of him afterward, I thought of "the Yesero." Now I've looked it up in a Spanish dictionary; it means lime-burner—a kind of work I had never heard of, of which I knew nothing. One of our tanks came riding up the incline. We stood up and, with our rifles under our arms, walked behind it, to the highest point on the ridge of the hill. From there I had a view of a little valley where, beside a river, lay one of those towns that are shown on colored posters in the waiting rooms of stations. I had never expected to see one this way.

The Germans fired at us from all directions. I had already lost the Yesero. I descended slowly, straight through a nearly ripe vineyard. I crept and jumped over the soldiers that had been killed. But the Germans were by no means all dead, though three of our tanks had already reached the top of the hill. I did not know where all the missiles came from. It seemed as if nothing could be done about it. I knelt, crept, clutched the tendrils of the vines so as not to slide down with my heavy pack. And then to have to shoot too. From time to time I forgot everything and crammed my mouth full of sour grapes.

Late in the afternoon I was walking on a road along the river. From a house near a bend, built against a declivity, came firing. I dropped on my stomach close to the water. My rifle lay on the asphalt road. The sergeant and two others crept in the brush against the declivity, with the intention of getting above the house. I waited. No one was on that road but me. Nothing could be seen at the house. The Germans did not fire any more because they could not see me. There was a large tobacco pipe painted on the side wall of the house. It was quiet everywhere. I did not move, yet I lived a hundred times as fast as usual. Then I heard the sound of three explosions. The roof flew up in a swarm of black slates. Smoke began billowing from the windows in a much slower tempo than mine. A German came out and ran toward the road. I shot him. Also a second, a third, a fourth. They folded double like a butterfly that is pinned up; I stuck them dead with a pin two hundred meters long. I did not succeed in hitting the fifth one before he jumped in the river. I shoved a new magazine in my rifle, and when I had shot it empty, I thought that I did not see the German's head above water any longer. I stood up and rushed forward. While I walked, I thought of everything. Possibly one of the Germans was not dead. He could shoot me with his pistol. Or there had been more inside the house; there were still a couple of them there. Or they had run out at the back, while I was aiming at the swimmer, and had hidden themselves in the bushes against the slope. They could not possibly miss when I went by. But I did not know what to do other than run. There would come an end to it, finally an end. I pulled my head in with fright. And like that I jumped over the bodies on the road without looking at them longer than was necessary to keep from tripping. But nothing happened. Houses appeared between me and the river. The nails in my shoes scraped over the cobblestones, the little street wound its way up to a square where our tank was standing.

I saw no Germans. Partisans stood in groups in front of a café, with bottles in their hands. I slung my rifle over my shoulder—I had kept it ready for action—and wanted to go inside too. But the sergeant came forward and held me back. He was bareheaded; he looked at me like an enemy. "Booby trap!" he said. He also said a lot more that I did not understand. "Booby trap!" He pushed me away. He pointed farther into the town and gave me a slap on the shoulder that pushed me at once in the right direction. From rage I felt no longer tired. But the street rose higher. At a corner I squatted by the iron nozzle of a fountain that spouted water. I held my whole head under it; the water ran under my clothes and down my back.

It tasted of sulphur, and was slightly effervescent. The trail over which it had reached the gutter for centuries was marked on the ground by a spotless precipitate of light yellow. Apparently it came from a natural spring; at all the street corners were the same eternally running fountains. And then suddenly I knew it: this was a spa, a de luxe spa. I was certain of it when I had climbed from the oldest part of the town and saw hotels standing surrounded by parklike gardens.

There was no one here except myself. The inhabitants must have fled or been evacuated. Two dogs came toward me. I put my hand out to them, but they ran after each other and took no notice of me.

It made me feel as if I were dead, as if I could see them but they could not see me. I was unable to get rid of the idea that they had run right through me instead of past me. I heard nothing but their panting and the ticking of their nails on the stones. The deserted houses stood on the point of moving and grouping themselves around me, offering themselves as the women in travel stories from India do.

The war had never really taken place; as long as I was not wounded, nothing had happened. There never were other people, never as long as I had lived, nowhere in the world. I stood still and took off my pack. I kept only my rifle, my helmet, my bayonet, my cartridges and my grenades with me. With these I walked along a low stone balustrade below which lay three red tennis courts. I did not know any more how tennis was played; I did not know what the net, the white lines, the high white chair, the heavy roller in a corner were for. The sun went down behind my back. It was reflected in the large window panes of a house diagonally across from me. With every step I took, one of the windows changed into an immense sheet of polished red copper. And then they shone only a deep black. I stood directly across from them.

The house itself was not large, but its subsidiary parts were large. The windows were of a solid piece of plate glass; the door frame had a height of two stories; there was a balcony along the whole width. In front lay a deep green, sloping lawn, with a large plane tree to one side. The top had been polled repeatedly so that the tree looked like a gallows with room for a whole family. The front door, which was of glass and metalwork, stood ajar.

Go look inside. I had time enough. I was given orders, I was sent somewhere. I did not know where, but nevertheless I could not just go back to the sergeant. I would construe the orders in my own manner. . . . Who knew what would come of it?

When I entered the garden and went slowly up toward the front steps, I realized that this would be the first time in ages that I would set foot in a real house, a private house. I had slept in jails, in barracks, on straw in school buildings, once under a truck, in haystacks, in freight trains. For three years now I had slept only in shelters where people work, wait, or are imprisoned: railway stations, police stations, sheds; also a week in a hospital. I looked inside through the open door; it was not dark, the corridor led to an outside door at the back. My hands broke into a sweat when I stood at the top of the steps and looked back before going inside. Imagine you've never been anywhere other than here, or make yourself believe you have captured this house and this hill as the solution to a puzzle; this, out of everything else that exists in the world. I was so impressed with the idea that I wiped my feet in the vestibule. Only then did I push the heavy door shut with my two hands. That shifted the atmosphere of the house, and it penetrated my nose. My mouth watered and I slid my tongue over my lips as I went to the back door. Some doctors declare that love at first sight is awakened not by what is seen but by what is smelled. Man knows well enough that he can never believe another, that what is said or shown never convinces. Smell, which works the weakest at a distance, which can be overpowered by perfume but never killed, cannot deceive because it continuously renews itself. Stench is always there, unchangeable. Smell is the only thing that tells the truth.

A lady's coat lay on the sofa. It spoke as the objects in a detective novel do. It said: I am lying carelessly crumpled, though I am expensive. Someone threw me here who was on the point of putting me on and going out. But she noticed that she had forgotten something. She is still in the house. Be careful, you are not alone. Two elk heads on the wall said nothing. I looked out through the back doors, across a long rectangular French garden. At the back stood a summerhouse. I put my rifle under my arm and began, nearly at a trot, to search as quickly as possible. I left all doors open behind me. I paid no attention to where I stepped. Booby traps!

This house would not collapse on my head. It did not smell like it. I was like a man, who, having recovered something, touches it continually to make sure it is within his reach. My searching did not look at all like an examination. I only wanted to absorb everything; I was not afraid.

In the downstairs rooms I saw no one. I even looked under the rug that hung from a large grand piano. Nothing. Yet I could not get rid of the feeling that someone had been here a short while ago. Biting one of my fingers, I stood in the middle of the salon and thought. On the wall hung painted portraits which gave no answer. On the mantelpiece were candelabra with half-burned candles in them; there was ash in the ashtrays, and a small crystal tumbler containing cigarettes. No, those things could have been here three months as well as three hours. Suddenly I knew what it was: nowhere was there dust. As long as a house is not dusty, it lives, as a body is not dead as long as it perspires.

I left the rooms, went into the kitchen. A pan of soup was steaming softly on a smoldering coal range. I did not see anyone. I went into the hall on my way to the upper stories. A staircase with a richly sculptured, gilded balustrade was thrown upward like a boomerang.

Perhaps, I thought, when I put my foot on the top step, all the booby traps in the whole house will explode. A woman was here to set them, just before she fled and left her coat behind. There was a room with bookcases and a writing desk. One room was locked. "Anyone here?" I called, while I banged on the door with the butt of my rifle. I only heard my own breathing and then my heart beat. Force the door? No, a waste of time. I went to a large bedroom which was separated by a heavy curtain from a still larger bathroom. The bathtub was knee high in the middle of the marble floor. Two bronze hydras held their heads over the rim. I opened the taps, both of them.

The water from one was immediately hot. A warm-water tap out of which warm water really runs! That had not happened during the whole war! I was so excited that I took off my clothes and let the bathtub fill up. Whoever might be hidden in the house could come out; I would not do anything. Yes, I had understood the sergeant's orders damned well! He had said: "I don't want to see your black face any longer! I don't want to smell your stinking hide! Beat it and scrub your paunch!" That is what that Bulgarian, Montenegrin, Slevene, or whatever he was, had said. Booby traps! Nowhere booby traps!

I stepped over the low rim of the bathtub and lay down. My high spirits quieted. Some of the water ran into my mouth. It tasted like the water that spouted from the fountains at the street corners. When I had lain in it for some minutes, I had the impression that it possessed a benumbing effect. I would slowly fall asleep. All the feeling in my body would gradually recede, from outside inward; it would concentrate at one point and then disappear into nothing. First my skin would become insensitive and finally I would not even hear my heart beat any longer. If people had no feeling, many things in the world would be improved. They could lose an arm or a leg without noticing; it would feel no different from paring nails. They could bleed to death without feeling it, smiling. Even at an early age! Babies could go on sucking their thumbs while they were boiled in bath water that was too hot. Who would pay any attention to a hole in his head if it did not cause any pain? Who would lie in bed if he felt no sleepiness? People should have been feelingless! Then there never would have been so many! Then so many would never have been left over! But they become more easily blind or deaf than feelingless. Because of such paltry inconspicuous tricks, the world goes on existing. I looked at my body to see if it was not engaged in the process of changing into a sulphur-yellow mummy. But I did not

even fall asleep. Behind a high window I saw the polled top of the
plane tree, spotted white like a primed door. Outside it was quiet;
there was no firing and I heard no motors. The piece of sky that I
could see became red and later purple. The objects in the room very
soon lost their shapes. I did not hurry. Not to leave anything untried,
I pulled the cord of an electric switch. We ourselves were accustomed to connecting a land mine to an electric wire here and there in
the houses of the places we evacuated. But nothing happened here,
no explosion. No light either, as a matter of fact. Now I remembered
again that everywhere in the rooms and halls were half-burned candles. Probably there had been no electricity in this town for some
time. I was safe, I solved puzzles with ease. I could lie in my bath as
long as I liked.

Only when a bomb suddenly exploded not far away, making the
water splash, did I get out to dress again. I dried myself, went to the
bedroom for a candle and screwed a Gillette together which, like
everything, stood in readiness over the washstand. More bombs kept
falling. I also heard machine guns, but could not see anything unusual from the window. Before a mirror in which I could see myself
from top to bottom, I shaved. I could always remain in a room completely lined with mirrors, without ever becoming bored, like Robin-
son Crusoe on his island. He who only thinks has but a partial contact with himself. Seeing has more value; seeing is everything. To see
yourself as another does would mean salvation, but you are always
on the wrong side.

I was especially attentive. Now that I was so clean, I expected to
discover almost anything. I discovered nothing. What I had experienced had disappeared, leaving no marks behind. Memory cannot
keep up with outward events. A man of eighty who looks in the
mirror does not have the impression that when he was eight he saw
another there.

Yet so much in me had changed at that moment that I could not
bring myself to put on my dirty underclothes and uniform again. I
went to a closet in the bedroom. A row of suits was hanging there
with shirts and ties on a shelf above them. While I was trying to
fasten trousers that were too wide for me, but also too short, heavy
motors raced by on the other side of the house. I did not consider
what they could mean. I had heard noise enough for my whole life. I
felt hungry and remembered the soup I had found. When I was
ready (the white shirt was as crisp and delightful as cake) I went to
the kitchen and ate the soup with a ladle from the pan.

After I had eaten everything, I lay on the sofa in the salon, propped with cushions, and smoked a cigarette. I looked at the ceiling, which represented the sky with golden angels. I flipped the ash on the carpet, but not without inner disapproval—I who had blown my nose on my shirt, who never washed my hands any more before eating, not to speak of brushing my teeth; I who had spit for three years wherever I felt like it, and had not wiped my hole for weeks.

It seemed to me that I must behave with decency again, though the owner of the house should be grateful to me if I did not plunder. His servant had made soup while I squirmed on the ground with thirst. Before I left, I would surely look in the cellar. That would make everything all right. A good bottle for the sergeant. He should never think that I did not understand his orders. I crushed the cigarette out underneath the sofa. I thought of everything I had seen in the house and felt that I was everywhere at the same time. You know exactly where things are, because you can easily go back to see if you have made a mistake. To be alone in a house where no one can come to remove anything or to change anything; it is enough with which to make a success of life. But I had not been everywhere in this house; I could not get in that one room. Perhaps I was not even alone. Still I heard no rustling or creaking anywhere.

I looked straight in the face of my mother, who pointed reproachfully at the carpet, where my footprints lay in white mud. "But you are dead," I answered, though she had said nothing. "Weren't you to be buried today?"

I was awakened by the chiming of a large clock. It came from the interior of the house. The candle was burned out.

Still it was not dark in the room. A red glow from big fires wavered on and off. The chiming stopped then started again. I got up from the sofa. Then I understood that the tinkling came from the doorbell. It would be useless not to open. Who could be at the door other than one of our own partisans? I walked to the corridor. Someone flashed an electric torch across the wall. I did not avoid it. When it fell on me it went out. Through the metalwork of the door, I could clearly see the person who had used it standing there.

But only when I had opened the door, and stepped immediately outside, did I see that it was a German. With his helmet pulled low over his eyes he looked like a lamppost without a light. He saluted with a gloved hand and asked: "Do you occupy this house?" I looked over his head at his motorcycle, which stood against the plane tree, I looked at the fire, of which I could see three focuses. "Yes," I said then. "I am ill. I was sleeping."

"Ah so! That shows more spirit than running away like the

others in this confounded place. How many rooms has your house?"

From something that was burning against the horizon sprang a broom of long-lasting sparks. I gave no answer.

"We would like to house a number of officers here."

"I congratulate the German Army on liberating us so quickly," I answered. "Heil Hitler!"

In the meantime I considered. How many rooms had the house? I did not even know how many stories.

The German made a gesture signifying that the recapture had cost him no difficulty. He walked back to his motorcycle when I said that the officers would be welcome.

I slammed the door, lit a candle and began going through the house, step by step so that the flame would not blow out. I did not want to run away, yet I would have to while it was still possible. How long had I not been running away? Only I really did not know where now. And when I saw my uniform in the bathroom, looking like a heap of rags by the candlelight, like the clothes of someone who had been murdered, I felt even less like putting them on than I had a couple of hours ago. Besides, where would that leave me? If the Germans found me I would be taken prisoner, and then they would find out soon enough who I really was. Or perhaps they shot partisans at once. So I hid everything in the closet. But I put my rifle under the bed with my cartridges and grenades. Then I thought: Now I must search the whole house, so that I know it completely; then they will not doubt that it is my lawful property.

But I did not get time enough. I heard the bell again. The candle blew out when I opened the door. The officers flashed their lights on me. Therefore I could not observe their faces.

"Heil Hitler," I said. "I am the son of the house. My parents and my two sisters have fled. Probably they are at my uncle's in Breslau. You may look upon this house as yours. But I count on it that nothing will be damaged."

"Oh no! We will not trouble you if it is not necessary."

"You have plenty of room. You may sit in the downstairs apartments. You may also play the piano, but not after eleven. I am very weak. I go to bed early."

I went upstairs ahead of them. They walked behind me with their electric torches. My shadow curled over the stairs.

"These," I said, pointing to the bathroom, the large bedroom, the library, and the room that was locked, "are the rooms I use myself."

"Naturally, naturally. We understand."

"And upstairs," I said, "are also some rooms which you may use if you find it necessary. Now I must wish you good night." Before they answered, I gave them my hand and went into the bedroom. I heard one go downstairs; the others remained there talking. They were busy for some hours. Cases were carried up the stairs. Autos rode back and forth. Heavy cannon fire coughed in the distance. I lay with my clothes on, diagonally across the twin beds. I had left the curtains open. The light in the room varied continually with the blazing of the fires which no one extinguished.

Our sergeant would arrest me. "What did you think you would do?" he would ask. "What did you really think? That the Germans would stay? You see, in two days we have kicked them out again. What did you really want: to stay in that house? Pay no more attention to us? Where is your uniform?" But perhaps the Germans would stay. The war could not last much longer. I would stay here, take a rest at last. Unless one of those officers came to me with his hand full of anti-German pamphlets. "You are the son of the house, are you not? We found these. What does it mean? You are not sick at all. You, the only one who remained behind in a town where everyone fled. You are a spy, admit it. Come, go with me to the back of the garden. We will put an end to it with a final shot."

How could I prove that I was not the son of the house—by getting out my Russian uniform, perhaps?

Then I remembered the locked room. Before leaving the house the owners had put all the damning evidence there. I only had to keep the Germans away. Then I was safe.

I, the son of the house, I thought, when I awoke the next morning and it was quiet everywhere. I have always lived here. It is my house.

Dirty underwear lay in a heap in the hall. They had taken a wild boar's head from the wall and used the tusk to hang things on. The cellar door had been broken open. Fine, then I did not have to do it myself. I went downstairs. The cellar was so full of all kinds of provisions, sacks of beans and sugar, cans and glasses of preserves on shelves, racks filled with bottles of wine, that I really could not tell if anything had been taken. But I would not stand for it. I, the son of the house!

When I saw a colonel coming home in the afternoon, I went to him and complained.

"The men were very tired," the colonel answered. "Then one does not look too closely." He took off his cap and rubbed his hand over his head. His neck and the back of his head had not been shaved for a long time and they were covered with a mossy white fuzz.

"They were not too tired to break open the cellar," I said.

The colonel put on his cap again, grew furious, and exclaimed that it would not happen again. When he walked on, I bowed my head, as if that could help me to put him entirely out of my mind. I wished to be alone, quite alone.

In the evening a corporal gunsmith brought me two new keys. He had put another lock on the cellar.

"How many keys have you kept for yourselves?" I asked.

"You like to joke," he answered. I never found any evidence that he kept one, nor did they make any more messes in the house. A week later two of them were busy beating carpets in the garden. They played only classical music on the piano. Always the same: Für Elise of Beethoven and the Turkish March.

A paper was shoved under my door, signed and stamped. All civilians were forbidden to remain in the town, but I was given a permit. The war moved rather far away from the vicinity. It was quiet on the street. There was no fighting in the neighborhood; there were only a few German soldiers, and no one else. Once in a while I walked in a park nearby, where a deserted Kurhaus stood, a nineteenth-century building with yellow columns from which the plaster was flaking off. An explosion had shattered the glass from the doors and windows; I went inside. There was a large rest room, with red plush divans along the walls and a round balustrade in the middle of the tiled floor. Below it lay an open cellar with a nickel and glass installation built around the mouth of the spring. The cellar was gradually filling with water; the installation was half under when I went there for the first time. The following day the water was streaming out the cellar windows. For the time being it could not flow away; it formed a moat around the building. A cat sat on a window sill. I waded out to him; he arched his back like a whip. He looked as if he were made of a piece of steel cable, spliced over and over again: in tail, head, and paws, in nails and whiskers. I picked him up and took him home; he clung to me like a burr.

He only let loose after I had gone in the house and upstairs. His tail rose slowly when he was on all four legs and he stole to the door of the room which had not yet been opened. He miaowed and rubbed his head against the doorpost. I dropped to my hands and knees to see if there was a crack above the threshold. There was one, but I could not smell whatever it was the cat smelled. I stayed on the floor with him and stroked his back. "It is nothing," I said, "and if it is, we cannot get in anyway. Come here." I had already tried all the keys I could find in the house, but none of them fitted. I picked the animal up and took him to my room. When I wanted to go to the

garden, I met the colonel again in the downstairs hall. He asked if I
still had complaints about anything. "No," I answered, "as a matter
of fact, it was not so bad, considering the unusual circumstances. In
wartime one cannot always comport oneself with the best of behavior." I will overlook everything, I thought, but leave me alone as
soon as possible.

"Unusual circumstances!" he exclaimed. "I recognize no unusual
circumstances!" It was clear, sunny weather. We heard only the
chirping of birds. He began with deliberation to tap a cigarette on a
silver case.

"As long as I have been in service," he said, "I have shaved myself
every morning, precisely at half-past six, with warm water. Today I
have been exactly forty years in service. Shaved with warm water,
war or no war! That is what I understand by culture!"

Though he was taller than I he kept balancing himself up and
down on his toes, so that his boots creaked.

"Culture grants no pardon! Culture is unity! Unusual circumstances only serve as an excuse! Whoever gives in to unusual circumstances, nàh! is simply no longer a person of culture!"

I said nothing. You give me a pain, I thought. He stood more at
ease now on one leg, rolling the other on its heel, and talked on.

"During the last war, the English drum fire began one morning at
a quarter-past six. At half-past six I shaved. It was too dark in the
trench. I went up to a higher spot. That cost me half of my little
finger. But at half-past seven I sat at my breakfast!" He stopped and
looked at me; he did not show me the little finger that was half shot
off. I did not care what he thought about culture. I did not care what
he thought about any subject whatsoever. I made up my mind to
avoid him, to avoid everyone. What good would talking do? I had
not talked for a long time; now that I had the opportunity, it might
only bring me misfortune.

I went out the back door, across the marble terrace and down
into the garden as I had so often done. I looked up at the two windows which, according to my calculations, belonged to the locked
room. There was nothing to be seen. The blackout blinds were let
down as usual. Nothing had changed. Walking up and down, I observed all the projections on the rear gable: window frames, rain-
pipes. I saw no possibility of climbing these without special contriv-
ances. I could not even get there from the window of another room.

When I was back in the house and went to my bedroom, I had to
push the cat back with the door, against which he was lying. He
wanted to slip past me and go to the locked door, but I was able to

grab him by the scruff of the neck. I lay with him on the bed, hugging him in my arms.

"Nothing must change," I whispered in his ear. "We will stay here. Everything must remain as it is. One day the war will be over. The Germans will go away. And we will stay here, always." He shook his head so that his ears made a clacking sound.

"No one is allowed in this town except the Germans and myself," I said. "The Germans will never find out that I am not the owner. And the war will never come to an end. This town will always be forbidden ground, except for me." I picked him up with my hands under his shoulders. I felt his small heart beating against my right thumb with the tempo of a clock. He did not look at me; he held his head stretched aslant. His eyes, with so little power to turn in their velvet casket, stared as if, with resignation, they could see the consequences of an inevitable but cruel judgment.

I let him go. He sprang to the floor with a thud and went to lie by the door.

After I had lived there somewhat longer, I hardly ever went out. Only as far as the summerhouse at the back of the garden. I felt no need for any occupation whatsoever. I was mostly in the bedroom, in bed. I never awakened till afternoon and was sometimes asleep again before it was dark. I only did things that I did not have to think about. Every day I stayed in the bath until the salts in the water had sunk to the bottom. The bathtub grew thickly coated, but it was large enough. Then I walked up and down, touching objects without examining them. On medicine bottles and powder boxes, on handkerchiefs and on the border of sheets, names were written which I did not try to pronounce. I completely stripped the clothes closets. I threw silk, velvet, and fur in a heap. My cat slept on it. I rummaged around in it myself, deeply sniffing in the scents. I looked carefully at twenty-five pairs of shoes, one by one. For shoes are the only things that retain something of a person if he is absent. A shoe always has the same form, even though there is no foot in it. Shoes do not collapse into shapeless rags as soon as they are taken off. I felt the back of them and the smooth high heels with the palm of my hand. I put them in pairs around the room. Twenty-five women encircled me. If they were naked or invisible that was not at all proof that they were not standing there, perhaps even with their hips swaying, their arms waving above their heads; they could do anything as long as they kept their feet still.

One day when I had slept longer than usual, I felt so energetic that I went to the library to read something. But all the books were written in a language that I did not know, except a number of German scientific works. They were large, old-fashioned volumes, with sticky, colored illustrations; loose leaves of oiled paper were placed on these for protection. They dealt exclusively with the subject of fish. When I realized this I threw them in the bookcase and never returned again to the library. *All those books in pisciculture.* Then the owner was a piscophile! At last I had discovered something about the person who had furnished and fitted this house. A lover of fishes! I knew something, but I did not want to know anything, not his name, nor how he looked, nothing! He had never existed, that was the truth! He was the intruder, not I. He would be dead at the end of the war, I would always remain here.

But sometimes my cat miaowed for hours at night. I let him go wherever he wanted, but he went and miaowed before the door of the room which had not been opened. He arched his back and dug his nails in the fitted carpet; he wanted to break open the floor to get there. He gave me no rest. I was afraid the Germans would hear it and come to ask what was the matter, why the cat remained sitting there.

And that is why, one sunny morning when I heard no noise anywhere and there was no auto before the door, so that I was sure that not one German was at home, I went to the pantry for a ladder and placed it against the rear gable, under the windows of the room. Looking up at the white stones, in which millions of suns smaller than pinheads glittered, I climbed the rungs, a screwdriver and pliers in my trousers pocket. My shadow followed a little below me, like a monkey.

"Hallo! Are you the window washer?" I turned around, let my whole body lean against the ladder, and looked down.

A man, with hands on his hips, held his head back to look at me.

Blinded as I was, I saw him three times over each other, like a careless color print. He spoke German with an accent I did not know. I had never seen the man.

"What do you want?"

"I want to speak to you!"

He kept his hands on his hips, legs spread wide apart.

When I came down, he had lit a cigarette and was gazing in the distance.

"Who are you?" I asked. "Where are your papers?"

He wore a rucksack and had two cameras, one hanging on each hip. His eyes were black, as was his thin mustache. He looked me up and down and then let his glance rest on my trousers as he handed me a folded paper. I opened it. It was precisely the same kind of permit that I had, with exactly the same stamps. I did not take the trouble to read his name. I was no longer the only civilian allowed in this town! That was the only thing that concerned me. I returned his paper.

"I have still another paper," he said, and handed it to me.

It was a letter signed by a major-general. The letter affirmed that he was the owner of a house (I did not recognize the address) and that he had permission to move into this house again.

I looked him straight in the eyes and said: "I do not know that address. I do not know this place so well."

"I do," he said. "Just come along with me."

"No. I forbid you entrance to these grounds. It has been requisitioned by the German Army. I am the owner. I am the only one who is permitted here." Stupid lie; he had in any case lived in the town, he would surely know the real owner. I knew even while I was uttering the words that they would not help.

He turned around, took a few steps away, looked at me and walked to the back door. I went after him, his paper still in my hand. Then he stopped suddenly and took a step back.

"Those trousers you are wearing do not fit you. They are exactly my size, not yours."

Now I tried earnestly to read the name that had been filled in on the papers. I had the impression that it looked like the names that appeared on the medicine bottles, the powder boxes and the sheets. He went inside the house, looked for a moment in the salons and then walked upstairs as if I did not exist.

In the bedroom he opened and closed the closets. I waited to see if he would go to the locked room. But he went and sat by the open window, so that his rucksack hung outside.

"So that is the way you are treated by your allies," he said. "That is how officers are! Steal clothes!"

He stuck his hand outside and threw his cigarette away in the garden. I had fallen on the bed. I looked at him silently, as if he were a film being shown for me.

"Your accent is peculiar," he continued. "I cannot imagine that you are a German officer. I cannot imagine that a German officer would put on civilian clothes that he finds in a requisitioned house and then claim to be the owner of the house. That is difficult for me to imagine!"

"And in what way does that concern me?"

"I will just consider that. In the meantime I will leave this here."

He stood up, put his rucksack down, snatched the major-general's declaration from my hand, and walked out of the room.

I remained sitting. The walls had resounded with his voice; the eyes in the portraits had turned toward him; he was the owner! A little later I thought that I heard him in the garden. I stared at his rucksack. *He was the owner*. Then I took my rifle from under the bed and crawled on my hands and knees to the window. He stood with his back to the house, at the edge of the lawn, near high rhododendron bushes which had long since left off flowering. At that period many more cats had strayed to the house. Nearly every day a new, starved one appeared. Now they all lay sunning in the grass; the black one I had taken from the Kurhaus, a striped one, a red one. They slept without moving. The man smoked a cigarette. He held his arm bent upward like a V. Blue smoke appeared now and then in front of his head. I aimed my rifle. The man's head, the bead, and the sight in one straight line . . .

There was a scream, quite close, nearly in my ear, when I fired the shot. I let the rifle go. It fell on the window seat with a bang, but I picked it up again at once.

A woman came from the bathroom while I was still on my knees. She called something in a language I did not understand. "Do not get excited," I said in German. "I was inspecting my rifle. Then it went off." I felt in my trousers for a handkerchief, but found only the screwdriver and pliers. With the screwdriver in one hand I made a couple of sham movements toward the rifle in the other. The woman had on a raincoat, buttoned up to her chin. She wore a hat.

Suddenly I burst into laughter, holding the rifle near my foot and beating myself softly on the thigh with the screwdriver.

"Where is my husband?" she asked in German. "Where is my husband? I have not seen him!"

My fit of laughter was now more like the hiccups; it gave me cramps in my abdomen muscles. I wished desperately that it would stop.

"But you surely heard him!" I said. "You were in the bathroom!"

"Where is my husband? I beg your pardon. I came in without asking. I beg your pardon."

She took a step toward me. Her thin bleached hair was combed back straight on her head.

"Keep away from the window! Away from the window!" I pulled up my rifle, let it loose and gripped it again near the lock.

No, no, she shook her head, as she recoiled in the direction of the

bathroom. She grabbed hold of the curtain and shot behind it. I took
such a deep breath that I could feel the air in my groin. Then I
stooped and shoved the rifle and screwdriver under the bed and took
out my bayonet. Sunlight lay in oblong patches on the part of the
floor that I had to cross to get to the bathroom. I did not know how I
should hold the bayonet: in front of me, gripped in my fist, or behind my back. When the sun went away, the original colors of the
carpet were there again, and I went into the bathroom. She stood in
the farthest corner, near the window that looked out on the plane
tree in the front garden. The greasy red filling was sticking out of a
gold lipstick holder that she held in her hand. She shoved it in with
her thumbnail and put it in her bag, without looking, without closing
the bag. She only looked at me, her mouth half open like the shel-
lacked mouth of a papier-mâché mask.

"What have I done, what have I done, why do you scream at
me?" she asked in a choking voice.

I walked around the bathtub, holding the bayonet behind me.
Her perfume came toward me in clouds, as though her skin were
white hot and evaporated everything at once. I threw down the bayonet, flung my hands around her neck and wrung. I pushed myself
away from her, in the corner, without looking at her. She did nothing back. I did not even breathe. I wanted to become congealed, so
that she could never free herself again. That is what I thought while
I stared outside, motionless. One of those German trucks with rattling iron caterpillar tires was riding by. The more I squeezed, the
more feeling I got in my fingers. The cartilage of her larynx would
leave a Röentgen photo on my hands. Her skin crushed between my
nails. The German auto disappeared behind the window post. A
sparrow came and sat on the window sill, flicked his tail, flew away,
and left a plaster gulden behind. But the woman was not yet dead.
She wanted to kick me. I pushed her down and hit the back of her
head against the rim of the bathtub until I heard something burst.
She did not move any more.

Then I looked at the woman and let her fall on the floor. Her
eyes were half closed, her pale tongue bulged out from between her
lips. I pulled her over the rim of the bathtub, turned on the cold
water, and sprinkled her face. But I was not able to close her mouth.
Her coat became spotted. Her bleached hair got wet and stuck to her
head. It looked as though much of it had already fallen out. I laid her
on the marble tiles and went back to the bedroom to look out the
window.

The sun broke out again across the back garden. The cats had not moved. The man lay face down in the rhododendrons. In fact, only his feet could be seen. I thought: The Germans hardly ever go there. They will not notice him. He must stay there for the present. If I go to hide now and the Germans come home and see me, they will know that I am involved. But if they find him like that, and I am not around, they will not think of me. But they will not find him, they never go in the back garden. Tonight they will be tired.

A heavy bomber flew low overhead. The shadow of its wing touched the man's feet as if to lift him up.

I withdrew from the window and went to stand on the sill of the bathroom door. Nearest to me lay the bayonet. Then, a little further, her bag and then she herself, half visible. I went to her, took her under the arms, dragged her to the bedroom and laid her on the left one of the twin beds.

Then I picked up the bayonet and her bag, which I closed. There was nothing left in the bathroom to show what had happened. I laid the bayonet by the rifle and put her bag on a chair, as if she had been sitting there and got up for a moment. I did not look to see what was in it. I left the man's rucksack where he had put it.

I lay down on the other bed and felt her cheek. I pushed her eyes closed; they closed farther than those of someone who is sleeping. Then I sat up with my back to her, my forehead in my hands. This shell of bone with its covering of mobile skin, everything comes from there: the other people, the world, war, the dreams, the words, the actions, which occur so completely of their own accord that one cannot imagine ever having been capable of consideration; so completely of their own accord, as though one's actions were the thoughts of the world. You would have to have a second head to understand what that one head is, but I only have one, here it is in my hands, I am holding it the way one never holds anything else. Yet, if it were not asserted by the learned, you would not know that the head is any different from a hand or a foot.

Explosions could now be heard, with the sound of the rattling chains on armored trucks cutting through them.

When it was dark enough I went to the back garden. Not one of the Germans had as yet come home. If they should just ride into the garden at this moment, they would not notice me in the dark. On the horizon I saw the dun-colored light of cannons.

I pulled the man by his feet from the bushes, until he lay entirely on the lawn. His cameras shored up above his head. I turned him around, held him under the arms, and dragged him to the summer-house. I laid him down behind it. Whoever found him would wonder for a moment how it had happened, rob him, shrug, and perhaps look after having him buried.

The house was as dark as when I had left it. The Germans had still not returned. I could forget the strain of that day; I would take the woman down and lay her beside her husband. And tomorrow morning it would seem as if nothing had happened. I looked up at the stars, the rumble of firing in my ears. Remain here always, I thought, nothing can happen here. I will not mind if the whole world disappears, if only this house, this lawn, everything that I see around me remains the same.

But when I had reached the upstairs hall, I saw a light shining. And that light came from the room which had always been locked. Then I knew suddenly that I had been walking around with a dagger in my stomach all the time and that dagger was now pushed straight up into my heart. My blood left its usual streams and swirled around as in a barrel.

I held tight to the hand rail of the staircase. The door of the room stood ajar. I heard nothing. Perhaps someone was there, perhaps someone had only been there and left the light on. With my hands stretched out before me, I walked toward the door. A key, attached to a key ring with other keys, was sticking in the lock. I was unarmed. I approached the end. It had always been in that room and now the time had come, like a case of dynamite. I took the key from the lock and pushed the door wider open. A cat that I had hurt screeched. I saw its eyes in the midst of glimmering lights as in a black tunnel of coal; light came from everywhere. But it all came from one lamp and that lamp was held by a man. The man stood on a pair of steps with his back toward me. He did not hear me walking. He raised his oil lamp and put his other hand into something. I saw what it was. It was an aquarium. The walls were all lined with racks, supporting aquariums.

"Who are you?" I screamed.

But the man did not even turn his head. I only heard the spluttering of water and firing in the distance. Then I took a couple of steps, until I stood right next to him, and pulled on his trouser.

"Are you deaf?"

He showed no fright, but turned around shakily on his narrow steps, pulling back his hand. Drops of water fell from his fingers on my face. The cat jumped up to him; the man stooped and pushed it away. He took no notice of me. It looked as if I had always walked in and out of here and it was not necessary for him to say anything to me.

"Answer! Answer!" I grabbed his wet hand. Only then did he come down and hold the lamp between our faces. He did not have a beard, though the stubble of many days showed up. He was older than I had ever seen anyone.

"I have many fishes," he said suddenly in an inquiring tone, "many, many fishes, Herr Hauptmann. They are hungry, but they are not yet dead."

He held the lamp near an aquarium and motioned for me to come and look.

"Don't play deaf!" I yelled. "How long have you been in the house? You heard everything, the shooting, the screaming!"

He pointed to the glass, where I could see nothing but the reflection of his lamp. "I have cultivated twenty-six other pairs with this one pair. No one else in Europe has been able to do that. They are only to be found in Mexico at an altitude of forty-five hundred meters above sea level. But the water there is not frozen, because it comes from a volcanic spring. Then I discovered that our St. Catharina spring here is exactly the same temperature. Thirty years ago there were no electric thermostats. I had a pipe with spring water. . . ."

"I shoot crazy people on sight!" I screamed, cupping my hands at his ear.

"Oh, it was quite a lot of work." He continued with his argumentation. And then I heard hundreds of bombers. The thumping of the anti-aircraft artillery came nearer.

"Herr Hauptmann! I have only bored you with my stories in order to let you know that this house has kept a unique article of culture hidden. You have respected it!"

His hand was so tired that the lamp swung back and forth. "I wish to proclaim my veneration for the manner in which you have served culture."

"She is lying dead in the bedroom," I said, while I gripped him by the arms. "And he is lying behind the summerhouse! You know it all. But you are afraid of me! You think that I'll kill you and cut you to pieces!"

"Let me stay here, Herr Hauptmann! I cannot live without my fishes, and my fishes cannot live without me. When I am no longer here, this unique collection will die. I have worked on it for eighty years. I began when I was sixteen."

As long as I had been in the town there had never been such heavy shooting as now. How could I tell if he heard it?

"Herr Hauptmann, I have been fourteen days under way. I have not eaten, but I have food for the little animals with me, here in this sack!" He picked up a cotton sack from the floor and rummaged in it with his hand. "Fourteen different kinds! You have no idea how difficult it is to get in these times. My son and daughter-in-law were hit by a shell on the way."

"You lie!" I took the lamp away from him and held it near my mouth. If he could not hear then he could at least read lips:

"Du lügst." I whispered very slowly.

"I am ninety-six and quite alone in the world, Herr Hauptmann. . . ."

He pulled out all the stops together: his fishes, unique collection, culture, alone in the world, daughter-in-law. It was like an octopus playing an organ in a motion-picture theater.

"Herr Hauptmann! Germany is winning on all the fronts. The secret weapon. The war will . . ."

He still talked when a bomb fell near by. He went on when I pushed the lamp in his hand again and took his keys out of my pocket. I pursed my lips and tapped them with my index finger, picked up the cat and left the room backward. I locked him in. There was nothing to do but let him stay here. Perhaps he would start to call and hammer on the door. If the Germans heard it, I could always find a way out. I could say that he was insane; my insane, unhappy grandfather who did not recognize me and therefore insisted that he had never seen me before. I would say that. The bombs fell close now. I could hear them whistling. Everything that was thin, everything that was loose, trembled. Perhaps a bomb would fall on the house presently. I believed that I would be quite contented if it did.

I pulled open the curtains in the bedroom. It looked as if the whole surrounding area was aflame. The anti-aircraft artillery did not fire any longer.

I could see the dead woman clearly. I went and sat by her on the bed and felt her face with the tips of my fingers. It was cold now. I put my hand under her coat, under her dress, and laid it on her thigh. Cold; a thing; water and proteins; something chemists have studied, nothing more. I tried to bend her leg. Carry her in my arms. No, put her over my shoulder and keep one hand free to open doors, hold on to the end rail of the staircase. And then walk through the garden; lay her down next to her husband, behind the summerhouse. It would not be dark in the garden. I got up, wondering how I could get her on my shoulder.

Then I heard walking on the stairs. The Germans screamed at

one another; I heard the thudding of heavy objects. I ran to the door
and held the knob tight, at once thinking that they would come in. I
remained standing like that until they had gone. Then I went and lay
on the bed next to the woman. I closed my eyes and laid my hand on
different parts of her body, expecting it to have remained living lo-
cally and to move slightly, shiver, or swell and shrink imperceptibly.
I was awakened in the midst of prolonged machine gun volleys. Yet
it was not that noise that brought an end to my sleep. Someone was
knocking on my door. I thought: "The old man has given an alarm.
The Germans have let him out. They have come to ask me what it all
means." I got out of bed. Why shouldn't I open the door? Yes, of
course, there stood the colonel.

"Verzeihen Sie," he said.

I did not see the old man standing in the hall. The colonel kept
clasping and unclasping his left thumb with his right hand.

"I came to inform you of the situation. The place is enclosed by
the bolshevists. I came to warn you. The other officers have been
killed. We are surrounded, surrounded."

"Thank you."

I stepped back, intending to shut the door as soon as possible.

"No, wait a moment. Perhaps we can do something together.
Perhaps we can escape."

"Yes, that is a fine idea! Wait here! One moment! I will be with
you directly!" I slammed the door and ran to the closet. I took out
my uniform, which I had kicked in a wad in the corner, and put it
on. While I was fastening my belt I stooped near the bed and
grabbed my rifle. I stuck the bayonet on the muzzle. I strapped my
helmet under my chin.

Then I went into the hall. The colonel put up his hands. I pushed
him down the stairs with my bayonet at his back. When we were in
the corridor, near to the doors that opened on the garden, he turned
toward me and said, with his arms still raised: "Be so kind as to allow
me to shave first." He had lowered his left arm slightly to look at his
watch. I saw his half-shot-off little finger. "It is exactly seven
o'clock. I have my shaving kit in my breast pocket. It will only take a
few moments." The tone in which he said it added to the words: I
know that it is the end. I ask a last favor.

He was quite certain that I had no other intention than to take
him to the back of the garden and shoot him.

"No," I said. "I shall decide what is to happen."

I pushed him away from the doors to the garden. I opened the
cellar door with my left hand and shoved him in. While I hung my

rifle on my back and put the key to the cellar in my pocket, I was thinking: There I stood, exactly as I had begun, a dirty soldier standing on the carpet between the marble walls of a strange house. Time could not make the grade and had rolled back.

When I went up to the old man, he sat on his steps by the window, from which he had removed the blackout blinds. He moved his finger back and forth before the glass of an aquarium. Two paradise fishes pressed their snouts against the other side of the glass as if they would like to kiss his fingers. He spoke to them in Hungarian.

I put a pot of cold coffee and a piece of bread in his hand.

"Good morning, Herr Hauptmann."

He did not show the least surprise; he could not tell the difference between the uniforms of the two parties.

"You take excellent care of an old man. Your hospitality does honor to the German Army."

The sky was red with the rising sun. The room also became red. Bullets whizzed in the garden. Short bursts glowed on a background of vague noise. I looked at the aquariums, where the fishes floated through the green as though on another planet.

"Herr Hauptmann, I have enough to keep them alive for three months!"

I went to him, took him by the hand and held him under the chin with my other hand. I brought my face close to his.

"Now you must pay careful attention!" I called.

He laughed.

"Of course, Herr Hauptmann. The glorious German Army! The defenders of our culture!"

He said it as if repeating it. They had impressed upon him that by saying such things you could appease the Germans, the way you can catch birds by putting salt on their tails. He thought only of culture.

I burst into laughter, but had to keep myself from hitting him.

"Now pay attention! Germans gone! Entirely gone! Never coming back!"

"Of course, Herr Hauptmann. War soon over. The secret weapon. Heil Hitler." While saying it he raised his hand.

I kneaded his shoulders as though I could convey my meaning to him through my fingers.

"No! Germans lost! Germans dead! Head cut off!"

I drew my hand back and forth across my neck.

"Naturally!" he said. "The principal evil-doers must be executed!"

I screamed till my vocal cords nearly split: "No, Russians here now! Never say Heil Hitler again!"

I pointed to him and again went through the movements of cutting my own throat. He raised his hands in horror.

"Oh no! I like Germany very much!"

"No! Germany lost. Germany broken! Hitler" (I stuck my hand up) "Hitler broken! Head cut off!"

He laughed, shaking his head, opened the bag of food for the fishes, and put his hand in it.

I heard heavy artillery riding through the streets. There was no more shooting. I had to hurry. If he did not understand it now I really could do nothing more. I walked out of the room and got a sheet of paper and a pencil from the library. I printed on it in German, in large letters:

"Germany beaten. Now the Soviets are coming. Never say Heil Hitler any more. Remember it, otherwise the Russians will kill you and gobble up your fishes."

I put the sheet of paper in his hands. I also gave him back his keys. He was still chuckling, and trying to see from which distance he could make out my letters the easiest, when I closed the door behind me.

I walked down the front steps, across the lawn, and out of the gate, and joined the partisans, who were singing as they marched behind covered wagons drawn by small horses.

Most of the houses in the town were on fire. Thick clouds of steam arose, caused by the little fountains that still spouted water on the street corners.

At the market square I looked around to see if they had not begun establishing a headquarters, where I could report. I knew exactly what I would say when they asked where I had been all these months. And then they would again give me an order to do something that I did not in the least understand. It did not matter. If they only understood me!

I stood on the same spot where I had last seen the sergeant, in front of a café, which had now collapsed. Yes, on precisely the same spot.

Who came along there? The Spaniard who spoke French, the Yesero! He recognized me immediately.

"Oh, amigo mi . . . mon ami! How are you? Where have you been?"

I told the same story as before.

"Taken prisoner by Germans. Here! Germans run away!"

"Fine! Good!"

"But they couldn't keep me! I escaped! Now I took German prisoner. Come with me!"

"Everything the same," he said. "First they, then you! Are you still thirsty?" He pulled a big bottle of prune brandy out of his pocket. I drank and thought: How will I get rid of him again? What can I do with him? I drew a deep breath and took another swallow.

He stayed with me. I walked on a way, he walked behind me. And a whole group of others followed, crowded around us, giving one another bottles.

"Women," said the Spaniard. "Hollander, don't you know any women?"

"Yes, there is one in the same house. For you and me. Good-looking woman. Send the others away."

He stood still and made a speech. I don't know what he said. It caused loud laughter. It did not have the least effect. They kept right on walking with us. "Hey, Spaniard, comrade! Send them away! Good-looking woman! Pour toi seulement!" But he gave me the bottle, from which I took a lot of drinks.

We went into the garden. On the front steps I turned around and put up my hand. I opened my mouth wide and screamed. In French, Spanish, German, Dutch; I made so many sounds that they surely must have included Montenegrin, Russian, Serbian, Bulgarian, and Rumanian. I overlooked the sloping garden at my feet, full of partisans. They crowded forward, they pushed me back and forth. I explained that my prisoner was not here at all. I said I had never taken a prisoner. He was gone, had vanished! But I heard the pieces of glass tinkling as they fell from the door behind me, and they pulled the lock open. They walked over me. They stood around me begging in broken German.

"Where is prisoner, Hollander?"

I let myself fall on the bench, gave them the key to the cellar, and remained sitting there.

The whole place was in uproar. They were walking on the staircase, in the upstairs halls. More soldiers kept crowding inside the hall. Then the Spaniard came back with a bloody razor in his hand. Two others held the colonel, who could hardly walk, by the collar. He had first shaved himself. Afterwards he had tried to cut his throat, but had just missed the artery.

He said nothing. I also said nothing. I handed him my handkerchief, which the Spaniard took and bound around his neck. The two others dragged him away to the salon, and the Yesero came and sat next to me.

"Hollander, where is that woman?"

He put his arm around my shoulders.

"You have everything. . . . House . . . German colonel . . . wine . . . food . . . everything. Where is woman! I three months no woman! Spanish can't stand that, no, Spanish can't, Hollander." He broke the neck of a bottle and threw the liquor over my face.

More partisans came back from the cellar. They had filled empty cases with bottles of wine. Jars of preserves were stamped open and eaten half empty with their hands. A smell of burning and blue smoke arose in the hall, caused by an attempt to light the stove, but those who tried to play cook could only make a mess of things.

What would the old man have done?

Was he still upstairs? Had he run away! Was he in the garden? I wanted to see if he was in the garden. But just at that moment a fight began on the stairs. At the same time someone started shooting at the elk heads on the wall. The gilded balustrade on the staircase cracked, gave way, and came down. The angels in the ceiling broke loose from their heaven and flew for the first time in their existence. In a haze of dust, half a company of partisans lay fighting on the floor. Two who could not move any more remained lying; the others went away. I walked around doing nothing.

Then it became rather quiet in the house. The conquerors had left in groups. Everything they could lay their hands on they had destroyed and soiled, each in the way that pleased him most. I had lost the Spaniard. But when I was going upstairs, I met him again. He held on to me.

"Come on," I said. "Good-looking woman. Upstairs."

"No, not upstairs."

I pulled him with me to the stairs. We staggered, stumbling over the balusters of the staircase, slipping on the muck of food that had been thrown away and the chunks of broken glass.

"No, not upstairs." He dragged me back.

"All right," I said, "then I'll go alone."

But he was so strong that I could not tear myself loose. I had no revolver, I had nothing, not even my helmet. He turned my wrists around and pulled me away from the stairs to the salon. He threw me on a sofa between two other partisans, who had cut the faces out of portraits and put them on as masks. The antique cupboards had been broken open, and someone was occupying himself by stamping the plates, cups, and saucers to fine pieces, one by one.

Others were playing a strange game. They tore the paper from the walls and compared who pulled the longest strip in one jerk. How was the winner rewarded? The colonel lay bound on the floor against the wainscot. They had put his head through a painting; the frame lay on his shoulders. The winner went and kicked him. Then he called something to three others who had been in the sun room relieving themselves in the flower vases, and, pulling up their pants, they came and stood beside him. They overturned the grand piano. The cover and sound board were kicked off. The piano rolled over, smashing a chair and a couple of small tables. They finally set it up straight, its legs against the wall, the keyboard on the floor. The strings were pulled from the frame one by one; they shot loose or broke, with a sharp snapping sound.

They used the thickest strings to bind the German in the gilded frame; they spanned him like the hide of an animal. He was not even unconscious, though he kept his eyes closed. But every now and then he opened them and looked around, and tried to blow away a corner of my handkerchief that was tickling him. His lips were pressed together as though tasting something, the way some people do when they have made a remark that seems striking to them. But he said nothing. He gave no sign of having seen me.

Then two soldiers came in with large wine glasses in their hands. They wore a lot of dresses, one on top of the other. Their faces were made up. They had pulled silk stockings, full of holes and heavily wrinkled, onto their bare legs. I looked at the antique rummers that they held in their hands. The glasses were filled to the brim with suffocating tropical fish. Soldiers rushed at them from everywhere. The two that held me on the divan let me loose. I was able to escape. I hoped that I could at least go upstairs. But it was again crowded on the staircase. I got the butt of a rifle on my lips. I was picked up and thrown into the garden. I lay face down with my arms around my head while I was kicked in the sides. When they stopped, I stood up and walked to the summerhouse with my mouth full and sat on the bench. I spat my teeth out between my feet.

The partisans left me alone after that. I looked up at the windows of the room with the aquariums. There was nothing to see. The windows were black as usual. The ladder that I had placed against them the morning before was still standing there. What is easier than breaking windows or throwing down a ladder? Yet just that had not happened. It still seemed as if it had not become useless to climb that ladder and break open the window; it was as though only an unimportant interruption had kept me from doing it.

Shots were falling everywhere. I saw soldiers going in and out of the house. I heard them singing and screaming. I gave up and lay dozing for a time. When it grew dark, I got up and stumbled to the house again. There was no more movement discernible now, neither in the halls nor in the rooms. Repeatedly striking matches, I went inside. Large puddles of spilled sugar glittered like ice. The hall was empty with the exception of the two partisans who had remained lying there after the balustrade broke. The doors of the rooms were closed. A radio was blaring in the salon but I heard nothing of people.

Water was streaming along the walls. My footsteps made a sloshing sound. Then I saw the black cat in a corner licking at the food that had been thrown away. I picked him up and said: "Now you know it. Now you know what was in that room. Now you have been there." I struck another match so I could see more than just his eyes. They looked like the eyes of the Chinese, which make the impression that they never should have opened. He squirmed. I had to throw the match away and then I pressed his head against my cheek. But he spat and scratched my hand with back paw. When I let him loose, he went back to his corner and continued eating with satisfaction.

I began climbing the stairs. I had to hold on to shreds of the runner.

The door to the aquarium room stood wide open. I struck a match. All the aquariums had been broken. Plants and fragments of glass lay in a debris on the floor. I saw no sign of the old man.

Tripping over the books of the library, that blocked the way in uncertain heaps, I went to the bedroom.

I felt among sopping wet mountains of mattresses, pillows, blankets, sheets. But I did not find the woman's body under them. The old man and the woman had both disappeared, as they had come: of their own accord; as everything happened: of its own accord. I believed it was possible, quite possible.

But as I was going to the bathroom, where I heard the taps continually running, and saw that the bathtub was full and flowing over, a horrible explanation of the old man's disappearance forced itself on me. The partisans' sense of humor had by then impressed me so strongly that I did not expect anything else than to find him drowned in the bathtub. They would have bound him and thrown him in. He who liked fishes so much must feel what it was like. I walked there, feeling my way. I stuck the whole length of my arm in the water, but I only found dirt, as everywhere.

I closed the taps, to have done something, at least. One did not grip and remained running.

Then I returned to the garden and went to lie on the bench in the summerhouse. It was not long before daybreak. A wind rose, and snow as fine as salt blew in horizontal gusts through the bushes.

As soon as it was light I got off the bench and walked to the back of the summerhouse. The owner of the house lay, just as I had left him, on wild grass and nettles; his mouth wide open, the half-burned cigarette having slid down his throat like the pistil in a flower. I sucked blood out of my toothless jaws and swallowed it. Squatting, I loosened his two cameras and hung them on my own shoulders. I also took his gold wrist watch.

And when the partisans were moving on and I came out to the lawn in front of the house, I saw what had happened to the old man. They had hanged him on the plane tree and pinned to his stomach the paper on which I had printed: "Deutschland kaputt. Jetzt kommen die Sowjets. Nie mehr Heil Hitler sagen. Sonst machen die Russen Sie tot und fressen Ihre Fische auf."

On another polled branch the colonel was hanging, with the naked corpse of the woman bound against him. They had hanged him with a piano string which had cut through to his spinal column.

I turned around and glanced at the house. It still looked whole even though the curtains in some of the windows were torn. I rushed back, went up the front steps, and threw a grenade in the rear of the corridor. We were marching out of the gate when the explosion was heard. The partisans looked upon this as the crowning joke of the whole thing. They began pushing and pulling at me; they asked if I would trade the cameras. I felt that I was becoming quite popular. I looked back at the house for the last time. All the panels had burst from the rabbets. I saw miserable, dead-looking thatch hanging down in bunches from the broken ceiling that had represented the heavens. I looked deep into the deathly sick throat of the house.

It was as if it had been playing a comedy the whole time and only showed itself now as it always was in reality: a hollow, draughty lump of stone, inwardly full of rubbish and filth.

*Translated from the Dutch by Estelle Debrot*

# Alberto Moravia

AGOSTINO

URING THOSE DAYS of early summer Agostino and his mother used to go out every morning on a bathing raft. The first few times his mother had taken a boatman, but Agostino so plainly showed his annoyance at the man's presence that from then on the oars were entrusted to him. It gave him intense pleasure to row on that calm, transparent, early morning sea; and his mother sat facing him, as gay and serene as the sea and sky, and talked to him in a soft voice, just as if he had been a man instead of a thirteen-year-old boy. Agostino's mother was a tall, beautiful woman, still in her prime, and Agostino felt a sense of pride each time he set out with her on one of those morning expeditions. It seemed to him that all the bathers on the beach were watching them, admiring his mother and envying him. In the conviction that all eyes were upon them his voice sounded to him stronger than usual, and he felt as if all his movements had something symbolic about them, as if they were part of a play; as if he and his mother, instead of being on the beach, were on a stage, under the eager eyes of hundreds of spectators. Sometimes his mother would appear in a new dress, and he could not resist remarking on it aloud, in the secret hope that others would hear. Now and again she would send him to fetch something or other from the beach cabin, while she stood waiting for him by the boat. He would obey with a secret joy, happy if he could prolong their departure even by a few minutes. At last they would get on the raft, and Agostino would take the oars and row out to sea. But for quite a long time he would remain under the disturbing influence of his filial vanity. When they were some way from the shore his mother would tell him to stop rowing, put on her rubber bathing cap, take off her sandals and slip into the water. Agostino would follow her. They swam round and round the empty raft with its floating oars, talking gaily together, their voices ringing clear in the silence of the calm, sunlit sea. Sometimes his mother would point to a piece of cork bobbing up and down a short distance from them, and challenge him to race her to it. She gave him a few yards' start, and they would swim as hard as they could toward the cork. Or they would have diving competitions from the platform of the raft, splashing up the pale, smooth water as they plunged in. Agostino would watch his mother's body sink down deeper and deeper through a froth of green bubbles; then suddenly he would dive in after her, eager to follow wherever she might go, even to the bottom of the sea. As he flung himself into the furrow his mother had made it seemed to him that even that cold, dense water must keep some trace of the passage of her beloved body. When their swim was over they would climb back onto the raft, and gazing all round her on the calm, luminous sea his mother would say: "How beautiful it is, isn't it?" Agostino made no reply, because he felt that his own enjoyment of the beauty of sea and sky was really due above all to his deep sense of union with his mother. Were it not for this intimacy, it sometimes entered his head to wonder what would remain of all that beauty. They would stay out a long time, drying themselves in the sun, which toward midday got hotter and hotter; then his mother, stretched out at full length on the platform between the two floats, with her long hair trailing in the water and her eyes closed, would fall into a doze, while Agostino would keep watch from his seat on the bench, his eyes fixed on his mother, and hardly breathing for fear of disturbing her slumber. Suddenly she would open her eyes and say what a delightful novelty it was to lie on one's back with one's eyes shut and to feel the water rocking underneath; or she would ask Agostino to pass her her cigarette case or, better still, to light one for her himself and give it to her. All of which he would do with fervent and tremulous care. While his mother smoked, Agostino would lean forward with his back to her, but with his head on one side so that he could watch the clouds of blue smoke which indicated the spot where his mother's head was resting, with her hair spread out round her on the water. Then, as she never could have enough of the sun, she would ask Agostino to row on and not turn round, while she would take off her brassière and let down her bathing suit so as to expose her whole body to the sunlight. Agostino would go on rowing, proud of her injunction not to look, as if he were being allowed to take part in a ritual. And not only did he never dream of looking around, but he felt that her body, lying so close behind him, naked in the sun, was surrounded by a halo of mystery to which he owed the greatest reverence.

One morning his mother was sitting as usual under the great beach umbrella, with Agostino beside her on the sand, waiting for the moment of their daily row. Suddenly a tall shadow fell between him and the sun. He looked up and saw a dark, sunburnt young man shaking hands with his mother. He did not pay much attention to him, thinking it was one of his mother's casual acquaintances; he only drew back a little, waiting for the conversation to be over. But the young man did not accept the invitation to sit down; pointing to the white raft in which he had come, he invited the mother to go for a row. Agostino was sure his mother would refuse this invitation as she had many previous ones; so that his surprise was great when he saw her accept at once, and immediately begin to put her things together—her sandals, bathing cap and purse—and then get up from her chair. His mother had accepted the young man's invitation with exactly the same spontaneity and simple friendliness which she would have shown toward her son; and with a like simplicity she now turned to Agostino, who sat waiting with his head down, letting the sand trickle through his fingers, and told him to have a sun bath, for she was going out for a short turn in the boat and would be back soon. The young man, meanwhile, as if quite sure of himself, had gone off in the direction of the raft, while the woman walked submissively behind him with her usual calm, majestic gait. Her son, watching them, could not help saying to himself that the young man must now be feeling the same pride and vanity and excitement which he himself always felt when he set out in a boat with his mother. He watched her get onto the float: the young man leaned backward and pushed with his feet against the sandy bottom; then, with a few vigorous strokes, lifted the raft out of the shallow water near the shore. The young man was rowing now, and his mother sat facing him, holding onto the seat with both hands and apparently chatting with him. Gradually the raft grew smaller and smaller, till it entered the region of dazzling light which the sun shed on the surface of the water, and slowly became absorbed into it.

Left alone, Agostino stretched himself out in his mother's deck chair and with one arm behind his head lay gazing up at the sky, seemingly lost in reflection and indifferent to his surroundings. He felt that all the people on the beach must have noticed him going off every day with his mother, and therefore it could not have escaped them that today his mother had left him behind and gone off with the young man of the bathing raft. So he was determined to give no sign at all of the disappointment and disillusion which filled him with such bitterness. But however much he tried to adopt an air of calm composure, he felt at the same time that everyone must be noticing how forced and artificial his attitude was. What hurt him still more was not so much that his mother had preferred the young man's company to his as the alacrity with which she had accepted the invitation—almost as if she had anticipated it. It was as if she had decided beforehand not to lose any opportunity, and when one offered itself to accept it without hesitation. Apparently she had been bored all those times she had been alone with him on the raft, and had only gone with him for lack of something better to do. A memory came back to his mind that increased his discomfiture. It had happened at a dance to which he had been taken by his mother. A girl cousin was with them who, in despair at not being asked by anyone else, had consented to dance once or twice with him, though he was only a boy in short trousers. She had danced reluctantly and looked very cross and out of temper, and Agostino, though preoccupied with his own steps, was aware of her contemptuous and unflattering sentiments toward himself. He had, however, asked her for a third dance, and had been quite surprised to see her suddenly smile and leap from her chair, shaking out the folds of her dress with both hands. But instead of rushing into his arms she had turned her back on him and joined a young man who had motioned to her over Agostino's shoulder. The whole scene lasted only five seconds, and no one noticed anything except Agostino himself. But he felt utterly humiliated and was sure everyone had seen how he had been snubbed.

And now, after his mother had gone off with the young man, he compared the two happenings and found them identical. Like his cousin, his mother had only waited for an opportunity to abandon him. Like his cousin, and with the same exaggerated readiness, she had accepted the first offer that presented itself. And in each case it had been his fate to come tumbling down from an illusory height and to lie bruised and wounded at the bottom.

That day his mother stayed out for about two hours. From under his big umbrella he saw her step onto the shore, shake hands with the young man and move slowly off toward the beach cabin, stooping a little under the heat of the midday sun. The beach was deserted by now, and this was a relief to Agostino, who was always convinced that all eyes were fixed on them. "What have you been doing?" his mother asked casually. "I have had great fun," began Agostino, and he made up a story of how *he* had been bathing too with the boys from the next beach cabin. But his mother was not listening; she had hurried off to dress. Agostino decided that as soon as he saw the raft appear the next day he would make some excuse to leave so as not to suffer the indignity of being left behind again. But when the next day came he had just started away when he heard his mother calling him back. "Come along," she said, as she got up and collected her belongings. "We're going out to swim." Agostino followed her, thinking that she meant to dismiss the young man and go out alone with him. The young man was standing on the raft waiting for her. She greeted him and said simply: "I'm bringing my son, too." So Agostino, much as he disliked it, found himself sitting beside his mother facing the young man, who was rowing.

Agostino had always seen his mother in a certain light—calm, dignified and reserved. During this outing he was shocked to see the change which had taken place, not only in her manner of talking but, as it seemed, even in herself. One could scarcely believe she was the same person. They had hardly put out to sea before she made some stinging personal remark, quite lost on Agostino, which started a curious, private conversation. As far as he could make out it concerned a lady friend of the young man who had rejected his advances in favor of a rival. But this only led up to the real matter of their conversation, which seemed to be alternately insinuating, exacting, contemptuous and teasing. His mother appeared to be the more aggressive and the more susceptible of the two, for the young man contented himself with replying in a calm, ironical tone, as if he were quite sure of himself. At times his mother seemed displeased, even positively angry with the young man, and then Agostino was glad. But immediately after she would disappoint him by some flattering phrase which destroyed the illusion. Or in an offended voice she would address to the young man a string of mysterious reproaches. But instead of being offended, Agostino would see his face light up with an expression of fatuous vanity, and concluded that those reproaches were only a cover for some affectionate meaning which he was unable to fathom. As for himself, both his mother and the young man seemed to be unaware of his existence; he might as well not have been there, and his mother carried this obliviousness so far as to remind the young man that if she had gone out alone with him the day before, this was a mistake on her part which she did not intend to repeat. In the future she would bring her son with her. Agostino felt this to be decidedly insulting, as if he was something with no will of its own, merely an object to be disposed of as her caprice or convenience might see fit.

Only once did his mother seem aware of his presence, and that was when the young man, letting go the oars for a moment, leaned forward with an intensely malicious expression on his face and murmured something in an undertone which Agostino could not understand. His mother started, pretending to be terribly shocked, and cried out, pointing to Agostino sitting by her, "Let us at least spare this innocent!" Agostino trembled with rage at hearing himself called innocent, as if a dirty rag had been thrown at him which he could not avoid.

When they were some way out from shore, the young man suggested a swim to his companion. Agostino, who had often admired the ease and simplicity with which his mother slipped into the water, was painfully struck by all the unfamiliar movements she now put into that familiar action. The young man had time to dive in and come up again to the surface, while she still stood hesitating and dipping one toe after another into the water, apparently pretending to be timid or shy. She made a great fuss about going in, laughing and protesting and holding on to the seat with both hands, till at last she dropped in an almost indecent attitude over the side and let herself fall clumsily into the arms of her companion. They dived together and came up together to the surface. Agostino, huddled on the seat, saw his mother's smiling face quite close to the young man's grave, brown one, and it seemed to him that their cheeks touched. He could see their two bodies disporting themselves in the limpid water, their hips and legs touching, and looking as if they longed to interlace with each other. Agostino looked first at them and then at the distant shore, with a shameful sense of being in the way. Catching sight of his frowning face, his mother, who was having her second dip, called up to him: "Why are you so serious? Don't you see how lovely it is in here? Goodness! what a serious son I've got"; a remark which filled Agostino with a sense of shame and humiliation. He made no reply, and contented himself with looking elsewhere. The swim was a long one. His mother and her companion disported themselves in the water like two dolphins, and seemed to have forgotten him entirely. At last they got back onto the raft. The young man sprang on at one bound, and then leaned over the edge to assist his companion, who was calling him to help her get out of the water. Agostino saw how in raising her the young man gripped her brown flesh with his fingers, just where the arm is softest and biggest, between the shoulder and the armpit. Then she sat down beside Agostino, panting and laughing, and with her pointed nails held her wet suit away from her, so that it should not cling to her breasts. Agostino remembered that when they were alone his mother was strong enough to climb into the boat without anyone's aid, and attributed her appeal for help and her bodily postures, which seemed to draw attention to her feminine disabilities, to the new spirit which had already produced such un-

pleasant changes in her. Indeed, he could not help thinking that his
mother, who was a naturally tall, dignified woman, resented her size
as a positive drawback from which she would have liked to rid herself; and her dignity as a tiresome habit which she was trying to replace by a sort of tomboy gaucherie.

When they were both back on the raft, the return journey
began. This time the oars were entrusted to Agostino, while the
other two sat down on the platform which joined the two floats. He
rowed gently in the burning sun, wondering constantly about the
meaning of the sounds and laughter and movements of which he was
conscious behind his back. From time to time his mother, as if suddenly aware of his presence, would reach up with one arm and try to
stroke the back of his neck, or she would tickle him under the arm
and ask if he were tired. "No, I am not tired," he replied. He heard
the young man say laughingly: "Rowing's good for him," which
made him plunge in the oar savagely. His mother was sitting with her
head resting against his seat and her long legs stretched out; that he
knew, but it seemed to him that she did not stay in that position;
once, for instance, a short skirmish seemed to be going on; his mother
made a stifled sound as if she were being suffocated and the raft
lurched to one side. For a moment Agostino's cheek came into contact with his mother's body, which seemed vast to him—like the sky
—and pulsing with a life over which she had no control. She stood
with her legs apart, holding on to her son's shoulders, and said: "I
will only sit down again if you promise to be good." "I promise,"
rejoined the young man with mock solemnity. She let herself down
again awkwardly onto the platform, and it was then her body
brushed her son's cheek. The moisture of her body confined in its
wet bathing suit remained on his skin, but its heat seemed to over-
power its dampness and though he felt a tormenting sense of uneasiness, even of repugnance, he persisted in not drying away the traces.

As they approached the shore the young man sprang lightly to the
rower's seat and seized the oars, pushing Agostino away and forcing
him to take the place left empty beside his mother. She put her arm
round his waist and asked how he felt, and if he was happy. She
herself seemed in the highest spirits, and began singing, another most
unusual thing with her. She had a sweet voice, and put in some pathetic trills which made Agostino shiver. While she sang she continued to hold him close to her, wetting him with the water from her
damp bathing suit, which seemed to exude a violent animal heat. And
so they came in to the shore, the young man rowing, the woman

singing and caressing her son, who submitted with a feeling of utter
boredom; making up a picture which Agostino felt to be false, and
contrived for appearance' sake.

Next day the young man appeared again. Agostino's mother insisted on her son coming and the scenes of the day before repeated
themselves. Then after a few days' interval they went out again. And
at last, with their apparently growing intimacy, he came to fetch her
daily, and each time Agostino was obliged to go too, to listen to their
conversation and to watch them bathing. He hated these expeditions,
and invented a thousand reasons for not going. He would disappear
and not show himself till his mother, having called him repeatedly
and hunted for him everywhere, succeeded at last in unearthing him;
but then he came less in response to her appeals than because her
disappointment and vexation aroused his pity. He kept completely
silent on the float, hoping they would understand and leave him
alone, but in the end he proved weaker and more susceptible to pity
than his mother or the young man. It was enough for them just to
have him there; as for his feelings, he came to see that they counted
for less than nothing. So, in spite of all his attempts to escape, the
expeditions continued.

One day Agostino was sitting on the sand behind his mother's
deck chair, waiting for the white raft to appear on the sea and for his
mother to wave her hand in greeting and call to the young man by
name. But the usual hour for his appearance passed, and his mother's
disappointed and cross expression clearly showed that she had given
up all hope of his coming. Agostino had often wondered what he
should feel in such a case, and had supposed that his joy would have
been at least as great as his mother's disappointment. But he was surprised to feel instead a vague disappointment, and he realized that the
humiliations and resentments of those daily outings had become almost a necessity of life to him. Therefore, with a confused and unconscious desire to inflict pain on his mother, he asked her more than
once if they were not going out for their usual row. She replied each
time that she didn't know, but that probably they wouldn't be going
today. She lay in the deck chair with a book open in her lap, but she
wasn't reading and her eyes continually wandered out to sea, as if
seeking some particular object among the many boats and bathers
with which the water was already swarming. After sitting a long
time behind his mother's chair, drawing patterns in the sand, Agostino came round to her and said in a tone of voice which he felt to be
teasing and even mocking: "Mamma, do you mean to say that we're

not going out on the raft today?" His mother may have felt the
mockery in his voice and the desire to make her suffer, or his few
rash words may have sufficed to release her long pent-up irritation.
She raised her hand with an involuntary gesture and gave him a
sharp slap on the cheek, which did not really hurt, probably because
she regretted it almost before the blow fell. Agostino said nothing,
but leaping up off the sand in one bound, he went away with his
head hanging down, in the direction of the beach cabin. "Agostino!
. . . Agostino! . . ." he heard his name called several times. Then
the calling stopped, and looking back he fancied he saw among the
throng of boats the young man's white raft. But he no longer worried about that, he was like someone who has found a treasure and
hastens to hide it away so that he may examine it alone. For it was
with just such a sense of discovery that he ran away to nurse his
injury; something so novel to him as to seem almost incredible.

His cheek burned, his eyes were full of tears which he could not
keep back; and fearing lest his sobs should break out before he got
into shelter, he ran doubled up. The accumulated bitterness of all
those days when he had been compelled to accompany the young
man and his mother came surging back on him, and he felt that if
only he could have a good cry it would release something in him and
help him to understand the meaning of all these strange happenings.
The simplest thing seemed to be to shut himself up in the beach
cabin. His mother was probably already out in the boat and no one
would disturb him. Agostino climbed the steps hurriedly, opened the
door and, leaving it ajar, sat down on a stool in the corner.

He huddled up with his knees tucked into his chest and his head
against the wall, and holding his face between his hands, started
weeping conscientiously. The slap he had received kept rising up before him, and he wondered why, when it seemed so hard, his
mother's hand had been so soft and irresolute. With the bitter sense
of humiliation aroused in him by the blow were mixed a thousand
other sensations, even more disagreeable, which had wounded his
feelings during these last days. There was one above all which kept
returning to his mind: the image of his mother's body in its damp
tricot pressed against his cheek, quivering with a sort of imperious
vitality. And just as great clouds of dust fly out from old clothes
when they are beaten, so, as the result of that blow to his suffering
and bewildered consciousness, there arose in him again the sensation
of his mother's body pressed against his cheek. Indeed, that sensation
seemed at times to take place of the slap; at others, the two became so
mixed that he felt both the throbbing of her body and the burning

blow. But while it seemed to him natural that the slap on his cheek should keep flaring up like a fire which is gradually going out, he could not understand why the earlier sensation so persistently recurred. Why, among so many others, was it just that one which haunted him? He could not have explained it, but he thought that as long as he lived he would only have to carry his memory back to that moment in his life in order to have fresh against his cheek the pulse of her body and the rough texture of the damp tricot.

He went on crying softly to himself so as not to interrupt the painful workings of his memory, at the same time rubbing away from his wet skin with the tips of his fingers the tears which continued to fall slowly but uninterruptedly from his eyes. It was dark and stuffy in the cabin. Suddenly he had a feeling of someone opening the door, and he almost hoped that his mother, repenting of what she had done, would lay her hand affectionately on his shoulder and turn his face toward her. And his lips had already begun to shape the word "Mamma" when he heard a step in the cabin and the door pulled to, without any hand touching his shoulder or stroking his head.

He raised his head and looked up. Close to the half-open door he saw a boy of about his own age standing in an attitude of someone on the lookout. He had on a pair of short trousers rolled up at the bottom, and an open sailor blouse with a great hole in the back. A thin ray of sunshine falling through a gap in the roof of the cabin lit up the thick growth of auburn curls round his neck. His feet were bare; holding the door ajar with his hands, he was gazing intently at something on the beach and did not seem to be aware of Agostino's presence. Agostino dried his eyes with the back of his hand and said: "Hello, what do you want?" The boy turned around, making a sign not to speak. He had an ugly, freckled face, the most remarkable feature of which was the rapid movement of his hard blue eyes. Agostino thought he recognized him. Probably he was the son of a fisherman or beach attendant, and he had doubtless seen him pushing out the boats or doing something about the beach.

"We're playing cops and robbers," said the boy, after a moment, turning to Agostino. "They mustn't see me."

"Which are you?" asked Agostino, hastily drying his eyes.

"A robber, of course," replied the other without looking around.

Agostino went on watching the boy. He couldn't make up his mind whether he liked him, but his voice had a rough touch of dialect which piqued him and aroused his curiosity. Besides, he felt instinctively that this boy's hiding in the cabin just at that moment was an opportunity—he could not have explained of what sort—but certainly an opportunity he must not miss.

"Will you let me play too?" he asked. The boy turned round and stared at him rudely. "How do you get into it?" he said quickly. "We're all pals playing together."

"Well," said Agostino, with shameless persistence, "let me play too."

The boy shrugged his shoulders. "It's too late now. We've almost finished the game."

"Well, in the next game."

"There won't be any more," said the boy, looking him over doubtfully, but as if struck by his persistence. "Afterwards we're going to the pine woods."

"I'll go with you, if you'll let me."

The boy seemed amused and began to laugh rather contemptuously. "You're a fine one, you are. But we don't want you."

Agostino had never been in such a position before. But the same instinct which prompted him to ask the boy if he might join their game suggested to him now a means by which he might make himself acceptable.

"Look here," he said hesitatingly, "if you . . . if you'll let me join your gang, I . . . I'll give you something."

The other turned round at once with greedy eyes.

"What'll you give me?"

"Whatever you like."

Agostino pointed to a big model of a sailboat, with all its sails attached, which was lying on the floor of the cabin among a lot of other toys.

"I'll give you that."

"What use is that to me?" replied the boy, shrugging his shoulders.

"You could sell it," Agostino suggested.

"They'd never take it," said the boy, with the air of one who knows. "They'd say it was stolen goods."

Agostino looked all round him despairingly. His mother's clothes were hanging on pegs, her shoes were on the floor, on the table was a handkerchief and a scarf or two. There was absolutely nothing in the cabin which seemed a suitable offering.

"Say," said the boy, seeing his bewilderment, "got any cigarettes?"

Agostino remembered that that very morning his mother had put two boxes of a very good brand in the big bag which was hanging from a peg; and he hastened to reply, triumphantly, "Yes, I have. Would you like some?"

"I *don't* think!" said the other, with scornful irony. "Are you stupid! Give them here, quick."

Agostino took down the bag, felt about in it and pulled out the two boxes. He held them out to the boy, as if he were not quite sure how many he wanted.

"I'll take both," he said lightly, seizing the boxes. He looked at the label and clicked his tongue approvingly and said: "You must be rich, eh?"

Agostino didn't know what to answer. The boy went on: "I'm Berto. What's your name?"

Agostino told him. But the other had ceased to pay any attention. His impatient fingers had already torn open one of the boxes, breaking the seals on its paper wrapping. He took out a cigarette and put it between his lips. Then he took a match from his pocket and struck it against the wall of the cabin; and after inhaling a mouthful of smoke and puffing it out through his nose, he resumed his watching position at the crack of the door.

"Come on, let's go," he said, after a moment, making Agostino a sign to follow him. They left the cabin one behind the other. When they got to the beach Berto made straight for the road behind the row of beach cabins.

As they walked along the burning sand between the low bushes of broom and thistles, he said: "Now we're going to the Cave . . . they've gone on past . . . they're looking for me lower down."

"Where is the Cave?" asked Agostino.

"At the Vespucci Baths," replied the boy. He held his cigarette ostentatiously between two fingers, as if to display it, and voluptuously inhaled great mouthfuls of smoke. "Don't you smoke?" he said.

"I don't care about it," said Agostino, ashamed to confess that he had never even dreamed of smoking. But Berto laughed. "Why don't you say straight out that your mother won't let you? Speak the truth." His way of saying this was contemptuous rather than friendly. He offered Agostino a cigarette, saying: "Go ahead, you smoke too."

They had reached the sea-front and were walking barefoot on the sharp flints between dried-up flower beds. Agostino put the cigarette to his lips and took a few puffs, inhaling a little smoke which he at once let out again instead of swallowing it.

Berto laughed derisively.

"You call that smoking!" he exclaimed. "That's not the way to do it. Look." He took the cigarette and inhaled deeply, rolling his sulky eyes all the while; then he opened his mouth wide and put it quite close to Agostino's eyes. There was nothing to be seen in his mouth, except his tongue curled up at the back.

"Now watch," said Berto, shutting his mouth again. And he puffed a cloud of smoke straight into Agostino's face. Agostino coughed and laughed nervously at the same time. "It's your turn now," said Berto.

A trolley passed them, whistling, its window curtains flapping in the breeze. Agostino inhaled a fresh mouthful and with a great effort swallowed the smoke. But it went the wrong way and he had a dreadful fit of coughing. Berto took the cigarette and gave him a great slap on the back, saying: "Bravo! There's no doubt about your being a smoker."

After this experiment they walked on in silence past a whole series of bath establishments, with their rows of cabins painted in bright colors, great striped umbrellas slanting in all directions, and absurd triumphal arches. The beach between the cabins was packed with noisy holiday-makers and the sparkling sea swarmed with bathers.

"Where is Vespucci?" asked Agostino, who had to walk very fast to keep up with his new friend.

"It's the last one of all."

Agostino began to wonder whether he ought not to turn back. If his mother hadn't gone out on the raft after all, she would certainly be looking for him. But the memory of that slap put his scruples to rest. In going with Berto he almost felt as if he were pursuing a mysterious and justified vendetta.

Suddenly Berto stopped and said: "How about letting the smoke out through your nose? Can you do that?" Agostino shook his head, and his companion, holding the stump of his cigarette between his lips, inhaled the smoke and expelled it through his nostrils. "Now," he went on, "I'm going to let it out through my eyes. But you must put your hand on my chest and look me straight in the face." Agostino went up to him quite innocently and put his hand on Berto's chest and fixed his eyes on Berto's, expecting to see smoke come out of them.

But Berto treacherously pressed the lighted cigarette down hard on the back of his hand and threw the butt away, jumping for joy and shouting: "Oh! you silly idiot! You just don't know anything." Agostino was almost blind with pain, and his first impulse was to fling himself on Berto and strike him. But Berto, as if he saw what was coming, stood still and clenched his fists, and with two sharp blows in the stomach almost knocked the breath out of Agostino's body.

"I'm not one for words," he said savagely. "If you ask for it you'll get it." Agostino, infuriated, rushed at him again, but he felt terribly weak and certain of being defeated. This time Berto seized him by the head, and taking it under his arm almost strangled him. Agostino did not even attempt to resist, but in a stifled voice, implored him to let go. Berto released him and sprang back, planting his feet firmly on the ground in a fighting stance. But Agostino had heard the vertebrae of his neck crack, and was stupefied by the boy's extraordinary brutality. It seemed incredible that he, Agostino, who had always been kind to everyone, should suddenly be treated with such savage and deliberate cruelty. His chief feeling was one of amazement at such barbarousness. It overwhelmed him, but at the same time fascinated him because of its very novelty and because it was so monstrous.

"I haven't done you any harm," he panted, "I gave you those cigarettes . . . and you . . ." He couldn't finish. His eyes filled with tears.

"Uh, you crybaby," retorted Berto. "Want your cigarettes back? I don't want them. Take them back to Mamma."

"It doesn't matter," said Agostino, shaking his head disconsolately. "I only just said it for something to say. Please keep them."

"Well, let's get on," said Berto. "We're almost there."

The burn on Agostino's hand was hurting him badly. Raising it to his lips he looked about him. On that part of the beach there were very few cabins, five or six in all, scattered about at some distance from each other. They were miserable huts of rough wood. The sand between them was deserted and the sea was equally empty. There were a few women in the shade of a boat pulled up out of reach of the tide, some standing, some lying stretched out on the sand, all dressed in antiquated bathing suits, with long drawers edged with white braid, all busy drying themselves and exposing their white limbs to the sun. A signboard painted blue bore the inscription: "Amerigo Vespucci Baths." A low green shack half-buried in the sand evidently belonged to the bath man. Beyond this the shore stretched away as far as the eye could see, without either cabins or houses, a solitude of windswept sand between the sparkling blue sea and the dusty green of the pine trees.

One entire side of the man's hut was hidden from the road by

sand dunes, which were higher at this point. Then, when you had
climbed to the top of the dunes, you saw a patched, faded awning of
rusty red, which seemed to have been cut out of an old sail. This
awning was attached at one end of two poles driven into the sand,
and at the other to the hut.

"That's our cave," said Berto.

Under the awning a man seated at a rickety table was in the act
of lighting a cigar. Two or three boys were stretched on the sand
around him. Berto took a flying leap and landed at the man's feet,
crying: "Cave!" Agostino approached rather timidly. "This is Pisa,"
said Berto, pointing to him. He was surprised to hear himself called
by this nickname so soon. It was only five minutes ago that he had
told Berto he was born at Pisa. Agostino lay down on the ground
beside the others. The sand was not so clean as it was on the beach;
bits of coconut shell and wooden splinters, fragments of earthenware
and all sorts of rubbish were mixed up in it. Here and there it was
caked and hard from the pails of dirty water which had been thrown
out of the hut. Agostino noticed that the boys, four in all, were
poorly dressed. Like Berto they were evidently the sons of sailors or
bath men. "He was at the Speranza," burst out Berto, without drawing breath. "He says he wants to play at cops and robbers too, but
the game's over, isn't it? I told you the game would be over."

At that moment there was a cry of "It's not fair! It's not fair!"
Agostino, looking up, saw another gang of boys running from the
direction of the sea, probably the cops. First came a thickset, stumpy
youth of about seventeen in a bathing costume; next, to his great
surprise, a Negro; the third was fair, and by his carriage and physical
beauty struck Agostino as being better bred than the others. But as
he got nearer his ragged bathing suit, full of holes, and a certain
coarseness in his handsome face with beautiful blue eyes, showed
that he too belonged to the people. After these three boys came four
more, all about the same age, between thirteen and fourteen. The
big, thickset boy was so much older than the others that at first it
seemed odd that he should mix with such children. But his pasty
face, the color of half-baked bread; the thick, expressionless features,
and an almost brutish stupidity were sufficient explanation of the
company he kept. He had hardly any neck, and his smooth, hairless
torso was as wide at the waist and hips as at the shoulders. "You hid
in a cabin," he shouted at Berto. "I dare you to deny it! Cabins are
out of bounds by the rules of the game."

"It's a lie!" retorted Berto, with equal violence. "Isn't it, Pisa?"
he added, suddenly turning to Agostino. "I didn't hide in a cabin, did

I? We were both standing by the hut of the Speranza, and we saw you go by, didn't we Pisa?"

"You did hide in my cabin, you know," said Agostino, who was incapable of telling a lie. "There, you see!" shouted the other, brandishing his fist under Berto's nose. "I'll bash your head in, you liar!"

"Spy!" yelled Berto in Agostino's face. "I told you to stay where you were. Go back to Mamma, that's the place for you." He was filled with uncontrollable rage, a bestial fury which amazed and mystified Agostino. But in springing to punish him one of the cigarette boxes tumbled out of his pocket. He stooped to pick it up, but the big boy was quicker still, and darting down he pounced on the box and waved it in the air, crying triumphantly: "Cigarettes! Cigarettes!"

"Give them back," shouted Berto, hurling himself upon the big boy. "They're mine. Pisa gave them to *me*. You just give them back."

The other took a step back and waited till Berto was within range. Then he held the box of cigarettes in his mouth and began to pummel Berto's stomach methodically with his two fists. Finally he kicked Berto's feet from under and brought him down with a crash. "Give me them back!" Berto went on shouting, while he rolled in the sand. But the big boy, with a stupid laugh, called out: "He's got some more . . . at him, boys." And with a unanimity which surprised Agostino all the boys flung themselves upon Berto. For a moment there was nothing to be seen but a writhing mass of bodies tangled together in a cloud of sand at the feet of the man, who went on smoking calmly at the table. At last, the fair boy, who seemed to be the most agile, disentangled himself from the heap and got up, triumphantly waving the second box of cigarettes. Then the others got up, one by one; and last of all Berto. His ugly, freckled little face was convulsed with fury. "Swine! Thieves!" he bellowed, shaking his fist and sobbing.

It was a strange and novel impression for Agostino to see his tormentor tormented in his turn, and treated as pitilessly as he himself had just been. "Swine! Swine!" Berto screamed again. The big boy went up to him and gave him a resounding box on the ear, which made his companions dance for joy. "Do you want any more?" Berto rushed like a mad one to the corner of the hut and, bending down, grabbed hold of a large rock with both hands and flung it at his enemy, who with a derisive whistle sprang aside to avoid it. "You swine!" yelled Berto again, still sobbing with rage, but withdrawing himself prudently behind a corner of the hut. His sobs were loud and furious, as if giving vent to some frightful bitterness, but his companions had ceased to take any interest in him. They were all stretched out again on the sand. The big boy opened one box of cigarettes, and the fair boy another. Suddenly the man, who had remained seated at the little table without moving during the fight, said: "Hand over those cigarettes."

Agostino looked at him. He was a tall, fat man of about fifty. He had a cold and deceptively good-natured face. He was bald, with a curious saddle-shaped forehead and twinkling eyes; a red, aquiline nose with wide nostrils full of little scarlet veins horrible to look at. He had a drooping mustache, which hid a rather crooked mouth, and a cigar between his lips. He was wearing a faded shirt and a pair of blue cotton trousers with one leg down to his ankle and the other rolled up below his knee. A black sash was wound round his stomach. One detail in particular added to Agostino's first feeling of revulsion, the fact that Saro—for this was his name—had six fingers instead of five on both hands. This made them look enormous, and his fingers like abbreviated tentacles. Agostino could not take his eyes off those hands; he could not make up his mind whether Saro had two first or two middle or two third fingers. They all seemed of equal length, except the little finger, which stuck out from his hand like a small branch at the base of a knotty tree trunk. Saro took the cigar out of his mouth and repeated simply: "What about those cigarettes?"

The fair boy got up and put his box on the table. "Good for you, Sandro," said Saro.

"And supposing I won't give you them?" shouted the elder boy defiantly.

"Give them up, Tortima; you'd better," called out several voices at once. Tortima looked all round and then at Saro, who with the six fingers of his right hand on the box of cigarettes, kept his half-closed little eyes fixed on him. Then, with the remark: "All right, but it isn't fair," he came over and put his box down on the table too.

"And now I'll divide them," said Saro, in a soft, affable voice. Without removing his cigar, he screwed up his eyes, opened one of the boxes, took out a cigarette with his stumpy, multiple fingers, which looked incapable of gripping it, and threw it to the Negro, with a "Catch, Homs!" Then he took another and threw it to one of the others; a third he threw into the joined palms of Sandro; a fourth straight at Tortima's stolid face—and so with all the rest. "Do you want one?" he asked Berto, who, swallowing back his sobs, had come silently back to join the others. He nodded sulkily, and was thrown one. When each of the boys had received his cigarette, Saro was about to shut the box, which was still half full, when he stopped and said to Agostino: "What about you, Pisa?" Agostino would have liked to refuse, but Berto gave him a dig in the ribs and whispered: "Ask for one, idiot, we'll smoke it together afterwards." So Agostino said he would like one, and he too had his cigarette. Then Saro shut the box.

"What about the rest? What about the rest?" shouted all the boys at once.

"You shall have the rest another day," replied Saro calmly. "Pisa, take these cigarettes and go and put them in the hut." There was complete silence. Agostino nervously took both boxes and, stepping over the boys' prostrate bodies, crossed to the shed. It appeared to consist of one room only, and he liked its smallness, which made it seem like a house in a fairy tale. It had a low ceiling with whitewashed beams, and the walls were of unplaned planks. Two tiny windows, complete with window sill, little square panes of glass, latches, curtains, even a vase or two of flowers, diffused a mild light. One corner was occupied by the bed neatly made up, with a clean pillowcase and red counterpane; in another stood a round table and three stools. On the marble top of a big chest stood two of those bottles which have sailboats or steamships imprisoned inside them. Sails were hung on hooks all round the walls, and there were pairs of oars and other sea tackle. Agostino thought how he should love to own a cottage as cozy and convenient as this. He went up to the table, on which lay a big, cracked china bowl full of half-smoked cigarettes, put down his two boxes and went out again into the sunlight.

All the boys were lying face downward on the sand around Saro, smoking with great demonstrations of enjoyment. And meanwhile they were discussing something about which they did not seem to agree. Sandro was just saying: "I tell you it *is* him."

"His mother's a real beauty," said an admiring voice. "She's the best looker on the beach. Homs and me got under the cabin one day to see her undress, but her chemise fell just above the crack we were looking through and we couldn't see anything at all. Her legs, gee, and her breasts. . . ."

"You never see the husband anywhere about," said a third voice.

"You needn't worry, she satisfies herself. . . . D'you know who with? That young guy from Villa Sorriso . . . the dark one. He takes her out every day on his raft."

"He's not the only one either. She'd take anyone on," said some-one maliciously.

"But I know it's not him," insisted another.

"Say, Pisa," said Sandro suddenly. "Isn't that your mother, that lady at the Speranza? She's tall and dark, with long legs, and wears a striped two-piece bathing suit . . . and she's got a mole on the left side of her mouth."

"Yes, why?" asked Agostino, nervously.

"It *is* her, it *is* her," cried Berto triumphantly. And then, in a burst of jealous spite: "You're just their blind, aren't you? You all go out together, her and you, and her gigolo. You're their blind, aren't you?" At these words everyone roared with laughter. Even Saro smiled under his mustache.

"I don't know what you mean," said Agostino, blushing and only half understanding. He wanted to protest, but their coarse jokes aroused in him a curious and unexpected sense of sadistic satisfaction. As if by their words the boys had, all unawares, avenged the humilia-tions which his mother had inflicted on him all these days past. At the same time he was struck dumb with horror at their knowing so much about his private affairs.

"Innocent little lamb," said the same malicious voice. "I'd like to know what they're up to; they always go a long way out," said Tor-tima with mock gravity. "Come on, tell us what they do. He kisses her, eh?" He put the back of his hand to his lips and gave it a smack-ing kiss.

"It's quite true," said Agostino, flushing with shame; "we do go a long way out to swim."

"Oh yes, to swim!" came sarcastically from several voices at once.

"My mother does swim, and so does Renzo."

"Ah, yes, Renzo, that's his name," affirmed the boy, as if recover-ing a lost thread in his memory. "Renzo that tall dark fellow."

"And what do Renzo and Mamma do together?" suddenly asked Berto, quite restored. "Is it this they do?" and he made an expressive gesture with his hand. "And you just look on, eh?"

"I?" questioned Agostino, turning around with a look of terror.

They all burst out laughing and smothered their merriment in the sand. But Saro continued to observe him attentively, without mov-ing. Agostino looked around despairingly, as if to implore aid.

Saro seemed to be struck by his look. He took his cigar out of his mouth, and said: "Can't you see he knows absolutely nothing?"

The din was immediately silenced. "How do you mean, he doesn't know?" asked Tortima, who hadn't understood.

"He just doesn't know," repeated Saro, simply. And turning to Agostino, he said in a softer voice: "Speak up, Pisa. A man and a woman, what is it they do together? Don't you know?"

They all listened breathlessly. Agostino stared at Saro, who continued to smoke and watch him through half-closed eyelids. He looked round at the boys, who were evidently bursting with stifled laughter, and repeated mechanically, through the cloud which seemed to cover his sight: "A man and a woman?"

"Yes, your mother and Renzo," explained Berto brutally.

Agostino wanted to say "Don't talk about my mother," but the question awoke in him a whole swarm of sensations and memories, and he was too upset to say anything at all. "He doesn't know," said Saro abruptly, shifting his cigar from one corner of his mouth to the other. "Which of you boys is going to tell him?" Agostino looked around bewildered. It was like being at school, but what a strange schoolmaster! What odd schoolfellows! "Me, me, me! . . ." all the boys shouted at once. Saro's glance rested dubiously on all those faces burning with eagerness to be the first to speak. Then he said: "You don't really know either, any of you. You've only got it from hearsay. . . . Let someone tell him who really knows." Agostino saw them all eyeing each other in silence. Then someone said: "Tortima." An expression of vanity lit up the youth's face. He was just going to get up when Berto said, with hatred in his voice: "He made it all up, himself. . . . It's a pack of lies. . . ."

"What d'you mean, a pack of lies?" shouted Tortima, flinging himself upon Berto. "It's you who tell lies, you bastard!" But this time Berto was too quick for him, and from behind the corner of the hut he began making faces and putting out his tongue at Tortima, his red, freckled face distorted by hatred. Tortima contented himself with threatening him with his fist and shouting: "You dare come back!" But somehow Berto's intervention had wrecked his chances, and the boys with one accord voted for Sandro. His arms crossed over his broad brown chest on which shone a few golden hairs, Sandro, handsome and elegant, advanced into the circle of boys stretched out on the sand. Agostino noticed that his strong, bronzed legs looked as if they were dusted over with gold. A few hairs also showed through the gaps in his bathing trunks. "It's quite simple," he said in a strong, clear voice. And speaking slowly with the aid of gestures which were significant without being coarse, he explained to Agostino what he now felt he had always known but had somehow forgotten, as in a deep sleep. Sandro's explanation was followed by other less sober ones. Some of the boys made vulgar gestures with their hands, others dinned into Agostino's ears coarse words which he had never heard before; two of them said: "We'll show him what they do," and gave a demonstration on the hot sand, jerking and writhing in each other's arms. Sandro, satisfied with his success, went off alone to finish his cigarette. "Do you understand now?" asked Saro, as soon as the din had died down. Agostino nodded. In reality he hadn't so much understood as absorbed the notion, rather as one absorbs a medicine or poison, the effect of which is not immediately felt but will be sure to manifest itself later on. The idea was not in his empty, bewildered and anguished mind, but in some other part of his being; in his embittered heart, or deep in his breast, which received it with amazement. It was like some bright, dazzling object, which one cannot look at for the radiance it emits, so that one can only guess its real shape. He felt it was something he had always possessed but only now experienced in his blood.

"Renzo and Pisa's mother," he heard someone say close beside him. "I'll be Renzo and you be Pisa's mother. Let's try." He turned suddenly and saw Berto, who with an awkward, ceremonious gesture was making a bow to another boy. "Madam, may I have the honor of your company on my raft? I'm going for a swim. Pisa will accompany us." Then suddenly blind rage took possession of him and flinging himself upon Berto he yelled: "I forbid you to talk about my mother." But before he knew what had happened he was lying on his back on the sand, with Berto's knee holding him down and Berto's fists raining blows on his face. He wanted to cry, but realizing that his tears would only be an opening for more jeers, he controlled them with great effort. Then, covering his face with his arm, he lay as still as death. Berto left him alone after a bit, and feeling very ill-treated he went and sat down at Saro's feet. The boys were already busy talking about something else. One of them suddenly asked Agostino: "Are you rich, you people?"

Agostino was so intimidated that he hardly knew what to say. But he replied: "I think so."

"How much? . . . A million? Two millions? . . . Three millions?"

"I don't know," said Agostino, feeling bothered.

"Got a big house."

"Yes," said Agostino; and somewhat reassured by the more courteous turn of the conversation, pride of possession prompted him to add: "We have twenty rooms."

"Bum . . ." came incredulously from someone.

"We've got two reception rooms and then there's my father's study . . ."

"Aha!" said a scornful voice.

"Or it *used* to be my father's," Agostino hastened to add, half hoping that this detail might make them feel a little more sympathetic towards him. "My father is dead."

There was a moment's silence. "So your mother's a widow?" said Tortima.

"Well, of course," came from several mocking voices. "That's not saying anything," protested Tortima. "She might have married again."

"No, she hasn't married again," said Agostino.

"And have you got a car?"

"Yes."

"And a chauffeur?"

"Yes."

"Tell your mother I'm ready to be her chauffeur," shouted someone.

"And what do you do in those reception rooms?" asked Tortima, on whom Agostino's account seemed to make more impression than on anyone else. "Do you give dances?"

"Yes, my mother has receptions," replied Agostino.

"Lots of pretty women, you bet," said Tortima, as if speaking to himself. "How many people come?"

"I don't really know."

"How many?"

"Twenty or thirty," said Agostino, who by now felt quite at his ease and was rather gratified by his success.

"Twenty or thirty . . . What do they do?"

"What do you expect them to do?" asked Berto ironically. "I suppose they dance and amuse themselves. They're rich . . . not like us. They make love, I suppose."

"No, they don't make love," said Agostino conscientiously, for the sake of showing that he knew perfectly well what they meant.

Tortima seemed to be struggling with an idea which he was unable to formulate. At last he said: "But supposing I was to appear at one of those receptions, and say: 'I've come too.' What would you do?" As he spoke he got up and marched forward impudently, with his hands on his hips and his chest stuck out. The boys burst out laughing. "I should ask you to go away," said Agostino simply, emboldened by the laughter of the boys.

"And suppose I refused to go away?"

"I should make our men turn you out."

"Have you got menservants?"

"No, but my mother hires waiters when she has a reception."

"Bah, just like your father." One of the boys was evidently the son of a waiter.

"And supposing I resisted, and broke that waiter's nose for him, and then marched into the middle of the room and shouted, 'You're a lot of rogues and bitches, the whole lot of you.' What would you say?" insisted Tortima, advancing threateningly upon Agostino, and turning his fist round and round, as if to let him smell it. But this time they all turned against Tortima, not so much from a wish to protect Agostino as from the desire to hear more details of his fabulous wealth.

"Leave him alone . . . they'd kick you out, and a good thing too," was heard on all sides. Berto said sneeringly: "What have you got to do with it? Your father's a boatman and you'll be a boatman too; and if you did turn up at Pisa's house you certainly wouldn't shout anything. I can see you," he added, getting up and mimicking Tortima's supposed humility in Agostino's house . . . " 'Excuse me, is Mr. Pisa at home? Excuse me . . . I just came . . . Oh, he can't? . . . Never mind, please excuse me . . . I'm so sorry . . . I'll come another time.' Oh, I can see you. Why, you'd bow down to the ground."

All the boys burst out laughing. Tortima, who was as stupid as he was brutal, didn't dare stand up to their taunts. But in order to get even he said to Agostino: "Can you make an iron arm?"

"An iron arm?" repeated Agostino.

"He didn't know what an iron arm is," said several voices, derisively. Sandro came over and took hold of Agostino's arm and doubled it up, and told him to stay with his hand in the air and his elbow in the sand. Meanwhile Tortima lay face downward on the sand and placed his arm in a similar position. "You push from one side," said Sandro, "and Tortima will push from the other."

Agostino took Tortima's hand. The latter at one stroke brought down his arm and got up triumphantly.

"Let me try," said Berto. He brought down Agostino's arm just as easily and got up in his turn. "Me too, me too!" cried all the others. One after another they all beat Agostino. At last it was the Negro's turn, and someone said: "If you let Homs beat you, well, your arm must be made of putty." Agostino made up his mind not to let the Negro beat him.

The Negro's arms were thin, the color of roasted coffee. He thought his own looked stronger. "Come on, Pisa," said Homs, with sham bravado, as he lay down facing him. He had a weak voice, like a woman's, and when he brought his face to within an inch of Agostino's, he saw that his nose, instead of being flat, as you might have expected, was almost aquiline, and curved in on itself like a black, shiny curl of flesh, with a pale, almost yellow mole above one nostril. Nor were his lips broad and thick like a Negro's, but thin and violet-colored. He had round eyes with large whites, on which his protuberant forehead with its great mop of sooty wool seemed to press. "Come on, Pisa, I won't hurt you," he said, putting his delicate hand with its thin, rose-nailed fingers in Agostino's. Agostino saw that by raising himself slightly on his shoulder he could easily have brought his whole weight to bear on his hand, and this simple fact allowed him at first to keep Homs under his control. For quite a while they competed without either of them getting the upper hand, surrounded by a circle of admiring boys. Agostino's face wore a look of great concentration; he was putting his whole strength into the effort; whereas the Negro made fearful grimaces, grinding his white teeth and screwing up his eyes. Suddenly a surprised voice proclaimed: "Pisa's winning!" But at that very moment Agostino felt an excruciating pain running from his shoulder right down his arm; he could bear no more, and gave in, saying: "No, he's stronger than me." "You'll beat me next time," said the Negro, in an unpleasantly honeyed voice, as he rose from the ground. "Fancy Homs beating you too, you're good for nothing," sneered Tortima. But the other boys seemed tired of ragging Agostino. "How about a swim?" said someone. "Yes, yes, a swim!" they all cried, and they set off by leaps and bounds over the hot sand to the sea. Agostino, trailing behind, saw them turning somersaults like fish into the shallow water, with shouts and screams of joy. As he reached the water's edge Tortima emerged, bottom first, like a huge sea-animal, and called out: "Dive in, Pisa. What are you doing?"

"But I'm dressed," said Agostino.

"Get undressed then," returned Tortima crossly. Agostino tried to escape, but it was too late. Tortima caught hold of him and dragged him along, struggling and pulled his tormentor over with him. He only let him go when he had almost suffocated him by holding his head under water. Then with a "Good-bye, Pisa," he swam off. Some way out Agostino could see Sandro standing in an elegant posture on a raft, in the middle of a swarm of boys, all trying to climb on to the floats. Wet and panting he returned to the beach and

stood a few moments watching the raft going further and further
out to sea, all alone under the blinding sunshine. Then hurrying
along the burnished sand at the water's edge, he made his way back
to the Speranza.

It was not so late as he feared. When he reached the bathing
place he found that his mother had not yet returned. The beach was
emptying; only a few isolated bathers still loitered in the dazzling
water. The majority were trailing languidly off in single file under
the midday sun up the tiled path which led from the beach. Agostino
sat down under the big umbrella and waited. He thought his mother
was staying out an unusually long time. He forgot that the young
man had arrived much later than usual with his raft and that it was
not his mother who had wanted to go out alone, but he who had
disappeared; and said to himself that those two had certainly profited
by his absence to do what Saro and the boys had suggested. He no
longer felt any jealousy about this, but experienced a new and
strange quiver of curiosity and secret approval, as if he were himself
an accomplice. It was quite natural for his mother to behave like that
with the young man, to go out with him every day on the float, and
at a safe distance from prying eyes to fling herself into his arms. It
was natural, and he was now perfectly well able to accept the fact.
These thoughts passed through his mind as he sat scanning the sea
for the return of the lovers. At length the raft appeared, a bright
speck on the sea, and as it drew rapidly nearer he could see his
mother sitting on the bench and the young man rowing. Every
stroke of the oars as they rose and fell left a glittering track in the
water. He got up and went down to the water's edge. He wanted to
see his mother land, and to discover some traces of the intimacy, at
which he had assisted so long without understanding, and which, in
the light of the revelations that Saro and the boys had made, must
surely be brazenly advertised in their behavior. As the raft came near
the shore his mother waved to him, then sprang gaily into the water
and was soon at his side. "Are you hungry? We'll go and have something to eat at once. . . . Good-bye, good-bye till tomorrow
. . . ." she added in a caressing voice, turning to wave to the young
man. Agostino thought she seemed happier than usual, and as he followed her across the beach he could not help thinking there had been
a note of joyous intoxication in her farewell to the young man; as if
what her son's presence had hitherto prevented had actually taken
place that day. But his observations and suspicions went no further
than this; for apart from her naïve joy, which was something quite

different from her customary dignity, he could not really picture
what might have happened while they were out together, nor imagine
what their relations actually were. Though he scrutinized her face,
her neck, her hands, her body with a new and cruel awareness, they
did not seem to bear any trace of the kisses and caresses they had
received. The more Agostino watched his mother the more dissatisfied he felt. "You were alone today . . . without me . . ." he
began, as they approached the cabin; almost hoping she would say:
"Yes, and at last we were able to make love." But his mother only
seemed to treat this remark as an allusion to the slap she had given
him, and to his running away. "Don't let's say any more about that,"
she said, stopping and putting her arm around his shoulders, and looking at him with her laughing, excited eyes. "I know you love me; give
me a kiss and we won't say any more about it, eh?" Agostino suddenly felt his lips against her neck—that neck whose chaste perfume
and warmth had been so sweet to him. But now he fancied he felt
beneath his lips, however faintly, a stirring of something new, as it
were a sharp quiver of reaction to the young man's kisses. Then she
ran up the steps to the cabin, and he lay down on the sand, his face
burning with a shame he could not comprehend.

Later, as they were walking back together, he stirred up these new
mysterious feelings in his troubled mind. Before, when he had been
ignorant of good and evil, his mother's relations with the young man
had seemed to him mysteriously tinged with guilt, but now that Saro
and his disciples had opened his eyes, he was, strange to say, full of
doubt and unsatisfied curiosity. It was indeed the frank jealousy of
his childish love for his mother which had first aroused his sensibilities; whereas now, in the clear, cruel light of day, this love, though as
great as ever, was replaced by a bitter, disillusioned curiosity compared with which those early, faint evidences seemed insipid and insufficient. Formerly, every word and gesture which he felt unbecom-
ing had offended without enlightening him, and he wished he had
not seen them. Now that he came to look back, those small, tasteless
gestures which used to scandalize him seemed mere trifles, and he
almost wished he could surprise his mother in some of the shameless
attitudes into which Saro and the boys had so recently initiated him.

He would never have hit so soon on the idea of spying on his
mother with the direct intention of destroying the halo of dignity
and respect which had hitherto enveloped her, had he not that very
day been driven by chance to take a step in that direction. When
they reached home mother and son ate their luncheon in silence. His
mother seemed distrait, and Agostino, full of new and, to him, in-

credible thoughts, was unusually silent. But after lunch he suddenly felt an irresistible desire to go out and join the gang of boys again. They had told him they met at the Vespucci bathing place early in the afternoon, to plan the day's adventures, and when he had got over his first fear and repugnance the company of those young hooligans began to exercise a mysterious attraction over him. He was lying on his bed with the shutters closed; it was warm and dark. He was playing as usual with the wooden switch of the electric light. Few sounds came to him from outside; the wheels of a solitary carriage, the clatter of plates and glasses through the open windows of the *pension* opposite. In contrast with the silence of the summer afternoon the sounds inside the house seemed to stand out more clearly, as if cut off from the rest. He heard his mother go into the next room and her heels tapping on the tiled floor. She went to and fro, opening and shutting drawers, moving chairs about, touching this and that. "She's gone to lie down," he thought suddenly, shaking off the torpor which was gradually invading his senses; "and then I shan't be able to tell her I want to go on the beach." He sprang up in alarm at the thought, and went out on the landing. His room looked over the balcony facing the stairs, and his mother's room was next to his. He went to her door, but finding it ajar, instead of knocking as he generally did, he gently pushed the door half open, moved perhaps by an unconscious desire to spy upon his mother's intimacy. His mother's room was much bigger than his, and the bed was by the door; directly facing the door was a chest of drawers, with a large mirror above it. The first thing he saw was his mother standing in front of the chest of drawers. She was not naked, as he had pictured and almost hoped when he went in so quietly; but she was partly undressed and was just taking off her necklace and earrings in front of the glass. She had on a flimsy chiffon chemise which only came halfway down her loins. As she stood leaning languidly to one side, one hip was higher and more prominent than the other, and below her solid but graceful thighs her slender, well-shaped legs tapered to delicate ankles. Her arms were raised to unfasten the clasp of her necklace and, through the transparent chiffon, this movement was perceptible all down her back, curiously modifying the contours of her body. With her hands raised thus, her armpits looked like the jaws of two snakes and the long, soft hair darted out of them like thin black tongues, as if glad to escape from the pressure of her heavy limbs. All her splendid, massive body seemed to Agostino's fascinated eyes to lose its solidity and sway and palpitate in the twilight of the room, as if nudity acted on it as a leaven and endowed it

with a strange faculty of expansion; so that at one moment it seemed
to billow outwards in innumerable curves, at another to taper upwards to a giant height, and to fill the space between floor and ceiling.

Agostino's first impulse was to hurry away again, but suddenly
that new thought, "It is a woman," rooted him to the spot, with wide-
open eyes, holding fast to the door handle. He felt his filial soul rebel
at this immobility and try to drag him back, but the new mind which
was already strong in him, though still a little timid, forced his reluctant eyes to stare pitilessly at what yesterday he would not have
dared to look upon. And during this conflict between repulsion and
attraction, surprise and pleasure, all the details of the picture he was
contemplating stood out more distinctly and forcibly: the movements of her legs, the indolent curve of her back, the profile of her
armpits. And they seemed to correspond exactly to his new conception, which was awaiting these confirmations in order to take complete sway over his imagination. Precipitated in one moment from
respect and reverence to their exact opposite, he would almost have
liked to see the improprieties of her unconscious nudity develop before his eyes into conscious wantonness. The astonishment in his
eyes changed to curiosity, the attention which riveted them and
which he fancied to be scientific in reality owed its false objectivity
to the cruelty of the sentiment controlling him. And while his blood
surged up to his brain be kept saying to himself: "She is a woman,
nothing but a woman," and he somehow felt these words to be lashes
of insult and contempt on her back and legs.

When his mother had taken off her necklace and put it down on
the marble top of the chest of drawers, she began with a graceful
movement of both hands to remove her earrings. In order to do so
she held her head slightly to one side, turning a little away from the
glass. Agostino was afraid she might catch sight of him in the big
standing mirror which was nearby in the bay window; for he could
see himself in it, standing furtively there, just inside the folding door.
He raised his hand with an effort, knocked at the doorpost and said:
"May I come in?"

"One moment, darling," said his mother calmly. Agostino saw
her disappear from sight and, after rummaging about for a while,
reappear in a long blue silk dressing gown.

"Mamma," said Agostino, without lifting his eyes from the
ground, "I am going down to the beach."

"Now?" said his mother, abstractedly. "But it's so hot. Hadn't
you better sleep a little first?" She put out one hand and stroked his

cheek, while with the other she rearranged a stray lock of her smooth black hair.

Agostino, suddenly become a child again, said nothing but remained standing, as he always did when any request of his had been refused, obstinately dumb, and looking down, his chin glued to his chest. His mother knew that gesture so well that she interpreted it in the usual way. "Well, if you really want to very much," she said, "go to the kitchen first and get them to give you something to take with you. But don't eat it now . . . put it in the cabin . . . and mind you don't bathe before five o'clock. Besides, I shall be out by then and we'll swim together." They were the same instructions she always gave him.

Agostino made no reply and ran barefooted down the stone stairs. He heard his mother's door close gently behind him. He put on his sandals in the hall and went out onto the road. The white blaze of the midday sun enveloped him in its silent furnace. At the end of the road the motionless sea sparkled in the remote, quivering atmosphere. In the opposite direction the red trunks of the pine trees bent under the weight of their heavy green cones.

He debated with himself whether to go to the Vespucci Baths by the beach or by the forest; but chose the former, for though he would be much more exposed to the sun he would be in no danger of passing the baths without seeing them. He followed the road as long as it ran by the sea, then hurried along as fast as he could, keeping close to the walls. Without his realizing it, what attracted him to the Vespucci, apart from the novel companionship of the boys, were their coarse comments on his mother and her supposed amours. He was conscious that his former disposition was changing into quite a different feeling, crueler and more objective, and he thought that their clumsy ironies, by the very fact that they hastened this change, ought to be sought out and cultivated. Why he so much wanted to stop loving his mother, why he even hated himself for loving her, he would have been unable to say. Perhaps because he felt he had been deceived and had thought her to be different from what she really was, or perhaps because, not being able to go on loving her simply and innocently as he had done before, he preferred to stop loving her altogether and to look on her merely as an ordinary woman. He was instinctively trying to free himself once and for all from the encumbrance of his old, innocent love, which he felt to have been shamefully betrayed; for now it seemed to him mere foolishness and ignorance. And so the same cruel attraction which a few minutes ago had kept his eyes fixed on his mother's back now drove him to seek out the humiliating and coarse companionship of those boys. Might not their scoffing remarks, like her half-revealed nakedness, help to destroy the old filial relationship which was now so hateful to him? When he came within sight of the baths he slowed down, and though his heart was beating violently so that he could hardly breathe, he assumed an air of indifference.

Saro was sitting as before at his rickety table, on which were a half-empty bottle of wine, a glass, and a bowl containing the remains of fish soup. But there seemed to be no one else about, though as he got nearer the curtain opened and he saw the black body of the Negro boy Homs lying on the white sand.

Saro took no notice at all of the Negro, but went on smoking meditatively, a dilapidated old straw hat rammed down over one eye. "Aren't they here?" asked Agostino in a tone of disappointment. Saro looked up and observed him for a moment, then said: "They've gone to Rio." Rio was a deserted part of the shore, a few kilometers further on, where a stream ran into the sea between sandbanks and reeds.

"Oh dear," said Agostino regretfully, "they've gone to Rio . . . what for?"

It was the Negro who replied. "They've gone to have a picnic there," and he put his hand to his mouth with an expressive gesture. But Saro shook his head and said: "You boys won't be happy till someone's put a bullet through you." It was clear that their picnic was only a pretext for stealing fruit in the orchards; at least, so it seemed to Agostino.

"I didn't go with them," put in the Negro obsequiously, as if to ingratiate himself with Saro.

"You didn't go because you didn't want to," said Saro calmly.

The Negro rolled in the sand, protesting: "I didn't go because I wanted to stay with you."

He spoke in a honeyed, singsong voice. Saro said contemptuously: "Who gave you permission to be so familiar, you little nigger? We're not brothers as far as I know."

"No, we're not brothers," said the other in an unruffled, even triumphant tone, as if the observation gave him profound satisfaction.

"You keep your place then," said Saro. Then, turning to Agostino: "They've gone to steal some corn. That's what their picnic'll be."

"Are they coming back?" asked Agostino anxiously. Saro said nothing but kept looking at Agostino and seemed to be turning something over in his mind. "They won't be back very soon," he replied slowly; "not till late. But if you like we'll go after them."

"But how?"

"In the boat," said Saro.

"Oh yes, let's go in the boat," said the Negro. He sprang up, all eagerness, and approached Saro, but the latter did not give him a glance.

"I have a sailboat . . . in about half an hour we shall be at Rio, if the wind's favorable."

"Yes, let's go," said Agostino happily. "But if they're in the fields how shall we find them?"

"Never you fear," said Saro, getting up and giving a twist to the black sash round his stomach. "We shall find them all right." Then he turned to the Negro, who was watching him anxiously, and added: "Come on, nigger, help me carry down the sail and mast."

"I'm coming, Saro, I'm coming," reiterated the jubilant Negro, and he followed Saro down to the boat.

Left by himself Agostino stood up and looked round him. A light wind had sprung up from the northwest, and the sea, covered now with tiny wavelets, had changed to an almost violet blue. The shore was enveloped in a haze of sun and sand, as far as the eye could see. Agostino, who did not know where Rio was, followed with a nostalgic eye that capricious indentation of the lonely coast line. Where was Rio? Somewhere out there, he supposed, where earth, sky and sea were mingled in one confused blackness under the pitiless sun. He looked forward intensely to the expedition, and would not have missed it for worlds.

He was startled from these reflections by the voices of the two coming out of the hut. Saro was carrying on one arm a pile of ropes and sails, while in the other he hugged a bottle. Behind him walked the Negro, brandishing like a spear a tall mast partly painted green. "Well, let's be *off*," said Saro, starting down the beach without glancing at Agostino. His manner seemed to Agostino curiously hurried, quite different from his usual one. He also noticed that those repulsive red nostrils looked redder and more inflamed than usual, as if all their network of little branching veins had suddenly become swollen with an inrush of blood. "*Si va . . . si va . . .*" intoned the Negro behind Saro, improvising a sort of dance on the sand, with the mast under his arm. But Saro had nearly reached the huts and the Negro slackened his pace to wait for Agostino. When he was near, the Negro signaled him to stop. Agostino did so.

"Listen," said the Negro, with an air of familiarity. "I've got to talk something over with Saro . . . please oblige . . . please . . . by not coming. Go away, please!"

"Why?" asked Agostino, much surprised.

"I told you I've got to talk something over with him . . . just the two of us," said the other impatiently, stamping his foot on the ground.

"I *must* go to Rio," replied Agostino.

"You can go another time."

"No—I can't."

The Negro looked at him, and his eyes and trembling nostrils betrayed a passionate eagerness which revolted Agostino. "Listen, Pisa," he said, "if you'll stay behind I'll give you something you've never seen before." He dropped the mast and felt in his pocket and brought out a sling shot made of a fork of pinewood and two elastics bound together. "It's lovely, isn't it," and the Negro held it up.

But Agostino wanted to go to Rio. Besides, the Negro's insistence aroused his suspicions. "No, I can't," he said.

"Take it," the other said again, feeling for Agostino's hand and trying to force the slingshot into his palm. "Take it and go away."

"No," repeated Agostino, "I can't."

"I'll give you the slingshot and these cards, too," said the Negro, feeling in his pocket again; and he drew out a small pack of cards with pink backs and gilt edges. "Take them all and go away. You can kill birds with the slingshot . . . the cards are quite new."

"I told you I won't," said Agostino.

The Negro turned on him an eye of passionate entreaty. Great drops of sweat shone on his forehead, his whole face was contorted in an expression of utter misery. "But why won't you?" he whined.

"I don't want to," said Agostino, and he suddenly ran toward the bath man, who was now standing by the boat. As he reached Saro he heard the Negro call after him: "You'll be sorry for this." The boat was resting on two rollers of unplaned fir a short way up the beach. Saro had thrown the sails into the boat and seemed to be waiting impatiently. "What's he up to?" he asked Agostino, pointing to the Negro.

"He's just coming," said Agostino.

And in fact the Negro came running over the sand with great leaps, holding the mast under his arm. Saro took hold of the mast with the six fingers of his right hand, and with the six fingers of his left reared it up and planted it in a hole in the middle seat. Then he got into the boat, fastened the sail and loosened the sheet. Saro turned to the Negro and said: "Now let's shove off from underneath."

Saro stood beside the boat, grasping the edges of the prow, while the Negro made ready to push from behind. Agostino, not knowing what to do, looked on. The boat was of medium size, part white and part green. On the prow, in black lettering, was written *Amelia.* "*Ah . . . issa,*" commanded Saro. The boat slid forward on its rollers over the sand. As soon as the keel passed over the hindmost roller the Negro bent down and took it in his arms, pressing it to his breast like a baby; then leaping over the sand as in a novel kind of ballet, he ran and placed it under the prow. "*Ah . . . issa,*" repeated Saro.

The boat slid forward again quite a distance, and again the Negro gamboled and caracoled from stern to prow, with the roller in his arms; one last shove, and the prow of the boat dipped into the water and it was afloat. Saro got in and placed the oars in the rowlocks; then, grasping one in each hand, he motioned for Agostino to jump in, excluding the Negro as if by prearrangement. Agostino entered the water up to his knees and tried to climb in. He would never have succeeded had not the six fingers of Saro's right hand seized him firmly by one arm and pulled him up like a cat. He looked up. Saro was lifting him with one arm, without looking in his direction, for he was busy adjusting the left-hand oar. Agostino, in disgust at being grasped by those fingers, went off and sat in the stern. "Good," said Saro, "you stay there; now we are going to take her out."

"Wait for me, I'm coming too!" shouted the Negro from the shore. Exhausted by his effort he sprang into the water and seized the edge of the boat. But Saro said: " No, you're not coming."

"What am I to do?" cried the boy, in an agony of disappointment. "What am I to do?"

"You can take the trolley," answered Saro, standing up in the boat and pulling hard. "You'll get there before us, see if you don't."

"But why, Saro?" wailed the Negro, thrashing along in the water beside the boat. "Why, Saro? I want to go too."

Without a word Saro dropped his oars, bent over and covered the Negro's face with his enormous hand. "I've told you you're not coming," he said quietly, and with one push sent the Negro over backward in the water. "Why, Saro?" he went on wailing. "Why, Saro?" and his melancholy voice, mingled with the splashing of the oars, made an unpleasant impression on Agostino and aroused in him an uneasy sense of pity. He looked at Saro, who smiled and said: "He's such a nuisance. What do we want with him?"

The boat was already some way from the shore. Agostino looked round and saw the Negro get out of the water and, as he thought, shake his fist threateningly at him.

Saro silently took out the oars and laid them down in the bottom of the boat. Then he went to the prow, undid the sail and fastened it to the mast. The sail fluttered uncertainly for a moment, as if the wind were blowing on both sides of it at once; then suddenly, with a violent shock swelled in the wind and leaned over to the left. The boat obediently settled down on its left side too, and began to skim over the waves, driven by the light breeze. "Good," said Saro, "now we can lie down and rest a bit." He settled down in the bottom of the boat and invited Agostino to lie beside him. "If we sit in the bottom," he explained, "the boat goes faster." Agostino obeyed, and lay down beside Saro.

The boat made swift progress in spite of its heavy build, rising and falling with the little waves and occasionally rearing up like a foal which feels the bit for the first time. Saro lay with his head resting against the seat, and one arm behind Agostino's neck, controlling the rudder. For a while he said nothing; then: "Do you go to school?" he asked at last.

Agostino looked up. Saro was half lying and seemed to be exposing his wide, inflamed nostrils to the sea air, as if to refresh them. His mouth was open under his mustache, his eyes half shut. His unbuttoned shirt revealed the dirty, gray, ruffled hair on his chest. "Yes," said Agostino, suddenly trembling with fear.

"What class are you in?"

"The third."

"Give me your hand," said Saro; and before Agostino could refuse he seized hold of it. To Agostino his grasp felt like a vise. The six short, stumpy fingers encircled his whole hand and met below it. "What do they teach you?" Saro went on, stretching himself out more comfortably and sinking into a kind of ecstasy.

"Latin . . . Italian . . . geography . . . history . . ." stammered Agostino.

"Do they teach you poetry . . . lovely poetry?" asked Saro, in a low voice.

"Yes," said Agostino, "poetry as well."

"Recite some to me."

The boat plunged, and Saro shifted the rudder without changing his beatific attitude. "I don't know what . . ." began Agostino, feeling more and more embarrassed and frightened. "I learn a lot of poetry . . . Carducci . . ."

"Ah yes, Carducci," repeated Saro mechanically. "Say a poem by Carducci."

"*Le fonti del Clitunno*," suggested Agostino, terrified by that hand which would not let him go, and trying little by little to escape from it.

"Yes, *Le fonti del Clitunno*," said Saro in a dreamy voice.

> *Ancor dal monte che di foschi ondeggia*
> *frassini al vento mormoranti e lunge*

began Agostino in a shaky voice.

The boat sped on, and Saro, still stretched at full length with closed eyes and his nose to the wind, began to move his head up and down as if scanning the lines. Agostino clung to poetry as the only means of escape from a conversation which he intuitively felt to be dangerous and compromising, and went on reciting slowly and clearly. Meanwhile, he kept trying to release his hand from those six imprisoning fingers; but they held him more tightly than ever. With terror he saw the end of the poem drawing near, and not knowing what to do he joined the first line of *Davanti a San Guido* on to the last line of *Fonti del Clitunno*. Here would be proof, if any were needed, that Saro didn't care a bit about the poetry but had something quite different in view; *what*, Agostino could not understand. The experiment succeeded. "*I cipressi che a Bolgheri alti e schietti*" suddenly began without Saro giving the faintest sign of noticing the change. Then Agostino broke off and said in an exasperated voice: "Let go, please," and tried at the same time to pull his hand quite away.

Saro started, and without letting go of him, opened his eyes and turned to look at him. He must have read such violent antipathy and such obvious terror on Agostino's face that he suddenly realized that his plan, for he certainly had a plan, was a complete failure. He slowly withdrew one finger after another from Agostino's aching hand and said in a low voice, as if speaking to himself: "What are you afraid of? We're going ashore now."

He dragged himself to his feet and pulled round the rudder. The boat turned its prow towards the shore.

Still rubbing his cramped fingers, Agostino got up from the bottom of the boat without a word and went to sit in the prow. By now the boat was not far from the shore. He could see the whole beach, the white stretch of sun-bleached sand which at that point was very wide, and beyond the beach the dense, brooding green of the pines. Rio was at a gap in the high dunes, overhung by a greenish-blue mass of reeds. But before they got to Rio, Agostino saw a group of people on the beach, and from the center of this group there rose a long thread of black smoke. He turned to Saro, who was sitting in the stern controlling the rudder with one hand. "Is this where we get out?"

"Yes, this is Rio," replied Saro indifferently.

As the boat drew nearer and nearer to the shore, Agostino saw the group gathered round the fire suddenly break up and start running down to the water's edge, and he at once saw that it was the boys. He could see them waving and probably calling out, but the wind carried their voices away. "Is it them?" he asked nervously.

"Yes, it's them," said Saro.

The boat drew nearer still and Agostino could clearly distinguish the boys. They were all there: "Tortima, Berto, Sandro, and the others. And there was the Negro Homs, leaping along the shore and shouting with the others, a discovery which for some reason gave him a very uncomfortable feeling.

The boat made straight for the shore where with a rapid turn of the rudder, Saro brought it in crosswise, and throwing himself upon the sail clasped it in both arms and lowered it to the deck. The boat swung motionless in the shallow water. Saro took a small anchor from the bottom and threw it into the water. "Let's go ashore," he said. He climbed over the edge of the boat and waded through the water to meet the boys who were waiting on the beach.

Agostino saw the boys crowding around him and apparently offering him congratulations, which Saro received with a shake of his head. Still louder applause greeted his own arrival, and for a moment he was deceived into thinking they were welcoming him cordially. But he soon realized he was mistaken. Their laughter was mocking and sarcastic. Berto called out: "Good old Pisa, he enjoys going out for a sail," while Tortima, putting his fingers into his mouth, gave a rude whistle. The others imitated him. Even Sandro, usually so reserved, looked at him with contempt. As for the Negro, he did nothing but jump about around Saro, who went on ahead towards the fire the boys had lit on the beach. Surprised and vaguely alarmed, Agostino went and sat down among the others around the fire.

The boys had made a sort of rough oven out of damp compressed sand. Inside was a fire of dried pine cones, pine needles and twigs. Heaped up in the mouth of the oven were about a dozen ears of corn, slowly roasting. Spread out on a newspaper near the fire were masses of fruit and a watermelon. "He's a fine one, is our Pisa," said Berto, when they had sat down. "You and Homs are buddies now, you ought to be sitting together . . . you're brothers, you two; he's black, you're white . . . that's all there is to it . . . and you both like going for a sail."

The Negro chuckled appreciatively. Saro was bending down to give the corncobs another turn in front of the fire. The others laughed derisively. Berto went so far as to give Agostino a push which sent him against Homs, so that for a moment their backs were touching; one chuckling with depraved self-satisfaction, the other bewildered and disgusted. "But I don't know what you mean," said Agostino suddenly. "I went out in the boat; what harm is there in that?"

"Aha, what harm is there in that? He went out in the boat. What harm is there in that?" repeated many scoffing voices. Some were holding their sides with laughter.

"Yes, indeed, what harm?" repeated Berto, turning to him again. "No harm at all! Why, Homs think it's grand, don't you, Homs?"

The Negro assented ecstatically. And now the truth began dimly to dawn on Agostino, for he couldn't help seeing some connection between their taunts and Saro's odd behavior in the boat. "I don't know what you mean," he declared. "I didn't do anything wrong in that boat. Saro made me recite some poems, that's all."

"Ah, ah, those poems," was heard on all sides.

"Isn't it true what I say, Saro?" cried Agostino, red in the face.

Saro didn't say yes or no; he contented himself with smiling, watching him all the while with a certain curiosity. The boys interpreted his air of pretended indifference, which was really a cloak for his treachery and vanity, as giving the lie to Agostino. "Oh, of course," they all struck up together: "He asks the host if the wine is good, eh, Saro? That's a good one! Oh, Pisa, Pisa!" The Negro was having his revenge, and enjoying himself particularly. Agostino suddenly turned on him, trembling with rage, and said: "What is there to laugh at?"

"I'm not laughing," he replied, edging away.

"Now, don't you two quarrel," said Berto. "Saro will have to see about making you friends again." But the boys lost all interest when the issue seemed to be settling itself peacefully, and were already talking of other things. They were telling how they had crept into a field and stolen corn and fruit; how they had seen the enraged farmer coming towards them with a gun; how they had run away, and the farmer had fired salt at them without hitting anyone. Meanwhile, the ears were ready, beautifully toasted on the embers. Saro took them out of the oven and with his usual fatherly air parceled out one to each. Agostino took advantage of a moment when they were busy eating, and sprang across to Sandro, who was sitting a little apart, eating his corn grain by grain.

"I don't understand," he began. The other gave him a knowing look and Agostino felt he need say no more. "The Moor came by trolley," said Sandro slowly, "and he said you and Saro had gone sailing."

"But what harm is there in that?"

"It's no business of mine," replied Sandro, casting down his eyes. "It's up to you . . . you and the Moor. But as far as Saro—" He stopped and looked at Agostino.

"Well?"

"Well, I wouldn't have gone out alone with Saro."

"But why?"

Sandro looked carefully round him, then in a low voice gave the explanation which Agostino somehow expected, without being able to say why. "Ah," he said . . . but he could say no more and went back to the others. Squatting in the middle of the boys, with his imperturbable, good-natured head on one side, Saro had the air of a kind pater-familias surrounded by his sons. But Agostino felt a deep loathing when he looked at him, greater in fact than he felt for the Negro. What made Agostino hate him more was his silence when appealed to, as if he wanted the boys to believe that what they had accused him of had really taken place. Besides, he could not help noticing that their scorn and derision had set a wide gulf between him and his companions—the same gulf which he now realized separated them from the Negro; only the Negro, instead of being humiliated and offended, as he himself was, seemed somehow to relish it. He tried more than once to turn the conversation on to the subject which so tormented him, but was met with laughter and an insulting indifference. Moreover, in spite of Sandro's only too clear explanation, he still could not quite grasp what had really happened. Everything seemed dark around him and within him, as if instead of beach, sea and sky, there were only shadows and vague, menacing forms.

Meanwhile, the boys had finished eating their roasted corn and tossed the bare cobs away in the sand. "Let's go swim at Rio," suggested someone, and the proposal was immediately accepted. Saro went with them, for it was agreed that he should take them all back to Vespucci in the boat.

As they walked along the sand Sandro left the others and came over to Agostino. "If you're offended with the Moor," he said, "why don't you put the fear of God into him?"

"How?" asked Agostino, in a discouraged tone.

"Give him a good hiding."

"But he's stronger than me," said Agostino, remembering the duel of the iron arm. "Unless you will help me."

"Why should I help you? It's your concern . . . yours and his." Sandro pronounced these words in such a way as to make it quite clear that he took the same view as the others as to the reason for Agostino's hatred of the Negro. A sense of terrible bitterness pierced Agostino to the heart. So Sandro, the only one who had shown him any kindness, believed that calumny too. After giving him this advice Sandro went off to rejoin the others, as if he were afraid of being seen with Agostino. From the beach they had passed through a forest of young pines; then they crossed a sandy path and entered the reed beds. The reeds grew thick and tall, and many had a white, plumy crest; the boys appeared and disappeared between their long green spears, slipping about on the damp earth and pushing the stiff, fibrous leaves aside with a dry, rustling sound. At last they came to a place where the reed bed widened around a low, muddy bank; at sight of them big frogs leaped from all sides into the opaque, glassy water; and there they began to undress, all together, under the eyes of Saro, who sat fully clothed on a rock overlooking the reeds, and appeared to be absorbed in his cigar, but was really watching them all the time through his half-closed eyelids. Agostino was ashamed to join them, but he was so afraid of being laughed at that he too began unbuttoning his trousers, taking as long as he could about it and keeping an eye on the others. The rest seemed to be overjoyed at getting rid of their clothes, and bumped into each other shouting with glee. They looked very white against the background of green reeds, with an unpleasant, squalid whiteness from groin to belly, and this pallor only emphasized a sort of graceless and excessive muscularity which is especially to be found in manual workers. The graceful, well-proportioned Sandro, whose pubic hair was as fair as that on his head, was the only one who hardly seemed to be naked, perhaps because his skin was equally bronzed over his whole body; in any case his nakedness was quite different from that repulsive nakedness displayed in the public baths.

Before diving in, the boys played all sorts of obscene pranks; opening their legs wide, poking and touching each other with a loose promiscuity which astounded Agostino, to whom this sort of thing was quite new. He was naked too, and his feet were black from the cold, filthy mud, but he would have liked to have hidden himself in the reeds, if only to escape the looks which Saro, who sat hunched up motionless like one of those huge frogs native to the reed bed, darted at him through half-closed eyes. But as usual his repugnance was less strong than the mysterious attraction which bound him to the gang; the two were so indissolubly mixed up together that it was impossible for him to distinguish between his horror and the pleasure which underlay it. The boys displayed themselves each in turn, boasting of their virility and bodily prowess. Tortima, the vainest of all, and in spite of his disproportionate strength the most squalid and plebeian looking, was so elated as to call out to Agostino: "Suppose I was to appear before your mother, one fine morning, naked like this, what would she say? Would she go along with me?"

"No," said Agostino.

"And I tell you that she'd come along at once," said Tortima. "She'd just give me one good look over, to see what I was good for, and then she'd say: 'Come along, Tortima, let's be off.' " The gross absurdity of his suggestion made them all laugh, and at his cry: "Come, Tortima, let's be off!" they flung themselves one after another into the water, diving in head over heels, just like the frogs whom their coming had disturbed.

The shore was so entirely surrounded by reeds that only a short stretch of the river was visible. But when they got into the middle of the stream they could see the whole river which, with an imperceptible motion of its dark, dense waters, flowed toward the mouth further down among the sandbanks. Upstream the river continued between two lines of large silvery bushes which cast delightful reflections in the water; till one came to a little iron bridge, beyond which the reeds, pines and poplars were so dense as to prevent further passage. A red house, half-hidden among the trees, seemed to keep guard over this bridge.

For a moment Agostino felt happy, as he swam in that cold, powerful water which seemed to be trying to bear his legs away with it; he forgot for a moment all his wrongs and crosses. The boys swam about in all directions, their heads and arms emerging from the smooth green surface. Their voices resounded in the limpid, windless air; seen through the transparency of the water their bodies might have been the white shoots of plants blossoming out of the depths and moving hither and yon as the current drew them. Agostino swam up to Berto, who was not far off, and asked: "Are there many fish in this river?"

Berto looked at him and said: "What are you doing here? Why don't you keep Saro company?"

"I like swimming," replied Agostino, feeling miserable again; and he turned and swam away.

But he was not so strong or experienced a swimmer as the others; he soon got tired, and let the current carry him towards the mouth of the river. He had soon left the boys and their clamor behind him; the reeds grew thinner; through the clear, colorless water he could see the sandy bottom over which gray eddies flowed continually. At last he came to a deeper green pool, the stream's transparent eye as it were; and when he had passed this his feet touched the sand, and after struggling a moment against the force of the water, he climbed out on to the bank. Where the stream flowed into the sea it curled round itself and formed a knot of water. The stream then lost its compactness and spread out fanwise, growing thinner and thinner till it was no more than a liquid veil thrown over the smooth sands. The tide flowed up into the river with tiny foam-flecked wavelets. Here and there in the watery sand, pools forgotten by the stream reflected the bright sky. Agostino walked about for a little, naked on the soft, mirroring sand, and enjoyed stamping on it with his feet and seeing the water suddenly rise to the surface and flood his footprints. There arose in him a vague and desperate desire to ford the river and walk on and on down the coast, leaving far behind him the boys, Saro, his mother and all the old life. Who knows whether, if he were to go straight ahead and never turn back, walking, walking on that soft white sand, he might not at last come to a country where none of these horrible things existed; a country where he would be welcomed as he longed to be, and where it would be possible for him to forget all he had learned and then learn it again without all that shame and horror, gently and naturally as he dimly felt it might be possible. He gazed at the dark, remote horizon which enclosed the utmost boundaries of sea and shore and forest and felt drawn to that immensity as to something which might set him free from his bondage. The shouts of the boys racing across the shore to the boat roused him from his melancholy imaginings. One of them was waving his clothes in the air, and Berto was calling: "Pisa, we're off!" He shook himself and walked along at the edge of the sea to join the gang.

The boys were thronging together in the shallow water. Saro was warning them in fatherly tones that the boat was too small to hold them all, but he was clearly only teasing them. Screaming, the boys flung themselves like mad upon the boat: twenty hands at once clutched the sides, and in a twinkling the boat was filled with their gesticulating bodies. Some lay down on the bottom, others sat in a heap in the stern around the rudder, some in the prow, others on the seats; others again sat on the edge and let their feet dangle in the water. The boat really was too small for so many, and the water came almost to the top.

"We're all here then, are we?" said Saro in great good humor. He stood up, let out the sail, and the boat sped out to sea. The boys cheered its departure loudly.

But Agostino did not share their happy mood. He was looking out for a favorable opportunity to prove his innocence and remove the unjust stigma which oppressed him. He took advantage of a moment when the other boys were deep in some discussion, to scramble up to the Negro who was sitting alone in the bow and resembled in his blackness a new kind of figurehead. Squeezing one arm hard, Agostino demanded: "What did you go and say about me just now?"

It was a bad moment to choose, but it was Agostino's first opportunity of getting near the Negro, who had taken good care to keep at a distance while they were on shore. "I spoke the truth," said Homs, without looking at him.

"What is the truth?"

The Negro's reply terrified Agostino. "It's no good your squeezing my arm like that. I only spoke the truth. But if you go on setting Saro against me I shall tell your mother everything. So look out, Pisa."

"What!" cried Agostino, seeing an abyss open beneath his feet. "What do you mean? Are you crazy? I . . . I . . ." He stammered, unable to follow up in words the frightful vision his imagination suddenly summoned up. But he had no time to continue. Shouts of derision broke out all over the boat.

"Look at them both side by side," laughed Berto. "Look at them! What a shame we haven't got a camera to take them both together." Agostino turned round, his face burning, and saw them all laughing. Even Saro was smiling under his mustache, as with half-closed eyes he puffed at his cigar. Agostino drew back from the Negro, as from the touch of a reptile, and with his arms around his knees sat watching the sea, his eyes full of tears.

On the horizon the sun was setting in clouds of fire above a violet sea, shot with pointed, glassy rays. The wind had risen and the boat made slow progress, listing heavily to one side under its load of boys. The prow of the boat was turned out to sea and seemed to be directed towards the dark profiles of far-off islands which rose among the red smoke of sunset like mountains at the end of a distant plateau.

Saro, holding firmly between his knees the boys' stolen watermelon, split it open with his seaman's knife and cut off large slices which he distributed to them paternally. They passed the slices and bit into them greedily, spitting out the seeds and tearing off pieces of the flesh. Then one after another the sections of red, close-gnawed rind flew overboard into the sea. After the melon it was the turn of the wine flask, which Saro solemnly produced from under the stern. The bottle made the round of the boat, and even Agostino was obliged to swallow a mouthful. It was warm and strong and at once went to his head. When the empty bottle had returned to its place Tortima sang an indecent song, and they all joined in the refrain. Between verses they pressed Agostino to sing too, for they had noticed his black mood; but no one spoke to him except to tease him and incite him to sing. Agostino felt within him a heavy weight of pent-up grief which the windy sea and magnificent fires of sunset on the violet waters only made more bitter and unbearable. It seemed to him horribly unjust that it was on such a sea under such a sky that a boat like theirs should be sailing, so crowded with malice, cruelty, falsehood and corruption. That boat, overflowing with boys gesticulating like obscene monkeys, with the fat and blissful Saro at the helm, was to him an incredible and melancholy sight in the midst of all that beauty. At moments he wished it would sink; he would have liked to die himself, he thought, and no longer be infected and stained by all that impurity. How far away seemed the morning when he had for the first time looked upon the red awning of the Vespucci Baths; far away and belonging to an age already dead. Each time the boat rose on an unusually high wave they gave a yell which made him shudder; each time the Negro addressed him with his revolting and hypocritically slavish humility, he tried not to listen and drew back still further into the prow. He was dimly conscious of having on that fatal day entered upon an age of difficulties and miseries from which he could see no way of escape. The boat made a long trip, going as far as the port and then turning back again. When they at last touched land Agostino ran off without saying good-bye to anyone. But he had not gone far before he slackened his pace and looking back saw the boys helping Saro pull the boat up on the beach. It was already getting dark.

That day was the beginning of a dark and troubled time for Agostino. On that day his eyes had been opened for him by force, but what he had learned was too much for him, a burden greater than he could bear. It was not so much their novelty as the quality of the things he had learned which oppressed and poisoned him; they were too appalling and too portentous for him to assimilate. He thought, for example, that after that day's disclosures about his mother his relations with her would have become clarified; that the uneasiness, distaste and even disgust which, after Saro's revelations, her caresses awoke in him would somehow, as if by enchantment, be resolved and reconciled in a new and serene consciousness. But it was not so; the uneasiness, distaste and disgust remained, rising in the first instance from the shock and bewilderment to his filial love occasioned by his obscure realization of his mother's femininity, and after that morning in Saro's tent rising from a bitter sense of guilty curiosity which his traditional and abiding respect for his mother rendered intolerable to him. At first he had unconsciously tried to break loose from that affection by an unjustified dislike, but now it seemed to him a duty to separate his newly won reasoned knowledge from his sense of blood relationship with someone whom he wanted to consider only as a woman. He felt that if only he could see in his mother what Saro and the boys did—just a beautiful woman—then all his unhappiness would disappear; and he tried with all his might to seek out occasions which would confirm him in this belief. But the only result was that his former reverence and affection gave place to cruelty and sensuality.

At home his mother did not hide herself from him any more than she had before, and was unaware of any change in his attitude towards her. As his mother, she had no sense of shame; but to Agostino it seemed that she was wantonly provocative. He would hear her calling him, and would go to her room to find her at her toilet, in negligee and with her breasts half uncovered. Or he would wake to find her bending over him to give him his morning kiss, with her dressing gown open so that he could clearly see the shape of her body through her fragile, crumpled nightgown. She would go to and fro in front of him as if he were not there; putting on or taking off her stockings, putting on her clothes, applying perfume or make-up; and all those acts which Agostino had once thought so natural now seemed to him the outward and visible signs of a much more embracing and more dangerous reality, so that his mind was torn between curiosity and pain. He kept saying to himself: "She's only a woman," with the objective indifference of a connoisseur. But a moment later, unable to endure either her maternal unselfconsciousness or his own watchfulness, he would have liked to shout: "Cover yourself up, go away, don't let me see you any more, I'm not the same as I used to be." But his hope of judging his mother as a woman and nothing more almost immediately suffered shipwreck. He soon saw that even if she had become a woman she remained in his eyes all the more his mother; and he realized that the cruel sense of shame which he had at first attributed to the novelty of his feelings would now never leave him. He saw in a flash that she would always remain for him the person he had loved with such a free and pure love; she would always mix with her most feminine gestures those purely affectionate ones which for so long had been the only ones he knew; never would he be able to separate his new conception of her from his now wounded memory of her former dignity. He did not for a moment doubt that the facts of her relationship with the young man really were as reported by the boys in Saro's tent. And he wondered secretly at the change which had taken place in him. At first he had only felt jealousy of his mother and antipathy towards the young man; both feelings being rather veiled and indefinite. But now, in his effort to remain objective and calm, he would have wished to feel sympathy for the young man and indifference towards his mother. But this sympathy seemed somehow to make him an accomplice, and his indifference to make him indiscreet. He very seldom went out with them now on the raft, for he generally contrived to avoid being invited. But whenever he went he was conscious of studying the young man's gestures and words almost as if he wanted him to over-step the limits of permitted social gallantry, and of studying his mother almost in the hope of having his suspicions confirmed. At the same time these sentiments were intolerable to him because they were the exact opposite of what he wanted to feel, and he would almost have liked to feel again the pity which his mother's foolish behavior had once aroused in him; it was more human and affection-ate than his present merciless dissection.

Those days of inner conflict left him with a confused sense of impurity. He felt that he had exchanged his former state of inno-cence, not for the manly calm he had hoped for but a dark, indeter-minate state in which he found no compensating advantages, but only fresh perplexities in addition to the old. What was the good of seeing clearly, if this clarity only brought with it deeper shades of darkness? Sometimes he wondered how older boys than himself managed to go on loving their mothers when they knew what he knew; and he concluded that such knowledge must at once destroy their filial affection, whereas in his own case the one did not banish the other, but they existed side by side in a dreary tangle.

As sometimes happens, the place which was the scene of these discoveries and conflicts—his home—became almost intolerable to

him. The sea, the sun, the crowd of bathers, the presence of many
other women at least distracted him and deadened his sensibilities.
But here, between the four walls of his home, alone with his mother,
he felt exposed to every kind of temptation, beset by every kind of
contradiction. On the beach his mother was one among many other
sun bathers; here she seemed overpowering and unique. Just as on a
small stage the actors seem larger than life, so here every gesture and
word of hers stood out with extraordinary definition. Agostino had a
very lively and adventurous sensibility in regard to the familiar things
of his home. When he was a child every passage, every nook and
corner, every room had had for him a mysterious and incalculable
character; they were places in which you might make the strangest
discoveries and live through the most fantastic adventures. But now,
after his meeting with those boys in the red tent, these adventures
and discoveries were of a quite different kind, so that he did not
know whether to be more attracted or frightened by them. Formerly he used to imagine ambushes, shadows, spirits, voices in the
furniture and in the walls; but now his fancy, even more actively
than in his exuberant childhood, attached itself to the new realities
with which the walls, the furniture, the very air of the house seemed
to him to be impregnated. And in place of his old innocent excitement which his mother's good-night kiss and dreamless sleep could
always calm, he was tormented by a burning and shameful curiosity
which at night grew to giant proportions and seemed to find in darkness more food for its impure fire.

Everywhere in the house he seemed to spy out traces of a woman's presence, the only woman whom he had ever known intimately;
and that woman was his mother. When he was with her he felt as if
he were somehow mounting guard over her; when he approached
her door he felt he was spying on her; if he touched her clothes he
felt as if it was herself he was touching, for she had worn these
clothes, they had held her body. At night he dreamed with his eyes
open, and had agonizing nightmares. He would sometimes imagine
himself to be a child again, afraid of every sound, of every shadow,
and would spring up to run and take refuge in his mother's bed; but
as soon as his feet touched the ground he realized, sleepy and bewildered though he was, that his fear was only a cunning mask for curiosity and that directly he was in his mother's arms his nocturnal vision would reveal its true purpose. Or he would wake suddenly and
wonder whether by chance the young man of the raft were there at
that very moment in his mother's room on the other side of the wall.
Certain sounds seemed to confirm this suspicion, others to contradict

it; he would toss restlessly in bed for a while, would find himself in the passage in his nightshirt, listening and spying outside his mother's room. Once he could not resist the temptation of going in without knocking, and he stood motionless in the middle of the room in the diffused moonlight which entered through the open window, his eyes fixed on the bed where he could distinguish his mother's black hair spread out over the pillow, and her long, softly rounded limbs. "Is that you, Agostino?" she asked, waking up. Without saying a word he turned and hurried back to his room.

His reluctance to remain alone with his mother drove him more and more to Vespucci. But here other torments awaited him, and made the place as odious to him as his home. The boys' attitude towards him after he had been out alone in the boat with Saro had not changed at all; it had in fact assumed a definite and final form, as if founded on an unshakable conviction. For he was the one who had accepted that signal and sinister favor from Saro; it was impossible to get that idea out of their minds. So that, in addition to the jealousy and contempt they had felt for him from the first on account of his being rich, was now added another source of contempt . . . his supposed depravity. And in the minds of those young savages the one seemed to justify the other, the one to grow out of the other. They seemed by their humiliating and cruel treatment of him to imply that he was rich and therefore naturally depraved. Agostino was quick to perceive the subtle relation between these two charges, and he dimly felt that they were making him pay for being different from them and superior to them. His social difference and superiority were expressed in his clothes and his talk about the luxury of his home, in his tastes and manner of speech; his moral difference and superiority impelled him to refute the charge of having had any such relations with Saro, and kept showing itself in open disgust at the boys' manners and habits. So at last, prompted by the humiliating position in which he found himself rather than exercising any definite choice of his own, he decided to be what they seemed to want him to be . . . that is, just like themselves. He began wearing his oldest and dirtiest clothes, to the great surprise of his mother, who noticed that he no longer took any pride in his appearance; he made a point of never mentioning his luxurious home, and he took an ostentatious pleasure in ways and habits which up to that time had disgusted him. But worst of all, and it needed a great effort to nerve himself to it, one day when they were making their usual jokes about his going out alone with Saro, he said that he was tired of denying it, and that what they accused him of had really happened,

and that he didn't care whether they knew it or not. Saro was startled by these assertions, but perhaps from fear of exposing himself
did not deny them. The boys were also very much surprised to hear
him admitting the truth of gossip which had seemed to torment him
so much before. He was so timid and shy that they would never have
given him credit for so much courage, but they very soon began
raining down questions on him as to what had really happened; and
then he lost heart, got red in the face and refused to say another
word. Naturally the boys interpreted his silence in their own way, as
being due to shame and not, as it really was, to his ignorance and
incapacity to invent. And the usual load of taunts and low jokes became heavier than ever.

But in spite of this breakdown he really had changed. Without
being conscious of it himself, without really trying to, he had, by
dint of spending so much time with the boys every day, ended by
becoming very like them, and had lost his old tastes without really
acquiring any new ones. More than once, in a mood of revolt against
Vespucci, he had joined in the more innocent games at Speranza,
seeking out his playmates of earlier in the summer. But how colorless
and dull those nicely brought-up boys now seemed to him, how boring their regulation walks under the eye of parents or tutors, how
insipid their school gossip, their stamp collections, books of adventure and such-like. The fact is that the company of the gang, their
talk about women, their thieving expeditions in the orchards, even
the acts of oppression and violence of which he had himself been a
victim, had transformed him and made him intolerant of his former
friendships. It was during this time that something happened which
brought this home to him more strongly. One morning when he arrived late at Vespucci he found no one there. Saro was off on some
business of his own, and there were no boys to be seen. He wandered
gloomily to the water's edge and seated himself on a float. Suddenly,
as he was watching the beach in the hope of seeing at least Saro come
in sight, a man and a boy about two years younger than himself appeared. He was a small man, with short, fat legs under a protruding
stomach, a round face and pointed nose confined by pince-nez. He
looked like a civil servant or professor. The boy was thin and pale, in
a suit too big for him, and was hugging a large and evidently new
leather ball to his chest. Holding his son by the hand, the man came
up to Agostino and looked at him doubtfully for some time. At last
he asked if it was possible to go for a row.

"Of course," replied Agostino, without hesitation.

The man considered him rather suspiciously over the top of his glasses, then asked how much it would cost to go out for an hour on a bathing raft. Agostino knew the prices and told him. Then he realized that the man had mistaken him for the bath man's son or for one of his boys, and that somehow flattered him. "Very well," said the man, "we will go."

Agostino didn't need telling twice. He at once took the rough pine log which served as roller, and placed it under the prow of the boat. Then, grasping the ends of the two floats in both hands, his strength redoubled by this singular spur to his pride, he pushed the raft into the water. He helped the boy and his father to get on, sprang after them and seized the oars.

For a while Agostino rowed without speaking. At that early hour the sea was quite empty. The boy hugged his ball to his chest and kept his pale eyes fixed on Agostino. The man sat awkwardly, with knees apart to make room for his paunch. He kept turning his fat neck to look about him, and seemed to be enjoying the outing. At last he asked Agostino who he was, the bath man's son, or employed by him. Agostino replied that he was employed by him. "And how old are you?" asked the man.

"Thirteen," replied Agostino.

"There," said the man, turning to his son, "this boy is almost the same age as you, and he's already at work." Then to Agostino: "And do you go to school?"

"I should like to, but how can I, sir?" he answered, assuming the hypocritical tone which he had heard the boys put on when asked a question like that. "We've got to live, sir."

"There, you see," said the father to his son. "This boy can't go to school because he has to work, and you have the face to make a fuss about your lessons."

"There's a lot of us in the family," said Agostino, rowing vigorously, "and we all work."

"And how much can you earn a day?" asked the man.

"It depends," replied Agostino. "If many people come, about twenty or thirty lire."

"Which of course you give to your father," interposed the man.

"Of course," replied Agostino, without a moment's hesitation, "except what I make in tips."

This time the man didn't think it necessary to point him out as an example to his son, but he nodded his head approvingly. His son said nothing, but hugged his ball still closer and kept his pale, watery eyes fixed on Agostino. "Would you like to have a leather ball like that, boy?" the man suddenly asked Agostino. Now Agostino had two identical balls, which had been lying about for a long time in his room with his other toys. But he said: "Of course I should, but how am I to get one? We have to buy necessities first." The man turned to his son and said to him, probably half in fun: "There now, Peter, give your ball to this boy who hasn't got one." The boy looked first at his father and then at Agostino, and greedily hugged his ball tighter; but still he didn't say a word. "Don't you want to?" asked his father gently. "Don't you want to?"

"It's my ball," said the boy.

"Yes, it's yours, but if you like you may give it away," persisted the father. "This poor boy has never had one in all his life; now, don't you want to give it up to him?"

"No," said his son emphatically.

"Never mind," interposed Agostino at this point, with a sancti-monious smile, "I don't really want it. I shouldn't have time to play with it . . . it's different for him."

The father smiled at these words, pleased at having found such a useful object lesson for his son. "He's a better boy than you," he went on, stroking his son's head. "He's poor, but he doesn't want to take away your ball, he leaves it to you; but whenever you want to grumble and make a fuss, I hope you'll remember that there are lots of boys like this in the world, who have to work, and who have never had balls or any toys of their own."

"It's my ball," repeated the boy obstinately.

"Yes, it's yours," sighed his father, absent-mindedly. He looked at his watch and said in a tone of command: "It's time we went back; take us in, boy." Without a word Agostino turned the prow towards the beach.

As they approached the shore he saw Saro standing in the water watching his maneuvers attentively, and he was afraid the bath man would give him away. But Saro didn't say a word; perhaps he under-stood, perhaps he didn't care; he gravely helped Agostino pull the boat up the beach. "This is for you," said the man, giving Agostino the sum agreed on and something over. Agostino took the money and gave it to Saro. "But I'm going to keep the tip," he added, with an air of self-satisfied bravado. Saro said nothing; scarcely even smil-ing, he put the money inside the sash bound around his stomach and walked off slowly across the beach to his hut.

This little incident gave Agostino a definite feeling of not belong-ing any more to the world in which boys of that sort existed, and by now he had got so used to living with the poor that the hypocrisy of any other kind of life bored him. At the same time he felt regretfully that he wasn't really like the boys of the gang. He was still much too sensitive. If he had really been one of them, he thought sometimes, he would not have suffered so much from their coarse and clumsy jokes. So it seemed that he had lost his first estate without having succeeded in winning another.

One day, towards the end of the summer, Agostino went with the boys to the pine woods to chase birds and look for mushrooms. This was what he enjoyed most of all their exploits. They entered the forest and walked for miles upon its soft soil along natural aisles, between the red pillars of the tree trunks, looking up in the sky to see if somewhere between those tall trunks there was anything moving among the pine needles. Then Berto or Tortima or Sandro, who was the most skillful of all, would stretch the elastic of his slingshot and aim a sharp stone in the direction they thought they had seen a movement. Sometimes a sparrow with a broken wing would come hurtling down, and go fluttering lamely along with pitiful little chirps till one of the boys seized it and twisted its neck between his fingers. But more often the chase was fruitless, and the boys would go wandering on deeper and deeper into the forest, their heads thrown back and their eyes fixed on some point far above them; going ever farther and farther till at last the undergrowth began and a tangle of thorny bushes took the place of bare, soft soil covered with dry husks. And with the undergrowth began their hunt for fungi. It had been raining for a day or two and the leaves of the undergrowth were still glistening with wet, and the ground was damp and covered with fresh green shoots. In the thick of the bushes . . . there were the yellow fungi, glittering with moisture; sometimes magnificent single ones, sometimes families of little ones. The boys put their fingers through the brambles and picked them delicately, holding the head between two fingers and taking care to bring the stalk away too, with earth and moss still clinging to it. Then they threaded them on long, pointed sprigs of broom. Wandering thus from patch to patch of undergrowth, they would collect several kilos for Tortima's dinner, for he, being the strongest, confiscated their finds. That day their harvest had been a rich one, for after wandering about a good deal they had found some virgin undergrowth where the fungi were growing closely packed together in their bed of moss. It was getting late before they had even half-explored this undergrowth; so they began to tramp slowly homeward, with several long spits laden with fungi and two or three birds.

They generally followed a path which led straight down to the shore; but this evening they were led farther in pursuit of a teasing sparrow which kept fluttering along among the boughs and continually gave the illusion of being just within reach, so that they ended by walking the whole length of the forest, which to the east came to an end just behind the town. It was dusk as they emerged from the last pine trees on to the piazza of a remote suburb, with rubbish heaps and thistles and broom scattered about and a few ill-defined paths winding over it. Stunted oleanders grew at intervals around the edge; there were no pavements, and the dusty gardens of the few little villas which bordered it alternated with waste ground enclosed by bits of fencing. These little villas were placed at intervals all round the piazza and the wide expanse of sky over the great square added to the impression of loneliness and squalor.

The boys cut diagonally across the piazza, walking two and two like a religious order. At the end of the procession came Tortima and Agostino. Agostino was carrying two long spits of fungi and Tortima held a couple of sparrows in his great hands, their bloody heads dangling.

When they had reached the far end of the piazza Tortima nudged Agostino with his elbow and, pointing to one of the little villas, said cheerfully: "Do you see that? Do you know what that is?"

Agostino looked. The villa was very like all the others; a little bigger perhaps, with three stories and a sloping slate roof. Its façade was gloomy and smoke-grimed, with white shutters tightly closed; while the dense trees in the garden almost hid it from view. The garden did not look very big; the wall around it was covered with ivy, and through the gate one could see a short path with bushes on either side, and a double-paneled door under an old-fashioned porch. "There's no one there," said Agostino, stopping.

"No one, eh?" laughed the other; and he explained to Agostino in a few words who it was lived there. Agostino had several times heard the boys talking about houses where women lived alone, and how they shut themselves in all day, and at night were ready to welcome anyone who came, in return for money; but he had never seen one of these houses before. Tortima's words roused in him to the full the sense of strangeness and bewilderment which he had felt when first he heard them discussing it. And now as then he could hardly believe that there really existed a community so singular in its generosity as to disperse impartially to all that love which seemed to him so far away and so hard to come by; so he now looked with incredulous eyes on the little villa, as if he hoped to read on its walls some trace of the incredible life that went on inside it.

Compared with his imaginary picture of rooms on each of which a naked woman shed her radiance, the house looked singularly old and grimy. "Oh yes," he said, with pretended indifference, but his heart had already begun to beat faster.

"Yes," said Tortima, "it's the most expensive in the town." And he added a number of details about the place and the number of women, the people who went there and the time you were allowed to stay. This information was almost displeasing to Agostino, substituting as it did sordid details for the confused, barbaric image he had formed when he first heard tell of these forbidden places. But assuming a tone of idle curiosity he put a great many questions to his companion. For, after the first moment of surprise and disappointment, an idea had suddenly sprung up in his mind and soon laid fast hold of him. Tortima, who seemed to be well informed, gave him all the information he needed. Deep in conversation they crossed the piazza and joined the others on the esplanade. It was now almost dark and the party broke up. Agostino gave his fungi to Tortima and started home.

The idea which had come to him was clear and simple enough, however complicated and obscure its origin. He had made up his mind to go to that villa this very night and sleep with one of the women. This was not just a vague desire, it was an absolutely firm, almost desperate resolution. He felt that this was the only way he could escape from the obsession that had caused him such intense suffering all that summer. If he could only possess one of those women, he said to himself, it would forever prove the boys' calumny to have been ridiculous, and at the same time sever the thin thread of perverted and troubled sensuality which still bound him to his mother. Though he did not confess it to himself, his most urgent aim was to feel himself forever independent of his mother's love. A simple but significant fact had convinced him of this necessity only that very day.

Up to now he and his mother had slept in separate rooms; but that night a friend of his mother's was arriving to spend a week with them. As the house was small it had been arranged that their guest should have Agostino's room, while a cot was to be made up for him in his mother's room. That very morning he had been disgusted to see the cot set up beside his mother's, which was still unmade and covered with bedclothes. His clothing and books and washing things had been carried in with the cot.

The fact of sleeping together only made Agostino hate still more that promiscuity with his mother which was already so hateful to him. He thought this new and still closer intimacy must suddenly reveal to him, without hope of escape, all that up to now he had only dimly suspected. Quickly, quickly he must find an antidote, and set up between his mother and himself the image of another woman to whom he could turn his thoughts if not his eyes. And the image which was to screen him from his mother's nakedness, and which would restore her dignity by removing her femininity . . . one of those women in the villa on the piazza was to supply that image.

How he was to get himself received in that house and how he would choose the woman and go off with her were matters to which Agostino did not give a thought—indeed, even if he had wanted to, he would never have been able to picture it. In spite of Tortima's information, the house and its inmates and everything belonging to it were surrounded by a dense atmosphere of improbability, as if one were not dealing with reality but with the most daring hypothesis which might at the last moment prove fallacious. The success of his undertaking depended on a logical calculation; if there was a house, then there were women too, and if there were women there was the possibility of meeting one of them. But it was not quite clear to him that the house and the women really were there; and this was not so much because he doubted Tortima's word as because he was totally lacking in terms of comparison. Nothing he had ever done or seen bore the faintest resemblance to what he was about to undertake. Like a poor savage who has heard about the palaces of Europe, and can only picture them as a slightly large version of his own thatched hut, so he is trying to picture those women and their caresses, could only think, with slight variations, of his mother; the love-making could only be conjecture and vague desire.

But, as so often happens, his very inexperience led him to busy himself with practical aspects of the question, as if once these were settled he could also solve its complex unreality. He was particularly worried by the question of money. Tortima had explained to him in great detail exactly how much he would have to pay and to whom; and yet he could not quite grasp it. What was the relation between money, which is generally used for acquiring quite definite objects with recognizable qualities, and a woman's caresses, a woman's naked flesh? Was there really a price, and was that price really fixed, and not different in each particular case? The idea of giving money in exchange for that shameful and forbidden pleasure seemed to him cruel and strange, an insult which the giver might find pleasant but which must be painful for the one who received it. Was it really true that he would have to pay the money directly to the woman, and in her very presence? He somehow felt he ought to hide it and leave her with the illusion of a disinterested relationship. And then, wasn't the sum Tortima had mentioned too small? No money would be enough, he thought, to pay for such an experience . . . the end of one period of his life and the beginning of another.

Faced with these doubts he decided to keep strictly to what Tortima had told him, even if it turned out to be false, for he had nothing else on which to base his plan of action. He had found out from his friend how much it cost to visit the villa, and the figure did not seem higher than the amount he had been saving for a long time in his terracotta money box. With the small coins and paper money it contained he must surely be able to get the amount together, and it might even prove to be more. His plan was to take the money out of the money box, then wait till his mother had gone to the station to meet her friend, when he would go out in his turn, fetch Tortima and set off with him to the villa. He must have enough money for Tortima too, for he knew him to be poor and certainly not in the least disposed to do him a favor unless he was going to get something out of it himself.

This was his plan, and though it still seemed to him desperately remote and improbable he resolved to prepare for it with the same care and certainty as if it had only been an outing in a boat or some expedition into the pine woods.

Eager and excited, freed for the first time from the poison of remorse and impotence, he almost ran all the way home from the distant piazza. The front door was locked, but the French windows of the drawing room stood open, and through them came the sound of music. His mother was at the piano. He went in; the two subdued lights over the piano lit up her face while the rest of the room was in darkness. His mother was sitting on the piano stool, and beside her, on another, sat the young man of the raft. It was the first time that Agostino had seen him in their house, and a sudden presentiment took his breath away. His mother seemed to divine his presence, for she turned her head with a calm gesture of unconscious coquetry, a coquetry of which Agostino felt the young man to be the object rather than himself. She at once stopped playing when she saw him, and called him to her. "Agostino, what do you mean by coming in at this hour? Come here."

He went slowly up to the piano, full of revolt and embarrassment. His mother drew him to her and put her arm around him. He noticed that his mother's eyes were extraordinarily bright and young and sparkling. Laughter seemed to be on the brink of bubbling up through her lips, making her teeth glitter. She quite frightened him by the impetuosity, almost violence, with which she drew him to her, as if she were trembling with joy. He was sure that these manifestations had nothing to do with him personally. And they reminded him strangely of his own excitement of a few minutes before, as he ran through the streets in his eagerness to fetch his savings and go with Tortima to the villa and possess a woman.

"Where have you been?" his mother went on, in a voice which was at once tender, cruel and gay. "Where have you been all this time, you naughty boy?" Agostino made no reply; he did not feel his mother really expected one. That was just how she sometimes spoke to the cat. The young man was leaning forward, clasping his knees with both hands, with eyes as sparkling and smiling as her own. "Where have you been?" repeated his mother. "How naughty of you to play truant like that." She rumpled up his hair on his forehead and then smoothed it again with her warm, slender hand, with a tender but irresistible violent caress. "Isn't he a handsome boy?" she said proudly, turning to the young man.

"As handsome as his mother," the young man replied. She smiled pathetically at this simple compliment. Full of shame and irritation, Agostino made an effort to free himself from her embrace. "Go and wash yourself," said his mother, "and make haste, because we are soon going in to supper." Agostino bowed slightly to the young man and left the room. Behind him, he immediately heard the music taken up again at the very point where he had interrupted it.

But once in the passage he stood still and listened to the sounds his mother's fingers were drawing from the keys. The passage was dark, and at the end of it he could see through the open door into the brightly lit kitchen, where the cook, dressed in white, was bustling about between the table and the kitchen range. His mother went on playing, and the music sounded to Agostino gay, tumultuous, sparkling, exactly like the expression in her eyes while she held him to her side. Perhaps that really was the character of the music, or perhaps his mother read into it some of her own fire and sparkle and vivacity. The whole house resounded to the music, and Agostino found himself thinking that out in the road lots of people must be stopping to listen, wondering at the scandalous wantonness which seemed to pour from every note.

Then, all at once, in the middle of a chord, the sounds stopped, and Agostino was convinced—he could not have told how—that the passion which had found expression in the music had suddenly found another outlet. He took two steps forward, and stood still on the threshold of the drawing room. What he saw did not much surprise him. The young man was standing up, and kissing his mother on the lips. She was bending forward over the low stool, which was too small to hold her body; one hand was still on the keyboard and the other was round the young man's neck. Even in the dim light he could see how her body was arched as it fell backward, with her chest thrust forward, one leg folded beside her, and the other stretched out toward the pedal. In contrast to her attitude of passionate surrender, the young man preserved his usual easy and graceful carriage. As he stood, he held one arm round the woman's neck, but apparently more from fear lest she might fall over than from any deep emotion. His other arm hung at his side and he still had a cigarette between his fingers. His white-trousered legs, planted far apart, expressed deliberation and complete mastery of the situation.

The kiss lasted a long time and it seemed to Agostino that whenever the young man wanted to interrupt it his mother clung to his lips more insatiably than ever. He really could not help feeling that she was hungry . . . famished for that kiss, like someone who has been starved too long. Then, at a casual movement of her hand two or three solemn, sweet notes sounded in the room. Suddenly they sprang apart. Agostino took a step forward and said: "Mamma." The young man wheeled about, and standing with his legs apart and his hands in his pockets, pretended to look out the window.

"Agostino!" said his mother.

Agostino went to her. She was breathing so violently that he could distinctly see her breasts rising and falling through her silk dress. Her eyes were brighter than ever, her mouth was half-open, her hair in disorder; and one soft, pointed lock, like a live snake, hung against her cheek.

"What is it, Agostino?" she repeated, in a low, broken voice, doing her best to arrange her hair. Agostino felt a sudden oppression of pity mingled with distaste. He would have liked to cry out to her: "Calm yourself, don't pant like that . . . don't speak to me in that voice." But instead, he put on a childish voice and said, with exaggerated eagerness: "Mamma, can I break open my money box? I want to buy a book."

"Yes, dear," she answered, putting out a hand to stroke his brow. At the touch of her hand Agostino could not help starting back. His movement was so slight as to be almost imperceptible, but to him it seemed so violent that he felt everyone must notice it. "Very well

then, I'll break it," he said. And he left the room quickly, without
waiting for a reply. The sand on the stairs made a gritty sound as he
ran up to his room. The idea of the money box had really only been
a pretext; the fact was he didn't know what to say when he saw his
mother looking like that. It was dark in his room; the money box was
on a table at the far end. Through the open window a street lamp lit
up its pink belly and great black smiling mouth. He turned on the
light, picked up the money box and flung it on the ground with an
almost hysterical violence. It broke at once and from the wide opening poured a quantity of money of every description. There were
several notes mixed with the coins. He went down on hands and
knees and frantically counted the money. His fingers were trembling
and, while he counted, the image of those two down in the drawing
room kept getting mixed up with the money that was lying scattered
over the floor—his mother, hanging backwards over the piano stool,
and the young man bending over her. But when he had finished
counting he discovered that the money did not amount to the sum he
needed.

What was he to do? It flashed through his mind that he might
take it from his mother, for he knew where she kept it, and nothing
would have been easier; but this idea revolted him and he decided
simply to ask her for it. But what excuse could he make? He suddenly thought of one, but at that moment he heard the gong sound-
ing for supper. He hastily hid his treasure in a drawer and went
downstairs.

His mother was already at the table. The window was wide open
and great velvety moths flew in from the courtyard and beat their
wings against the white lampshade. The young man had gone and his
mother had again assumed her usual dignified serenity. Agostino, as
he looked at her, wondered why her mouth bore no trace of the kisses
which had been pressed on it a few minutes before, just as he had
wondered that first time, when she went out on the raft with the
young man. He could not have defined what feelings this thought
awoke in him. A sense of pity for his mother to whom that kiss
seemed to be so disturbing and so precious; and at the same time a
strong feeling of repulsion, not so much for what he had seen as for
the memory which remained with him. He would have liked to ex-
pel that memory, to forget it altogether. How was it possible that
such troublous and changing impressions could enter through one's
eyes? He foresaw that the sight would be forever stamped on his
memory.

When they had finished, his mother rose from the table and went upstairs. Agostino thought he would never find such an opportune moment to ask for the money. He followed her up and went into her room with her. His mother sat down at the dressing-table and silently studied her face in the glass.

"Mamma," said Agostino.

"What is it?" she asked absent-mindedly.

"I want twenty lire."

"What for?"

"To buy a book."

"But didn't you say you were going to break open your money box?" asked his mother, gently passing the powder puff over her face.

Agostino purposely made a childish excuse.

"Yes, but if I break it I shan't have any money left. I want to buy a book without opening my money box."

His mother laughed fondly. "What a baby you are." She studied herself a moment more in the glass, then she said: "You'll find my purse in the bag on my bed. Take out twenty lire, and put the purse back again." Agostino went to the bed, opened the bag, took out the purse and took twenty lire from it. Then clutching the two notes in his hand he flung himself on the cot beside his mother's. She had finished her make-up and came over to him. "What are you going to do now?"

"I'm going to read this book," he said, taking a book of adventures at random from the bed table, and opening it at an illustration.

"Very well, but remember before you go to sleep to put out the light." His mother was still moving about the room, doing one thing and another. Agostino lay watching her, with his head pillowed on his arm. He obscurely felt that she had never been so beautiful as on that evening. Her dress of glossy white silk showed off brilliantly her brown coloring and the rich rose of her complexion. By an unconscious reflowering of her former character she seemed to have recovered all the sweet, majestic serenity of bearing she used to have; but with an indefinable breath of happiness. She was tall, but Agostino had never seen her look so imposing before. Her presence seemed to fill the room. White in the shadow of the room, she moved majestically about, with head erect on her beautiful neck, her black eyes calm and concentrated under her smooth brow. Then she put out all the lights except the bed-table lamp, and bent down to kiss her son. Agostino drank in again the perfume he knew so well, and as he touched her neck with his lips he could not help wondering if those women . . . out there in the villa . . . would be as beautiful and smell as sweet.

Left alone, Agostino waited about ten minutes to give his mother time to have gone. Then he got up from the cot, put out the light, and tiptoed into the next room. He felt about in the dark for the table by the window, opened the drawer and filled his pockets with coins and notes. He felt with his hand in every corner of the drawer to see if it was really empty, and left the room.

When he was on the road he began to run. Tortima lived at the other end of the town, in the caulkers' and sailors' quarter, and though the town was small he had a long way to go. He chose the dark alleys bordering on the pine woods, and walking fast and occasionally running, he went straight ahead until he saw, appearing between the houses, the masts of the sailboats in the drydock. Tortima's house was just above the dock, beyond the movable iron bridge which spanned the canal leading to the harbor. By day this was a forgotten, dilapidated spot with tumble-down warehouses and ships bordering its wide, deserted, sun-baked quays, pervaded by the smell of fish and tar, with green, oily water, motionless cranes and barges laden with shingle. But now the night made it like every other part of the town, and only a ship whose bulging sides and masts overhung the footpath, revealed the presence of the harbor water lying deep in between the houses. Agostino crossed the bridge and headed toward a row of houses on the opposite side of the canal. Here and there a street lamp irregularly lit the walls of these little houses. Agostino stopped in front of an open lighted window, from which came the sounds of voices and clatter of plates, as if they were having a meal. Putting his fingers to his mouth he gave one loud and two soft whistles, which was the signal agreed upon between the boys of the gang. Almost at once someone appeared at the window. "It's me, it's Pisa," said Agostino, in a low, timid voice. "I'm coming," answered Tortima. He came down, still eating his last mouthful, red in the face from the wine he had been drinking. "I've come to go to that villa," said Agostino. "I've got the money here . . . enough for both of us." Tortima swallowed hard and looked at him. "That villa the other side of the piazza," Agostino repeated. "Where the women are."

"Ah," said Tortima, understanding at last. "You've been thinking it over. Bravo, Pisa. I'll be with you in a moment." He ran off and Agostino walked up and down, waiting for him, his eyes fixed on Tortima's window. He was kept waiting a long time, but at last

Tortima reappeared. Agostino scarcely recognized him. He had always seen him as a big boy with trousers tucked up, or half-naked on the beach and in the sea. Now he saw before him a young working man in dark holiday clothes: long trousers, waistcoat, collar and tie. He looked older too, because of the brilliantine with which he had plastered down his usually unruly hair; and his spruce, ordinary clothes brought out for the first time something ridiculous and vulgar in his appearance.

"Shall we go now?" said Tortima as he joined him.

"But is it time yet?" asked Agostino, hurrying along beside him as they crossed the bridge.

"It's always time there," said Tortima with a laugh.

They took a different road than the one Agostino had come by. The piazza was not far away, only about two turnings further on. "But have you been there before?" asked Agostino again.

"Not to that one."

Tortima did not seem to be in any hurry and kept his usual pace. "They'll hardly have finished supper and there'll be no one there," he explained. "It's a good moment."

"Why?" asked Agostino.

"Why, don't you see, we can choose the one we like best."

"But how many are there?"

"Oh, about four or five."

Agostino longed to ask if they were pretty, but refrained. "What do we have to do?" he asked. Tortima had already told him, but the sense of unreality was so strong in him that he felt the need of hearing it reaffirmed.

"What does one do?" said Tortima. "Nothing simpler. You go in . . . they come and show themselves . . . you say: 'Good evening, ladies,' you pretend to talk for a bit, so as to give yourself the time to look them well over . . . then you choose one. It's your first time, eh?"

"Well," began Agostino rather shamefacedly. "Go along!" said Tortima brutally. "You're not going to tell me it isn't the first time. Tell that to the others, if you like, but not to me. But don't be afraid. She does it all for you. Leave it to her."

Agostino said nothing. The image evoked by Tortima of the woman initiating him into love pleased him . . . it had something maternal about it. But in spite of these facts he still remained incredulous. "But—but do you think they'll want *me*?" he asked, standing still suddenly and looking down at his bare legs.

The question seemed to embarrass Tortima for a moment. "Let's

go on," he said, with feigned self-assurance. "Once there, we'll manage to get you in."

They came through a narrow lane to the piazza. The whole of it
was in darkness, except for one corner where a street lamp shone
peacefully down on a stretch of uneven sandy earth. In the sky
above the piazza the crescent moon hung red and smoky, cut in two
by a thin filament of mist. Where the darkness was thickest Agostino
recognized the villa by its white shutters. They were closed, and no
ray of light showed through them. Tortima, without hesitation,
crossed over to the villa. But in the middle of the piazza, under the
crescent moon, he said to Agostino: "Give me the money, I'd better
keep it."

"But I . . ." began Agostino, who did not quite trust Tortima.
"Are you going to give it me or not?" persisted Tortima harshly.
Agostino was ashamed of all that small change, but he obeyed and
emptied his pockets in Tortima's hands.

"Now keep your mouth shut, and come along with me," said his
companion.

As they came near to the villa, the darkness grew less dense, and
they could see the two gateposts, the garden path and the front door
under the porch. The gate was not locked, and Tortima pushed it
open and entered the garden. The front door was ajar. Tortima
climbed the steps and went in, motioning to Agostino not to make a
sound. Agostino, looking curiously about him, saw a quite empty
hall, at the end of which was a double door, with brightly lit panes of
red and blue glass. Their entrance was the signal for a ringing of
bells, and almost immediately the massive shadow of someone seated
behind the glass door rose against the glass, and a woman appeared in
the doorway. She was a kind of servant, middle-aged and very stout,
with a capacious bosom, dressed in black with a white apron tied
round her waist. She came forward, sticking out her stomach, and
with her arms hanging down. She had a swollen face and sulky eyes
which looked out suspiciously from under a mass of hair.

"Here we are," said Tortima. Agostino saw from his voice and
manner that even he, who was usually so bold, felt intimidated.

The woman scrutinized them hostilely for a moment; then she
made a sign, as if inviting Tortima to pass inside. Tortima smiled
with renewed assurance, and hastened toward the glass door. Agostino made as if to follow him. "Not you," said the woman, putting
her hand on his shoulder.

"What!" cried Agostino, at once losing all his fear. "Why him
and not me?"

"You've really neither of you any business to be here," said the woman firmly; "but he will just pass, you won't."

"You're too little, Pisa," said Tortima mockingly. And he pushed the door open and disappeared. His stunted shadow stood out for a moment against the panes of glass; then it vanished in the brilliant light.

"But what about me?" insisted Agostino, exasperated by Tortima's treachery.

"You get off, boy, go away home," said the woman. She went to the front door, opened it wide, and found herself face to face with two men who were just coming. "Good evening . . . good evening," said the first, who had a red, jolly face. "We're agreed, eh?" he added, turning to his companion, a pale, thin young man. "If Pina's free, I'm to have her . . . and no nonsense about it."

"Agreed," said the other.

"What's this little fellow doing here?" the jovial man asked the woman, pointing to Agostino.

"He wanted to come in," said the woman. A flattering smile framed itself on her lips.

"So you wanted to go in, did you?" cried the man, turning to Agostino. "At your age, home's the place at this hour. Home with you," he cried again, waving his arms.

"That's what I told him," the woman said.

"Suppose we let him come in?" remarked the young man. "At his age I was making love to the maid."

"Well, I'm blest! Get away home . . . home . . . *home*," shouted the other, scandalized. Followed by the fair man he entered the folding door, which banged-to behind him. Agostino, hardly knowing how he got there, found himself outside in the garden.

How badly it had all turned out; he had been betrayed by Tortima, who had taken his money, and he himself had been thrown out. Not knowing what to do, he went up the garden path, looking back all the time at the half-open door, the porch, the façade with its white shutters closed. He felt a burning sense of disappointment, especially on account of those two men who had treated him like a child. The laughter of the jovial man, the cold, experimental benevolence of his companion, seemed to him no less humiliating than the dull hostility of the woman. Still walking backward, and looking round at the trees and shrubs in the garden, he made his way to the gate. Then he noticed that the left side of the villa was illuminated by a strong light coming from an open window on the ground floor. It occurred to him that he might at least have a glimpse of the inside of the villa through that window; and making as little noise as possible he went towards the light.

It was a window open wide on the ground floor. The windowsill was not high; very quietly, and keeping to the corner where there was less chance of his being seen, he went up to the window and looked in.

The room was small and brilliantly lighted. The walls were papered with a handsome design of large green and black flowers. Facing the window a red curtain, hanging on wooden rings from a brass rod, seemed to conceal a door. There was no furniture visible, but someone was sitting in a corner by the window for he could see crossed legs with yellow shoes stretched out into the room. Agostino thought they must belong to someone lying in an armchair. Disappointed at not seeing more, he was going to leave his post when the curtain was raised and a woman appeared.

She had on a full gown of pale blue chiffon which reminded Agostino of his mother's nightgown. It was transparent and reached to her feet; looking at her long, pale limbs through that veil was almost like seeing them float indolently in clear sea water. By a vagary of design the neck of her gown was cut in an oval reaching almost to her waist; and from it her firm, full breasts seemed to be struggling to escape, so closely were they pressed together by the dress, which was gathered round them into the neck with many fine pleats. Her wavy brown hair hung loosely on her shoulders; she had a large flat, pale face, at once childish and vicious, and there was a whimsical expression in her tired eyes and mouth, with its full, painted lips. She came through the curtain with her hands behind her back and her bosom thrust forward, saying nothing and standing quietly, in an expectant attitude. She looked at the corner where the man with the crossed legs was lounging; then, silently as she had come, she turned and disappeared, leaving the curtain wide open. At the same time the man's legs vanished from the sight of Agostino. He heard someone get up and withdrew from the window in alarm.

He returned to the path, pushed the garden gate open, and came out on the piazza. He felt a keen sense of disappointment at the failure of his attempt, and at the same time a feeling almost of terror at what awaited him in days to come. Nothing had happened, he had not possessed any woman. Tortima had gone off with all his money, and tomorrow the same old jokes would begin again and the torment of his relations with his mother. Years and years of emptiness and frustration lay between him and that act of liberation. Meanwhile he had to go on living just as before, and his whole soul rebelled at the bitter thought that what he had hoped for had become a definite impossibility. When he got home, he went in without making any noise; he saw the visitor's luggage in the hall and heard voices in the sitting room. He went upstairs and flung himself on the cot in his mother's room. He tore off his clothes in the dark, and throwing them on the floor got into bed naked between the sheets. . . .

After a little he became drowsy and at last fell asleep. Suddenly he woke with a start. The lamp was lit and shone on his mother's back. She was in her nightgown and with one knee on the bed was just going to get in. "Mamma," he said suddenly, in a loud, almost violent voice.

His mother came over to him. "What is it?" she asked. "What is it, darling?" Her nightgown was transparent, like the woman's at the villa; the lines and vague shadows of her body were visible, like those of that other body. "I want to go away tomorrow," said Agostino, in the same loud, exasperated voice, trying to look not at his mother's body but at her face.

His mother sat down on the bed and looked at him in surprise. "But why? . . . What is the matter? Aren't you happy here?"

"I want to go away tomorrow," he repeated.

"Let us see," said his mother passing her hand gently over his forehead, as if she were afraid he was feverish. "What is it? Aren't you well? Why do you want to go away?"

His mother's nightgown reminded him so much of the dress of that woman at the villa: the same transparency, the same pale, indolent, acquiescent flesh; only the nightgown was creased, which made this picture even more intimate and secret. And so, thought Agostino, not only did the image of that woman not interpose itself as a screen between him and his mother, as he had hoped, but it actually seemed to confirm the latter's femininity. "Why do you want to go away?" she asked again. "Don't you like being with me?"

"You always treat me like a child," said Agostino abruptly, without knowing why.

His mother laughed and stroked his cheek. "Very well, from now on I'll treat you like a man. . . . Will that be all right? But you must go to sleep now, it's very late." She stooped and kissed him. Then she put out the light and Agostino heard her get into bed.

"Like a man," he couldn't help thinking before he fell asleep. But he wasn't a man. What a long, unhappy time would have to pass before he could become one.

*Translated from the Italian by Beryl de Zoete*

# Tommaso Landolfi

## GOGOL'S WIFE

$A$T THIS POINT, confronted with the whole complicated affair of Nikolai Vassilevitch's wife, I am overcome by hesitation. Have I any right to disclose something which is unknown to the whole world, which my unforgettable friend himself kept hidden from the world (and he had his reasons), and which I am sure will give rise to all sorts of malicious and stupid misunderstandings? Something, moreover, which will very probably offend the sensibilities of all sorts of base, hypocritical people, and possibly of some honest people too, if there are any left? And finally, have I any right to disclose something before which my own spirit recoils, and even tends toward a more or less open disapproval?

But the fact remains that, as a biographer, I have certain firm obligations. Believing as I do that every bit of information about so lofty a genius will turn out to be of value to us and to future generations, I cannot conceal something which in any case has no hope of being judged fairly and wisely until the end of time. Moreover, what right have we to condemn? Is it given to us to know, not only what intimate needs, but even what higher and wider ends may have been served by those very deeds of a lofty genius which perchance may appear to us vile? No indeed, for we understand so little of these privileged natures. "It is true," a great man once said, "that I also have to pee, but for quite different reasons."

But without more ado I will come to what I know beyond doubt, and can prove beyond question, about this controversial matter, which will now—I dare to hope—no longer be so. I will not trouble to recapitulate what is already known of it, since I do not think this should be necessary at the present stage of development of Gogol studies.

Let me say it at once: Nikolai Vassilevitch's wife was not a woman. Nor was she any sort of human being, nor any sort of living creature at all, whether animal or vegetable (although something of the sort has sometimes been hinted). She was quite simply a balloon.

Yes, a balloon; and this will explain the perplexity, or even indignation, of certain biographers who were also the personal friends of the Master, and who complained that, although they often went to his house, they never saw her and "never even heard her voice." From this they deduced all sorts of dark and disgraceful complications—yes, and criminal ones too. No, gentlemen, everything is always simpler than it appears. You did not hear her voice simply because she could not speak, or to be more exact, she could only speak in certain conditions, as we shall see. And it was always, except once, in tête-à-tête with Nikolai Vassilevitch. So let us not waste time with any cheap or empty refutations but come at once to as exact and complete a description as possible of the being or object in question.

Gogol's so-called wife was an ordinary dummy made of thick rubber, naked at all seasons, buff in tint, or as is more commonly said, flesh-colored. But since women's skins are not all of the same color, I should specify that hers was a light-colored, polished skin, like that of certain brunettes. It, or she, was, it is hardly necessary to add, of feminine sex. Perhaps I should say at once that she was capable of very wide alterations of her attributes without, of course, being able to alter her sex itself. She could sometimes appear to be thin, with hardly any breasts and with narrow hips more like a young lad than a woman, and at other times to be excessively well-endowed or—let us not mince matters—fat. And she often changed the color of her hair, both on her head and elsewhere on her body, though not necessarily at the same time. She could also seem to change in all sorts of other tiny particulars, such as the position of moles, the vitality of the mucous membranes and so forth. She could even to a certain extent change the very color of her skin. One is faced with the necessity of asking oneself who she really was, or whether it would be proper to speak of a single "person"—and in fact we shall see that it would be imprudent to press this point.

The cause of these changes, as my readers will already have understood, was nothing else but the will of Nikolai Vassilevitch himself. He would inflate her to a greater or lesser degree, would change her wig and her other tufts of hair, would grease her with ointments and touch her up in various ways so as to obtain more or less the type of woman which suited him at that moment. Following the natural inclinations of his fancy, he even amused himself sometimes by producing grotesque or monstrous forms; as will be readily understood, she became deformed when inflated beyond a certain point or if she remained below a certain pressure.

But Gogol soon tired of these experiments, which he held to be "after all, not very respectful" to his wife, whom he loved in his own way—however inscrutable it may remain to us. He loved her, but which of these incarnations, we may ask ourselves, did he love? Alas, I have already indicated that the end of the present account will furnish some sort of an answer. And how can I have stated above that it was Nikolai Vassilevitch's will which ruled that woman? In a certain sense, yes, it is true; but it is equally certain that she soon became no longer his slave but his tyrant. And here yawns the abyss, or if you prefer it, the Jaws of Tartarus. But let us not anticipate.

I have said that Gogol obtained with his manipulations *more or less* the type of woman which he needed from time to time. I should add that when, in rare cases, the form he obtained perfectly incarnated his desire, Nikolai Vassilevitch fell in love with it "exclusively," as he said in his own words, and that this was enough to render "her" stable for a certain time—until he fell out of love with "her." I counted no more than three or four of these violent passions —or, as I suppose they would be called today, infatuations—in the life (dare I say in the conjugal life?) of the great writer. It will be convenient to add here that a few years after what one may call his marriage, Gogol had even given a name to his wife. It was Caracas, which is, unless I am mistaken, the capital of Venezuela. I have never been able to discover the reason for this choice: great minds are so capricious!

Speaking only of her normal appearance, Caracas was what is called a fine woman—well built and proportioned in every part. She had every smallest attribute of her sex properly disposed in the proper location. Particularly worthy of attention were her genital organs (if the adjective is permissible in such a context). They were formed by means of ingenious folds in the rubber. Nothing was forgotten, and their operation was rendered easy by various devices, as well as by the internal pressure of the air.

Caracas also had a skeleton, even though a rudimentary one. Perhaps it was made of whalebone. Special care had been devoted to the construction of the thoracic cage, of the pelvic basin and of the cranium. The first two systems were more or less visible in accordance with the thickness of the fatty layer, if I may so describe it, which covered them. It is a great pity that Gogol never let me know the name of the creator of such a fine piece of work. There was an obstinacy in his refusal which was never quite clear to me.

Nikolai Vassilevitch blew his wife up through the anal sphincter with a pump of his own invention, rather like those which you hold down with your two feet and which are used today in all sorts of mechanical workshops. Situated in the anus was a little one-way valve, or whatever the correct technical description would be, like the mitral valve of the heart, which, once the body was inflated, allowed more air to come in but none to go out. To deflate, one unscrewed a stopper in the mouth, at the back of the throat.

And that, I think, exhausts the description of the most noteworthy peculiarities of this being. Unless perhaps I should mention the splendid rows of white teeth which adorned her mouth and the dark eyes which, in spite of their immobility, perfectly simulated life. Did I say simulate? Good heavens, simulate is not the word! Nothing seems to be the word, when one is speaking of Caracas! Even these eyes could undergo a change of color, by means of a special process to which, since it was long and tiresome, Gogol seldom had recourse. Finally, I should speak of her voice, which it was only once given to me to hear. But I cannot do that without going more fully into the relationship between husband and wife, and in this I shall no longer be able to answer to the truth of everything with absolute certitude. On my conscience I could not—so confused, both in itself and in my memory, is that which I now have to tell.

Here, then, as they occur to me, are some of my memories.

The first and, as I said, the last time I ever heard Caracas speak to Nikolai Vassilevitch was one evening when we were absolutely alone. We were in the room where the woman, if I may be allowed the expression, lived. Entrance to this room was strictly forbidden to everybody. It was furnished more or less in the Oriental manner, had no windows and was situated in the most inaccessible part of the house. I did know that she could talk, but Gogol had never explained to me the circumstances under which this happened. There were only the two of us, or three, in there. Nikolai Vassilevitch and I were drinking vodka and discussing Butkov's novel. I remember that we left this topic, and he was maintaining the necessity for radical reforms in the laws of inheritance. We had almost forgotten her. It was then that, with a husky and submissive voice, like Venus on the nuptial couch, she said point-blank: "I want to go poo poo."

I jumped, thinking I had misheard, and looked across at her. She was sitting on a pile of cushions against the wall; that evening she was a soft, blonde beauty, rather well-covered. Her expression seemed commingled of shrewdness and slyness, childishness and irresponsibility. As for Gogol, he blushed violently and, leaping on her, stuck two fingers down her throat. She immediately began to shrink and to turn pale; she took on once again that lost and astonished air which was especially hers, and was in the end reduced to no more than a

flabby skin on a perfunctory bony armature. Since, for practical reasons which will readily be divined, she had an extraordinary flexible
backbone, she folded up almost in two, and for the rest of the evening she looked up at us from where she had slithered to the floor,
in utter abjection.

All Gogol said was: "She only does it for a joke, or to annoy me,
because as a matter of fact she does not have such needs." In the
presence of other people, that is to say of me, he generally made a
point of treating her with a certain disdain.

We went on drinking and talking, but Nikolai Vassilevitch
seemed very much disturbed and absent in spirit. Once he suddenly
interrupted what he was saying, seized my hand in his and burst into
tears. "What can I do now?" he exclaimed. "You understand, Foma
Paskalovitch, that I loved her?"

It is necessary to point out that it was impossible, except by a
miracle, ever to repeat any of Caracas' forms. She was a fresh creation every time, and it would have been wasted effort to seek to find
again the exact proportions, the exact pressure, and so forth, of a
former Caracas. Therefore the plumpish blonde of that evening was
lost to Gogol from that time forth forever; this was in fact the tragic
end of one of those few loves of Nikolai Vassilevitch, which I described above. He gave me no explanation; he sadly rejected my proffered comfort, and that evening we parted early. But his heart had
been laid bare to me in that outburst. He was no longer so reticent
with me, and soon had hardly any secrets left. And this, I may say in
parenthesis, caused me very great pride.

It seems that things had gone well for the "couple" at the beginning of their life together. Nikolai Vassilevitch had been content
with Caracas and slept regularly with her in the same bed. He continued to observe this custom till the end, saying with a timid smile
that no companion could be quieter or less importunate than she. But
I soon began to doubt this, especially judging by the state he was
sometimes in when he woke up. Then, after several years, their relationship began strangely to deteriorate.

All this, let it be said once and for all, is no more than a schematic
attempt at an explanation. About that time the woman actually began to show signs of independence or, as one might say, of auton-
omy. Nikolai Vassilevitch had the extraordinary impression that she
was acquiring a personality of her own, indecipherable perhaps, but
still distinct from his, and one which slipped through his fingers. It is
certain that some sort of continuity was established between each of
her appearances—between all those brunettes, those blondes, those

redheads and auburn-headed girls, between those plump, those slim, those dusky or snowy or golden beauties, there was a certain something in common. At the beginning of this chapter I cast some doubt on the propriety of considering Caracas as a unitary personality; nevertheless I myself could not quite, whenever I saw her, free myself of the impression that, however unheard of it may seem, this was fundamentally the same woman. And it may be that this was why Gogol felt he had to give her a name.

An attempt to establish in what precisely subsisted the common attributes of the different forms would be quite another thing. Perhaps it was no more and no less than the creative afflatus of Nikolai Vassilevitch himself. But no, it would have been too singular and strange if he had been so much divided off from himself, so much averse to himself. Because whoever she was, Caracas was a disturbing presence and even—it is better to be quite clear—a hostile one. Yet neither Gogol nor I ever succeeded in formulating a remotely tenable hypothesis as to her true nature; when I say formulate, I mean in terms which would be at once rational and accessible to all. But I cannot pass over an extraordinary event which took place at this time.

Caracas fell ill of a shameful disease—or rather Gogol did—though he was not then having, nor had he ever had, any contact with other women. I will not even try to describe how this happened, or where the filthy complaint came from; all I know is that it happened. And that my great, unhappy friend would say to me: "So, Foma Paskalovitch, you see what lay at the heart of Caracas; it was the spirit of syphilis."

Sometimes he would even blame himself in a quite absurd manner; he was always prone to self-accusation. This incident was a real catastrophe as far as the already obscure relationship between husband and wife, and the hostile feelings of Nikolai Vassilevitch himself, were concerned. He was compelled to undergo long-drawn-out and painful treatment—the treatment of those days—and the situation was aggravated by the fact that the disease in the woman did not seem to be easily curable. Gogol deluded himself for some time that, by blowing his wife up and down and furnishing her with the most widely divergent aspects, he could obtain a woman immune from the contagion, but he was forced to desist when no results were forthcoming.

I shall be brief, seeking not to tire my readers, and also because what I remember seems to become more and more confused. I shall therefore hasten to the tragic conclusion. As to this last, however, let there be no mistake. I must once again make it clear that I am very sure of my ground. I was an eyewitness. Would that I had not been!

The years went by. Nikolai Vassilevitch's distaste for his wife became stronger, though his love for her did not show any signs of diminishing. Toward the end, aversion and attachment struggled so fiercely with each other in his heart that he became quite stricken, almost broken up. His restless eyes, which habitually assumed so many different expressions and sometimes spoke so sweetly to the heart of his interlocutor, now almost always shone with a fevered light, as if he were under the effect of a drug. The strangest impulses arose in him, accompanied by the most senseless fears. He spoke to me of Caracas more and more often, accusing her of unthinkable and amazing things. In these regions I could not follow him, since I had but a sketchy acquaintance with his wife, and hardly any intimacy—and above all since my sensibility was so limited compared with his. I shall accordingly restrict myself to reporting some of his accusations, without reference to my personal impressions.

"Believe it or not, Foma Paskalovitch," he would, for example, often say to me: "Believe it or not, *she's aging!*" Then, unspeakably moved, he would, as was his way, take my hands in his. He also accused Caracas of giving herself up to solitary pleasures, which he had expressly forbidden. He even went so far as to charge her with betraying him, but the things he said became so extremely obscure that I must excuse myself from any further account of them.

One thing that appears certain is that toward the end Caracas, whether aged or not, had turned into a bitter creature, querulous, hypocritical and subject to religious excess. I do not exclude the possibility that she may have had an influence on Gogol's moral position during the last period of his life, a position which is sufficiently well known. The tragic climax came one night quite unexpectedly when Nikolai Vassilevitch and I were celebrating his silver wedding—one of the last evenings we were to spend together. I neither can nor should attempt to set down what it was that led to his decision, at a time when to all appearances he was resigned to tolerating his consort. I know not what new events had taken place that day. I shall confine myself to the facts; my readers must make what they can of them.

That evening Nikolai Vassilevitch was unusually agitated. His distaste for Caracas seemed to have reached an unprecedented intensity. The famous "pyre of vanities"—the burning of his manuscripts—had already taken place; I should not like to say whether or not at the instigation of his wife. His state of mind had been further inflamed by other causes. As to his physical condition, this was ever more pitiful, and strengthened my impression that he took drugs. All the same, he began to talk in a more or less normal way about Belinsky, who was giving him some trouble with his attacks on the *Selected Correspondence.* Then suddenly, tears rising to his eyes, he interrupted himself and cried out: "No. No. It's too much, too much. I can't go on any longer," as well as other obscure and disconnected phrases which he would not clarify. He seemed to be talking to himself. He wrung his hands, shook his head, got up and sat down again after having taken four or five anxious steps round the room. When Caracas appeared, or rather when we went in to her later in the evening in her Oriental chamber, he controlled himself no longer and began to behave like an old man, if I may so express myself, in his second childhood, quite giving way to his absurd impulses. For instance, he kept nudging me and winking and senselessly repeating: "There she is, Foma Paskalovitch; there she is!" Meanwhile she seemed to look up at us with a disdainful attention. But behind these "mannerisms" one could feel in him a real repugnance, a repugnance which had, I suppose, now reached the limits of the endurable. Indeed . . .

After a certain time Nikolai Vassilevitch seemed to pluck up courage. He burst into tears, but somehow they were more manly tears. He wrung his hands again, seized mine in his, and walked up and down, muttering: "That's enough! We can't have any more of this. This is an unheard of thing. How can such a thing be happening to me? How can a man be expected to put up with *this?*"

He then leapt furiously upon the pump, the existence of which he seemed just to have remembered, and, with it in his hand, dashed like a whirlwind to Caracas. He inserted the tube in her anus and began to inflate her. . . . Weeping the while, he shouted like one possessed: "Oh, how I love her, how I love her, my poor, poor darling! . . . But she's going to burst! Unhappy Caracas, most pitiable of God's creatures! But die she must!"

Caracas was swelling up. Nikolai Vassilevitch sweated, wept and pumped. I wished to stop him but, I know not why, I had not the courage. She began to become deformed and shortly assumed the most monstrous aspect; and yet she had not given any signs of alarm —she was used to these jokes. But when she began to feel unbearably full, or perhaps when Nikolai Vassilevitch's intentions became plain to her, she took on an expression of bestial amazement, even a little beseeching, but still without losing that disdainful look. She was afraid, she was even committing herself to his mercy, but still she could not believe in the immediate approach of her fate; she could not believe in the frightful audacity of her husband. He could not see her face because he was behind her. But I looked at her with fascination, and did not move a finger.

At last the internal pressure came through the fragile bones at the base of her skull, and printed on her face an indescribable rictus. Her belly, her thighs, her lips, her breasts and what I could see of her buttocks had swollen to incredible proportions. All of a sudden she belched, and gave a long hissing groan; both these phenomena one could explain by the increase in pressure, which had suddenly forced a way out through the valve in her throat. Then her eyes bulged frantically, threatening to jump out of their sockets. Her ribs flared wide apart and were no longer attached to the sternum, and she resembled a python digesting a donkey. A donkey, did I say? An ox! An elephant! At this point I believed her already dead, but Nikolai Vassilevitch, sweating, weeping and repeating: "My dearest! My beloved! My best!" continued to pump.

She went off unexpectedly and, as it were, all of a piece. It was not one part of her skin which gave way and the rest which followed, but her whole surface at the same instant. She scattered in the air. The pieces fell more or less slowly, according to their size, which was in no case above a very restricted one. I distinctly remember a piece of her cheek, with some lip attached, hanging on the corner of the mantelpiece. Nikolai Vassilevitch stared at me like a madman. Then he pulled himself together and, once more with furious determination, he began carefully to collect those poor rags which once had been the shining skin of Caracas, and all of her.

"Good-by, Caracas," I thought I heard him murmur, "Good-by! You were too pitiable!" And then suddenly and quite audibly: "The fire! The fire! She too must end up in the fire." He crossed himself— with his left hand, of course. Then, when he had picked up all those shriveled rags, even climbing on the furniture so as not to miss any, he threw them straight on the fire in the hearth, where they began to burn slowly and with an excessively unpleasant smell. Nikolai Vassilevitch, like all Russians, had a passion for throwing important things in the fire.

Red in the face, with an inexpressible look of despair, and yet of sinister triumph too, he gazed on the pyre of those miserable remains. He had seized my arm and was squeezing it convulsively. But those traces of what had once been a being were hardly well alight when he seemed yet again to pull himself together, as if he were suddenly remembering something or taking a painful decision. In one bound he was out of the room.

A few seconds later I heard him speaking to me through the door in a broken, plaintive voice: "Foma Paskalovitch, I want you to promise not to look. *Golubchik*, promise not to look at me when I come in."

I don't know what I answered, or whether I tried to reassure him in any way. But he insisted, and I had to promise him, as if he were a child, to hide my face against the wall and only turn round when he said I might. The door then opened violently and Nikolai Vassilevitch burst into the room and ran to the fireplace.

And here I must confess my weakness, though I consider it justified by the extraordinary circumstances. I looked round before Nikolai Vassilevitch told me I could; it was stronger than me. I was just in time to see him carrying something in his arms, something which he threw on the fire with all the rest, so that it suddenly flared up. At that, since the desire to *see* had entirely mastered every other thought in me, I dashed to the fireplace. But Nikolai Vassilevitch placed himself between me and it and pushed me back with a strength of which I had not believed him capable. Meanwhile the object was burning and giving off clouds of smoke. And before he showed any sign of calming down there was nothing left but a heap of silent ashes.

The true reason why I wished to see was because I had already glimpsed. But it was only a glimpse, and perhaps I should not allow myself to introduce even the slightest element of uncertainty into this true story. And yet, an eyewitness account is not complete without a mention of that which the witness knows with less then complete certainty. To cut a long story short, that something was a baby. Not a flesh-and-blood baby, of course, but more something in the line of a rubber doll or a model. Something which, to judge by its appearance, could have been called *Caracas' son*.

Was I mad too? That I do not know, but I do know that this was what I saw, not clearly, but with my own eyes. And I wonder why it was that when I was writing this just now I didn't mention that when Nikolai Vassilevitch came back into the room he was muttering between his clenched teeth: "Him too! Him too!"

And that is the sum of my knowledge of Nikolai Vassilevitch's wife. In the next chapter I shall tell what happened to him afterwards, and that will be the last chapter of his life. But to give an interpretation of his feelings for his wife, or indeed for anything, is quite another and more difficult matter, though I have attempted it elsewhere in this volume, and refer the reader to that modest effort. I hope I have thrown sufficient light on a most controversial question and that I have unveiled the mystery, if not of Gogol, then at least of his wife. In the course of this I have implicitly given the lie to the insensate accusation that he ill-treated or even beat his wife, as well as other like absurdities. And what else can be the goal of a humble biographer such as the present writer but to serve the memory of that lofty genius who is the object of his study?

*Translated from the Italian by Wayland Young*

# Ramón Sender

## THE TERRACE

In Miss Slingsby's house lived a dog with a mother-of-pearl collar, a castrated Siamese cat, and a parrot that knew how to say "Come again" to callers as they were departing. For Miss Slingsby these three animals represented nature.

But Miss Slingsby died. With her hatred of extremes she would have preferred to give the impression that she was dying only a little, but she died, totally and forevermore. Four days later Miss Slingsby's remains had been cremated and there, on the jasper mantelpiece beside the Dresden clock, was a small gold box with the inscription: "Ellen Slingsby.—1887-1945.—Laus Deo." Under this inscription was the name of the funeral home responsible for the cremation: "The Elysian Fields, Inc."

When the cook called for the ashes she was told that they were usually kept at the mortuary until they were cold. Otherwise as they cooled small particles might move inside the box, making some slight sound, which sensitive people could associate with the soul of the deceased.

Insisting that this did not matter, the cook left with the still tepid ashes of Miss Slingsby.

About midday the lawyer, Mr. Arner, arrived at Miss Slingsby's home. He was a middle-aged man, blond and lean, with a silhouette that somehow reminded one of a kangaroo. He was scraping off the soles of his shoes on the felt mat when the door opened.

The house was hushed. Mr. Arner took out a visiting card and presented it to the maid. She read: "Froilan Arner, Attorney-at-Law." She handed the card to the cook, the cook passed it on to the chauffeur who, not knowing what to do, returned it to the lawyer. Evidently a man of orderly habits, he put it back in his cardcase. Then he sat down, blew his nose, apologetically, opened his brief case and said:

"The dog, cat and parrot are also required to be present."

They were brought in at once. The attorney asked:

"This is the dog named Merlin?"

Upon hearing his name the dog tried to wag his tail but, since he had none, he started moving his hind quarters with a discreet acceleration.

"This is the cat called David?"

The cat turned its head and contemplated the attorney with little interest.

"This is the parrot named George?"

The parrot screeched:

"Come again."

Mr. Arner announced that he was going to read Miss Slingsby's last will and testament. The maid was seated on the edge of her chair, her feet crossed, her knees together and bent to one side. The chauffeur looked at her, thinking: "She does look like a lady."

In the silence the cat occasionally heard a sound somewhere, pricked up his ears and looked around intrigued. The cook suspected that he was hearing the ashes inside the box.

Mr. Arner read the preamble and then the executive part of the will. "To the dog Merlin, who in all probability will not live over seven years, I bequeath ten thousand dollars. To the cat David, who may also live six or seven years, I bequeath fifteen thousand dollars. To the parrot George, whose life may yet be prolonged for more than forty years, I bequeath thirty thousand dollars. These sums are for veterinary fees, when necessary, as well as living expenses and entertainment, since the general upkeep of the house, which will continue to be cared for by the maid so long as any of the three animals shall live, is provided for in section B-3. I recommend frequent renovation of the tropical décor in the bridge room where the parrot feels so contented, and I suggest that he be made to forget the phrase *come again* and learn another more in keeping with the new circumstances of his life." Upon hearing his name the parrot repeated the expression, accompanying it by a slight trill.

The chauffeur was hoping the maid would look at him, but aware of this she continued looking "nowhere," and wondering what new phrase they should teach George.

Mr. Arner went on reading: "To the servants I bequeath, in turn, the following sums: To Jane, the maid, ten thousand dollars. To Herbert, the chauffeur, five hundred dollars." (The chauffeur allowed an exclamation of quite impertinent disgust to escape him and the others held their breath.) To Bertha, the cook, eight thousand dollars."

The chauffeur conjectured: "Why five hundred to me?" He

could discover no reasons for so unjust a difference. But Mr. Arner was still reading: "To the sanatorium for mental diseases on Coronado Avenue, two hundred thousand dollars to be distributed as follows: fifty thousand for the construction of a chapel of the same faith as the church of my grandparents. The rest to cover the expenses of a party to take place every month in said sanatorium. It is my wish that a monthly celebration with dancing be held for the mentally ill of the masculine sex, to be attended by girls from the city as well as by the women servants of my household. Another party for the women patients to which men will be invited, I shall expect Herbert the chauffeur to attend. With these parties it is my desire to give the poor sick people a little social life to make their sad situation more bearable.

"Trustee and administrator of these funds will be Mr. Froilan Arner."

The will caused a sensation. The maid looked through the windows at the high cement walls visible beyond the residential section, and the terrace overlooking them. There was the sanatorium. "But why should Miss Slingsby want the insane people to dance?" she wondered.

The attorney finished the reading and rose, ready to take his leave. As the door opened the parrot cried out: "Come again." The maid ordered him to be quiet, her finger on her lips. Then she looked at the others and asked:

"What new phrase shall we teach him?"

Lowering her eyes, the cook proposed a pious theme: *Rest in Peace*. Herbert suggested a patriotic one: *Viva Massachusetts!* which was Miss Slingsby's native state although she had always lived in Cibola.

The cook was resting her elbow on the table and meditating on why Miss Slingsby obliged her to dance once a month with the insane in the sanatorium. She did not know the meaning to give this wish of her mistress. She stood up, sighed, took the small box from the mantel with both hands, as one holds a sacred object, and prepared to leave. In the street she met a priest who asked in a pained tone if the body of the poor lady was still in the house. The cook pointed to her pocketbook and said: "No, poor dear, I have her here."

She walked to the neighborhood church still pondering: "Forgive me, God, but why do the insane need to dance?"

Half an hour later when she returned home, she surprised the maid sitting on the chauffeur's knees, his arms around her waist. The startled maid jumped up, began screaming and, covering her mouth with her hand, ran off in the direction of the garden. The chauffeur went after her, pleading, and after him the dog Merlin, barking.

Herbert and the maid were married three weeks later. The cook thought: "This would have pleased Miss Slingsby."

Two months later the first dance in the sanatorium was held. The director, Dr. Smith, presented the estimate before the party and Arner wrote him a check. The only expenses were for an orchestra and the cold buffet supper served the guests. Miss Slingsby's will was being carried out. Mr. Arner figured that the remaining hundred and fifty thousand dollars, after giving fifty thousand for the building of the chapel, could bring in five percent annually, well administered, or seven thousand, five hundred dollars. And he hesitated.

He had not intended going to the dance, although he did feel a certain curiosity about the women suffering from mental disorders, especially if they were young and pretty. This was not an unhealthy curiosity. So he went to the sanatorium. The night was cool and mild, with a yellowish desert moon. The moon of the desert of Cibola.

As he entered the vestibule and found himself surrounded by marble over which his own shadow glided smoothly, he remembered that he had had a shoeshine and haircut, important details when one is going to a party, even a party for madmen.

He moved forward feeling his feet sink into the thick carpeting and thinking of poor Miss Slingsby who wanted the insane to dance after her death.

It was certainly a pleasant place. Marble that was not marble, rugs of coco fiber that was not coco, aluminum murals that were not aluminum. But everything clean and tidy. In the air welcoming him was the odor of wax and freshly cut grass intermingled, not the typical hospital smell.

It suddenly occurred to him that, thanks to Miss Slingsby and to him, the poor patients in the sanatorium were going to have a delightful evening. Arner felt like an instrument of providence.

In the elevator he met the director, Dr. Smith. A physician fifty years old with modern ideas, although he was in the habit of speaking of them as if he were not quite sure. Other people were in the elevator, among them the good bourgeois of Germanic air and gold-rimmed glasses that one is likely to find in elevators and who, as the elevator goes up, appears to be thinking: "Just watch me raising myself by my own merits."

"In what part of the building is the dance?" Arner asked.

"On the terrace," replied the director, at the same time bowing to another guest.

The director's profile had something about it that suggested certain fishing birds. As the elevator stopped the doors opened quietly. They entered a corridor like the one on the ground floor. Arner remarked that he knew the name of one of the patients: Matilda Strolheim. He had been a friend of her husband, an aviator who made a reputation for himself during the Second World War. He still flew in jet planes now and then. He was quite rich, Strolheim. Thinking of the aviator's wealth, Arner asked himself if it would not be a good thing to invest Miss Slingsby's money in air transport stock.

As he looked toward the terrace he heard the director say: "Yes, Matilda Strolheim. You see? The party is outdoors, so people can smoke. But," he added, "I don't have much faith in such things."

The terrace was spacious and above the balustrade was a grating supporting a heavy wire mesh. In a whisper Arner asked if all the women there were insane and the director replied:

"In any case, only those who are tranquil may come to the party, don't worry."

"No, I'm not worried," Arner hastened to say.

"And don't use the word *insane* here. They are not insane, they are ill."

Everything seemed natural and with no signs of violence. Only the silence was extraordinary as if they were in a temple. Suddenly music broke the silence and lightened the atmosphere. Afraid of their own nerves the patients lowered their voices. The men imitated them, unconsciously. They were townspeople who had been carefully chosen before receiving invitations.

"They say that you psychiatrists are slightly abnormal too," ventured Arner. "Is this so?"

"Yes," laughed the doctor. "Choosing this profession would seem to be an indication."

"A symptom?"

"No, no, only an indication."

The orchestra was playing seated on a small platform.

"Percussion instruments are exciting," the director remarked. "Stringed instruments, on the other hand, are soothing and tranquilizing."

Everything on the terrace was gray and neutral. A guest approached Dr. Smith, saying:

"I'm going to San Francisco tomorrow. You know my heart is a

little . . . well, do you think I can fly? I ask because people do die
in airplanes."

"People also die in bed," countered the doctor, raising his bird-
like head.

The guest boldly made his way out onto the terrace. The attorney Arner thought: "I didn't believe Dr. Smith had a sense of humor." He asked if Miss Slingsby's chauffeur was attending the dance
and the director assured him he was. Then Mr. Arner wished to find
out which patient was Mrs. Strolheim and the doctor said:

"The one there to the right of the dance floor, and who is just
now touching her necklace. Don't look at her. She realizes we're
talking about her."

At the table beside Matilda another patient was crying like a
child while a nurse, who was trying to calm her, offered her a cigarette, lighting it for her. Arner asked:

"Do they behave rationally?"

"Yes, don't worry."

"I told you before that I'm not worried, doctor."

At the table level the air on the terrace was the same quiet air of
the inside rooms. But a little higher, wild outdoor breezes were blowing.

Many small tables were scattered about the terrace, each with a
little lamp. These lights in the declining paleness of evening had a
cold fluid quality. In the middle of the terrace the dance floor
gleamed, freshly. At the back a nurse was preparing refreshments
behind a wide table covered with a cloth.

The attorney was prying around discreetly, playing at discrimi-
nating between the insane women who revealed some symptoms and
those who seemed completely normal. From time to time Arner's
eyes sought the noble solitary figure of Matilda.

The attorney remembered how the Arabs consider the madman a
supernatural being, venerating and reverencing him. Glancing at
some of the women he noticed that their expressions became sweeter
under the influence of the waltz the orchestra was playing. Those
madwomen awakened in him, even though he was not an Arab, a
strange, superstitious inclination.

Arner imagined he saw Miss Slingsby—her lovable ghost—in the
center of the dance floor, presiding over the dancing with her silver
cane.

Above the terrace hung an immense violet sky with here and
there a star. The moon was hidden behind the high wall topped by
the television antenna.

Arner was aware of an animal taciturnity in some women. He said so and Dr. Smith agreed, adding that instinctive life was very strong in these patients.

"Stronger than in you or in me," he observed.

"What does Dr. Smith know about my instinctive life?" Arner mused, slightly uncomfortable. And again he wondered what he could do with Miss Slingsby's money. It didn't seem right to keep it immobilized in the bank.

Arner's financial ideas were sometimes very original and he dared not mention them to his banker friends.

Years ago it had occurred to him that the manufacture of masks of delicate and fine artificial skin, reproducing the features of movie stars, would be a great success. All men are in love with some movie star. The mask of that heroine on the wife's face would be charming on occasion. Every time he thought about it he felt slightly ashamed and said to himself: "That's a perverse idea. Like hypocritically rationalizing adultery." He rejected it but the seed stayed in his mind.

It was now dark. Above the balustrade the vertical bars of the grating supporting the heavy mesh were visible. At the top these bars were bent toward the inside, to prevent anyone who might climb up the grating from peering over and maybe falling or deliberately throwing himself down into the street.

Reflections from the small table lamps were coloring the mesh red and yellow.

The director and the attorney sat down at an unoccupied table near the dance floor. Mr. Arner looked with some insistence at Matilda who, realizing this, returned his glance in a natural and friendly way. She had a pure, oval face, a warm complexion, and wide blue eyes.

"I think you ought to dance with her," the physician suggested.

Arner invited Matilda to dance. She was rather stiff despite her youth and he could not lead her easily. Arner decided to let her do the leading, but they did not get along that way either. Then he apologized and asked; laughing: "Do you want to be a good girl and obey me?"

She smiled: "I have always wanted to obey. Since they brought me here, at least."

"Not before?"

"That's what they say. But now I'm a good girl."

As he passed near them, the director flattered Arner:

"Eh, doctor, where in the devil did you learn how to dance so well?"

Some people called Arner doctor because he had a doctorate in jurisprudence from Yale. But Matilda misunderstood:

"As soon as I saw you I knew you were a doctor," she said.

Arner dared not undeceive her. A windblown lock of her hair tickled his forehead, reminding him that they were out in the open. Matilda added:

"I like doctors from outside the sanatorium better than those inside."

"That's natural, I suppose."

"Not so natural. But in reality the sanatorium doctors aren't human. The director Smith looks like one of those stuffed birds you see in museums. And pardon the extravagance, but it's true."

"Yes, a fishing bird," said Arner.

At that moment the orchestra was playing softly, with muted instruments, and Arner kept still. Not a voice could be heard on the terrace and the attorney admitted that it was true, the director did look like a bird. But why stuffed?

Just then the director was thumbing his way through some papers which he had removed from a small portfolio, and between his lips he was holding a silver pencil, crosswise. Now he did have the profile of a bird with a fish in its beak.

Arner and Matilda continued dancing. The corner of a tablecloth swaying in the breeze gave a sensation of pleasant abandon. Matilda spoke:

"Since you are a doctor I'm going to confide in you."

Arner was about to tell her that he was not a medical doctor, but she was speaking again:

"I am not insane," Matilda assured him.

Arner started talking about the errors of science. She shook her head:

"No, that's not it. I am actually as sick as anybody else, but at this moment I am as sane as you. I am only insane three or four days every month. You can tell a doctor everything, can't you? I'm only insane on my *lunar* days."

Arner was thinking that here was the first misunderstanding of the evening. It was doubtless inevitable at a party of mental patients, and this remark about lunar days must be common among nurses and doctors. He looked at her eyes and saw in her an immense trust. At that moment he heard an echo—the echo of the orchestra—in some distant corner of the terrace, in some fold of the high night.

Matilda waited for Arner to say something.

"Doesn't my sickness seem odd to you?" she asked.

"But what?"

Arner had never found himself in a situation like this before either, talking as a physician to a beautiful madwoman. Her eyes were still questioning and Arner could do no less than reply:

"The son you might have could be someone, understand? I am an ordinary man. There are millions like me. But some men in our time have had a great influence, like Freud, Gandhi, Lenin, and especially Einstein. Nevertheless nature does not stop with them. It can never stop with anybody. It goes ahead with its desires and necessities, which we still don't understand, nor will we probably ever succeed in understanding. Yet nature has its ideal. And searches for it, in one way or another. You beautiful women are the agents of this natural miracle."

She was looking solemn, although she had an urge to laugh. She was probably thinking that the doctor was also slightly insane.

"What can nature's ideal be?" she insisted.

Arner was growing weary, feeling that Matilda was pushing him to confused and brilliant fields in which he feared he might lose his way. Oh, those faces where intelligence slumbers, how they can stir up ours at times! But he maintained a calm exterior.

"I don't know what nature's ideal is," he said. "Only a man of genius could imagine that. And I am just an *homo vulgaris*."

She laughed and this encouraged Arner to continue along the same line:

"An *homo simplicissimus*."

Now she was shaking her head:

"That's not true. No one is sincere when he says something like that. Neither are you."

The attorney thought: "Here we have an intelligent opinion." And she went on with her inquisitiveness:

"You believe that nature expects so much of me?"

"That's what I dare to assume, seeing the reactions imposed upon you by nature. Nature does not protest with other women. Just assume that if the men who can destroy this world have already been born" (he was referring to the specialists in nuclear physics), "the world may not want to die and is waiting for those who could save it. One of those men could be born any day. And he will have to be born to some woman. I only want to make it clear to you that, for all these reasons, your case is a state of natural tension rather than a disease. You understand. Men now exist who can disintegrate matter, who are already speculating with *anti-matter*. Creation may need other men who can reintegrate it, forming higher syntheses. The world cannot stand still, passively. It must go on evolving or die. And we can't forget that the man who may save us will be born to a woman. Understand? Nothing that lives must stop living, if we can help it. On those lunar days when you cry in your room . . ."

"I don't cry. Scream, that's what I do, scream. You should hear me."

"All right, when you feel yourself falling into that well, and you scream and want to throw yourself against the wall and tear open your veins with your teeth, it isn't you alone, but the entire planet that is falling ino the darkness because it sees its hope endangered. The savior might be born to you."

After saying the words "planet" and "savior," he was sorry. He should not let himself be so utterly carried away. For the first time, however, she appeared capable of understanding. Yet what she said was somewhat out of line:

"You must be a rather queer doctor. But I like queer people. My second husband was like that too—Bob, I mean. And as for me, well, I had the reputation of a freak, have no doubt of that. Before coming here I was something like a savage and dangerous wildcat. Now, as you see, I'm a gentle little lamb. I listen to you and begin to think you might be right. If so, isn't my case tremendous?"

At that instant someone overturned an ice bucket and the ice cubes spilled merrily over the floor. Here even the slightest incident had enormous repercussions. On some of the cubes the lamp light played delicately. Several people formed a kind of safety cordon, so that no one would slip on the ice and fall. Meanwhile they were all picking it up. The director himself, Dr. Smith with his fish face, got down on all fours to gather up some ice cubes underneath a table.

A nurse grabbed her skirts on seeing a little piece of ice slide over the floor, as if it were a mouse.

Arner and his partner continued dancing. When the music ended, Matilda led Arner to the buffet. She served two plates, which they carried to a free table. As he passed near the orchestra Arner's foot brushed the enormous mass of the base viol, which vibrated for some seconds. Arner glanced around for Dr. Smith, but did not see him. And he reflected: "This party alone cost eight hundred and twenty-three dollars and twenty cents. If Miss Slingsby's money were invested, it could earn substantial profits. For the sanatorium patients, of course."

On the terrace the night appeared to be more dense. Outside the enclosure things were black and remote.

"You know," Matilda remarked with a rather childlike coquetry,

"I wish this night could be longer than the others. As long as some nights I knew before coming to the sanatorium. An interminable night, shall we say?"

"Oh," said Arner with alarm.

"There are long nights and short nights. Some can last ten hours, twenty hours, two weeks. And more. I believe there could be a night without end."

Arner listened with misgiving and said nothing. Matilda was gazing at an ice cube on the tablecloth. Its angles decomposed the light and blue, rose, and green tints appeared. The table lamp had a shade with red and black designs. Arner spun it around to see the complete figure of one of those birds the Indians weave into their rugs and paint on ceramic objects. Arner was realizing that the calls of the universe for hope had led her on to the "infinite night." Such exaltations were contagious. And he said, prudently straying from the subject:

"That bird on the lampshade is not the storm thunderbird, because if it were it would have the form of a cross and be a front view with spread wings. This is a profile. See? The Zuñi bird is always a profile, I believe. As painted by the Indians, I mean."

Lowering his voice, he added:

"It looks a little like Dr. Smith, true enough. But the bird of the Zuñis, like the thunderbird, is sacred. All birds are sacred among the Indians because they come down from the sky where the rain is made. In that, their sacredness, they differ from Dr. Smith."

"Don't you believe it. For some patients the director is also sacred and that is understandable, don't you think so, Dr. Arner?"

The orchestra was playing again, but they remained seated at their table. The director was eyeing them from a distance. He no longer had the silver pencil in his mouth.

Pursuing the neutral theme, Arner remarked that the Zuñis have not only abandoned nomadism and the hunting of wild animals, but they also have household gods like the Greeks and Romans do. Before dwelling in a room the Zuñis wait for the Indian lares to bless it. The most important of those lares is the one they call Shalako.

"I can't go into a new house either," she said, "unless somebody else, a relative or friend, is there to receive me. The same thing happens to me as to the Zuñis. But that doesn't matter. I have confidence in things, really. When a serious problem comes up and there seems to be no solution, everything can still be arranged. Everything can always be arranged."

"How?" Arner asked, uneasily.

"Very simple. By making the night longer. Because time is elastic and nothing is easier than to stretch or shrink time."

She said this lightly, looking at the lamp and thinking about the profile of the Zuñi bird.

Just then Miss Slingsby's former chauffeur came up to invite Matilda to dance. Arner thought: "Dr. Smith has sent him over to keep Matilda from being too long with me, or with the same person, at least." But it was not true. Dr. Smith himself came over shortly and sat down at Arner's table. Matilda and the chauffeur were dancing.

"Have you talked to Mrs. Strolheim about her husband?" asked the director.

"No, no."

Out on the dance floor the chauffeur was saying to his partner:

"I will always come to these dances and my wife will come to those organized for the men. Out of respect to Miss Slingsby's memory. We won't miss a single party. My wife and I have always had the best opinion of you, I want you to know. We never believed you ever tried to poison anybody. Miss Slingsby didn't think so either."

Matilda made a strange movement and broke away from him.

"Maybe," said the chauffeur, "I have stirred up the ashes of your old memories, without meaning to. Please excuse me."

Matilda said that she did not feel well and would prefer to return to Arner's table. The chauffeur accompanied her. She sat down beside the attorney, thinking about her husband Bob who had suffered the effects of the poison she had given him some time back. He suffered the effects, but did not die.

Meanwhile the two men—the director and Arner—were still talking about the Zuñi Indians.

"For the Indians water is also a divine element," said Arner and added, looking at his friend's nose: "And also fishing birds."

Matilda remembered, in spite of the fact that the chauffeur did not believe it, that she had indeed tried to poison both her husbands. But that had happened during her lunar days. Maybe she could be forgiven if what Dr. Arner had told her were true. At that moment they called Dr. Smith from another table and the physician left. The attorney continued with the Indian theme.

At another table nearby a patient was lowering her head and raising her shoulders from time to time with a convulsive movement. Matilda said that the poor dear heard airplanes in the air and thought that they were passing dangerously near her head. Then Mrs. Strolheim fell silent, thinking about her second husband Bob. She had not

received any flowers from him for some time. And she said in a loud
voice:

"He usually sends them to me from the most faraway places. In
special plastic boxes. From Holland, Spain, Turkey."

She sighed and said that her husband had gone somewhere with
his elastic night and a small tube of cyanide of mercury in his pocket,
but he sent her flowers and sometimes books along with the flowers.
She did not read them. She gave them to the sanatorium library and
they wrote her name inside the cover.

"What a calm night!" said Arner.

The moon was now rising over the television antenna and was no
longer yellow but blue.

"Don't think that our beautiful sanatorium is always so calm. If
there were only women, maybe, but there are men and once in a
while something unexpected and terrible happens. For instance, last
year a madman escaped. A friend of mine. Well, although I consider
him a friend of mine, I have never talked to him. Dr. Smith, who is a
little pedantic, says that our friendship is a case of telesympathy. The
madman escaped, misbehaved in some way, and seeing himself pursued hid in the factory you see yonder. Don't you see the smokestack? To flee from the orderlies and police he started climbing up
the spikes in the smokestack until he reached the very top, over two
hundred feet high. When he got up there he stripped and there he
was, cool as a cucumber, sometimes seated, sometimes standing.
Leaning on the lightning rod. The poor fellow could not flee horizontally as they would have caught him at once with their automo-
biles and motorcyles, and so he tried to escape vertically by climbing
up the smokestack. But vertical flight isn't for living beings, is it? It's
only for the dead. He stayed on top of that smokestack for three
days. Meanwhile the factory couldn't operate because they didn't
want to suffocate him with the smoke. And the whole city talked
about the case, in the streets, restaurants, churches. Yes, in the
churches, too. They photographed him and published the pictures in
the papers."

She had one of the pictures, but only the negative. And suddenly
she decided to show it to Arner. "You'll see." She took out of her
purse a sheet of dark film and handed it to him. Arner held it against
the light. The chimney top was visible and on top a small nude man
leaning on the lightning rod. Naked, up so high, the madman
looked like the statue of Neptune with his trident. "It's like the
counterfigure of Bob," she said. "See? Behind him all the infinite

night." And this she said with a great complacency. "Although Bob didn't have the night behind but in front of him," she added.

Arner was surprised and somewhat to blame, he felt, for Mrs. Strolheim's excitement, with the counterfigure of Bob and the infinite night. A patient passing by bent over Arner's hand, which was resting on the edge of the table. She acted as if she were going to kiss it, but she merely gazed at it closely and attentively. Then she said: "The veins."

"Don't pay any attention," said Matilda. "It's a game. An innocent game. I'm thinking about what you said before. I believe you're right. Maybe if I had had a son things would have been different. And now I would not be ill. But I think Bob is sterile. Flying at great heights makes some pilots sterile, understand? But, do you see the counterfigure of Bob in the picture? Don't you see it?"

She showed it to him again. Arner wanted to distract her and started making trivial observations. For example, that in the land of Cibola there were more painters per square mile than any place else on earth. Furthermore, there was a desert with a sphinx. The sphinx was a stone camel to the left of the highway going north from Santa Fe. A camel made by natural erosion. The peculiar characteristics of Cibola did not end there, however. The dogs of the Indians spend day and night burying bones for the anthropologists of the future—Matilda snickered. Indians sometimes have three names: one Spanish, another Indian, and another English, and they carefully conceal all three—she laughed more openly. Strangers their first year in Cibola learn six Spanish words which they pronounce in French. Finally the second year they buy a guitar. She laughed outright at this and Arner felt gratified. "I'm a skillful man," he reflected, although modestly.

But Matilda forgot about these pleasantries and was gazing at the top of the enclosed grating above the balustrade, thinking: "They've put up that grating to keep me from jumping off head first down into the street." And she felt grateful to the administration for its foresight.

Mr. Arner wanted to go back to his joking and his definitions of Cibola: "This is the most cosmopolitan state in the union. Here one can find Spaniards, Englishmen, Argentinians, Frenchmen, Canadians, Russian exiles, Italians, Greeks. And even people from Brooklyn."

This, said with comical emphasis, made Matilda smile still, but the first effect had worn off. And she was brooding: "Bob hasn't sent me any flowers for exactly eighteen days." Arner wanted to return to his jesting:

"Do you know how to dance the Varsoviana, Mrs. Strolheim?"

"No."

"Have you ever seen a saucer fly, in other words, a flying saucer?"

"No, I haven't, doctor."

"Did you ever pass a truck in the highway carrying an atomic bomb?"

"I don't know. You know we almost never leave the sanatorium."

But Bob was on her mind and she could not see any connection between her own presence in the sanatorium and the poison mentioned by her recent dancing partner. When she attempted it she wrinkled her brow, thinking: "Why was I going to do a thing like that to Bob? To my first husband, I understand, but why on earth to Bob?"

Still mulling this over she removed the shade from the lamp with the pretext of putting it on at a better angle and the harsh light fell on both their faces. She was motionless for a short while as if posing for her portrait. A moth struck against the electric bulb with a slight tinkling sound. Her eyes were fixed on something above the head of the attorney whose face in the harsh light had the color of a sweet potato. Just to be doing something Arner picked up the negative and held it against the light. She seemed to wake up and started talking again about the fugitive madman:

"He climbed up that distant smokestack. Don't you see it? From here you can see it, way over there above the neon lights. And the firemen made him come down. Meanwhile the factory was paralyzed and then the workers demanded their wages and went on strike. That man caused great confusion in the city. And behind the photo, you see?"

Arner thought, surprised: "Yes, behind, the infinite night. On the other hand, Bob had it in front of him." He turned his chair sideways, facing the dance floor. Between Matilda and the girls around them he was becoming aware of subtle relationships. One of them also removed the lampshade, leaving the bulb uncovered. At the next table another did likewise. They all wanted to have the light in their faces.

Arner was puzzled. He wanted to dance again and the girl rose indolently. Always girls who go to dances rise indolently.

Arner asked Matilda why she didn't get a copy of the picture, and she said she preferred the negative with the body black and hair and eyes white. She continued talking and it was evident that the subject obsessed her:

"He is on the other side of the sanatorium, in the men's pavilion, on the fourth floor. He has only seen me once and from a distance. During the lunar days when I fall into the black well he knows, from far away, what's happening to me and in his pavilion he starts howling and moaning. They have to tie him up and put him in a padded cell, like they do to me. Even so his screams are heard all over the sanatorium at night. The doctors don't understand. That's the bad thing about medicine. You doctors fix up everything with drugs, baths and injections, but you can't understand. About what happens to us women, you don't understand a thing. Pardon me for talking like this. I say so thinking of the doctors who work in the sanatorium."

All the table lamps were now shadeless. Supposing that the medical director was following them with his fishing bird's look, he avoided holding Matilda too close. And as they danced she was saying:

"The more I think about it the more convinced I am that maybe I could be the mother of that creature the planet needs. But it would be more difficult than you realize. With Bob, I mean, because Bob is far away. Always far away. Of course they do artificial insemination now but even so . . ."

At that moment her white shawl caught on the hard twigs of a boxwood sphere. One of those potted shrubs stood at each corner of the dance floor. They stopped to disentangle it and then began dancing again. Over Matilda's shoulder Arner could see the physician seated, smoking. He was exhaling the smoke in wide clouds that rose slowly above the terrace wall where they were torn apart and dissolved in the breeze. Arner asked Matilda, referring to the man on the smokestack:

"What did he do before coming to the sanatorium?"

"He was an engineer, I believe. A generating engineer," she replied tranquilly.

In the glare of the naked electric bulbs the patients' faces changed expression, according to the music. With the bolero they all became dreamy.

"Do you believe," she asked, "that the man on the smokestack could be the right father? To create the new being humanity is waiting for, I mean."

"Ah, that . . . one never knows. That is a mystery."

Arner fell silent and she said:

"Everything is a mystery. Bob knows how to make the nights elastic. I'm serious. Nights fifty and sixty hours long. And even longer. I understand this is hard for you to believe, but I can explain it, if you like."

The music stopped and they returned to their table.

"Do you want me to explain it to you?"

The electric bulbs had been covered with their shades again. Before Arner could answer Matilda, a nurse approached saying:

"You are wanted on the telephone."

There were vases on some tables, and in each vase a flower. On the piano was another and very large vase, but empty. Matilda hated empty vases and was staring at that one, sometimes uncomfortably.

Arner answered the telephone. It was his wife asking him not to be late. Arner returned to the terrace and, his back to the street, leaned against the balustrade, for Mrs. Strolheim was not where he had left her. He thought of the explanations she had given him about the elasticity of the night, and then he started making new calculations regarding the beauty mask business. Again he wondered if the use of such masks would not in the end produce neuroses.

Matilda hastened to his side, speaking very animatedly:

"Don't run away, doctor. I was thinking about the contradictions on this terrace. Don't you agree? There are rugs as in a bedroom and wild storms too, I would say. But talk to me because a man dressed in black is looking my way, as if he wanted to come over. He must be a protestant minister and I don't like any kind of priests for dancing. They're too good and I'm afraid of them. I don't know how to talk to those men."

She had a piece of toast in one hand and her fine small teeth were making a crunching sound. A sound that habitually annoyed Arner because in it he heard something like the inner resonance of the skull Such an allusion to the non-erotic anatomy of a woman was an offense to her. However, the crunching toast did not echo inside Matilda's skull and was not unpleasant.

She offered him the negative and once more Arner looked at it against the light and remarked that the man was handsome. Matilda smiled:

"He wrote me a love letter."

She took a folded paper out of her purse saying that she had made a copy to send to Bob, since she did not wish to keep secrets of any kind from him. In the end Bob had not divorced her. Arner said nothing and Matilda, seeing Miss Slingsby's chauffeur pass by, re-called his remarks to her as they were dancing. And she felt the need to talk: "You can poison a man, but that's not deceiving him, is it?" She said this hoping for Arner's reaction, but he was at a loss for words. Then Matilda gave him the letter where the man on the smokestack spoke to her about the "fountain mother," the "circle of origins," the "capital breath" and the "cordial breath." Matilda was the nucleus of the cosmic night. And she said to Arner:

"It's a strange language. How to answer him? I don't know how to write such things. You could answer him with your theory of the needs of the universe."

For a moment Arner thought that Matilda might be mocking him. The music stopped. A paper blown by the wind brushed against the strings of the violincello, making them vibrate. Arner saw Dr. Smith in the distance and suddenly decided to treat Matilda naturally and without any precaution whatsoever. As if she were a normal woman. Maybe she was.

"I knew your husband, Bob Strolheim," he told her. "We were good friends at college."

But she did not answer. Her silence again made Arner feel that he was in a false situation. A cement terrace on top of a hospital is al-ways a little bit out of this world. He asked Matilda if she had actu-ally been in love with either of her husbands.

"With Bob," she answered without hesitation.

And she added that she was going to explain how Bob, who was truly a genius, lengthened the night whenever he wished. First she told him the rather painful circumstances of her disagreement with her first husband. About her break with him. More than painful they were dramatic. Or tragic. That is to say, tragi-grotesque.

On a summer afternoon two years ago Bob had been waiting for her in a hotel bar. At the time he was trying out jet planes. Thanks to his fortune, and to a special authorization of the AAF, he had one of the latest models, which he kept in a private hangar. With that plane he could fly over one thousand miles an hour easily and this was the luxury of his life.

Before being secluded in the sanatorium Matilda—she herself said so—was violent, eccentric and confused. Suddenly she would break off relations with a girl friend because, as she said, she had discovered that her friend had the feet of a dead person. Or that the expression on her friend's lips did not match that of her eyes when she smiled. She was married to her first husband and hated him, but she was faithful. Although she met Bob under equivocal circumstances, there was no adultery. The only liberty she ever took was to speak ill of her husband, but this was not so ominous because, as she said, adulterous wives do just the opposite. They speak well of their husbands to everybody, especially their lovers.

Among other extravagant things, Matilda told Bob that when her husband became tender he smelled of asphalt, and that he had a sense of prudence which she found intolerable.

That memorable night in the hotel bar Matilda arrived and said to Bob:

"Don't speak to me, Bob. Be still and wait till I'm more calm. Then I'll talk to you. Don't ask me anything."

Bob, the athletic and serious, almost taciturn, man, looked at her, thinking once more: "Nothing's wrong with her. Nerves. She hates her husband but doesn't divorce him. I wonder why she doesn't divorce him?"

Matilda, glancing at her sanatorium companions, was musing: "They all know I'm only periodically insane and that the rest of the time I'm well behaved. And they envy me, and they're right, because it's as if I lived in two different countries."

Again she remembered that night in the bar with Bob, while still married to her first husband. After a sip of cognac she asked:

"Don't you notice anything strange about me, Bob?"

She took out her cigarette case, opened it, hesitated a moment, closed it again, evidently deciding not to smoke, and added:

"Don't look at me, for I'm going to say something barbarous. I believe I've killed him, my husband I mean. Don't say anything to me yet. Don't speak to me, please."

On the sanatorium terrace she reflected: "All these men who have come to the party have their past, too. Arner, among them. Mine is more distant, even though I am so young. It's more distant because they say I'm mad." Then she returned to the scene in the bar.

Bob stood up, left two bills on the table and said:

"Let's go somewhere else. Let's get out of here, but be calm."

It was useless advice because she was calm. Now also on the terrace of the sanatorium she was calm. She looked at the sky and thought of the infinite night.

They left the bar. Something odd was happening. Bob began telling himself that Matilda was quite capable of having killed her husband. "If so," it suddenly dawned on him, "I'm going to lose her before I've made her mine." This gave him a certain dejected feeling.

It was hot that night, but the air is dry and light in the nights of

Cibola. They climbed into the car and by the avenue running parallel to the river they drove down to a little desert. On the sanatorium terrace Matilda recalled that this night, which later became elastic, was for the moment very rigid. That's the way it seemed to her, at least.

She said to Bob:

"I've killed him, but when the police find out I won't be alive. I am determined to kill myself before morning."

She opened her purse and showed him the revolver with a very short barrel and a very wide breech. The cartridges were intact. Incredulous Bob asked:

"Your husband . . . is he dead?" She nodded. "And you say you killed him? But how did you kill him?"

Matilda said that her husband took two pills before going to bed every day. That night instead of those he ordinarily took, she had put two others on the table, from a bottle marked with a double poison sign. The pills looked the same and he took them. They were not pills, however, but capsules. Matilda justified herself in a shocking manner:

"I swear to you that I could stand no more, Bob. I looked at my husband and felt the roots of my hair turn cold. When I returned home at night he would say to me, smiling in a horrible way: 'Did you have fun, Matty?' He never said Matilda but Matty, which does not suit me because that's the nickname for Martha. When he wanted to feel protecting he caressed me with his open hand, patting me on the back the way he would a dog. And sometimes he moved his left ear like a cat. But he was not a cat or a dog either. He belonged to another species, to one of those species they call extinguished. Or extinct. Don't they say extinct?"

Bob nodded uncomprehending and she went on:

"Besides he had secret vices. He never drank anything but boiled water. Do you believe that a man who never drinks anything but boiled water can be honest? A type like that is hiding some moral deformity, that's what I say. In short, whatever happened, it's done now and can't be helped. I know that if they catch me I am lost, but they won't catch me. And in any case, I don't care. Don't you believe I've lived long enough?"

"How long?"

"Twenty-one years."

That had been the most dramatic night in Matilda's life. And she remembered it as she watched Dr. Smith, who also resembled those examples of extinct species, walking around the terrace. The orchestra was playing softly and Matilda returned to the unforgettable night without the slightest sensation of guilt. She put the revolver back in her purse and said to Bob: "If you had a memory you would recall what we talked about one day. We were talking about my husband and you asked: 'Why don't you divorce him?' What did I answer? Do you remember what I answered?"

Bob was looking for a place with a public telephone. When he found it he stopped the car, got out and called Matilda's home. After the second ring the husband answered. His voice revealed nothing beyond the indolence of a man who has taken the trouble to drop his newspaper to answer the telephone. Twice he repeated: "Who is it?" Bob, holding his breath, slowly hung up the receiver without saying a word and returned to the car, filled with doubts. He repeated what had happened. She asked:

"A man's voice?" Bob nodded. "It must have been the police. Or some neighbor. That means they already know. When he felt bad he must have gone to the stairs calling for help."

The car was racing along a broad avenue where blue and violet fluorescent lights had recently been installed.

"Where are we going?" she asked.

"To my house."

"No, not to your house, Bob. You know that."

Matilda's moral sense was indeed original. She could poison a husband but go to Bob's bachelor apartment, that she could not do.

Recalling all this, Matilda paid attention to the silence on the terrace, a silence fraught with nerves. "If I screamed," she thought, "all the women would scream."

In her memories she returned to the spot in the city suburbs where she had been with Bob. The river ran close by and on that side the bank was over fifty feet high. The moon was full. "That's the difference," said Matilda. "Now I can look at the moon. When I have committed suicide and am dead, the moon will look at me."

After a slight pause she suddenly exclaimed:

"I am not to blame for everything that happened."

"Then who is?"

"My husband."

"Why?"

"Because he told me one or two weeks ago that those tablets caused almost instant death."

"Let's get this straight. Were they pills, capsules or tablets?"

"You're right. Tablets. Anyway, it's too late now, and this must be the last night of my life. You know me and you also know that I am not saying this just to be talking. There's only one thing I would like: for this night to last a little longer than the others, since it is the last one in my life. I can't bear the idea of the sun's coming up in a few hours. I don't want to see it. I don't want to be alive when the daylight appears. Have you noticed how ugly people are in the sunlight? Their wide foolish faces, with hairs in their noses. By daylight the streets, houses, cities, too, are ugly. Everywhere there are a thousand horrible little things: dead men in elevators. Dead and standing. Strange things that walk on all fours and bark. And a lot of poverty with a clean shirt. And a lot of hatred."

"Also a little love, Matilda. Also a great deal of love, I would say."

"Everything is dusty and dry and dirty. Or too bright. Haven't you noticed? Little trivial things to make you laugh and suffer at the same time. Haven't you seen those streets with rubber patches on the sidewalk? And people recently shaved with sleep-swollen faces? Haven't you noticed that people are uglier in the summertime than in winter? They all have too fat ankles and pimply noses. I'll be gone before daylight. I don't want to see those things again. But I would like for the night to be longer, I wish this night would last for two or three days, because I am rather cowardly and afraid of suicide. No more afraid than anybody else. Anyway, I will do it."

With the drowsy tone he was wont to use for important revelations, Bob said:

"Listen, Matilda, I can make this night last as long as you wish. Six hours? A hundred? How long do you want me to stretch out the night for you and put off the hour of dawn, dear?"

"This is no time for joking, Bob."

She was far from imagining, she told herself there on the terrace, that Bob was serious. She recalled that they crossed over a rather high bridge, and that on one side there was a sign which read: "Throwing objects into the river prohibited."

That night long ago Bob had the sudden idea that Matilda could be right, and that in spite of everything her husband was dead. The man who answered the telephone must have been a policeman or neighbor.

"To those who are about to die," he said solemnly, "you give whatever they wish. I can give it to you, my darling. I mean it. How many hours do you want me to add to the night?"

Bob accelerated as if in a hurry to arrive somewhere and on passing a drug store he stopped, saying that he wanted to buy something.

But again he went to the telephone and called Matilda's home. This time nobody answered and he was really frightened.

Nevertheless as he took the wheel again he muttered:

"Listen, darling. And if there were no crime?"

"How many times do I have to tell you? If he isn't dead yet, he will die. That doesn't keep me," she added hastily, "from being an honest woman. I have never offended my husband. To kill a man is not to offend him, is it?"

Then she repeated that she would commit suicide that very night. Bob looked up at the sky:

"Don't worry," he said, "there's no sign of dawn yet."

They went to the airport, which she always insisted on calling air course instead of airport. Everybody there knew Bob. He signed some papers in an office with a strange swiftness and without paying any attention to Matilda. Then a passport, which he took from a leather jacket kept in a cupboard, was duly stamped and signed.

When he appeared to have forgotten Matilda, he put his arm around her and led her to a kind of wardrobe beside the hangars. There he had her put on an uncomfortable, coarse jacket. Soon they were installed in the plane which took off. "This is something I hadn't counted on," Matilda commented. Bob reminded her that it was not the first time she had flown with him. "That isn't what I meant," she admonished.

The airplane rose. Immediately they were flying above the clouds which they could see underneath illumined by the moon. She said: "Maybe my husband is dead and his ghost is wandering around up here." Bob, in a less lugubrious mood, repeated:

"The night will be as long as you wish."

Underneath them the earth was a confused mass, the cities looked like small handfuls of yellow, white, and green lights.

They reached San Francisco before midnight. It was still eleven o'clock there. The mechanics refueled the plane. Matilda was excited by the adventure and Bob asked her:

"Do you want to rest?"

He was referring to the rest rooms. She said no and they returned to the plane. Matilda remarked: "I've heard there are Chinese in San Francisco, but I don't see any."

Again they were airborne, over the sea.

"I don't know what all this is for," she remarked.

"Yes, you do," he said. "Now we're on our way to Honolulu."

They were flying very high and Bob had her put on a mask connected to a tank of compressed oxygen. The taciturn Bob then initiated one of those monosyllabic dialogues which were his specialty.

"All right?"

"Yes."

"Dizzy?"

"No."

"Your ears?"

"All right."

"What are you thinking of?"

"Nothing."

"Really nothing?"

"Really, why?"

Bob sighed:

"No matter. I'm thinking for both of us."

They reached Honolulu in less than three hours and as they climbed out of the plane Bob again asked Matilda: "Do you want to rest?"

"No," she answered, slightly impatient.

In Honolulu it was not yet midnight. "Here," Matilda noted, "are dark-skinned women with low buttocks who wiggle their hips when they dance, but I don't see any." Her remark about the low buttocks made Bob laugh.

In Honolulu Matilda had the impression that the night had begun to expand like the cupola of an immense umbrella. It was six o'clock by her watch, with still no sign of dawn.

They ate a light supper at the airport bar before returning to the plane. Matilda drank only a sip of mineral water. She drank nothing alcoholic because she wanted to be wide awake and alert when the final instant arrived. That's what she said.

The next stop was in the Marshall Islands. It was terribly hot and they shed so much clothing they were almost nude. Seeing her awake, fresh and vigorous, and without fatigue or drowsiness, Bob decided that she owed half her beauty to her excellent health. The healthiness of a precious animal. Bob felt highly stimulated and filled with hope. She repeated: "It's obscenely hot." This expression, which she had learned from a waitress in the bar, appealed to her.

They reached Luzon in the Philippines. People dressed neatly in white and, according to Matilda, had turtle eyes. They all seemed affable and polite, but Matilda thought that they stared at her too hard.

Then Calcutta, in India. Here they had difficulties because the police asked for Matilda's passport which, naturally, she did not have. Uncomfortably she said: "What are these people looking for?" Bob whispered in her ear: "Maybe they suspect you."

"But why? Whatever I've done in my own country is my affair and is nobody's business, much less theirs with their absurd laws. They are laws for coolies who speak with an Oxford accent. That's incongruent."

It was still midnight. By Matilda's watch it was three in the afternoon and yet it was midnight, just as in the Philippines.

They flew to Karachi and then on to Cairo. In Karachi Matilda saw Americans dressed in shorts like the English wear. Matilda observed: "In this country they used to cremate the widow along with the body of her husband." In her remark about cremation a great respect for the country was apparent. Back in the plane Bob returned—he seemed to be sleepy—to his short-phrased dialogues:

"Shall we wait for the dawn here?" he asked. "Or do you still mean to kill yourself?"

"Yes. Before sun-up."

"All right. Then the sun will never come up."

"And who are you to keep the sun from rising?" she asked, offended.

Bob turned his head, burst out laughing—just a little chortle— and kissed her. Then he became taciturn again.

When they reached Cairo it was twelve five. The night was broad and stretchable, still. They had been flying for thirteen hours and always it was midnight. The dawn did not appear. Bob's airplane pulled the night and spread it over the planet. In Cairo the police also questioned Matilda. She refused to answer without the presence of her lawyer. Or so she said. They left her alone on realizing that the plane was about to take off for the Sahara. Matilda continued as fresh as a rose of Alexandria, a city over which they flew.

In Tunis only Bob left the plane, because Matilda was sleepy and distrusted the Arabs who, according to her, were treacherous and sanguinary. She called them "Tuaregs," acting as if she knew everything there was to be known on the subject. Bob gave Matilda a long kiss, but she pushed him away saying she had the impression that her husband was peering through the windows in the cabin roof and making remarks.

"What?"

"Practical things. The names of the hotels and their prices. The exchange rate of money and the maximum and minimum temperature."

"How strange in a dead man!"

"That's what husbands usually say, dead or alive."

When they reached Lisbon it was only twelve forty by the airport clock. Matilda liked what she saw from there and wanted to go into the city, but Bob refused. "If we go," he said, "the dawn will trap you there, the light of day, I mean, and you know what will happen." But just in case he asked:

"Or have you changed your mind?"

"About suicide? No."

They flew to the Azores, and from there to Bermuda and St. Louis, and finally Cibola again. Always it was night. There they were in the city where Matilda believed she had killed her husband. Flexing his numb legs, Bob declared:

"What do you think of that? We've been flying for twenty-four hours now without ever seeing daylight."

He started giving instructions for continuing the flight and said to Matilda:

"We'll continue on to Seattle and from there we'll go to Japan in a direct flight. I can keep on giving you an elastic night, an interminable night. But don't you want to rest?"

She said yes and went to the rest room. When she returned she expressed a rather unexpected desire. Timidly she said that she would like to go to her house for a moment, in other words, to the scene of the crime.

Bob looked for a telephone and called her husband for the third time. The "dead" man answered immediately. Bob announced their call—of the two of them—and the husband seemed surprised but not displeased. His tone was affable.

When they reached Matilda's house her husband was wearing pajamas and gray bathrobe with a green print and his hair was tousled. Matilda looked at him, absolutely nonplussed, and the husband began mixing highballs:

"I was worried," he said with a natural calm, "because Matty took the revolver, but I see that everything has gone well, fortunately."

She opened her purse and there was a moment of stupefaction in both men when they saw her with the revolver in her hand. But Bob took the gun and handed it to the husband who, gesticulating with it, said to his wife:

"May I ask where you have been, my dear?"

"We have made a trip around the world,' she said with an innocent expression.

"You see?" commented the husband, addressing Bob.

Bob thought he detected a whiff of asphalt. He confirmed Matilda's words, stating that they had just flown around the planet. The husband looked at both of them with a perturbed expression.

"Well, in any case you know, my dear, that I can give you a divorce whenever you wish," he said, more affable than ever.

While he was speaking Bob thought he saw his left ear move. The three of them were standing and laughing foolishly. The husband added several amiable and vague phrases, which Bob answered in the same tone, and shortly afterward Matilda said that she was ready to leave and went out leading Bob by the hand.

In a few minutes they were at the bar. They sat down at their usual table, almost in the dark. "I'm worried," she remarked. "It must not be easy to divorce a dead man."

"But your husband is alive!"

"Ah," she said, "that's what you think."

Bob felt sure that the poisoning had been a trick of the husband. He had wanted to try out Matilda and see how far her dangerousness would go. He put two harmless tablets in the cyanide tube and warned his wife to be careful with them, as they would cause instant death. A trick of daring prudence indeed. It turned out all right, that is to say, badly.

Bob took Matilda's hand and asked her:

"Will you come to my house, now?"

Before replying Matilda remembered the tablets. She did not answer. Bob was meditating, stirring his whiskey with a swizzle stick.

On the sanatorium terrace Matilda was dancing again with Arner, unable to recall anything more. There it all ended. That is to say, she vaguely supposed that she had married Bob, and then he became ill, and scandalous and unpleasant things happened to her. The only thing she knew for certain was that Bob was not coming to see her at the sanatorium, although he sent her flowers and books from New York, Florida, Bermuda, and even from Paris. The flowers from Paris seemed to bring with them some kind of intelligent roguishness.

The music on the terrace stopped and they returned to their table. Matilda glanced up at the sky frequently and a neighbor came up to her and said:

"The plane will not come."

"What plane?" she asked a little frightened.

Arner smiled and also looked at the sky. The night was turning cold and some of the patients were retiring, accompanied by nurses. Matilda's paper napkin slipped off her lap and Arner bent over to pick it up. In the spaces between the rugs the floor of red stone slabs looked hardened and meteorized. They stood up and went over to the balustrade nearest the orchestra.

They saw a woman enter the terrace with uncertain steps, walk over to a table, take a glass of orangeade and leave again, after bowing slightly to Matilda. Matilda explained:

"The poor dear's on the fourth floor. Did you notice how she walks? Sideways. She was born that way, they say. Like that, diagonally. One might say she lives a diagonal life."

Matilda began talking about Bob, who still loved her, she said, in spite of their separation. Arner felt that it must be easy to love this woman. Again she asked:

"Now do you understand about the infinite night?"

"Yes."

"You believed it was madness. I thought that everything about the exceptional man who can redeem the universe was madness, too, and nevertheless I realize that it is possible. Isn't it?"

"Yes, of course."

"And I am the potential mother. Isn't that what you call it?"

Arner gazed at the television antenna on the roof, in the form of an S. It looked like Miss Slingsby's initial.

Again the orchestra was playing and several couples were dancing. Near the entrance the sanatorium director and several nurses were examining a small notebook.

"Dr. Smith must be talking about my lunar calendar," Matilda commented, smiling. "Maybe the black days are approaching. Know something? Just before each crisis I can feel my own skeleton vibrating like the wires on telephone poles. Haven't you heard those wires vibrating out in the country on windy days?"

No sooner had Matilda said this than she began imitating the humming of the telephone lines. Then the humming increased until it became a sad lowing. A great and sorrowful lowing. An immense, desolate and muffled bellowing, like that of a calving cow.

Two nurses came running with Dr. Smith to lead Matilda away, but without violence, as if she were a delicate child. She turned to glance back at the attorney who was also feeling—he acknowledged later—his own bare skeleton, dry and vibrating.

On the terrace the dancing continued.

*Translated from the Spanish by Florence Sender*

# Jorge-Luis Borges

## TLÖN, UQBAR, ORBIS TERTIUS

I owe the discovery of Uqbar to the conjunction of a mirror and an encyclopedia. The mirror troubled the depths of a corridor in a country house on Gaona Street in Ramos Mejía; the encyclopedia is fallaciously called *The Anglo-American Cyclopaedia* (New York, 1917) and is a literal but delinquent reprint of the *Encyclopaedia Britannica* of 1902. The event took place some five years ago. Bioy Casares had had dinner with me that evening and we became lengthily engaged in a vast polemic concerning the composition of a novel in the first person, whose narrator would omit or disfigure the facts and indulge in various contradictions which would permit a few readers—very few readers—to perceive an atrocious or banal reality. From the remote depths of the corridor, the mirror spied upon us. We discovered (such a discovery is inevitable in the late hours of the night) that mirrors have something monstrous about them. Then Bioy Casares recalled that one of the heresiarchs of Uqbar had declared that mirrors and copulation are abominable, because they increase the number of men. I asked him the origin of this memorable observation and he answered that it was reproduced in *The Anglo-American Cyclopaedia*, in its article on Uqbar. The house (which we had rented furnished) had a set of this work. On the last pages of Volume XLVI we found an article on Upsala; on the first pages of Volume XLVII, one on Ural-Altaic Languages, but not a word about Uqbar. Bioy, a bit taken aback, consulted the volumes of the index. In vain he exhausted all of the imaginable spellings: Ukbar, Ucbar, Ooqbar, Ookbar, Oukbahr . . . Before leaving, he told me that it was a region of Iraq or of Asia Minor. I must confess that I agreed with some discomfort. I conjectured that this undocumented country and its anonymous heresiarch were a fiction devised by Bioy's modesty in order to justify a statement. The fruitless examination of one of Justus Perthes' atlases fortified my doubt.

The following day, Bioy called me from Buenos Aires. He told me he had before him the article on Uqbar, in Volume XLVI of the encyclopedia. The heresiarch's name was not forthcoming, but there was a note on his doctrine, formulated in words almost identical to those he had repeated, though perhaps literarily inferior. He had recalled: *Copulation and mirrors are abominable.* The text of the encyclopedia said: *For one of those gnostics, the visible universe was an illusion or (more precisely) a sophism. Mirrors and fatherhood are abominable because they multiply and disseminate that universe.* I told him, in all truthfulness, that I should like to see that article. A few days later he brought it. This surprised me, since the scrupulous cartographical indices of Ritter's *Erdkunde* were plentifully ignorant of the name Uqbar.

The tome Bioy brought was, in fact, Volume XLVI of the *Anglo-American Cyclopaedia*. On the half-title page and the spine, the alphabetical marking (Tor-Ups) was that of our copy, but, instead of 917, it contained 921 pages. These four additional pages made up the article on Uqbar, which (as the reader will have noticed) was not indicated by the alphabetical marking. We later determined that there was no other difference between the volumes. Both of them (as I believe I have indicated) are reprints of the tenth *Encyclopaedia Britannica*. Bioy had acquired his copy at some sale or other.

We read the article with some care. The passage recalled by Bioy was perhaps the only surprising one. The rest of it seemed very plausible, quite in keeping with the general tone of the work and (as is natural) a bit boring. Reading it over again, we discovered beneath its rigorous prose a fundamental vagueness. Of the fourteen names which figured in the geographical part, we only recognized three—Khorasan, Armenia, Erzerum—interpolated in the text in an ambiguous way. Of the historical names, only one: the impostor magician Smerdis, invoked more as a metaphor. The note seemed to fix the boundaries of Uqbar, but its nebulous reference points were rivers and craters and mountain ranges of that same region. We read, for example, that the lowlands of Tsai Khaldun and the Axa Delta marked the southern frontier and that on the islands of the delta wild horses procreate. All this, on the first part of page 918. In the historical section (page 920) we learned that as a result of the religious persecutions of the thirteenth century, the orthodox believers sought refuge on these islands, where to this day their obelisks remain and where it is not uncommon to unearth their stone mirrors. The section on Language and Literature was brief. Only one trait is worthy of recollection: it noted that the literature of Uqbar was one of fantasy and that its epics and legends never referred to reality, but to the two imaginary regions of Mlejnas and Tlön . . . The bibliography enumerated four volumes which we have not yet found, though the third—Silas Haslam: *History of the Land Called Uqbar*, 1874—figures in the catalogues of Bernard Quaritch's book shop.[1] The first, *Lesbare und lesenswerthe Bemerkungen über das Land Ukkbar in Klein-Asien*, dates from 1641 and is the work of Johannes Valentinus Andreä. This fact is significant; a few years later, I came upon that name in the unsuspected pages of De Quincey (*Writings*, Volume XIII) and learned that it belonged to a German theologian who, in the early seventeenth century, described the imaginary community of Rosae Crucis—a community that others founded later, in imitation of what he had prefigured.

That night we visited the National Library. In vain we exhausted atlases, catalogues, annuals of geographical societies, travelers' and historians' memoirs: no one had ever been in Uqbar. Neither did the general index of Bioy's encyclopedia register that name. The following day, Carlos Mastronardi (to whom I had related the matter) noticed the black and gold covers of the *Anglo-American Cyclopaedia* in a bookshop on Corrientes and Talcahuano . . . He entered and examined Volume XLVI. Of course, he did not find the slightest indication of Uqbar.

II

Some limited and waning memory of Herbert Ashe, an engineer of the southern railways, persists in the hotel at Adrogué, amongst the effusive honeysuckles and in the illusory depths of the mirrors. In his lifetime, he suffered from unreality, as do so many Englishmen; once dead, he is not even the ghost he was then. He was tall and listless and his tired rectangular beard had once been red. I understand he was a widower, without children. Every few years he would go to England, to visit (I judge from some photographs he showed us) a sundial and a few oaks. He and my father had entered into one of those close (the adjective is excessive) English friendships that begin by excluding confidences and very soon dispense with dialogue. They used to carry out an exchange of books and newspapers and engage in taciturn chess games . . . I remember him in the hotel corridor, with a mathematics book in his hand, sometimes looking at the irrecoverable colors of the sky. One afternoon, we spoke of the duodecimal system of numbering (in which

[1] Haslam has also published *A General History of Labyrinths*.

twelve is written as 10). Ashe said that he was converting some kind
of tables from the duodecimal to the sexagesimal system (in which
sixty is written as 10). He added that the task had been entrusted to
him by a Norwegian, in Rio Grande do Sul. We had known him for
eight years and he had never mentioned his sojourn in that region
. . . We talked of country life, of the *capangas*, of the Brazilian
etymology of the word *gaucho* (which some old Uruguayans still
pronounce *gaúcho*) and nothing more was said—may God forgive
me—of duodecimal functions. In September of 1937 (we were not at
the hotel), Herbert Ashe died of a ruptured aneurysm. A few days
before, he had received a sealed and certified package from Brazil. It
was a book in large octavo. Ashe left it at the bar, where—months
later—I found it. I began to leaf through it and experienced an astonished and airy feeling of vertigo which I shall not describe, for this is
not the story of my emotions but of Uqbar and Tlön and Orbis
Tertius. On one of the nights of Islam called the Night of Nights,
the secret doors of heaven open wide and the water in the jars becomes sweeter; if those doors opened, I would not feel what I felt
that afternoon. The book was written in English and contained 1001
pages. On the yellow leather back I read these curious words which
were repeated on the title page: *A First Encyclopaedia of Tlön. Vol.
XI. Hlaer to Jangr.* There was no indication of date or place. On the
first page and on a leaf of silk paper that covered one of the color
plates there was stamped a blue oval with this inscription: *Orbis Tertius.* Two years before I had discovered, in a volume of a certain
pirated encyclopedia, a superficial description of a nonexistent country; now chance afforded me something more precious and arduous.
Now I held in my hands a vast methodical fragment of an unknown
planet's entire history, with its architecture and its playing cards,
with the dread of its mythologies and the murmur of its languages,
with its emperors and its seas, with its minerals and its birds and its
fish, with its algebra and its fire, with its theological and metaphysi-
cal controversy. And all of it articulated, coherent, with no visible
doctrinal intent or tone of parody.

In the "Eleventh Volume" which I have mentioned, there are
allusions to preceding and succeeding volumes. In an article in the
*N. R. F.* which is now classic, Néstor Ibarra has denied the existence
of those companion volumes; Ezequiel Martínez Estrada and Drieu
La Rochelle have refuted that doubt, perhaps victoriously. The fact is
that up to now the most diligent inquiries have been fruitless. In vain
we have upended the libraries of the two Americas and of Europe.
Alfonso Reyes, tired of these subordinate sleuthing procedures, pro-

poses that we should all undertake the task of reconstructing the many and weighty tomes that are lacking: *ex ungue leonem*. He calculates, half in earnest and half jokingly, that a generation of *tlönistas* should be sufficient. This venturesome computation brings us back to the fundamental problem: Who are the inventors of Tlön? The plural is inevitable, because the hypothesis of a lone inventor— an infinite Leibniz laboring away darkly and modestly—has been unanimously discounted. It is conjectured that this brave new world is the work of a secret society of astonomers, biologists, engineers, metaphysicians, poets, chemists, algebraists, moralists, painters, geometers . . . directed by an obscure man of genius. Individuals mastering these diverse disciplines are abundant, but not so those capable of inventiveness and less so those capable of subordinating that inventiveness to a rigorous and systematic plan. This plan is so vast that each writer's contibution is infinitesimal. At first it was believed that Tlön was a mere chaos, an irresponsible license of the imagination; now it is known that it is a cosmos and that the intimate laws which govern it have been formulated, at least provisionally. Let it suffice for me to recall that the apparent contradictions of the Eleventh Volume are the fundamental basis for the proof that the other volumes exist, so lucid and exact is the order observed in it. The popular magazines, with pardonable excess, have spread news of the zoology and topography of Tlön; I think its transparent tigers and towers of blood perhaps do not merit the continued attention of *all* men. I shall venture to request a few minutes to expound its concept of the universe.

Hume noted for all time that Berkeley's arguments did not admit the slightest refutation nor did they cause the slightest conviction. This dictum is entirely correct in its application to the earth, but entirely false in Tlön. The nations of this planet are congenitally idealist. Their language and the derivations of their language—religion, letters, metaphysics—all presuppose idealism. The world for them is not a concourse of objects in space; it is a heterogeneous series of independent acts. It is successive and temporal, not spatial. There are no nouns in Tlön's conjectural *Ursprache*, from which the "present" languages and the dialects are derived: there are impersonal verbs, modified by monosyllabic suffixes (or prefixes) with an adverbial value. For example: there is no word corresponding to the word "moon," but there is a verb which in English would be "to moon" or "to moonate." "The moon rose above the river" is *hlör u fang axaxaxas mlö*, or literally: "upward behind the on-streaming it mooned."

The preceding applies to the languages of the southern hemisphere. In those of the northern hemisphere (on whose *Ursprache* there is very little data in the Eleventh Volume) the prime unit is not the verb, but the monosyllabic adjective. The noun is formed by an accumulation of adjectives. They do not say "moon," but rather "round airy-light on dark" or "pale-orange-of-the-sky" or any other such combination. In the example selected the mass of adjectives refers to a real object, but this is purely fortuitous. The literature of this hemisphere (like Meinong's subsistent world) abounds in ideal objects, which are convoked and dissolved in a moment, according to poetic needs. At times they are determined by mere simultaneity. There are objects composed of two terms, one of visual and another of auditory character: the color of the rising sun and the faraway cry of a bird. There are objects of many terms: the sun and the water on a swimmer's chest, the vague tremulous rose color we see with our eyes closed, the sensation of being carried along by a river and also by sleep. These second-degree objects can be combined with others; through the use of certain abbreviations, the process is practically infinite. There are famous poems made up of one enormous word. This word forms a *poetic object* created by the author. The fact that no one believes in the reality of nouns paradoxically causes their number to be unending. The languages of Tlön's northern hemisphere contain all the nouns of the Indo-European languages—and many others as well.

It is no exaggeration to state that the classic culture of Tlön comprises only one discipline: psychology. All others are subordinated to it. I have said that the men of this planet conceive the universe as a series of mental processes which do not develop in space but successively in time. Spinoza ascribes to his inexhaustible divinity the attributes of extension and thought; no one in Tlön would understand the juxtaposition of the first (which is typical only of certain states) and the second—which is a perfect synonym of the cosmos. In other words, they do not conceive that the spatial persists in time. The perception of a cloud of smoke on the horizon and then of the burning field and then of the half-extinguished cigarette that produced the blaze is considered an example of association of ideas.

This monism or complete idealism invalidates all science. If we explain (or judge) a fact, we connect it with another; such linking, in Tlön, is a later state of the subject which cannot affect or illuminate the previous state. Every mental state is irreducible: the mere fact of naming it—i.e., of classifying it—implies a falsification. From which it can be deduced that there are no sciences on Tlön, not even reasoning. The paradoxical truth is that they do exist, and in almost uncountable number. The same thing happens with philosophies as happens with nouns in the northern hemisphere. The fact that every philosophy is by definition a dialectical game, a *Philosophie des Als Ob*, has caused them to multiply. There is an abundance of incredible systems of pleasing design or sensational type. The metaphysicians of Tlön do not seek for the truth or even for verisimilitude, but rather for the astounding. They judge that metaphysics is a branch of fantastic literature. They know that a system is nothing more than the subordination of all aspects of the universe to any one such aspect. Even the phrase "all aspects" is rejectable, for it supposes the impossible addition of the present and of all past moments. Neither is it licit to use the plural "past moments," since it supposes another impossible operation . . . One of the schools of Tlön goes so far as to negate time: it reasons that the present is indefinite, that the future has no reality other than as a present hope, that the past has no reality other than as a present memory.[1] Another school declares that *all time* has already transpired and that our life is only the crepuscular and no doubt falsified and mutilated memory or reflection of an irrecoverable process. Another, that the history of the universe—and in it our lives and the most tenuous detail of our lives—is the scripture produced by a subordinate god in order to communicate with a demon. Another, that the universe is comparable to those cryptographs in which not all the symbols are valid and that only what happens every three hundred nights is true. Another, that while we sleep here, we are awake elsewhere and that in this way every man is two men.

Amongst the doctrines of Tlön, none has merited the scandalous reception accorded to materialism. Some thinkers have formulated it with less clarity than fervor, as one might put forth a paradox. In order to facilitate the comprehension of this inconceivable thesis, a heresiarch of the eleventh century [2] devised the sophism of the nine copper coins, whose scandalous renown is in Tlön equivalent to that of the Eleatic paradoxes. There are many versions of this "specious reasoning," which vary the number of coins and the number of discoveries; the following is the most common:

*On Tuesday, X crosses a deserted road and loses nine copper*

---

[1] Russell (*The Analysis of Mind*, 1921, page 159) supposes that the planet has been created a few minutes ago, furnished with a humanity that "remembers" an illusory past.

[2] A century, according to the duodecimal system, signifies a period of a hundred and forty-four years.

*coins. On Thursday, Y finds in the road four coins, somewhat rusted by Wednesday's rain. On Friday, Z discovers three coins in the road. On Friday morning, X finds two coins in the corridor of his house.* The heresiarch would deduce from this story the reality—i.e., the continuity—of the nine coins which were recovered. *It is absurd* (he affirmed) *to imagine that four of the coins have not existed between Tuesday and Thursday, three between Tuesday and Friday afternoon, two between Tuesday and Friday morning. It is logical to think that they have existed—at least in some secret way, hidden from the comprehension of men—at every moment of those three periods.*

The language of Tlön resists the formulation of this paradox; most people did not even understand it. The defenders of common sense at first did no more than negate the veracity of the anecdote. They repeated that it was a verbal fallacy, based on the rash application of two neologisms not authorized by usage and alien to all rigorous thought: the verbs "find" and "lose," which beg the question, because they presuppose the identity of the first and of the last nine coins. They recalled that all nouns (man, coin, Thursday, Wednesday, rain) have only a metaphorical value. They denounced the treacherous circumstance "somewhat rusted by Wednesday's rain," which presupposes what is trying to be demonstrated: the persistence of the four coins from Tuesday to Thursday. They explained that *equality* is one thing and *identity* another, and formulated a kind of *reductio ad absurdum:* the hypothetical case of nine men who on nine successive nights suffer a severe pain. Would it not be ridiculous —they questioned—to pretend that this pain is one and the same?[1] They said that the heresiarch was prompted only by the blasphemous intention of attributing the divine category of *being* to some simple coins and that at times he negated plurality and at other times did not. They argued: if equality implies identity, one would also have to admit that the nine coins are one.

Unbelievably, these refutations were not definitive. A hundred years after the problem was stated, a thinker no less brilliant than the heresiarch but of orthodox tradition formulated a very daring hypothesis. This happy conjecture affirmed that there is only one sub-

---

[1] Today, one of the churches of Tlön Platonically maintains that a certain pain, a certain greenish tint of yellow, a certain temperature, a certain sound, are the only reality. All men, in the vertiginous moment of coitus, are the same man. All men who repeat a line from Shakespeare *are* William Shakespeare.

ject, that this indivisible subject is every being in the universe and that these beings are the organs and masks of the divinity. X is Y and is Z. Z discovers three coins because he remembers that X lost them; X finds two in the corridor because he remembers that the others have been found . . . The Eleventh Volume suggests that three prime reasons determined the complete victory of this idealist pantheism. The first, its repudiation of solipsism; the second, the possibility of preserving the psychological basis of the sciences; the third, the possibility of preserving the cult of the gods. Schopenhauer (the passionate and lucid Schopenhauer) formulates a very similar doctrine in the first volume of *Parerga und Paralipomena*.

The geometry of Tlön comprises two somewhat different disciplines: the visual and the tactile. The latter corresponds to our own geometry and is subordinated to the first. The basis of visual geometry is the surface, not the point. This geometry disregards parallel lines and declares that man in his movement modifies the forms which surround him. The basis of its arithmetic is the notion of indefinite numbers. They emphasize the importance of the concepts of greater and lesser, which our mathematicians symbolize as $>$ and $<$. They maintain that the operation of counting modifies quantities and converts them from indefinite into definite sums. The fact that several individuals who count the same quantity should obtain the same result is, for the psychologists, an example of association of ideas or of a good exercise of memory. We already know that in Tlön the subject of knowledge is one and eternal.

In literary practices the idea of a single subject is also all-powerful. It is uncommon for books to be signed. The concept of plagiarism does not exist: it has been established that all works are the creation of one author, who is atemporal and anonymous. The critics often invent authors: they select two dissimilar works—the *Tao Te Ching* and the *1001 Nights*, say—attribute them to the same writer and then determine most scrupulously the psychology of this interesting *homme de lettres* . . .

Their books are also different. Works of fiction contain a single plot, with all its imaginable permutations. Those of a philosophical nature invariably include both the thesis and the antithesis, the rigorous pro and con of a doctrine. A book which does not contain its counterbook is considered incomplete.

Centuries and centuries of idealism have not failed to influence reality. In the most ancient regions of Tlön, the duplication of lost objects is not infrequent. Two persons look for a pencil; the first finds it and says nothing; the second finds a second pencil, no less real, but closer to his expectations. These secondary objects are called *hrönir* and are, though awkward in form, somewhat longer. Until recently, the *hrönir* were the accidental products of distraction and forgetfulness. It seems unbelievable that their methodical production dates back scarcely a hundred years, but this is what the Eleventh Volume tells us. The first efforts were unsuccessful. However, the *modus operandi* merits description. The director of one of the state prisons told his inmates that there were certain tombs in an ancient river bed and promised freedom to whoever might make an important discovery. During the months preceding the excavation the inmates were shown photographs of what they were to find. This first effort proved that expectation and anxiety can be inhibitory; a week's work with pick and shovel did not manage to unearth anything in the way of a *hrön* except a rusty wheel of a period posterior to the experiment. But this was kept in secret and the process was repeated later in four schools. In three of them the failure was almost complete; in the fourth (whose director died accidentally during the first excavations) the students unearthed—or produced— a gold mask, an archaic sword, two or three clay urns and the moldy and mutilated torso of a king whose chest bore an inscription which it has not yet been possible to decipher. Thus was discovered the unreliability of witnesses who knew of the experimental nature of the search . . . Mass investigations produce contradictory objects; now individual and almost improvised jobs are preferred. The methodical fabrication of *hrönir* (says the Eleventh Volume) has performed prodigious services for archaeologists. It has made possible the interrogation and even the modification of the past, which is now no less plastic and docile than the future. Curiously, the *hrönir* of second and third degree—the *hrönir* derived from another *hrön*, those derived from the *hrön* of a *hrön*—exaggerate the aberrations of the initial one; those of fifth degree are almost uniform; those of ninth degree become confused with those of the second; in those of the eleventh there is a purity of line not found in the original. The process is cyclical: the *hrön* of twelfth degree begins to fall off in quality. Stranger and more pure than any *hrön* is, at times, the *ur*: the object produced through suggestion, educed by hope. The great golden mask I have mentioned is an illustrious example.

Things become duplicated in Tlön; they also tend to become effaced and lose their details when they are forgotten. A classic example is the doorway which survived so long as it was visited by a beggar and disappeared at his death. At times some birds, a horse, have saved the ruins of an amphitheater.

*Postscript (1947).* I reproduce the preceding article just as it appeared in the *Anthology of Fantastic Literature* (1940), with no omission other than that of a few metaphors and a kind of sarcastic summary which now seems frivolous. So many things have happened since then . . . I shall do no more than recall them here.

In March of 1941 a letter written by Gunnar Erfjord was discovered in a book by Hinton which had belonged to Herbert Ashe. The envelope bore a cancellation from Ouro Preto; the letter completely elucidated the mystery of Tlön. Its text corroborated the hypotheses of Martínez Estrada. One night in Lucerne or in London, in the early seventeenth century, the splendid history has its beginning. A secret and benevolent society (amongst whose members were Dalgarno and later George Berkeley) arose to invent a country. Its vague initial program included "hermetic studies," philanthropy and the cabala. From this first period dates the curious book by Andreä. After a few years of secret conclaves and premature syntheses it was understood that one generation was not sufficient to give articulate form to a country. They resolved that each of the masters should elect a disciple who would continue his work. This hereditary arrangement prevailed; after an interval of two centuries the persecuted fraternity sprang up again in America. In 1824, in Memphis (Tennessee), one of its affiliates conferred with the ascetic millionaire Ezra Buckley. The latter, somewhat disdainfully, let him speak —and laughed at the plan's modest scope. He told the agent that in America it was absurd to invent a country and proposed the invention of a planet. To this gigantic idea he added another, a product of his nihilism:[1] that of keeping the enormous enterprise secret. At that time the twenty volumes of the *Encyclopaedia Britannica* were circulating in the United States; Buckley suggested that a methodical encyclopedia of the imaginary planet be written. He was to leave them his mountains of gold, his navigable rivers, his pasture lands roamed by cattle and buffalo, his Negroes, his brothels and his dollars, on one condition: "The work will make no pact with the impostor Jesus Christ." Buckley did not believe in God, but he wanted to demonstrate to this nonexistent God that mortal man was capable of conceiving a world. Buckley was poisoned in Baton Rouge in 1828; in 1914 the society delivered to its collaborators, some three hundred

[1] Buckley was a freethinker, a fatalist and a defender of slavery.

in number, the last volume of the *First Encyclopedia of Tlön*. The edition was a secret one; its forty volumes (the vastest undertaking ever carried out by man) would be the basis for another more detailed edition, written not in English but in one of the languages of Tlön. This revision of an illusory world, was called, provisionally, *Orbis Tertius* and one of its modest demiurgi was Herbert Ashe, whether as an agent of Gunnar Erfjord or as an affiliate, I do not know. His having received a copy of the Eleventh Volume would seem to favor the latter assumption. But what about the others?

In 1942 events became more intense. I recall one of the first of these with particular clarity and it seems that I perceived then something of its premonitory character. It happened in an apartment on Laprida Street, facing a high and light balcony which looked out toward the sunset. Princess Faucigny Lucinge had received her silverware from Poitiers. From the vast depths of a box embellished with foreign stamps, delicate immobile objects emerged: silver from Utrecht and Paris covered with hard heraldic fauna, and a samovar. Amongst them—with the perceptible and tenuous tremor of a sleeping bird—a compass vibrated mysteriously. The Princess did not recognize it. Its blue needle longed for magnetic north; its metal case was concave in shape; the letters around its edge corresponded to one of the alphabets of Tlön. Such was the first intrusion of this fantastic world into the world of reality.

I am still troubled by a stroke of chance which made me the witness of the second intrusion as well. It happened some months later, at a country store owned by a Brazilian in Cuchilla Negra. Amorim and I were returning from Sant' Anna. The River Tacuarembó had flooded and we were obliged to sample (and endure) the proprietor's rudimentary hospitality. He provided us with some creaking cots in a large room cluttered with barrels and hides. We went to bed, but were kept from sleeping until dawn by the drunken ravings of an unseen neighbor, who intermingled inextricable insults with snatches of *milongas*—or rather with snatches of the same *milonga*. As might be supposed, we attributed this insistent uproar to the store owner's fiery cane liquor. By daybreak, the man was dead in the hallway. The roughness of his voice had deceived us: he was only a youth. In his delirium a few coins had fallen from his belt, along with a cone of bright metal, the size of a die. In vain a boy tried to pick up this cone. A man was scarely able to raise it from the ground. I held it in my hand for a few minutes; I remember that its weight was intolerable and that after it was removed, the feeling of oppressiveness remained. I also remember the exact circle it pressed into my palm. This sensation of a very small and at the same time extremely heavy object produced a disagreeable impression of repugnance and fear. One of the local men suggested we throw it into the swollen river; Amorim acquired it for a few pesos. No one knew anything about the dead man, except that "he came from the border." These small, very heavy cones (made from a metal which is not of this world) are images of the divinity in certain regions of Tlön.

Here I bring the personal part of my narrative to a close. The rest is in the memory (if not in the hopes or fears) of all my readers. Let it suffice for me to recall or mention the following facts, with a mere brevity of words which the reflective recollection of all will enrich or amplify. Around 1944, a person doing research for the newspaper *The American* (of Nashville, Tennessee) brought to light in a Memphis library the forty volumes of the *First Encyclopedia of Tlön*. Even today there is a controversy over whether this discovery was accidental or whether it was permitted by the directors of the still nebulous *Orbis Tertius*. The latter is most likely. Some of the incredible aspects of the Eleventh Volume (for example, the multiplication of the *hrönir*) have been eliminated or attneuated in the Memphis copies; it is reasonable to imagine that these omissions follow the plan of exhibiting a world which is not too incompatible with the real world. The dissemination of objects from Tlön over different countries would complement this plan . . .[1] The fact is that the international press infinitely proclaimed the "find." Manuals, anthologies, summaries, literal versions, authorized re-editions and pirated editions of the Greatest Work of Man flooded and still flood the earth. Almost immediately, reality yielded on more than one account. The truth is that it longed to yield. Ten years ago any symmetry with a semblance of order—dialectical materialism, anti-Semitism, Nazism—was sufficient to entrance the minds of men. How could one do other than submit to Tlön, to the minute and vast evidence of an orderly planet? It is useless to answer that reality is also orderly. Perhaps it is, but in accordance with divine laws—I translate: inhuman laws—which we never quite grasp. Tlön is surely a labyrinth, but it is a labyrinth devised by men, a labyrinth destined to be deciphered by men.

The contact and the habit of Tlön have disintegrated this world. Enchanted by its rigor, humanity forgets over and again that it is a rigor of chess masters, not of angels. Already the schools have been invaded by the (conjectural) "primitive language" of Tlön; already the teaching of its harmonious history (filled with moving episodes)

[1] There remains, of course, the problem of the *material* of some objects.

has wiped out the one which governed in my childhood; already a fictitious past occupies in our memories the place of another, a past of which we know nothing with certainty—not even that it is false. Numismatology, pharmacology and archaeology have been re-formed. I understand that biology and mathematics also await their avatars . . . A scattered dynasty of solitary men has changed the face of the world. Their task continues. If our forecasts are not in error, a hundred years from now someone will discover the hundred volumes of the *Second Encyclopedia of Tlön.*

Then English and French and mere Spanish will disappear from the globe. The world will be Tlön. I pay no attention to all this and go on revising, in the still days at the Adrogué hotel, an uncertain Quevedian translation (which I do not intend to publish) of Browne's *Urn Burial.*

*Translated from the Spanish by James E. Irby*

# Dazai Osamu

## VILLON'S WIFE

I WAS AWAKENED by the sound of the front door being flung open, but I did not get out of bed. I knew it could only be my husband returning dead drunk in the middle of the night.

He switched on the light in the next room and, breathing very heavily, began to rummage through the drawers of the table and the bookcase, searching for something. After a few minutes there was a noise that sounded as if he had flopped down on the floor. Then I could hear only his panting. Wondering what he might be up to, I called to him from where I lay. "Have you had supper yet? There's some cold rice in the cupboard."

"Thank you," he answered in an unwontedly gentle tone. "How is the boy? Does he still have a fever?"

This was also unusual. The boy is four this year, but whether because of malnutrition, or his father's alcoholism, or sickness, he is actually smaller than most two-year-olds. He is not even sure on his feet, and as for talking, it's all he can do to say "yum-yum" or "ugh." Sometimes I wonder if he is not feeble-minded. Once, when I took him to the public bath and held him in my arms after undressing him, he looked so small and pitifully scrawny that my heart sank, and I burst into tears in front of everybody. The boy is always having upset stomachs or fevers, but my husband almost never spends any time at home, and I wonder what if anything he thinks about the child. If I mention to him that the boy has a fever, he says, "You ought to take him to a doctor." Then he throws on his coat and goes off somewhere. I would like to take the boy to the doctor, but I haven't the money. There is nothing I can do but lie beside him and stroke his head.

But that night, for whatever reason, my husband was strangely gentle, and for once asked me about the boy's fever. It didn't make me happy. I felt instead a kind of premonition of something terrible, and cold chills ran up and down my spine. I couldn't think of anything to say, so I lay there in silence. For a while there was no other sound but my husband's furious panting.

Then there came from the front entrance the thin voice of a woman, "Is anyone at home?" I shuddered all over as if icy water had been poured over me.

"Are you at home, Mr. Otani?" This time there was a somewhat sharp inflection to her voice. She slid the door open and called in a definitely angry voice, "Mr. Otani. Why don't you answer?"

My husband at last went to the door. "Well, what is it?" he asked in a frightened, stupid tone.

"You know perfectly well what it is," the woman said, lowering her voice. "What makes you steal other people's money when you've got a nice home like this? Stop your cruel joking and give it back. If you don't, I'm going straight to the police."

"I don't know what you're talking about. I won't stand for your insults. You've got no business coming here. Get out! If you don't get out, I'll be the one to call the police."

There came the voice of another man. "I must say, you've got your nerve, Mr. Otani. What do you mean we have no business coming here? You amaze me. This time it is serious. It's more than a joke when you steal other people's money. Heaven only knows all my wife and I have suffered on account of you. And on top of everything else you do something as low as you did tonight. Mr. Otani, I misjudged you."

"It's blackmail," my husband angrily exclaimed in a shaking voice. "It's extortion. Get out! If you've got any complaints I'll listen to them tomorrow."

"What a revolting thing to say. You really are a scoundrel. I have no alternative but to call the police."

In his words was a hatred so terrible that I went goose flesh all over.

"Go to hell," my husband shouted, but his voice had already weakened and sounded hollow.

I got up, threw a wrap over my nightgown, and went to the front hall. I bowed to the two visitors. A round-faced man of about fifty wearing a knee-length overcoat asked, "Is this your wife?," and, without a trace of a smile, faintly inclined his head in my direction as if he were nodding.

The woman was a thin, small person of about forty, neatly dressed. She loosened her shawl and, also unsmiling, returned my bow with the words, "Excuse us for breaking in this way in the middle of the night."

My husband suddenly slipped on his sandals and made for the door. The man grabbed his arm and the two of them struggled for a moment. "Let go or I'll stab you!" my husband shouted, and a jack-knife flashed in his right hand. The knife was a pet possession of his, and I remembered that he usually kept it in his desk drawer. When he got home he must have been expecting trouble, and the knife was what he had been searching for.

The man shrank back and in the interval my husband, flapping the sleeves of his coat like a huge crow, bolted outside.

"Thief!" the man shouted and started to pursue him, but I ran to the front gate in my bare feet and clung to him.

"Please don't. It won't help for either of you to get hurt. I will take the responsibility for everything."

The woman said, "Yes, she's right. You can never tell what a lunatic will do."

"Swine! It's the police this time! I can't stand any more." The man stood there staring emptily at the darkness outside and muttering, as if to himself. But the force had gone out of his body.

"Please come in and tell me what has happened. I may be able to settle whatever the matter is. The place is a mess, but please come in."

The two visitors exchanged glances and nodded slightly to one another. The man said, with a changed expression, "I'm afraid that whatever you may say, our minds are already made up. But it might be a good idea to tell you, Mrs. Otani, all that has happened."

"Please do come in and tell me about it."

"I'm afraid we won't be able to stay long." So saying the man started to remove his overcoat.

"Please keep your coat on. It's very cold here, and there's no heating in the house."

"Well then, if you will forgive me."

"Please, both of you."

The man and the woman entered my husband's room. They seemed appalled by the desolation they saw. The mats looked as though they were rotting, the paper doors were in shreds, the walls were beginning to fall in, and the paper had peeled away from the storage closet, revealing the framework. In a corner were a desk and a bookcase—an empty bookcase.

I offered the two visitors some torn cushions from which the stuffing was leaking, and said, "Please sit on the cushions—the mats are so dirty." And I bowed to them again. "I must apologize for all the trouble my husband seems to have been causing you, and for the terrible exhibition he put on tonight, for whatever reason it was. He has such a peculiar disposition." I choked in the middle of my words and burst into tears.

"Excuse me for asking, Mrs. Otani, but how old are you?" the man asked. He was sitting cross-legged on the torn cushion, with his elbows on his knees, propping his chin on his fists. As he asked the question he leaned forward toward me.

"I am twenty-six."

"Is that all you are? I suppose that's only natural, considering your husband's about thirty, but it amazes me all the same."

The woman, showing her face from behind the man's back, said, "I couldn't help wondering, when I came in and saw what a fine wife he has, why Mr. Otani behaves the way he does."

"He's sick That's what it is. He didn't used to be that way, but he keeps getting worse." He gave a great sigh, then continued, "Mrs. Otani, my wife and I run a little restaurant near the Nakano Station. We both originally came from the country, but I got fed up dealing with penny-pinching farmers, and came to Tokyo with my wife. After the usual hardships and breaks, we managed to save up a little and, along about 1936, opened a cheap little restaurant catering to customers with at most a yen or two to spend at a time on entertainment. By not going in for luxuries and working like slaves, we managed to lay in quite a stock of whisky and gin. When liquor got short and plenty of other drinking establishments went out of business, we were able to keep going.

"The war with America and England broke out, but even after the bombings got pretty severe, we didn't want to be evacuated to the country, not having any children to tie us down. We figured that we might as well stick to our business until the place got burnt down. Your husband first started coming to our place in the spring of 1944, as I recall. We were not yet losing the war, or if we were we didn't know how things actually stood, and we thought that if we could just hold out for another two or three years we could somehow get peace on terms of equality. When Mr. Otani first appeared in our shop, he was not alone. It's a little embarrassing to tell you about it, but I might as well come out with the whole story and not keep anything from you. Your husband sneaked in by the kitchen door along with an older woman. I forgot to say that about that time the front door of our place was shut, and only a few regular customers got in by the back.

"This older woman lived in the neighborhood, and when the bar where she worked was closed and she lost her job, she often came to our place with her men friends. That's why we weren't particularly surprised when your husband crept in with this woman, whose name was Akichan. I took them to the back room and brought out some gin. Mr. Otani drank his liquor very quietly that evening. Akichan paid the bill and the two of them left together. It's odd, but I can't forget how strangely gentle and refined he seemed that night. I wonder if when the devil makes his first appearance in somebody's house he acts in such a lonely and melancholy way.

"From that night on Mr. Otani was a steady customer. Ten days later he came alone and all of a sudden produced a hundred-yen note. At that time a hundred yen was a lot of money, more than two or three thousand yen today. He pressed the money into my hand and wouldn't take no for an answer. 'Take care of it, please,' he said, smiling timidly. That night he seemed to have drunk quite a bit before he came, and at my place he downed ten glasses of gin as fast as I could set them up. All this was almost entirely without a word. My wife and I tried to start a conversation, but he only smiled rather shamefacedly and nodded vaguely. Suddenly he asked the time and got up. 'What about the change?' I called after him. 'That's all right,' he said. 'I don't know what to do with it,' I insisted. He answered with a sardonic smile, 'Please save it until the next time. I'll be coming back.' He went out. Mrs. Otani, that was the one and only time that we ever got any money from him. Since then he has always put us off with one excuse or another, and for three years he has managed without paying a penny to drink up all our liquor almost singlehanded."

Before I knew what I was doing I burst out laughing. It all seemed so funny to me, although I can't explain why. I covered my mouth in confusion, but when I looked at the lady I saw that she was also laughing unaccountably, and then her husband could not help but laugh too.

"No, it's certainly no laughing matter, but I'm so fed up that I feel like laughing, too. Really, if he used all his ability in some other direction, he could become a cabinet minister or a Ph.D. or anything else he wanted. When Akichan was still friends with Mr. Otani she used to brag about him all the time. First of all, she said, he came from a terrific family. He was the younger son of Baron Otani. It is true that he had been disinherited because of his conduct, but when his father, the present baron, died, he and his elder brother were to divide the estate. He was brilliant, a genius in fact. In spite of his youth he was the best poet in Japan. What's more, he was a great scholar, and a perfect demon at German and French. To hear Akichan talk, he was a kind of god, and the funny thing was that she didn't make it all up. Other people also said that he was the younger son of Baron Otani and a famous poet. Even my wife, who's getting along in years, was as enthusiastic about him as Akichan. She used to tell me what a difference it makes when people have been well brought up. And the way she pined for him to come was quite unbearable. They say the day of the nobility is over, but until the war ended I can tell you that nobody had his way with the women like that disinherited son of the aristocracy. It is unbelievable how they fell for him. I suppose it was what people would nowadays call 'slave mentality.'

"For my part, I'm a man, and at that a very cool sort of man, and I don't think that some little peer—if you will pardon the expression —some member of the country gentry who is only a younger son, is all that different from myself. I never for a moment got worked up about him in so sickening a way. But all the same, that gentleman was my weak spot. No matter how firmly I resolved not to give him any liquor the next time, when he suddenly appeared at some unexpected hour, looking like a hunted man, and I saw how relieved he was at last to have reached our place, my resolution weakened, and I ended up by giving him the liquor. Even when he got drunk, he never made any special nuisance of himself, and if only he had paid the bill he would have been a good customer. He never advertised himself and didn't take any silly pride in being a genius or anything of the sort. When Akichan or somebody else would sit beside him and sound off to us about his greatness, he would either change the subject completely or say, 'I want some money so I can pay the bill,' throwing a wet blanket over everything.

"The war finally ended. We started doing business openly in black-market liquor and put new curtains in front of the place. For all its seediness the shop looked rather lively, and we hired a girl to lend a little charm. Then who should show up again but that damned gentleman. He no longer brought women with him, but always came in the company of two or three writers for newspapers and magazines. He was drinking even more than before, and used to get very wild-looking. He began to come out with really vulgar jokes, which he had never done before, and sometimes for no good reason he would hit one of the reporters he brought with him or start a fist fight. What's more, he seduced the twenty-year-old girl who was working in our place. We were shocked, but there was nothing we could do about it at that stage, and we had no choice but to let the matter drop. We advised the girl to resign herself to bearing the child, and quietly sent her back to her parents. I begged Mr. Otani not to come any more, but he answered in a threatening tone, 'People who make money on the black market have no business criticizing others. I know all about you.' The next night he showed up as if nothing had happened.

"Maybe it was by way of punishment for the black-market business we had been doing that we had to put up with such a monster. But what he did tonight can't be passed over just because he's a poet or a gentleman. It was plain robbery. He stole five thousand yen from us. Nowadays all our money goes for stock, and we are lucky if we have five hundred or one thousand yen in the place. The reason why we had as much as five thousand tonight was that I had made an end-of-the-year round of our regular customers and managed to collect that much. If I don't hand the money over to the wholesalers immediately we won't be able to stay in business. That's how much it means to us. Well, my wife was going over the accounts in the back room and had put the money in the cupboard drawer. He was drinking by himself out in front but seems to have noticed what she did. Suddenly he got up, went straight to the back room, and without a word pushed my wife aside and opened the drawer. He grabbed the bills and stuffed them in his pocket.

"We rushed into the shop, still speechless with amazement, and then out into the street. I shouted for him to stop, and the two of us ran after him. For a minute I felt like screaming 'Thief!' and getting the people in the street to join us, but after all, Mr. Otani is an old acquaintance, and I couldn't be too harsh on him. I made up my mind that I would not let him out of my sight. I would follow him wherever he went, and when I saw that he had quieted down, I would calmly ask for the money. We are only small business people, and when we finally caught up with him here, we had no choice but to suppress our feelings and politely ask him to return the money. And then what happened? He took out a knife and threatened to stab me! What a way to behave!"

Again the whole thing seemed so funny to me, for reasons I can't explain, that I burst out laughing. The lady turned red, and smiled a little. I couldn't stop laughing. Even though I knew that it would have a bad effect on the proprietor, it all seemed so strangely funny that I laughed until the tears came. I suddenly wondered if the phrase "the great laugh at the end of the world," that occurs in one of my husband's poems, didn't mean something of the sort.

And yet it was not a matter that could be settled just by laughing about it. I thought for a minute and said, "Somehow or other I will make things good, if you will only wait one more day before you report to the police. I'll call on you tomorrow without fail." I carefully inquired where the restaurant was, and begged them to consent. They agreed to let things stand for the time being, and left. Then I sat by myself in the middle of the cold room trying to think of a plan. Nothing came to me. I stood up, took off my wrap, and crept in among the covers where my boy was sleeping. As I stroked his head I thought how wonderful it would be if the night never ended.

My father used to keep a stall in Asakusa Park. My mother died when I was young, and my father and I lived by ourselves in a tenement. We ran the stall together. My husband used to come now and then, and before long I was meeting him at other places without my father's knowing it. When I became pregnant I persuaded him to treat me as his wife, although it wasn't officially registered, of course. Now the boy is growing up fatherless, while my husband goes off for three or four nights or even for a whole month at a time. I don't know where he goes or what he does. When he comes back he is always drunk; and he sits there, deathly pale, breathing heavily and staring at my face. Sometimes he cries and the tears stream down his face, or without warning he crawls into my bed and holds me tightly. "Oh, it can't go on. I'm afraid. I'm afraid. Help me!"

Sometimes he trembles all over, and even after he falls asleep he talks deliriously and moans. The next morning he is absent-minded, like a man with the soul taken out of him. Then he disappears and doesn't return for three or four nights. A couple of my husband's publisher friends have been looking after the boy and myself for some time, and they bring money once in a while, enough to keep us from starving.

I dozed off, then before I knew it opened my eyes to see the morning light pouring in through the cracks in the shutters. I got up, dressed, strapped the boy to my back and went outside. I felt as if I couldn't stand being in the silent house another minute.

I set out aimlessly and found myself walking in the direction of the station. I bought a bun at an outdoor stand and fed it to the boy. On a sudden impulse I bought a ticket for Kichijoji and got on the streetcar. While I stood hanging from a strap I happened to notice a poster with my husband's name on it. It was an advertisement for a magazine in which he had published a story called "François Villon." While I stared at the title "François Villon" and at my husband's name, painful tears sprang from my eyes, why I can't say, and the poster clouded over so I couldn't see it.

I got off at Kichijoji and for the first time in I don't know how many years I walked in the park. The cypresses around the pond had all been cut down, and the place looked like the site of a construction. It was strangely bare and cold, not at all as it used to be.

I took the boy off my back and the two of us sat on a broken bench next to the pond. I fed the boy a sweet potato I had brought from home. "It's a pretty pond, isn't it? There used to be many carp and goldfish, but now there aren't any left. It's too bad, isn't it?"

I don't know what he thought. He just laughed oddly with his mouth full of sweet potato. Even if he is my own child, he did give me the feeling almost of an idiot.

I couldn't settle anything by sitting there on the bench, so I put the boy on my back and returned slowly to the station. I bought a ticket for Nakano. Without thought or plan, I boarded the streetcar as though I were being sucked into a horrible whirlpool. I got off at Nakano and followed the directions to the restaurant.

The front door would not open. I went around to the back and entered by the kitchen door. The owner was away, and his wife was cleaning the shop by herself. As soon as I saw her I began to pour out lies of which I did not imagine myself capable.

"It looks as if I'll be able to pay you back every bit of the money tomorrow, if not tonight. There's nothing for you to worry about."

"Oh, how wonderful. Thank you so much." She looked almost happy, but still there remained on her face a shadow of uneasiness, as if she were not yet satisfied.

"It's true. Someone will bring the money here without fail. Until he comes I'm to stay here as your hostage. Is that guarantee enough for you? Until the money comes I'll be glad to help around the shop."

I took the boy off my back and let him play by himself. He is accustomed to playing alone and doesn't get in the way at all. Perhaps because he's stupid, he's not afraid of strangers, and he smiled happily at the madam. While I was away getting the rationed goods for her, she gave him some empty American cans to play with, and when I got back he was in a corner of the room, banging the cans and rolling them on the floor.

About noon the boss returned from his marketing. As soon as I caught sight of him I burst out with the same lies I had told the madam. He looked amazed. "Is that a fact? All the same, Mrs. Otani, you can't be sure of money until you've got it in your hands." He spoke in a surprisingly calm, almost explanatory tone.

"But it's really true. Please have confidence in me and wait just this one day before you make it public. In the meantime I'll help in the restaurant."

"If the money is returned, that's all I ask," the boss said, almost to himself. "There are five or six days left to the end of the year, aren't there?"

"Yes, and so, you see, I mean—oh, some customers have come. Welcome!" I smiled at the three customers—they looked like workmen—who had entered the shop, and whispered to the madam, "Please lend me an apron."

One of the customers called out, "Say, you've hired a beauty. She's terrific."

"Don't lead her astray," the boss said, in a tone which wasn't altogether joking, "she cost a lot of money."

"A million-dollar thoroughbred?" another customer coarsely joked.

"They say that even in thoroughbreds the female costs only half-price," I answered in the same coarse way, while putting the sake on to warm.

"Don't be modest! From now on in Japan there's equality of the sexes, even for horses and dogs," the youngest customer roared. "Sweetheart, I've fallen in love. It's love at first sight. But is that your kid over there?"

"No," said the madam, carrying the boy from the back room in her arms. "We got this child from our relatives. At last we have an heir."

"What'll you leave him besides your money?" a customer teased.

The boss, with a dark expression, muttered, "A love affair and debts." Then, changing his tone, "What'll you have? How about a mixed grill?"

It was Christmas Eve. That must have been why there was such a steady stream of customers. I had scarcely eaten a thing since morning, but I was so upset that I refused even when the madam urged me to have a bite. I just went on flitting around the restaurant as lightly as a ballerina. Maybe it is only conceit, but the shop seemed exceptionally lively that night, and there were quite a few customers who wanted to know my name or tried to shake my hand.

But I didn't have the slightest idea how it would all end. I went on smiling and answering the customers' dirty jokes with even dirtier jokes in the same vein, slipping from customer to customer, pouring the drinks. Before long I got to thinking that I would just as soon my body melted and flowed away like ice cream.

It seems as if miracles sometimes do happen even in this world. A little after nine a man entered, wearing a Christmas tricornered paper hat and a black mask which covered the upper part of his face. He was followed by an attractive woman of slender build who looked thirty-four or thirty-five. The man sat on a chair in the corner with his back to me, but as soon as he came in I knew who it was. It was my thief of a husband.

He sat there without seeming to pay any attention to me. I also pretended not to recognize him, and went on joking with the other customers. The lady seated opposite my husband called me to their table. My husband stared at me from beneath his mask, as if he were surprised in spite of himself. I lightly patted his shoulder and asked, "Aren't you going to wish me a merry Christmas? What do you say? You look as if you've already put away a quart or two."

The lady ignored this. She said, "I have something to discuss with the proprietor. Would you mind calling him here for a moment?"

I went to the kitchen, where the boss was frying fish. "Otani has come back. Please go and see him, but don't tell the woman he's with anything about me. I don't want to embarrass him."

"If that's the way you want it, it's all right with me," he consented easily, and went out front. After a quick look around the restaurant, the boss walked straight to the table where my husband sat. The beautiful lady exchanged two or three words with him, and the three of them left the shop.

It was all over. Everything had been settled. Somehow I had believed all along that it would be, and I felt exhilarated. I seized the wrist of a young customer in a dark-blue suit, a boy not more than twenty, and I cried, "Drink up! Drink up! It's Christmas!"

In just thirty minutes—no, it was even sooner than that, so soon it startled me, the boss returned alone. "Mrs. Otani, I want to thank you. I've got the money back."

"I'm so glad. All of it?"

He answered with a funny smile, "All he took yesterday."

"And how much does his debt come to altogether? Roughly— the absolute minimum."

"Twenty thousand yen."

"Does that cover it?"

"It's a minimum."

"I'll make it good. Will you employ me starting tomorrow? I'll pay it back by working."

"What! You're joking!" And we laughed together.

Tonight I left the restaurant after ten and returned to the house with the boy. As I expected, my husband was not at home, but that didn't bother me. Tomorrow when I go to the restaurant I may see him again, for all I know. Why has such a good plan never occurred to me before? All the suffering I have gone through has been because of my own stupidity. I was always quite a success at entertaining the customers at my father's stall, and I'll certainly get to be pretty skillful at the restaurant. As a matter of fact, I received about five hundred yen in tips tonight.

From the following day on my life changed completely. I became lighthearted and gay. The first thing I did was to go to a beauty parlor and have a permanent. I bought cosmetics and mended my dresses. I felt as though the worries that had weighed so heavily on me had been completely wiped away.

In the morning I get up and eat breakfast with the boy. Then I put him on my back and leave for work. New Year's is the big season at the restaurant, and I've been so busy my eyes swim. My husband comes in for a drink once every few days. He lets me pay the bill and then disappears again. Quite often he looks in on the shop late at night and asks if it isn't time for me to be going home. Then we return pleasantly together.

"Why didn't I do this from the start? It's brought me such happiness."

"Women don't know anything about happiness or unhappiness."

"Perhaps not. What about men?"

"Men only have unhappiness. They are always fighting fear."

"I don't understand. I only know I wish this life could go on forever. The boss and the madam are such nice people."

"Don't be silly. They're grasping country bumpkins. They make me drink because they think they'll make money out of it in the end."

"That's their business. You can't blame them for it. But that's not the whole story, is it? You had an affair with the madam, didn't you?"

"A long time ago. Does the old guy realize it?"

"I'm sure he does. I heard him say with a sigh that you had brought him a seduction and debts."

"I must seem a horrible character to you, but the fact is that I want to die so badly I can't stand it. Ever since I was born I have been thinking of nothing but dying. It would be better for everyone concerned if I were dead, that's certain. And yet I can't seem to die. There's something strange and frightening, like God, which won't let me die."

"That's because you have your work."

"My work doesn't mean a thing. I don't write either masterpieces or failures. If people say something is good, it becomes good. If they say it's bad, it becomes bad. But what frightens me is that somewhere in the world there is a God. There is, isn't there?"

"I haven't any idea."

Now that I have worked twenty days at the restaurant I realize that every last one of the customers is a criminal. I have come to think that my husband is very much on the mild side compared to them. And I see now that not only the customers but everyone you meet walking in the streets is hiding some crime. A beautifully dressed lady came to the door selling sake at three hundred yen the quart. That was cheap, considering what prices are nowadays, and the madam snapped it up. It turned out to be watered. I thought that in a world where even such an aristocratic-looking lady is forced to resort to such tricks, it is impossible for anyone alive to have a clear conscience.

God, if you exist, show yourself to me! Toward the end of the New Year season I was raped by a customer. It was raining that night, and it didn't seem likely that my husband would appear. I got ready to go, even though one customer was still left. I picked up the boy, who was sleeping in a corner of the back room, and put him on my back. "I'd like to borrow your umbrella again," I said to the madam.

"I've got an umbrella. I'll take you home," said the last customer, getting up as if he meant it. He was a short, thin man about twenty-five, who looked like a factory worker. It was the first time he had come to the restaurant since I started working there.

"It's very kind of you, but I am used to walking by myself."

"You live a long way off, I know. I come from the same neighborhood. I'll take you back. Bill, please." He had only had three glasses and didn't seem particularly drunk.

We boarded the streetcar together and got off at my stop. Then we walked in the falling rain side by side under the same umbrella through the pitch-black streets. The young man, who up to this point hadn't said a word, began to talk in a lively way. "I know all about you. You see, I'm a fan of Mr. Otani's and I write poetry myself. I was hoping to show him some of my work before long, but he intimidates me so."

We had reached my house. "Thank you very much," I said. "I'll see you again at the restaurant."

"Good-bye," the young man said, going off into the rain.

I was wakened in the middle of the night by the noise of the front gate being opened. I thought that it was my husband returning, drunk as usual, so I lay there without saying anything.

A man's voice called, "Mrs. Otani, excuse me for bothering you."

I got up, put on the light, and went to the front entrance. The young man was there, staggering so badly he could scarcely stand.

"Excuse me, Mrs. Otani. On the way back I stopped for another drink and, to tell the truth, I live at the other end of town, and when I got to the station the last streetcar had already left. Mrs. Otani, would you please let me spend the night here? I don't need any blankets or anything else. I'll be glad to sleep here in the front hall until the first streetcar leaves tomorrow morning. It it wasn't raining I'd sleep outdoors somewhere in the neighborhood, but it's hopeless with this rain. Please let me stay."

"My husband isn't at home, but if the front hall will do, please stay." I got the two torn cushions and gave them to him.

"Thanks very much. Oh, I've had too much to drink," he said with a groan. He lay down just as he was in the front hall, and by the time I got back to bed I could already hear his snores.

The next morning at dawn without ceremony he took me.

That day I went to the restaurant with my boy as usual, acting as if nothing had happened. My husband was sitting at a table reading a newspaper, a glass of liquor beside him. I thought how pretty the morning sunshine looked, sparkling on the glass.

"Isn't anybody here?" I asked. He looked up from his paper. "The boss hasn't come back yet from marketing. The madam was in the kitchen just a minute ago. Isn't she there now?"

"You didn't come last night, did you?"

"I did come. It's got so that I can't get to sleep without a look at my favorite waitress's face. I dropped in after ten but they said you had just left."

"And then?"

"I spent the night here. It was raining so hard."

"I may be sleeping here from now on."

"That's a good idea, I suppose."

"Yes, that's what I'll do. There's no sense in renting the house forever."

My husband didn't say anything but turned back to his paper. "Well, what do you know. They're writing bad things about me again. They call me a fake aristocrat with Epicurean leanings. That's not true. It would be more correct to refer to me as an Epicurean in terror of God. Look! It says here that I'm a monster. That's not true, is it? It's a little late, but I'll tell you now why I took the five thousand yen. It was so that I might give you and the boy the first happy New Year in a long time. That proves I'm not a monster, doesn't it?"

His words didn't make me especially glad. I said, "There's nothing wrong with being a monster, is there? As long as we can stay alive."

*Translated from the Japanese by Donald Keene*

# Tadeusz Borowski

## THIS WAY FOR THE GAS, LADIES AND GENTLEMEN

ALL OF US walk around naked. The delousing is finally over, and our striped suits are back from the tanks filled with a solution of Zyklon B, an efficient killer of lice in clothing and of men in gas chambers. Only the inmates in the blocks cut off from ours by the "Spanish goats"* still have nothing to wear. But all the same, all of us walk around naked: the heat is unbearable. The camp has been sealed off tight. Not a single prisoner, not one solitary louse, can sneak through the gate. The labor Kommandos have stopped working. All day, thousands of naked men shuffle up and down the roads, cluster around the squares, or lie against the walls and on top of the roofs. We have been sleeping on plain boards, since our mattresses and blankets are still being disinfected. From the rear blockhouses we have a view of the FKL—*Frauen Konzentration Lager*—there too the delousing is in full swing. Twenty-eight thousand women have been stripped naked and driven out of the barracks. Now they swarm around the large yard between the blockhouses.

The heat rises, the hours are endless. We are without even our usual diversion: the wide roads leading to the crematoria are empty. For several days now, no new transports have come in. Part of "Canada." † has been liquidated and detailed to a labor Kommando—one of the very toughest—at Harmenz. For there exists in the camp a special brand of justice that rests on envy: when the rich and mighty fall, their friends see to it that they fall to the very bottom. And Canada, our Canada, which smells not of maple forests but of French perfume, has amassed great fortunes in diamonds and currency from all over Europe.

Several of us sit on the top bunk, our legs dangling over the edge.

* Crossed wooden beams wrapped in barbed wire.
† "Canada" designated wealth and well-being in the camp. More specifically, it referred to the members of the labor-gang, or Kommando, who helped unload the incoming transports of people destined for the gas chambers.

We slice the neat loaves of crisp, crunchy bread. It is a bit coarse to the taste, the kind that stays fresh for days. Sent all the way from Warsaw—only a week ago my mother held this white loaf in her hands . . . dear Lord, dear Lord . . .

We unwrap the bacon, the onion, we open a can of evaporated milk. Henri the fat Frenchman, dreams aloud of the French wine brought by the transports from Strasbourg, Paris, Marseilles . . . Sweat streams down his body.

"Listen, *mon ami*, next time we go up on the loading ramp, I'll bring you real champagne. You haven't tried it before, eh?"

"No. But you'll never be able to smuggle it through the gate, so stop teasing. Why not try and 'organize' some shoes for me instead, you know, the perforated kind, the kind with a double sole, and what about that shirt you promised me long ago?"

"*Patience, patience*, when the new transports come, I'll bring all you want. We'll be going on the ramp again!"

"And what if there aren't any more 'cremo' transports?" I say spitefully. "Can't you see how much easier life is becoming around here: no limit on packages, no more beatings? You even write letters home. . . . One hears all kind of talk, and, dammit, they'll run out of people!"

"Stop talking nonsense." Henri's serious fat face moves rhythmically; his mouth is full of sardines. We have been friends for a long time, but I do not even know his last name. "Stop talking nonsense," he repeats, swallowing with effort. "They can't run out of people or we'll starve to death in this damned camp. All of us live on what they bring."

"All? We have our packages . . ."

"Sure, you and your friends, and ten other friends of yours. Some of you Poles get packages. But what about us, and the Jews, and the Russkis? And what if we had no food, no '*organization*' from the transports, do you think you'd be eating those packages of yours in peace? We wouldn't let you!"

"You would, you'd starve to death like the Greeks. Around here, whoever has grub, has power."

"Anyway, you have enough, we have enough, so why argue?"

Right, why argue. They have enough, I have enough, we eat together and we sleep on the same bunks. Henri slices the bread, he makes a tomato salad. It tastes good with the commissary mustard.

Below us, naked, sweat-drenched men crowd the narrow barracks aisles or lie packed in eights and tens in the lower bunks. Their nude, withered bodies stink of sweat and excrement, their cheeks are hollow. Directly beneath me, in the bottom bunk, lies a rabbi. He has covered his head with a piece of rag torn off a blanket and reads from a Hebrew prayer book (there is no shortage of this type of literature at the camp), wailing loudly, monotonously.

"Can't somebody shut him up? He's been raving as if he'd caught God himself by the feet."

"I don't feel like moving. Let him rave. They'll take him to the oven that much sooner."

"Religion is the opium of the people," Henri, who is a Communist and a rentier, says sententiously. "If they didn't believe in God and eternal life, they'd have smashed the crematoria long ago."

"Why haven't you done it then?"

The question is rhetorical; the Frenchman ignores it.

"Idiot," he says simply, and stuffs a tomato in his mouth.

Just as we finish our snack, there is a sudden commotion at the door. The Moslems* scurry in fright to the safety of their bunks, a messenger runs into the Block Elder's shack. The Elder, his face solemn, steps out at once.

"Canada! *Antreten!* But fast! There's a transport coming!"

"Great God!" yells Henri, jumping off the bunk. He swallows the rest of his tomato, snatches his coat, screams *"Raus"* at the men below, and in a flash is at the door. We can hear a scramble in the other bunks. Canada is leaving for the ramp.

"Henri, the shoes!" I call after him.

*"Keine Angst!"* he shouts back, already outside.

I proceed to put away the food. I tie a piece of rope around the suitcase where the onions and the tomatoes from my father's garden in Warsaw mingle with Portuguese sardines, bacon from Lublin (that's from my brother), and authentic sweetmeats from Salonika. I tie it all up, pull on my trousers, and slide off the bunk.

*"Platz!"* I yell, pushing my way through the Greeks. They step aside.

At the door I bump into Henri.

*"Was ist los?"*

"Want to come with us on the ramp?"

"Sure, why not?"

"Come along then, grab your coat! We're short a few men. I've already told the Kapo," and he shoves me out the barracks door.

We line up. Someone has marked down our numbers, someone

---

* Moslem was the camp name for a prisoner who had been destroyed physically and spiritually, and who had neither the strength nor the will to go on living—a man ripe for the gas chamber.

up ahead yells, "March, march," and now we are running toward the gate, accompanied by the shouts of a multilingual throng that is already being pushed back to the barracks. Not everybody is lucky enough to be going on the ramp . . . We have almost reached the gate. *Links, zwei, drei, vier! Muetzen ab!* Erect, arms stretched stiffly along our hips, we march past the gate briskly, smartly, almost gracefully. A sleepy SS man with a large pad in his hand checks us off, waving us ahead in groups of five.

"*Hundert!*" he calls after we have all passed.

"*Stimmt!*" comes a hoarse answer from out front.

We march fast, almost at a run. There are guards all around, young men with automatics. We pass Camp II B, then some deserted barracks and a clump of unfamiliar green, apple and pear trees. We cross the circle of watchtowers and, running, burst onto the highway. We have arrived. Just a few more yards. There, surrounded by trees, is the ramp.

A cheerful little station, very much like any other provincial railroad stop: a small square framed by tall chestnuts and paved with yellow gravel. Not far off, beside the road, squats a tiny wooden shed, uglier and more flimsy than the ugliest and flimsiest railroad shack; farther along lie stacks of old rails, heaps of wooden beams, barracks parts, bricks, paving stones. This is where they load freight for Birkenau: supplies for the construction of the camp, and people for the gas chambers. Trucks drive around, load up lumber, cement, people—a regular daily routine.

And now the guards are being posted along the rails, across the beams, in the green shade of the Silesian chestnuts, to form a tight circle around the ramp. They wipe the sweat from their faces and sip out of their canteens. It is unbearably hot, the sun stands motionless at its zenith.

"Fall out!"

We sit down in the narrow streaks of shade along the stacked rails. The hungry Greeks (several of them managed to come along, God only knows how) rummage underneath the rails. One of them finds some pieces of mildewed bread, another a few half-rotten sardines. They eat.

"*Schweinedreck*," spits a young, tall guard with corn-colored hair and dreamy blue eyes. "For God's sake, any minute you'll have so much food to stuff down your guts, you'll bust!" He adjusts his gun, wipes his face with a handkerchief.

"Hey you, fatso," his boot lightly touches Henri's shoulder. "*Pass mal auf*, want a drink?"

"Sure, but I haven't got any Marks," replies the Frenchman with a professional air.

"*Shade*, too bad."

"Come, come, *Herr Posten*, isn't my word good enough any more? Haven't we done business before? How much?"

"One hundred. *Gemacht?*"

"*Gemacht.*"

We drink the water, lukewarm and tasteless. It will be paid for by the people who have not yet arrived.

"Now you be careful," says Henri turning to me. He tosses away the empty bottle. It strikes the rails and bursts into tiny fragments. "Don't take any money, they might be checking. Anyway, who the hell needs money, you've got enough to eat. Don't take suits, either, or they'll think you're planning to escape. Just get a shirt, silk only, with a collar. And an undershirt. And if you find something to drink, don't bother calling me. I know how to shift for myself, but you watch your step or they'll let you have it."

"Do they beat you up here?"

"Naturally. You've got to have eyes in your ass. *Arschaugen.*"

Around us sit the Greeks, their jaws working greedily, like huge human insects. They munch on stale lumps of bread. They are restless, wondering what will happen next. The sight of the large beams and the stacks of rails has them worried. They dislike carrying heavy loads.

"*Was wir arbeiten?*" they ask.

"*Niks. Transport kommen, alles Krematorium, compris?*"

"*Alles verstehen*," they answer in crematorium Esperanto. All is well—they will not have to move the heavy rails or carry the beams.

In the meantime, the ramp has become increasingly alive with activity, increasingly noisy. The crews are being divided into those who will open and unload the arriving cattle cars and those who will be posted by the wooden steps. They receive instructions on how to proceed most efficiently. Motorcycles drive up, delivering SS officers, bemedaled, glittering with brass, beefy men with highly polished boots and shiny, brutal faces. Some have brought their briefcases, others hold thin, flexible whips. This gives them an air of military readiness and agility. They walk in and out of the commissary—for the miserable little shack by the road serves as their commissary, where in the summertime they drink mineral water, *Sudetenquelle*, and where in winter they can warm up with a glass of hot wine. They greet each other in the state-approved way, raising an arm Roman fashion, then shake hands cordially, exchange warm smiles, discuss mail from home, their children, their families. Some stroll majestically on the ramp. The silver squares on their collars glitter, the gravel crunches under their boots, their bamboo whips snap impatiently.

We lie against the rails in the narrow streaks of shade, breathe unevenly, occasionally exchange a few words in our various tongues, and gaze listlessly at the majestic men in green uniforms, at the green trees, and at the church steeple of a distant village.

"The transport is coming," somebody says. We spring to our feet, all eyes turn in one direction. Around the bend, one after another, the cattle cars begin rolling in. The train backs into the station, a conductor leans out, waves his hand, blows a whistle. The locomotive whistles back with a shrieking noise, puffs, the train rolls slowly alongside the ramp. In the tiny barred windows appear pale, wilted, exhausted human faces, terror-stricken women with tangled hair, unshaven men. They gaze at the station in silence. And then, suddenly, there is a stir inside the cars and a pounding against the wooden boards.

"Water! Air!"—weary, desperate cries.

Heads push through the windows, mouths gasp frantically for air. They draw a few breaths, then disappear; others come in their place, then also disappear. The cries and moans grow louder.

A man in a green uniform covered with more glitter than any of the others jerks his head impatiently, his lips twist in annoyance. He inhales deeply, then with a rapid gesture throws his cigarette away and signals to the guard. The guard removes the automatic from his shoulder, aims, sends a series of shots along the train. All is quiet now. Meanwhile, the trucks have arrived, steps are being drawn up, and the Canada men stand ready at their posts by the train doors. The SS officer with the briefcase raises his hand:

"Whoever takes gold, or anything at all besides food, will be shot for stealing Reich property. Understand? *Verstanden?*"

"*Jawohl!*" we answer eagerly.

"*Also los!* Begin!"

The bolts crack, the doors fall open. A wave of fresh air rushes inside the train. People . . . inhumanly crammed, buried under incredible heaps of luggage, suitcases, trunks, packages, crates, bundles of every description (everything that had been their past and was to start their future). Monstrously squeezed together, they have fainted from heat, suffocated, crushed one another. Now they push toward the open doors, breathing like fish cast out on the sand.

"Attention! Out, and take your luggage with you! Take out everything. Pile all your stuff near the exits. Yes, your coats too. It is summer. March to the left. Understand?"

"Sir, what's going to happen to us?" They jump from the train onto the gravel, anxious, worn-out.

"Where are you people from?"

"Sosnowiec, Będzin. Sir, what's going to happen to us?" they repeat the question stubbornly, gazing into our tired eyes.

"I don't know, I don't understand Polish."

It is the camp law: people going to their death must be deceived to the very end. This is the only permissible form of charity. The heat is tremendous. The sun hangs directly over our heads, the white, hot sky quivers, the air vibrates, an occasional breeze feels like a sizzling blast from a furnace. Our lips are parched, the mouth fills with the salty taste of blood, the body is weak and heavy from lying in the sun. Water!

A huge, multicolored wave of people loaded down with luggage pours from the train like a blind, mad river trying to find a new bed. But before they have a chance to recover, before they can draw a breath of fresh air and look at the sky, bundles are snatched from their hands, coats ripped off their backs, their purses and umbrellas taken away.

"But please, sir, it's for the sun, I cannot . . ."

"*Verboten!*" one of us barks through clenched teeth. There is an SS man standing behind your back, calm, efficient, watchful.

"*Meine Herrschaften*, this way, ladies and gentlemen, try not to throw your things around, please. Show some good will," he says courteously, his restless hands playing with the slender whip.

"Of course, of course," they answer as they pass, and now they walk alongside the train somewhat more cheerfully. A woman reaches down quickly to pick up her handbag. The whip flies, the woman screams, stumbles, and falls under the feet of the surging crowd. Behind her, a child cries in a thin little voice "*Mamele!*"—a very small girl with tangled black curls.

The heaps grow. Suitcases, bundles, blankets, coats, handbags that open as they fall, spilling coins, gold, watches; mountains of bread pile up at the exits, heaps of marmalade, jams, masses of meat, sausages; sugar spills on the gravel.

Trucks, loaded with people, start up with a deafening roar and drive off amidst the wailing and screaming of the women separated from their children, and the stupefied silence of the men left behind. They are the ones who had been ordered to step to the right—the healthy and the young who will go to the camp. In the end, they too will not escape death, but first they must work.

Trucks leave and return, without interruption, as on a monstrous conveyor belt. A Red Cross van drives back and forth, back and forth, incessantly: it transports the gas that will kill these people. The enormous cross on the hood, red as blood, seems to dissolve in the sun.

The Canada men at the trucks cannot stop for a single moment, even to catch their breath. They shove the people up the steps, pack them in tightly, sixty per truck, more or less. Nearby stands a young, cleanshaven "gentleman," an SS officer with a notebook in his hand. For each departing truck he enters a mark; sixteen trucks gone means one thousand people, more or less. The gentleman is calm, precise. No truck can leave without a signal from him, or a mark in his notebook: *Ordnung muss sein*. The marks swell into thousands, the thousands into whole transports, which afterwards we shall simply call "from Salonika," "from Strasbourg," "from Rotterdam." This one will be called "Sosnowiec-Będzin." The new prisoners from Sosnowiec-Będzin will receive serial numbers—131-132—thousand, of course, though afterwards we shall simply say 131-132, for short.

The transports swell into weeks, months, years. When the war is over, they will count up the marks in their notebooks—all four and a half million of them. The bloodiest battle of the war, the greatest victory of the strong, united Germany. *Ein Reich, ein Volk, ein Führer*—and four crematoria.

The train has been emptied. A thin, pock-marked SS man peers inside, shakes his head in disgust and motions to our group, pointing his finger at the door.

"*Rein.* Clean it up!"

We climb inside. In the corners amid human excrement and abandoned wrist watches lie squashed, trampled infants, naked little monsters with enormous heads and bloated bellies. We carry them out like chickens, holding several in each hand.

"Don't take them to the trucks, pass them on to the women," says the SS man, lighting a cigarette. His cigarette lighter is not working properly; he examines it carefully.

"Take them, for God's sake!" I explode as the women run from me in horror, covering their eyes.

The name of God sounds strangely pointless, since the women and the infants will go on the trucks, every one of them, without exception. We all know what this means, and we look at each other with hate and horror.

"What, you don't want to take them?" asks the pock-marked SS man with a note of surprise and reproach in his voice, and reaches for his revolver.

"You mustn't shoot, I'll carry them." A tall, gray-haired woman takes the little corpses out of my hands and for an instant gazes straight into my eyes.

"My poor boy," she whispers and smiles at me. Then she walks away, staggering along the path. I lean against the side of the train. I am terribly tired. Someone pulls at my sleeve.

"*En avant*, to the rails, come on!"

I look up, but the face swims before my eyes, dissolves, huge and transparent, melts into the motionless trees and the sea of people . . . I blink rapidly: Henri.

"Listen, Henri, are we good people?"

"That's stupid, why do you ask?"

"You see my friend, you see, I don't know why, but I am furious, simply furious with these people—furious because I must be here because of them. I feel no pity, I am not sorry they're going to the gas chamber. Damn them all! I could throw myself at them, beat them with my fists. It must be pathological, I just can't understand . . ."

"Ah, on the contrary, it is natural, predictable, calculated. The ramp exhausts you, you rebel—and the easiest way to relieve your hate is to turn against someone weaker. Why, I'd even call it healthy. It's simple logic, *compris?*" He props himself up comfortably against the heap of rails. "Look at the Greeks, they know how to make the best of it! They stuff their bellies with anything they find. One of them has just devoured a full jar of marmalade."

"Pigs! Tomorrow half of them will die of the shits."

"Pigs? You've been hungry."

"Pigs!" I repeat furiously. I close my eyes. The air is filled with ghastly cries, the earth trembles beneath me, I can feel sticky moisture on my eyelids. My throat is completely dry.

The morbid procession streams on and on—trucks growl like mad dogs. I shut my eyes tight, but I can still see corpses dragged from the train, trampled infants, cripples piled on top of the dead, wave after wave . . . freight cars roll in, the heaps of clothing, suitcases and bundles grow, people climb out, look at the sun, take a few breaths, beg for water, get into the trucks, drive away. And again freight cars roll in, again people . . . The scenes become confused in my mind—I am not sure if all of this is actually happening, or if I

am dreaming. There is a humming inside my head, I feel that I must
vomit.

Henri tugs at my arm.

"Don't sleep, we're off to load up the loot."

All the people are gone. In the distance, the last few trucks roll
along the road in clouds of dust, the train has left, several SS officers
promenade up and down the ramp. The silver glitters on their collars. Their boots shine, their red, beefy faces shine. Among them
there is a woman—only now I realize she has been here all along—
withered, flat-chested, bony, her thin, colorless hair pulled back and
tied in a "Nordic" knot; her hands are in the pockets of her wide
skirt. With a ratlike, resolute smile glued on her thin lips she sniffs
around the corners of the ramp. She detests feminine beauty with the
hatred of a woman who is herself repulsive, and knows it. Yes, I have
seen her many times before and I know her well: she is the commandant of the FKL. She has come to look over the new crop of
women, for some of them, instead of going on the trucks, will go on
foot—to the concentration camp. There our boys, the barbers from
Zauna, will shave their heads and will have a good laugh at their
"outside world" modesty.

We proceed to load the loot. We lift huge trunks, heave them
onto the trucks. There they are arranged in stacks, packed tightly.
Occasionally somebody slashes one open with a knife, for pleasure or
in search of vodka and perfume. One of the crates falls open, suits,
shirts, books drop out on the ground . . . I pick up a small, heavy
package. I unwrap it—gold, about two handfuls, bracelets, rings,
brooches, diamonds . . .

"*Gib hier*," an SS man says calmly, holding up his briefcase already full of gold and colorful foreign currency. He locks the case,
hands it to an officer, takes another, an empty one, and stands by the
next truck, waiting. The gold will go to the Reich.

It is hot, terribly hot. Our throats are dry, each word hurts. Anything for a sip of water! Faster, faster, so that it is over, so that we
may rest. At last we are done, all the trucks have gone. Now we
swiftly clean up the remaining dirt: there must be "no trace left of
the *Schweinerei*." But just as the last truck disappears behind the
trees and we walk, finally, to rest in the shade, a shrill whistle sounds
around the bend. Slowly, terribly slowly, a train rolls in, the engine
whistles back with a deafening shriek. Again weary, pale faces at the
windows, flat as though cut out of paper, with huge, feverishly burning eyes. Already trucks are pulling up, already the composed gen-

tleman with the notebook is at his post, and the SS men emerge from
the commissary carrying briefcases for the gold and money. We unseal the train doors.

It is impossible to control oneself any longer. Brutally we tear
suitcases from their hands, impatiently pull off their coats. Go on, go
on, vanish! They go, they vanish. Men, women, children. Some of
them know.

Here is a woman—she walks quickly, but tries to appear calm. A
small child with a pink cherub's face runs after her and, unable to
keep up, stretches out his little arms and cries: "Mama! Mama!"

"Pick up your child, woman!"

"It's not mine, sir, not mine!" she shouts hysterically and runs on,
covering her face with her hands. She wants to hide, she wants to
reach those who will not ride the trucks, those who will go on foot,
those who will stay alive. She is young, healthy, good-looking, she
wants to live.

But the child runs after her, wailing loudly: "Mama, mama, don't
leave me!"

"It's not mine, not mine, no!"

Andrei, a sailor from Sevastopol grabs hold of her. His eyes are
glassy from vodka and the heat. With one powerful blow he knocks
her off her feet, then, as she falls, takes her by the hair and pulls her
up again. His face twitches with rage.

"Ah, you bloody Jewess! So you're running from your own
child! I'll show you, you whore!" His huge hand chokes her, he lifts
her in the air and heaves her onto the truck like a heavy sack of
grain.

"Here! And take this with you, bitch!" and he throws the child
at her feet.

"*Gut gemacht*, good work, that's the way to deal with degener-
ate mothers," says the SS man standing at the foot of the truck.
"*Gut, gut, Russki.*"

"Shut your mouth," growls Andrei through clenched teeth and
walks away. From under a pile of rags he pulls out a canteen, un-
screws the cork, takes a few deep swallows, passes it to me. The
strong vodka burns the throat. My head swims, my legs are shaky,
again I feel like throwing up.

And suddenly, above the teeming crowd pushing forward like a
river driven by an unseen power, a girl appears. She descends lightly
from the train, hops onto the gravel, looks around inquiringly, as if
somewhat surprised. Her soft, blond hair has fallen on her shoulders
in a torrent, she throws it back impatiently. With a natural gesture

she runs her hands down her blouse, casually straightens her skirt. She stands like this for an instant, gazing at the crowd, then turns and with a gliding look examines our faces, as though searching for someone. Unknowingly, I continue to stare at her, until our eyes meet.

"Listen, tell me, where are they taking us?"

I look at her without saying a word. Here, standing before me, is a girl, a girl with enchanting blond hair, with beautiful breasts, wearing a little cotton blouse, a girl with a wise, mature look in her eyes. Here she stands, gazing straight into my face, waiting. And over there is the gas chamber: communal death, disgusting and ugly. And over in the other direction is the concentration camp: the shaved head, the heavy Soviet trousers in sweltering heat, the sickening, stale odor of dirty, damp female bodies, the animal hunger, the inhuman labor, and later the same gas chamber, only an even more hideous, more terrible death . . .

Why did she bring it, I think to myself, noticing a lovely gold watch on her delicate wrist. They'll take it away from her anyway.

"Listen, tell me," she repeats.

I remain silent. Her lips tighten.

"I know," she says with a shade of proud contempt in her voice, tossing her head. She walks off resolutely in the direction of the trucks. Someone tries to stop her; she boldly pushes him aside and runs up the steps. In the distance I can only catch a glimpse of her blond hair flying in the breeze.

I go back inside the train, I carry out dead infants, I unload luggage. I touch corpses, but I cannot overcome the mounting, uncontrollable terror. I try to escape from the corpses, but they are everywhere: lined up on the gravel, on the cement edge of the ramp, inside the cattle cars. Babies, hideous naked women, men twisted by convulsions. I run off as far as I can go, but immediately a whip slashes across my back. Out of the corner of my eye I see an SS man, swearing profusely. I stagger forward and run, lose myself in the Canada group. Now, at last, I can once more rest against the stack of rails. The sun has leaned low over the horizon and illuminates the ramp with a reddish glow; the shadows of the trees have become elongated, ghostlike. In the silence that settles over nature this time of day, the human cries seem to rise all the way to the sky.

Only from this distance does one have a full view of the inferno on the teeming ramp. I see a pair of human beings who have fallen to the ground locked in a last desperate embrace. The man has dug his fingers into the woman's flesh and has caught her clothing with his teeth. She screams hysterically, swears, cries, until at last a large boot comes down over her throat and she is silent. They are pulled apart and dragged like cattle to the truck. I see four Canada men lugging a corpse: a huge, swollen female corpse. Cursing, dripping wet from the strain, they kick out of their way some stray children who have been running all over the ramp, howling like dogs. The men pick them up by the collars, heads, arms, and toss them inside the trucks, on top of the heaps. The four men have trouble lifting the fat corpse onto the car, they call others for help, and all together they hoist up the mound of meat. Big, swollen, puffed-up corpses are being collected from all over the ramp; on top of them are piled the invalids, the smothered, the sick, the unconscious. The heap seethes, howls, groans. The driver starts the motor, the truck begins rolling.

"*Halt! Halt!*" an SS man yells after them. "Stop, damn you!"

They are dragging to the truck an old man wearing tails and a band around his arm. His head knocks against the gravel and pavement, he moans and wails in an uninterrupted monotone: "*Ich will mit dem Herrn Kommendanten sprechen*—I wish to speak with the commandant . . ." With senile stubbornness he keeps repeating these words all the way. Thrown on the truck, trampled by others, choked, he still wails: "*Ich will mit dem . . .*"

"Look here, old man!" a young SS man calls, laughing jovially. "In half an hour you'll be talking with the top commandant! Only don't forget to greet him with a *Heil Hitler!*"

Several other men are carrying a small girl with only one leg. They hold her by the arms and the one leg. Tears are running down her face, she whispers faintly: "Sir, it hurts, it hurts . . ." They throw her onto the truck on top of the corpses. She will burn alive along with them.

The evening has come, cool and clear. The stars are out. We lie against the rails. It is incredibly quiet. Anemic bulbs hang from the top of the high lampposts; beyond the circle of light stretches an impenetrable darkness. Just one step, and a man could vanish forever. But the guards are watching, their automatics ready.

"Did you get the shoes?" asks Henri.

"No."

"Why?"

"My God, man, I am finished, absolutely finished!"

"So soon? After only one transport? Just look at me, I . . . since Christmas, at least a million people have passed through my hands. The worst of all are the transports from around Paris—one is always bumping into friends."

"And what do you say to them?"

"That first they will have a bath, and later we'll meet at the camp. What would you say?"

I do not answer. We drink coffee with vodka; somebody opens a tin of cocoa and mixes it with sugar. We scoop it up by the handful, the cocoa sticks to the lips. Again coffee, again vodka.

"Henri, what are we waiting for?"

"There'll be another transport."

"I'm not going to unload it! I can't take any more."

"So, it's gotten you down? Canada is nice, eh?" Henri grins indulgently and disappears into the darkness. In a moment he is back again.

"All right. Just sit here quietly and don't let an SS man see you. I'll try to find you your shoes."

"Just leave me alone. Never mind the shoes." I want to sleep. It is very late.

Another whistle, another transport. Freight cars emerge out of the darkness, pass under the lampposts, and again vanish in the night. The ramp is small, but the circle of lights is smaller. The unloading will have to be done gradually. Somewhere the trucks are growling. They back up against the steps, black, ghostlike, their searchlights flash across the trees. *Wasser! Luft!* The same all over again, like a late showing of the same film: a volley of shots, the train falls silent. Only this time a little girl pushes herself halfway through the small window and, losing her balance, falls out onto the gravel. Stunned, she lies still for a moment, then stands up and begins walking around in a circle, faster and faster, waving her rigid arms in the air, breathing loudly and spasmodically, whining in a faint voice. Her mind has given way in the inferno inside the train. The whining is hard on the nerves: an SS man approaches calmly, his heavy boot strikes between her shoulders. She falls. Holding her down with his foot, he draws his revolver, fires once, then again. She remains face down, kicking the gravel with her feet, until she stiffens. They proceed to unseal the train.

I am back on the ramp, standing by the doors. A warm, sickening smell gushes from inside. Ths mountain of people filling the car almost halfway up to the ceiling is motionless, horribly tangled, but still steaming.

"*Ausladen!*" comes the command. An SS man steps out from the darkness. Across his chest hangs a portable searchlight. He throws a stream of light inside.

"Why are you standing about like sheep? Start unloading!" His whip flies and falls across our backs. I seize a corpse by the hand; the fingers close tightly around mine. I pull back with a shriek and stagger away. My heart pounds, jumps up to my throat. I can no longer control the nausea. Hunched under the train I begin to vomit. Then, like a drunk, I weave over to the stack of rails.

I lie against the cool, kind metal and dream about returning to the camp, about my bunk, on which there is no mattress, about sleep among comrades who are not going to the gas tonight. Suddenly I see the camp as a haven of peace. It is true, others may be dying, but one is somehow still alive, one has enough food, enough strength to work . . .

The lights on the ramp flicker with a spectral glow, the wave of people—feverish, agitated, stupefied people—flows on and on, endlessly. They think that now they will have to face a new life in the camp, and they prepare themselves emotionally for the hard struggle ahead. They do not know that in just a few moments they will die, that the gold, money, and diamonds which they have so prudently hidden in their clothing and on their bodies are now useless to them. Experienced professionals will probe into every recess of their flesh, will pull the gold from under the tongue and the diamonds from the uterus and the colon. They will rip out gold teeth. In tightly sealed crates they will ship them to Berlin.

The SS men's black figures move about, dignified, businesslike. The gentleman with the notebook puts down his final marks, rounds out the figures: fifteen thousand.

Many, very many, trucks have driven today to the crematorium.

It is almost over. The dead are being cleared off the ramp and piled into the last truck. The Canada men, weighed down under a load of bread, marmalade and sugar, and smelling of perfume and fresh linen, line up to go. For several days the entire camp will live off this transport. For several days the entire camp will talk about "Sosnowiec-Będzin." "Sosnowiec-Będzin" was a good, rich transport.

The stars are already beginning to pale as we walk back to the camp. The sky grows translucent and opens high above our heads—it is getting light.

Great columns of smoke rise from the crematoria and merge up above into a huge black river which very slowly floats across the sky over Birkenau and disappears beyond the forests in the direction of Trzebinia. The "Sosnowiec-Będzin" transport is already burning.

We pass a heavily armed SS detachment on its way to change

guard. The men march briskly, in step, shoulder to shoulder, one mass, one will.

"*Und morgen die ganze Welt* . . ." they sing at the top of their lungs.

"*Rechts ran!* To the right march!" snaps a command from up front. We move out of their way.

*Translated from the Polish by Barbara Vedder*

# Slawomir Mrozek

## ON A JOURNEY

Just after B—— the road took us among damp, flat meadows. Only here and there the expanse of green was broken by a stubble field. In spite of mud and potholes the chaise was moving at a brisk pace. Far ahead, level with the ears of the horses, a blue band of the forest was stretching across the horizon. As one would expect at that time of the year, there was not a soul in sight.

Only after we had traveled for a while did I see the first human being. As we approached his features became clear; he was a man with an ordinary face and he wore a Post Office uniform. He was standing still at the side of the road, and as we passed he threw us an indifferent glance. No sooner had we left him behind than I noticed another one, in a similar uniform, also standing motionless on the verge. I looked at him carefully, but my attention was immediately attracted by the third and then the fourth still figure by the roadside. Their apathetic eyes were all fixed in the same direction, their uniforms were faded.

Intrigued by this spectacle I rose in my seat so that I could glance over the shoulders of the cabman; indeed, ahead of us another figure was standing erect. When we passed two more of them my curiosity became irresistible. There they were, standing quite a distance from each other, yet near enough to be able to see the next man, holding the same posture and paying as much attention to us as road signs do to passing travelers. And as soon as we passed one, another came into our field of vision. I was about to open my mouth to ask the coachman about the meaning of those men, when, without turning his head, he volunteered: "On duty."

We were just passing another still figure, staring indifferently into the distance.

"How's that?" I asked.

"Well, just normal. They are standing on duty," and he urged the horses on.

The coachman showed no inclination to offer any further eluci-
dation; perhaps he thought it was superfluous. Cracking his whip
from time to time and shouting at the horses, he was driving on.
Roadside brambles, shrines and solitary willow trees came to meet us
and receded again in the distance; between them, at regular intervals,
I could see the now familiar silhouettes.

"What sort of duty are they doing?" I inquired.

"State duty, of course. Telegraph line."

"How's that? Surely for a telegraph line you need poles and
wires!"

The coachman looked at me and shrugged his shoulders.

"I can see that you've come from far away," he said. "Yes, we
know that for a telegraph you need poles and wires. But this is wireless telegraph. We were supposed to have one with wires but the
poles got stolen and there's no wire."

"What do you mean, no wire?"

"There simply isn't any," he said, and shouted at the horses.

Surprise silenced me for the moment but I had no intention of
abandoning my inquiries.

"And how does it work without wires?"

"That's easy. The first one shouts what's needed to the second,
the second repeats it to the third, the third to the fourth and so on
until the telegram gets to where it's supposed to. Just now they
aren't transmitting or you'd hear them yourself."

"And it works, this telegraph?"

"Why shouldn't it work? It works all right. But often the message gets twisted. It's worst when one of them has had a drink too
many. Then his imagination gets to work and various words get
added. But otherwise it's even better than the usual telegraph with
poles and wires. After all live men are more intelligent, you know.
And there's no storm damage to repair and great saving on timber,
and timber is short. Only in the winter there are sometimes interrup-
tions. Wolves. But that can't be helped."

"And those men, are they satisfied?" I asked.

"Why not? The work isn't very hard, only they've got to know
foreign words. And it'll get better still; the postmaster has gone to
Warsaw to ask for megaphones for them so that they don't have to
shout so much."

"And should one of them be hard of hearing?"

"Ah, they don't take such-like. Nor do they take men with a lisp.
Once they took on a chap that stammered. He got his job through

influence but he didn't keep it long because he was blocking the line.
I hear that by the twenty-kilometers stone there's one who went to a
drama school. He shouts most clearly."

His arguments confused me for a while. Deep in thought, I no
longer paid attention to the men by the road verge. The chaise was
jumping over potholes, moving towards the forest, which was now
occupying most of the horizon.

"All right," I said carefully, "but wouldn't you prefer to have a
new telegraph with poles and wires?"

"Good heavens, no." The coachman was shocked. "For the first
time it's easy to get a job in our district—in the telegraph, that is. And
people don't have to rely only on their wages either. If someone expects a cable and is particularly anxious not to have it twisted, then
he takes his chaise along the line and slips something into the pocket
of each one of the telegraph boys. After all a wireless telegraph is
something different from one with wires. More modern."

Over the rattle of the wheels I could hear a distant sound, neither
a cry nor a shout, but a sort of sustained wailing.

"Aaaeeeaaauuueeeaaaeeeaayayay."

The coachman turned in his seat and put his hand to his ear.

"They are transmitting," he said. "Let's stop so that we can hear
better."

When the monotonous noise of our wheels ceased, total silence
enveloped the fields. In that silence the wailing, which resembled the
cry of birds on a moor, came nearer to us. His hand cupped to his
ear, the telegraph man nearby made ready to receive.

"It'll get here in a moment," whispered the coachman.

Indeed. When the last distant "ayayay" died away, from behind
a clump of trees came the prolonged shout:

"Fa . . . th . . . er dea . . . d fu . . . ner . . . al Wed . . . nes-
. . . day."

"May he rest in peace," sighed the coachman and cracked his
whip. We were entering the forest.

*Translated from the Polish by Konrad Syrop*

# Alexander Solzhenitsyn

## MATRYONA'S HOME

A HUNDRED AND EIGHTY-FOUR kilometers from Moscow trains were still slowing down to a crawl a good six months after it happened. Passengers stood glued to the windows or went out to stand by the doors. Was the line under repair, or what? Would the train be late?

It was all right. Past the crossing the train picked up speed again and the passengers went back to their seats.

Only the engine-drivers knew what it was all about.

The engine-drivers and I.

In the summer of 1953 I was coming back from the hot and dusty desert, just following my nose—so long as it led me back to Russia. Nobody waited or wanted me at any particular place, because I was a little matter of ten years overdue. I just wanted to get to the central belt, away from the great heats, close to the leafy muttering of forests. I wanted to efface myself, to lose myself in deepest Russia . . . if it was still anywhere to be found.

A year earlier I should have been lucky to get a job carrying a hod this side of the Urals. They wouldn't have taken me as an electrician on a decent construction job. And I had an itch to teach. Those who knew told me that it was a waste of money buying a ticket, that I should have a journey for nothing.

But things were beginning to move. When I went up the stairs of the N—— Oblast Education Department and asked for the Personnel Section, I was surprised to find Personnel sitting behind a glass partition, like in a chemist's shop, instead of the usual black leather-padded door. I went timidly up to the window, bowed, and asked, "Please, do you need any mathematicians somewhere where the trains don't run? I should like to settle there for good."

They passed every dot and comma in my documents through a fine comb, went from one room to another, made telephone calls. It was something out of the ordinary for them too—people always wanted the towns, the bigger the better. And lo and behold, they found just the place for me—Vysokoe Polye. The very sound of it gladdened my heart.

Vysokoe Polye did not belie its name. It stood on rising ground, with gentle hollows and other little hills around it. It was enclosed by an unbroken ring of forest. There was a pool behind a weir. Just the place where I wouldn't mind living and dying. I spent a long time sitting on a stump in a coppice and wishing with all my heart that I didn't need breakfast and dinner every day but could just stay here and listen to the branches brushing against the roof in the night, with not a wireless anywhere to be heard and the whole world silent.

Alas, nobody baked bread in Vysokoe Polye. There was nothing edible on sale. The whole village lugged its victuals in sacks from the big town.

I went back to Personnel Section and raised my voice in prayer at the little window. At first they wouldn't even talk to me. But then they started going from one room to another, made a telephone call, scratched with their pens, and stamped on my orders the word "*Torfoprodukt.*"

Torfoprodukt? Turgenev never knew that you can put words like that together in Russian.

On the station building at Torfoprodukt, an antiquated temporary hut of gray wood, hung a stern notice, BOARD TRAINS ONLY FROM THE PASSENGERS' HALL. A further message had been scratched on the boards with a nail, *And Without Tickets*. And by the booking-office, with the same melancholy wit, somebody had carved for all time the words, *No Tickets*. It was only later that I fully appreciated the meaning of these addenda. Getting to Torfoprodukt was easy. But not getting away.

Here too, deep and trackless forests had once stood, and were still standing after the Revolution. Then they were chopped down by the peatcutters and the neighboring kolkhoz. Its chairman, Shashkov, had razed quite a few hectares of timber and sold it at a good profit down in Odessa oblast.

The workers' settlement sprawled untidily among the peat bogs —monotonous shacks from the 'thirties, and little houses with carved façades and glass verandas, put up in the 'fifties. But inside these houses I could see no partitions reaching up to the ceilings, so there was no hope of renting a room with four real walls.

Over the settlement hung smoke from the factory chimney. Little locomotives ran this way and that along narrow-gauge railway lines, giving out more thick smoke and piercing whistles, pulling loads of dirty brown peat in slabs and briquettes. I could safely assume that in the evening a loudspeaker would be crying its heart out over the door of the club and there would be drunks roaming the streets and, sooner or later, sticking knives in each other.

This was what my dream about a quiet corner of Russia had brought me to . . . when I could have stayed where I was and lived in an adobe hut looking out on the desert, with a fresh breeze at night and only the starry dome of the sky overhead.

I couldn't sleep on the station bench, and as soon as it started getting light I went for another stroll around the settlement. This time I saw a tiny market-place. Only one woman stood there at that early hour, selling milk, and I took a bottle and started drinking it on the spot.

I was struck by the way she talked. Instead of a normal speaking voice she used an ingratiating singsong, and her words were the ones I was longing to hear when I left Asia for this place.

"Drink, and God bless you. You must be a stranger round here?"

"And where are you from?" I asked, feeling more cheerful.

I learned that the peat workings weren't the only thing, that over the railway lines there was a hill, and over the hill a village, that this village was Talnovo, and it had been there ages ago, when the "gypsy woman" lived in the big house and the wild woods stood all round. And farther on there was a whole countryside full of villages —Chaslitsy, Ovintsy, Spudni, Shevertni, Shestimirovo, deeper and deeper into the woods, farther and farther from the railway, up towards the lakes.

The names were like a soothing breeze to me. They held a promise of backwoods Russia. I asked my new acquaintance to take me to Talnovo after the market was over, and find a house for me to lodge in.

It appeared that I was a lodger worth having: in addition to my rent, the school offered a lorry-load of peat for the winter to whoever took me. The woman's ingratiating smile gave way to a thoughtful frown. She had no room herself, because she and her husband were "keeping" her aged mother, so she took me first to one lot of relatives, then to another. But there wasn't a separate room to be had and both places were crowded and noisy.

We had come to a dammed-up stream that was short of water and had a little bridge over it. No other place in all the village took my fancy as this did: there were two or three willows, a lop-sided house, ducks swimming on the pond, geese shaking themselves as they stepped out of the water

"Well, perhaps we might just call on Matryona," said my guide, who was getting tired of me by now. "Only it isn't so neat and cozy-like in her house, neglects things she does. She's unwell."

Matryona's house stood quite nearby. Its row of four windows looked out on the cold backs, the two slopes of the roof were covered with shingles, and a little attic window was decorated in the old Russian style. But the shingles were rotting, the beam-ends of the house and the once mighty gates had turned gray with age, and there were gaps in the little shelter over the gate.

The small door let into the gate was fastened, but instead of knocking my companion just put her hand under and turned the catch, a simple device to prevent animals from straying. The yard was not covered, but there was a lot under the roof of the house. As you went through the outer door a short flight of steps rose to a roomy landing, which was open to the roof high overhead. To the left, other steps led up to the top room, which was a separate structure with no stove, and yet another flight down to the basement. To the right lay the house proper, with its attic and its cellar.

It had been built a long time ago, built sturdily, to house a big family, and now one lonely woman of nearly sixty lived in it.

When I went into the cottage she was lying on the Russian stove under a heap of those indeterminate dingy rags which are so precious to a working man or woman.

The spacious room, and especially the best part near the windows, was full of rubber-plants in pots and tubs standing on stools and benches. They peopled the householder's loneliness like a speechless but living crowd. They had been allowed to run wild, and they took up all the scanty light on the north side. In what was left of the light, and half-hidden by the stove-pipe, the mistress of the house looked yellow and weak. You could see from her clouded eyes that illness had drained all the strength out of her.

While we talked she lay on the stove face downwards, without a pillow, her head towards the door, and I stood looking up at her. She showed no pleasure at getting a lodger, just complained about the wicked disease she had. She was just getting over an attack; it didn't come upon her every month, but when it did, "It hangs on two or three days so as I shan't manage to get up and wait on you. I've room and to spare, you can live here if you like."

Then she went over the list of other housewives with whom I should be quieter and cozier, and I wanted me to make the round of them. But I had already seen that I was destined to settle in this dimly lit house with the tarnished mirror in which you couldn't see yourself, and the two garish posters (one advertising books, the other about the harvest), bought for a ruble each to brighten up the walls.

Matryona Vasilyevna made me go off round the village again, and when I called on her the second time she kept trying to put me off, "We're not clever, we can't cook, I don't know how we shall suit. . . ." But this time she was on her feet when I got there, and I thought I saw a glimmer of pleasure in her eyes to see me back. We reached agreement about the rent and the load of peat which the school would deliver.

Later on I found out that, year in year out, it was a long time since Matryona Vasilyevna had earned a single ruble. She didn't get a pension. Her relatives gave her very little help. In the kolkhoz she had worked not for money but for credits, the marks recording her labor days in her well-thumbed workbook.

So I moved in with Matryona Vasilyevna. We didn't divide the room. Her bed was in the corner between the door and the stove, and I unfolded my camp-bed by one window and pushed Matryona's beloved rubber-plants out of the light to make room for a little table by another. The village had electric light, laid on back in the 'twenties, from Shatury. The newspapers were writing about "Ilyich's little lamps," but the peasants talked wide-eyed about "Tsar Fire."

Some of the better-off people in the village might not have thought Matryona's house much of a home, but it kept us snug enough that autumn and winter. The roof still held the rain out, and the freezing winds could not blow the warmth of the stove away all at once, though it was cold by morning, especially when the wind blew on the shabby side.

In addition to Matryona and myself, a cat, some mice, and some cockroaches lived in the house.

The cat was no longer young, and gammy-legged as well. Matryona had taken her in out of pity, and she had stayed. She walked on all four feet but with a heavy limp: one of her feet was sore and she favored it. When she jumped from the stove she didn't land with the soft sound a cat usually makes, but with a heavy thud as three of her feet struck the floor at once—such a heavy thud that until I got used to it, it gave me a start. This was because she stuck three feet out together to save the fourth.

It wasn't because the cat couldn't deal with them that there were mice in the cottage: she would pounce into the corner like lightning, and come back with a mouse between her teeth. But the mice were usually out of reach because somebody, back in the good old days, had stuck embossed wallpaper of a greenish color on Matryona's walls, and not just one layer of it but five. The layers held together all right, but in many places the whole lot had come away from the wall, giving the room a sort of inner skin. Between the timber of the walls and the skin of wallpaper the mice had made themselves runs where they impudently scampered about, running at times right up to the ceiling. The cat followed their scamperings with angry eyes, but couldn't get at them.

Sometimes the cat ate cockroaches as well, but they made her sick. The only thing the cockroaches respected was the partition which screened the mouth of the Russian stove and the kitchen from the best part of the room.

They did not creep into the best room. But the kitchen at night swarmed with them, and if I went in late in the evening for a drink of water and switched on the light the whole floor, the big bench, and even the wall would be one rustling brown mass. From time to time I brought home some borax from the school laboratory and we mixed it with dough to poison them. There would be fewer cockroaches for a while, but Matryona was afraid that we might poison the cat as well. We stopped putting down poison and the cockroaches multiplied anew.

At night, when Matryona was already asleep and I was working at my table, the occasional rapid scamper of mice behind the wallpaper would be drowned in the sustained and ceaseless rustling of cockroaches behind the screen, like the sound of the sea in the distance. But I got used to it because there was nothing evil in it, nothing dishonest. Rustling was life to them.

I even got used to the crude beauty on the poster, forever reaching out from the wall to offer me Belinsky, Panferov, and a pile of other books—but never saying a word. I got used to everything in Matryona's cottage.

Matryona got up at four or five in the morning. Her wall-clock was twenty-seven years old, and had been bought in the village shop. It was always fast, but Matryona didn't worry about that—just so long as it didn't lose and make her late in the morning. She switched on the light behind the kitchen screen and moving quietly, considerately, doing her best not to make a noise, she lit the stove, went to milk the goat (all the livestock she had was this one dirty-white goat with twisted horns), fetched water and boiled it in three iron pots: one for me, one for herself, and one for the goat. She fetched potatoes from the cellar, picking out the littlest for the goat, little ones for herself and egg-sized ones for me. There were no big ones, because her garden was sandy, had not been manured since the war and was always planted with potatoes, potatoes, and potatoes again, so that it wouldn't grow big ones.

I scarcely heard her about her morning tasks. I slept late, woke up in the wintry daylight, stretched a bit and stuck my head out from under my blanket and my sheep-skin. These, together with the prisoner's jerkin round my legs and a sack stuffed with straw underneath me, kept me warm in bed even on nights when the cold wind rattled our wobbly windows from the north. When I heard the discreet noises on the other side of the screen I spoke to her, slowly and deliberately.

"Good morning, Matryona Vasilyevna!"

And every time the same good-natured words came to me from behind the screen. They began with a warm, throaty gurgle, the sort of sound grandmothers make in fairy-tales.

"M-m-m . . . same to you too!"

And after a little while, "Your breakfast's ready for you now."

She didn't announce what was for breakfast, but it was easy to guess: taters in their jackets or tatty soup (as everybody in the village called it), or barley gruel (no other grain could be bought in Torfoprodukt that year, and even the barley you had to fight for, because it was the cheapest and people bought it up by the sack to fatten their pigs on it). It wasn't always salted as it should be, it was often slightly burnt, it furred the palate and the gums, and it gave me heartburn.

But Matryona wasn't to blame: there was no butter in Torfoprodukt either, margarine was desperately short, and only mixed cooking fat was plentiful, and when I got to know it I saw that the Russian stove was not convenient for cooking: the cook cannot see the pots and they are not heated evenly all round. I suppose the stove came down to our ancestors from the Stone Age because you can stoke it up once before daylight, and food and water, mash and swill, will keep warm in it all day long. And it keeps you warm while you sleep.

I ate everything that was cooked for me without demur, patiently putting aside anything uncalled-for that I came across: a hair, a bit of peat, a cockroach's leg. I hadn't the heart to find fault with Matryona. Afer all, she had warned me herself.

"We aren't clever, we can't cook—I don't know how we shall suit. . . ."

"Thank you," I said quite sincerely.

"What for? For what is your own?" she answered, disarming me with a radiant smile. And, with a guileless look of her faded blue eyes, she would ask, "And what shall I cook you for just now?"

For just now meant for supper. I ate twice a day, like at the front. What could I order for just now? It would have to be one of the same old things, taters or tatty soup.

I resigned myself to it, because I had learned by now not to look for the meaning of life in food. More important to me was the smile on her roundish face, which I tried in vain to catch when at last I had earned enough to buy a camera. As soon as she saw the cold eye of the lens upon her Matryona assumed a strained or else an exaggeratedly severe expression.

Just once I did manage to get a snap of her looking through the window into the street and smiling at something.

Matryona had a lot of worries that winter. Her neighbors put it into her head to try and get a pension. She was all alone in the world, and when she began to be seriously ill she had been dismissed from the kolkhoz as well. Injustices had piled up, one on top of another. She was ill, but not regarded as a disabled person. She had worked for a quarter of a century in the kolkhoz, but it was a kolkhoz and not a factory, so she was not entitled to a pension for herself. She could only try and get one for her husband, for the loss of her breadwinner. But she had had no husband for twelve years now, not since the beginning of the war, and it wasn't easy to obtain all the particulars from different places about his length of service and how much he had earned. What a bother it was getting those forms through! Getting somebody to certify that he'd earned, say, 300 roubles a month; that she lived alone and nobody helped her; what year she was born in. Then all this had to be taken to the pensions office. And taken somewhere else to get all the mistakes corrected. And taken back again. Then you had to find out whether they would give you a pension.

To make it all more difficult the Pensions Office was twenty kilometers east of Talnovo, the Rural Council Offices ten kilometers to the west, the Factory District Council an hour's walk to the north. They made her run around from office to office for two months on end, to get an *i* dotted or a *t* crossed. Every trip took a day. She goes down to the rural district council—and the secretary isn't there today. Secretaries of rural councils often aren't here today. So come in tomorrow. Tomorrow the secretary is in, but he hasn't got his rubber stamp. So come again the next day. And the day after that back she goes yet again, because all her papers are pinned together and some cock-eyed clerk has signed the wrong one.

"They shove me around, Ignatich," she used to complain to me after these fruitless excursions. "Worn out with it I am."

But she soon brightened up. I found that she had a sure means of putting herself in a good humor. She worked. She would grab a shovel and go off to lift potatoes. Or she would tuck a sack under her arm and go after peat. Or take a wicker basket and look for berries deep in the woods. When she'd been bending her back to bushes instead of office desks for a while, and her shoulders were aching from a heavy load, Matryona would come back cheerful, at peace with the world and smiling her nice smile.

"I'm on to a good thing now, Ignatich. I know where to go for it" (peat she meant), "a lovely place it is."

"But surely my peat is enough, Matryona Vasilyevna? There's a whole lorry-load of it."

"Pooh! Your peat! As much again, and then as much again, that might be enough. When the winter gets really stiff and the wind's battling at the windows, it blows the heat out of the house faster than you can make the stove up. Last year we got heaps and heaps of it. I'd have had three loads in by now. But they're out to catch us. They've summoned one woman from our village already."

That's how it was. The frightening breath of winter was already in the air. There were forests all round, and no fuel to be had anywhere. Excavators roared away in the bogs, but there was no peat on sale to the villagers. It was delivered, free, to the bosses and to the people round the bosses, and teachers, doctors, and workers got a load each. The people of Talnovo were not supposed to get any peat, and they weren't supposed to ask about it. The chairman of the kolkhoz walked about the village looking people in the eye while he gave his orders or stood chatting, and talked about anything you liked except fuel. He was stocked-up. Who said anything about winter coming?

So just as in the old days they used to steal the squire's wood, now they pinched peat from the trust. The women went in parties of five or ten so that they would be less frightened. They went in the daytime. The peat cut during the summer had been stacked up all over the place to dry. That's the good thing about peat, it can't be carted off as soon as it's cut. It lies around drying till autumn, or, if the roads are bad, till the snow starts falling. This was when the women used to come and take it. They could get six peats in a sack if it was damp, or ten if it was dry. A sackful weighed about two poods and it sometimes had to be carried over three kilometers. This was enough to make the stove up once. There were two hundred days in the winter. The Russian stove had to be lit in the mornings, and the "Dutch" stove in the evenings.

"Why beat about the bush?" said Matryona angrily to someone invisible. "Since there've been no more horses, what you can't heave around yourself you haven't got. My back never heals up. Winter you're pulling sledges, summer it's bundles on your back, it's God's truth I'm telling you."

The women went more than once in a day. On good days Matryona brought six sacks home. She piled my peat up where it could be seen, and hid her own under the passageway, boarding up the hole every night.

"If they don't just happen to think of it, the devils will never find it in their born days," said Matryona smiling and wiping the sweat from her brow.

What could the peat trust do? Its establishment didn't run to a watchman for every bog. I suppose they had to show a rich haul in their returns, and then write off so much for crumbling, so much washed away by the rain. . . . Sometimes they would take it into their heads to put out patrols and try to catch the women as they came into the village. The women would drop their sacks and scatter. Or somebody would inform and there would be a house-to-house search. They would draw up a report on the stolen peat, and threaten a court action. The women would stop fetching it for a while, but the approach of winter drove them out with sledges in the middle of the night.

When I had seen a little more of Matryona I noticed that apart from cooking and looking after the house, she had quite a lot of other jobs to do every day. She kept all her jobs, and the proper times for them, in her head and always knew when she woke up in the morning how her day would be occupied. Apart from fetching peat, and stumps which the tractors unearthed in the bogs, apart from the cranberries which she put to soak in big jars for the winter ("Give your teeth an edge, Ignatich," she used to say when she offered me some), apart from digging potatoes and all the coming and going to do with her pension, she had to get hay from somewhere for her one and only dirty-white goat.

"Why don't you keep a cow, Matryona?"

Matryona stood there in her grubby apron, by the opening in the kitchen screen, facing my table, and explained to me.

"Oh, Ignatich, there's enough milk from the goat for me. And if

I started keeping a cow she'd eat me out of house and home in no time. You can't cut the grass by the railway track, because it belongs to the railway, and you can't cut any in the woods, because it belongs to the foresters, and they won't let me have any at the kolkhoz because I'm not a member any more, they reckon. And those who are members have to work there every day till the white flies swarm, and make their own hay when there's snow on the ground—what's the good of grass like that? In the old days they used to be sweating to get the hay in at midsummer, between the end of June and the end of July, while the grass was sweet and juicy. . . ."

So it meant a lot of work for Matryona to gather enough hay for one skinny little goat. She took her sickle and a sack and went off early in the morning to places where she knew there was grass growing—round the edges of fields, on the roadside, on hummocks in the bog. When she had stuffed her sack with heavy fresh grass she dragged it home and spread it out in her yard to dry. From a sackful of grass she got one forkload of dry hay.

The farm had a new chairman, sent down from the town not long ago, and the first thing he did was to cut down the garden-plots for those who were not fit to work. He left Matryona fifteen hundredths of sand—when there were ten hundredths just lying idle on the other side of the fence. Yet when they were short of working hands, when the women dug in their heels and wouldn't budge, the chairman's wife would come to see Matryona. She was from the town as well, a determined woman whose short gray overcoat and intimidating glare gave her a somewhat military appearance. She walked into the house without so much as a good morning and looked sternly at Matryona. Matryona was uneasy.

"Well now, Comrade Vasilyevna," said the chairman's wife, drawing out her words. "You will have to help the kolkhoz! You will have to go and help cart muck out tomorrow!"

A little smile of forgiveness wrinkled Matryona's face—as though she understood the embarrassment which the chairman's wife must feel not being able to pay her for her work.

"Well—er," she droned, "I'm not well, of course, and I'm not attached to you any more . . ." Then she hurried to correct herself. "What time should I come, then?"

"And bring your own fork!" the chairman's wife instructed her. Her stiff skirt crackled as she walked away.

"Think of that!" grumbled Matryona as the door closed. "Bring your own fork! They've got neither forks nor shovels on the kolkhoz. And I don't have a man who'll put a handle on for me!"

She went on thinking about it out loud all evening.

"What's the good of talking, Ignatich. I must help, of course. Only the way they work it's all a waste of time—don't know whether they're coming or going. The women stand propped up on their shovels and waiting for the factory hooter to blow twelve o'clock. Or else they get on to adding up who's earned what and who's turned up for work and who hasn't. Now what I call work, there isn't a sound out of anybody, only . . . oh dear, dear, dinner time's soon rolled round—what, getting dark already. . . ."

In the morning she went off with her fork.

But it wasn't just the kolkhoz—any distant relative, or just a neighbor, could come to Matryona of an evening and say, "Come and give me a hand tomorrow, Matryona. We'll finish lifting the potatoes."

Matryona couldn't say no. She gave up what she should be doing next and went to help her neighbor, and when she came back she would say without a trace of envy, "Ah, you should see the size of her potatoes, Ignatich! It was a joy to dig them up. I didn't want to leave the allotment, God's truth I didn't."

Needless to say, not a garden could be plowed without Matryona's help. The women of Talnovo had got it neatly worked out that it was a longer and harder job for one woman to dig her garden with a spade than for six of them to put themselves in harness and plow six gardens. So they sent for Matryona to help them.

"Well—did you pay her?" I asked sometimes.

"She won't take money. You have to try and hide it on her when she's not looking."

Matryona had yet another troublesome chore when her turn came to feed the herdsmen. One of them was a hefty deaf mute, the other a boy who was never without a cigarette in his drooling mouth. Matryona's turn only came round every six weeks, but it put her to great expense. She went to the shop to buy tinned fish, and was lavish with sugar and butter, things she never ate herself. It seems that the housewives showed off in this way, trying to outdo each other in feeding the herdsmen.

"You've got to be careful with tailors and herdsmen," Matryona explained. "They'll spread your name all round the village if something doesn't suit them."

And every now and then attacks of serious illness broke in on this life that was already crammed with troubles. Matryona would be off her feet for a day or two, lying flat out on the stove. She didn't complain, and didn't groan, but she hardly stirred either. On these days, Masha, Matryona's closest friend from her earliest years, would come to look after the goat and light the stove. Matryona herself ate nothing, drank nothing, asked for nothing. To call in the doctor from the clinic at the settlement would have seemed strange in Talnovo, and would have given the neighbors something to talk about—what does she think she is, a lady? They did call her in once, and she arrived in a real temper and told Matryona to come down to the clinic when she was on her feet again. Matryona went, although she didn't really want to; they took specimens and sent them off to the district hospital—and that's the last anybody heard about it. Matryona was partly to blame herself.

But there was work waiting to be done, and Matryona soon started getting up again, moving slowly at first and then as briskly as ever.

"You never saw me in the old days, Ignatich. I'd lift any sack you liked, I didn't think five poods was too heavy. My father-in-law used to say, 'Matryona, you'll break your back.' And my brother-in-law didn't have to come and help me lift on the cart. Our horse was a war-horse, a big strong one. . . ."

"What do you mean, a war-horse?"

"They took ours for the war and gave us this one instead—he'd been wounded. But he turned out a bit spirited. Once he bolted with the sledge right into the lake, the men-folk hopped out of the way, but I grabbed the bridle, as true as I'm here, and stopped him. . . . Full of oats that horse was. They liked to feed their horses well in our village. If a horse feels his oats he doesn't know what heavy means."

But Matryona was a long way from being fearless. She was afraid of fire, afraid of "the lightning," and most of all she was for some reason afraid of trains.

"When I had to go to Cherusti the train came up from Nechaevka way with its great big eyes popping out and the rails humming away—put me in a proper fever. My knees started knocking. God's truth I'm telling you!" Matryona raised her shoulders as though she surprised herself.

"Maybe it's because they won't give people tickets, Matryona Vasilyevna?"

"At the window? They try to shove first-class tickets on to you. And the train was starting to move. We dashed about all over the place. 'Give us tickets, for pity's sake.'

"The men-folk had climbed on top of the carriages. Then we found a door that wasn't locked and shoved straight in without tickets . . . and all the carriages were empty, they were all empty, you could stretch out on the seat if you wanted to. Why they wouldn't give us tickets, the hard-hearted parasites, I don't know. . . ."

Still, before winter came Matryona's affairs were in a better state than ever before. They started paying her at last a pension of eighty rubles. Besides this she got just over a hundred from the school and me.

Some of her neighbors began to be envious.

"Hm! Matryona can live forever now! If she had any more money she wouldn't know what to do with it at her age."

Matryona had herself some new felt boots made. She bought a new jerkin. And she had an overcoat made out of the worn-out railway-man's greatcoat given to her by the engine-driver from Cherusti who had married Kira, her foster-daughter. The humped-backed village tailor put a padded lining under the cloth and it made a marvelous coat, such as Matryona had never worn before in all her sixty years.

In the middle of winter Matryona sewed two hundred rubles into the lining of this coat for her funeral. This made her quite cheerful.

"Now my mind's a bit easier, Ignatich."

December went by, January went by—and in those two months Matryona's illness held off. She started going over to Masha's house more often in the evening, to sit chewing sunflower seeds with her. She didn't invite guests herself in the evening out of consideration for my work. Once, on the feast of the Epiphany, I came back from school and found a party going on and was introduced to Matryona's three sisters, who called her "nan-nan" or "nanny" because she was the oldest. Until then not much had been heard of the sisters in our cottage—perhaps they were afraid that Matryona might ask them for help.

But one ominous event cast a shadow on the holiday for Matryona. She went to the church five versts away for the blessing of the water, and put her pot down among the others. When the blessing was over the women went rushing and jostling to get their pots back again. There were a lot of women in front of Matryona and when she got there her pot was missing, and no other vessel had been left behind. The pot had vanished as though the devil had run off with it.

Matryona went around the worshipers asking them, "Has any

of you girls accidentally mistook somebody else's holy water? In a pot?"

Nobody owned up. There had been some boys there, and boys got up to mischief sometimes. Matryona came home sad.

No one could say that Matryona was a devout believer. If anything, she was a heathen, and her strongest beliefs were superstitious. You mustn't go into the garden on the fast of St. John or there would be no harvest next year. A blizzard meant that somebody had hanged himself. If you pinched your foot in the door you could expect a guest. All the time I lived with her I didn't once see her say her prayers or even cross herself. But, whatever job she was doing, she began with a "God bless us," and she never failed to say "God bless you," when I set out for school. Perhaps she did say her prayers, but on the quiet, either because she was shy or because she didn't want to embarrass me. There were icons on the walls. Ordinary days they were left in darkness, but for the vigil of a great feast, or on the morning of a holiday, Matryona would light the little lamp.

She had fewer sins on her conscience than her gammy-legged cat. The cat did kill mice. . . .

Now that her life was running more smoothly, Matryona started listening more carefully to my radio. (I had, of course, installed a speaker, or as Matryona called it, a peeker.)

When they announced on the radio that some new machine had been invented, I heard Matryona grumbling out in the kitchen, "New ones all the time, nothing but new ones. People don't want to work with the old ones any more, where are we going to store them all?"

There was a program about the seeding of clouds from airplanes. Matryona, listening up on the stove, shook her head, "Oh dear, dear, dear, they'll do away with one of the two—summer or winter."

Once Chaliapin was singing Russian folk songs. Matryona stood listening for a long time before she gave her emphatic verdict, "Queer singing, not our sort of singing."

"You can't mean that, Matryona Vasilyevna . . . just listen to him."

She listened a bit longer, and pursed her lips. "No, it's wrong. It isn't our sort of tune, and he's tricky with his voice."

She made up for this another time. They were broadcasting some of Glinka's songs. After half a dozen of these drawing-room ballads,

Matryona suddenly came from behind the screen clutching her apron, with a flush on her face and a film of tears over her dim eyes.

"That's our sort of singing," she said in a whisper.

So Matryona and I got used to each other and took each other for granted. She never pestered me with questions about myself. I don't know whether she was lacking in normal female curiosity or just tactful, but she never once asked if I had been married. All the Talnovo women kept at her to find out about me. Her answer was, "You want to know—you ask him. All I know is he's from distant parts."

And when I got round to telling her that I had spent a lot of time in prison she said nothing but just nodded, as though she had already suspected it.

And I thought of Matryona only as the helpless old woman she was now, and didn't try to rake up her past, didn't even suspect that there was anything to be found there.

I knew that Matryona had got married before the Revolution and come to live in the house I now shared with her, that she had gone "to the stove" immediately. (She had no mother-in-law and no older sister-in-law, so it was her job to put the pots in the oven on the very first morning of her married life.) I knew that she had had six children and that they had all died very young, so that there were never two of them alive at once. Then there was a sort of foster-daughter, Kira. Matryona's husband had not come back from the last war. She received no notification of his death. Men from the village who had served in the same company said that he might have been taken prisoner, or he might have been killed and his body not found. In the eight years that had gone by since the war Matryona had decided that he was not alive. It was a good thing that she thought so. If he was still alive he was probably in Brazil or Australia, and married again. The village of Talnovo, and the Russian language, would be fading from his memory.

One day, when I got back from school, I found a guest in the house, A tall, dark man, with his hat on his lap, was sitting on a chair which Matryona had moved up to the Dutch stove in the middle of the room. His face was completely surrounded by bushy black hair with hardly a trace of gray in it. His thick black mustaches ran into his full black beard, so that his mouth could hardly be seen. Black side-whiskers merged with the black locks which hung down from his crown, leaving only the tips of his ears visible; and broad black eyebrows met in a wide double span. But the front of his head as far as the crown was a spacious bald dome. His whole appearance made an impression of wisdom and dignity. He sat squarely on his chair, with his hands folded on his stick, and his stick resting vertically on the floor, in an attitude of patient expectation, and he obviously hadn't much to say to Matryona, who was busy behind the screen.

When I came in he eased his majestic head round towards me and suddenly addressed me, "Master, I can't see you very well. My son goes to your school. Grigoriev, Antoshka . . ."

There was no need for him to say any more. . . . However strongly inclined I felt to help this worthy old man I knew and dismissed in advance all the pointless things he was going to say. Antoshka Grigoriev was a plump, red-faced lad in 8-D who looked like a cat that's swallowed the cream. He seemed to think that he came to school for a rest and sat at his desk with a lazy smile on his face. Needless to say, he never did his homework. But the worst of it was that he had been put up into the next class from year to year because our district, and indeed the whole oblast and the neighboring oblasts, were famous for the high percentage of passes they obtained, and the school had to make an effort to keep its record up. So Antoshka had got it clear in his mind that however much the teachers threatened him they would put him up in the end, and there was no need for him to learn anything. He just laughed at us. There he sat in the eighth class, and he hadn't even mastered his decimals and didn't know one triangle from another. In the first two terms of the school year I had kept him firmly below the pass line and the same treatment awaited him in the third.

But now this half-blind old man, who should have been Antoshka's grandfather rather than his father, had come to humble himself before me—how could I tell him that the school had been deceiving him for years, and that I couldn't go on deceiving him, because I didn't want to ruin the whole class, to become a liar and a fake, to start despising my work and my profession.

For the time being I patiently explained that his son had been very slack, that he told lies at school and at home, that his mark-book must be checked frequently, and that we must both take him severely in hand.

"Severe as you like, master," he assured me, "I beat him every week now. And I've got a heavy hand."

While we were talking I remembered that Matryona had once interceded for Antoshka Grigoriev, but I hadn't asked what relation of hers he was and I had refused to do what she wanted. Matryona was standing in the kitchen doorway like a mute suppliant on this

occasion too. When Faddei Mironovich left saying that he would
call on me to see how things were going, I asked her, "I can't make
out what relation this Antoshka is to you, Matryona Vasilyevna."

"My brother-in-law's son," said Matryona shortly, and went out
to milk the goat.

When I'd worked it out I realized that this determined old man
with the black hair was the brother of the missing husband.

The long evening went by, and Matryona didn't bring up the
subject again. But late at night, when I had stopped thinking about
the old man and was working in a silence broken only by the rustling
of the cockroaches and the heavy tick of the wall-clock, Matryona
suddenly spoke from her dark corner, "You know, Ignatich, I nearly
married him once."

I had forgotten that Matryona was in the room. I hadn't heard a
sound from her—and suddenly her voice came out of the darkness,
as agitated as if the old man were still trying to win her.

I could see that Matryona had been thinking about nothing else
all evening.

She got up from her wretched rag bed and walked slowly towards me, as though she were following her own words. I sat back in
my chair and caught my first glimpse of a quite different Matryona.

There was no overhead light in our big room with its forest of
rubber-plants. The table lamp cast a ring of light round my exercise
books, and when I tore my eyes away from it the rest of the room
seemed to be half-dark and faintly tinged with pink. I thought I
could see the same pinkish glow in her usually sallow cheeks.

"He was the first one who came courting me, before Yefim did
. . . he was his brother . . . the older one. . . . I was nineteen
and Faddei was twenty-three. . . . They lived in this very same
house. Their house it was. Their father built it."

I looked round the room automatically. Instead of the old gray
house rotting under the faded green skin of wallpaper where the
mice had their playground, I suddenly saw new timbers, freshly
trimmed, and not yet discolored, and caught the cheerful smell of
pine-tar.

"Well, and what happened then?"

"That summer we went to sit in the coppice together," she whispered. "There used to be a coppice where the stable-yard is now.
They chopped it down. . . . I was just going to marry him, Ignatich. Then the German war started. They took Faddei in the army."

She let fall these few words—and suddenly the blue and white
and yellow July of the year 1914 burst into flower before my eyes:

the sky still peaceful, the floating clouds, the people sweating to get the ripe corn in. I imagined them side by side, the black-haired Hercules with a scythe over his shoulder, and the red-faced girl clasping a sheaf. And there was singing out under the open sky, such songs as nobody can sing nowadays, with all the machines in the fields.

"He went to the war—and vanished. For three years I kept to myself and waited. Never a sign of life did he give. . . ."

Matryona's round face looked out at me from an elderly threadbare head-scarf. As she stood there in the gentle reflected light from my lamp her face seemed to lose its slovenly workaday covering of wrinkles, and she was a scared young girl again with a frightening decision to make.

Yes. . . . I could see it. . . . The trees shed their leaves, the snow fell and melted. They plowed and sowed and reaped again. Again the trees shed their leaves, and snow fell. There was a revolution. Then another revolution. And the whole world was turned upside down.

"Their mother died and Yefim came to court me. You wanted to come to our house, he says, so come. He was a year younger than me, Yefim was. It's a saying with us—sensible girls get married after Michaelmas, and silly ones at midsummer. They were short-handed. I got married. . . . The wedding was on St. Peter's day, and then about St. Nicholas' day in the winter he came back . . . Faddei, I mean, from being a prisoner in Hungary."

Matryona covered her eyes.

I said nothing.

She turned towards the door as though somebody were standing there. "He stood there at the door. What a scream I let out! I wanted to throw myself at his feet! . . . But I couldn't. If it wasn't my own brother, he says, I'd take my axe to the both of you."

I shuddered. Matryona's despair, or her terror, conjured up a vivid picture of him standing in the dark doorway and raising his axe to her.

But she quieted down and went on with her story in a singsong voice, leaning on a chairback, "Oh dear, dear me, the poor dear man! There were so many girls in the village—but he wouldn't marry. I'll look for one with the same name as you, a second Matryona, he said. And that's what he did—fetched himself a Matryona from Lipovka. They built themselves a house of their own and they're still living in it. You pass their place every day on your way to school."

So that was it. I realized that I had seen the other Matryona quite often. I didn't like her. She was always coming to my Matryona to complain about her husband—he beat her, he was stingy, he was working her to death. She would weep and weep, and her voice always had a tearful note in it. As it turned out, my Matryona had nothing to regret, with Faddei beating his Matryona every day of his life and being so tight-fisted.

"Mine never beat me once," said Matryona of Yefim. "He'd pitch into another man in the street, but me he never hit once. . . . Well, there was one time . . . I quarreled with my sister-in-law and he cracked me on the forehead with a spoon. I jumped up from the table and shouted at them, 'Hope it sticks in your gullets, you idle lot of beggars, hope you choke!' I said. And off I went into the woods. He never touched me any more."

Faddei didn't seem to have any cause for regret either. The other Matryona had borne him six children (my Antoshka was one of them, the littlest, the runt) and they had all lived, whereas the children of Matryona and Yefim had died, every one of them, before they reached the age of three months, without any illness.

"One daughter, Elena, was born and was alive when they washed her, and then she died right after. . . . My wedding was on St. Peter's day, and it was St. Peter's day I buried my sixth, Alexander."

The whole village decided that there was a curse on Matryona.

Matryona still nodded emphatic belief when she talked about it. "There was a *course* on me. They took me to a woman as used to be a nun to get cured, she set me off coughing and waited for the *course* to jump out of me like a frog. Only nothing jumped out. . . ."

And the years had run by like running water. . . . In 1941 they didn't take Faddei into the army because of his poor sight, but they took Yefim. And what had happened to the elder brother in the first war happened to the younger in the second . . . he vanished without out trace. Only he never came back at all. The once noisy cottage was deserted, it became old and rotten, and Matryona, all alone in the world, grew old in it.

So she begged from the other Matryona, the cruelly beaten Matryona, a child of her womb (or was it a spot of Faddei's blood?), the youngest daughter, Kira.

For ten years she brought the girl up in her own house, in place of the children who had not lived. Then, not long before I arrived, she had married her off to a young engine-driver from Cherusti. The only help she got from anywhere came in dribs and drabs from Cherusti: a bit of sugar from time to time, or some of the fat when they killed a pig.

Sick and suffering, and feeling that death was not far off, Matryona had made known her will: the top room, which was a separate frame joined by tie-beams to the rest of the house, should go to Kira when she died. She said nothing about the house itself. Her three sisters had their eyes on it too.

That evening Matryona opened her heart to me. And, as often happens, no sooner were the hidden springs of her life revealed to me than I saw them in motion.

Kira arrived from Cherusti. Old Faddei was very worried. To get and keep a plot of land in Cherusti the young couple had to put up some sort of building. Matryona's top room would do very well. There was nothing else they could put up, because there was no timber to be had anywhere. It wasn't Kira herself so much, and it wasn't her husband, but old Faddei who was consumed with eagerness for them to get their hands on the plot at Cherusti.

He became a frequent visitor, laying down the law to Matryona and insisting that she should hand over the top room right away, before she died. On these occasions I saw a different Faddei. He was no longer an old man propped up by a stick, whom a push or a harsh word would bowl over. Although he was slightly bent by backache, he was still a fine figure; he had kept the vigorous black hair of a young man in his sixties; he was hot and urgent.

Matryona had not slept for two nights. It wasn't easy for her to make up her mind. She didn't grudge them the top room, which was standing there idle, any more than she ever grudged her labor or her belongings. And the top room was willed to Kira in any case. But the thought of breaking up the roof she had lived under for forty years was torture to her. Even I, a mere lodger, found it painful to think of them stripping away boards and wrenching out beams. For Matryona it was the end of everything.

But the people who were so insistent knew that she would let them break up her house before she died.

So Faddei and his sons and sons-in-law came along one February morning, the blows of five axes were heard and boards creaked and cracked as they were wrenched out. Faddei's eyes twinkled busily. Although his back wasn't quite straight yet he scrambled nimbly up under the rafters and bustled about down below, shouting at his assistants. He and his father had built this house when he was a lad, a long time ago. The top room had been put up for him, the oldest son, to move in with his bride. And now he was furiously taking it apart, board by board, to carry it out of somebody else's yard.

After numbering the beam-ends and the ceiling boards they dismantled the top room and the storeroom underneath it. The living room, and what was left of the landing, they boarded up with a thin wall of deal. They did nothing about the cracks in the wall. It was plain to see that they were wreckers, not builders, and that they did not expect Matryona to be living there very long.

While the men were busy wrecking, the women were getting the drink ready for moving day—vodka would cost a lot too much. Kira brought a pood of sugar from Moscow oblast, and Matryona carried the sugar and some bottles to the distiller under cover of night.

The timbers were carried out and stacked in front of the gates, and the engine-driver son-in-law went off to Cherusti for the tractor.

But the very same day a blizzard, or "a blower" as Matryona called it, began. It howled and whirled for two days and nights and buried the road under enormous drifts. Then, no sooner had they made the road passable and a couple of lorries gone by, than it got suddenly warmer. Within a day everything was thawing out, damp mist hung in the air and rivulets gurgled as they burrowed into the snow, and you could get stuck up to the top of your knee-boots.

Two weeks passed before the tractor could get at the dismantled top room. All this time Matryona went around like someone lost. What particularly upset her was that her three sisters came and with one voice called her a fool for giving the top room away, said they didn't want to see her any more, and went off. At about the same time the lame cat strayed and was seen no more. It was just one thing after another. This was another blow to Matryona.

At last the frost got a grip on the slushy road. A sunny day came along and everybody felt more cheerful. Matryona had had a lucky dream the night before. In the morning she heard that I wanted to take a photograph of somebody at an old-fashioned hand-loom. (There were looms still standing in two cottages in the village; they wove coarse rugs on them.) She smiled shyly and said, "You just wait a day or two, Ignatich, I'll just send the top room there off and I'll put my loom up, I've still got it, you know, and then you can snap me. Honest to God!"

She was obviously attracted by the idea of posing in an old-fashioned setting. The red, frosty sun tinged the window of the curtailed passageway with a faint pink, and this reflected light warmed Matryona's face. People who are at ease with their consciences always have nice faces.

Coming back from school before dusk I saw some movement

near our house. A big new tractor-drawn sledge was already fully loaded, and there was no room for a lot of the timbers, so old Faddei's family and the helpers they had called in had nearly finished knocking together another home-made sledge. They were all working like madmen, in the frenzy that comes upon people when there is a smell of good money in the air or when they are looking forward to some treat. They were shouting at one another and arguing.

They could not agree whether the sledges should be hauled separately or both together. One of Faddei's sons (the lame one) and the engine-driver son-in-law reasoned that the sledges couldn't both be taken at once because the tractor wouldn't be able to pull them. The man in charge of the tractor, a hefty fat-faced fellow who was very sure of himself, said hoarsely that he knew best, he was the driver, and he would take both at once. His motives were obvious: according to the agreement the engine-driver was paying him for the removal of the upper room, not for the number of trips he had to make. He could never have made two trips in a night—twenty-five kilometers each way, and one return journey. And by morning he had to get the tractor back in the garage from which he had sneaked it out for this job on the side.

Old Faddei was impatient to get the top room moved that day, and at a nod from him his lads gave in. To the stout sledge in front they hitched the one which they had knocked together in such a hurry.

Matryona was running about amongst the men, fussing and helping them to heave the beams on to the sledge. Suddenly I noticed that she was wearing my jerkin and had dirtied the sleeves on the frozen mud round the beams. I was annoyed, and told her so. That jerkin held memories for me: it had kept me warm in the bad years.

This was the first time that I was ever angry with Matryona Vasilyevna.

Matryona was taken aback. "Oh dear, dear me," she said. "My poor head. I picked it up in a rush, you see, and never thought about it being yours. I'm sorry, Ignatich."

And she took it off and hung it up to dry.

The loading was finished, and all the men who had been working, about ten of them, clattered past my table and dived under the curtain into the kitchen. I could hear the muffled rattle of glasses and, from time to time, the clink of a bottle, the voices got louder and louder, the boasting more reckless. The biggest braggart was the tractor-driver. The stench of hooch floated in to me. But they didn't go on drinking long. It was getting dark and they had to hurry.

They began to leave. The tractor-driver came out first, looking pleased with himself and fierce. The engine-driver son-in-law, Faddei's lame son and one of his nephews were going to Cherusti. The others went off home. Faddei was flourishing his stick, trying to overtake somebody and put him right about something. The lame son paused at my table to light up and suddenly started telling me how he loved Aunt Matryona, and that he had got married not long ago, and his wife had just had a son. Then they shouted for him and he went out. The tractor set up a roar outside.

After all the others had gone Matryona dashed out from behind the screen. She looked after them, anxiously shaking her head. She had put on her jerkin and her head-scarf. As she was going through the door she said to me, "Why ever couldn't they hire two? If one tractor had cracked up the other would have pulled them. What'll happen now, God only knows!"

She ran out after the others.

After the booze-up and the arguments and all the coming and going it was quieter than ever in the deserted cottage, and very chilly because the door had been opened so many times. I got into my jerkin and sat down to mark exercise books. The noise of the tractor died away in the distance.

An hour went by. And another. And a third. Matryona still hadn't come back, but I wasn't surprised. When she had seen the sledge off she must have gone round to her friend Masha.

Another hour went by. And yet another. Darkness and with it a deep silence had descended on the village. I couldn't understand at the time why it was so quiet. Later I found out that it was because all evening not a single train had gone along the line half a verst from the house. No sound was coming from my radio and I noticed that the mice were wilder than ever. Their scampering and scratching and squeaking behind the wallpaper was getting noisier and more defiant all the time.

I woke up. It was one o'clock in the morning and Matryona still hadn't come home.

Suddenly I heard several people talking loudly. They were still a long way off, but something told me that they were coming to our house. And sure enough I heard soon afterwards a heavy knock at the gate. A commanding voice, strange to me, yelled out an order to open up. I went out into the thick darkness with a torch. The whole village was asleep, there was no light in the windows, and the snow had started melting in the last week so that it gave no reflected light. I turned the catch and let them in. Four men in greatcoats went on towards the house. It's a very unpleasant thing to be visited at night by noisy people in greatcoats.

When we got into the light, though, I saw that two of them were wearing railway uniforms. The older of the two, a fat man with the same sort of face as the tractor-driver, asked, "Where's the woman of the house?"

"I don't know."

"This is the place the tractor with a sledge came from?"

"This is it."

"Had they been drinking before they left?"

All four of them were looking around them, screwing up their eyes in the dim light from the table-lamp. I realized that they had either made an arrest or wanted to make one.

"What's happened, then?"

"Answer the question!"

"But . . ."

"Were they drunk when they went?"

"Were they drinking here?"

Had there been a murder? Or hadn't they been able to move the top room? The men in greatcoats had me off balance. But one thing was certain: Matryona could do time for making hooch.

I stepped back to stand between them and the kitchen door. "I honestly didn't notice. I didn't see anything." (I really hadn't seen anything—only heard.) I made what was supposed to be a helpless gesture, drawing attention to the state of the cottage: a table-lamp shining peacefully on books and exercises, a crowd of frightened rubber-plants, the austere couch of a recluse, not a sign of debauchery.

They had already seen for themselves, to their annoyance, that there had been no drinking in that room. They turned to leave, telling each other this wasn't where the drinking had been then, but it would be a good thing to put in that it was. I saw them out and tried to discover what had happened. It was only at the gate that one of them growled, "They've all been cut to bits. Can't find all the pieces."

"That's a detail. The express at 21:00 hours nearly went off the rails. That would have been something." And they walked briskly away.

I went back to the hut in a daze. Who were "they"? What did "all of them" mean? And where was Matryona?

I moved the curtain aside and went into the kitchen. The stink of hooch rose and hit me. It was a deserted battlefield: a huddle of stools and benches, empty bottles lying around, one bottle half-full, glasses, the remains of pickled herring, onion, and sliced fat pork.

Everything was deathly still. Just cockroaches creeping unperturbed about the field of battle.

They had said something about the express at 21:00. Why? Perhaps I should have shown them all this? I began to wonder whether I had done right. But what a damnable way to behave—keeping their explanations for official persons only.

Suddenly the small gate creaked. I hurried out on to the landing. "Matryona Vasilyevna?"

The yard door opened, and Matryona's friend Masha came in, swaying and wringing her hands. "Matryona . . . our Matryona, Ignatich . . ."

I sat her down and through her tears she told me the story.

The approach to the crossing was a steep rise. There was no barrier. The tractor and the first sledge went over, but the tow-rope broke and the second sledge, the home-made one, got stuck on the crossing and started falling apart—the wood Faddei had given them to make the second sledge was no good. They towed the first sledge out of the way and went back for the second. They were fixing the tow-rope—the tractor-driver and Faddei's lame son, and Matryona, heaven knows what brought her there, was with them, between the tractor and the sledge. What help did she think she could be to the men? She was forever meddling in men's work. Hadn't a bolting horse nearly tipped her into the lake once, through a hole in the ice?

Why did she have to go to the damned crossing? She had handed over the top room, and owed nothing to anybody. . . . The engine-driver kept a look-out in case the train from Cherusti rushed up on them. Its headlamps would be visible a long way off. But two engines coupled together came from the other direction, from our station, backing without lights. Why they were without lights nobody knows. When an engine is backing, coal-dust blows into the driver's eyes from the tender and he can't see very well. The two engines flew into them and crushed the three people between the tractor and the sledge to pulp. The tractor was wrecked, the sledge was matchwood, the rails were buckled, and both engines turned over.

"But how was it they didn't hear the engines coming?"

"The tractor engine was making such a din."

"What about the bodies?"

"They won't let anybody in. They've roped them off."

"What was that somebody was telling me about the express?"

"The nine o'clock express goes through our station at a good speed and on to the crossing. But the two drivers weren't hurt when their engines crashed, they jumped out and ran back along the line waving their hands and they managed to stop the train. . . . The nephew was hurt by a beam as well. He's hiding at Klavka's now so that they won't know he was at the crossing. If they find out they'll drag him in as a witness. . . . Don't know lies up, and do know gets tied up. Kira's husband didn't get a scratch. He tried to hang himself, they had to cut him down. It's all because of me, he says, my auntie's killed and my brother. Now he's gone and given himself up. But the mad-house is where he'll be going, not prison. Oh, Matryona, my dearest Matryona. . . ."

Matryona was gone. Someone close to me had been killed. And on her last day I had scolded her for wearing my jerkin.

The lovingly drawn red and yellow woman in the book advertisement smiled happily on.

Old Masha sat there weeping a little longer. Then she got up to go. And suddenly she asked me, "Ignatich, you remember, Matryona had a gray shawl. She meant it to go to my Tanya when she died, didn't she?"

She looked at me hopefully in the half-darkness . . . surely I hadn't forgotten?

No, I remembered. "She said so, yes."

"Well, listen, maybe you could let me take it with me now. The family will be swarming in tomorrow and I'll never get it then." And she gave me another hopeful, imploring look. She had been Matryona's friend for half a century, the only one in the village who truly loved her.

No doubt she was right.

"Of course . . . take it."

She opened the chest, took out the shawl, tucked it under her coat and went out.

The mice had gone mad. They were running furiously up and down the walls, and you could almost see the green wallpaper rippling and rolling over their backs.

In the morning I had to go to school. The time was three o'clock. The only thing to do was to lock up and go to bed.

Lock up, because Matryona would not be coming.

I lay down, leaving the light on. The mice were squeaking, almost moaning, racing and running. My mind was weary and wandering, and I couldn't rid myself of an uneasy feeling that an invisible Matryona was flitting about and saying good-bye to her home.

And suddenly I imagined Faddei standing there, young and black-haired, in the dark patch by the door, with his axe uplifted. "If it wasn't my own brother I'd chop the both of you to bits."

The threat had lain around for forty years, like an old broadsword in a corner, and in the end it had struck its blow.

When it was light the women went to the crossing and brought back all that was left of Matryona on a hand-sledge with a dirty sack over it. They threw off the sack to wash her. There was just a mess . . . no feet, only half a body, no left hand. One woman said, "The Lord has left her her right hand. She'll be able to say her prayers where she's going. . . ."

Then the whole crowd of rubber-plants was carried out of the cottage . . . these plants that Matryona had loved so much that once when smoke woke her up in the night she didn't rush to save her house but to tip the plants on to the floor in case they were suffocated. The women swept the floor clean. They hung a wide towel of old homespun over Matryona's dim mirror. They took down the jolly posters. They moved my table out of the way. Under the icons, near the windows, they stood a rough unadorned coffin on a row of stools.

In the coffin lay Matryona. Her body, mangled and lifeless, was covered with a clean sheet. Her head was swathed in a white kerchief. Her face was almost undamaged, peaceful, more alive than dead.

The villagers came to pay their last respects. The women even brought their small children to take a look at the dead. And if anyone raised a lament, all the women, even those who had looked in out of idle curiosity, always joined in, wailing where they stood by the door or the wall, as though they were providing a choral accompaniment. The men stood stiff and silent with their caps off.

The formal lamentation had to be performed by the women of Matryona's family. I observed that the lament followed a coldly calculated age-old ritual. The more distant relatives went up to the coffin for a short while and made low wailing noises over it. Those who considered themselves closer kin to the dead woman began their lament in the doorway and when they got as far as the coffin, bowed down and roared out their grief right in the face of the departed. Every lamenter made up her own melody. And expressed her own thoughts and feelings.

I realized that a lament for the dead is not just a lament, but a kind of politics. Matryona's three sisters swooped, took possession of the cottage, the goat, and the stove, locked up the chest, ripped the two hundred rubles for the funeral out of the coat lining, and drummed it into everybody who came that only they were near relatives. Their lament over the coffin went like this, *"Oh nanny, nanny! Oh nan-nan!* All we had in the world was you! You could have lived in peace and quiet, you could. And we should always have been kind and loving to you. Now your top room's been the death of you. Finished you off it has, the cursed thing! Oh why did you have to take it down? Why didn't you listen to us?"

Thus the sisters' laments were indictments of Matryona's husband's family: they shouldn't have made her take the top room down. (There was an underlying meaning too: you've taken the top room all right but we won't let you have the house itself!)

Matryona's husband's family, her sisters-in-law, Yefim and Faddei's sisters, and various nieces lamented like this, *"Oh poor auntie, poor auntie!* Why didn't you take better care of yourself! Now they're angry with us for sure. Our own dear Matryona you were, and it's your own fault! The top room has nothing to do with it. Oh why did you go where death was waiting for you? Nobody asked you to go there. And what a way to die! Oh why didn't you listen to us?" (Their answer to the others showed through these laments: we are not to blame for her death, and the house we'll talk about later.)

But the "second" Matryona, a coarse, broad-faced woman, the substitute Matryona whom Faddei had married so long ago for the sake of her name, got out of step with family policy, wailing and sobbing over the coffin in her simplicity, *"Oh my poor dear sister!* You won't be angry with me, will you now? Oh-oh-oh! How we used to talk and talk, you and me! Forgive a poor miserable woman! You've gone to be with your dear mother, and you'll come for me some day for sure! Oh-oh-oh-oh! . . ."

At every "oh-oh-oh" it was as though she were giving up the ghost. She writhed and gasped, with her breast against the side of the coffin. When her lament went beyond the ritual prescription the women, as though acknowledging its success, all started saying, "Come away now, come away."

Matryona came away, but back she went again, sobbing with even greater abandon. Then an ancient woman came out of a corner, put her hand on Matryona's shoulder, and said, "There are two riddles in this world: how I was born I don't remember, how I shall die I don't know."

And Matryona fell silent at once, and all the others were silent, so that there was an unbroken hush.

But the old woman herself, who was much older than all the

other old women there and didn't seem to belong to Matryona at all, after a while started wailing, "Oh my poor sick Matryona! Oh my poor Vasilyevna! Oh what a weary thing it is to be seeing you into your grave!"

There was one who didn't follow the ritual, but wept straight-forwardly, in the fashion of our age, which has had plenty of prac-tice at it. This was Matryona's unfortunate foster-daughter, Kira, from Cherusti, for whom the top room had been taken down and moved. Her ringlets were pitifully out of curl. Her eyes looked red and bloodshot. She didn't notice that her head-scarf was slipping off out in the frosty air and that her arm hadn't found the sleeve of her coat. She walked in a stupor from her foster-mother's coffin in one house to her brother's in another. They were afraid she would lose her mind, because her husband had to go for trial as well.

It looked as if her husband was doubly at fault: not only was he moving the top room, but as an engine-driver he knew the regula-tions about unprotected crossings, and should have gone down to the station to warn them about the tractor. There were a thousand people on the Urals express that night, peacefully sleeping in the upper and lower berths of their dimly lit carriages, and all those lives were nearly cut short. All because of a few greedy people, wanting to get their hands on a plot of land, or not wanting to make a second trip with a tractor.

All because of the top room, which had been under a curse ever since Faddei's hands had started itching to take it down.

The tractor-driver was already beyond human justice. And the railway authorities were also at fault, both because a busy crossing was unguarded and because the coupled engines were traveling without lights. That was why they had tried at first to blame it all on the drink, and then to keep the case out of court.

The rails and the track were so twisted and torn that for three days, while the coffins were still in the house, no trains ran—they were diverted on to another line. All Friday, Saturday, and Sunday, from the end of the investigation until the funeral, the work of re-pairing the line went on day and night. The repair gang was frozen, and they made fires to warm themselves and to light their work at night, using the boards and beams from the second sledge which were there for the taking, scattered around the crossing.

The first sledge just stood there, undamaged and still loaded, a little way beyond the crossing.

One sledge, tantalizingly ready to be towed away, and the other perhaps still to be plucked from the flames—that was what harrowed the soul of black-bearded Faddei all day Friday and all day Saturday. His daughter was going out of her mind, his son-in-law had a criminal charge hanging over him, in his own house lay the son he had killed, and along the street the woman he had killed and whom he had once loved. But Faddei stood by the coffins clutching his beard only for a short time, and went away again. His tall brow was clouded by painful thoughts, but what he was thinking about was how to save the timbers of the top room from the flames and from Matryona's scheming sisters.

Going over the people of Talnovo in my mind I realized that Faddei was not the only one like that.

Property, the people's property, or my property, is strangely called our "goods." If you lose your goods, people think you disgrace yourself and make yourself look foolish.

Faddei dashed about, never stopping for a sit-down, from the settlement to the station, from one official to another, stood there with his bent back, leaning heavily on his stick, and begged them all to take pity on an old man and give him permission to recover the top room.

Somebody gave permission. And Faddei gathered together his surviving sons, sons-in-law and nephews, got horses from the kolkhoz and from the other side of the wrecked crossing, by a roundabout way that led through three villages, brought the remnants of the top room home to his yard. He finished the job in the early hours of Sunday morning.

On Sunday afternoon they were buried. The two coffins met in the middle of the village, and the relatives argued about which of them should go first. Then they put them side by side on an open sledge, the aunt and the nephew, and carried the dead over the damp snow, with a gloomy February sky above, to the churchyard two villages away. There was an unkind wind, so the priest and the deacon waited inside the church and didn't come out to Talnovo to meet them.

A crowd of people walked slowly behind the coffins, singing in chorus. Outside the village they fell back.

When Sunday came the women were still fussing around the house. An old woman mumbled psalms by the coffin, Matryona's sisters flitted about, popping things into the oven, and the air round the mouth of the stove trembled with the heat of red-hot peats, those which Matryona had carried in a sack from a distant bog. They were making unappetizing pies with poor flour.

When the funeral was over and it was already getting on towards evening, they gathered for the wake. Tables were put together to make a long one, which hid the place where the coffin had stood in the morning. To start with they all stood round the table, and an old man, the husband of a sister-in-law, said the Lord's Prayer. Then they poured everybody a little honey and warm water, just enough to cover the bottom of the bowl. We spooned it up without bread or anything, in memory of the dead. Then we ate something and drank vodka and the conversation became more animated. Before the jelly they all stood up and sang "Eternal Remembrance" (they explained to me that it had to be sung before the jelly). There was more drinking. By now they were talking louder than ever, and not about Matryona at all. The sister-in-law's husband started boasting, "Did you notice, brother Christians, that they took the funeral service slowly today? That's because Father Mikhail noticed me. He knows I know the service. Other times it's saints defend us, homeward wend us, and that's all."

At last the supper was over. They all rose again. They sang "Worthy Is She." Then again, with a triple repetition of "Eternal Remembrance." But the voices were hoarse and out of tune, their faces drunken, and nobody put any feeling into this "eternal memory."

Then the main guests went away, and only the near relatives were left. They pulled out their cigarettes and lit up, there were jokes and laughter. There was some mention of Matryona's husband and his disappearance. The sister-in-law's husband, striking himself on the chest, assured me and the cobbler who was married to one of Matryona's sisters, "He was dead, Yefim was dead! What could stop him coming back if he wasn't? If I knew they were going to hang me when I got to the old country I'd come back just the same!"

The cobbler nodded in agreement. He was a deserter and had never left the old country. All through the war he was hiding in his mother's cellar.

The stern and silent old woman who was more ancient than all the ancients was staying the night and sat high up on the stove. She looked down in mute disapproval on the indecently animated youngsters of fifty and sixty.

But the unhappy foster-daughter, who had grown up within these walls, went away behind the kitchen screen to cry.

Faddei didn't come to Matryona's wake—perhaps because he was holding a wake for his son. But twice in the next few days he walked angrily into the house for discussions with Matryona's sisters and the deserting cobbler.

The argument was about the house. Should it go to one of the sisters or to the foster-daughter? They were on the verge of taking it to court, but they made peace because they realized that the court would hand over the house to neither side, but to the rural district council. A bargain was struck. One sister took the goat, the cobbler and his wife got the house, and to make up Faddei's share, since he had "nursed every bit of timber here in his arms," in addition to the top room which had already been carried away, they let him have the shed which had housed the goat, and the whole of the inner fence between the yard and the garden.

Once again the insatiable old man got the better of sickness and pain and became young and active. Once again he gathered together his surviving sons and sons-in-law, and they dismantled the shed and the fence, and he hauled the timbers himself, sledge by sledge, and only towards the end did he have Antoshka of 8-D, who didn't slack this time, to help him.

They boarded Matryona's house up till the spring, and I moved in with one of her sisters-in-law, not far away. This sister-in-law on several occasions came out with some recollection of Matryona, and made me see the dead woman in a new light. "Yefim didn't love her. He used to say, 'I like to dress in an educated way, but she dresses any old way, like they do in the country.' Well then, he thinks, if she doesn't want anything, he might as well drink whatever's to spare. One time I went with him to the town to work, and he got himself a madam there and never wanted to come back to Matryona."

Everything she said about Matryona was disapproving. She was slovenly, she made no effort to get a few things about her. She wasn't the saving kind. She didn't even keep a pig, because she didn't like fattening them up for some reason. And the silly woman helped other people without payment. (What brought Matryona to mind this time was that the garden needed plowing and she couldn't find enough helpers to pull the plow.)

Matryona's sister-in-law admitted that she was warm-hearted and straightforward, but pitied and despised her for it.

It was only then, after these disapproving comments from her sister-in-law, that a true likeness of Matryona formed itself before my eyes, and I understood her as I never had when I lived side by side with her.

Of course! Every house in the village kept a pig. But she didn't. What can be easier than fattening a greedy piglet that cares for nothing in the world but food! You warm his swill three times a day, you live for him—then you cut his throat and you have some fat.

But she had none. . . .

She made no effort to get things round her. . . . She didn't struggle and strain to buy things and then care for them more than life itself.

She didn't go all out after fine clothes. Clothes, that beautify what is ugly and evil.

She was misunderstood and abandoned even by her husband. She had lost six children, but not her social ways. She was a stranger to her sisters and sisters-in-law, a ridiculous creature who stupidly worked for others without pay. She didn't accumulate property against the day she died. A dirty-white goat, a gammy-legged cat, some rubber-plants. . . .

We had all lived side by side with her and never understood that she was that righteous one without whom, as the proverb says, no village can stand.

Nor any city.

Nor our whole land.

*Translated from the Russian by H. T. Willetts*